Climbing the Ranks 3

A Tower Climber Epic Fantasy

By

Tao Wong

Copyright

This is a work of fiction. Names, characters, businesses, places, events, and incidents are either the products of the author's imagination or used in a fictitious manner. Any resemblance to actual persons, living or dead, or actual events is purely coincidental.

No part of this publication may be reproduced, distributed, or transmitted in any form or by any means, including photocopying, recording, or other electronic or mechanical methods, without the prior written permission of the publisher, except in the case of brief quotations embodied in critical reviews and certain other non-commercial uses permitted by copyright law.

No part of this book may be used or reproduced in any manner for the purpose of training artificial intelligence technologies or systems.

Published by Starlit Publishing

PO Box 30035

High Park PO

Toronto, ON, Canada M6P 3K0

www.starlitpublishing.com

Ebook ISBN: 9781778552458

Paperback ISBN: 9781778552694

Hardcover ISBN: 9781778552700

Books in the Climbing the Ranks Series

Other Series by Tao Wong

The System Apocalypse Universe

The Hidden Universe

Table of Contents

Chapter 1

Arthur felt the world lurch, his body pulled apart and reformed, or just transported so fast it felt like that. He was pretty sure he was being torn apart, transformed, and reformed on the other end. Like those Star Trek transporters. Which, of course, came with all kinds of morality questions of whether they really were people, and if they could do this pulling apart, was it possible to create clones? All kinds of crazy questions.

Except for the fact that the Tower only ever created a single individual. And the way they could manage power, the memories and the way they could control things, the idea of cultivation and the notices... it spoke of souls. Others had attempted, using Tower abilities, to replicate the division process. In other words, cloning in the outside world. The closest to success merely created undifferentiated blobs of cells, the kind that gave nightmares because they just . . . sat there. Stem cells, but not really, that had no face or shape. Some believed that it was clear evidence that a soul existed, was needed to create the right form.

Others said that the cloners had just done it wrong, that they hadn't figured out how to transport memory properly.

Arguments for philosophers and scientists and university kids in their ivory towers. As for Arthur, he was here; he had his spear, and he was looking out at the sixth floor.

The good news on the sixth floor? The rest of his team were coming into being next to him, forming up. They weren't being split into separate groups since they had all entered the same portal.

Better news? There were safe spots, Tower buildings, scattered throughout this floor. There wasn't a climber village, a central location where others congregated, though some had built small buildings next to the Tower-administrated ones. Places they could stop, recuperate, and even buy new gear.

All of which was great, except for the fact that the bad news was . . . this floor. Someone had decided to make the entire layout a vertical one, making the idea of climbing a Tower a reality. You started at the bottom, jumped, climbed, leapt or walked, and thus ascended a circular column. The fact that it was over two hundred levels upwards, give or take a score or two, was one thing.

The other was the constant rain of death.

"Left!" Arthur called out and the group shuffled away, watching as a large stone, a bouncing ball of doom, careened into the earth where they had been and ploughed into it.

Death from above by bouncing balls that sometimes went upwards or sideways was the least of the dangers of the sixth floor. But still a massive one. Arthur wiped at his face where mud had splattered. He sighed, looked upward, and judged for further bouncing balls, then called out.

"We need overwatch." A moment's hesitation, then he added, "Rick?"

"On it." The shooter, the only member other than Casey who utilised ranged weapons well, tilted his head up, checking for incoming danger.

"Everyone good? Ready to move? Remember the problems of this floor?" Arthur asked.

"One . . . second." Leia, the last to exit, was holding a hand to her head, trying to deal with the transition.

"Maybe we can talk things through? Know what's coming again?" Casey said, her bow held down by her side.

"Usual rule of three." Arthur complied immediately, looking around as he searched. "For monsters, that is. Traps too. Three kinds: balls, stakes, and swinging death traps. The monsters are weird: Swinging, eating plant monster with big fanged petals and grasping vines. An exploding, camouflaged, creeping piece of grass of some form. And finally, the only really mobile one. A moving mushroom."

"Weirdest part," Rick said, still looking up. "There's a platform floor of one form or another in all the Beginner towers. Many of them rather reminiscent of this one. And there's a game like this in the real world."

"Eh, if you can call a game. So boring, *lah*. Sifu used to make us watch it, and it was always bad," Eric said.

"It's a classic," Rick snapped.

"Classic of its kind, yes," Mel piped up. "The kind that's trash and boring and only considered good because it's old."

"Hey!" Rick said, looking hurt. He couldn't look away from staring above, watching for the bouncing balls. Thankfully, they weren't that common, only two or three in sight at any one time. Sometimes, they got stuck, all the energy they used to bounce sucked up and jammed away. It was part of the reason why things got worse as you went higher, because the number of death balls increased.

"At least it isn't *Cobra*," Lam said.

The silence that greeted that random pronouncement had the man look around. "What? You all never heard of it?"

"I . . . sort of?" Rick was frowning. "I have some memory . . ."

"Wiki mention. I saw a few pictures," Arthur offered. "It's supposedly a very hard game. Not really relevant though. They say it's only tangentially related to the platform floors."

"It's a good game. Hard. Very hard to beat," Lam said. "Not like modern games. They all hold your hand."

"Right?" Rick said, glad to have someone agreeing with him. "I mean, not the Rings saga, though."

"Easy," Lam scoffed. Casey was looking at her bodyguard in new light.

"Boring . . ." Eric said.

"Enough," Leia interrupted, straightening. "I'd rather climb and maybe die than listen to a bunch of nerds whine about their video games." She waved a hand around. "As though all this isn't hard enough."

"Hey!" Eric said, hurt. "I wasn't—"

Arthur clapped his hands together, looked up, judged the falling ball, and pointed down a short distance. "We start there. Use simple vines to climb. Casey, take out the gripper with your bow, will you?"

She frowned, barely seeing the plant and its petals in question at this angle. Still, she nodded, heading left while the rest of the team approached the overhang. An arrow, drawn and loosed and curving through space, struck the creature; half the hanging vines were now jerking and spasming. The group slowed down a little, staring at the moving vines, some of which they might have unwittingly grabbed to pull themselves up, and a few gulped.

Another arrow, drawn and loosed, put a stop to the spasming. The group moved forward, taking hold of non-monster vines and began climbing, Rick and Casey watching for further trouble. Yao Jing and Eric were the first up, both of them reaching the top at the same time as they tried to outrace one another. Arthur just rolled his eyes at the competitiveness but figured it didn't hurt.

Someone had to be on top.

As he climbed, he couldn't help but reiterate his warnings, since they had started him on this. "Remember, we want to do this floor fast. It's one of the floors where we can save on time, which means trying to tackle it all in one big push. We'll keep heading up, as far and as fast as possible, but that doesn't mean we take risks.

"Slow and steady, just like the hare."

"Turtle," Casey corrected.

"What?" Arthur said, puzzled as he got onto the first level. He formed a Refined Energy Dart in his mind, looking upwards as he gestured for Uswah to take overwatch. On the ground, they'd had a lot of space to run. Now, on the small column of rock and earth that made this platform, if a ball came careening down, they needed to start moving. Which was, of course, why he was also trying to chart a path upwards that gave them the most options.

"It's a turtle, not a hare, that was slow but won the race."

"Eh, boss. What's all this about hair?" Yao Jing said, ruffling his own.

"Hare. H. A. R. E." Lam, by the side, explained. "Not hair."

"Oh . . ."

"You sure it was the hare not the turtle?"

"Why would a hare be slow?"

Arthur shrugged. Not as though he'd ever seen a real one.

"Whatever. That way." He pointed to the right and a platform that was a short hop upwards. "There and then up via the vines. Kill the mushrooms lingering there." He flicked his gaze over the group; Casey and Rick were finally up. "Uswah, Lam, and Jan. Go."

They went. While he didn't want them too spread out, the platform they were on was small enough that it was getting crowded as it stood. Best to get moving, before they all got squashed.

After all, they still had one last boss to handle above.

Chapter 2

Ascending the sixth floor could almost be considered routine. With the team forced to move diagonally and vertically to ascend, keeping an eye on where they could jump to, which platform jutting out of the walls was viable to climb to, and how to get to them was the trick. Arthur had to keep a 3D map of the place in mind at all times, with the occasional bouncing ball, monsters, and other traps in play. All of which meant that he made mistakes.

"Go left, left!" Arthur waved his hand in the direction he meant, even as everyone scrambled. Not all in the right direction, what with the team being turned one way or the other, chatting, looking out for threats, or breaking down a spike trap, or firing at a creeping camouflaged creature climbing upwards.

All of which meant that Jan, Casey, and Yao Jing chose to move right—as per Arthur's facing—instead of left. At which point, Lam, Uswah, and then Eric grabbed the three and yanked them the right way as they scrambled away from the falling rock. It came slamming into the ground a half-dozen feet next to the sprawled group.

Arthur shaded his eyes a little as he waited for the ball to careen away. Once the dust had settled, he jumped up sideways and then again, using his Cloud Step rather than bothering with the longer passage the others had to use to get to the same area. He managed to get a hand around the platform edge and hauled himself upward, grunting a moment later as he reached the majority of the group. Leia was right at the top with Rick at the moment, the pair leading the charge as Rick took potshots at mushrooms high above.

"Oy!" Arthur called, waited for Rick to stop shooting, then waved at them all.

"New rule." He pointed upwards, to where a line of brown basalt was: the sun was beginning to set. "Sunward." Then, he turned and pointed down the other side of the canyon. "Canyonward. I scream sunward, we all go that way. I scream canyon, we go this way. Got it?"

"I . . . maybe?" Casey said.

More frustrated looks. They understood the point, but shifting to new words and orientations in the middle of the day was going to be difficult.

"Let's try it. And let's keep moving. Rick, more mushies."

So warned, Rick turned and scanned for the bouncing creatures, raising his pistol. Casey joined him moments later, even as Arthur bounced up to the top level so he could continue charting the way.

"Tiu!" Yao Jing snarled, rearing back from the swinging scythe of death. Those often hung or fell down from other platforms, swinging through areas randomly and nearly bisecting climbers who might be caught. The only way to catch sight of them was to watch for the telltale glint in platforms above.

In this case, Arthur had nearly missed it. If Yao Jing had been only a little faster, he'd have been bisected. As it was, the damn thing kept swinging back and forth, its speed increasing as the arc decreased. Eventually, it'd be retracted, reset, and fired off again. Which was a delay, but not an unexpected one.

The bigger problem was the spikes right ahead on this platform. They needed to cross this bridge to the other side, just so they could jump, climb, and cross over the series of platforms ahead. And while the spike could be broken when they came up, they also had a bad habit of regenerating.

Sometimes at the most inconvenient of times.

"Boss?" Yao Jing called.

"Shit, shit, shit . . ." Arthur cast around for options. They could push ahead, maybe, but with the timing they might not get all their people through. Jumping and timing the spikes that rose out of the ground was child's play, except you still had to time it. And they'd lose quite a few minutes, waiting for the swinging scythes. Never mind waiting around for giant balls to bounce in or the mushrooms, which were all coming to close in on them.

"That way." A hand on his arm, Casey turned him to look down. He watched her finger as she pointed out the way she'd picked out. "Works?"

"Mostly." He spotted a few more issues that way, more carpet monsters from the first level where they had to switch over and some grasping vines right next to the carpet monsters on a platform they weren't going to take, which was why he had avoided it in the first place. Then again . . .

"Bombardment on three." He was already forming an Exploding Energy Dart as he called out. "Back down. Two platforms, head canyonward and to the other edge, then up. We'll mark where you need to go."

The group scrambled, Yao Jing jumping down near him moments later, firing an explosive off.

"Ready?" Arthur asked, only to find Casey already loosing arrows. He snorted, checked where she aimed at, and released his own attack. He'd bounce ahead, using Cloud Step over the open air. One advantage of his technique and having progressed it farther than the others.

Monsters, dozens of them. All swarming around, the tiny mushroom figures bouncing downwards. Tiny, because they'd found a variant that exploded when they got struck but became even smaller copies of themselves. There were dozens, but it felt like hundreds as they scrambled all around Arthur's group, spears swinging and blocking. More than once, Arthur was nearly knocked over by another spear, the damn creatures finding them at the worst time, when they were all grouped close together on two different platforms while waiting for a series of swinging scythes of doom to reset and for Lam to get the timing right.

Arthur was smacked in the back and thrown off, forced to stagger and catch his balance by forming a Cloud Step beneath his foot. He threw himself back onto the platform, knocked into Mel, and had to grab her armour by the nape to stop her from falling. Making a decision, he dropped his spear to the ground and snatched out his kris as he shuffled to the side.

"Parangs. Close-ranged weapons only!" he cried.

It filled him with some pride to see that the group had already made the decision to do so themselves, jumping to the very same conclusion long before him. They kept fighting and, thankfully, only managed to lose one person—as Uswah, blown back by an unhappy explosion, fell down.

She slammed into a surface, two platforms down, half off and hurt. Arthur winced, even as Jan leapt downwards to go to her aid.

Hopefully, she wasn't too badly injured.

"Inside!" Arthur called, waving the group into the administrative center. They'd made it halfway there, which was decent progress for their first day. But night had fallen, and while the luminescent biome of the canyon walls and monsters shed enough light for the team to continue, albeit more dangerously, the group was injured and sore from their ascent.

Most especially Uswah who was still groggy and concussed, having hit her head when she fell. She also had managed to wrench her back, so she was currently on the need-to-heal list. Unfortunately, they hadn't been able to stop long enough for her to heal properly, forced to keep moving by the traps and monsters. Thankfully, the passive healing effects of their technique had certainly helped relieve some of the issues.

On the other hand, considering how hard they'd pushed, they had done well. Even if there was more planning to do.

"Everyone in?" Arthur said, then double-checked his own count. Mel was doing the same and gave him an affirmative nod shortly before he managed his own confirmation.

Then, and only then, did he relax. Slumped against the edge of the door, he looked outside and watched the bouncing balls that rained down around them, the constant slamming like a thunderstorm that never stopped rolling. A drumbeat by an over-enthusiastic god, all of which had made shouting commands for the last half-hour a pain.

They needed a new method for tomorrow. Something to think about.

Shaking aside those thoughts, Arthur waved to the fox creature that acted as the Tower Administrator. The rest of the team had splayed out, resting, though he noted Rick searching in his pack, ready to make a trade. Not a problem for him to worry about, but he had first dibs.

Arthur made his way over as quickly as possible, offering the creature his token and waited. After all, he'd gotten used to the routine by now.

The only question was if the Chins had any building they could take here. After all, they'd come across more than one shattered building as they ascended the sixth floor.

Time and the Administrator would tell.

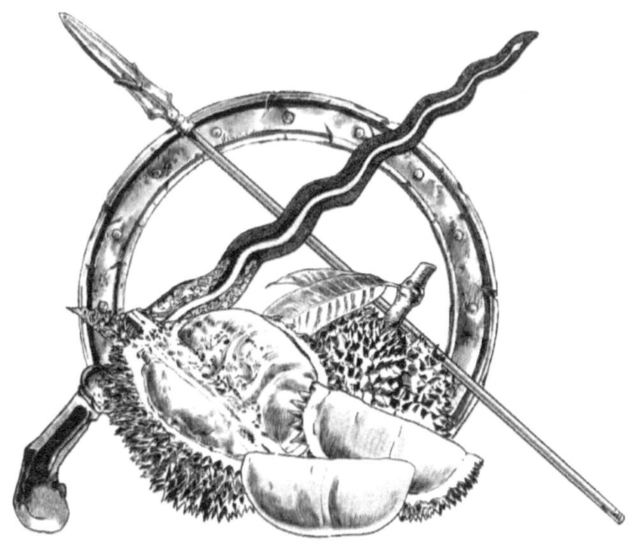

Chapter 3

The Tower blared its usual notification about ascending to a new floor, noting his presence here and indicating it had updated its own records. All kinds of random administrative aspects that Arthur cared little for. It had no real bearing on him, though the next notification was of much more interest.

The Benevolent Durians Clan Status
Organizational Ranking: 182,742
Number of Towers Occupied: 1
Number of Clan Buildings: 4
Number of Clan Members: 312
Overall Credit Rating: F-
Aspect: Guardianship
Sigil: The Flame Phoenix

More members. A lot more. Arthur's eyes bulged a little at the sudden increase, wondering what the hell happened. He knew he'd picked up at least forty or fifty in the floor below. And he was sure that numbers had also increased on the fourth floor as people realised that what he could offer was significant. What he could offer in time, that is.

No, even a minor prod of his mind was enough to clarify the truth of the matter. He was, once again, getting a lot of recruits on the first floor. His organisation was growing incredibly lopsided, with a supremely wide base. Not too surprising, since so many people had no formal organisation to join when they first entered the Tower. And beating the tongs and other gangs likely contributed to that number, made it so that the Durians looked brighter and better.

Or just the winning group at that moment. Too many just joined whichever looked the best. And he was fine with Amah Si picking up anyone who needed help—that was the point of the Durians after all. He just hoped that within that group there were some true companions.

Because the good times only rolled for so long.

"Got to have the good, if you want to know what the bad feels like. Got to be in the mood, to do it right." Arthur muttered to himself, dismissing the Clan Status information at last. He ignored the look the fox was giving him, turning to Casey. "Your turn?"

"Yes, yes . . ." She stepped closer to the fox, waving her token at him. A few moments later, she waved Arthur to come forward. He placed his seal back in the fox's hand and then allowed the prompt to blossom in his mind, wincing a little as the details crept up.

"So..."

"Nothing on this level. One at the top and another much further canyonward, but we'd have to make our way there and it's about fifty feet down. The next closest place is another hundred feet up," Casey said as she raised a finger, pointing up. "Beside the next administrative center. And we'd still have to head sunward to get there, which means we'd be severely restricted on paths."

"Exactly." Getting to this building which they'd managed to spot half by chance rather than any actual planning, what with the random locations people were teleported into on this level, had taken a significant portion of time on their climb. It had also been dangerous, what with them having to actually fight and kill a couple of the grasping ivy monsters rather than just avoid them.

All in all, annoying. And potentially dangerous.

"Not sure it's worth getting the top place either though," Arthur pointed out. "Might as well just head to the seventh floor." Which, being a rest floor, meant they weren't going to be attacked immediately. In fact, the large town built on the seventh floor was a great place to cultivate and they'd be able to build up what they'd need there.

"It's not all curry and gold, you know?" Casey said, softly. "All the major groups are on the seventh floor, and by now, they know who you are."

"You mean, more politics and maybe fighting?" Arthur said.

"And assassinations."

Arthur grunted. He remembered being singled out, being forced to fight on the first floor. On the last few floors none of their enemies had tried to corner them. But from what she said, that might just change again. If they made it to the seventh floor and were underpowered—and he knew he still was underpowered, what with this damn rush—he'd be in trouble.

"Balancing the needs of now, with the needs of the future, really sucks," Arthur said. "*Wo hen bu xiang.*"

Casey winced at the bad Mandarin but had to nod in agreement. "No one likes it. But that's the way it works." She frowned and added. "We should also talk about getting your Mandarin better."

"What?" Arthur said, surprised.

"Mmmm, my family can be a bit, umm . . ." she searched for the word, frowning.

"Racist?"

"No, classist? Sinophist? Whatever. We have a lot of dealings with China, and they get on our families case. So, they do it to the rest of us," she explained. "Cantonese just won't do. Or your accent."

Arthur grunted, running a hand through his hair. Damn Chinese. But . . . "Future. Future. What do we do now?"

Casey shrugged. "Your call. It's your Clan."

"But you've got to have thoughts on this," Arthur said.

"Ask Mel?"

Arthur rolled his eyes but, since they didn't actually need to make a decision immediately, went to get his second-in-command. He still felt, sometimes, that she was the one who should have been chosen as clan head. But then again, that was life. The deserving didn't always get it, just the lucky. Or the foolish. Or the fated.

End of the day, it was what you chose to do with your fortune. The Chinese even had a saying about that: how the first members of a family made the money, the second generation maintained it, and the third wasted it away. Fortune and results were as much a question of choice and making the most of one's opportunities.

"We could use a place to rest up. Maybe power up in the middle of the road, grow stronger," Mel said. "It won't hurt us to stop in the middle and get stronger before we head up. We also don't have to wait around when we do reach the top."

"Or we can just spend as long as we want at the top. We'll have more stones by then," he said and patted his pouch, where the sixth-floor stones they'd been gathering rested. "Easier to cultivate with more of them."

"It's not like we're going out of our way to acquire stones," Mel pointed out. "Not really the floor for it, you know?"

Arthur understood. There were monsters here, but they weren't swarm monsters like the leech swarms. On top of that, some—like the ivy monsters—were really annoying to kill. After all, murdering a plant if you didn't have insecticide and a lot of time was a matter of dealing enough damage for its sap and other properties to stop working. And while some of them had explosive techniques, those cost energy to use. Never mind the stones they lost when someone knocked a monster off its perch and it fell, along with its stone.

"Point. We could farm the top?" Arthur paused, thought about what that would entail, with giant boulders appearing, and then snorted. "Yeah, never mind."

The moment he finished confirming what he wanted from the Tower Administrator, Arthur felt a pricking in his head. He could feel where their new Clan Hall was located. He was not the only one as he watched the majority of his people turn that way too. For a moment, they shared a look of bemusement at the Tower dumping information into their head. If you really thought about it, it could get kind of scary.

Which was the reason most Tower climbers got very, very good at not thinking about the various incongruities, exploitations, and problems there were with the entire Tower experience. Sort of like how Americans figured having non-public healthcare was a good idea, or how dangerous life had gotten, when the person seated next to you on public transportation might just snap and—being a Tower climber and you not being one—could raze through the entire bus before help arrived.

Most people were practical. They focused on survival, not philosophizing.

"Okay, okay. Next!" Arthur turned to the fox. "We got stuff to sell, from the floor below. You buying?"

The fox nodded, though Casey put a hand on his arm. "I wouldn't."

"Why?"

"Prices are better on the next floor."

"Sure, sure. But, our *kawan* here must be bored, right?" Arthur found himself switching into a more casual vernacular, trying to buddy-buddy the Administrator by calling the fox "friend." Not that it was likely to work, but he figured it couldn't hurt. "Won't hurt to see our stuff. Maybe make a better offer? You don't mind, right?"

"It is my function," said the fox.

"Perfect! Let's show him." Arthur waved the group over, whereby they began to unload the various drops. Not that they had a lot, since it was still a Beginner Tower. But they certainly had more drops than on the lower levels. Arthur nodded to Mel who was discreetly taking notes of prices and commentary.

In the end, they chose only to sell the bulkiest of their drops, the ones that were making it difficult to climb. Or the grossest; luckily, the heart and sap of ivy creatures was an actual quest acquisition here. The rest, as per Mel's suggestion, they kept for the next level.

"Will that be all, sirs?"

"One more thing. Map?" Arthur asked.

Perhaps the creature truly had been bored, or perhaps it did look upon Arthur favorably. Regardless the fox provided the next piece of information free of charge. "Not worth buying, but I can show it to you."

"Why?" Now Mel and Arthur and Casey were looking interested.

"The floor changes. The platforms shift, slowly."

"Really?" Arthur said, surprised. Then, he considered the maps that he'd seen, the ones that were sold on eBay and the like at a really cheap price. And how people complained none of these maps were very good, even the hand-drawn ones that people swore were real. It explained a lot. But still . . . "Why doesn't anyone know this?"

To that, of course, the fox had no answer. And even Casey, who usually had some inside information, could not answer him.

In the end, all Arthur could only assume was that it was one of those secrets that the real players kept to themselves. A way to make others waste funds, while keeping themselves in power.

In other words, a way for them to be *ben dan* to everyone else. Real asses.

Chapter 4

They crashed, either inside the administrative center or near it. Once they worked out that there was a small amount of space that was safe from falling rocks—mostly by looking at where other rocks had struck before and the clear space around—the group settled down. Of course they were not just trusting in the impact locations and had someone on watch. After all, the mushroom movers and even the camouflage grass had a tendency to move, if very slowly in the second case.

Arthur was one of the first to crash, woken later in the evening by Jan who happily took his place, curling up in the laid-out blanket and extra clothing that worked as their bedding. Sleeping bags and other comforts like blowup sleeping mats were things that most climbers brought with them, early on.

It rarely took more than a few floors before these items were sold off or lost to the vagaries of climbing for the serious climbers, or left behind at settlements for later. When you had to run in the middle of the night from a fight, when you had to blow up a sleeping mat and then squeeze the air out every day, such creature comforts were much less important. Especially when the added weight could draw the line between life and death.

Not that this kind of mindset was held by all, of course, but it was more common than not. You could have luxuries when you got back to your base, especially if you were making only overnight or two-night trips at most into the wilderness. The rest of the time, you could sleep comfortable.

Out here, a little discomfort might even keep you alive, keep your sleep light in case something snuck up on you.

Back against the wall, Arthur's gaze roamed over the night sky. There were stars up there and a trio of moons, though one was barely thrice the size of a twinkling star. It was just a little more steady, a little more textured than the planets that lay in the distance. The constellations were nothing at all that he recognised, though to be fair he'd only learnt to spot a few and mostly for navigation purposes. They'd not spent much time with that though, what with the alien geography of the Towers that mostly dominated the floors.

Mostly.

A half-hour later, Arthur found Mel slipping in beside him, leaning her head back to watch their right. They sat in companionable silence for a few minutes before Arthur could not help but ask.

"You know, I can't help but wonder how far I've come. How I—we— stack up against the seventh floor." He touched the armour he had slipped back on for his watch. "I've got better equipment now, but not that much better . . ."

"Better than what we have," Mel said, though there was no rancour in her voice.

"Yeah, but compared to our competitors? Everyone else on the seventh?" Arthur grimaced. Their choice to rush ahead was dangerous, so damn dangerous. They were underleveled, underpowered. Even if they'd grinded for cultivation levels and were at the minimum needed, they lacked the various techniques and equipment those who had spent more time in the Tower would have gotten. "How far behind am I?"

Mel smiled a little, then shook her head. "Less than you think. You've improve a lot. Gotten some actual experience under all that training, and that makes you even more deadly." She turned her head and nodded to his seniors who were sleeping, propped up on the other side of the door. "Look at them."

"Exactly! They're three quarters of the way to the second threshold, third transformation. Much more rounded out than I am." He waggled his hand. "I'm still . . . not there yet."

"You've got 17, 18, in Body?" Mel asked.

"18," Arthur replied. He'd managed to eke out another point in the time they'd spent to get up here, and he would have been even closer if he hadn't pushed another point into Spirit to speed up his cultivation.

"Right. Two more points to another Trait. And you've chosen them well, to back up what you need." She continued, slowly, "By now you're as strong as the rest of us who followed you from the first floor, I'd say." She smiled, ruefully. "Except maybe Uswah. Your Yin Body, the better cultivation techniques, they all help."

"Really?" he said, surprised.

"You can't see it because you're so close, but you've come a long way." Mel frowned. "Just don't forget the rest of us, when you start overtaking us."

"I wouldn't. "

"I know you don't think so. But . . . it's easy." Something in her voice made him look at her more closely. She turned away, looking upward as her voice dropped. "I had … a friend. Someone who I was close to. Then, her family, they . . . she changed. Grew colder, grew critical about me, about my family." A shake of her head. "I'm messing this up. A relative of hers, an uncle, got lucky. Joined one of the bigger groups, TG, because he did someone a favour in the Tower. He became someone important there, and he helped his family."

Appropriate. Normal, of course. Pulling up the extended family via your connections and opportunities was a time-honoured tradition. Meant that you had someone to fall back on, someone to help solidify your position. Mutual aid when things got rough for one person. In-built loyalty via blood.

She never even noticed his thoughts, her mind on a distant past. "Started laughing at the rest of us, being a bitch. She thought she was better than us, because she had the chance to get proper training now, get taught an actual cultivation method before even entering the Tower. When she did, she'd be ahead. She'd leave the rest of us behind, so what did we matter anymore?

"Not that she said it that way. She even offered, you know? To help us. Get us jobs, get us contracted. Maybe be mules."

Arthur grimaced. Dangerous jobs, but an opportunity. Not necessarily a bad thing, but . . . "Not much of a help is it? Unless they were offering better contracts?" Because often, the families of slain mules or those who failed to bring the goods over were the ones under the kris.

"I never checked. She just stopped being who I knew, stopped being a friend because she started thinking of what we could do for her." Mel sighed. "So, when you really start being the boss, don't forget about us, eh? We're not just tools."

"I won't," Arthur repeated, just as firmly. He nodded to his two seniors, then at the snoring Rick. "Why do you think I have the Durians, or you guys at all? The goal is to keep growing, together. To make something, of ourselves, of this world. To give people . . . options."

"Good." Then, she elbowed him in the side. "So why are you still talking?"

"What?"

"Why aren't you cultivating? We have a few hours. Pull out a stone and get to it. You might even get somewhere." This time, he was sure she was laughing at him. Not that she was wrong; he should probably get back to utilising the stones to boost himself. After all, for all his complaining, there was quite a bit of energy in the sixth-floor stones. Enough that a few hours at it and he'd be most of the way towards getting a new point.

Worries for later, cultivating for now. End of the day, if he was afraid he didn't have enough strength to beat those on the seventh floor, he just needed to get stronger.

Chapter 5

Cultivation on a higher floor was significantly faster than on the first floor. The sheer density of Tower energy allowed one to pull energy in faster here, though it was not a six-times multiplicative effect. Or even five. It was closer to something like twice as effective as the first floor, which meant that in a less than a half hour, Arthur had enough Tower energy to refine into fractions of a point of refined energy. Well, slightly more, since his trait From the Dregs allowed him to keep a little more energy and refine a little better. Since his overall ability to refine energy was significantly higher, the ideal situation was if he could actually attempt to refine and cultivate at the same time. It would ensure he'd have a constant flow of Tower energy and refined energy.

Of course, his first attempts at that hadn't been cultivating and refining, but drawing from beast stones. The stones were significantly more powerful here, providing refined energy directly. He could draw in significant amounts of refined energy from the stones these days, but this meant that he could—if he was not careful—run his stores of them down faster than the team could collect new stones.

It was why, in the end, most people fell back on Tower energy and cultivating it. It was why, rather than directly cultivating immediately, Arthur was chasing the idea of cultivating and refining at the same time. The problem was, it was not as simple as thinking and doing it.

The process of cultivating Tower energy was governed by the cultivation method he had studied. It focused on efficiently making Tower energy his own, controlling the energy that seeped into his body, that made up parts of the body and that permeated his meridians. It did so by pushing existing energy—his personal chi stores, if you wish—through his meridians and, in the process, drawing Tower energy in. Like a stream, rushing down and drawing in water that flowed along its banks, mixing it together till it became all the same.

Or something like that. Arthur would be the first to admit that the theory of cultivation escaped him beyond the most basic levels. He had always been more interested in the practical aspects—how to do it, how to make it work. And the Night Emperor Cultivation Technique worked very, very well.

The problem was, while the Night Emperor scroll had some minor things to say about refining, the technique left that portion mostly alone. It gave Arthur enough knowledge to improve his refinement a little, but it also highlighted the way it conflicted with his current flow of energy. During cultivation, Tower energy was rushed through the meridians before finally being deposited in the lower dantian. This was a circular flow overall, but it did need the use of the meridians leading to the lower dantian. The same channels that refining energy required.

Now, Arthur had learnt how to coach energy through his body, bypassing meridian flows, pooling or combining streams of energy as needed for his various techniques. It was sort of like rubbing your head and drumming the fingers of that same hand, on time, to two separate beats. You didn't need to learn how to control the individual nerves but the mind itself to make it work.

Well, okay, you also had to learn to control the muscles and grow so conscious of their movements that you could force those muscles to contract and move as you wanted them to, to get the most efficiency from this act. But, you could, theoretically, not bother.

Theoretically, then, Arthur figured it should be possible to both refine and cultivate at the same time. Unfortunately, each time he got started on it, he fell over with a spike of pain. Didn't matter if he started refining first or started cultivating first; the pain would arrive almost immediately as the two disparate energies clashed within his body.

After the fourth and most painful time, as he'd tried to keep forcing it to happen, Arthur lay slumped against the wall, staring into the sky while waiting for his body to finish healing. Thankfully, whatever damage he was doing to himself was being fixed by the Tower—he could tell.

At least here, there was no permanent damaging of cultivation bases like in *xianxia* novels. Oh, it could happen, but it generally required some really stupid things done. And, you know, not having a healing technique. Which, Arthur had to admit, he'd been lucky to stumble onto figuring out. Even if, he was still in the beginning stages of improving his healing technique.

"Is it not possible?" Arthur asked, absently.

"What not possible?" Mel said, raising an eyebrow. She'd left him to squeal and fall over without questioning his motives, though she was obviously curious. Given an opening, she leapt at it like a taxi driver at a *gweiloh*—a Westerner—stumbling out of KL International Airport. Poor sucker was going to get taken for a ride. Literally.

"Cultivating and refining at the same time."

"Are you—!" She hesitated, then shook her head. Mel had seen enough of Arthur to know he really was crazy to some extent. Then again, by experimentation, he'd also managed to figure out a healing technique by chance and effort. But still. "What's the problem?"

Arthur explained, indicating the shooting pain, the damage he felt and when it kept happening. When he was done, she offered a simple solution.

"Why not try another dantian?"

"What?"

"We have three, right?" she said. "So use another one to refine."

"Well, that's because we need to store the refined energy where we have space, in the lower dantian. That's where we have the most space, for Tower energy and refined energy, and . . ." Arthur slowly stopped as he tried to explain why it didn't work. Not just because of the fact that he did store both Tower and refined energy in his dantian—though Tower Energy also suffused the body—but also, there was no reason it had to be stored there. On the other hand . . .

"I don't really know how to open or use the middle or upper dantian," he said. The middle dantian, in the chest, was near the heart and if mismanaged could damage the heart itself. A stopped heart or frozen lungs was never fun. The upper dantian, meanwhile, was where Arthur occasionally built his Refined Energy Darts for the third eye. Again, for the same reason, he didn't build Exploding Energy Darts there when he wasn't certain; he wasn't going to mess around with the exploding variant of his technique. He might survive a heart attack or bloody lungs. But a brain bleed was a lot to ask of the Tower to fix, even if it could.

"Good thing we're at a place where you could maybe buy a cultivation technique that might help with that, no?" Mel said.

Arthur hesitated, then laughed. "Point." Pushing himself up and then failing, clutching at his stomach, he waved a hand at her. "Maybe in a few minutes."

She was kind enough not to laugh.

Once inside the administrative center and speaking softly to the fox attendant who was, surprisingly, still awake, Arthur outlined his needs.

"Do you want a new cultivation technique or a cultivation method?" the attendant asked.

"Technique, not method." He already had a cultivation method and wasn't intending on changing it. Well, perhaps a little, depending on how things worked. Maybe he could alter it a little, but it'd hurt, so a technique was probably better, since techniques like his Refined Energy Dart generally also had secondary effects. He just needed to open and use his dantian; after that, he could figure out the rest, he hoped.

"There are no techniques that open or store energy in the middle or upper dantian directly." A slight pause. "There are techniques that utilise an already opened location, but the opening and utilisation of multiple dantian are the purview of cultivation methods."

"Right, right, but I don't want a new method. Isn't there, I don't know, a cultivation technique that lets me store extra energy in those dantian? Or store an attack or something?" He grinned. "I could store a fully formed Refined Exploding Energy Dart in my upper dantian then."

"What techniques we have still require you to have formed and made full use of them."

"So you do have such techniques!" Arthur said, grinning. "Just sell me one of them, I'll figure out the rest."

"I cannot until you have the required dantian available."

"Oh come on . . . surely you can bend the rules."

"Once you informed me that you did not have an open dantian, I am expressly forbidden from selling techniques that will harm or kill a climber."

"*Tiu!*" Arthur cursed.

"You don't need a cultivation method to open a dantian, though," Lam said, walking over. He looked tired and annoyed, having been woken from his sleep in the administrative center by Arthur's conversation. He made sure to keep his voice low as he added, "Just buy a dantian-breaking pill."

"A what?" Arthur said.

"I can sell that," the fox replied, holding a hand out. "You will not be able to utilise the dantian, of course, till you study a proper cultivation method or technique, but the opening of a second or third dantian is considered an acceptable risk."

Arthur narrowed his eyes, noting that it was an acceptable risk. Still, he handed over his token and then a handful of stones to help cover the cost of the purchase. He had enough contribution points after his time on the fifth floor, though barely. Buying the armour and now this was painful. In fact, he was certain he'd be borrowing someone else's points to buy the technique after.

For now, though, the cultivation pill that was dropped in his hand was a green-yellow marble that swirled in hypnotic patterns.

"So, just eat it?"

"I'd sit down," Lam said, gesturing to a nearby position on the floor. "It's rather painful."

Arthur took his seat on the floor next to the table, glanced at the pill, at Lam, and then shrugged. "Well, in for a penny, in for a pill. At least he's not a shill."

Then, without further ado, he swallowed it.

47

Chapter 6

The process of opening a dantian wasn't like how they described it in xianxia novels. It wasn't as though you were trying to light a fire in your body or break through numerous clogged portions of the body, trying to free up a section of your existence that had not been used. There were no impurities to clean out, because the dantian was always in use.

The process of opening the middle dantian was more akin to building an underused muscle. First, you had to locate it, which required multiple attempts at moving your body part in action until you finally located it. The degree one could do that, and how quickly an individual picked up that particular muscle was dependent upon a few factors, from talent and body awareness to how much time said individual contemplated and reviewed their body.

Once you had found the dantian, you had to work it to grow the dantian. The core was like any muscle, and while the lower core or dantian was the largest by virtue of its location and years of practice and use, it was possible to increase the size of other storage areas through focused effort.

The working of these dantian were a matter of flooding said location with energy, then squeezing it out, expanding the dantian slowly. The more energy one forcibly stored within, the better. Of course, you could damage yourself doing these exercises, and the process of forcing energy through specific meridians into dantian was tightly controlled, or should be. Thus the existence of cultivation methods.

However, the Tower had given them extremely robust bodies with the assumption that mistakes were going to be made. Or so Arthur figured, because one of the simplest ways to create a new cultivation method was a process of elimination. Of trying and testing till it stopped working, or worked better than ever.

The dantian-breaking pill simplified the process. It did it in three parts. Firstly, it contained energy that radiated and moved towards the three dantian in Arthur's body. He no longer needed to strain to locate them; he could tell where they were by the increasing amount of heat within those spots. A simple but effective method of locating the centers in his body.

The second way it aided him was that, in the movement of energy to each of those locations, he also noticed where and how the energy flowed through his various meridians to reach the location. It happened a little too fast in the beginning for him to do anything beyond vaguely note which portions were warmer, but it was there. He could, if he paid attention, locate the meridians as energy coursed through them.

Not that he had a lot of time. Because his upper and middle dantian were getting really, really warm. That was the part that was considered painful. He could sense the growing pain, and instinctively, Arthur squeezed down on those sections. Most of his attention was on the middle dantian, the place he intended to test his theory, and squeezing on this dantian relieved the pain immediately.

It was like getting hold of a three-part bladder that was slowly filling up with water. By squeezing down on the bags, you shifted and made the water within flow around, relieving the pressure. To keep the pain regulated, he just needed to squeeze on both his lower dantian and middle one at the same time, regularly. Doing so relieved the pain, allowing the pill energy to collect at more reasonable locations.

That was where the third benefit of the pill came into play. It was how the energy slowly dissipated, as it accelerated the healing process of the body, specifically the meridians and the core. After all, to "break" a dantian open, he needed to make it large enough, make himself conscious enough of its location, that the dantian could then be used for other things. Which meant a process of slowly enlarging the core over months and years had to be done quickly.

So. Let it fill, keep an eye on where the energy flowed when it entered and left each section. When it grew too painful, when his body felt too stretched, he would squeeze and force the energy out, like a sponge being wrung. Then wait, as the exhausted muscles soaked in healing energy from the pill, grew larger and stronger, before he proceeded to repeat the entire process over again.

Instinctively, Arthur knew that the longer he could hold out on squeezing the energy, the better off he would be. Since the pill itself had a specific duration, he needed to make best use of the pill before it faded away, at which point he would be back to doing this the old way. Though he would be better off now, because he at least knew which cultivation streams to bring to the middle dantian, if he paid attention.

Even so, it was not easy.

Like slowly filling hot pockets in his body, coals glowing. He felt like he had a pair of balloons within him that were blowing up with warm air; and if he didn't squeeze some of the air out now, they'd pop. Luckily, squeezing into the surrounding tissues and meridians didn't seem to appreciably increase the tension around a non-squeezed dantian. Arthur knew it had something to do with energy density, the difference between second and third and future transformations, where the energy held within a body was just not as compact as they could be.

Not that he was paying attention to that right now, not with the pain filling him. Just that it did mean he wasn't going to pop the upper dantian by squeezing the middle one. Luckily, freeing up space in other two dantian pulled energy into them, relieving the pressure of his upper dantian at the same time.

Again, Arthur recalled reading about a cultivation method that made use of this phenomenon, that made full use of all three dantian, because it was so effective at pulling energy through the body. Supposedly, the cultivation method was a three-star one. It was even purchasable on the open market outside, but the price and need to have three dantian open meant there were almost no adherents. At least not at the Beginner level.

Arthur was no stranger to pain, no stranger to the constant ache of the body that pushing oneself to the limit entailed. He'd spent more than one day standing in a supermarket store freezer, utilising it as a poor man's ice bath for a little extra help moving goods back and forth later on. He understood pain.

And even with all that experience, all that knowledge, all the mental and emotional callouses he'd grown, he was not sure he would voluntarily take another dantian-opening pill.

Squeeze. Relax. Breathe, wait with patience. Grit your teeth as the pain grew, as the body struggled to heal itself. Some people thought healing was painless, but they'd never had nerves reawaken as the body patched itself together.

Hold. Hold. Hoooold.

Squeeze.

Do it all over again.

And again.

By the time Arthur had sense to pick himself off the ground, wiping away the sweat and the spit that had dribbled down his mouth, the day was well underway. Seated not far from him, cultivating with a watchful eye out, was Uswah.

"Report?" Arthur croaked, then gratefully accepted the bottle of water to clear his dry throat.

"Rick, Casey, and Mel are hunting. The others are inside, cultivating. We're ready to go, and I'll signal the others once you're good." She looked up, eyeing the sun that was headed directly overhead. "Best get moving, no?"

"Yeah, we got a long way to go to the clan building." He gestured outwards. "Get them to come in. I got to get one thing sorted, then we're good to go."

"*Boleh*," she affirmed.

Slipping in, Arthur glanced at the notification he finally let bloom, grinning a little.

Middle Dantian Opened!
Additional (+6) Tower Energy or (+3) Refined Energy may be stored.

Now, he just had to figure out how to make use of it.

Chapter 7

The swinging vines high above their heads kept coming, even though they'd already sliced a half-dozen of the vines away. A pair of spears were hanging in the air, being swung around by vines and nearly clipping the group. Luckily, the vine creature was blind to its own attacks and so any attacks were coming in with the blunt end of the spears, the creature not seeming to grasp the idea of using the pointy end against its opponents.

In fact, the spears were less dangerous than the actual vines themselves. The variant vine, more common now as they climbed higher and across the canyon to their resting spot, had sharpened steel vines and leaves. Catching a face full of vine no longer simply stung or left thin cuts from sharpened and roughened edges but could now lay open faces and necks.

Normally, the group would have avoided the creatures entirely, but chance and luck had brought them to this particular platform series. There was no way up except through and across the ledge they were trying to sneak past, bouncing ahead canyonward and then turning around to strike at the mutated vine. All well and good, but they had to get through the lashing vines first.

"Shoot it, will you?" Arthur growled, as he ducked another spear and stabbed upwards. He felt his spear head grate along the vine, then puncture through suddenly and tear into the vine. It stopped swinging around as much, at which point Yao Jing jumped and grabbed the spear shaft and yanked, hard. He managed to reacquire it at the cost of nearly bowling over Jan who had switched to a parang and was swinging the edged blade into vines that threatened Arthur from the back.

"Oy! Careful, *lah*," she cried.

"I'm. Trying!" Casey snarled. Back two platforms, she was forced to draw and fire her arrows, lobbing them up and across to land onto the vines. Not only did she have to fire blindly because she couldn't actually see where the main body was, with the angle of a swinging trap ahead; she had to time her attacks or else see her arrows get knocked off course.

Even so, she at least could hit it. Rick's bullets moved in a much straighter line, which meant that he was mostly useful for blowing up or tearing apart vines that hung over the edge. He had switched out his pistols for the shotgun in this case, the big slugs a better fit for the problem right now. Even so, the quiet boom of the weapon had slowed down as he reloaded and tried to conserve ammunition.

"One . . . moment!" Uswah grunted, her hand raised high as she yanked downwards with shadow tendrils formed right under the overhanging platform. They swept up and grabbed a bunch of the vines, holding them tight together and constraining their movements. She strained, all three of her shadow tendrils gripping the bunch of tentacles together, her face covered in sweat.

Luckily, she didn't need to hold it for long as Rick's shotgun boomed, tearing apart the vines. A moment later, Lam jumped high and swung his parang, forming an edge and extending the weapon and then using a Focused Strike to sever the rest of the tendrils. His attack was not without cost though, for one of the other swinging vines slammed into him, sending him away from his landing spot. Out into open air.

Luckily, Mel was watching for this. She jumped, straight out into the air, and then formed a cloud beneath her foot. Kicking sideways on the cloud, she reversed trajectory, slamming into Lam and sending the pair of them onto the platform again, only for their legs to clip the edge. They crashed to the ground, cursing, but the attacks had created the necessary opening.

Both Leia and Eric had been waiting for this opportunity. Together, the pair raced across the area. Eric went high and ahead, swinging his pair of parang, tearing into the few remaining vines that hung in the way. He was infusing his body with energy, similar to Arthur's own Heavenly Sage's Mischief but it was a short-lived technique. On the other hand, it had the advantage of having a much higher increase and minimum. One of the reasons he was going high, because each swing cut through the steel-like vines with ease, even hanging in air.

A couple of steps behind, Leia raced across the falling vines, free to make the leap across space to the platform above. She managed it with ease, spun, and then leaned backwards before lurching forward. She threw her spear like a javelin, arcing it high and down. As it flew, a light gathered around its tip, a light that exploded that when the spear touched down inside the vine.

Now the vine creature tossed and turned, twisting around. Moments later, following the smoke and the thrashing, an arrow from Casey's bow landed in the midst. Then, another. More thrashing. The creature pulled damaged vines backwards into its core to protect against the attacks, leaving only a couple behind to continue to attempt to grab at its attackers.

A spear was flung away, Mel crying out as she watched her weapon plunge into the depths of the canyon.

Taking the momentary break, Arthur and Jan jumped across to the other side, joining Eric, while Yao Jing kept an eye out for more lashing vines, ready to sweep it all aside with his weapon.

Arthur grunted, finally no longer directly beneath the creature. He could see parts of it, the spear stuck in its body, the energetic arrows that were fading and leaving behind wounds that leaked yellow sap like alien blood. He leapt straight upwards, formed a cloud beneath his feet as he reached the top of his range, and leapt again.

Now, he was looking down and could see they'd all been missing the center of the creature by a bit. The main cluster had been so protected by vines that all the attacks had been the equivalent of wounding its limbs. Not anymore. He released a Refined Exploding Energy Dart from his third eye. Right through the gaps, coming down at an angle the mutated vine had not expected.

It tore through a flailing vine, exploded moments later, and tore a giant hole in the main body, a hole that had begun to leak. Then, he could not see further as he landed. Raising his hand, he called out to the group.

"Hold! Don't waste energy, it's nearly dead." He knew it just needed to finish dying. Damn plants were the worst at that. You could land a fatal blow but it'd still keep thrashing for a bit till all the sap had leaked out and it could no longer move. Between all the severed vines, the open wounds, and his last blow, it was dead.

It just needed time to figure that out.

In the meantime, Arthur scanned the surroundings, grunted, and waved a hand around. "Mushrooms incoming. Also, pretty sure that's camograss coming up on you, Eric." He pointed behind Eric who jumped forward and away before spinning around, eyes wide. No one wanted to get grabbed by those. It hurt—a lot—since the camograss had razorblades for its grass and collapsed inwards, turning and grinding at the body. While not necessarily deadly immediately, it could wear a climber down.

Well, a team that wasn't made up of healers like them, at least.

"Rick. Casey. No playing around, get over here!" He watched as the pair stopped killing the mushrooms that were coming at them and made their way over gingerly. Yao Jing was still on the bottom platform along with Uswah.

They'd regather, finish killing the monsters, grab the big beast stone— and he was certain it was a big—

from the variant vine and then keep going. He could see their new base, not far away. And then, finally, he'd get to read the cultivation technique he'd purchased.

To say he was a little impatient was an understatement.

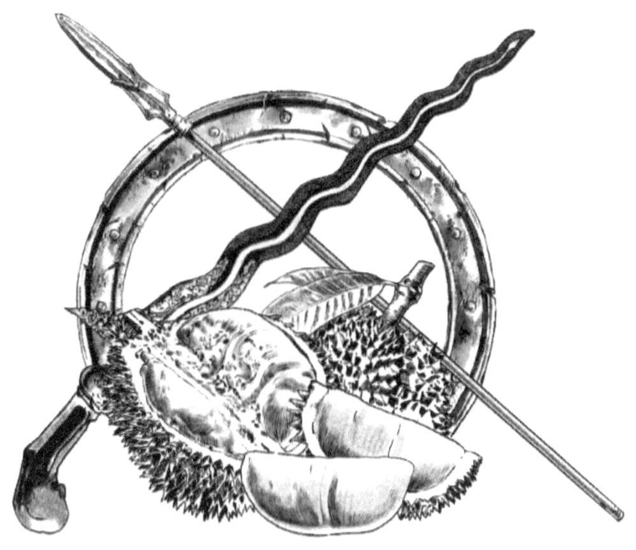

Chapter 8

Even seeing it in person, Arthur still found the residence they'd picked out a little hard to believe. Knowing from the Administrator that the platforms moved a little, he wondered how long this one was going to last, what with it being half-built into a cave. He wondered if the cave was attached to the platform, or if they had just lucked out. When he asked, Casey could only shrug.

"Don't know. Maybe they bought it from the Tower?" she said. It was a possibility, though the kind of farming that would have been needed to make a permanent change like that in the Tower was outside the range and possibility for ordinary individuals. It would take thousands of points, literal years of work.

And what cultivator would do that, just to get a place they'd literally leave behind the next time they progressed? Especially when they couldn't even take it with them, or ever visit it again? Unless they were stuck and unable or unwilling to go further, it would make no sense.

"Where you get wood, ah?" Jan asked, staring at the structure. Even if most of it was in the cave, a large awning and opening was made of wood, with gaps covered by cloth and plastic tarps.

"Again, I don't know," Casey said, exasperated. "It's not something I studied." She paused, then looked at Lam. "Do you?"

He shrugged and waved the others in. With the wide opening, there was no way to stop mushrooms from coming in. "We're going to need a guard."

Arthur stepped in under the wide awning and received the usual notification.

Clan Head Confirmed

Control of Benevolent Durians Clan Building (Sixth Floor, Tower 2895) Confirmed

Type: Residence

Building Bonus Chosen: Security (Town Guard assigned)

Total Number of Floors: 5

Total Number of Residents: 04

Total Number of Rooms: 1

He grunted, glancing to the side where a Tower Guard was forming. Then he pointed. "Don't think that's gonna be good enough."

Lam scratched his head. "Let's see how they do against the mushrooms first, eh? If they get overwhelmed..."

"Tower Guard beaten?" Eric snorted. "You dumb or what?" He strolled right past the man, even as Arthur busied himself with giving both Casey and Lam guest rights. Once that was done, he surveyed his new domain. No need to poke at the wireframe design, what with it being a single room, albeit gigantic. The cave itself was lost to darkness further ahead, such that he was forced to squint and the others to pull out various lamps.

"Anyone got wood? I start a fire, okay?" Yao Jing called out from within.

"Oy! You *nak mati?*" Jan raged. "We choke to death, you idiot."

In the meantime, others who actually wanted sleep or rest had headed deeper in. This included Mel and Uswah, and Arthur soon joined them. The darkness didn't bother him, though the lack of fresh air probably would become a problem as the accumulated stink arrived.

But that was a problem for future Arthur.

Present Arthur had a cultivation technique to study.

Poket Simpanan Tua

Storage pocket for discrete cultivation techniques.

Effect: Allows storage of a discrete cultivation technique in the upper or middle dantian that may then be unleashed without further expansion of energy. Stored techniques can last up to a maximum of seven days before breaking down.

Arthur sighed at the name. Old person's storage pocket. Someone up in the Tower had a sense of humour. Not a good one, but at least a sense of humour. More importantly, the scroll allowed him to understand how to use the dantian, how to store things within it, how to push and separate energy within. He just had a few questions.

Would there be other energy forms in there when he stored it? If he did store this technique in his dantian, would the additional storage amounts mentioned when he first opened the dantian go away? Was he somehow cramming this in there as well or was it a replacement? He could already feel his body mixing the energies together, making use of the extra space he'd created. If he had to shove it all out, he had a feeling it'd hurt again.

On top of that, he also wanted to know how this Poket managed to keep an entire technique stored in a dantian. The Tower specified this would be a "discrete technique," so he needed to test that out a lot more. He figured the Refined Energy Dart would be something similar to that, or perhaps even Focused Strike. However, it was possible that full-body techniques might not work, but that was his guess. Unfortunately, there wasn't any handy wiki on hand to consult nor was the technique something he'd ever studied. There was, after all, only so much he could learn, and opening a dantian had not been high on his list of skills.

"You keep sighing," Uswah said.

"I'm wondering why I didn't just bring a tablet with a full download of the wiki with me," Arthur said, grumpily. "I bet we could make some good money just offering access to it."

"Tried. The electronics break down," Uswah said. "Lasts about six months, sometimes less. The bigger players keep some, and people occasionally buy access but it's not worth it."

"Oh?" Arthur said.

"Other more advanced Towers possibly, but we're a Beginner Tower. How many techniques do you have?" she said.

Arthur paused, considered, and then nodded. He saw the point. There was only so much time you could spend learning techniques, never mind there being an upper limit when the study of such techniques got in the way of one another. It took a long time before things became unconscious habits, and unlearning old techniques were a pain. It was why most beginners tried not to purchase too many techniques. Even if you weren't pushing to ascend, having just a few techniques that you knew how to use well and could pull out at a moment's notice was generally the best way.

Still, he did wish he had access to one right now. Perhaps he might have been able to find the perfect technique, though "perfect" was always going to be subjective. And dependent on what the floor had to offer.

"Okay, okay. Time to cultivate." He pushed aside the thoughts, squinting as he read over the cultivation technique once again. He needed it memorised before he could really begin practise. Luckily, he could see well enough between his traits, his Yin Body, the flames that Yao Jing had started near the entrance, and a nearby lamp.

After scanning through the document and then carefully reading it over twice more, Arthur could not help but break out into a wide grin. This was even more perfect than he could have imagined. The process of storing a cultivation technique required him to pull it apart, shelter it in a separate bubble of energy and intent, and then keep it stored away until it was ready to be unleashed. The actual usage of the stored technique was quite simple, barely even a fifth of the document itself.

However, the majority of the work was teaching the climber how to separate and store this cultivation technique. Which made sense, of course, but what had Arthur grinning like a loon—and what, exactly, was a loon and why was the bird grinning so much, he had no idea—was the way the document taught how to store a technique.

Specifically, it began the process by teaching the climber to break apart a small portion of energy—generally, refined energy—and use it as a "bundle" that could then be contained. The basic principle was to learn to contain this bubble of energy in his upper or middle dantian for the full seven-day period before he placed a full cultivation technique within.

It was an incredibly safe method, since the backlash from losing a bundle of refined energy in the wrong location was minimal. However, it also meant that, for Arthur's purpose, he could not only learn how to store and prise apart energy; eventually, he should be able to focus his dantian and cultivate using separate processes. Or at least, that was the idea.

After all, while all this training would let him understand how to use his energy, how to store and separate it, and even gave him some idea about why the energy conflicted when he tried to channel and cultivate them at the same time, it still didn't mean he could do it.

He would have to just try, but at least, this new technique was a way forward. One that he delved into immediately, beginning the laborious process of teasing refined energy from his system into his middle dantian.

And hey, worst case scenario, in the long run, he might even have a new technique he could use.

Chapter 9

By unspoken agreement, the team had stayed in their new clan building for nearly a week. Arthur managed to get quite a decent degree into learning his new technique, the Poket Simpanan Tua. He was able to contain a bundle of energy in his middle dantian, though right now he was practicing keeping it contained and running. The biggest problem was whenever he tried to do anything beyond sitting still and concentrating on the containment.

At the same time, while he would have loved to progress in refining and cultivating at the same time, he had hit a dead end. Even if he had a second open dantian—and he could, with some degree of focus shift energy around—he was still struggling to keep the energies separated enough to allow him to refine and cultivate at the same time. The monster core energy was just too foreign, and the necessary shift from Tower energy to his own refined energy required him to pass it through meridians in his lower dantian. Till he worked out how to shift the refinement process and alter his Night

Emperor cultivation practice to use the middle dantian as well, he could not do both at the same time.

Frustrating, but the continual process of pulling refined energy apart, bundling it, and containing it was awarding him progress in other things. Funnily enough, the Tower was giving him additional percentage points on his Simultaneous Flow technique and his Night Emperor—which hinted that he was learning something, even if he wasn't sure how it all fit together just yet.

Sort of like sorting jigsaw puzzle pieces while missing the big picture and doing it wearing welding goggles. Everything was a blur, viewed through tiny slits, but something was coming together.

Kind of like the Benevolent Durians.

Now it was time to get moving, to finishing off this level. So far, things had gone pretty well, and even if he wasn't as strong as he wished to be, Casey had gotten that impatient look in her eyes. So long as they stayed together though, they should be fine. Cultivating on next floor would also be more useful anyway, since there would be a higher density of energy up there. And it's not as though he was totally weak . . .

A twitch of his eye and a thought had his latest stats pull up.

Cultivation Speed: 2.573 Yin
Energy Pool: 27/27 (Yin) + (6/6)
Refinement Speed: 0.1421
Refined Energy: 2.41 (30) + (0/3)

Attributes and Traits
Mind: 15 (Multi-Tasking, Quick Learner, Perfect Recall)
Body: 19 (Enhanced Eyesight, Yin Body, Swiftness, Fast Twitch Faster)

Spirit: 12 (Sticky Energy, From the Dregs)

Techniques

Night Emperor Cultivation Technique

Focused Strike

Accelerated Healing – Refined Energy (Grade IV)

Heavenly Sage's Mischief

Refined Energy Dart

Bark Skin

Seven Cloud Stepping Technique

Partial Techniques

Simultaneous Flow (137.8%)

Yin-Yang Energy Exchange (72.8%)

Pocket Simpanan Tua (72%)

Quite the expansion from when he started. It annoyed him that the Yin-Yang Energy Exchange never seemed to clear itself off his board of partially-learned techniques. If he ever had the time to practise, he would want to get it done. However, it degraded each time he progressed in any of his attributes or cultivation techniques, as his Yin Body altered even further and made it more difficult to make the technique work. He feared that even if he did ever learn it fully, it would eventually degrade anyway.

In the meantime, he had two full points to use. The first attribute point available he'd sunk in the moment they had arrived, upgrading his Body attribute so that he had a week to get used to it while they were in a safe environment. No reason to make it more difficult, especially as they took small jaunts outside to collect monster cores and break up the monotony.

Now, he had only one more point left to sink it into Body before getting another trait. So far, he'd leaned into a fast, nimble build. When he found the time, he'd probably look more into maneuverability options too, something to boost his speed even further—and strength, because speed came from strength too, like the Heavenly Sage's Mischief.

The question, as always, was to shore up weaknesses or to double-down on his strengths.

Swiftness made him generally faster, an overall boost. He had seen its effects, the equivalent of a few points of Body compared to others of his level. Add in his training and he was generally faster than opponents at his level, just because he didn't waste as much time moving what was unnecessary. Economy of movement.

Always an advantage.

Fast-twitch reflexes gave him explosive power. It wasn't like some of the other traits like Cat-like Reflexes that sped up how fast he reacted to things by shortening and speeding up the neutron impulses between muscles and brains. People who had those traits were great at the ruler-snatching, buzzer-smacking competitions. Fast-twitch instead made him more explosive when the signals reached his brain. It meant he could harness more energy, more explosive power. It basically made him hit faster and harder.

So, not just speed.

The obvious answer to all this was add Lightning Reflexes, Cat-like Reflexes, or Smoother Neuron Pathways or any of the other traits that did mostly the same thing. Add one of those traits to his Fast-Twitch Reflexes and he would be reacting and moving well before the majority of people on his level, especially those who didn't focus on speed.

He would even be faster than most of those who had gone through their third transformation, probably. He'd have to test it out himself to be certain, but it was a possibility. Even if he only matched their speed, it would keep him alive and then, it was a matter of skill. And techniques.

On the other hand, he could also make himself tougher, stronger, or more perceptive. Relying on his sight had a net negative, when so many creatures used techniques to blend themselves into the background or warped the very light around themselves. He knew that was a common method of hiding; so the options were, again, to double down on his sensing strategies—either expanding on them to add better hearing, for example— or upgrading Enhanced Eyesight further. Night Vision or Infrared Vision would add a weird halo effect to his sight, he knew, but would become even more useful at night. Night Vision just expanded his ability to discern in low-light conditions, while Cat Eyes was both disturbing and useful. It literally altered the shape of the face and eyes, which allowed the climber to take in more light like a cat's eyes did. It was a subtle difference, but this trait came with an obvious physical tell.

In the end, Arthur could not help but think he should lean on pushing himself forward on the same pathway: speed. Eventually, he'd focus on upping his Spirit, adding to his cultivation speed and making it easier to manipulate energy. But . . . for now, greater speed was the way to go.

Pouring the refined energy into his Body attribute, feeling it ripple through him and affect his soul and nerves, and then choosing Lightning Reflexes had him shuddering a little, as the Tower rebuilt him. He knew the effects would be most stark now, but it would take a whole few hours to settle down as his Tower-made body completed its integration.

Before he could second-guess himself, he poured another point into Spirit, upping his ability to manipulate energy. He could feel its effects almost immediately as controlling the energy within him was made simpler. It did bring up the question if certain techniques were barred from use based off attribute minimums. Not directly, of course, but practically.

Something to think about for later. For now, he pulled up his stats once more.

Cultivation Speed: 2.673 Yin

Energy Pool: 27/28 (Yin) + (6/6)

Refinement Speed: 0.1421

Refined Energy: 0.48 (32) + (0/3)

Attributes and Traits

Mind: 15 (Multi-Tasking, Quick Learner, Perfect Recall)

Body: 20 (Enhanced Eyesight, Yin Body, Swiftness, Fast Twitch Faster, Lightning Reflexes)

Spirit: 13 (Sticky Energy, From the Dregs)

Not a lot of Refined Energy left, but he would make do. He was nearly out of stones, so he'd just have to rely on other techniques. Perhaps, with his rather immense Energy Pool, he should consider learning the basic Energy Dart, which relied on Tower energy. It wasn't as damaging as his Refined Energy Dart, of course, but it had the advantage of making use of his large pool of non-refined energy.

Later. He'd worry about that later.

"We good to go?" he asked those around.

The team was looking fit. He could see the subtle changes of refined energy poured into their bodies. Sometimes a smoother flow of energy, sometimes in the spring of a step or a gleam in the eye. In Yao Jing's case, even more brawn. Seriously, he was beginning to look like Bolo Yeung, if he'd been fed on a diet of steroids and Tower energy since young.

Which, you know, don't do that.

"Waiting for you, boss." Jan as usual was the first to answer, grinning cockily. Something was different around her, and it took Arthur a moment to realise what it was. An aura, gathered around her, that made the air spark.

Oh, that'd be interesting.

"Then let's go."

Chapter 10

They went through the next few platforms like hawker food through the intestines of a newly arrived *gweilo*. Or, like a katana goes through the neck of an unarmed civilian, waiting to be dropped into a mass grave in a school. A little too racist? Maybe; but then again, Arthur had never promised not to be racist. Or, for that matter, had the Japanese ever apologised or even acknowledged the atrocities they'd committed in Malaysia or other parts of South East Asia in the previous century. Then again, why would they?

The Westerners might decry racism within their countries—and it was bad, or so he'd heard—but it was nothing like the way a whole country hated another. When you had thousands of years of stored animosity, all of it recorded and remembered, from personal tales to long history lessons at school, it was hard to let go. Especially when one side or the other failed to acknowledge or even think they had done anything wrong.

Which was why Arthur was quite happy to acknowledge he was a massive, raging erection. But at least knowing he was one gave him a starting point to improving. If he wanted to improve.

More importantly, and more pertinently to the matter at hand, his new Lightning Reflexes trait—in combination with Fast Twitch, Swiftness, and his ability to pick out minute changes in musculature or landscape—was having some weird feedback effects. In particular . . .

He watched as the vine swung towards him, moving at what he knew was objectively at the same speed it had been before they had arrived in the clan building. But to his newly improved Body and senses, the vine might as well have been moving through slow motion.

It wasn't exactly like those speedster movies, where the hero had all the time in the world to look things over, make a decision, and act. On the other hand, it wasn't that far from it. He could feel himself making quicker decisions, feel as though he had more time to move out of the way as he saw the beginning of an attack long before it transmitted all the way. A minor shift in weight, a twitch in the vine starting near its base. He saw it all.

When he did decide to move, though, things went a little haywire.

It should have been simple. Lean backwards, let the vine pass over his head, missing him by an inch. Then, move forwards, throwing his body into a lunge with his spear leading the way, tear a hole in the gap between two vines he knew would appear in half a second.

Except, when he leaned backwards, he moved not an inch and a half like he meant to. He moved nearly half a foot. The vine that should have just passed by him had swung far away. And as he shoved himself forward, he nearly collided with the vine's trailing ends as he moved too fast.

Also, too fast was his retaliation. Instead of finding a gap between swinging vines that should have appeared like he'd planned, he'd pinned the other vine in place, his tip punching all the way through with barely any effort. That was, of course, the other side effect of moving faster than ever—the greater force he could apply.

He managed to hit his target and kill the vine monster, even if it was much more sloppily than he had ever expected. He still had to dodge a half-dozen more swings as he widened the initial wound, but that was easy enough. Even if he did feel like a jerking marionette managed by an amateur puppeteer.

"Eh, boss. You okay, ah?" Yao Jing asked, wandering over and reaching in, tearing apart vines to dig into the creature they belonged to. These higher-level plants had a nasty set of thorns on them, but Yao Jing had added to his knowledge of Wood Body and combined it with a greater defense trait, allowing him to grab hold of the plants barehanded and not bleed.

Much.

"Getting used to my new Body and traits." Breaching the 20-point attribute level seemed to have been a whole new explosion in energy, and the traits working together were even more synergistic than he'd expected. It was going to take him a bit to get used to.

"Heh. You look like a second-year student, trying to ape his seniors," Leia called out from above. She had moved ahead of the group, intercepting with Rick a bunch of mushroom men before they managed to disrupt the team.

"Whatever," Arthur said, grumpily. "I took care of the vine myself, you know." Of course, there were two vines on this platform, each of them covering for one another, and if not for the rest of the team, he'd have to step back and blast away from a distance. As it was, with its attention focused on Yao Jing and Eric, he had managed to slip through close enough to finish the creature without being subjected to two vine monsters.

Though . . .

"I'd like to try both next time."

"My turn next!" Uswah called out. "I only need one, though. And only at the start. Someone can have the second."

"That'd be me," Lam said, firmly. "Though, I don't have much to test. I only need the one."

Arthur looked around, searching for objections. There were none, so he waved the team on. Uswah moved ahead of him along with Lam, so he fell back to join Mel at the back, keeping an eye out for more trouble and more traps. Now that they had actually spotted the traps, it had grown quite boring dodging them. Even if they came down faster and were more numerous the higher they climbed, they were only a real concern when the monsters started arriving.

Arthur and Mel managed another couple of platforms, literally jumping upwards on cloud steps in one case, before they broke the silence.

"What did you get?" Arthur asked.

"From cultivating?"

"No. When you slept with Rick," he said sarcastically.

The sudden silence and blush made Arthur jerk his head to the side and nearly fall over. He could not, would not believe it. Except, of course, it was true.

"YOU DID SLEEP WITH HIM!" he whisper-shouted in horror. "HOW? WHEN?"

"It happened," she said, then fell silent. Shrugging, she continued, "When we were out gathering stones. And it wasn't anything."

"But why?"

"He's rather good looking? A woman has needs?" Mel shrugged. "I don't see how this is your business."

"As your . . ." Arthur shook his head, cutting himself off. "No, I can't do this. Won't do this. It's just not the kind of miss I'd take." He grimaced. "Whatever. Sleep with who you want."

"I will." She paused, then added, "Anyway, I didn't get much of an upgrade. I'm focusing on Mind and Body mostly." She grinned a little. "I like the Refined Energy Darts, but they're a lot of energy to use. So if I can speed up and process energy faster, it will be better." She smiled slightly. "Anyway, not as though I'm being fed a ton of monster cores."

Arthur grunted, but he forced himself not to hunch inwards. He knew the reason he was being given the majority of cores; without him, the entire clan would crumble. So, he was not going to feel guilty about it. Or at least, he'd try to tell himself he wasn't going to feel guilty.

"Any good traits?"

"Recaptured Energy," Mel said. "Makes my workings more refined, so that when I use a technique, a small portion of it comes back to me."

"Sounds like one of mine, From the Dregs."

"You pull energy from your stores, from your body to fuel your actions," she explained. "It's broad ranging and always working, even making it cheaper for you to exist. Useful for when you exit the Tower even. I recover spent energy, which is only useful if you're using a technique. On the other hand . . ."

"It's more." Arthur paused, considered his options and chose not to use his Cloud Stepping method. Instead he backed off two steps and took off running, jumping to catch the edge of the next platform that reared all too far away and then swinging himself up. He landed in a crouch, feeling the earth give way only slightly beneath his fingers.

"Right. Yours doesn't even bother giving a percentage amount to your return, but mine does." Mel chuckled. "Only a few percent, but it's there."

Arthur nodded in reply, then looked at both Uswah and Lam. Neither one seemed to have added to their number of techniques, or even significantly increased their attributes. At least on first glance. Then Lam took a blow to the chest, head-on from one of the bunched vines—a spear by any other name—and just shrugged it off. Now, he was wearing a breastplate, but still . . .

"*Wah lau!*" Arthur shouted in surprise. He exclaimed again a moment later, when a dark tendril managed to slip in between a wound, pierce deep into the vine that Uswah was fighting, and then explode in a flurry of spike shadow tendrils.

"I guess they've improved." Arthur grinned.

It was always nice to see people power up.

Chapter 11

Making their way to the top was the simple part of this platform, once they had taken a moment to power up and understand the system. Spending an extra day, having to occasionally wake up and move away from a falling rock or deal with creepgrass, was annoying, and none of them were their best; but it did mean they managed to make it to the top rested.

For various definitions of rested, at least.

The most annoying bit was the last portion, where the swinging axes that went vertically across the canyon walls became horizontal axes, utilizing wood and cane arms that swung endlessly. There was barely a gap between the moving axes, such that you had to time things with utmost care or get bisected.

Or take other precautions.

"Move, move, move!" Rick called out.

Arthur would have chosen to speak, but he was currently pre-occupied with holding an axe still. He wasn't the only one, being shoulder-carried by

Yao Jing who was acting as his legs. Much like a pair of medieval acrobatic fools. Together, they were holding at bay the axe that was meant to be swinging, legs and arms trembling as they strained.

"Give us more space then!" Mel snapped, as she helped the others to jump upwards, lacing her fingers together to boost them over the cliff.

Arthur could, intellectually, understand her point. After all, the gap he and Yao Jing and Leia and Eric had created by holding separate axes apart was barely large enough for one person to be tossed upward. Carefully, of course. He could understand it, but he certainly wasn't going to contradict Rick either.

After all, even with the Heavenly Sage running through him, giving him additional strength, both he and Yao Jing and his seniors on the other side were struggling to hold back the axes. With each moment, the amount of pressure increased and the chance grew of them slipping and letting the axes swing, catching themselves—or one of their friends.

One after the other, their teammates grew in number at the top of the cliff. Until Rick, jumping and then engaging his technique and literally being dragged upwards by the expelled energy in a weird, almost frozen pose, was up there, leaving only the four of them behind.

"Seniors, you first!" Arthur called.

"No, you. Go!" The grunting strain brooked little argument. Not that Arthur intended to, because a moment of consideration told him why he should be moving. If he got caught, it was over; and Yao Jing, the person clamped to him and holding his legs, was not as skilled with a movement technique.

Which did leave the question of how to vacate the space, but he had some time to consider the problem.

"HOLD ON!" Arthur called out below, clamping his legs firmly around Yao Jing's upper body. The man gripped tighter, not understanding but following orders anyway. And then, to his surprise, Arthur lifted him upwards, by curling his body up and then inwards, beginning to swing Yao Jing under a swinging wooden arm.

Immediately, of course, the arm began moving, adding to the momentum. Rotating in the opposite direction with his empowered curl, Arthur lifted Yao Jing inwards and upwards even as he swung him under the axe. It was a dangerous maneuver, though, because the swinging arm would enter the gap in the cliff face soon enough, smashing Arthur into the wall if he did not move fast enough.

Doing the world's most dangerous levered curl and plank, Arthur used all the momentum given to him and everything that the Tower had enabled his body to do, along with the explosive energy from his fast-twitch muscles, to almost throw Yao Jing into the air. He then finished the rotation, curling up on the other side of the axe arm as he let it go, no longer needing the pivot point. By that point, he'd released Yao Jing, who, unfortunately, was a touch too slow in releasing Arthur.

That left him tumbling weirdly, and only the formation of a cloud under his arm, just above where the swinging axe head popped out, kept him from getting skewered. Yao Jing, still in the air and much higher, had an easier time of it as he righted himself and then was grabbed by Rick who yelped at Yao Jing's weight but pulled him to safety.

Arthur just threw himself into a sideways cartwheel, off the cloud and onto the cliff. He missed sticking his landing with his foot, sliding a little on the wet grass but managing to not sprawl on his face. All in all, as far as he was concerned, it was a successful operation. Maybe not cool, but effective.

Again, kind of like the Durians.

Grinning, Arthur took back his spear from Mel when she handed it to him, rotating his shoulders as he ignored the complaining Yao Jing, and wandered over to the edge of the cliff. His seniors had dropped their own swinging axe, though they had chosen not to be flashy about coming up. Instead, he watched as Leia held a hand up, a glowing green tangle of energy in it.

"What's that?" Arthur called out.

"New technique. Or old. Sort of." Leia shrugged. "Finally got it working at range. I think." Eyes narrowed, she counted for a few seconds and then tossed the energy upwards. She caught the swinging handle as it passed overhead, the tangle of green energy bursting into a snare of barbed vines that held the axe.

Before anyone could react or question her use of it, Eric had grabbed hold of Leia and leapt upwards, easily clearing the space by activating his own body-empowering technique. The man made it look easy, though Arthur couldn't help but wonder how many points he had to sacrifice to make it look that easy.

Moments later, there was a popping noise as the green thorns were broken, the technique fading and allowing the axe to return to its swinging.

No big surprise why they'd used their bodies rather than rely on the energy-based technique. Especially since this was likely the first time she had ever attempted the technique. It was a good test, to see how long her new snare method worked; though once the pair had settled themselves, he could not help but ask.

"What do you mean new and old?" Arthur said.

"It's a variation of the defensive technique I use." When everyone looked at Leia, she shrugged. "Or used to use. Don't need it as much with the group and it's expensive. It uses refined energy. It moves around my body, hurts those who hit me or grabs at their weapons, which slows it down." Now, Leia grimaced. "It's actually not as good as it sounded."

Eric nodded in agreement. "It supposedly is the base technique that the Killing Ivy uses." He shrugged. "But that might be a lie, or if it is, she's upgraded it a lot. It grabs things, but only if it's slow enough. Better with blunt instruments, but cutting ones are only slowed a bit."

"So I've been working on something else, figured if I could throw it . . ." She waved downwards, to indicate what she'd done. "I couldn't make it work before, but I had some time to really test it. It's still slow, and I can only throw it around ten feet away from me, but . . ."

"If you could fit that with your Energy Dart . . ." Mel said, excited.

"Trapping Energy Dart." Leia nodded. "Though I might need to make it out of refined energy."

Now Arthur was excited, because he would love to learn how to do it. But, he had rather enough stuff on his plate. He forced himself to temper his excitement, scanning the surroundings instead. Now that they were up here, there was only one last thing to do, which was to pass through the portal.

And over there, he could see the portal stones that indicated where they were meant to be.

All they had to do was hike the kilometer or so to the location.

Oh, and kill the boss that was hovering there, flapping its wings, feeding a nest of baby Rocs.

Chapter 12

Taking on a dungeon boss was always a tricky thing. They were stronger, tougher, and smarter than your average monster. Of course, the fact that the monsters they fought earlier on this floor were all dumb as rocks was not a good indication of intelligence. After all, the jenglot were dangerous and smart; and they were only on the first floor.

No, the giant Roc that hovered over the battlefield was more than just smart and tough; it also had the advantage of being able to fly. Fighting it would require them to shower it with long-range attacks until it fell upon them, at which point the melee fighters could at last contribute to the battle.

However, the thing was massive and their slings weren't going to do much to it. After all, it might suck to get hit by a stone, but when you were the size of a house, it mattered a lot less than when you were the size of, say, an elephant. Which meant they were mostly going to be relying heavily on teammates with ranged techniques that could actually do real damage.

"Add in to that, we're going to have to deal with those," Arthur growled, waving at the stand of grasping vines. It was clear, now that they had crept in closer, that that the damn Roc was being protected by the Tower. They'd attempted to lure it out by firing upon it, but all they had done was waste the energy from Casey's bow and their time setting up a trap.

"So, the plan?" Mel asked, curiously.

He hesitated, glanced at his seniors for confirmation. Leia shook her head, refusing to answer and Eric clamped his own mouth shut when he saw her not speaking. Realising they were going to make him do the talking, Arthur slowly spoke.

"We need to get in, close." Arthur looked around the group, assessing them, and sighed. "We split into three groups. Ranged group to take the Mama Roc. Another group to take the vines. Lastly, a baby Roc group. The vine group will be our fast and heavy hitters. Their job is to clear out the environmental hazards so we can fight without worrying about being randomly eaten. That group is going to be me, Uswah, Yao Jing, and Jan."

Arthur made himself not look enquiring or worried.

"For ranged, we have Rick and Casey. I'll join ranged group the moment I'm done." He hesitated, then added, "Leia and Eric, you have the baby Rocs. I know there are three Rocs to your two, but I'm going to assume you can snare one. If not, Uswah . . ." She nodded, understanding his point. "Lam, you're free-floating. You hit whoever or whatever needs dealing with, but I want your focus mostly on the Mama Roc." He grimaced. "When it comes winging down, smash it."

Arthur hesitated, then continued, "While it'd be nice to ground the damn Mama Roc, the Tower might not allow us to. Or, more likely, it'll fade out the skill faster than ever, so Uswah and Leia?" They perked up, looking at him. "Try to snare it when you're both free. Do it together."

"The Tower don't allow?" Jan asked. "What, you read about this?"

"I did, but it's been a while. Also, the sixth floor boss varies, and not just in what's up here but the skills it has. Previous bosses included a giant vine trap; a portal in the middle of a village filled with, well, gremlins; and a mushroom area that had poisonous spore clouds." He made a face at that because that last boss had spiked the kill rate for a bit before the Tower had chosen to get rid of the mushroom field. "The Roc has been popular for the last two years, with it rotating in every . . . three? Three bosses. But it's not always there."

Then, Arthur shrugged. "I worked out that I was better off sneaking past it than actually trying to fight it, if I was going alone. And if I wasn't . . ." He sighed. "I thought I'd be with people who actually would have spent time memorising shit too."

"Nerd!" Eric taunted, good-naturedly.

"Still beat you at spears." Arthur grinned at the dual-wielding fighter before he waved the distraction away. "Any other questions?"

Of course there were. Since they had nothing better to do, they talked it over until everyone was settled in their positions.

After all, they had some time to waste. And no one wanted to face the Roc's special attack, not if they had a choice.

Arthur was trying something new, and it was not going well. Not in the "oh god, oh god, we're all going to die" way, but in the "this is going to suck a lot till it's over" way. In this case, what Arthur was doing was testing out creating two different forms of the same technique.

In this case, the pair of Refined Exploding Energy Darts were held in either hand as they crept close to where the ivies were. They knew that the boundary of whatever was keeping the Roc from pulling out was almost certainly going to be crossed before they neared the thrashing, grasping vine monsters. It made no sense otherwise, or else they'd just cheese the level and blow all the vines out.

They could have tested exactly where the range was, but it made more sense to just get into range and when the Roc decided to start it up, that was when they'd rush the rest of the way in. Presumably, by that point, the thrashing vines and the creepgrass that they'd finally spotted, now that they were closer, would be close enough that they'd have to deal with them.

Now, it was possible they could attack and run away. And that had been plan A, but no one was particularly surprised that the same barrier that stopped the Roc from venturing far sprung into existence, blocking *them* from running away.

All in all, it meant they were committed. It was just a prolonged staring game right now, as the group slowly drew closer. Whoever was the first to blink . . .

Or soar, in this case. The beating of the Roc's massive wings blew up sand and grit, causing the group to squint. The smell of something dry and musky filled the air, a little bit rotten as well. It was not the humid, musky smell of a horse or other mammal, but something cleaner and yet alien. The creature let out a loud squawk as it pulled upwards, the predatory, streamlined face with its sharp, curved beak reminiscent of a falcon or hawk.

Or maybe Arthur really had no idea what he was talking about. Because, really, you didn't get those kind of large birds of prey in Malaysia; instead you had plenty of crows. So many crows, lining the streets around hospitals or hanging around open dumpsters. They were even more ubiquitous than pigeons, who mostly didn't stand a chance in Malaysia.

More to the point, now that the Roc was making its move, so did the group. Releasing the pair of Refined Exploding Energy Darts one after the other, he watched them shoot away faster than an arrow but certainly not as fast as a bullet. Releasing the Darts relieved him immediately of a mental burden, causing him to move and breathe easier. Holding the pair, even if he had formed them one after the other, had been more difficult than running two disparate techniques.

No idea why, but something to consider and train in the future. He'd probably figure it out soon enough, but it felt like it might have to do with the way the techniques burdened his mind and meridians.

By the time he finished contemplating all that—which is another way of saying within seconds—his attacks arrived. The first didn't manage to make its way completely through the lazily waving vines, instead exploding and shredding a vine it had impacted and just a couple more nearby. But they opened the way for his next Dart, coming in hot from behind to explode against the body of the vine monster. Wood and bark greenery showered the surroundings while sap began to dribble out. Enough of that lost, and the creature would die.

It wasn't enough to kill a vine monster right away, but Arthur was already forming another Refined Exploding Energy Dart as he ran forward. Once he was done, he'd hold it in reserve while he chopped his way in and begin engaging Heavenly Sage's Mischief. He knew he'd need the strength, though right now, reaching the thrashing vines was his first priority.

Not that he was the vanguard of the charge. That was Jan and Yao Jing. The big man was just wading in, grabbing at vines and tearing them apart with his hands, coating his Wood Body with his greater strength so that he could do damage that way. Meanwhile, Jan's aura of flame actually pushed the vines back. Even the vines that came in contact with her started having trouble, control being lost within seconds. It meant that the deeper she went in, the worse it got for the vines.

Eventually, they'd probably die just from her presence—if she didn't fall first.

The only one not charging in on the vine party was Uswah. She was just hunched down near where Arthur had been, eyes narrowed in concentration. Near his own target, a series of shadow vines had erupted from the ground, slamming and spearing into the vine creature itself. Against a captive, unmoving audience, she was the first to manage an actual kill, the sudden spiky death from within more than sufficient to put the vine monster down.

Which meant the rest of the teams could rush in, to finish the battle on the other adds.

And before the incoming Mama Roc could mess with their day.

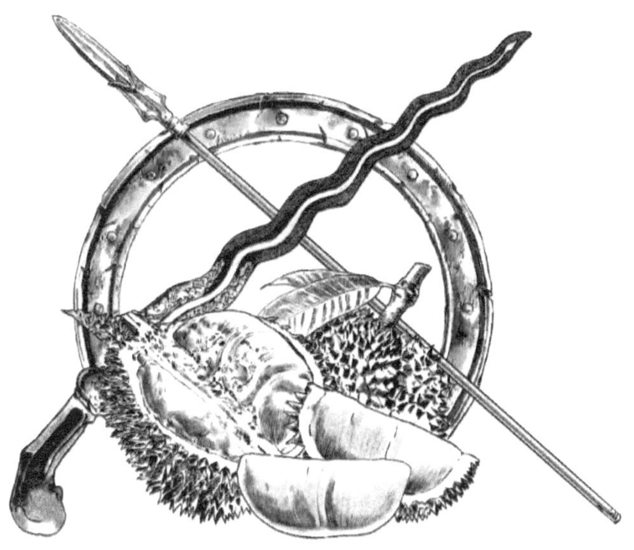

Chapter 13

The thrum of a bowstring being pulled and loosed filled the air as Casey went to work. It could barely be heard—or not at all—against the boom of Rick's shotgun as he braced himself, stock firmly against his shoulder as he fired at the Roc. A shotgun wasn't the most effective weapon, not at the ranges they needed, but it was slightly more accurate with the slugs than his pistol and were more likely to do effective damage. The Roc's size worked against it in this case, though Rick's ability to hit it with a tight grouping was significantly degraded compared to Casey.

Of course, once they got close, the shotgun was going to do a lot more damage; which was why he seemed to be taking his time firing, lining up shots rather than slamming shells out. Or perhaps it was because he was running out of ammunition.

Hard to say, and not really Arthur's job.

He only had a few moments to check things over before he was in among the vines once again. He dodged and tore his way through, using the spear he wielded to smack against vines and allowing his body to block the others, letting the vines glance off his armour. The few that managed to get hold of him, he used his greater strength to tear apart before they could get a good hold on him. It was never easy, but so long as he kept moving, kept cutting them apart before enough of them gripped him tight and strung him up, he was safe enough. The razor edges hurt if they found an opening in his armour, but that was the thing about good armour—the razors couldn't get to him otherwise.

Deeper and deeper he dug in. Unfortunately, the closer he got, the denser the vines waving before him grew. Soon enough, he couldn't even swing his spear properly and cut his way through.

Again, not unexpected.

He released the Refined Exploding Energy Dart and jumped backwards, hopping again as fast as he could to retreat. The outer edge of the explosion still caught him, making his ears ring and his sight darken for a moment before he reoriented himself. At the point of impact though, various vines had been torn apart, many of them blasted away.

A more-than-sufficient gap for him to heave back and throw, sending his spear arcing in to plunge deep into the monster's main body. He left the spear there as he grabbed at his kris and waded right back in, cutting at each of the vines that came in close. He watched as the thrashing vine monster's own movements widened the gap that his spear, still embedded in the body, had created. One of the things about such creatures was that the plants just weren't smart enough to grab and pull weapons out, so it just thrashed around.

The combination of his Refined Exploding Energy Darts, his strength, and his cursed kris was more than sufficient to kill one of the vine creatures. In fact, he was one of the fastest to deal with them; though fast was not something any of them really did, other than Uswah. Plant creatures were just stupidly tough.

The grunts and shouts, the cries of his companions, and the smell of sweet sap filled his senses, roaring into place and then disappearing in between the careful, deep breaths he took. After all, one of the greatest dangers about battles, especially large scale ones like this, was running out of energy and breath at the wrong time. It was too easy to go in all blazing and gas oneself.

So. Breath control, taking a moment to relax muscles when you had a moment, was important. He backed off a little, knowing he needed to catch his breath. Not that far that he was out of range, but enough that the few vines coming at him could be struck and parried with the kris easily.

Already, he could see the way the kris was affecting the vine creature, making it slower, making its thrashing subside. Before he could make his final move, though, a shadow tendril reached up, grabbed and held his spear and pivoted it. The large wound it caused as it tore the spear out made even more sap fall out and caused the nearest still-functioning vines to droop. A moment later, he was catching his spear as the shadow tendril disappeared.

"Yeah, yeah, I get it. No need to smash it." Heading away from to tackle the next vine creature in line, knowing that the current plant would die off sooner rather than later even if it tried to chase after them, he started the process all over again. Rush in, utilize a Refined Exploding Energy Dart, tear apart vines till they bunched together, and then finish it off.

All the while, he fell back a little, using his kris to block and defend just to get a view of what was happening elsewhere, to check that everyone was fine.

He caught when the Roc, having gained enough air, did its dive bomb attack. The way Rick and Casey scattered, leaving the creature to grasp at nothing. Except, rather than sweep upwards and flap its wings to rise again, the Roc instead crashed hard enough to throw both of them onto the ground again as the earth itself cracked. Then, as they tried to stand up, the wing flared outwards, knocking Casey to the ground once more and nearly slapping Rick in the face.

Only Lam, rushing in with his spear, kept them from being eviscerated as he threatened the Roc's eyes. Of course, that put him right across its face, and the sudden pecking motion nearly caught him out. As it stood, the spray of blood as his arm was caught by the razor-sharp attack was vivid in the air.

On the other side, the rest of the vine team was doing good work. Jan had shifted targets without asking, going after the creepgrass that was threatening the other team, using her aura to catch them out and then stabbing them to death in short order the moment they curled up. In the meantime, Uswah was doing the most damage, though Arthur knew that wouldn't last. Her shadow techniques used a lot of energy, which meant she would need to fall back and try to recuperate soon enough. Yao Jing, on the other hand, didn't have to worry about that, since his Wood Body was a low-cost approach; for attacks he relied simply on his strength and his parang. It meant Yao Jing was the slowest of the group, but the eight vine plants that formed the ring were less than half active now.

The last team, the ones going after the baby Rocs, were having the hardest time. Even though they were not full grown, each was the size of a horse and had a beak sharp enough to pierce armour if it wasn't blocked right. No surprise then that the pair of spear users—Leia and Eric—were keeping back, harrying the Rocs rather than going for a direct, immediate kill.

The good news was that, of the three smaller rocs, one was trapped. Bad news was, whether it was an instinctive flock behavior or just something they had been told to do, the pair that were free weren't leaving their sibling to be attacked. They clustered close, forcing his seniors to attack around them, stabbing and twisting to keep the birds moving, the squawk of the creatures continuing to ring through the air. Unlike the mother, the babies weren't as versatile in their attacks, not really grasping how to use their wings better.

A portion of Arthur's mind was cursing, wanting to get involved in the main fight. He wanted to be part of the battle against the Mama Roc, against the babies—not the plants. He wanted to plunge his spear in them and act like the big hero. All children dreamed about being the protagonist, the one standing in the middle of a war, the one who held the attention of the big bad. Arthur was the same.

The big difference? He wasn't a child anymore. He had a job taking on the vine plants.

He shifted away from his most recent kill, leaving it for Yao Jing to finish off, and took a moment to assess. His skill set, the techniques he had, was quite wide ranging, allowing him to support in a variety of ways. He could hit at range, get in close, and even maneuver better than most. He couldn't stall people, yet, but he knew he'd learn a technique for that eventually.

It didn't make him good at any one area. But he could spot problems coming while he was pulled back and also deal with the issues as they arose.

Uswah was cultivating, spending the time to pull energy into her core. She was keeping an eye out for the fights too, ready to try to web the Mama Roc if needed. Which was a good thing, because Lam was looking the worse for wear. He was wielding his spear one-armed now, even as Casey and Rick fired at the Roc from either side.

"Web!" Arthur shouted, waving his hand back and forth to get the attention of the team. He moved towards the baby Rocs, knowing that Leia would need to back off to assist Uswah. In the meantime, he shouted again: "Uswah, one attempt. NOW!"

Pulling herself out of the brief moment of cultivation, she concentrated. As the Mama Roc tried to step forward, clawed feet sinking into the earth with ease, a series of shadowy tendrils reached up and grabbed at it. They held the monster still, causing it to stumble and face-plant on the ground, beak slamming into the earth not far from Lam who had thrown himself backwards when he saw the creature falling.

Scrambling back to his feet, the bodyguard threw a quick thrust with his single uninjured arm, the blade scoring a line of blood along the twitching head but missing the eye he had been targeting. On the other side though, Casey didn't miss, her conjured arrow plunging deep within the other eye and causing the monster to thrash about, wings beating against the ground and legs and tearing free of shadow and earth itself.

Spinning around and around, a wing knocked Lam senseless. Thankfully, it missed seeing him vulnerable on the ground. The massive bird, blood pouring out from another wound that exploded with feathers and skin as Rick fired, took to the skies once more. Even if the shotgun shell blasts were doing a ton of damage, the size of the thing meant that it was not dying just yet, even if it shed blood all over the surroundings, causing the group to squint.

"Shit. Boss!" Leia said, skidding to a halt. She was halfway between both groups, looking puzzled as the creature rose up, unable to hit it with her own web system. She was without an effective long-range technique unless she shifted to her less deadly techniques. She hesitated, uncertain of what was best.

Arthur, glancing back, shouted, "Group up! Let it hit you all together."

Then, he had no more time to worry about them, because he was next to Eric and had his own problems to deal with.

Chapter 14

Arthur ducked low, sticking his arm upwards. The edge of the kris scraped along the tip of the wing that tried to bat at him, ineffectually. It was almost cute, the way the baby Rocs fought. They were definitely juveniles, for they had a lack of elegance, a clumsiness that was over and above the fact that they were birds on the ground. It made fighting them somewhat easy, though Arthur was focused not on killing them but poisoning.

It was why he was holding his spear low and to the ground, grip shortened so he could thrust when he needed to or deflect the beak, but mostly, he cut and stabbed, again and again. The kris would work a lot better with a living creature whose hot blood pumped the poison through the body. Get a half-dozen good stabs or cuts in and they would fall over.

More than what it had taken to take down Mel earlier, but then again, they were multiple levels up. The effectiveness of the kris was decreasing as the monsters and individuals increased their body and their natural resistance to such things. Eventually, it would be worth no more than a normal knife. Eventually, he'd sell it off.

But that was not now.

Focused as he was, only a glimpse as he ducked back and turned his head gave him warning. The cries of surprise were just rising, but he reacted without thought. He swung his weapon sideways, smacking Eric away with the haft of his spear even as he threw himself to the side.

A touch too slow, as the descending claws closed, grabbing hold of his outstretched arm and piercing part of his chest and arm as it grabbed him. This time, the Mama Roc did not land, instead beating its wings and pulling upwards with a shriek. Air and wings buffeted him, knocking Arthur around and his helm askew as it rose, pain and the attacks disorienting him for precious moments.

By the time he managed to figure out what was happening, he was in the air, dangling from one arm that was threatening to break, an arrow flashing by his face to lodge in the body above him. He swung his free arm in an attempt to cut the creature. Too far, he realised. No body to cut, and its legs were bunched up and gripping tight. The movement itself sent bolts of agony down his arm as Arthur realised that the damn creature had broken something important.

He pushed past the pain, stabbing into the leg holding him, again and again. He would have sawed against a tendon or something, but the kris was not really meant to be a cutting weapon; its thin, pointed edge really meant for stabbing and then widening the wounds. Even as he did so, he began the process of changing the flow of power, dropping the Heavenly Sage's Mischief for another full-body technique. As he stabbed, he tried to get the weapon into the bony, tendony claws that gripped him; though from his experience, it would take a bit to poison the creature with the appendages having so little blood flow, so far away from its body.

It did, however, manage to do one other thing.

It annoyed the Mama Roc.

Flapping a half-dozen times more, rising with each flap, the Mama Roc chose to drop him. He could hear the silence from below, the almost continuous boom of Rick's shotgun having ceased. Whether he was reloading again or scared to hit Arthur, no way to tell. Casey had slowed down too, only a single arrow flickering past him to embed itself in the creature as he dropped.

The Mama Roc waited a brief moment, just long enough for Arthur to start dropping, turning as it did so and rising upwards and away. Arthur could see its intention and knew he didn't have time. He could feel the weaves of energy forming within him, the necessary pull of power coming together. Quickly, but not quickly enough as the creature tucked its wings close.

That was when Arthur released the Refined Exploding Energy Dart, his back to the ground and arms and legs splayed. He had managed to get himself into fall position through all this, stabilized just about enough to send it in the right direction. It didn't hit the Mama Roc's directly in its open, screeching mouth, but it struck the top of its beak and that explosion of energy was enough.

The initial dive ended, the bird throwing its wings back, squawking loud and surprised as it rolled its head to the side and twisted. One eye partially blinded, the other blinking and upset as an arrow flashed past Arthur's tumbling form. Then the bark of a shotgun shell, the warm spray of blood, and the shower of feathers and bone falling around him.

Arthur grinned a little and spun in the air, twisting to spot the ground rushing up to him. All too close, shadows forming beneath his falling spot to catch him. No time to explain he didn't need help, all he had to do was . . .

Form a cloud and jump.

What he hadn't considered was how fast he was falling. The cloud he formed was shattered, broken almost immediately as his foot came down upon it. He felt a jolt of pain run through him, like stomping particularly hard on a concrete floor. He tried to form a second cloud, but he was still falling and had never mastered it, so all he got was wisps of mist that slowed him down a little.

Then, the shadowy tendrils were there. Like falling through particularly spongy branches, he shattered the tendrils that reached for him, that cushioned his fall. Only problem was, he had no idea where the ground was, so that when he hit it, it was a surprise. He rolled with the fall anyway, the same injured leg taking the brunt of the damage.

More sharp, shooting pain as he tucked himself and rolled forwards, bleeding off energy and momentum with each moment. It still hurt, it still sucked, and his ribs felt bruised beneath the armour. He didn't even manage to put together the rest of the technique he was intent on building, so much tumbling and moving around there had been.

Still, Arthur managed to get onto his foot, though he found himself heavily lopsided. One leg not wishing to bear his weight, one arm broken and hanging uselessly by his side, his spear lost somewhere in the commotion. He still had his kris though, but the Mama Roc was still up there.

Or . . . not?

Jerking his head around, he searched for the monster. Couldn't find it in the air. Then, he realised of most of the team was moving in another direction. So large was the creature that its thrashing body was easy to spot.

As he tried to limp over, he found Uswah sliding under the arm of his injured side to give him aid.

"What happened?" He waved a hand at the Mama Roc.

"We downed it. I think your attack concussed it. Add in blood loss and a lucky shot, and it tumbled to the ground. We're trying to finish it," Uswah said, gesturing around before lowering her voice. "I'm almost out though."

"Energy?"

She nodded.

Arthur checked his own stores, grimaced. He was fine on Tower energy, had quite the decent store. Refined energy, however, was low. Always his problem, because he had a tendency to use that more than his other forms. Maybe he should spend some time learning a basic healing technique, one that used normal energy.

He discarded the idle thought, knowing how poor those were. It wasn't as if he didn't have enough work anyway.

Her words did have him check over his people. They had burnt hot, utilising their skills and resources without stop, burning through energy to take down monsters. He could see the signs everywhere. Jan no longer utilized her aura, having switched instead to her sling so that she could strike at the still-living Roc from a distance. Casey had put her bow away, edging around the sides in an attempt to attack the bird though she refused to get too close. Even Rick was careful about his fire, switching out his shotgun and its percussive booms for the sharper snap of his pistols as he unloaded into the massive monster.

Only Yao Jing and Lam seemed to be going strong, the pair having been more circumspect about their energy use. He also knew they had pushed towards a more enduring use of their energy, allowing them to outlast their opponents. For Yao Jing, it was just a consequence of his greater use of passives, Arthur assumed. Lam was more reasoned, for what use was a bodyguard who was too tired to guard his charge?

Eric was the other fighter who seemed to be doing well, though he was still fighting the last remaining baby Roc with the help of Mel. She had switched out with Yao Jing at some point, though—when, Arthur wasn't sure. It felt like he had lost bits and pieces of time, almost like people had teleported or made decisions without his input.

Fights were sometimes like that, when you lost track of what was happening. He might have, he figured, lost a few moments when he was grabbed, when he rolled. Hard to say, except by virtue of what was happening.

The Mama Roc was still alive by the time the pair limped over, pushing itself around on one last wing, twisting its body and head. It would not be long now though, for Jan had snuck up on the dead wing side with her spear, ready to plunge it deep in and finish the job.

Arthur almost felt sorry for the creature. Sorry for the piteous cries it released, for the fading light in its eyes. It was hurt, bleeding from numerous wounds, furious at the death of its children, at being disturbed when it just tried to live its life. Or at least, Arthur thought he saw all those emotions in its large, remaining eye.

He pushed the feelings aside, refusing to acknowledge them. That was how the Tower caught you, making you think the monsters were real. Making you hesitate. Better not to feel, better not to acknowledge what they were doing. Even if it was, in a way, truly barbaric.

There was no other way, after all.

"What?" Uswah said.

Arthur blinked, realised he had spoken aloud that last sentence. Shook his head, trying to clear it, realised maybe he was a little loopier and more concussed than he realised. By the time he focused on the bird again, it was dead. Unmoving.

And just like that, they were free to make their way to the seventh floor. The final rest floor before it was just a punishing run.

Chapter 15

It was not so easy as that, leaving the floor. There were injuries. Arthur remembered his own all too well, thankful at least that the deep cut that had shredded his breastplate had clotted already. He still had to pull the armour off with help, holding back the shouts of agony as his broken arm was maneuvered to allow the breastplate to be extracted so that the rest of his wounds could close. The parts that had been torn apart had to be pushed back away, hammered back into place, and then duct-taped over till a proper fix could be completed. His broken arm had to be straightened and splinted, his boots taken off, and his foot checked over to ensure that it did not swell too much before his healing caught up with it all.

Lam was just as injured. Moments after the Mama Roc had died, the man had taken a half-dozen steps back and then collapsed onto his back. He now lay asleep, his body in a vegetative and healing state. When asked, Casey had just shrugged and said "Chin family secret technique" and refused to answer more, beyond the fact that he'd be fine.

It did highlight some other aspects of the previous battles, how Lam had looked more lethargic after particularly intense battles, or how he'd managed to keep up with the team even without having a healing technique of his own. Or, in this case, seemingly had a combined berserk and healing technique.

Arthur wasn't jealous, not at all.

There were other injuries, big and small. More than that, though, the team needed time to harvest all the stones and refill their energy stores. Going onto the seventh floor without any energy at all was a bad idea, which was why not even Casey begrudged the time everyone took to rest up and cultivate.

Of course, it didn't stop Mel from coming over to bother Arthur as he sat propped up and waiting for the shooting pain that ran through his body to go away while his injuries healed.

"You nearly died there," she said without preamble.

"Not really," Arthur said, raising a hand and waggling it side to side. "I had the Cloud Stepping technique. Even if I hit the ground without Uswah's help, I probably would have only broken my feet."

She shook her head, pointing to his wounds in the side. "And that?"

"I dodged it." A slight pause. "Most of it."

"Because you were trying to save someone else. When you should have been saving yourself."

Arthur shrugged. He would not explain his instinctive reactions. They were, by virtue of being instinctive, not something he could do much about. "Nor did you plan to back-up with you."

"We needed all hands on deck."

"Did we?" Mel looked around at the injured and cultivating. She shrugged. "I'd say we pulled this off without anyone dying or coming close to it other than you and Lam. If we had one of us watching you, I doubt it would have changed much."

Arthur shook his head. "Me and Lam. That's two. And if it hadn't gone after me, it would have been someone else. And I'm the best with Cloud Step. So other than Uswah or Casey . . . I don't know if any of you would have survived the grab."

"Maybe no one else would have been grabbed." She shook her head. "It coming for you, after you killed its children, that was to be expected. If someone was watching your back, maybe you could have dodged it. Either way, if one of us dies, it's sad. But if you die—"

"It's tragic." Arthur sighed. "I know. I just . . . this was the best choice I could see. We all survived." He fixed Mel with a firm gaze. "I won't take chances, and I didn't; but I won't baby myself too. Because we have to climb, and without some risk, there's no point. Sooner or later, I'll be alone again. And if I don't get some experience this way, I'll freeze up. And then where will we be?"

Mel grimaced, then nodded. "Fine. Just . . . stop scaring us, will you?"

"My journey to become the OP protagonist continues," Arthur replied and that made Mel grin a little.

He certainly seemed to have some of it. His ability to think clearly in the middle of the fight, the way he could assess things; it was trained for sure. But the Yin Body was another aspect to it. It did dampen his desires a little— well, a lot—but he had never been that focused on the physical side anyway. One day, perhaps, but it was hard to worry about such things when you were surviving day to day and moving towards a goal.

Though, now that goal had shifted. Which perhaps made the idea of living for tomorrow a bit of a joke.

Something to think about.

"Going to see if I can focus enough to finish healing, if you don't mind . . ."

Mel nodded, propping the weapon by her side. "Go ahead. I'll keep watch."

After their previous conversation, he didn't even have the heart to object. Not that there was anything to guard against, considering how well they'd razed the surroundings of life. But it made her feel better, and that was good enough for him.

The faster he got to healing and refining, the faster they could leave anyway.

They chose to rest the night, not just because they all had a lot of energy to recover but also because no one wanted to enter the seventh floor half-asleep. They had all heard the rumours. The so-called resting floor of the Malaysian Tower might be safe—as these things went—from monsters, but it was not in any way and shape and form actually, you know, safe. Not like walking down the streets of Bangsar, or in KLCC Mall where armed guards kept the *gweilo* and other tourists safe.

No, safety was a varying concept and one that none of them were going to take for granted. Better to arrive on the seventh floor ready for the tricks and traps that might arise, rather than wander into it unknowing.

It would be the floor they stayed the longest on, other than the first floor, for they would recover and recuperate, cultivate and study more techniques, before making the push for the last three floors. The last three were both easy and hard.

Hard, because they were set up to bring individuals through—not teams—and so there was no helping one another. Not unless you were the Chins with their Tower-enchanted items.

Easy, because the floors themselves weren't considered super challenging for individual Tower climbers. You had to do them alone, but it wasn't like the Labyrinth in Athens that nearly two thirds of beginner cultivators got lost within or the chilling frozen tundra of the Swedish dungeon's final floor, where you had to keep moving or risk becoming a popsicle.

Easy and hard.

The seventh floor would be where Casey would get a chance to make full use of the Tower, to build up her body and cultivation faster than anyone could expect. It would be where the cumulative advantage of her clan would make a difference for her and hopefully justify all the expenses.

It would also be the last floor where Arthur would easily acquire stones to cultivate.

A lot of hopes and dreams lived on that floor, some never leaving.

"Penny for your thoughts?" Casey asked, as she watched Yao Jing slip through the portal. They would be one of the last to step through, their people making sure it was safe on the other side. At least, in theory.

"One more floor, then I guess I'll see you outside," Arthur said.

"Yes." She glanced to the side where Rick had been, then sighed. "I don't like you allying with him."

"He's a clan member now."

"Don't." She shook her head, facing Arthur firmly. "Don't try to justify what you can't. You know what you did. And I don't like it." She exhaled.

"But I can accept it. Just remember, I offered first. And we can do better for you than he can."

"Nothing about how he can't be trusted?" Arthur said, wryly.

"Rick himself may be fine . . ." Casey said. "But you're going to be dealing with his parents. And you know how I feel about them. About what they did."

"I do." He remembered. Buying up factories, breaking their word. Putting people on the streets by automating work that didn't need to be automated yet. He remembered. "I'll keep it in mind."

"Then, also remember this. You'll get more offers, meet more people on the seventh floor. This is their last chance to make a deal, before you emerge and become a power." She tapped her bow against her leg. "And last chance to kill you before you become a public problem. Watch yourself."

With Lam gone, it was her turn. She didn't hesitate, leaving him with that dire warning. Leaving him to stand there, on the sixth floor, on the cusp of the next stage.

Unsure of what he might face, but knowing he still had a clan to grow and a Tower to conquer.

"Good thing I'm ready and all kinds of steady."

Chuckling to himself, Arthur stepped through.

Chapter 16

Once more, the world turned on Arthur as he transferred between floors, his body compressing and then expanding. For some reason, he could smell nutmeg and star anise, donuts and fried *sambal*, even as all the colours in the rainbow and some that weren't pivoted around him.

As the world shifted again, he felt his footing alter and he instinctively adjusted. Eyes snapped open and Arthur clutched the hilt of his kris in one hand, his spear in the other. His backpack was on him, weighed down by the necessities of travel, as was damaged armour that he wore. The last battle with the giant roc had seen the armour near his left shoulder pierced, leaving it now vulnerable and rather uncomfortable to wear even after their makeshift patches.

Too bad this wasn't a game with a repair function they could use to make things more comfortable.

Eyes flicking from left to right, he checked over what dangers there might be. The room they were in was the size of a Malaysian school gymnasium—

so just about big enough for a basketball court and some space along the sides. No space for bleachers or anything like that. What parent had the time to come watch their kids play, at least back when there were jobs and the schools were still being constructed? These days, it was all most of the schools could do to keep the facilities intact and functioning, what with the decreased tax base.

This room was bare and open, filled with tiny teleportation pedestals. The open space near the main doors were in the direction he faced, though obviously there were others who could appear behind him. However, guards stood around, watching for trouble. Real guards, meant to actually stop problems instead of allowing betting like on the last floor that had a proper teleportation platform.

What made him actually relax and step off the teleportation platform was the sight of his friends and Clanmates.

It seemed that everyone had survived the trip and managed to arrive without issue. Mel was over on the side, her lightly tanned skin covered with a sheen of sweat and dirt like the rest of them, arguing with a man holding a tablet like a clipboard.

Arthur had a sudden flicker of fear and concern run through him at that sight. Men with clipboards—or in this case an actual working table. Never a good thing.

He hurried over, his mind running through rhymes. Clipboard, slipboard. Ripping broad. Slipshod.

"Oh, that was a good one," he said as he came up to the two.

"Good what?" Clipboard Man was sporting a pair of glasses on the top of his head, rather than on his nose where it would have been useful. He looked unperturbed, even as Mel stood there fuming.

"Rhyme." Seeing the blank look on the man's face which Arthur knew would soon turn to anger if he continued this line of inanity, he waved it off. "Don't worry about it. So, what can I help you with?"

"Payment for the use of the teleportation center." He turned the tablet aside slightly so that Arthur could see it. "I just need to finish inspection of what you've brought along, total up duties, and then I will have your total expenses."

"Payment for what?" Arthur said, dumbfoundedly. Irritation at the blatant shakedown began to grow in him, as he continued. "The teleportation platforms are run by the Tower, not you. Whoever you are."

Mel by his side was nodding, gripping her spear shaft tight. The guards by the side looked over, their attention focused on Arthur's group. Two of the guards with modern crossbows by their side were paying very careful attention to Rick who had his arms crossed, glaring about him.

"We are a coalition of concerned groups that manage the teleportation platforms and the buildings involved. Do you think the guards and the platforms have no cost?" The man jerked his chin up, as though dismissing the topic. Amusingly, it almost made the precariously perched glasses on his balding pate bob and threaten to fall off. "Among us are the Prime Group, TG, other *interested parties*, and the government." He looked pointedly at Mel's grip of the spear and then Arthur's hand that still rested on the hilt of the kris and added. "So if you think you can just fight your way out of here without consequences…"

"It's comfortable here…" Arthur said, which it was. However, he did shift his hand so that he leaned his wrist on the hilt rather than lightly clasping it. "But you said the Prime Group?"

"Yes."

"Perfect..." he purred. Clipboard Man started looking worried but Arthur did not give him time to ask. Or ready himself.

"Casey!" Arthur roared.

A loud sigh as she strolled over. Her armour—fit together at the sides via Velcro straps so that it was easier to put on and take off—had been undone so that it could shift easier. All of which helped her pull a necklace out from under the breastplate, giving a brief glimpse of sweaty and clinging silk that made Arthur turn away abruptly.

Not that she noticed. Finally free of the encumbrance, with Lam trailing along and holding her backpack, she waved the ID card in front of Clipboard Man.

"Casey Chin."

"My apologies! I did not recognize you. It's been many years since we received an updated dossier..." The man was bobbing-bowing now, tablet clutched before him as he continued. "If they had just said that, well, we would have..."

"What's this about a customs tax?" Casey asked, leaning forwards. "The entrance fee is known—

and acceptable—" The glare she shot Mel and Arthur to keep them quiet said that it had better be. "But I've never heard of this customs tax. On what we bring?"

"A new council motion. It is, of course, waived for those members affiliated with the council." A hesitation as his gaze took in Arthur's disparate group, and he added, "And their entourage."

"Entourage!" Mel hissed.

Arthur actually smiled, finding it amusing, but Casey was not to be diverted.

"How new?" Casey snapped.

"Two months ago. I could get you the…"

Flicking her hair, she turned to Lam. "Pay him." Then, she stalked out of the room, right past Clipboard Man, who still clutched his tablet to him, a sickening smile growing on his face as Lam loomed over him, nearly fumbling the grab as the bodyguard shoved Casey's backpack at him to hold.

In fact he did fumble the tablet, letting it drop on the ground where it thumped into the pressed earth floor.

Arthur, bemused, looked around only to jerk a little as Casey snarled from just outside the entrance.

"Coming?"

Well. Now he knew what Casey Chin looked like when she was on a warpath.

Chapter 17

The building they exited was impressive—in the paranoid, prison-complex kind of way. It was a pair of concentric circles, with a moat dug in between each set of walls. It was basically a building inside a moated, walled complex, with guards on both sides. Of course, the guards themselves had a variety of ranged weapons hanging on the wall, ranging from slings to bows and crossbows and even a few conveniently placed stacks of rocks.

Not that Arthur was discounting what a good thrown rock, empowered by a skill and the stats of a Tower Climber, could do to an unlucky recipient. He was thus doubly grateful he hadn't had to fight his way out or subject him and his Clanmates to a search.

That, however, didn't make him any happier to be rushing after Casey as she stomped along the thin bridge, the entire thing wobbling and bouncing as she literally pounded her way across it. Considering that right under the bridge were a bunch of stakes, he really thought it would have been smart to be a little more considerate about the infrastructure, but hey.

He wasn't the one currently raging.

Which was a nice change.

"So... exactly why are you angry?" he asked as he finally caught up to her at the gates. He caught up mostly because it was taking a while for the gates to swing open, the guards in charge being a touch too slow.

"Because my idiot aunt is getting greedy. Again," she growled, under her breath. She was at least keeping her voice low. "Her job is supposed to be running the floor, collecting our share of the beast stones and passing it on. That's it. Don't cause trouble, don't overreach, don't make a mess of things."

Arthur was about to ask a little more, only to actually catch a glimpse of the world outside as he stepped out. The seventh floor's settlement was a proper town, a place of residence for thousands. Even if few people managed to make it here each month, the inflow of Climbers over the past twenty-plus years was enough to populate the Tower itself. If not for the forced sterilisation that every Climber basically underwent—outside of some rather specific techniques and pills supposedly—the entire place would have been filled with little brats.

As it was, it was still busy with quite a broad range of ages, though the oldest still only capped out around late fifties or early sixties would be Arthur's guess. Which tracked, considering most people older than their thirties or so wouldn't have risked the Tower. The occasional midlife crisis notwithstanding, those who didn't train didn't manage to ascend.

Still, having a bunch of strong, powerful, and disciplined individuals in a small space had pushed the building out of the town quite a bit. There were actual roads—not just paths people walked, but pressed earth roads with a mixture of crushed gravel and packed earth—leading away from the building.

There were road signs hanging high above, indicating where people should go and signposts indicating major points of interest.

The Tower administrative center. The teleportation center. The baths. The supermarket. The auction house. Prime Group's Banking Service. Mosque.

And the buildings. Quite a variety, though many were made of wood, with a few a mixture of mud and brick, and all of them with simple thrush and tile roofs. Most had big windows, though few had actual glass within them and those that did were mostly cloudy and warped. Instead, the majority of the windows were covered by either paper or pressed leaf, or were just wooden windows with slits in place.

It was rather jarring in that sense, the entire place. The occasional flicker of modern living—a bicycle there, solar panels on those roofs, metal gutters leading to a couple of barrels for collecting rainwater—and then the rather more rustic majority; people wandering around in dirty or torn clothing, furs here and there; men not even bothering with shirts in other cases. The flow of commerce up a Tower was hard after all, especially this far up; what resources had made it through were carefully hoarded and practical.

In between all that, the magical. Lamps that hung outside windows, a few glowing even now as the processed monster cores—also known as beast stones—drew upon their internal power and as well as Tower energy to shed light without end. Enchanted scrollwork on window frames that blocked entry of bugs or warded an entire house against them. Weapons with a glyph or two, glowing and pulsing with the energy of the Tower.

Oh, yeah. That was the other major shift.

Weapons, everywhere. Just like every other floor, but those here carried their weapons like it was a third set of limbs.

"Oy! Move already, *lah*," Yao Jing called behind Arthur.

Waking up from his startlement, realising he was blocking the exit, Arthur stepped outwards and away. His self-professed bodyguard stepped through moments later, the big bodybuilder scanning the surroundings and moving ahead of the group to ward off the curious. Not that they got more than a glance.

"It's something," Arthur grunted, then looked at Casey who had stepped aside, tapping her lips in thought. "So what now?"

"I'm thinking."

Arthur just grunted again, watching as the rest streamed out. Mel joined him a moment later while Uswah waved a hand, her only one, and walked on without stopping.

"Where you going?" he called after her.

"Mosque," she called out behind her.

He frowned but didn't stop her as she paused only long enough to check the signposts before turning down another road. Arthur could have suggested she take a moment to clean herself in their new Clan building, but really... he had no right to dictate her schedule. Not as though they were leaving anytime soon.

"I'm going to get a drink," Rick said, his words making Yao Jing perk up and then look sad as he glanced at the unmoving Arthur. Giving them all a nod, still holding onto his backpack, Rick strolled off.

Eyes narrowing, Arthur sighed and waved to Yao Jing. "Keep him out of trouble."

"You sure, boss?"

"Yes." He waved at Jan who looked like she wanted to join them and added, "I got her. And it's not like this floor is actually supposed to be casually deadly."

"Only for monsters," Mel muttered under her breath, but it didn't stop Yao Jing or Rick from heading off, the pair throwing arms over one another. "You know, those two could really get into trouble..."

"Drunk?" Arthur said, then snorted. "With what alcohol?" He chuckled softly. "Imported stuff is stupidly expensive, and the local brewed amounts taste like turpentine, so I'm told, and are just as expensive." He shrugged. "They'll get tipsy but I doubt they'll get into real trouble."

Jan was nodding along, adding. "Jing's not that *bodoh*."

But no one mentioned Rick not being stupid enough to cause trouble. Other than Casey, Rick was the only one who had enough funds to actually get drunk, if they took real cash. Which was not always a guarantee.

"We should get you the Clan building first," Casey said, suddenly.

"Tower administrative center then?" Arthur said, gesturing down to the road to their left. He grunted after a moment, watching the flow of traffic and those who were watching them or the area around. He wasn't surprised to see a few watchers. It always paid to know who might be arriving, and seeing some of them hurry off soon after he emerged from the teleportation center was one thing.

Watching a pair of watchers trail after his own people, not so much.

Still...

"Leia. Eric. " He jerked his chin, and his two seniors nodded. They didn't need any further information. Then, looking at Casey, he gave her a firm nod. "Let's go."

Time to get the Clan building and establish themselves. And hopefully make it clear for predators on the floor that the Durians really did have sharp thorns they didn't want to be pricked by.

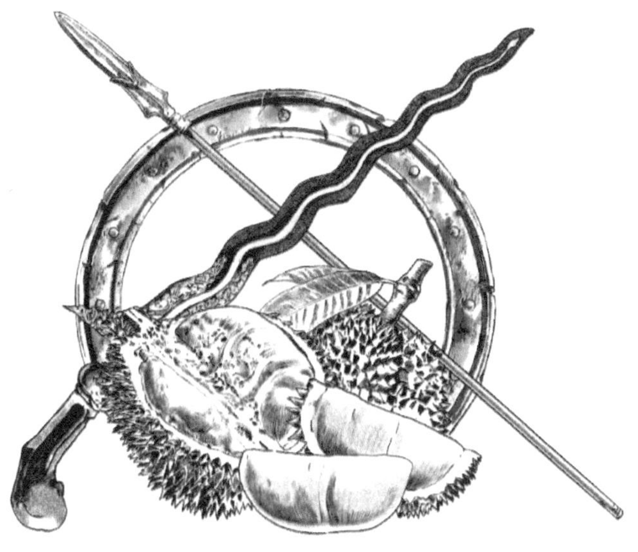

Chapter 18

The smaller group sauntered down the street, getting a few glances as they passed by but only major interest from the roadside hawkers and street merchants who cried out for attention. Most were selling basic items—combs, clean underwear and socks, razors—or services, like the man with the whetstone and the girl with a full set of manicure, pedicure, and scissors by her side.

That got the attention of the women, especially when she started talking about the kinds of nails she had left, and it was with reluctance that Casey moved on.

Almost all of them were offering to buy items within their purview or, in a few cases, men and merchants hurrying alongside with their avaricious eyes focused on their backpacks and the monster bits attached.

"Best price, I promise. Don't think the corporations who buy from you give good pricing. Trust me *lah*, I'll give you the best... urk!" A shove by Lam, forcing a mustached man back.

On the other side, a woman, shorter and darker skinned was trotting beside them, carefully out of range of Jan's arm. "Just let me look, okay? Look only. Five minutes and I can tell you what we can do with it."

"We got nothing."

"But you have something," the woman said, firmly. "Items you haven't identified? Loot? I can do it."

"Not now," Jan snapped.

"Mel, get her information," Arthur said, after a moment. "We can meet up with them later." A glance to the mustached man and he added, "And his too."

"You know I can get you the friends and family price, right?" Casey said, a slight frown marring her face.

"Yes. For now." He gestured around him. "But everyone keeps reminding me I'm the boss, so I got to start thinking outside of just a single alliance." A slight hesitation, then he added, "Also, recruit new people. Can't ever have too many hard workers."

"Mmm, not always. Sometimes what you want in your organisation is a ..." She trailed off, seeing the amused look Arthur was giving her. "You don't want a lecture on management practices, do you?"

"Actually, I wouldn't mind." Arthur admitted. "But perhaps not right now. Busy taking in the town."

"It's something, isn't it?" she said in agreement.

After that, they kept silent for the rest of the walk. It was a companionable one, no longer strained after months of time together. Arthur still wasn't sure if he trusted her, not fully, but at the least she wasn't intending to stab him in the back. Or kill him. Which, all things considered, was a damn good start.

The sight of the only stone building in the town was more than sufficient to clue them in that they'd found the Tower administrative center. More than a few Climbers traversed the grounds before it, entering and exiting in a sparse but constant stream. Not far away, in the simple square that had been dug out, a number of merchant stalls stood.

A quick glance at the building and the stalls before he spoke. "Mel, with me? Jan, you can keep an eye on things out here, chat with the others." He glanced at Lam and shrugged, knowing it wasn't his place to command him. "Let's go."

Casey followed. They slipped into one of the three queues after a moment's review, ignoring the one that was meant for quests and getting in behind the shorter of the two that seemed to involve general administrative matters. Most of which, Arthur knew, involved buying and selling and registration of contribution points and access to the Tower's library and stores.

No surprise that this building was busy. This was the last major chance for a Climber to upgrade before they tried the final few floors. It was the last place that you could give yourself an edge. Arthur knew he'd be back purchasing more than just armour or equipment or identifying the various weapons they might have acquired. He'd be looking at techniques. Upgrades to his current skill set, though he would have to work out what gaps he might have.

Area control or damage over time would be his guess, what with the other areas currently filled. Of course, he could upgrade his strengths too, find a stronger version of his generic body buff or explore the Refined Energy Dart further; but he had been learning and expanding upon that skill himself.

Better to find techniques that he couldn't get as easily, techniques you couldn't obtain on your own without purchasing. Then, he could turn his understanding of energy and skills on said techniques, see if he could improve them.

"It's fine. We have quite a few buildings here," Casey said softly to him.

"What?" he blinked down at her. "Why are you trying to console me?"

"You're frowning."

"About something else." He hesitated, then seeing her confusion he explained. "My build."

"Ah." Silence, the woman visibly weighing something further to say. Eventually, after a few false starts, she offered, "I can help talk you through some options, if you want. We get training on choosing optimal builds."

"Even for my case?" Arthur said, raising an eyebrow. This Yin Body he had sometimes felt like it did little. Other times, he realised how much it had changed him. How he seemed to be chiller overall, not as easily worked up. How his libido, never that huge before, had shrunk. Not that he didn't enjoy the view, but it had become similar to watching a sunset. Beautiful, easy to enjoy, but not something he coveted or felt the need to own.

Made his life simpler. Easier too, considering just how many women— some of them extremely fit and toned—he was around.

"Not as much, but the theories are the same," she said.

"Mm-hmm..." He chose not to object. Stepped forward again, watched as the man before him dropped a dozen stones off, had them registered. He listened in on the numbers and qualities and made note of it for future reference. Then, it was their turn.

When he handed over his seal, muttered the usual requests, got the Administrator to come out, he was not surprised to see the usual bloom of information moments later as he let the Tower push the notification to him.

The Benevolent Durians Clan Status

Organizational Ranking: 182,721

Number of Towers Occupied: 1

Number of Clan Buildings: 5

Number of Clan Members: 398

Overall Credit Rating: F

Aspect: Guardianship

Sigil: The Flame Phoenix

No surprise at the sudden increase in noise around him. He ignored the curious looks from those within the building, ignored all the fellas trampling their way in to catch a glimpse of the person who had registered a Clan. Instead, he kept his eye on the current number of Clan members, noted how little it had gone up, relatively speaking.

Amah Si and the others below were probably hitting the end of the easy pickings. Only so many people who weren't already allied, who were trustworthy, and whom they wanted. It would be a few more months of consolidation before they would begin pulling in people without issue, new regular members who might join them just for the basics of their Clan seal but who might never contribute much.

That was fine with him. He wasn't trying to build a small, tightknit group of friends and family who could carry him to the heights of the world. He just wanted to help people, to give others another viable path beyond the gangs and triads and the corporations. Of course, there was only so much good work they could do before things crashed down if they didn't demand some aid and benefits from their members.

Clan taxes, payment for resources and information, usage of the Clan buildings. All of those things that he had talked with Amah Si and Mel about, over and over again.

But here and now, well...

"Your turn." He stepped aside and waved to Casey, who offered her own token. Listened to the usual spiel, even as he ignored all the blatant eavesdroppers.

Not as though what was going to happen was at all that easy to hide. Especially when the Administrator was hovering before him, pulling out details about the various buildings they had on offer. If he was a little surprised by the sheer number, well, it certainly showed on his face.

"Told you," Casey said.

He could only grunt in reply. Eyes flicking over the options, listening to her caution him about which ones he really should not take, not without angering her and the actual controller of the floor, her aunt.

Debated, once again, what he could do. Warehouse, residence, and retail-residential townhouse were his main options. In terms of a residence, there was even something equivalent to an apartment complex.

These locations were scattered around, ranging from close to the main teleportation complex to the forests.

Options. He asked, of course, for Mel's opinion. But in the end, he made his decision.

Not that there had been that much choice, if you thought about it.

Chapter 19

"Apartment building?" Jan said, as she followed him along.

"That's the best choice," Mel said. "Only real one."

"Why?" Jan replied. "Why not something like that?" A hand waved at a retail store-and-residence combo.

"Not enough space," Mel replied. "Also, the building bonus."

"Security, *ya*?"

"Yes," Arthur replied, glancing back. "Means we get a Tower Guard. How much business you think we're going to get, with one of those things staring at our customers? Never mind having to pull security in or let people in individually."

"High-end stores are like that, right?" Jan offered. She looked at Casey, probably the only person in their group who actually had an experience at a high-end store.

The heiress glanced back at Jan, shrugged. "Not unless you sell really expensive jewelry or something. I mean, mostly, people just don't go there. It's too much, you know?"

Arthur grunted. Of course, in Kuala Lumpur it also was true that many of those kinds of stores were in the same areas, places a little more exclusive than Bangsar or Bukit Bintang. Old money places like Bukit Tunku or yuppie places like Damansara Heights. Areas that had security guards even on the roads coming in, whether or not you were supposed to, because there were different laws for different classes.

"Down this street?" Arthur said into the silence.

Lam was the one who answered, confirming Arthur's guess. His gaze swept left and right, taking in the surroundings with eyes narrowing. He tensed and the group did too, taking a cue from his body language. Moments later, he spoke, tersely.

"Gangers, straight ahead."

It took Arthur a moment to spot them, another to frown. Six, just a few too many for his liking. Worst part, they were lounging outside their new Clan apartment building, a building that had a number of other, angry Climbers standing outside it now. He slowed his footsteps, even as the lounging gangers straightened as they spotted Arthur's group.

"Spotted us," Mel said.

"So did the crowd." Casey frowned. "Who are they?"

"Shit," Arthur muttered moments later. "I know." He paused, sighed. "It's the previous occupants. Look, over there, there's a guy holding a real pillow."

"Really? Silk, feather?" Casey said, curiously.

"I don't think that's the point," Lam muttered. He glanced at Casey, then slowed down a tiny bit, hand held out sideways to make her slow with him. "I feel this is something that Clan Head Chua and his people should settle."

"Oof, Brutus," Arthur said.

"Eh?" Lam said.

"Julius Caesar, gets stabbed by his friend?" He sighed when few of his entourage nodded. "No one watches the classics anymore." He watched the crowd coming, flicked his glance between the two groups and made a quick decision. "Mel, you're on the gangers. Probably the Ghee Hin." Easy call since they were all Chinese, while other groups like the Double Sixes were often more varied in racial composition.

"I with you," Jan muttered.

Arthur nodded, figuring he needed more help. If they got into a fight, that was understandable and perhaps Mel would need their aid. But if they were fighting a whole apartment block of annoyed residents, they were doing something seriously wrong.

"What can I offer them?" Mel, ever practical, asked.

"Nothing," he said simply. "Find out what they want, don't promise anything."

Mel nodded and then Arthur turned to Casey. "They're mostly short-term residents, right?" Casey nodded. One of the reasons he picked this apartment block. "Then that gives me a plan."

Moments later, they no longer had time to plan as the angry group of residents made their way over. Mel had caught the eye of the triad members, waving them over to the side of the road discreetly so that they could converse. Lam and Casey had fallen back, heading over to a nearby merchant store and stepping in rather than get involved directly.

Arthur let the wash of voices roll over him and listened to the shouting group. He parsed together their comments soon enough, the words coming to him in a thick wash of Manglish, Malay, Cantonese, and Mandarin and even the occasional Hindi or Tamil or Punjabi. With the Indian languages, he could never really distinguish one from the other. The smaller the ethnic group, the fewer outsiders learned their language other than a few words here and there.

In the end, he raised his hand to get them to quiet. Then he waved it back and forth, but all he received was more shouting. It was Jan who managed to shut them up, releasing a loud "Oy!" that silenced the group briefly.

Rather than let the momentary silence go to waste, Arthur broke in.

"I hear you. You're upset you were kicked out. I understand you paid the Chins." He raised a hand again. "I get you're angry at me. But they were the ones who sold it to us, so if you want or need a refund, get it from them."

That, of course, didn't make them any happier. More shouting, more words of recriminations, more threats. He glared at the few who tried the threats, not letting himself be intimidated even though a part of him knew that they likely out-leveled him.

One danger of rushing. However, they didn't know that and so long as they didn't, he could bluff.

"You kicked us out!" A finger, pointing towards him. He didn't move, even if it did feel uncomfortable to have something so sharp almost prodding at him. Weird how a single finger, even if it was the least dangerous and probably dumbest threatening move, could still set the hind brain on edge. "So I think you should let us back in!"

"And I can't do that. I don't know who you people are, which rooms you lived in, nothing. What agreements you had with the Chins, that's with them."

He hesitated, then continued, "We can, however, discuss potentially renting some of those rooms out. To a select few."

"Oh, now you're going to rent me my home? Going to sell me back my furniture now? All my equipment?" the finger-pointer snarled. Arthur took him in now. Pudgy hick was surprising for a Climber, florrid, angry. The finger that now poked at him was part of the most calloused part of his body, the hands stained and with minor nicks and a lot of callouses.

"What are you doing, keeping a lot of stuff in a short-term rental area? Isn't that, like, the opposite of what you should do?" Arthur asked, curiously.

"I was in between places," the man retorted. Something in the way he said that, the defensive tone of voice, made Arthur curious.

He looked around, judged the group as he thought it over. Ignored other people complaining about leaving things behind, before he waved a hand at them. "Alright, alright. Enough. You all have keys to your own rooms?" Nods from all around. "Fine. Here's what we do. We get the Prime Group manager over here, you can shout at them about what they owe you still. Get a refund or something. And..." More shouting, but he kept staring in silence, waiting until they realised he had more to say.

"And I'll let you all in, one way or the other, under supervision, to take what you want. After we confirm that's your room. We'll be renting a few of the rooms out on a weekly basis. Great for cultivation, but for the short term only. Don't expect to stay long. Long-term stay only for friends of the Durians or members."

"*Tiu nei!*"

"*Cibai!*"

Again, the curses washed over him. He had a feeling this might take a bit, what with the sheer anger that was being exhibited. Almost, almost, he wanted to push ahead, to ignore them, but he knew this would cause more trouble. Some of the smarter ones, though, they had grown silent at the mention of the Benevolent Durians.

"I can't let you stay, damn it. It's not safe for you or us. The Tower Guard sentry we have, he needs renewal regularly. I miss it, you miss it, he chops your head off. You think I want that?" Arthur shook his head. "I'm sure you don't. So. No long-term guests. Anyway, I'll rent to those who do come by with valid reason and aren't asses and who have been here longest or paid longest, at the same rate as before."

That really shut the smart ones up, an avaricious gleam in their eyes. No one was dumb enough not to realise what a Clan building could do for their cultivation. How much denser the energy within it would be, especially on the seventh floor. Of course, for those who had to use short-term housing, such luxuries were generally considered an impossibility to acquire.

A luxury that only the rich or the great managed. Now, perhaps, their ill luck had turned.

He saw some of the smarter ones backing off, heading for the Prime Group manager who had been attempting to sneak off if not for a few Climbers who had kept him contained rather than rush over to deal with the Durians. Once they started leaving, the energy in the crowd started fading.

It still wasn't going to be that easy, of course, and he'd still need to calm down the angriest of the group; but at least it hadn't resulted in blows. Which, in his view, was an overall win.

Chapter 20

By the time Rick, Yao Jing, and his seniors managed to make their way back late at night, Arthur was in a significantly less than charitable mood. Having to deal with irate Climbers who had just been tossed out of their home did that to you, especially when he had to tell some of them that he just wasn't going to rent a place to someone who just threatened to gut him and dance on his entrails.

After telling the third person that threatening him was not going to get them a place—and having them removed by the Tower Guard—the rest of the discussions had grown a lot less strident. Then again, they should never have let him start the conversation inside the lobby of the building, even if it was more comfortable.

A strategic error on their part, though Arthur assumed he was going to have to watch his back a little when he did go out. Not that being careful about potential threats to his life and limb had not been something he'd had to consider before. But random Climbers had not been this high on his list of dangers before.

"Had fun, all of you?" Arthur said angrily to the quartet as they stumbled in. His eyes narrowed a little, noting fresh bruises and cuts on their faces. "Do I want to know?"

It was Leia who moved first, pushing Eric towards the stairs. Uswah, who had slunk downstairs, waved them upwards while muttering about the rooms that had been set aside for them. The building was a set of similar apartments, all of them nothing more than a large room with places to store armour and goods and a washroom. No kitchen needed, though there was a large one on the ground floor for the few times people needed, or rather wanted, to cook.

The boys dealt with, Leia wandered over to Arthur. "We got into a fight. Some idiot has a cultivator technique that makes everyone in the bar drunk."

"Seriously?" Arthur said.

"Yeah. Add in the actual alcohol and it makes for a good time. Till someone heard we were Durians."

"How?" Arthur was suddenly envisioning a lot of individuals singing songs featuring durians in some capacity.

"Someone spotted Yao Jing's crest on his shoulder." Leia sighed. "He took his jacket off. Someone wanted to know more, we started talking, then another person wanted to talk with us and then we had a few more people. Someone got into it, angry about what they'd heard about us before."

"Heard about us?"

"We're a bit of the talk of the town. Rumors, you know."

"Anything useful?"

"We're owned by others. Branch family of the Chins. Or a subset of the Double Sixes. Or the Suey Ying. We killed all the Suey Ying on the first floor or third. Or fifth."

"Fifth?" Arthur said, surprised.

"Rumors. They don't have to be real, right." Leia waved a hand as she flopped into a chair beside him. "Lots of questions, people who want to join us, or are angry with us. A few people wanting to tell us things."

"Sounds about right, really." Arthur sighed. "How did that become a fight?"

"Someone got into it with Yao Jing, about the Suey Ying. They wouldn't believe we didn't kill more of them, blamed us for the fact their little brother who was in there hasn't made it up. He was…"

"Drunk." Arthur sighed.

"Yes. He kept pushing, Yao Jing said something rather stupid—don't ask." She cut him off before he could. "And well, he threw a punch. Then Yao Jing threw him. And then…"

"It became a brawl. And everyone got involved."

"Exactly." He frowned. "So what took so long?"

"Well, I mean, after the fight and the cleanup, we had to find a place to relax."

"Not here?"

"Well, we didn't really—"

"You were avoiding this place!" Arthur said, seeing the tells, the way she had spoken. "You heard about the trouble and you guys were avoiding work!"

"It sounded like you had everything under control. The rest was just…"

"Paperwork. Bureaucracy."

Leia smiled guiltily. "You know I hate that."

"And of course, all of you decided it was best to stay away."

He snorted. "Well, I'll figure out a way to make you all pay."

"Wouldn't expect otherwise."

He grinned, and then she narrowed her eyes at the empty lounge. "What are you doing here, alone?"

"Work." Arthur muttered. "Just work. Go to bed, I just need to look at some things." He waved her off, waited till she was gone before he turned back to his status screen. A pull in that weird mental direction brought forth the information he needed.

Cultivation Speed: 2.573 Yin

Energy Pool: 28/28 (Yin) + (6/6)

Refinement Speed: 0.1421

Refined Energy: 0.18 (32) +(0/3)

Attributes and Traits

Mind: 15 (Multi-Tasking, Quick Learner, Perfect Recall)

Body: 20 (Enhanced Eyesight, Yin Body, Swiftness, Fast Twitch Faster, Lightning Reflexes)

Spirit: 13 (Sticky Energy, From the Dregs)

Techniques

Night Emperor Cultivation Technique

Focused Strike

Accelerated Healing – Refined Energy (Grade III)

Heavenly Sage's Mischief

Refined Energy Dart

Bark Skin

Seven Cloud Stepping Technique (189%)

Partial Techniques

Simultaneous Flow (141.8%)

Yin-Yang Energy Exchange (79.4%)

Pocket Simpanan Tua (72.7%)

A lot to upgrade. He had done well with the Seven Cloud Stepping Technique, though the new percentage numbers he had willed into it gave him an understanding—or the Tower's understanding of his understanding—of how much further he had to go before he could form a second cloud step on the regular. That last eleven percent, though, that was going to be a pain and a half.

He did like the variety of techniques he had now, the way he had both a defense, a buff, a movement, and a couple of attack techniques. He still needed, as he'd considered briefly, a debuff and an area control technique, though a more powerful attack technique or buff was important too. Both if he could do it.

On the other hand, his black spear had done well for him so far, and if he took the time to get it enchanted he might be able to skip getting a powerful attack technique since he could have a technique imbued in the weapon itself. A rather important consideration, since learning new techniques and sustaining them was the biggest issue.

He still couldn't really run more than two techniques at a time, and they had to be two different techniques that were active and passive—not two full-body techniques like the Seven Cloud and his Accelerated Healing, for example. He needed a lot more practise to get there, and while he thought he had an idea, he was sure there were other ways around it that he was not seeing. His methodology was likely the most convoluted method, but it worked for him.

And gave him access to the middle dantian, to store more energy. In fact, with the Pocket Simpanan Tua, he might even be able to store a cultivation technique within. So long as he kept it mildly powered up, he could give himself a quick boost or release an attack via his Refined Energy Dart within moments.

A huge advantage, especially as a surprise attack.

Talking of his Refined Energy Dart, it was rather surprising to him how much it had become his mainstay weapon. He couldn't afford to use it too much, because of how expensive it was to utilize; every time he released a Dart it was hours of meditation dribbling away. However, he'd managed to refine and alter the flow so much that he had a variety of attacks now and, hopefully, even more in the future.

If anything, he felt that continuing to utilize and expand upon the Refined Energy Dart would give him a major advantage. It helped him learn about Tower energy, his own techniques, and how it all worked together. Never mind the advantage of having a ranged attack that did so much damage too, of course.

"So, do I finish the Pocket Simpanan first or work on the other options?" He really did need that area effect or area control method. He could probably buy something from the Tower shop here.

But the cheapskate part of him that had never had a lot growing up was wondering if he could do something else. He could not help but let his eyes drift upwards, to look at his attributes and their traits. Specifically, the one that had changed him the most, the one he had yet to explore much.

A recent conversation with Uswah came to mind and he reached sideways, took the kris out of his side. His first enchanted weapon, his trusty knife and stabbing tool. Its Yin poison was powerful and had saved his life more than once.

And he'd been thinking, he needed to expand his ranged attacks after all, get a debuff running.

So what if he combined the two? A Yin-based ranged attack that could sink into his opponents? And more, if he could make it stick to his spear, add an enchantment that helped him damage the opponent more, what would happen?

He had to admit, for the first time in a while, Arthur was looking forward to finding out.

Chapter 21

As much as he wanted to be focused upon exploring the various methodologies and techniques and his new Yin Body further, Arthur was, in the end, the Clan Head. He had responsibilities and as much as he tried to shift them to others, delegating like any smart manager did, there were just some things that only he could handle.

Including the all-hands meeting the next morning, held in the corner of the lobby with Eric glaring at those other residents who were coming down, curious about what was happening.

"We need a real meeting room." Mel said, sighing as Eric shooed off the next lookie-loo. "We can't talk Clan business in the lobby."

"No meeting room," Arthur said. "I checked. This place is barebones."

"We could break a room down, make one?" Yao Jing offered.

"Great. If you can do that without breaking the building," Arthur said. "I can't exactly tell if a wall is load-bearing. Can you?"

"Load bearing...?"

"The walls that make sure the building doesn't come down," Leia said with a sigh. "I can ask around, see if anyone knows. But most of the walls are pretty thin. It should be fine."

"Probably." Arthur shrugged. "I'd still like to know first before we break anything."

A few confirming nods, before he dismissed the topic. It wouldn't help them now anyway. "Right. So, we have three things." A slight pause. "At least, in my view. Anyone have anything to add, add it after I'm done. First up, our new residents." He waved upwards. "We collected their payments, after the Chins finally coughed up refunds, so those that are here are here." He chuckled a little. "Didn't have to even kick out that many, what with the place not being full." In fact, they actually had more rooms than they needed, especially with a few of his group doubling up, including Jan with Yao Jing and Eric with Leia. "That being said, we should get a proper document set up and make sure those who are meant to be leaving are. Need someone in charge of that."

"You're not letting them stay afterwards?" Leia asked, curiously.

"No," Arthur said, firmly. "Not at these rates at least, and while there might be a few—" He stopped at Leia's look and added, "I'll tell you later. While there might be a few who are interesting, we don't let them in if they don't join the Clan. There's not enough space once we start recruiting, I'd bet. So those who want long-term residence, even Clan members, are going to need to show they're worth it."

"Eh, boss. This a big building, what," Yao Jing said. "You sure we need worry that much, *ah*?"

"Definitely. We need to keep at least a few rooms free for those ascending and give them time to get their feet under them, and then a few rooms for the Chins and a few for long-termers as perks. Space is going to run out, fast. So, we need a plan and someone managing this. Volunteers?"

No one offered themselves up, so Arthur stared at Leia. She winced but nodded eventually, accepting her fate. As much as she disliked such work, he knew she'd be decent at it. And decent was all they needed, at least till he found his Floor Boss.

"Next. The Thorned Lotuses." Mel and Uswah both perked up. "They're yours, of course. Just get to them soon, and let's set up a meeting. Hopefully they like us well enough and it's less of a headache getting them to join and agree."

"And if it is?" Mel said, carefully.

"Then we work it out. You know the Lotuses have first call."

She smiled happily and he snorted, turning away. Sometimes, his Vice Clan Head could get real touchy. "Thirdly, the Chins. Getting payment and all that." He shrugged. "That's for me to deal with, but Casey's been pretty good at getting us payment quick. Once it comes in, I'll take payment." A slight hesitation, then he nodded to Jan. "We'll also be dealing with the merchants and whatnot. Shouldn't take long; not like we have a lot to trade for yet."

Murmured agreements, before he finished. "That's it *lah*, ya?"

"Ghee Hin." Mel offered.

"*Celaka*. I forgot. Right, what did they want?"

"They want to talk."

"Talk?"

"Just talk, they said," Mel replied with a shrug. "Seemed respectful enough."

"Huh." Arthur frowned, considering. The triads were always tricky to work with, and he'd hoped to avoid them this floor, but obviously it wasn't going to happen.

"Eh, Arthur? Maybe *we* should, you know?" Leia waved at herself and Eric. "We just worked with them. Know how they think, we could feel them out to start at least."

"And avoid dealing with this building?" he said with a smirk.

She grinned. "It makes sense, *lah*."

"Uh huh." She was right, but he was still reluctant.

Rick, silent until now, coughed. "I could do it." Then, hurrying to clarify, he added, "The building. Not the gangsters. I know how to do this—take money, take notes, feel people out. It's what my father had me do before, really. It's not that hard."

"Says you."

Arthur hesitated, still not entirely sure he could trust the man all that far. Then again, this might be a good first step. He was the heir of a multi-million-dollar business empire. He must have the relevant skills, Arthur figured. And how badly could he screw up the recruitment and management of a bunch of Climbers and their apartments anyway? It was not as though anyone else was voluteering.

"Fine." He sighed, rubbed his face. "Last thing."

"I though you said there were only three?" Mel said, teasingly.

"Funny. But seriously, last thing. This is the last rest floor. When we head up, there's no guarantee we'll be together. The last floors, you know how it is." Nods all around, and he continued. "So. While setting up the Durians is important, most important is making sure you're all ready for what's above." He firmed his voice as he added, "No dying."

They echoed the words back, some seriously, a few like Yao Jing with a smile. It was Uswah who fixed him with a look till he paid attention to her.

"You especially, Arthur," Uswah said. "We will take as much of these meetings as we can, because you need to practise and grow stronger. You most of all."

Arthur hesitated, before he bobbed his head in acknowledgement. He had been thinking the same thing last night after all, that he needed to work on his techniques. As much as he could, he intended to do that, and he said the same out loud.

Some other minor conversations continued, discussions of places to eat, or buildings the group had seen. Even a brief mention of the altercation last night.

Then, they split off, everyone with their own jobs.

"So what now, boss?" Jan said, hovering by his side.

"You find our merchants, let's talk to them. Maybe we can sell something, maybe we can recruit them. I want to know what we can get." He turned slightly, touched the spear he had brought down and propped up against the wall near him. "I want enchanters, if possible."

She nodded, hesitated, then added, "Then you cultivate, *lah*. This for me to do."

"But..."

"You don't need to be down here, *lah*. Ah Jing and I, we can do it enough."

"I'm sure you do it enough..."

She snorted, not even blushing. Yao Jing grinned, puffing up a bit till she smacked him in the stomach with the back of her hand as she continued. "Once we know something, we tell you. But you go cultivate."

Again, he considered protesting but eventually nodded. She was right. Casey wasn't going to be back with any new stones anytime soon, but he had some from their recent ascent. And a lot of experimenting to do either way. What he needed, most of all, was time. She was offering, so why was he resisting?

In the end, he shook his head and dismissed his reluctance. "Okay. Go."

Jan nodded, took a few steps away, frowned and turned around, leveling a finger at him. "You. Stay inside, okay?"

"Yeah, yeah." He waved a hand, dismissing her concerns. He knew better than to leave the building. In fact, grabbing his spear, he turned to head for the stairs right away. If he was going to experiment, his room was the best option.

Whistling as he strode up the stairs, he could not help but wonder what he'd learn today.

Chapter 22

Arthur flopped himself on the bed, winced as he bounced a little off the hard wooden bedframe underneath. Made note not to do that again before he pulled his legs towards him. First things first, he was going to finish with this Pocket Simpanan Tua. He figured a few days of constant practise would get him there, especially if he actually focused only on practising the cultivation technique rather than playing around with dual cultivating or healing himself or whatever other jazz.

Sometimes, multi-tasking really wasn't more efficient. Especially as he needed to actually complete some of these techniques. Though, in a while he was going to have to practise the Poket Simpanan anyway, because the last portion of making the technique work was learning to store a technique within, without it breaking on him.

First things first, though. He crossed his legs, went into lotus position, and placed his hands between his legs, cupping them loosely. He breathed, slowly, letting his mind relax. After so many years practising, it only took him a few breaths to clear his mind entirely, finding that peace of mind necessary to delve within.

Then, inside, he turned to his middle dantian. Not his lower one, which everyone utilized because it was the largest and safest to work with, but the one higher up in his chest. He felt the energy that was stored within, the thrum of Tower energy that was waiting to be compressed and turned into refined energy.

He ignored it, letting the energy gather as he manipulated the space. Energy pulsed, pouring through his meridians, channeled through various meridian points and twisted and wrung out, such that it was properly channelled and in a state ready to be manipulated. Then, he wove that net into a cloth made of power that was permeable for energy flowing in but not the other way. At least, that was the theory.

Thus far, the entire technique patterning was him learning how to manipulate his energy, creating the right kind of energy within, and then weaving the cloth in the right manner. Practise, practise, practise. He could try most of this in the quiet of the night or when he was safe. Due to the chance of backlash when he did wrong, it wasn't a technique he dared to do while in danger.

So, right now, he was focused all the way in, pushing at the Poket Simpanan, testing it and tightening the weave. He managed to get the weave of power down, or so he thought after time interminable. Then, with an exhalation, he released it all and watched it dissipate.

All to do it again.

Twice more, each time trying for accuracy before speed. Each time he tried to speed up, he could hear his *sifu*'s voice, the harsh admonition to "Slow down. Do it right." Or "Get it right, first; before you eat their fist next." Perfection was the enemy of progress; so many people would say. But what they didn't tell you was that perfection, or the striving for it, was how you got good. So many other schools pushed for the easy wins, and those easy wins were great; until you had to dodge a half-dozen monsters or fists and you had an inch or half-inch to move in. Then, every shred of perfection was needed.

Arthur knew, in the end, it was that pursuit of perfection that had gotten him through so far. He might not have started with plain battle sense, that ability to cold-read opponents and know what they were going to do. He was never the best duellist in the school, never the best fighter. Too small, too short, too wiry.

He only ever had two advantages. A willingness to take the hits when necessary. And the ability to dance in chaos better than any of the others. Some of his fellow students, they hated the mass fights, the two or three or four-on-ones that happened at times. Arthur? He thrived on them.

Chaos, he loved it. It loved him, because somehow things fell into place there. A place where his ability to think and react and choose fast made all the sense.

Not that any of that mattered right now, as he released the latest pocket weave and stood up. Stretched, got ready to start again; only for a knock on the door to stop him.

He frowned, gripped the kris as he slid over, to the side of the door. Called out, knowing he was being paranoid.

"Who is it?"

"Jan." She wiggled the door, noted it was locked, and waited. He unlocked and swung it open, frowning as she looked around, flicking her gaze up and down him and not seeing anything problematic.

"So?"

"You were right. Those merchants, they might be good," she said, reporting in.

"Can any of it wait?" he asked.

"Uhh…" Jan hesitated, but she nodded.

"Then, tonight." He moved to close the door. "Unless it can't, tonight. I need practise." A pause, a glance, then he added, "Tell the others?"

"Okay." She sounded doubtful and almost he asked, almost got involved right away. But at some point, he needed to get this technique done. Closing on the door on her and pushing aside his worries, he got back onto his bed gingerly after a quick series of stretches.

Back to working on the Poket Simpanan Tua. He was, mostly, happy with how far he'd come and it was time for the harder, more dangerous part. The portion that he was not looking forward to. Now he split his attention, attempted to put together the technique while he built out another.

Failed. Felt the backlash and winced as his body thrummed with unreleased power.

Fought down the pain, waited for his body to settle.

Failed again.

Tried again, as he pulled together both techniques together at the same time. It wasn't that he couldn't do it, but building a new technique he wasn't entirely familiar with and another technique like his Refined Energy Dart was difficult when he was trying to do it fast and smooth.

But he had it. So next step was to slide the Dart in the pocket, get it stored away.

Failed, as the energy mixed. He fell over, clutching his chest, forced himself to concentrate as he smoothed out the energies, dispersed some of it. Rubbed at his nose, wondering why he was smelling mint and perfume.

Something light and floral and a remembrance of a late night in a club after a delivery job, when a young lady had pulled him aside and...

Well. Maybe he was getting a little antsy, even with the Yin Body.

Focused again. Sat down, allowing energy to course through him as he pulled everything together into separate techniques. Adjusted the Poket Simpanan as he began to pull the Dart through. Made it two thirds of the way in, much better than before; but another failure.

Less of a backlash, less pain.

It hurt, but what was pain but a transient emotion. Like lust or jealousy or desire. He felt his mind calm after a few breaths, marveled at how much easier it was with the Yin Body, that calmness and lack of push. Tried again. And again. And eventually, he figured it out.

Enough, at least, to hold the Dart within the walls of the cloth, the woven net of energy. Then, he needed the next step, to connect the two together, such that the Poket Simpanan took over the running, the management; feeding the finished technique the necessary energy to keep it running even as it bled a little energy off just by existing, but not by much.

That was when he realised there was a marked difference between the kinds of techniques and how well each was put together. He sensed it now that he was looking, how the Refined Energy Dart bled off excess energy, used itself up as he held it in him. Fractions of points each moment, gaps that needed filling, or parts that were unrefined and bleeding energy.

His concentration wavered, a part of him wanting to fix it, to do better. Perfection dragged at him, knowledge that if he did better, it might be faster to put things together, smoother. Cost less energy, which was important, oh so damn important. On the other hand...

He had other things to do, a technique he had to finish.

Forced himself to concentrate, to remember what he was here for. Made note of his imperfections though, before he began the process of detaching the technique. The technique was mostly ready, just needing a little bit of direction and will, needing those controlling inputs and...

It was not that easy. Never was.

Lying on the ground, clutching his chest, rubbing at it as he pulled energy back into his core and recombined it. He took a few moments to cultivate and refine, just to clear the dregs of rampant, uncontrolled power coursing through that sent electric shocks through him. Thankfully, it was all his own energy; so the pain was more akin, after the initial shock, to having a leg or limb fall asleep. Incredibly annoying, numbing and tingly, but not the end of the world.

Not unless he messed up really badly.

And that wasn't worth thinking about, so he rolled himself back onto his feet. Breathed deep.

Got back to training.

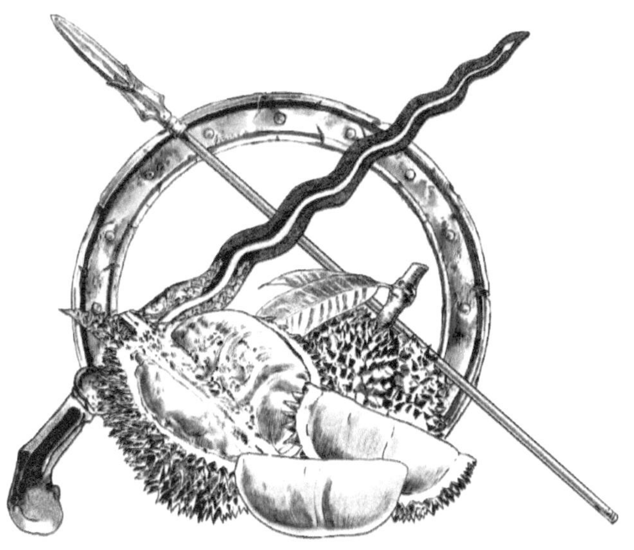

Chapter 23

Arthur stumbled down the stairs, searching for water. He had forgotten to pack enough in his bags, didn't refill the bottles he had upstairs, and the water coming out of the taps was rather funky-tasting. Not that he was going to complain, what with the fact that they had actual running water in the building, but perhaps some strainers or something to get the taste out would help. If he had to guess, it was likely just rainwater gathered from the barrels on the rooftop, with some assistance from a few barrels carried up and dumped into the water tower to keep it filled. He doubted they had an actual motor or enchantment pulling water from a citywide water system.

He had been a little surprised to find neither Jan nor Yao Jing outside his door, but then they were technically safe in this building. Still, it would have been convenient to send someone to get him some water…

"You're out," Leia said, a tinge of surprise.

"Why are you so surprised?" He hesitated, then added, "I wasn't in there for a week or something, right?"

"Just a day." A hand gestured outside where the sun had set and the room was only lit by various enchanted beast stone lamps. The lamps always gave off a weird color to Arthur's eyes, just a little too yellow and dark. A mental note to see about getting—or trading—for solar panels if they could. Getting electronics here would be helpful, though it generally required Tower-grade equipment. Which, amusingly, was simpler equipment, requiring fewer tiny microchips and connections and bigger wires because the varying temperatures and the Tower itself did less damage to such things. It wasn't all like that, of course, but mobiles, computers, and anything that seemed to carry around information got targeted.

Which kind of led to the theory that the Towers were alive. And jealous about their secrets.

"Oh, thank god. What time is it?" Arthur said, or croaked. Reminded himself of what he needed to do, so went to grab some water as he listened.

"Early morning. So, any luck?"

"So-so, *lah*." He even managed a little head bobble to add emphasis and grinned back at her as she snorted. Wandered over, took a seat, and let out a long yawn as he lay his head on the table, glass of water still beside him. "What you doing up?"

"Couldn't sleep. Eric started snoring again."

"Ooooh"…" He remembered that. The man snored a little, but mostly the small, soft cute snoring type. Occasionally though, when he had drunk too much, was too tired, or was getting a cold he managed to locate his chainsaw and got to work cutting down the sandman's forest. "So. You and Eric."

"Don't," she warned.

He grinned unrepentantly till she sighed and answered him. "It just, I couldn't let him die, right? And then we started spending more time together. And he's kind of sweet, if you look at him in the right way."

"Right way."

Then she grinned wickedly. "Also, you know most of you all are pretty damn hot, right? All that exercise, all those abs. And he's got great control of his hips. He does this thing where he rolls his hips when—"

"Lalalalala!" Sticking his fingers in his ears, Arthur couldn't hide the smile he returned as she stopped talking at last. It wasn't really as bad as hearing a sibling describe their sex life, but it was comparable. After all, they'd grown up together and even if hooking up in the class was not uncommon, it still wasn't something you discussed. At least, between sexes and between the men.

He made no promises of what happened between women, especially considering how blatant some of the older women could get at times. That brought a very real shudder, especially in the last few years when they started trying to set him up with their daughters. A man just wanted to go shopping for new shorts without being offered to be set up on a date sometimes.

"So, it work?"

"Yeah, yeah it did." He touched his chest, sensing again the churning mass of energy within him. "I got it working."

"What was it again? Something to do with your middle dantian?" Disapproval in her voice, for obvious reasons. He ignored it, since he did survive opening the damn thing.

"Holding technique for, uhhh, techniques." He chuckled a little sheepishly. "Lets me keep something contained in the dantian."

"Like a healing?"

"No, no full-body things. Or not the start at least." He waved his hands, trying to describe it. "Full-body techniques, they need to work all at the same time, right? You can't just contain them and then expect them to spread out. You're actively working those techniques into you. So healing, buffs, that kind of thing doesn't work. But something more contained? You could do that. Like your Energy Dart. Or Focused Strike. A bundle of energy."

"OK. So nothing continuous?"

"Can't store the energy you need to keep it running, but you could store the starting amount and then start feeding it, I guess."

"You guess?"

Arthur shrugged. "I just figured it out like... thirty minutes ago. Been testing and re-testing it, and now I'm going to try carrying around my technique for a few days, see if it works." Rubbed his temples. "It's also good training for splitting my flows, you know."

Leia nodded. Almost every cultivator eventually got to the point of needing to split their energy flows. In fact, it was the only way to progress after a point, since you needed protective techniques, attacking techniques, and sensing ones active if you wanted to survive advanced towers.

For all that, you'd think there would be more information about such techniques on the Internet; but so far no one had leaked a technique that was worth shit. Most of the techniques available publicly were like half-star techniques at the best and most serious Climbers read them over, but made sure to buy proper training manuals in the Tower. Or, like Arthur, just figured it out themselves.

One of the difficulties was that it was rather individual, what with multiple traits and physiologies getting involved. Some methodologies were just easier for others, and while Arthur had considered buying one himself... well, he had enough things to learn and was progressing well enough.

If nothing else, he didn't need to split into three parts. Not yet.

"So, what's happened while I was gone?" he asked, shifting a little to find a more comfortable part of his arm to lie on.

"Not much. Jan talked to Mel when she got back, they interviewed some of the merchants. Made an offer to sell our stuff, they're looking into enchanters and getting bulk deals for us." She ticked her fingers off. "Mel says we've got lousy timing. The big boss of the Lotuses isn't around, they're training or something outside. But she made an open invitation for the other girls to use the living room, just so they can train a bit if they want and talk to us."

Arthur grunted, looking around the empty space in the lobby. They'd need to fix it up a little from its spartan appearance if people were going to actively be cultivating down here. Some privacy screens or something. Almost made him think of those massage centers run by blind masseurs who'd work on you in a wide open area, while others lay just beside you.

"Rick's on it. Jan asked the merchants to get us some screens and some seats for people to cultivate. Or rest." She grunted. "We're going to need shifts, to watch over things down here." She raised an eyebrow and she shrugged. "They can't hurt us, but doesn't mean they can't steal."

True enough. Once they were let in, the Tower Guard probably wouldn't care. Or it might. He wasn't entirely sure the Guards cared within a building. Then again, if he didn't know, maybe everyone else didn't either.

"Rick?" he asked instead.

"He has a book started. Names, dates, all that jazz. Also, he took inventory of the building and the rooms, damage, all that kind of thing." She grinned. "Casey helped, had her manager hand over his bookm now that they didn't need it anymore." Rubbed her chin. "Rick was talking of hiring him, if we can."

"Because he's good?"

"He knows the building. Seemed competent enough."

"Spy."

She waved up to the ceiling. "We literally have a Chin living here and she's one of your closest confidantes."

"Not that close..." At the smirk, he sighed. "Okay, but she knows a lot. And is smart."

"And cute."

Arthur smiled. It didn't hurt. "I'll think about it. How about you?"

"Not much to report. The Ghee Hin are posturing. They want you to come, we're saying you're busy, we have a meeting in two days, just me and Eric. We'll see what we come to in an agreement about meetings and feel out what they want."

Arthur sighed but was at least grateful that he didn't have to get involved yet. Leia watched as his eyes drooped, head nuzzling into his own arm. She reached out, shook him, and gestured upstairs when he stared at her.

"What?"

"Sleep. In your room."

"Urgh." He sighed and pushed himself upwards, grabbed his cup and downed it, frowned as Leia took it from him and gestured for him to head back upstairs again. Letting out a long-suffering sigh, he stumbled over to the stairs, realising how exhausted he was. It was one thing cultivating, another putting yourself through the wringer with constant cultivation backlashes while studying a technique. It hurt and was tiring, and he just...

Well, maybe it was time to rest. After all, it seemed everyone else had it well in hand.

For now.

Chapter 24

The next couple of days were a grind, interspersed with brief forays outside. He set up regular meetings with the others so that he could speak with his team, getting updates and making sure they rotated through downtime too and begin resting themselves. He couldn't just work his people to the bone, letting them take over his job or work for the Clan without giving them time to train. Or else they might not ever make it out of the Tower, which would be a real tragedy.

Balancing training and how far everyone was coming along was important, which was why he was grateful most of the team had alternates. Mel and Uswah, Jan and Yao Jing, Eric and Leia. Rick was about the only one who didn't, but it seemed the man also had the easiest job once he was settled. Most days, he was found downstairs, chatting with the residents or in his room. Though, Arthur thought he felt a growing sense of impatience in the man, one that he knew he'd have to deal with eventually.

As for himself, well...

Perhaps the most important was the Poket Simpanan Tua technique that finally was complete. It was a minor shift, but one that he was quite proud of. As expected, the process of splitting the flows and then holding them within him while doing other forms of training had been difficult, but it further improved his Simultaneous Flow Cultivation technique. He still had a long way to go, but he could feel the progress in the way it was easier to work things.

Now, carrying the Refined Energy Dart within him, he got to work on his next plan for improvement. Rather than purchasing a new cultivation technique, Arthur's focus was on the Yin energy within him. And the kris.

After extracting the wavy dagger-sword weapon out of its sheath, he had begun the process of studying the energy within. At first, he'd intended on doing it the smart and patient way: pay attention to the enchantments and the energy within the kris itself.

It took him all of twenty minutes to realise that he was only inching forward on his progress and understanding. At that point, he chose to take a shortcut. One that he knew others would be annoyed with, if they knew, which was why he was grateful for the locked door.

He took off his pants to start, then carefully pricked an outer side of his leg. He'd considered the inside but knew that could get dangerous. Even if it was less likely to scar and chaff when he walked. The edge of the kris, sharpened with a whetstone beforehand, cut through his flesh with only the lightest push, blood welling within moments as he removed the blade.

Arthur cursed, realising he forgot to get a bandage and had to scramble to find one in his bag, even as blood seeped out from the deeper-than-expected wound. Not as though he had a lot of experience with self-harm. Training was tough, but it wasn't that tough.

All this was hindered by his need to keep focused on the flow of poison entering him. It wasn't a liquid but an enchanted chi poison, a flow of energy that stained his own. Or tried to. As he'd learnt on the first floor, having a Yin Body gave him a natural resistance, but the question was why.

Now he found out.

Or tried to, at least.

"I should turn off my healing…" Arthur muttered ten minutes later as he finished wiping down his thigh with the damp and bloody cloth. Beneath the blood-streaked area was smooth skin, his passive healing technique having finished the simple fix. Which was great and probably did a little for his on-going use and improvement of the technique, especially as he was focused quite hard at that area but it did mean he had to cut himself again. So maybe keeping it running was the way to go.

Even before the wound was healed, his body had shaken off the poison chi. Too bad leaving the kris blade unbared on unblemished skin did absolutely nothing. Whatever enchantment there was that gave the kris its poisonous nature, it only activated or penetrated his natural defenses when it breached his skin. Possibly, it just wasn't strong enough otherwise.

Magic theory had never been his strong suit.

Another breath, another prick. Bandage on the wound, as he focused on the strange and foreign chi coursing through him, the way it stilled the muscles, slowed the flow of his own chi. There was almost a seeking element to it, as it found Yang energy within him—and yes, even in a Yin Body, there was Yang—

and attacked it. Neutralised the Yang energy, causing his body and the elements of it to slow and freeze.

He teased at the energy, trying to understand the difference between his own and the kris's, tried to understand how it affected him in such a way and how his own energy neutralised the enchantment. It wasn't just that he had less Yang energy and needed it less to function with a Yin Body, which had been his first guess. He wanted to understand the way the two Yin energies interacted.

His own was subsuming the foreign, transforming it to something similar, something more in line with his own chi. He couldn't explain why it was different, just that it was and that the more he pushed and prodded at it, the more he could feel the differences between the two.

If he had to describe it, Arthur would have likened it to feeling the shape of a Lego block with his eyes closed. Everyone had the same pieces probably, or close enough; the building blocks themselves were all the same after all. The difference was how these pieces were structured and put together. There were parts that needed to be left open for future attachments, other parts that shifted or changed or came apart as different meridians and meridian points interacted with it.

His goal, as he studied the foreign Yin energy was to work out how and why it was different. And then, eventually, how to make his own Yin energy similar to the invading energy, at least in part.

When the knock came, halfway through the afternoon, it startled Arthur. He blinked, sitting up, staring at his leg and then around, at the mess he had made. He'd washed and cleaned some bandages, over and over again to help with the work, but even then…

Bloody bandages, bloody blade, scattered clothing and stained bedding. Streaks of sweat and blood on his arms and legs, and of course, pantless.

A real stable kind of look.

Chapter 25

"Arthur!"

Another call, louder this time, by Mel. It startled Arthur out of his stupor and had him moving. First things first, he grabbed his pants and started pulling them on. Calling out, he asked her to wait. Once his pants were on, belt cinched, he kicked the bandages and bloody bits under the bed before walking over to the door.

Pulled it open, a little, keeping one foot behind and leaning around it.

"Yes?"

Immediately, her eyes narrowed. "What's wrong?"

"What do you mean?" he asked.

"You're being weird. What's wrong?"

"Nothing. It's just a mess in here, I was training," Arthur said, mostly truthfully. "What do you want?"

"I have the Chins here."

"So, let Casey know."

"They're here for you." A slight pause, then Mel added, "Both of you."

"Ah, hmm…" he hummed for a moment, looking entirely unhappy about the idea of actually having to step outside. Then again… "Do they have our beast stones?"

"They do."

"*Celaka.*" Arthur sighed and leaned back, intending to close the door. "Just give—"

He never finished as Mel, seeing her opportunity, pushed the door open and bumped him, causing Arthur to scramble to get his balance as she squeezed in. And then froze.

"Arthur—!" her voice rose.

"It doesn't look like what you think it looks like?" Arthur tried.

"So you weren't playing surgery on yourself in here in an attempt to make your healing technique advance?" Mel said, spinning to glare at Arthur.

"I… actually, no, I wasn't." He expected more hysterics or anger, not an actual considered and plausible scenario coming out of her mouth. Which, to be fair to Mel, was always going to be her likely reaction if he had thought about it. Prone to hysterics was not something he had ever considered her to be. Then again, anyone prone to hysterics probably hadn't made it off the first floor.

"Then what were you doing?" she said.

"Working on my Yin chi."

Eyes scanned the room, alighted on the kris. She shook her head after a moment, muttering, "I should have guessed," before she fixed him with a disappointed look.

"I was being safe. Only cutting a little. I actually don't need a lot of the enchantment to work things out. It just… had to happen a lot."

"Masochist," she muttered.

That was the other reason he hadn't wanted anyone else involved. Once things like that got around, it was really hard to live down. Or squash. After all, John "Poo Pants" Lee still hadn't squashed that name, even if it had been because he'd been kicked a little too hard during a bout.

"Look, it had to be done." Making sure the door was closed, Arthur leaned back on it. "I was nearly there too. Until, you know, you interrupted me."

"Nearly there at . . . making the poison?" Now she was intrigued.

"Sort of? I think I can make a version of it, inside me. Problem is, I don't think I want the exact same thing."

"Why not?"

"Because the exact same poison attacks me. I want something that's like it but doesn't hurt me.," Arthur explained.

"Hmm. *Susah.*"

He sighed, agreeing with her: it would be difficult indeed. But... "Anyway. Don't tell anyone. I don't need people learning about this, till I actually need to use it. Or first, figure it out." He raised a hand, before Mel could ask. "And yes, I'll talk to Uswah. But no one else. And none about..."

"You stabbing yourself like you're getting *siew yoke* ready? Okay." Mel turned and waved him away from the door, glancing at the room one last time. "But make sure to clean up. I'll delay them."

It was when she was mostly out, that he remembered to say it, "Thanks."

"Don't sweat it."

Meeting the Chin entourage downstairs reminded Arthur once again how inconvenient using the apartments were for a Clan building. Great for storing a bunch of people, but the lobby was the only place he could hold a meeting, and not without making friends in ways he wasn't ready for yet.

Especially considering how hard it was to bathe regularly.

As he got close to the group, he debated if he could remove any rooms to make space for a proper meeting room.

Benevolent Durians Clan Building (Seventh Floor, Tower 2895)

Type: Residence

Building Bonus Chosen: Security (Town Guard assigned)

Total Number of Floors: 5

Total Number of Residents: 32

Total Number of Rooms: 68

Probably. If he was willing to accept that. Now, it was time to focus on his allies. Or whatever this group was.

"Ms. Chin," Arthur greeted the older woman standing there. Casey's aunt, he assumed. She was in her forties maybe, though such things were hard to tell with the Tower messing up ages and aging and stats a little. It didn't give people immortality, but the more you cultivated, the longer your lifespan. There were even a few formulas that had been created to estimate the lifespan of a Climber, though with only twenty years of data it was very much a series of competing hypotheses and formulas. "Welcome to the Benevolent Durians Clan House."

"No need to welcome me. I've been here before," the older woman said. "And it's not Chin. It's Wen."

"Ah, my apologies Ms. Wen. Then, you married into the family?" After all, Chinese women generally did not take the last name of their husband's family, keeping their own family name. Even if they were part of the husband's family officially, they were—and would always be—an outsider too.

"I did. And then, when he died in the Tower, I was sent to take the place he was supposed to have had," Ms. Wen said. "The Chins are nothing if not practical. And unforgiving of mistakes."

A warning? Or just the complaints of an angry woman? He was beginning to understand a little of why she might have grown greedy. Without a fortune or power of her own, she was vulnerable to the whims of those above. Better, then, to take what one could.

"Casey's been a decent companion so far," Arthur said, diplomatically. "Can I offer you some tea? Cookies?" Looking around, he spotted Jan and raised an eyebrow, at which she disappeared to look for refreshments.

"About time," Ms. Wen muttered under her breath even as he gestured for them to take a seat further back. He ignored the various guards and other personnel as he waited for his guest to sit, plopping down beside her as did Casey moments later.

Soon enough, a battered teapot and a handful of mildly smashed cookies graced the tiny tea table before them, and Arthur gestured for the woman to eat. They'd passed the time with basic small talk and enquiries to health, Casey silent and non-committal.

When refreshments had been consumed, only then did Arthur speak, barely even hesitating at the usage of the familiar as he did. "Did Auntie have a reason for visiting me, then?"

"I wanted to see my niece, of course. And meet the boy who had so charmed her."

"Mmm, I fear it's the other way."

"Really? Little Casey seduced you?" An eye raked over the other girl's form critically, a light sneer appearing on her face. "I guess some people like their women thin and without a butt."

"Auntie!" Casey hissed, scandalized.

"It's true, though. All you Chin women have no bums. I know how hard you all work, but sometimes, you just have to accept genetics for what it is. At least your sister has nice breasts though."

"They're fake!"

"But good ones, no?" Ms. Wen said.

Arthur's head turned from one lady to the other. For all her initial outrage, it seemed that Casey was on the backfoot dealing with the older lady. And recalling which side the *kaya* was spread on in his toast, he spoke up.

"Eh, Casey's got a nice body. Very hourglass and Climber-hot you know?"

What used to be a fitness model ideal for healthiness and sexiness had transformed, moving towards more practical fitness. Rather than bodybuilder ideals of male or female beauty, Climbers had become the focus. And the natural consequence of never having to eat, a Tower-energy induced system, and a combination of cultivation and genes had led towards a more practical, if still strong-looking, body type. You were more likely to see barrel-chested and thick-legged men stared at than the bodybuilder V-shape of before; and with women, a slimmer but stronger gymnast build had become the default.

None of which helped Casey, who glared at Arthur and his helpful addition.

"Auntie Wen. Did you bring Arthur's stones? In a bag perhaps?" The words were sweet and vicious.

A head turned, fingers crooking sideways. A man stepped forward, a literal briefcase offered and opened. Inside were plastic cases, dozens of beast stones sorted.

"As your man requested." Ms. Wen's lips turned up. "I'll want the cases returned, of course." Her eyes roamed over Arthur and then she leaned forward, propping a hand on her chin. "By the Clan Head himself."

"Why me?" he asked, curiously.

"Because I asked you to? Can you not indulge an old woman?" She gestured upstairs. "Not yet, of course. You need to cultivate, gain some strength." Eyes dropped lower. "And stamina."

"AUNTIE!"

"What?" Ms. Wen said, standing up smoothly. She smoothed her dress down, wiggling a little sensuously in a way that made the men—and a few women—follow her hands and hips. "You want to climb, you got to have stamina. This floor, it can be exhausting." Then, wickedly, she added, "As can I."

With those words, she swept past the front door, leaving a rather stunned group behind.

Yao Jing, watching her go, muttered, "What a woman."

And Arthur could only concur.

Chapter 26

It took some time to calm Casey after she had been ambushed by her own aunt. After muttering about disgraceful older women, she had eventually left to visit the Chin family home on this floor, intent on discussing matters with her aunt in private. How she intended that conversation to play out, Arthur had no idea and, quite firmly, really did not need to know.

Instead, he turned to the next job, one he was suddenly glad was being done in public. The kind of rumors that would be created, as he handed out cases of the beast stones for cultivating to his various Clan members was perfect recruitment bait. Of course, there were negatives to such actions; but being in one of the safest buildings on this floor allayed most of that.

Still, he did caution his people to watch where they stored their new stones and not to walk around with them in public. The Tower Guard's protection only extended to the building itself after all.

Finally, when all that had been sorted and a quick discussion with the returned Eric and Lcia confirmed he had another appointment tomorrow with the Ghee Hin leadership, he was able to scurry back upstairs to continue his period of testing and practise. As he had promised Mel, his period of self-mutilation was over. Mostly.

Instead, he spent his time lying on the bed, focused inside as he turned energy around and around in his meridians, trying to form a poisonous Yin energy combination that was both effective at nullifying Yang chi and yet was stable within himself. A somewhat contradictory set of requirements, he had to admit.

But hey, if wasn't challenging, everyone would have done it already.

"So, remind me again why we're meeting with the Ghee Hin?"

"And the Double Sixes," Leia replied Arthur.

"And the Sixes. And the United Nations," Arthur confirmed. "As though we want to deal with all of the damn gangs at the same time."

"You want to ignore them, can also," Eric said. "But then, *susah* for us."

"I know, I know. We're not big enough to deal with them, and they're all big enough to crush our people in the various places. And even if we were the size of Prime Group or whatever, they'd still be someone we have to appease a bit." Arthur sighed. "Everyone wants to bother us."

"Normal, right?" Leia pointed out. His seniors were flanking him as they walked down the street, Yao Jing ahead of the group and Jan already watching the meeting spot.

"Because we have something they all want?" Arthur sighed. Access to the Clan rooms, to the potential powers and strength as they grew. "Still stupid. We're nothing yet."

"Don't forget the government also, eh?" Eric added.

Arthur let out another sigh at that. How could he forget. The Clan's good luck, a little maneuvering by Casey and Mel, the general laziness of the government bureaucrats, and the Durians' fast ascent had kept the greedy hands of the government personnel at bay. That, and the fact that the few bureaucrats who were semi-permanently stationed in the Tower just weren't the cream of the crop, had left them somewhat undisturbed.

It was not going to last. Either this floor or when he exited, he had to deal with them.

The problem with dealing with the government—with any government—as an individual, was a matter of disparate strength. Even the most powerful Climber could not, alone, defy a government. At least, not successfully in the long term and not become a criminal. Sure, they could retreat to a Tower. In a Tower, the advantages of a government—the significant difference in resources, the numbers and the various apparatus to leverage against the individual and their loved ones—were curtailed, but that was not defiance that could last in the long term and in the outside world.

For many of the Guilds in the west or the Clans in the East, the most powerful gained an uneasy alliance with their governments, balancing their needs with the government's own need and desire for strong Climbers, the outflow of enchanted material and goods and stones to provide for Climbers that had exited, and of course, the training of personnel.

Beginner Towers were notoriously unreliable for providing materials. Even now, the Malaysian Tower had basically offered very little in loot drops. On exit, they might be able to acquire some small number of goods; but mostly, the exiting Climbers would only emerge from the Tower with increased stats, their cultivation skills, and a host of stones—many collected in the last few floors that they could then utilize to sell to ex-Climbers or to extend their own stay in the outside world.

By entering and clearing another Beginner Tower, they would necessarily gain a second or third or more surplus of beast stones to sell onwards. Which was, in the end, the most common methodology of survival and progress for a large number of Climbers before they were themselves required to progress to Intermediate Towers by the accumulation of Tower energy in their body.

A smaller number of cultivators, of course, chose to progress through Beginner Towers quicker to move towards intermediate locations. Not an official designation, of course, but one utilized by the governments to indicate Towers which were not only harder but also more likely to provide material gains.

It was these Towers and their resources that powered the Tower economy and, at the highest level of progress, Earth technology and luxury goods. With basic automation having overtaken the necessity for labour, the Towers made for a necessary relief valve for the population and, also, a series of luxury items that could not be acquired anywhere else. As always, scarcity drove demand, especially among the elite.

In this sense, Clans and Guilds were both in high demand for their ability, theoretically, to train and create a powerful and consistent source of new Climbers exiting Towers. These were Climbers who not only survived the first few Towers but progressed to Intermediate Towers and emerged with rarer materials and goods.

Of course, on top of all that, there were other considerations like military might, utilisation of Climbers against other countries, and the like—most commonly exemplified by series of bad movies like *Tower Force 1, 2, 3*, and *4*. Or TV shows like *Vigilance* or *Death by Climbers*.

All of which was to say, at some point, he'd have to deal with the government. He could only hope that their Clan's small size would allow them to skate under the radar. For while rare, Clans or Guilds weren't exactly uncommon at all. Just not usually formed on the very first floor of a Beginner Tower.

Heck, there were two other Clan buildings on this very floor, including the one dedicated for the Bumikasih. Government-sponsored and -trained Climbers were, for the most part, elites that the rest of them left alone— even Casey. Most were old money; others had contacts or were related to powerful individuals or royalty. None of them were people worth antagonising under fear of being tossed into prison when one exited a Tower. Or fear of being visited in the Tower by someone paid to showcase the government's significant disapproval.

"Whatever. So, the triads want to meet. What for?"

"Tell us not to steal their people?" Eric offered.

"Maybe."

"Probably want to talk about how you can work together," Leia said. "With three of them here, can't be more than that, no?"

"Well, it'd be unusual for them to all agree to kill us. Especially after we did well with the Sixes," Arthur said.

"Oh... you think maybe," Eric made some stabbing motions, low down as though he expected to slip a kris into a kidney or two.

"Betray us all?" Arthur considered the words, glancing around the city again idly. While he was becoming well known, at least by reputation, few enough people actively recognised him. Though the way people prodded and poked and pointed, he doubted that would last too long. "Be very brave to do that, to the other groups."

"Unless they kill us and the Sixes too."

"Still a danger of retaliation outside of this floor."

"No *lah*," Eric said. "Mostly fights stay on each floor, you know? At least among the triads."

"What do you mean?" Arthur said, curiously. He hadn't heard of that before, not that there was a reason he should have.

"Can't have all-out war just because one person started it on one floor, so we normally keep retaliation to each floor. At most, in one Tower. Don't bring it outside, unless they step too far," Eric said.

Now Arthur looked confused, so Leia explained.

"It's about timing. If the gangs start fighting, by the time word gets back that a fight has been resolved or a peace agreement or treaty formed, it might be too late. The fight might have spread outside or to another Tower. There's too much time and distance, so generally they keep it to the floor. If it's really bad, the Tower."

"Oh, that's smart." He frowned. "How about Guilds and Clans?"

"Same *lah*, but sometimes you can communicate faster."

That, Arthur knew of. Guilds that had communication means through Towers were generally only one-way or of limited use. Still, even limited real-time communication gave them a huge advantage over informal organisations, which was why Tower-made organisations were so valued.

Before he could ask further, he realised they had arrived. It was easy to tell, what with the dozen or so thugs hanging around outside, glowering at anyone who even looked like they intended to come close.

Chapter 27

Arthur could not tell if it was stereotypical or practical. Or maybe a little of both. Meeting in a restaurant—an expensive restaurant—when none of the parties involved needed to eat seemed foolish, but it also had the advantage of giving the speakers things to play with, a conversation piece, and a large room that allowed full vision and made sneaking up on the group difficult.

It also meant that he had a chance to dine on the restaurant foodstuff, all of which was quite tasty, if a little canned. After all, bringing fresh foodstuff all the way to the seventh floor was nearly impossible and so the cooks made do with canned goods and local ingredients.

It left familiar recipes tasting a little different, a touch too sour, too sweet, too salty.

Not that a single eater complained, as they finished their meal in companionable silence. Arthur kept an eye on the other leaders, taking a read of them.

The Ghee Hin boss was frustratingly handsome, a tall, well-built man that might have been better off getting a job as a sugar baby or a male model than take part in the gang. He moved with a predator's grace, though he was quick to smile and answer and flirt, most especially with the United Nations boss.

The UN leader was very tall for a woman, rail thin, and pretty in a severe way. She sat with a leg propped up on her chair, glowered at the Ghee Hin boss whenever he opened his mouth and tried to flirt, and otherwise tried to out-macho the men in the room at every opportunity.

As for the Double Sixes boss, unusually, he was an Indian. Lighter of skin, with a florid mustache and a shirt half-unbuttoned to showcase the hair rug beneath, he was the most politely reserved of the group. However, he was also the only one to greet Arthur in any form of familiarity or genuine happiness, and as such, Arthur had made sure to take a seat beside him.

Now, finally, the dessert was placed on the table. It made Arthur smile, as he saw what it was.

"How did you get a durian in here?" He could not help but ask the smirking Ghee Hin boss, who was justifiably proud of himself. It was only a single durian, and split open, the bright yellow colour of the contents showed that it was an older variety, a D24. Venerable and tasty, but nothing like the newer XO or ZT crop.

"We grew it," Fang Chien said. "This is the first crop. Not got many, but it's good." A magnanimous hand waved. "Eat, eat."

The group fell on the fruit after quick thanks, Arthur sucking on the smooth and slightly slimy flesh, expertly peeling skin off the bulbous, oval seed with his tongue. Maybe that's why Malaysian men were good with their mouths, having to use them so much for such food.

"So. I'm hoping this isn't too symbolic," Arthur said, wiping his face and taking one of the slices and waiting for the waiter to fill it water. Tilting one side up, he sipped on it, allowing the slightly bitter and sweet liquid flow into him. It was an old trick, to help wash the water down and reduce the "heatiness" of the fruit.

"What?" the woman asked, frowning. "What you mean?"

"Jean, right?" A scowling nod confirmed his guess, and he gestured at their plates. "The durian being split open and consumed, shared by all of you."

"You got a big head *lah*. This is good," she gestured at the food. "Fresh!"

A hesitation, then Arthur nodded in acknowledgement. Still, the way Fang Chien looked, he could not help but assume that the dessert choice was more than chance.

"Then, what is it that you wanted from us?" Arthur asked, tired of dancing around the issue.

"Nothing. Or, well, we just want to make sure, make clear we all understand things," Raj said, trying to mollify Arthur.

"Understand what?" he said, frustrated.

"What we do. What you should do," Jean said, flatly. "You better not interfere with us, got it?" She leveled a finger at him, glaring over it.

"Or what?" Arthur could not help but ask.

She clenched a fist, a clear threat. Before Arthur could answer her, Fang Chien waved a hand between the two, that big bright smile on his face.

"No, no. We're all friends here," Fang Chien said. "No threats, nothing like that." He waved between the two others and himself, adding. "We just want to make sure you understand, we have a good thing. Not like other floors. We don't fight, we don't quarrel. We all have our own things, our own places. And we don't want you all to mess it up, you know."

"Us?" Arthur said, cocking his head to the side. "What makes you think we're going to make more trouble for you than the Prime Group? Or TG? Or any others."

"You got a Clan *lah*." Fang Chien waggled a finger at Arthur. "Already we know, you have kicked out some people. Talking to the Lotuses. Soon, you'll start recruiting. Maybe buy up places?"

Arthur shrugged. "If we can afford it, in the future, maybe. But that's a long time away."

"Better to talk now, than talk later," Raj offered.

"Fine," Arthur said. "Tell me."

The next half-hour tested his patience as he was talked down to about how the city ran, explained to him over and over again as though he could not understand simple concepts like geographic and industrial boundaries. It did, at least, clarify for Arthur that they truly were serious about this, wanting to demarcate where and how the Durians could expand, who they could poach and what kind of buildings they could acquire.

Only two things stopped him from losing his temper. Firstly, the practical reality that while the Durians were entirely safe behind the walls of their Clan building—or at least, as safe as one could be—that protection did not extend outside of the building. The gangs could easily make the lives of their members miserable, harming them long before they could reach the Clan residence or any time they left, including to ascend.

The second reason was the way they were talking. A little patronising towards him. They were, in the end, treating the Clan like an actual equal, one that they had to pacify to some extent and discuss problems with. They might not be a threat, now, but the gangs were all clear that could change all too fast.

Which was, of course, why they were trying to clip the Durians' wings before they could spread. It was the reason none of the other players—the corporations and the government—were involved. This was a political maneuver, but a strange one to Arthur. After all, anything he agreed to could be rescinded; none of them had anything but his word to go on.

Even so, if they were here to test how far they could push the new Clan Head; he could see it somewhat. And if that was the case…

"I understand your points," Arthur said, slowly. "All of them. However, it seems that you've divided the city up almost completely, both geographically and industry-wise. There's nothing else for us to do."

"That doesn't matter, right? You're a Clan. You should be pushing people to ascend and training them, not running businesses or buying up restaurants and the like," Raj said.

"We still need income. And while there are mobs out there on the fringes, the real income comes from the businesses, no?" Arthur said.

"We never said you can't have business. Just, you have to pay like everyone," Jean said.

"And do the other big businesses have to pay?" Silence was the answer he received, which was answer enough. "Then, why us?"

"Because you're no Prime Group. You want to fight us? Can also." Jean grinned.

Again, Fang Chien spoke up. "No, no. We don't want to fight the Durians, not unless you want to force it." He smiled, traded looks between the group. "We can work out a deal for you all. If it's cores, you have space, right? In your Clan building?"

Arthur hesitated, seeing what was happening now. A single gang he might be willing to pit the Durians against. However, that was only so long as he and the main team were here. Unless he killed or seriously hurt the gang they were fighting, they would eventually recover. That was, of course, the problem with fighting international organisations. It didn't matter how much damage you did locally; eventually, they'd reinforce and you had to start all over again.

With all three gangs agreed on this, it would be a real problem. Better for Arthur to comply. More importantly, something that Jean had said had given him an idea. In fact…

"In that case, whatever business we build outside of whatever you agreed on, no honing in. No protection money, no blocking us off, all of it," Arthur said. "Agreed?"

"Wait, what kind of—"

Before Fang Chien could agree, Jean spoke up. "Agreed."

"You can't agree," Fang Chien protested at Jean.

Raj was slower, flicking his gaze between the arguing pair. He met Arthur's gaze, then smirked and offered a slight nod.

"Agreed," he said.

"I… you too?" Now Fang Chien looked angry, but outvoted, he grated a low, "agreed."

"Great, then I got a need for a place to buy," Arthur said. "Or have built. You guys do construction, right?"

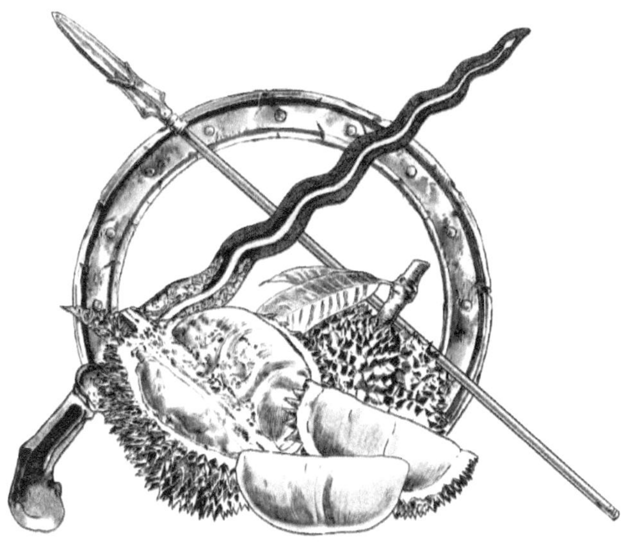

Chapter 28

Arthur chuckled softly, hands in his pockets as he strolled away from the restaurant. His companions followed behind him, heads tilted curiously to the side as they watched him. They knew better than to ask though, not until the group was far enough away that their conversation could not be overheard by the gang members.

"You *gila* ah?" Eric said, angrily.

"What?" Arthur said.

"You bought their building and then paid for them to upgrade it and then took a loan!" he snapped. "You took a loan from the triads!"

"Eh, pretty sure the..." He winced as he was struck in the side. "Fine, no being pedantic. It's worth it. And I split it among all three, so that it wasn't like we owe any one gang too much. And the interest rates are actually reasonable." He raised a finger. "Between what Casey will be providing us, and what I have, we should be able to cover it to start."

"To start," Leia said. "That's still a lot of interest!"

"We'll get it paid," Arthur said firmly. "Once we get more people, we will have a better income. And the building will pay for itself once it's finished."

"Doing what *lah*? You already agreed, it's not open to their businesses. And why so much space?" Eric asked.

"I'll tell you guys when we're back." He hesitated, then added, "When everyone is here. In the meantime, you're not wrong. We do need more cores."

A long, low groan rose from the pair. Eventually, of course, Arthur would need to visit the Tower administrative center to take control of the building officially; right now everything was being done on a handshake. So, letting people know of his plans was dangerous and for now he was going to play it close.

"I barely got time to cultivate, *lah*," Eric said.

"But the two of you are still our strongest. So you'll need the least cores." He hesitated, then added, "It's important. And I'm not asking you to grind stones for us without pushing ahead. But I need you to do this, Seniors."

"Fine..." Leia said, eventually. "Once you get back, we'll get our gear."

Eric looked unhappy but nodded along, allowing Leia to make the decisions. Good thing too, since Arthur didn't want to beg. Never mind the fact that his plan was very much reliant on the pair.

Inside, a quick check showed that not much new had happened. Nothing, at least, that needed him. The Thorned Lotuses still hadn't returned, so for now, it was time to get back to cultivating. Working on his own strength, even if it pushed back and increased their loan amount, was more important.

Especially since he thought he was actually getting close.

Night and coming down for a break had Arthur spotting Rick, the man seated on one of the lobby couches, a small note held in hand. When he spotted Arthur, he hid the note automatically, and then after a moment, relaxed and placed it back down.

"Something I should know?" Arthur said.

"No." A glance at the staircase, seeing no one else around this late in the evening. "Yes."

"Problem with a tenant?"

"No. Though... one of them's an enchanter. He's... ummm... different."

"What do you mean different?"

"A kook. He's supposedly good, but also a kook. He's blown up, like, two offices so far, which is why he was kicked out of his last place. He works and sleeps in the same place which..."

"Which means he's doing his experiments in our apartment complex," Arthur said, angrily.

Rick held a hand up, waited until he had Arthur's attention, and added. "I have it handled. He's on the top floor now, and right under the rain barrels. If he blows anything up..."

"The rain barrels will rain right down onto his room?" Arthur shook his head. "I still don't like the idea of our place blowing up."

"Even for free enchanted equipment? For us and the Clan?" Rick said.

That made Arthur hesitate. Those crafters who were willing to live in Towers and get good enough to enchant things were rare, mostly by virtue of the artificial place they existed within. After all, you had to be strong enough to get to a certain floor. And if you were strong enough, you often spent your time training or fighting, not practising crafting. Which left many crafters either on the first few floors or nowhere.

No surprise then that using the Tower administrative services was the most common way to get enchanted equipment.

"Fine, but he joins us," said Arthur.

"Already agreed." Rick tapped the paper. "But this isn't that."

"Oh?" Curious now, Arthur took the offered note, scanning it. He shook his head after a moment. " '*A gift. Love Mom & Dad.*' What's it mean?"

"Restock."

"Re-… oh. Ohhhhh!" Arthur's eyes widened. Now he could see the need for secrecy and Rick's hesitation. Getting and keeping the necessary restock for Rick's guns must have been difficult, if not deadly. Guns and ammo were rare, nearly impossible to acquire in the Tower in Malaysia and, of course, any in the Tower was at a premium—if it didn't get stolen or used up first.

Most people wouldn't have a gun anyway.

Which meant that if the bearer of Rick's restock had been waylaid, then a trap laid to bring Rick out—

along with his weapons—might result in quite the profit. They wouldn't even have to kill him, just stab or beat him enough to take his weapons. Even Arthur's new allies probably wouldn't consider it too much of a strain to do that.

"You need backup," Arthur said. "When, where?" Rick looked taken aback at the sudden offer of help. When he was silent, Arthur smirked as he continued, "You're Clan now. Which means you get to ask and even if you don't, we're helping."

"Okay. Yeah, okay. Thanks." Rick recovered from his surprise. "There was also a verbal message, saying to meet at noon."

"Where?"

"A restaurant. Roadside stall, really. Down south and closer to the forest."

Arthur nodded, considered. "We'll get Jan and Yao Jing and maybe Uswah if she's around. They'll be the obvious, she'll be behind and quiet. If she's not there..."

"I—"

Ignoring Rick, he continued. "I'll take her place. But better if she's there." He sighed. "I'm probably a little too famous these days, and just as likely to attract attention."

"Yeah," Rick agreed. He ran a hand through his dark floppy haircut, the ends a little too long so that they brushed against his nose when he didn't pay attention. Unlike the rest of them, he hadn't gone for the easy and common fix of taking a dagger to his hair. Aided by a friend—or not, in some cases.

"Thank you."

"No need." A wave of his hand, dismissive, and then Arthur was standing. "You can ask them yourself, or you want me to do it for you?"

"I... I can do it," Rick said, taken aback at the casual distribution of responsibility.

Getting a cup and pouring himself water from a jug, Arthur finished the glass and wandered back up, waving goodbye. Hopefully, the pickup would go well with little problem.

Either way, he had his own focus.

Chapter 29

Slow, careful breathing as he teased the energy through his body. He watched as it floated before him, a morass of Yin energy contained and separated, different from the usual that existed within him. Like an extra cold spot or a slight ache that he held in hand. Yet, it stayed still, breaking down a little as time went by but not otherwise interacting with him or his body or, more importantly, the Yang energy within him.

Three days. It had taken him three days to get this far and not a damn notification from the Tower other this one.

Internal Energy Manipulation (58%)

Not that he was complaining about getting a new skill and some acknowledgement of the work he had done. Did make him wonder why the notification had taken so long to show up, but he theorised it probably had something to do with how most climbers had some form of control and ability. No need to make a skill known until it started becoming a technique, and that required—like all good techniques—a system and process.

Something he hadn't realised was a necessity till two days in, when he had to start keeping notes outside of his head of the variations of energy he kept manipulating. How he pulled energy, at what speeds, adjusting again and again as energy drained away or dispersed or transformed too fast.

All till he got here, and this bundle of Yin energy.

Now, the question was what to do about it. The obvious answer: make a Refined Energy Dart.

He really wanted to do that, though there were two problems. Firstly, the energy he had created was Tower energy, not refined energy. That meant that he would have to learn how to do this again with the refined energy, pushing his progress even further back. It might be simple, but somehow, instinctively, Arthur knew it wasn't going to be.

Now, he could, potentially break the Refined Energy Dart technique down, or even just buy the basic Energy Dart technique and then learn that before modifying it. Again, it would take a ton of time and give him another technique that he barely used. Especially since basic Energy Darts were significantly less powerful.

The other problem with all that was, well, he was out of time.

"Sorry, I'm late." Arthur waved to the group as he trundled down the stairs, nodding to Mel and Uswah and then eyeing the half-dozen women who had gathered in the lobby. He didn't recognise a single one of them, but they all had that air he'd come to realise belonged to the true survivors. The kind who weren't going to be content just existing day-to-day on this floor.

Murmured agreements. He stuck his hand out, shaking hands and doing his best to glad-hand the group, plastering on as friendly a face as he could as they made the introductions.

"Why were you late?" An older woman, Li Sun, asked with an angry glare. She was the oldest and by the fact that she hadn't bothered to rise or take his hand, he assumed she was either their leader or just a natural contrarian.

"Training," Arthur said, completely truthfully. "I was working on a cultivation technique."

"Tower-bought?"

He shook his head. "Something derived from an enchantment, actually." He tapped the kris by his side.

To his surprise, it actually made the woman soften a little. "So you're one of those?"

"Uhhh, not sure what those you're talking about."

"An experimenter. Someone making their own techniques."

Arthur nodded. "It's not that hard..."

Li Sun leaned forward then, nodding in agreement. "Yes! Exactly. It's like they want you to try making things. The pain isn't that bad even, it's just a little bit. These kids, they just spend their cores and contribution points buying techniques all the time rather than putting in some real effort! Why, in my time..."

"You were not able to afford the techniques," interjected Noor, who was not much younger than Li Sun, "because you could only spend them on building yourself up and because it cost too much. So you had to learn how to do it yourself. We know already *lah*." Noor laughed ruefully. "We're not here to recreate your past."

"You..." Li Sun sighed. "Fine. But what's there to talk? It's a Clan. That means we might actually get ahead."

The others looked unhappy at Li Sun's forthright admission, Noor poking her in the side. "What if he gives us a bad deal?"

"What deal?" Arthur said. "There's no deal. You join, you become a member, you get access and contribute. No differences between you all and everyone else in the Clan." That made the group look a little unhappy, but he pointed to Mel. "On the other hand, you all are trusted already, which means almost all our floor leaders will come from you guys. Which means you all dictate the treatment you get and can make sure it's fair."

"You said 'almost all' your floor leaders?" Noor asked.

"I did. Not all of your people have agreed, or were trustworthy," Arthur said. "I value individuals that come in and work for it. Not whatever seniority you all had before. Think of it as a new start." He shrugged. "If you manage to keep the same level of authority and trust, even without a formal designation, all the better."

Some looked angry, a few considered his words thoughtfully. Li Sun didn't seem annoyed or angry at all but almost cunning. He could almost see the future, just by looking at the way they glanced at one another, at her, and their body language. He'd have to check, but he would have bet that woman was going to try to weasel out of anything official, even if she was their leader now.

All the more reason to get her, if he could. Guilt was a useful tool, weaponised incompetence another. Again, something to check with Mel, that he was reading things right. But he didn't think he wasn't. After multiple floors and the politics within, he was beginning to get a feel for these things.

Didn't mean there weren't other complications he was bound to run into.

It wasn't that easy, of course, and eventually food and drinks had to be brought out. They had questions, queries about the Clan, about what the Sigil and Aspect did.

The Aspect of Guardianship was the most quietly important, its minor bonuses were passive but powerful—affecting everything from healing and shielding to precision techniques, as well as the increased cultivation speed when other Clan members were nearby.

The Sigil of the Flame Phoenix, on the other hand, was perhaps the biggest direct benefit. An Advanced Healing Technique, available to the entire clan, that boosted low-level healing could offer significant improvements in survivability. Not to mention the increase in recovery times and the long-term potential of regeneration.

Though, Arthur knew he was a long way from that. In a more advanced Tower, he might even consider picking up a healing technique scroll to aid him; right now a Beginner Tower's limited resources meant that there wasn't a scroll significantly better than what he already had.

"Fire Phoenix? Aren't they all fire?" A puzzled speaker, mousy with a pair of glasses on her nose, one of its temples broken and held together by what looked like tree sap and cloth.

"Flame Phoenix," Arthur corrected gently. He'd forgotten her name already, which would be annoying but he'd long ago learnt not to bother him. He'd work it out, later. "And no, I don't know if there's a difference."

Still, answering questions like these did remind him that he hadn't done anything about the Sigil. If they could have one linked skill because he had studied it, perhaps he should look into flame-based techniques himself. Of course, being Yin bodied, that might be... well, interesting. What little exploration he'd done about using a flame aura and even many Yang-oriented techniques had shown that he was going to struggle with it.

One of the reasons Jan was the one with a flame aura and not him. Never mind other considerations.

He'd tack it on to his long list of things to do. Speaking of...

In one of the breaks, he held a hand up as others looked to ask more questions. "Look, Mel and Jan and Uswah can answer most of your questions, so you don't need for me for that. In fact, all you need me to do is add you to the Clan, or add someone as the floor boss and they can do that. Now, I'm not choosing anyone yet, so unless anyone wants to join immediately..."

He let his voice trail off, expecting no one to agree and was thus surprised when Li Sun nodded to him.

"You sure?"

"Yeah."

"Huh." Arthur shrugged, then added, "Do you swear to abide by the rules of the Clan, to protect it and its people like your own, to promote the well-being of the Clan and its people?"

"Yeah." Again, no hesitation from the older woman.

He prodded the Tower in that way he had learnt to do, pushing his mental request to it and watching a moment later when the offer appeared before her. She barely even read it, acknowledging the agreement and adding to his numbers a moment later. Within seconds, he had a flood of new applicants. The dam had broken, much to the annoyance of the more cautious Lotuses.

Finally, the Benevolent Durians got going on the seventh floor.

Chapter 30

He managed to escape after twenty minutes, leaving Mel and Jan to answer questions from the newly added Clan members. Not that he didn't value them, but his mind was still on his previous training and they were better at dealing with people than he was. If nothing else, they weren't going to snap at the speaker for asking the same question he'd just answered five minutes ago to another.

Maybe they could write up a FAQ on a brochure or something and hand it out when people joined, so they could avoid all this.

What kind of Aspect do we have? What does it do?

Why are we called Benevolent Durians?

How do we get Clan contribution points? How's it recorded?

Can I really stay in the Clan hall for free?

What kind of techniques do you offer?

And more. Amusingly, he was not the only one to escape and he stopped before opening the door to his own room, staring at the woman who had followed him up.

"What do you want?" Arthur asked Li Sun. He could have made a joke about not being interested, but it just wasn't in him to do it. Especially if it started rumors about his taste. It was bad enough that rumors of him being a eunuch because he had a Yin Body kept being floated around by Jan.

"To talk," Li Sun said. "You're working on your technique, right? I want to know more." She saw his eyes narrowing and she held a hand up. "I was hoping I could help."

Now he had to ask. "Why?"

"I'm not stupid," Li Sun said, gesturing at Arthur. "You're weak right now. New to this floor. And based off how fast you've climbed, you can't be that strong either." Eyes narrowed, gesturing down the hallway. "The Chins might have given you a deal, but there's nothing like time." He idly noted she was entirely wrong about where Casey's apartment was, the woman having chosen to take one higher up because water pressure was better than down here, though it was less convenient to climb more flights of stairs. "Or training. You don't have the first, so..."

"Doesn't explain why you want to help, though."

"Because you're the boss. Stronger you are, stronger we are," Li Sun said. "The others might not realise it, or maybe they're nice enough not to mention, but if you die, we lose the Clan. And all those good things are gone."

"Only until we get big enough to start acquiring more Clan bonuses," Arthur said.

"And when's that?" she asked. When he didn't have an answer, she nodded as though she had confirmed something she had been thinking of. "Right. So you're our best bet for now."

Still, he didn't move. After the silence dragged on for a bit, Li Sun eventually broke first. "What?"

"You've got another reason."

"How...?" she frowned, shook her head. "Fine. I'm also bored. I like studying techniques, have a few myself. But the rest of them..." She gestured downwards, shrugged. "They don't care. They have what they need, most of them. They don't need more so they don't push for more. The ones who do, they often aren't interested in what I have to teach because buying from the Tower's easier."

"You're lonely," Arthur said, surprised.

Now the older woman raised her chin, almost glaring at his blunt assessment. She didn't acknowledge his words, which was more than fair. He probably wouldn't have admitted it himself either. Still, it didn't make it wrong.

"How'd you know? That I had a second reason."

"I didn't," Arthur admitted, just because it amused him a little. She glared at the back of his head, but he ignored that too as he threw the door open. "Come on in then, let's talk." He hesitated, then added, "But you show me yours, first."

That got a laugh from the older woman, though like him, she didn't take the words in a sexual direction. A good thing too, because Arthur hadn't really meant it that way and only realised what he'd said when it came out of his mouth.

It didn't take long for the show and tell and overview on both sides to end. Not that Arthur had told her all his various skills—he didn't trust her enough—but neither Focused Strike, his Refined Energy Dart, or the new kris-originated Yin energy were things he expected to keep hidden for long. And he almost definitely needed help with some techniques.

"So, I'm thinking, I can bundle the Yin energy and basically use the container from the Refined Energy Dart and combine it with Focused Strike. Either expanding Focused Strike to give it a poison element, or better, make it a new system that lets me layer the energy to work as a poison," he said.

"You use a spear, right?" Li Sun looked at the rather obvious weapon propped to the side.

"Yeah...?"

"Focused Strike is decent then," she said. "Lets you throw your energy upwards. Better than some of the others, though not as good as one of the imbued attacks."

Arthur grunted. "Imbued attacks?"

"Fire, water, ice, all those," she said, making a stabbing motion. "Put the element into the attack."

"Those are hard," Arthur said, knowing how difficult it was to create the necessary element. Easier, much easier, to just imbue the attack with Tower energy. Shaping or refining or concentrating it, rather than transforming it.

"But more effective. And it lets you do what you want," she said, making a gesture with her hands. "Puts it in a container, that lets you deposit into the other."

"Isn't that what the Refined Energy Dart does?"

"No, no..."

After a few minutes of technical discussion with a few drawn examples on scrap paper, Arthur had a better understanding of what she meant. He was fast realising that her knowledge of the various forms of the chi and Tower energy exercises was greater than his by far. It probably helped that for all the disdain of the Tower techniques, she actually had quite a few to her name.

"So, you think I shouldn't bother learning a new technique?" Arthur said, clarifying.

"Not all of one. I'll sketch out the one I use, for the Energy Dart and Imbue Weapon. Once you figure that one out, you can adapt it to your container and just use that," Li Sun was saying, waving her hands around excitedly. "Then you should have a container for strikes with your spear that hits harder, drives the poison in. And Imbue Weapon is a persistent skill, not like Focused Strike. So if you use that, you can just keep it running and recharge the weapon."

"I like it." Arthur tapped the little drawing she had made of what the Energy Dart looked like to her and the mana flows she had to use to build it. The shorthand she had used for the various meridian points was a well-known one, what with many of the same points studied and utilized in acupuncture and qigong, so it was simple enough for him to grasp.

The container and the way you manipulated basic Energy Darts was, surprisingly, somewhat more complicated. Unlike his expectation, the two types of Energy Darts actually utilized entirely different containers. If he had to describe it, the Refined Energy Dart was more an actual container, like a dart, whereas the basic Dart was more a contained sphere of energy.

He wasn't entirely certain why Li Sun, who had never studied the more costly Refined Energy Dart herself, was intrigued enough to start experimenting herself.

It did, however, lead him to a rather obvious question after they'd finished their initial discussion.

"Why are you not out of the Tower?" he asked.

"Hmmm?" Staring down at the jotted notes Arthur had offered on the Refined Energy Dart, Li Sun looked up, puzzled.

"Why aren't you out of the Tower?" he repeated.

"I'm waiting for someone," she said.

Something in her voice, something in her tone had him clamp his mouth shut. At her strength, she could easily leave the Tower. At her age, anyone she was waiting for... well. But well-honed instinct had Arthur keep his mouth shut.

Sometimes, hope was all you had.

Chapter 31

The next week flowed fast. With the new recruits—and the majority of the Thorned Lotuses chose to become just that—filling the apartment block, things got busy. A pair of first-floor rooms had their walls broken down, a couple of the new recruits able to confirm that it was safe to do so. With more membership taxes being paid now, Arthur was less worried about paying for his loan from the gangs, though he had to mollify Casey when she learnt about his further entanglement. He assumed she was just angry that she hadn't gotten a chance to offer a loan herself and bother him further.

Rick and the team, not at all surprisingly, ended up with their own adventure. Thankfully, it was one that happened entirely without him, Arthur only learning about the incident days later, having completely forgotten about Rick's restock rendezvous while pursuing his own cultivation exploration. It made him feel a little guilty, but everyone had survived and they'd only left three corpses behind.

Of course, that was going to cause its own problems, but the small gang involved—well, technically a corporation that hired a gang—was holding off on causing further trouble.

For now.

In fact, with everything calming down for the moment, Arthur was able to keep focused on building up his techniques. He soon learnt why refined energy and basic Tower energy required different containers. It had to do with the attractive and structural properties of the two, with refined energy actually willing to be shaped, sort of like dragon candy that could be mixed while warmed but hardened after a bit. Basic Tower energy, on the other hand, was the equivalent of slapping together a bunch of mud and lobbing it at someone. You had to compress it really hard and hope strongly that it would hold together.

Still, once he worked that out and figured out how to use Imbue Weapon, which was marginally familiar to him thanks to Focused Strike and the expulsion of energy to his aura, it had been a short step from there to actually creating his new techniques. He now had two, which were both recognised on his status sheet.

Imbued Strike - Yin Poison (28%)
Yin Poison Darts (37.3%)

Arthur had to admit he'd spent more time on the modified Energy Darts, as having the ranged equivalent to use was more important than a close-range debuff. He still needed to learn the basics first though, which was why he even had the Imbued Strike, especially when he practised utilizing it on Li Sun.

She had been a real revelation. And tragedy.

"Her younger sister. They came up together, or were supposed to. She never made it," Noor explained one evening when he cornered her to ask. "It's been years, but Li Sun keeps expecting her to show up. Said they promised they would join up in the Tower. And when she came across this floor..."

"She never pushed further because she hoped she'd turn up here and not the floors below." He got it. No one would stay on the fifth floor longer than they needed and the sixth was a death trap to hang around in. And the previous floors could be done solo. Though, he did wonder how long Li Sun had waited on the fifth.

"Don't ask her. She's... well, once a year, she gets drunk. Isn't much use that month."

He nodded, understanding. Someone else might have dug more, but it was clear Noor was done talking about it and Arthur... Arthur had no desire to delve into others' pasts. It was enough, for now, that she functioned.

Still, as much as he wanted to spend time on his cultivating and studying his techniques; there were some things even he couldn't put off. The opening and purchase of his new building being one of them, including the handing over of the big bag of monster cores. He had managed to get the majority of his management team to come along to that, both to act as muscle in case of a potential fight and then, when he led them to the updated and rebuilt building, to explain things.

"So, here it is."

He looked around the massive open space that was the former warehouse. It had been modified a bit since then, private rooms added down one side where the massive bay doors had been, additional lightning and windows on the top. No fans, of course, which would make the room sweltering and something he'd have to look into at some point, but at least they had magical lights up there.

"So what is?" Mel asked, looking around. "You wanted a warehouse? To sell what? What business do you want us to do?"

"No business. Or, well, no warehousing at least." He looked to Eric and Leia, seeing if they had gotten it yet. They still looked blank and he sighed. "I don't want to compete with the others about businesses. We're meant to be more than another thieving merchant. Remember what the Durians are?"

"A spiky fruit."

"Us?"

"Our Clan."

Shaking his head, Arthur tried again. "What did we want to achieve with the Durians?"

"To save the Lotuses," Mel said.

"To save everyone," Uswah said, moments later. "You wanted it to be a Clan for everyone."

"Exactly!" He grinned, waving a hand around. "And why do so many people not progress out of here?" He didn't look at Li Sun who had joined them, for her choices were different. For everyone else, though… "So we help them."

"You want to open up a training hall," Leia said. "A place like sifu has." She looked around the warehouse again as though she was seeing it anew. "That's why you wanted so much space."

"Exactly!" Arthur snapped his fingers. "You and Eric can start with teaching the basics, the physical fitness, the technique training. The how-to-fight that so many people don't actually know." He snorted. "If we did it right, we might even be able to do something sifu never managed." At their puzzled looks, he grinned. "Bring in real monsters."

"No way, *lah*." Eric crossed his arms. "We already got no time."

"Just to start, until we find other trainers," Arthur cajoled him. "I can help too, of course." He looked about; some of the others were looking excited, a few hesitant or unsure. Li Sun had a strange look on her face as she looked around.

"I can teach MMA," Yao Jing offered, grinning and subtly flexing.

Arthur nodded then looked at Mel, noting how his second-in-command was quiet. "We need space to train, right? Cultivation techniques, skills, all of that. And the seventh floor is a resting floor anyway. And it isn't messing with any of the other groups' businesses either, so they can't take anything from us." He hesitated, then added, "Heck, we could even train some of them, for a price."

"And make them more dangerous?" Mel said.

"Save some lives. And if we get all of them training here, we should make ourselves and the Durians safer." He added, after a moment, "If we get some cultivation techniques that we can write out, we can even teach some of those."

"Undercut the Tower?" An eyebrow rose. It happened, of course, when some individuals were willing to train others. But it wasn't usual for entire schools to set up in a Tower, mostly because people moved on. However, Mel looked over at Li Sun who had been silent. "Maybe..."

"You want me, don't you." Li Sun asked, softly.

"To train others, yeah. Even if it's stupid Tower techniques. But who knows, maybe you'll find some proper students too," Arthur offered.

"If..." A hesitation, then she added, "If my sister arrives, I will leave with her. You know that, right?"

"Of course," Arthur said. He made sure to keep his voice firm and without hesitation as he continued. "But she'll need to train too, if she comes up. And she's welcome to become a Durian."

Li Sun looked around again, then nodded slowly and again, more firmly.

"Arthur." Mel's voice cut in, making him look at her. She opened her mouth to say something, then shut it, shaking her head. He assumed she was going to complain about his secretiveness, but at least for now, she'd hold her complaints.

Fair enough, but sometimes, it seemed she forgot that he really was the boss. And it wasn't a bad idea, not at all.

No matter what she thought.

Chapter 32

It wasn't that easy, of course. There were still a bunch of questions, but once everyone got on board, it became much simpler. They started making plans of what to teach, where each of the teaching places would be, fighting rings and even exercise regions and the purchase of exercise equipment. Once Mel had gotten her quiet word in and requested that Arthur please not make decisions without at least consulting her, she had joined in wholeheartedly in the planning.

Eric and Leia's focus would be on fighting tactics and weapons, Yao Jing on close combat and unarmoured combat. Mel and Noor both had the most experience dealing with monsters, so they would focus on teaching tactics to deal with a variety of monsters and surviving them while Lin Su and Uswah would help others practise their cultivation techniques.

Rick and Arthur would help out where they could, though Rick's job was to play manager and sales person, getting in new customers. Of course, to start they were going to gateway entrance to just Clan members and iron out the basics of the training.

"Don't forget the Chins," Mel said. "They can come and train, maybe in exchange for helping fill out the warehouse. And then, later for a price."

Arthur nodded. He wasn't entirely sure they should be favoring Prime Group that much, but then again, they were already allied. Not giving them first chance would be insulting.

"No problem. The big question is what we're going to do about the building when we're not here," Arthur said. A quick glance at the building data, he sighed.

Benevolent Durians Building #2 (Seventh Floor, Tower 2895)

Type: Training Hall
Building Bonus: None

It would have been great if he had the funds to actually buy a building bonus like Security; but in this case the bonus was only for the main Clan building. Any upgrades he wanted, he'd have to pay. And right now, he was too poor to do that. Which meant that the building could be stolen from them at any time.

In the end, rather than set up a watch rotation, they chose to just schedule training sessions throughout the day. With the various magical stone lamps and lights set through the building, and the necessity anyway for night time training, it made sense to just make use of the facility 24/7. Having people active and in the building would be just as effective a deterrent from a thief as any security guard.

Of course, once all the bureaucracy was over, it was time for fun.

With all the space that they had, it made sense to have a mass combat. The group split, utilizing a series of short sticks to pick sides rather than a more chaotic, free-for-all battle. It was how Arthur found himself grouped with a motley crew of Noor, Eric, Rick and Yao Jing to face off against Mel, Uswah, Leia, Jan and Li Sun.

It amused him, a little, that it was all the men on one side against the women on the other. Not all of them, of course, what with the smaller numbers of men thus far, but he hoped, eventually, that'd change. Unfortunately, the equilibrium of climber society and the Towers meant that that level of equality might take a while to arrive.

All issues for the future. For the present...

"Rick, you've got Jan. Eric, Leia. I'll take Li Sun; and Noor, you have Uswah. Yao Jing, Mel." He gave the orders fast and firmly, choosing not to overthink matters too greatly. This was, after all, supposed to be fun. "Remember, only one technique!"

Li Sun, across and to the right of him just grinned as the group shifted a little, getting in position. He readied his staff, choosing to use that rather than his more deadly spear. At the same time, he pulled at the energy within him, getting it ready.

"When we start?" Jan asked.

In answer, Rick charged forward, yanking his bowie knife up. It was still in its sheath, the closest thing he had to a safe option for the weapon. Which, really, wasn't that safe but it was what they had. Anyway, none of them were intent on moving at full speed, and even though it wouldn't look so to a nonclimber, the entire group was going to limit themselves. Which was, after all, the reason why they were only using one technique.

In Arthur's case, he pulled on his energy within to begin the process of creating his newest technique. The Imbued Strike stretched outwards, swallowing the staff in its entirety. He focused on keeping it contained as he charged after his group, angling to the side to meet Li Sun.

He wondered what she intended to use. They were restricted to some extent; certain types of techniques like his Refined Exploding Energy Dart was just too dangerous to utilize, even if it might have done significant damage to his opponents. After all, the goal was not to kill each other, just win a sparring match.

Eyes narrowed, he watched for the flow of power through her. There was something, something in her external aura, but it wasn't fully visible. It was almost like it was pulsing, shifting each moment.

Then there was no more, as he reached her. She was wielding a pair of tonfa, the twisted nightsticks on either hand spinning outwards to block his staff as it came down. His aura pulsed, trying to wrap around hers, trying to impart the Yin effect and failing. His weapon hand ached, the staff vibrating at the contact.

A flurry of blows, he pushing forward, she backing away reluctantly. She tried to slip close, intent on using both of the tonfas to her advantage and land her strike. She failed as he wove a net of wood before him, the staff rebounding back faster and faster with each attack, his hands aching as he tried to control the increasingly erratic movement.

One last strike, rising from the center line, blocking a lunge. It was battered aside and the staff, already vibrating in a way that made it hard to hold spun away, his grip lost. She didn't give him time to recover, instead passing forwards and attacking with the tonfa in a lunge for his upper chest.

He collapsed backwards, voiding his body and hunching inwards to pull his chest aside even as he swung his backhand down. He struck, just the top of her hand and the top of the tonfa's handle. Felt his aura finally interact firmly with hers and pulse, the Yin energy he'd gathered flowing into her briefly.

Then contact, as she hammered her own strike into him. He fell back, chest aching, feeling like she had hit him not once, but a couple of times in short order. Off-balance already, he fell back and he tucked himself in, rolling and spinning, lifting himself off a little with arm and shoulder while swinging his leg into a sweep.

Contact, another pulse of Yin energy into her. Small drips, entering her system, this time more. Then, he was up on his feet again as Li Sun cursed. They squared off, only for their private fight to be interrupted.

Arthur cursed as he bowled over, Yao Jing's thrown body slamming into him. Caught by surprise, his aura and the Yin energy he converted flowed into the man unceasing until they managed to extricate themselves. The bodybuilder looked woozy, and Arthur's own technique staggered to a stop as the sudden expulsion of his Yin energy robbed him of what energy he had before.

Mel wasn't joining Li Sun, instead having chosen to help Jan beat on Rick who was already on the losing end of that fight. By the time he and Yao Jing were able to rejoin the battle and get around Li Sun, it was as good as over.

Of course, all that meant was that they had to do it again.

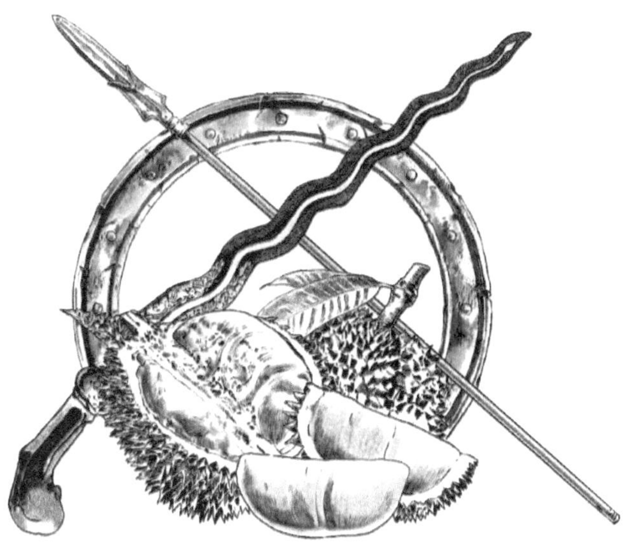

Chapter 33

"Well, that didn't work," Arthur groused, lying on his back. Not just once, but half a dozen times, his Imbued Strike had broken down. It had happened almost every time he had over-extended the amount of attacks in a short space, his body and energy techniques insufficient to keeping up with the expenditure.

"It does a lot of damage though, before you run out," Uswah said. "I might want to see if I can learn how to use that with my tentacles."

"Yeah, that'd be... scary." Just imagining shadow tentacles grabbing and holding people, forcing them to be drained by the Yin energy was scary. "Expensive though. Your techniques pretty costly already, no?"

"It is," Uswah admitted. "Have to take traits to make it cheaper, and even then..." She shook her head.

"No fair *lah*, using that," Eric grumbled. He had been victim of her tentacles more than once.

"It's because you're too dangerous to be allowed to run free," Uswah said. Her attempts at mollification worked, making the man grin a bit. Of course, Eric had nearly taken out his opponent the first time before being ganged up on, unlike the rest of the boys.

"What were you working on?" Arthur asked, curiously. "I couldn't tell."

"Nothing," Eric said.

"What? Why would you waste training time like that?" Rick asked.

"No, *lah*, wasn't wasting it. I working on using nothing, right?" Eric said. "Only martial arts, only skill." He clenched his fist and raised it upwards. "Real strength."

"Don't you start," Leia said warningly and Eric subsided. Mostly because Noor and some of the others were looking quite admiring already and, in Yao Jing's case, contemplative.

"It's not really fair, this training. I'm literally handicapped," Rick said. "None of my techniques really work without my guns."

"Maybe you should have thought about that first, eh?" Noor said. "Anyway, you got that weird skimming thing."

"My movement technique? The Gunslinger Slide?" Rick said. "It's good for dodging the first few times, but I don't have control of where I end up."

"Yet," Li Sun said. "You don't have control yet. Let me show you how, we'll fix that."

"Really?" Now Rick looked interested, while Li Sun was nodding.

Arthur listened as the others kept talking, then tuned out the conversations as he considered what he'd learnt. Li Sun had kept utilizing various techniques, pulling out three by the time they were done. He hadn't gotten a name for them yet, but he was more interested in what they could teach him.

The first had been that vibrating aura technique, basically adding a degree of resonance to what she hit. Painful and dangerous if she hit an individual too often, really good at cracking through armour or, as she said, giving concussions. Luckily, she'd mostly targeted his weapon rather than his chest and heart.

The second technique had been a movement one, allowing her to literally skate across the floor. She had used that one to traverse the floor and attack various members of the opposition, and she had kept that one up for a number of fights before everyone wised to her and started calling out her location.

After that, she'd utilized the least flashy technique, a simple buff that was similar to his own Heavenly Sage's Mischief. Unlike his, though, she seemed to be able to pulse or adjust the amount of energy and strength to her technique, varying how hard she hit or how far she'd move. It was an unpleasant experience, as she managed to overpower her opponents at times, but it also seemed the most taxing in terms of concentration. More than once, she had reacted too slow to a change in circumstance, whether it was an Energy Dart that blew them over or a new technique pulled on her.

Fascinating, and Arthur really wanted more time with Li Sun. But first, he had to figure out his own Imbued Strike. The first, and rather obvious refinement, was to work out how to keep the Yin energy flowing while he was striking. The second, and less obvious, was figure out why it had been so easy when he was unarmed to transfer his attacks to his opponents and not so much while using the staff.

Without thinking about it, he closed his eyes, replaying the feeling of each strike, the moment of contact. He tried to trace what had happened, how his own Yin energy in the aura had flowed through and over, and then compared it to when he was striking. It took him a few tries before he sat up, eyes flying open.

"That's it! I'm expecting it!" Arthur threw a punch, grinning. Then flushed, as everyone looked at him. "Sorry!"

"Worked something out, eh?" Jan said. "So, you volunteering, then?"

"Uh, for what?" Arthur said.

"To watch the place, tonight."

"What? No..." Arthur looked around, considered. No one had hit the place before because it was empty, other than some lights. And while the lamps were valuable, they weren't that valuable—and they were also hung high above, which made actually taking them down a pain and a half. Even with climber movement techniques, it still wouldn't be simple. "Why?"

"Better to get used to it," Mel said. "If we keep a watch now, even when there's nothing worth stealing, then no one will even think about breaking in."

Arthur grimaced but they weren't wrong. And it wasn't as though he needed his room to actually practise his techniques. If anything, the larger space might be useful. It was while he was getting used to the idea that he'd been voluntold that the rest of them had been prepping to leave, making him reluctantly ask.

"Can someone stay? We shouldn't be in here alone anyway." It probably wasn't very leaderlike to ask like this, but then again, these were just as much his friends as they were his subordinates.

"I'll stay," Rick offered. "I could use a night away from the building." That, of course, raised the question which he was happy to explain when asked. "No one cares what time it is if they've got a complaint. Broken sink, too loud neighbors, too quiet neighbors, funny smells..." He rolled his eyes.

"Huh," Arthur said. "That's... not great. Maybe we really should get Casey to lend her manager to us."

"Or we get someone else to work the night shift," Noor said. "One of my girls could."

"Or that." Arthur nodded. "Get Rick a list tomorrow, he can do interviews."

Noor grinned, happy to sneak another member of the Lotuses into power. Not that she was really sneaking it, if Arthur was being generous. Then again, her objectives had always been clear.

After that, the group broke off, some muttering about the need to get working showers and clothing together. As for Arthur, well, he got back to training.

Chapter 34

Tugging at his neckline, Arthur sighed as he walked beside Casey and Lam, somewhat grumpily complaining, "Exactly why do I have to come again?"

"Because my aunt has the next batch of stones and is refusing to release it until you make good on visiting her," Casey said with careful patience. "And I don't know about you, but it's a little slow to just cultivate with Tower energy, even with the Clan building."

Arthur grunted. He wasn't sure why she was complaining. Unlike him, she was spending and wasting less energy than he was training new techniques. Not that she wasn't training, of course. Her disappearing off to the private Prime Group training grounds on the regular was more than clear enough that she was doing her own upgrading.

It kind of made him sad, actually, that she and Lam had been less of a presence in the near month since they'd gotten the building. He had gotten used to having them around, but already, he felt the pair were drifting away.

It wasn't surprising, as their lives and what they were meant for were different. But it was sad.

On the other hand, without having to do as much socialising or dealing with others, outside of a few regular meetings, he had managed to push his cultivation and techniques much further.

Cultivation Speed: 2.773 Yin

Energy Pool: 21/27 (Yin) + (6/6)

Refinement Speed: 0.1421

Refined Energy: 0.32 (35) +(0/3)

Attributes and Traits

Mind: 15 (Multi-Tasking, Quick Learner, Perfect Recall)

Body: 20 (Enhanced Eyesight, Yin Body, Swiftness, Fast Twitch Faster, Lightning Reflexes)

Spirit: 15 (Sticky Energy, From the Dregs, Strengthened Aura)

Techniques

Night Emperor Cultivation Technique

Focused Strike

Accelerated Healing – Refined Energy (Grade III)

Heavenly Sage's Mischief

Refined Energy Dart

Bark Skin

Seven Cloud Stepping Technique (189%)

Poket Simpanan Tua (135%) (Refined Energy Dart - 84% Integrity)

Imbued Strike - Yin Poison

Partial Techniques

Simultaneous Flow (141.8%)

Yin-Yang Energy Exchange (79.4%)

Yin Poison Darts (37.3%)

Yin Aura (21.7%)

After all his work with his Yin aura, extending his techniques and making them wrap around his staff, or learning to more actively infuse his Yin poison energy through it, Arthur had realised exactly how powerful control and management of it could be. Because of that, when he had chosen to increase his Spirit, he had taken the Strengthened Aura trait. Unlike the more specific Flexible Aura or Imbued Aura or Yin Aura, the Strengthened Aura just made it easier for him to imbue the aura or control it. It reduced the amount of effort and concentration he required to make his various techniques work.

As a consequence of taking that trait, and the work he had done on his aura in general, he'd gained that new bottom line on his sheet. Arthur guessed that the 20% line of understanding was where the Tower chose to start displaying such information. At that point, it was not just an ancillary aspect that he had improved, but he was fast forming a technique or series of techniques to utilize it.

He wasn't ready to climb the next few floors, of course, and there was an argument that he was in many ways done with his agreement with Casey. After all, he couldn't help her through the next floors. Unlike Lam, he didn't have a companion ring to accompany her whenever she chose to move up, so there was nothing else the Durians could do for her.

Which meant, of course, that he could potentially just hang out here even longer.

"Remember, Auntie has a lot of supporters outside," Casey said. "So you can't insult her."

"Or you, no?" Arthur said with a little smirk.

That caused Casey to grimace. He didn't follow up, knowing that her stomping off to curtail her aunt's goal of grabbing more funds for herself had likely cost her. At least in face, if nothing else. Though it did raise the question.

"If she's so poor, how come she has so much support?" Arthur asked.

"Her husband was popular. And then she made herself popular." A moue of distaste crossed Casey's face.

"How?"

This time around, Casey didn't reply. He wondered, again, what she might have done, not just to get support but to make Casey annoyed with it. Lam was no help; the bodyguard had the usual studied neutrality on his face. Then again, he might not know. This seemed like a Chin family secret.

"We're here," Casey said, slowing down as they reached the mansion. Mansion it was, or at least the seventh floor Tower equivalent. Big, with three stories worth of space. There was an actual pavement with planters filled with flowers. It looked vaguely colonial, though the biggest flourish to the building was the use of stone for the building itself and white paint. Dragging that much stone, or buying it from the Tower, had to be expensive.

"Very nice. I should have taken this."

"As if." Casey hesitated, looked at Arthur and continued. "Be good."

Snorting, Arthur ignored her and walked up to the door. Before he could knock, it swung open, revealing the older gentleman standing behind it. He was dressed, of all things, in a butler's uniform. Traditional, old, stuffy, and entirely unpractical. Both for Malaysia and the Tower. For all his advanced age, and he was in the sixties or so at the least, there was a hardness to the man, a real deadliness. If he had both his legs, Arthur was certain he would have managed to clear the remaining floors.

And perhaps, even now, he might have finished the climb if he hadn't a job.

"Ms. Chin. Mr. Chua. The mistress is waiting for you sir. Ms. Chin, I have a missive for you here," the old man intoned the words with an upper crust, snooty British accent. Exactly like the kind you'd hear coming out of a British drama, which probably meant it was faker than an KTV girl's protestations of love.

Casey started, then brightened at the mention of a message.

"Thanks," Arthur said, stepping in. He looked sideways at the servant waiting within, their hand extended to him and he frowned. "I don't have a coat."

"Your weapon, sir." The girl that spoke was in a maid's outfit, a practical and long-skirted dress— not the kind that made weebs fall into palpitations but with similar themes, though.

"Ah, right." He glanced at Casey who had already walked past him and then shifted to Lam. Neither of whom had been asked to give their weapons away, though Casey had handed her sword over the moment she stepped in. After a little more thought, he offered the spear to the maid, glad that if they did take it, it wasn't his black spear. That one was in for enchantment right now, another huge drain on his resources.

"This way, sir," came that dry accented voice again. He started down the corridor, ignoring the main staircase that swept upwards that Casey had already ascended, leaving Arthur behind without a glance. Whatever the message was, it was clear she was happy to abandon him to her Aunt's not so tender ministrations to read it.

The building was a weird mixture of rustic and luxury that hurt Arthur's head to look at. They had vases filled with flowers from the flower beds outside, pieces of hanging art and tapestries that covered walls that were beginning to peel, the paint flaking off after years of lack of touch-ups. Everything was immaculately clean and tidy, but the number of decorations were few in comparison to the space available, making the place look sparse rather than minimalistic or rich. Given a choice, Arthur would likely have gone the other way, with even fewer non-useful items.

What did catch his attention, as he was led past the room, was the library. Books in the dozens, maybe hundreds, filling the room. He craned his neck as he walked, catching glimpses of titles. A lot of fiction and history, but also written works on various Towers too, a new brand of fiction category that often had its own section in bookstores. Sometimes two categories, depending if they decided to split it into Tower fiction and Tower non-fiction.

No surprise, since the Towers had come to dominate the social landscape, the escape valve of the colosseum or the army for many countries.

"Mr. Chua, Lady Wen," Snooty intoned, gesturing through the open door into what Arthur assumed would have been a drawing room.

Of course, the moment he stepped in, the polite smile on his face grew slack-jawed at what he saw within.

Chapter 35

Ms. Wen—that is, Auntie Wen—was splayed across the divan, the kind noblewomen once lay upon, one side raised for leaning against, the other wide open so you could let your feet hang off. She was dressed in home wear and entirely covered, but her clothes were rather tight fitting. Yoga or athletic wear was still a persistent happy place of fashion, especially with the advent of the athletic style of climbers. While she was fit and beautiful and yes, certainly eye-catching, that was not what caught Arthur's attention.

It was the creature sprawled across her.

Hand went for his kris, only to find an implacable grip dropping on it before he could draw. He would have turned to look at the butler, if his brain wasn't catching up. It took him a moment to understand that the snake, green and yellow with a body as thick as his forearm wasn't trying to eat Casey's aunt. It was just lounging.

"Lady Wen would be grateful if you did not harm her pet," Snooty said.

"Ah… right… okay…" Arthur hesitated, released his grip on the kris and waited for his arm to be freed. He walked further in, stood next to a seat far away from Ms. Wen, who looked highly amused by all this.

A hand raised, lifting the creature with casual ease as she continued. "Be a dear, Renard. Put Sammy away?"

"Of course, m'lady."

Once the snake was gone, she went back to sprawling, one hand thrown over the raised side of the divan. She looked at Arthur with hooded eyes. He had yet to sit down, and she frowned.

"Sit, sit. I didn't know you were that scared of snakes," she said.

"Not scared, just don't like them," Arthur said. "Had a few try to eat my face on the floors below."

She laughed at that. "Oh, Sammy isn't a Tower monster, just a normal python from our world. He's a dear, wouldn't hurt a fly." Grinned suddenly. "Doesn't have the strength, really."

"Oh, you're one of those," Arthur said, trying and failing to keep the disapproval from his voice. Some climbers had a bad habit, with their greater strength and riches, to start indulging themselves. Who cared about tigers or lions or bears being too dangerous to keep as pets, when you were now stronger and tougher. At a certain point, that strength made many climbers see things different and made many of them foolish with the kind of casual risks they took.

Which was why there had been a bloom in exotic animal sales. Still illegal in most countries that had any sense, of course, but there were sadly too many of those that didn't. The fact that such animals occasionally escaped or injured non-climbers was just a minor price to pay.

"You disapprove," Ms. Wen said.

"Not at all, Lady Wen."

"Trudy. You can call me Trudy," she said. "And here, I thought you'd be more fun than my niece. If you're going to be so stuffy, you can just leave."

"I'm still uncertain why you called me here," Arthur said, quietly. "Other than the fact that you were holding my beast stones hostage."

"Your beast stones"—she sat up now, angrily—"Your beast cores! I gathered them, I collected and stored them. They're not your stones, they're mine. Certainly not Casey's either."

Arthur shrugged. "Then you can argue that with Casey, of who has the right to split what. Though from what she told me, you were always meant to give her that portion. It's just being split between me and her."

"Is that what she told you?" Trudy laughed. "That girl, shading the truth. Of course she gets an allowance, but the amount she's asking for—it's being taken from the amount we were supposed to pass up. She's eating into the profits of the group, for your alliance."

Arthur shrugged, not sure why he should care. Oh, he understood it engendered some resentment; and it was easier to target him than Casey. But it was not new information after all, and she'd promised to shield him. If she couldn't, well, that was the reason why he was making nice with others too.

"To be so arrogant and young and cute," Trudy flopped back, her irritation suddenly gone. "Sit, sit. You think she's your friend, and you're wrong. She's, at best, an ally. And if you're not careful, she'll draw you in with promises of luxury and ease and the next thing you know, the Chins will have you. All wrapped up and you'll be wondering how you're here... alone, without friends."

Arthur took the seat, leaning forwards a little with hands on his knees. "Is that what you're looking for then? Friends?"

"Company, here." She smiled a little, tracing a finger down her stomach and then adding, "I can be a good ally outside, you know. A very good one."

"Aren't you stuck here?" he asked.

"And that's why I'm such a good one," she said with a laugh. "What I need isn't immediate, at least for a few more years. And after that, all I need is some security, some small help. What I can offer, though, in the immediate future…" She watched his eyes and then stopped her finger movements, seeming to realise that her play the coquette was getting her nowhere.

It wasn't that she wasn't good-looking or seductive, in that MILF way that had been all the rage about twenty years ago. Now, there was a push for GILFs, but it had never hit the same level of societal buy-in. Sadly, for the boomers and Gen X, they had just to accept that they weren't the trend of desirableness anymore. Again, climbers had managed to make their mark there with the wider variety of body forms and athletic scenarios.

In the end, for Arthur, his Yin Body just made it easier to ignore such temptations. It wasn't that he was cut off entirely, but it was more at a remove, a less driven need.

"I'm not against making new friends," Arthur said, ears twitching a little as he heard the footsteps approaching and then stopping as he spoke. He made sure to choose his next words carefully. "So long as my friends don't bring more trouble—more enemies—than they're worth." He smiled thinly. "And really, if it's not a transaction. I find that friendship, real friendship, isn't about the considered give or take, but just being there when it's needed."

"Without consideration for cost?" Now Trudy laughed. "It seems like you're being a hypocrite, asking for an alliance that favors you and, yet, holding off those who might be your friend, no?"

Now he shrugged. He had no answer to that, just his truthful thoughts. Moments later, that lurking shadow took a few more steps, revealing Casey.

"Auntie, are you bothering Arthur again?"

"Always bothering." Trudy sat up, glared at Casey. "I'm trying to make friends."

"I know the kind of friends you make." Casey's voice was frosty. "He's not interested."

"Oh, and you're so much better? He better be careful, before you all start adding more clauses and asking him to do things for you. Maybe he'll end up taking loans too, eh?" Then, Trudy cackled. "Or maybe he'll be smart and go to the triads. They're at least safer than the Chins."

"Auntie!"

Arthur had to admit, watching the self-assured Casey be put on the backfoot and devolve into a foot-stamping teenager was worth his visit. And, perhaps, the alliance with Trudy Wen. If she could handle the other Chins just as well, she might well be worth every dollar. Though, he doubted it, or else why would she be stuck here? Still...

"I can speak for myself, you know." Arthur glanced at Casey, then continued. "I am curious about what you can offer, outside the Tower. As someone has told me, things will change once we're out." Smiling triumphantly, Trudy made to speak, only for Arthur to talk over her. "But that's something we can discuss with Mel and some of my administrative team with me."

Now Trudy pouted, causing Casey to smirk. Till she registered everything he had to say and found herself looking at Arthur, doubt filling her eyes. He ignored the unvoiced question and hurt in her eyes, continuing. "In the meantime, Casey and I need the beast stones."

After all, that was the point of their visit. Whatever other reasons the others had.

Chapter 36

They walked in silence for a few streets, Lam and Arthur watching the surroundings with care. They had a couple of additional guards from the household with them, though the minor additional income on this round was significantly smaller than their first payment. Then again, it was still enough for some to kill for, especially considering there was no official rule of law.

On the other hand, rather than the lawless society some might posit, casual robbery and theft occurred much less often in the Tower than one might expect. There were a few reasons for that, from the fact that nearly every individual who had arrived on this floor was trained to fight and even kill, along with the sheer volume of Tower techniques available to track down a perpetrator.

No one was going to bother, unless they really were bored, with a small theft. However, murders and killings and maybe even brutal beatings were another thing. And if someone didn't have the money or skill to do it themselves, you could always hire the gangs who had a regular business conducting revenge beatings.

Add in the fact that the gangs themselves kept an eye on the streets, especially the ones in their sector to make sure that thefts were limited, if not entirely eliminated, in exchange for enforcement and protection fees—and well, it was relatively peaceful. But relative still meant that there were fights and killings, and so neither party were taking it easy.

Casey, on the other hand, while watching the surroundings ritually, was worrying something over in her mind. In the end, she spoke up when they were halfway back, crossing the sprawling seventh floor city.

"Do you really think we're that bad?" Casey said.

"No."

"Then why?" she asked.

"You're the one who told me to make nice," Arthur said. "And I wasn't going to sleep with her."

Casey snorted. "You wish. She's a tease, not a slut."

"Good to know," Arthur replied, then frowned. "Should you be using those words for your Aunt?"

"Auntie-in-law," Casey corrected. Then, added, "Probably not. Sorry. She's just so aggravating. She keeps saying all these things about the family, acting as though she didn't marry into us on purpose!"

"Maybe, but maybe she didn't know what it entailed." Arthur shrugged. "Anyway, I wasn't lying. Having her on our side, especially if what she wants isn't too bad, isn't a bad thing." A twitch of his lips. "Anyway, she's a Chin, right? You wanted me to be more like her."

Frosty silence greeted his statement.

"I am curious what she can offer. Here and outside. Helpful if someone would give some hints…"

"Oh, now you want my help," she snapped. "Not when you're taking out a loan and buying up real estate."

"Still angry about that?" Arthur said, quietly. "I needed to give them something, and sneaking it right by them was important. More than giving Prime Group a little win by selling an unused warehouse. Especially at a discount."

"You..." She shook her head. "You could have asked."

"Yeah, I could. But we don't tell each other everything, now do we?" When she opened her mouth to protest, he continued. "Like about a missive that you received and had you hurry away, even after you said you'd be with me on the meeting."

"That was different!" Casey said, heatedly.

"How?"

"That was private!"

Arthur blinked, noted the flush on red on her cheeks and then chose to drop it.

"Fine, I'll ask you next time if we have to buy something," Arthur said.

"Good."

"So." He watched her look at him and then continued. "We have to buy a bunch of weights. And some more cutlery. And I'd love to get a table and some office chairs."

"Why are you telling me that?" Casey said. Then, after a moment, growled. "Never mind. Stop. You know what I mean." Arthur chuckled instead and eventually Casey joined him. Eventually though, she sobered up and spoke softly. "Auntie Wen, she's got her supporters outside. Older men, some managers she helped move upwards. Her husband was well liked, and when he died..." Again, another shake of her head. "She managed to garner a lot of sympathy and used it well. Then, she volunteered to take this post, which got her even more approval." A slight frown, as she continued. "Though, I think it wasn't just purely altruistic. I think she received some promises, that if she came, they'd help her.

"Since then, her investments outside, the people she helped, have done well. She has a good feel for people."

"Well, of course," Arthur said, puffing out his chest, causing Casey to roll her eyes again. "So, what's the problem? Why are you all upset with her?" He hesitated, before adding, "Beyond her trying to get more money for herself."

"Because the people she has promoted, the industries she's involved in, they're… dodgy." She gestured to the side. "Some construction. Nail salons. Massage parlors. KTV lounges."

"Triad places."

"Exactly." Casey shook her head. "She pushes the boundaries. Uses our name to keep them away, keeps her people out from paying for protection."

"Smart."

"Dangerous. It causes trouble for us all. Gives us bad PR."

"So, why not stop her?"

"Her companies aren't directly affiliated with the Prime Group. And Grandpa still feels bad for her, so none of us can do anything. She just trades on it," Casey said. "It's not stable."

Arthur just nodded, choosing not to contradict her. Her words did illuminate matters further for him, but he found himself drawing a rather different conclusion.

After all, whether he liked it or not, he was dealing with the triads and gangs already. He wasn't big enough to stop them from preying on him, and while they were currently at abeyance, he had a feeling eventually they'd come in.

And as much as Casey might like to think her family's corporation was pure, he'd heard the rumors. Really, the same ones that involved any major corporation. That they'd paid off this government servant or that one, that they were affiliated with this gang or that one.

End of the day, grow large enough and you had to deal with the two devils of Malaysia.

The gangs and the government.

Chapter 37

Arthur had to admit, he enjoyed the nighttime training sessions in their new training hall. Weeks after its debut, it was now looking more like an actual gym, with a set of wooden dummies and the pair of canvas and leather punching bags in one corner, a heavy-duty set of weights and strap-on weights in another corner, a padded obstacle course that also doubled as a complicated fighting scenario space with requisite moving obstacle racks, and finally, a much larger, open space for generic training. Right now, they hadn't set up firing lanes and protection, so the ranged enthusiasts had to wait till the melee combatants cleared the floor, but it was on the list of things to improve.

Some of the more enthusiastic in the group were discussing putting a sprung floor, adding just enough spacing on a bunch of wood risers beneath so that when one was thrown or fell it hurt somewhat less. Arthur could not help but scoff at the idea, a sentiment shared by Eric but not Leia, who called them over-testosteroned masochists.

The training hall was also filling up on the regular, not just with Clan members who made use of the facility and the trainers, but also gradually with climbers purchasing memberships and classes. Rick was busy managing the membership plans and pricing, working with Mel and Yao Jing to build out various options that would work for their limited space. He was even talking about adding a second building on the floor and putting together a document to send down to the first floor when they exited, enthusiastically discussing how the Clan—and his family if necessary—could provide the funds and what not to build it.

In truth, Arthur was glad to see his idea was having fruit. He was even quietly making plans on how he could do the same in the real world, though training halls in the real world were, not surprisingly, quite numerous. It was likely that a more public one would have to wait, at least till a Clan-only one was filled.

Even with all the newcomers to the training hall, nighttime sessions were less popular. Even if night owls were not uncommon, many enjoyed the silence and peacefulness of the evening to themselves, cultivating or reading or recharging batteries in the darkness. As such, the training hall, especially in the late of the evening, was often at the quietest.

Breathing in a little deeply, his nose no longer smelling the slightly stale sweat of the warehouse—a factor that no amount of vinegar seemed to be able to remove entirely, no matter how often they cleaned the place—his gaze took in his other late-night companions. Uswah wasn't here, the pair having chosen to take alternate nights to give the hall more overlap. Which left him with Jan from the regular group and Noor here.

Like Li Sun, Noor was on the older side and she had allowed herself to slack on her training over the last few years. She had no intention of going further, seeming to have grown quite accustomed to life on the seventh floor, including having a husband, a house, and a garden. Still, perhaps it was the enthusiastic addition of the others that had her joining in the training sessions.

Though, late night was uncommon entirely for her. Though Arthur was curious, the pinched look on her face and silent tossing around of heavy weights was giving off real "don't talk to me" vibes. One that he was happy to listen to.

Especially since he had a trio of his own students here. His only in the sense that they showed up each evening and managed to convince him to help them out.

"Jai, knee." Long stick in hand, he pushed Jai's folding knee outwards so that it was in line. The African kid was one of the many children of immigrants who'd made their way to Malaysia in the early '00s before things took a turn. Still rare, though. "Remember, keep it in a straight line when you lunge; otherwise you're going to be in pain eventually."

Or at least, that was how it worked for normal humans. Who knew, between their healing technique and climber physique. It probably wouldn't matter as much, but it did reduce efficiency and effectiveness by fractions.

"Good," Arthur said to the other two students, who were working together, moving through a series of semi-static blocks. Inside right upper block, inside left upper block, inside right lower block, inside right lower block, then step to the right, turn and block with outside left arm. Turn again, outside right, cross body block, outside left, cross body block and so on, so forth. "Movements crisp, blocks fast but soft till contact. Don't tense till you need to. Watch where your hand is moving. Now, faster."

Zhiang Lin and Aman moved around one another, Aman only a little taller than Zhiang Lin—and she was only five foot three. Not tall at all, even for a Chinese woman, especially with the increased height of the population in the last couple of generations thanks to better nutrition, way too many growth hormones in meat and tofu, and just the combination of good genetics. Then again, he knew better than to mention Aman's shortness to the little Indian man. Height, like other sizes, were always a bit touchy.

The entire blocking routine used both inside and outside portions of the arms, meant to train the instinctive reactions. It was a favorite of his sifu's, taught to newbies until their arms were black and blue with bruises as they sped up. No pain, no gain, though; and eventually the bruises would fade, helped along with Chinese medicine rubbed on the arms. And with practice, they would begin to block instinctively.

Later, of course, there would be other techniques to add. High blocks, lower blocks, knee blocks, elbow and knee checks, slips and rolls. It all worked together, until you stopped thinking about what you were going to do and just reacted to the incoming fist or sword or monster.

Foot movement, too, positioning. That would be later, when they shifted to the one-step and two-step drills. The training to understand where you needed to be, when someone was coming at you. Then, speeding up the drills so that you could make those decisions quicker with other, fun little variations to make it interesting and challenging, like no hand, no trips, only hips, and so on.

Training was arduous and painful, but also fun, or it should be. At least, that's the way his master had trained him and how he tried to show his students now.

Though too many ran off at the disciplined and painful part and never learnt to embrace the pain.

"Aaargh!" Arthur tilted his head to the side at the thump and cry, looked over to see a girl rubbing her leg. She was one of his Clan members. In her mid-twenties, she had short hair and a determined look on her face as she stood up again to try once more.

"You're doing fine," Arthur called out encouragingly. "Most can't even do two steps, three is really hard."

"I know," she said, curtly. Then narrowed her eyes, readying herself to jump, even as she favored her injured foot.

Foolish, but who was he to criticize. He had his own tendency to be stubborn.

Finished with the review of the group, he walked off to a corner, content to let them run through the set. They'd switch out once the timer went off, practicing forms and punches, and then the various drills. As for himself, well, he was working on adding to his energy stores. Extracting the stone he had begun to draw from, he took a seat, cast one last look at everyone and began the process of draining the monster core.

Of course, it was only five minutes later when the building was attacked.

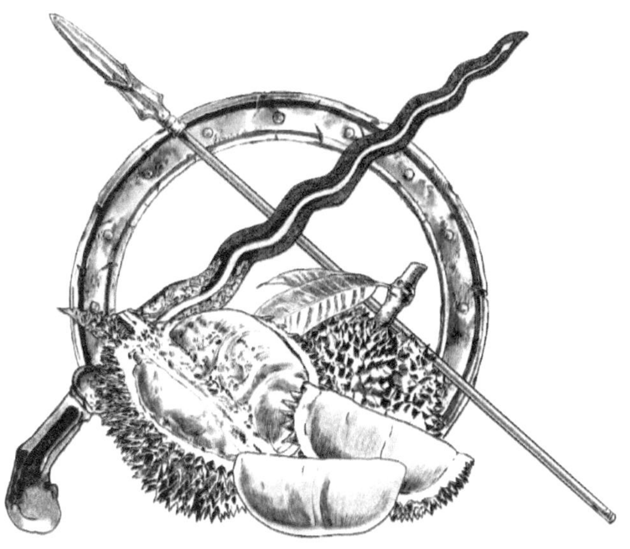

Chapter 38

The gang strode in without breaking stride, slamming the door open to announce their entry. Arthur cut off the flow of energy from the stone he was cultivating from, pulled the energy deeper within him as he smoothly stood up, and slipped the stone into his pocket. Ever since he learnt how to control two flows, moving and cultivating was a lot easier. He couldn't fight at the same time, and he wouldn't even want to try cultivating while having to do more than pay minor attention; but cutting off the flow and pulling the energy in was something he could handle.

Unless he got shot immediately, of course. But the way the gang was strutting around, spreading out to take up space at the entrance, it was clear this was more a show-off moment than a full-out assault.

"Oy! Don't get in the way, we won't hurt you. Got it or not?" The speaker, a mohawk hair-styled leader with dyed purple tips—and how he managed that in this environment, Arthur was really curious about—was swinging his parang around to punctuate his point.

Arthur reached sideways without taking his eyes off the speaker or his gang, grabbing his spear. He could see how Noor had dropped the bars, grabbed at her own shield and short spear combo. The trio of his students were less careful and had started inching towards their weapons, spreading out until they realised there was no way they'd reach them. What with their weapons and clothing near the front entrance.

Something to reconsider and look into.

"Who are you?" he called out once he had grip of his spear and the majority of the energy within him had been put away. He started up the Heavenly Sage's Mischief, figuring he'd need that soon enough. Though Bark Skin might make more sense. He still wasn't competent enough to run two full-body techniques yet. Once he was sure he was stabilized, he'd build another Refined Energy Dart.

"We're the 04," snapped the speaker, he and his fellow gang members waving their parangs around. They were all Indians, all but the single Chinese member hanging right in the back.

Arthur frowned, racking his brain and remembering details. The 04 weren't like the Ghee Hin or the Double Sixes who'd jumped into the Towers with abandon. Instead, they'd stuck to their usual businesses— murdering, extorting, kidnapping and dealing drugs—until they realised they'd been overshadowed. Now, while still strong in the real world, they were a significantly smaller power in the Towers.

Still, they should have avoided the Towers. Gang 04 was an old triad gang before they'd devolved into just being a brute thug group without the same level of connection to other groups like the Ghee Hin. Which was why the gang 04 generally listened to the Ghee Hin. Unless...

"Great," Arthur replied. "Counting past three is a big thing. You should be proud. Now, stop terrorising my people and get out."

"You think you such a big man, ah?" Sneering, the leader waved to two of his people on his left. They stopped the casual rifling of backpacks and clothing near the entrance where the members kept their goods and headed for Arthur.

"I'm going to give you all one last chance. Mostly because I don't want to be cleaning up the blood," Arthur said, slowly and carefully. He moved forward, seeing how his students came to flank him at a distance and Noor hurried from the weight area. Jan, he knew, was down at the obstacle course, though she'd been quiet for the last hour. "You don't want to start this. Even if you win, the Benevolent Durians are going to have hunt you down."

"You think you something, ah? Once we teach you a lesson, your people won't dare." Another gesture, another two on his right moving to flank Arthur on the other side. The leader himself moved forward now that it was clear everyone was committed.

"Okay." Arthur sighed. He wondered what they had to use, what they intended. How lethal they intended to be. How lethal he intended to be. Then, after a moment, he realised it didn't matter. Just like the 04 meant to make a statement, he needed to make one too.

He waited till they were ten feet away—and they were moving rapidly now. Then he released the first Refined Energy Dart, sending it right at the outermost thug who was trying to flank him. He waited a half-second, watched the man jerk and throw himself back to dodge the speeding attack, and released the Energy Dart from his Poket Simpanan.

Arthur didn't have time to pay attention to the outcome of his pair of surprise attacks, instead having to do his own dodging. The first Energy Dart shot outwards from the other flanker on his right—the gang leader's left—aimed at Arthur's head.

Fool.

He leaned sideways, letting it flow pass him as he dropped his weight and started a low-passing lunge. He saw the flicker of movement on the other side, a hand rising up to clench at him and he leapt without thought. Moments later, grasping tendrils of energy tried to grab him, missing by inches.

Hauling his spear back, he got ready to thrust it at the Energy Dart opponent only to be thrown back, his whole body cast away as a pulse of energy tore through the air centered around the boss. In the air, he had nothing to brace against and he found himself tumbling backwards.

Arthur hit the ground hard, rolling with the attack. He'd managed to hold onto his spear through long practise. He wasn't the only one hit, he noticed as he came up on his feet. Zhiang Lin was picking herself up and Jai was recovering, desperately throwing a block with his arm against the descending parang.

Arthur winced, looking aside, pouring the Heavenly Sage's Mischief through him as he formed another Refined Energy Dart. His first gambit had worked at least, his target down and clutching at his chest and the hole his attack had created. Then, he was too busy to pay attention, blocking the swinging pair of parang.

Two on one was never fun, but neither party were trained to work with one another. So after he backpedalled a bit, he managed to get them to foul up their own footsteps, putting the leader in front of his opponent. He'd been reserving how fast he was moving till then, exploding into a flurry of blows with his spear that culminated with an ankle hook using his lead leg.

As the 04 leader fell, Arthur thrust with his spear. The strike was perfect, catching the other in the neck. Only for it to bounce and bend a little as Tower energy reinforced skin refused to give away immediately. So instead of skewering the other in the neck, it just tore a wide hole through it.

It still put his opponent down as he rolled away, clutching his neck.

A couple of seconds of backing away gave Arthur enough time to take in the rest of the fight. Noor had her own opponent well in hand, weaving an impenetrable defense that kept hemming her opponent in and actually fouling up his footsteps and those of his others. She was angling him into their backline, forcing him to stumble and fall over others.

At the same time, Aman was actually rolling around on the floor, grappling his own opponent trying to see who would come out the winner. Luckily, neither had a weapon in hand so they were easy to dismiss. Whoever won that fight, it would be significantly later unless either party showed a degree of sudden and surprising competence.

Jai, on the other hand, was staggering back, holding onto his arm. Good news: he hadn't lost it. Bad news, it was a close thing and only exceptional Body stats and probably a Trait had stopped that. But he was bleeding all over the place. Only the fact that Zhiang Lin had chosen to get involved with Jai's attacker by sending a series of spinning lights that kept rotating around the other man and blinding him kept Aman alive. Unfortunately, without a weapon herself she wasn't doing very well, nor was one other Clan member against the two after her.

In other words, they were losing.

Cross-body block with the spear, pushing the parang off line. He angled it so that the weapon would slide and bounce away rather than keep sliding down into his fingers and then he stepped in, bumping his opponent with chest and hip. While the other man was falling back, and as the leader was staggering away, he roared.

"JAN!"

Chapter 39

The shout was enough of a distraction that his opponent wasn't ready for the sweep and strike by his spear. He managed to sink the butt of the spear deep into his opponent's stomach, causing him to cough and exhale, hard. Too bad it wasn't the other end, but needs must.

Then, Arthur was jumping back, pulling the leader to him, dodging another flashing Energy Dart, pulling an opponent to him and only barely managing to shift his body so that the thrown knife imbued with Focused Strike sunk into the top of Arthur's shoulder instead of his chest. It hurt a little, but adrenaline kept him in the fight as his spear kept darting around.

He waited, just long enough for the flashing lights to blind Jai's opponent, to loose his own Refined Energy Dart. He aimed at the man's head, watched as it exploded out of the side of the man's head because he was too busy with the flashing lights, and tried to keep his stomach from rebelling at getting splattered with warm blood and brain matter.

It cost him, as a parang slammed into his leg. He felt skin part, causing him to hiss in pain and causing his leg to buckle. Another strike caught his spear, and as the parang swept for his fingers, he was forced to let go or watch his fingers fly off. One-handed, another opponent grabbed at it, only for Arthur to gift it to him, point first.

Movement in the corner of his eyes, and a boot caught him in the chest, sending him sprawling backwards.

Too much going on, his opponents too fast. Other cultivation techniques were being thrown around. Someone had activated an Aura, one that slowed down the movement of Tower energy. He could feel his chi, his energy struggling to move properly, making the Heavenly Sage's Mischief less powerful, his body heavier. He found himself pushing back with his Yin Aura, helping to remove the pressure a little, grateful his new trait let him do so.

He kicked a few times, pushing his opponent back. Mindful of the swinging parang, nearly getting a toe lopped off but managing to smack the arm away. Then, he kipped himself up, using a shoulder and then arm to spring sideways in a weird capoeira-wushu kick mix that he made up on the spot. His flailing legs coming in at a high angle caught a face, throwing his opponent back with a bleeding nose and scratched chin before Arthur managed to finish the spin and recover.

No weapon though, his kris was with the rest of the gear at the front entrance of the training hall. He hadn't wanted to wear it while he was training, the sheath annoying when it banged against his thighs. Instead, he kept forming a Refined Exploding Energy Dart.

Movement behind his opponents, and he backed off, casting a glance back to check he wasn't running into anyone.

Meanwhile his opponent lunged for him, never realising that they'd left their back open.

Jan's spear erupted out of the boss's back, punching through as the full-speed sprint and lunge pushed the weapon through his ribcage and out his front. He staggered a step, then another, his own momentum pulling him off the weapon. Arthur stepped sideways, grabbed and stripped the parang from his hand.

Shock cut through the gang of 04 members at the violent death of their boss. The younger members literally froze. Moving swiftly, Arthur backed away, putting himself in front of the door and snarling one word.

"Surrender."

Sadly, things didn't go how he expected. Rather than dropping their weapons and taking the easy out, the remaining members fought even harder, two of them charging him at the same time.

Shoulders hunching, he set his feet.

One way or the other, they weren't leaving. Not after what they had done.

Arthur groaned, leaning against the wall and recalling what they said about desperate rats. The last minute of fighting had been even more furious. He had picked up more injuries then than the rest of the fight before, as he refused to back out of the door. He had dropped the Refined Energy Dart the moment he had created it into his Poket Simpanan, instead switching over to forming Bark Skin as he stopped feeding energy to Heavenly Sage.

After that, he just had to hang on long enough for his friends to finish off the others and come help him. The gang had fought until it was clear they weren't going to escape, and then the sole member left standing had dropped their parang. Right now, he was tied up with a bunch of rope and was kissing the ground as Noor and Jan finished bandaging the other members. Though, looking at one of them, Arthur wasn't sure if he'd survive.

Gut wounds were nasty, and while they were more resistant to infections, more resistant didn't mean immune.

One last look, as he triggered his own Accelerated Healing. He moved slow, making sure to put as little weight on his foot as possible, feeling blood still leaking outwards from it as he took a step. Painful to the extreme, but he could survive it. The problem was making sure he made it over to Jai where his friends had strapped a splint on the man's arm to keep it straight and in one direction.

"Don't keep messing with it," Arthur growled, sitting down beside them with blessed relief. He winced, reached sideways and pulled up the flap of skin by his side that flopped open, pressing his hand against it and waiting for it to gum up. "You need to make sure it's aligned mostly, then the Tower can do the rest."

"It... I'm going to lose my hand. Oh gods, oh gods, I'm done for. Shit... shit."

"You're not. Now, I need you to focus."

"I shouldn't. I blocked it. I didn't think. I just... blocked it. I'm so stupid, oh god, oh god."

"Oy!" Arthur considered reaching over to smack Jai with his one free hand but knew doing so would hurt. Instead he growled out the question, hoping it would get his attention. "You want to join us or not?"

A shove, and the mental prompt.

"What? Wah...?"

"Jai!" Zhiang Lai pushed on his arm, trying to get his attention. "Say yes! Yes."

"I…"

"You all too," Arthur said, cutting off the other two before they could ask. Or think about it. More pushing on the Tower, then he lapsed into silence as he waited to see what they'd do. He focused on his own healing a little more, tried to pull it through to the specific areas that needed fixing. Stopping his bleeding was the first and biggest step; he was leaking like a punctured sieve after moving again and reopening his wounds which was a bad idea.

"Shit!" Arthur cursed, suddenly.

"What?" He barely noted how everyone tensed, weapons raised. He shook his head, dismissing their worry as he continued. "I forgot to use my new technique!"

Of course, considering it wasn't meant for short battles but was better at taking out bigger monsters, perhaps it wasn't as big a mistake. Except, maybe he could have left a few more people alive.

Then, looking at the injured and the injuries, he dismissed that concern.

They'd made their decisions. As had he.

Regrets were for the late nights, not when everyone was still bleeding.

Chapter 40

Jai and his friends made sure to take the Clan invite, of course. Along with the help of the only actual nurse in the Clan, they'd managed to position Jai's near-detached arm such that there was a good chance it would actually be functional. Right now, he was pouring whatever energy he had into fixing it most of the way, though he had been cautioned to leave the remainder healing to natural Tower processes on the off-chance it would do a better job than a rushed one.

Truth be told, Arthur figured the nurse was being too cautious, but since it was a matter of days rather than weeks or months, he didn't say anything. Also, he didn't want her glaring at him. For such a tiny woman, she had quite the ferocious look as she hovered around the injured.

Which should have been him, but he'd managed to sneak away by pulling rank. And the need to finish interrogation.

A small but busy group of Clan members were dealing with the bodies, stripping them of goods and clothing before hauling them outside. The bodies would eventually be tossed outside the city perimeter to allow the beasts to deal with them, unless someone came by to claim them.

Which would have been rather daring, all things considered.

In the meantime, mops and buckets were in play, while the only conscious member of the gang was propped up in a corner, Jan seated before him, picking dried blood out from under her fingers with a knife.

Dramatic, but effective from the way he was sweating.

"So, who sent you?" Jan asked, again.

"I told you, it was the boss! He told us to come, so we come." The man half-sobbed out. "Please, don't kill me. I have a little brother!"

"So? So do I," Jan said. "I don't like mine though." Knife came out, pointed at him. "And I don't like liars."

"I'm not lying!"

Jan leaned forward with the knife pointed at the man's eye, forcing him to lean back. He couldn't back off, what with being strapped to a weight machine with its weight on the bar and his arms tied to it in a spread-eagle fashion.

"Stop." Arthur said, causing Jan to look over at him, knife hovering in front of the other man's face, mere inches from punching into the other's eye.

"Boss? He's lying."

"I know, but we're better than that," he said, disapprovingly. He waited for the man to slump a little in relief, before he continued. "Everyone just cleaned up this area. Don't force us to make a mess again here. So inconsiderate."

Yao Jing snorted. He was standing behind the prisoner and holding the barbell rack down with one hand just in case the other tried to jump up. Arthur bent low, waited for Jan to move the knife away so it wouldn't be near him as he continued, speaking to their prisoner.

"You know who I am, right?"

"Ya, ya, I know!"

"You know where we are, right?"

Confused, the man said. "Training hall?"

"In the Tower. Where there's no actual laws," Arthur said. "No Geneva Convention, no civil rights. We want to beat you, cut you, kill you... no one really says anything, you know?"

The man pled, "*Tolong, lah.* I don't know anything!"

"And I want to believe you, but I don't. You must know something. Otherwise, I'll let her get it out of you. And if you think I won't..." He shrugged, gestured backwards to the exit and where the clan was still cleaning the blood out of the floor and equipment.

"I... Please..."

Arthur sighed, leaned back and pointed to Jan. "Give him a few minutes. Let him think about what he can remember. And then, if he doesn't tell us anything, you know what to do."

He waited for her to nod, then turned to their prisoner. "Just so you know, we moved your other friends there." A gesture to the end of the hall where the other two injured and unconscious members lay. He would have to make his way over and put some of his Yin energy into them to make sure they stayed asleep. "Anything you tell us, it better be the truth. Because we'll be asking them. And anything they tell us, which you don't . . .?" Arthur smiled.

"I don't know anything!" the man blubbered again.

He ignored the man's shouting, limping over to check on the others. Sometimes, leaving someone to fill in the blanks was the best threat of all. He just hoped that Jan knew to only push it so far. As much as they might threaten torture, he didn't actually intend to use it. After all, it set a bad precedent and left any of his own people open to retaliation of the same sort.

There was a reason there were lines in war. You tried not to cross them, if you could.

Of course, the fact that the 04 were a crude gang and not an organized triad, well, maybe someone was willing to cross those lines. If that was the case, then Arthur was just going to have to dissuade them.

Uswah, gliding up beside him as he limped over, asked softly, "So?"

"Nothing yet. We'll get something." He hesitated, looked at her. "Can you find out more? About the 04? Ask Casey and her people. Maybe the Lotuses too. I need to know what we're against."

"You think it's not just one group?"

"I don't know," Arthur said. "And I'd rather not be forced to keep guessing."

"Okay, boss." A one-handed lazy salute and then she slunk off as they crossed into the obstacle course, moving to disappear. He wondered if it would be wrong to buy a ninja costume for the Yin-bodied sneak. After all, her usual head covering already kept her hair hidden. But it might be a little too on-point.

Dismissing idle speculation, he began the process of pulling energy into his body and transferring it to his hand. Both of the remaining members of the gang were here, both trussed up securely, one much more than the other mostly due to the injury of the second. But other than a big blue-black egg forming around one head and a deep cut down one arm, the second opponent was doing pretty good. Well enough that he was glaring at Arthur.

"He say anything?" Arthur asked the guard curiously. He didn't even recognise this Clan member of his, though the way she held her weapon and the fact she'd arrived with the rest of the Clan, he'd assumed it was someone he recently added.

"No."

"Okay, one second then." Making a quick decision, he went over to the more injured one, letting Yin energy slide into their body. Laboured breathing evened out as they slipped fully into unconsciousness, only for their other captive to thrash, spitting and swearing around the gag.

"Chill." He reached forwards, watched the man thrash and he pulled his hand back. "Chill, I said." Eventually, he managed to get the gag off without getting his fingers bit off, which was always a plus.

"If you—"

"I put him to sleep. Helped him be in less pain." Arthur smiled, trying for kind though he was pretty sure he just came off cold. Hard to find empathy for a man who'd recently cut you up and you still sported a few of the wounds. "We're not monsters."

"What do you want?"

"World peace, a lot of beast stones, and a dragon," Arthur said. "Barring that, how about your story?"

"Then what? You kill us?"

Arthur shook his head. "As I said, I'm not a monster. Your *tai kor* got killed. No need to add you to it. You're just a soldier, right?" A reluctant nod. "So, I get promises, hang onto you, and get a ransom. That's about it." He smiled. "If you tell me who your boss is and who ordered you here. The whole story, right?"

He watched a variety of emotions flicker across the man's face. Thought, consideration. Then he looked sideways, at the woman who had been guarding the man. His eyes widened and instinct had Arthur throwing himself sideways, a hand rising in a block. Spotting the parang, swinging sideways, meant for his neck.

Chapter 41

Arthur managed to angle his block enough such that when it came down, the momentum of his push and the hardness of his enhanced body had the parang slide sideways even as his hand slipped down the blade and met his attacker's hand. He felt the pressure, the deep wrongness of the blade slicing into flesh and skin, parting muscle and sending nerves ablaze. He gripped her hand, tight, the Yin energy from the Imbued Strike still running through his body and pulsing into her.

She jerked her hand back, yanking the blade out of his flesh, parting it further and almost sending the flap of cut flesh to the ground. At the same time, his fingers, already half-numb, slipped from hers as she pulled back. On his butt, he kicked a leg backwards to give himself room, the woman stalking forward with focused intensity.

No time to think or defend himself as the blade raised again, intent on chopping through his arm. The block wouldn't work the next time, even though his Yin energy began to slow her down. Instead, he tapped into the

Refined Energy Dart he'd stored so recently, releasing the attack out of his middle eye.

It tore through the air, and only a last-minute twist of the woman stopped it from punching through her heart but it did tear a line along her armour. Off-balance for a moment, Arthur capitalized on it as his flailing leg caught the ankle closest to him, causing her to tumble. He grabbed at her arm, battering it aside so that it was across his body, her back now turned to him. His other free hand clamped down, even as he noticed the captive thrash around, trying to free himself at last.

The pair squirmed and fought, Arthur desperate to keep her arm from coming free, grateful that the longer blade of the parang and its single edge meant that she could not just twist it around and cut him that easily. All the while, he kept the Imbued Strike running, yanking energy upwards with all the strength and force he could as he pumped it into her through the shared contact of their bodies.

Little grunts and cries, a warm body and a pained sob from the prisoner stabbed in the stomach behind him. Arthur kept fighting, keeping his head near hers and just to the side, avoiding the head slam that was tried, ignoring the hand that tried to lever itself away and then found his open wound, digging in deep, deep, deep. Squirming inside his body a little, pain so great it nearly tore his concentration away.

If not for the sticky energy of his own body that allowed him to more easily grasp it. If not for the Yin Body that gave him a degree of impervousness to the pain, a dulling of the agony. If not for hours and days and years spent training, slamming fist and leg into hard objects and getting slammed in turn, he might have given up.

Eventually though, that thrashing slowed, weakened. Stopped. He rolled her off, drew enough of a breath to scream, and then hesitated long enough to aim a kick at the tied prisoner who was nearly out of his bonds, slamming the other man's head back into the column he'd been tied to before he cried out for help.

Then, and only then, did he release the Imbued Strike and his control.

He tried, of course, to utilize his Accelerated Healing. But there was only so much that his damaged body could take, and he'd hit that limit as he reached inwards, questing for that energy.

Arthur never even realised he'd fainted.

He woke up, bound. After an initial jerking motion as he tried to move, Arthur stilled himself. Eyes opening a little, he tried to grasp what had happened, why he was tied up. There was motion on one side, voices low and murmuring, and a soft but not mattress-soft place he was resting upon. Right arm was actually free; it was just his left that was tied off, tight to his body. Legs were numb. More than that, though, he was in agony. Strained muscles, cuts, stabs, and a couple of broken bones he was sure.

"You're awake. Don't move, you'll just open up your wounds again," Mel said, exasperated. "Really. What did we say about going places without a bodyguard?"

Opening his eyes fully, Arthur let out a little relieved breath. Even that motion was enough to make his chest hurt, those broken ribs thrumming, that blasted knife attack that had gone inside him like a poker. Lucky that it hadn't made his lungs fill with blood or something like that.

"What happened?"

"They had a second plan, to get to you. Or maybe someone had an added plan," Mel said, frowning. "Or maybe it was all one plan, and they wanted you dead from the start and just didn't want to make it public."

"Or it was just an opportunity," Noor added.

"Sorry, boss. I should have been there," Yao Jing said, coming in from the other side with a grimace. "I shouldn't have left you…"

"Not your fault. Or Jan's. We were supposed to be safe, with half the Clan here." He sighed. "Was she, is she, one of us?"

"No. She just snuck in. With all the new additions, none of us realised she wasn't really part of the Clan," Mel said.

"Told you. Should have tattoos visible," Yao Jing said, patting his own shoulder where his was.

Mel shook her head, not wanting to get engaged in that argument. Instead, she continued, "We're questioning her, but she's keeping her mouth shut. And we're not exactly willing to torture people." Hands on her hips, she glared at him. "Right?"

"Of course not."

"Good, because I caught Jan dragging one of the men outside and about to cut his fingers off," she said. "She told me you okayed it."

"I didn't!" A pause. "Well, I did threaten to do it, but I didn't mean it…"

That had Noor snort. Yao Jing grinned triumphantly and said, "I told her."

"Maybe, but you didn't stop her." Mel sighed. "We'll try to get the other one to talk, but at least one of them gave us some information. The one you kicked in the head." He waited, content to gently pull at his refined energy. Weaving it slowly into the Accelerated Healing method to speed up the patching. "We got confirmation that the head of 04 gave the orders. Whether he chose to do it himself or not, we don't know." A darker look. "She's not part of them, I think. So either an add-on or..." a shrug.

"Why?" he asked, coughed. Yao Jing bent down, helped him up a little so he could sip at the cup. He found himself draining the entire thing, his body craving the liquid after all the blood loss. Accelerated Healing could do a lot, as did the Tower, but physical aid made a difference for sure.

Noor was the one who answered his question once he was able to focus. "They're not known to have women. In fact, they actively discount women. Send them off to us or the other gangs like the Sixes or the UN." She shrugged. "Not that the Sixes are big here anymore." At the look the others gave her, she answered simply. "Their best left a few months ago. We, the Lotuses, actually picked up a few new girls because of that. Though, how long they'll stay..."

Arthur understood. You didn't join a gang because you wanted to for the most part. You did it because they offered protection, a way forward. And the Lotuses in the real world were a non-entity.

"Then.... who?" he asked.

To that, no one had any answer. In the end, he dismissed them all, knowing that they'd do their best to get answers from their prisoners. In the meantime, all he could do was heal himself and get ready.

Because one thing was clear. Someone really didn't like them and the moves they'd made. And Arthur somehow doubted that this attempt on his life—or two attempts, depending on how you counted it—was the end of it.

Chapter 42

This meeting had been delayed for two days, long enough for him to heal up, thanks to Accelerated Healing. He'd have preferred more time, more time to interrogate their prisoners, more time to wear away their energy and willpower as they were badgered over and over again by the interrogators. Non-stop questions, always circling back.

Enhanced interrogation techniques indeed.

It worked, though. They managed to piece together some further information, from moments when one prisoner exploded in anger, from times when a quiet word and a sympathetic ear from the matronly Li Sun drew out other information. Slow, in dribbles. Which was why they wanted more time, but the 04 leaders had leveled one last threat, dragging their score or so members and that number again of hired help to stand outside the Durians' Clan hall to harass anyone going in and out.

After all that commotion, it was nearly impossible to keep it quiet. Arthur had agreed to the meeting, a short distance away in a nearby restaurant that had enough seats for everyone and a clear back exit that could be seen from the Clan hall. The seating area was large and open-air; no one was going to sneak up on them.

It also meant that much of the conversation wasn't going to be private, but at this point, it was clear there was no hiding the altercation. Not that either party was exactly trying to do that.

"Boss Harish," Arthur greeted congenially as he walked in. His people flared outwards, taking up one corner of the open-air restaurant, leaving the other side to be filled by the 04 gang members. With the kitchen, back exit, and a wall taking up the other sides of the rectangle, it meant that the restaurant was pretty crowded except near the wall. No point sitting there.

"Clan Head Chua." Harish was a bear of a man, a muscular individual who was hairy in all the places, never mind just the chest—as Arthur could see, since the 04 boss was wearing a white singlet. He had a big, bushy mustache too that he'd trimmed and oiled, along with his hair. There was the slight smell of coconut oil used to keep everything in place and oiled, but also gone slightly rancid with the lack of good bathing facilities around. "You finally came out, did you?"

Arthur shrugged. "I had things to do." He sat down, and then deliberately stuck one foot up on the chair, so that he was sitting with his leg upwards in an insolent manner as he continued. "Anyway, I didn't have anything to talk to you about. Yet."

Harish eyes narrowed at Arthur's studied insolence and more than a few of his people stirred. One of his dumber lieutenants snarled, stepping closer only for the one nearest Arthur to push that one back. Interesting, that the slight and shorter man had the strength to do so easily. A lot of Body points invested in that tiny compact frame.

"So you want keep my men, torture them more? That the way the Durians do things?" Harish said. "We won't let you."

"You admit the attackers were yours?" Arthur said, curiously.

"Yes."

A flicker of something in Harish's eyes.

Arthur blinked, rearranging the information in his mind. On second questioning, they'd learnt that the orders had come from above but not from Boss Harish. Just his second-in-command, the short man who had restrained his subordinate. The man's name was Jeet, but he was also known as JT, like that old pop singer who'd gotten caught in that Tower-climbing scandal.

"And you sent them?" Arthur asked. But no point pushing the matter, Harish was not going to admit he didn't have full control. Not in public, and he needed a win in public. In fact...

"JT." Harish voice snapped and the thin man stepped forward with a briefcase, an actual briefcase which raised all kinds of questions like why the hell someone would bring one all the way into the Tower. It was put on the table and snapped open and Arthur blinked, seeing the mishmash of leather and cloth pouches within.

"Uhhh..."

"Beast cores," Harish said. He gestured impatiently at Arthur who reached forward and picked a cloth up, only now seeing that each pouch had a marking on it. 4-12, or 7-11, and so on. Picking up the 4-12 one, he realised quickly that these were fourth floor stones, twelve of them.

"A good haul," Arthur said, suddenly feeling like he was entirely afloat. Uncertain of what he was bargaining for, or how much. He'd expected to be paid but how did you value a life. Could you? And was this amount, what with the various denominations and numbers a good thing or bad? To buy himself a little time, he started sifting his way through the pouches, doing a count on the number of pouches. Seven pouches all in, no surprise. Not a lot of first-floor stones, not surprisingly, and quite a few fifth-floor ones. More than even the seventh floor stones, which was a surprise.

He wanted, desperately, to look back at Noor, at Li Sun, at his people. Then again, he knew they might not have any clue either. They'd always had to grovel and ask and trade favors to get their people back when someone ran afoul. And they'd not had to bargain at these kind of levels.

Favors...

"So?" JT asked, butting in.

Ignoring the man, Arthur made a choice. He dropped the fourth-floor pouch inside, plucked the seventh floor pouch out and then added, "And a favor. For each man returned."

"Each one?" Harish scoffed. "One favor. For all of them." Then, he added, "There's still three alive, right?"

"Still three," Arthur confirmed. "Your last man actually pulled through. Our nurse is pretty good." Surprisingly, she was the one with a breakthrough in their healing technique. She had already been studying how to project healing to others, to aid them in healing faster. Before joining the Durians, what little she had learnt from the Tower techniques and then working with Li Sun had almost never been worth the cost. However, ever since Arthur's Accelerating Healing technique had passed on to her via membership, she'd been making great gains.

It was still not a formal technique yet but she was well on the way. Even the little she had managed to learn allowed her to suppress the infection, help drive the man's body to clean out the impurities and dirt and give him time to heal up. He'd probably recover, all things considered.

"Two favors." Arthur pushed the briefcase back, tossed the pouch over his shoulder to Li Sun. "Get them, will you?" he asked her. He took that moment to watch the others, everyone playing the hard-ass. The only one showing a degree of discomfort in all this being Rick, the man warring between dislike for the 04 and fear, hands caressing the grips of his pistols. Arthur figured he was fine, so long as no one started anything but he did catch Yao Jing's gaze and cut his eyes over to Rick, a silent warning.

The big man offered a nod and, content that someone had an eye on the nervous rich boy, he played his next card. Curious how the 04 would react.

"So, the girl yours too?" Arthur asked.

"What girl?" Genuine surprise on the gang leader's face. Arthur caught it, but his attention was fixed just past the other man's head. Watching his lieutenant who had bent over to grab the briefcase and the others in his group. He'd already assumed Harish was not involved; rather, someone—JT most likely—was cutting him out.

Except, JT was surprised too. Now wasn't that something?

"The one that tried to kill me." Arthur touched his neck, remembering how it had nearly been severed. His arm still ached, though he knew it was psychosomatic for the most part. Didn't stop it from hurting, mind you. But at least, he knew it wasn't real.

"I guess we keep her then?" Arthur said, indulgently. No reactions from the 04, not that he saw. Maybe someone else did. As Harish agreed to it, muttering how it was all just meant to be a shakedown, not a murder attempt. Soon enough, the group of injured prisoners were walked out into the not-so-loving embrace of the gang. More than a few muttered words of contempt and anger coming from those not involved, but no strikes.

Not yet.

Arthur didn't envy the poor bastards when they got back though. Getting involved in a war and getting beaten wasn't going to do them any favors. Still, the negotiation was over, and as Harish stood up, Arthur did too.

It was only when he was nearly about to leave did he lean in, lower his voice and add, "So, if you learn more about the attack, and the girl, you'll tell us, eh? Consider it a favor, even."

A single cutting look over to JT who had frozen as Arthur whispered. Harish sneered a little at Arthur's words, not even deigning to answer him. Waving the others off with him.

Now, all he had to see if the seed he planted sprouted.

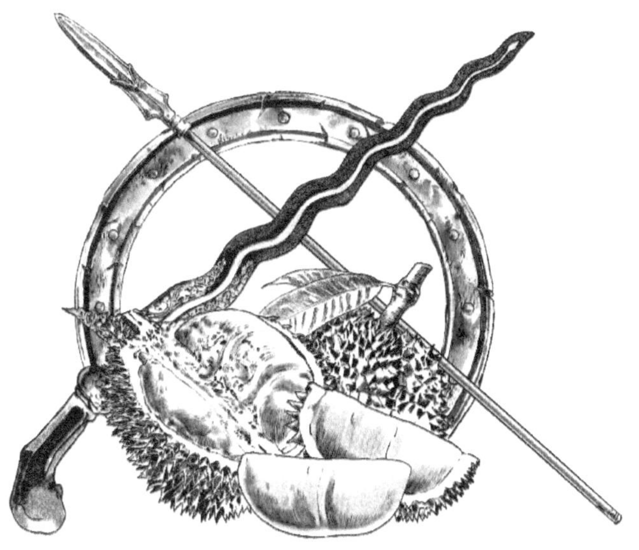

Chapter 43

Casey found him in the newly-made boardroom of the Clan hall. At least, it looked new by most standards. It was really just two rooms in the building with the separating wall knocked down, giving just enough space to fit a small table and a bunch of chairs within. The pair of windows set on either side and double doors made it a little incongruous, though they'd saved time by just leaving those alone.

"You let them go?" Casey said. "For only a dozen stones?"

"And information. And two favors," Arthur said. "Which means they won't be attacking us anytime soon."

"Also makes you look weak, which increases the chance of others coming for you," Casey argued.

"Killing half the attackers wasn't enough?" he said, then shook his head. "Anyway, any of the smaller players aren't my concern. At least, not here. Outside though..." He gestured upwards, indicating the other Towers. "The 04 aren't exactly small out there."

"They don't mess with climbers though, not outside."

Which was, generally, good practise. There were more than enough non-climbers to bother, and this way, they avoided bringing down trouble they couldn't manage. Even with their own climbers, they just didn't have the numbers or the infrastructure to keep their total numbers high.

That was another concern for Arthur when he finally exited the Tower. Sooner or later, he and the others who came with him would have to enter a more advanced Tower. In their absence, whatever they built in this first Tower might come down. Which was, of course, why Casey and Rick and everyone else warned him and told him to make alliances. Those alliances, that web of interconnected debt, it would keep his Clan and whatever he built functioning while he was gone.

Theoretically at least.

"They don't normally." He opened both his hands, palms up. "We're still small. And if we need help... "Again, that crooked smile. "Anyway, the point wasn't them."

"The girl."

"Yeah. A real hard case, that one." Arthur sighed. Luckily, even if some of the other Clan members were a little more bloodthirsty than others, no one had tried torturing her. On the other hand, having multiple people guarding her, waking her up, keeping her tied up in a room with bright lights and constantly, constantly being interrogated was diverting significant resources. Especially since he only trusted a few people to do it, and do it right.

Or as close to right as a bunch of amateurs could get.

"Still not talking?" she said, curiously.

"Nope." He shrugged. "So, maybe now, we'll see if someone tries to break her out. Or kill her. Or something."

"Not worried they'll kidnap one of your people to trade?"

Arthur hesitated, not sure he wanted to explain that he was worried but not hugely. All the people he truly cared about were staying close on hand. Everyone else was moving in groups of two or three. And if they were kidnapped and taken, at least it'd give him a lead. Not having one was driving him nuts.

"Maybe you'll do fine after all," Lam, her silent shadow, said.

Uncertain how to take that, Arthur switched topics. "You all hear anything new? Ms. Wen have anything?"

"No. She did say she was glad to get the letter from you." Eyes narrowed in suspicion, but he gave nothing away. "We just have rumors. Some of the triads are denouncing the attack. A few are even loudly looking for the culprit or have started pressuring the 04. They've lost a few places too, pushed back further."

"So, lose-lose for the 04. And no one else is willing to stick their necks out and come after us," Arthur sighed. Nothing more to be done about it then, not unless their unseen assailant made a mistake. He said as much and Casey changed the topic this time.

"How's your cultivation?"

"Decent." He waggled his hand from side to side. "Nowhere near second ascension, but I've been working on techniques, you know." She grimaced at his admission, and he knew she felt he should have pushed for his next transformation. Different philosophies at play, of course. "You?"

"I'm getting close to where I want to be, but I need more stones. In a week, I'll be farming them myself." She left the unspoken invitation hanging there.

"A week, you said?" Once confirmed, he nodded. "I'll get cultivating then."

They broke before she did. It wasn't that they let Arthur's attacker go, though Arthur was seriously considering doing so. They just stopped with the enhanced interrogation techniques, allowing her to sleep and rest, rather than keeping her awake and the cell filled with noise and questioning.

Arthur spoke as though it was a matter of making sure his personnel, the interviewers, had time to cultivate and continue to progress themselves. That was how he pitched it to everyone who asked. Few enough out there who did, but at least that was what got around.

The truth was simpler: they were good people. There was a point where you either decided to go true villain, go really bad and just torture people, or you stopped. Because it went from "enhanced interrogation" to straight out torture when the prisoner was slurring and bleary and hallucinating and nothing coming out was useful.

Unless Arthur really thought that an imaginary, stuffed bunny called Mr. Pinkie had asked for his death.

At a certain point, you just had to give up and realise that the longer, slower interrogation methods were all you had. And even then, Arthur wasn't certain how long they could do that. It wasn't as though the building itself was that secure. If they didn't have someone watching over her constantly, she could likely have punched her way through the walls and escaped. After all, the Tower Guard wasn't going to stop people from leaving, just from entering.

And she was, by definition, a guest.

Four days later, and accepting that he really wouldn't become an outright villain and even the idea of too long an interrogation made him squeamish, Arthur went in to speak with her one last time. One way or the other, they had to work this out. If that meant she was set free, so be it.

"Why did you try to kill me?" Arthur asked the assassin.

They hadn't even managed to get her real name. They had gotten multiple names. Which, Arthur assumed, was her trying to cover for the real name she had given at some point. He just wasn't sure when she had come up with that plan.

She certainly reacted to none of his questions:

"What did you expect to get out of it?"

"You know you could have—probably should have—died, right?"

"Who hired you?"

"Did you know that I wear my underwear on the outside, sometimes?"

That last one did get a reaction. A long, slow blink. Mel, unfortunately had even more of a reaction, which amused Arthur, but otherwise, not much else.

"You know, you should learn the Yin Body technique yourself. You're cold blooded enough to really benefit from it." He paused, then added, "Unless the addition caused a chain reaction that froze over the Tower. Too much for mortal man, when the lady with ice veins finally can, with the Yin and the Yang."

Still no reaction.

In the end, Arthur sighed. Stood up. "You give me no choice."

Now, just the slightest tightening of muscles. A miniscule reaction as she readied herself to fight. He stepped away, slipping the kris from his belt as he readied his techniques. He watched her watch him, even as Mel did the same on the other side. Then, he reached out, and opened the door.

"Go."

Surprise, now, as she hesitated. Outright suspicion dancing in her eyes. He didn't blame her.

"I won't kill you in cold blood. And since the only person you tried to kill was me, I get final say." He shrugged. "Maybe you'll come after me, maybe you won't. At least next time, I'll be watching. And I won't even try to interrogate you."

Silence. They walked with her, all the way to the entrance. She hesitated at the door, watching the traffic outside, and then took off running. Arthur turned to the Tower Guard, informed them the young lady was no longer a guest and closed the door.

Only to find Jan and Mel staring at him.

"What?"

"That was foolish," Mel said.

"She's gonna try again," Jan said.

"You're right," Arthur said. "But I'm not walking down that road. And she won't find it that easy, next time. Or even living on this floor." At Jan's puzzled look, he continued. "I got her description and a sketch to all our friends. They'll all be looking out for her and have promised not to work with her. So let me know if she works with anyone else." He shrugged. "It's a small enough town. She's either going to have to leave, or if she sticks around long enough, we'll know who she works for."

"And Uswah is tracking her?" Mel said.

"Nope. She's sleeping the night off."

"But…"

"Nah, I figure she's good enough to pick out Uswah if we tried to set her watching. Or smart enough to hide till daylight came and then lose our resident rogue." Arthur shrugged. "More importantly, you can't prove a negative."

"What? Oh..." Jan grinned evilly. "You want her to think that someone might be watching but she can't see. So she won't report in."

"Or waste a ton of time trying." He shrugged. "Either way, it's the best we can do." Then he pointed up at his room. "Now, don't bother me. I got more cultivating to do, before we leave."

Ignoring Mel's attempt at starting that conversation, Arthur made his way to his room, feeling a lot lighter. It seemed being a good person and a Clan leader was going to require some reassessment. And a few risks taken.

Chapter 44

There wasn't a good way for the group to leave the Clan building for their hunt without attracting attention. More than one restaurant had found themselves host to a number of consistent spies—though perhaps "paid watchers" was a better word. After all, it wasn't as though sitting outside, day in and day out, was exactly sneaky.

Even at night, there were those who watched the building. Arthur could have snuck away at night, but the group itself was not particularly discreet. Anyway, he did not feel like playing the rogue, instead choosing to head out while everyone was watching. Let them come, if they were going to attack them.

After all, his last gambit had not the effect he wanted. Whoever his opponent was now, they were careful enough to cover their tracks. Even Harish hadn't been able to provide further information to him after questioning his own lieutenant a little more vigorously than Arthur was willing to. Then again, Harish had been somewhat upset when he learnt that part of the deal had included his eventual death and deposition.

Either way, no more news regarding the assassin's employer. Or the assassin herself who had disappeared. Rumor was that she had left to actually finish the Tower, but Arthur wasn't going to drop his wariness till he confirmed that. He still was rather struck by that remarkably composed and, now that he thought of it, severely beautiful woman who'd nearly killed him.

What could he say? Growing up in a martial arts studio had given him proclivities towards strong women.

Right now, though, on the final walk out and no danger between the buildings and the rolling plains with their shin-high grasses, he took a moment to scan his status screen. He'd managed to get quite a bit of additional training down. With each seventh-floor core containing about 0.07 points of refined energy, he only needed about 14 hours and 14 cores to get a full point.

No, the limiting factor wasn't time right now but number of cores—of which there were too few, especially after being split with his core team—and cultivation speed. He could cultivate much faster now, especially with the overall higher density of energy on the seventh floor and in his room. Even outside, he could pull nearly three points every ten minutes easily, or nearly a full ten points in half an hour.

Unfortunately, he still had to refine all that energy and compress it down, which meant ten points or half an hour of cultivation to get the necessary Tower energy pool started. After which, with his faster refinement speed, it was another forty or so minutes to compress all that down.

Which meant that he needed roughly an hour and ten minutes for each 0.01 point of refined energy. Or about 116 hours, or six days, if he did nothing but cultivate and sleep for eight hours a day.

Which was, of course, the reason why people wanted rooms in his Clan building. Between the compressed energy on the floor, he could halve the amount of time needed for cultivating energy. He could literally filled his dantian with a full ten points of energy in ten minutes in his room.

Which was incredible, though his refinement speed only received a moderate boost in effectiveness. That was all internal mostly, though the environment offered some minor boost. Even so, shaving enough time off to make it 45 minutes rather than 70 minutes was huge. Put another way, he only needed, give or take, four days.

Two whole days might seem like much now, but it meant he could add two whole attribute points rather than one in the week he focused on this— with the aid of a few cores of course.

And like all advantages, it built upon one another.

Which was why, staring at his screen, Arthur couldn't help but be a little smug.

Cultivation Speed: 2.773 Yin

Energy Pool: 27/27 (Yin) + (6/6)

Refinement Speed: 0.1421

Refined Energy: 0.17 (37) +(0/3)

__Attributes and Traits__

Mind: 15 (Multi-Tasking, Quick Learner, Perfect Recall)

Body: 22 (Enhanced Eyesight, Yin Body, Swiftness, Fast Twitch Faster, Lightning Reflexes)

Spirit: 15 (Sticky Energy, From the Dregs, Strengthened Aura)

__Techniques__

Night Emperor Cultivation Technique

Focused Strike

Accelerated Healing – Refined Energy (Grade III)

Heavenly Sage's Mischief

Refined Energy Dart

Bark Skin

Seven Cloud Stepping Technique (189%)

Poket Simpanan Tua (135%) (Refined Energy Dart - 84% Integrity)

Imbued Strike - Yin Poison

Partial Techniques

Simultaneous Flow (168.4%)

Yin-Yang Energy Exchange (83.3%)

Yin Poison Darts (39.7%)

Yin Aura (32.8%)

"How close are you to third ascension?" Arthur asked, curiously. Thirty points in a single attribute was huge, and it sometimes happened a little later if you only focused on a single attribute. But supposedly, it was a major change in the body and physique again. That, and the fact that it was often the benchmark needed to cross the last three floors of this Beginner Tower.

Casey clanged at Arthur, hesitated before answering, softly, "I'm close. My family prefers a more balanced build, especially when we are looking to exit."

"Ah, the eternal question. Min-max or balanced builds," Arthur said, amusedly. Of course, you couldn't really go entirely min-max. None of the three attributes they had were really "dump" stats, so it was common that they were within a 20- to 30-point range. If not, one would either take all too long to refine and cultivate chi and thus never progress or be so delicate that death was but a moment away. Still, it was a matter of degrees.

"Close enough." Casey shrugged. "I'm not going for an entirely balanced one."

"So what do the Chins favor?" At the look she gave him, he amended it. "Or you?"

"What do *you* favor?"

"Body right now," Arthur replied without question. As her silent prompting gaze, he clarified further. "I might change later, but right now, I need the added survivability to keep up with you all."

She nodded in acceptance of that. Sooner or later, he'd want to shift to something a little more balanced. Ten points was pretty much the top line of a min-max build that was recommended and generally agreed upon. Once he got that, he figured he'd up his Mind attribute further. It was about time to emphasise and develop his willpower and gain a trait to aid his refinement, and if he hadn't already agreed to exit his building to hunt for beast stones, he would have likely dumped his newly acquired points there.

"You?" he prompted as they continued walking.

"Mind."

"Makes sense." Refinement speed was the most important thing for the rich since it helped them understand and eke out further advantages from their cultivation texts and compress their energy further. At a certain point, supposedly, the entire thing tipped over such that you were literally cultivating and refining at the same time. Of course, that was at higher level Towers, which were a non-issue for Arthur at the moment.

One day.

"So, what kind of monsters are we facing? Or hunting?" Arthur asked, curiously.

"Didn't do any research?" She sounded surprised, looking back at the trailing bodyguards. When they gave her impassive gazes as they entered the outer boundaries of the rolling grass plains, she turned back. Ahead of their small group, Clan scouts could be seen bobbing and weaving through the grass, the rolling nature of the land and the high grass making them appear and disappear as they kept walking.

"Three major monsters we have to worry about. We're going to hit a confusion of the wildebeests if we can," Casey said. "Though they're not really wildebeests…"

"They just look a little like them." Arthur confirmed, and she frowned at his interruption.

"Not dangerous individually, but very, very fast. Hard to capture, and there are no cliffs to run them off. So we'll have to sneak up on them at night if we can or trap whoever we can. Sonic attack that causes confusion, sharp horns, and occasional elemental attacks." A grimace. "Rumors are, if you wander far out enough, some of the female leaders have a blast attack too."

"So keep it ranged once we trap them, but get in close to pick off the edge if we can."

"Yes. Then, there are the packs. The ecological equivalent of hyenas. The *dubuk menara*." Tower hyenas, literally translated. Stupid name, but it worked. "They're fast, work in packs, we'll probably locate the wildebeests tracking them. Or maybe just find them, after they've taken a few down, feeding. Pack coordination, enhanced speed, and a knockback attack aura on the charge. Also, projected bites."

"Projected bites?" Arthur said, curiously.

"Their faces grow a… phantasm? A semi-solid mask that expands and chomps." Casey gnashed her teeth in display, then blushed as she realised what she had done. That made Arthur chuckle a little, before he waved her to continue. "All good cores, anyway."

And all group animals, which was the main reason why they were going out as a group. You didn't want to try to hunt these animals down yourself, because without an overwhelming strength advantage, multiple attackers trumped skill and strength. It wasn't a simple linear progression in difficulty but exponential.

"And the last?"

"That one we want to avoid. Solo hunter. Can you guess?"

"The seventh-floor equivalent of the lion, except not because lions aren't solo hunters." He frowned, running the details through his mind and winced. "A tiger."

"Yes. If we're lucky, we won't see one of those at all."

Chapter 45

Everything had gone well to start. Three days in, the team had managed to track down a pack of the *dubuk menara* and kill them. It had been a hard fight, the creatures faster than any Earth-based animal could ever have been, crossing dozens of feet in the blink of an eye. However, Arthur's team was stronger and faster now and had a wide array of techniques, including some that rooted and blocked off the straight-line approach of the creatures.

Those that tried to flank were pinned or attacked, driven back by ranged attacks even as people like Jan or Mel stayed in the rear to watch their backs. Killing them had been tough, but no one picked up any major injuries. After that, it was only a matter of following the trail of wildebeests who had stampeded away and running them down till they slowed to a stop. They fought the wildebeests and harvested their cores too.

Of course, those were two of the three major threats. There were other creatures on the plains, smaller monsters and wildlife that attacked the group and could inflict injuries if not found beforehand. Most were significantly weaker, equivalent to third- and fourth-floor monsters—some as weak as first-floor monsters—but only offered stones that were weaker too. Tiny little stones but still packed with dense energy as befitted the seventh floor.

There was, for instance, the grass snake, small and lounging on the floor. It had a venom that would kill. Arthur actually had one captured and tested on him, in hopes of leveling up his Accelerated Healing resistance to such venoms. While he did manage to understand and improve on the technique a little, he utterly refused to try again.

There was something incredibly painful and off-putting about watching your own skin rot and melt as the venom destroyed the flesh around a wound, and trying to combat it as searing agony ripped up your calf. Not fun at all. It didn't help that the looks he got from his team ranged from "you're an idiot" to "wow, you're a pervert masochist."

Other smaller monsters, like gophers, scorpion-like creatures, and a snapping turtle, were a lot easier to handle and kill. Though rarer in numbers.

No, everything had gone well for the first few days. Which was why, when calamity arrived, Arthur was entirely unsurprised.

The savannah tiger equivalent—and really, he should stop trying to relate these creatures to Earth animals so much—had six legs and an almost monochrome set of fur in varying shades of green to help it blend into the swaying grass. It was just over twelve feet long from head to haunch. It also had a trio of tails, each of which moved independently and were the length of half the tiger's body. Sharpened razor thorns on the tails spun through the air, striking at those who got too close, even as claws lashed out and that huge mouth threatened to bite and chomp.

It came bursting out of the grasslands, a single leap that crossed nearly a dozen feet in a single motion, preceded only by a shouted warning by Uswah. Her shadow tendrils had reached outwards, gripping at the body but only to break apart almost immediately as the monster's greater strength allowed it to power itself through the bindings.

No time to even think about it, Arthur ducked low and got his spear in place, braced as best he could against the ground. It tore into the side of the creature, releasing a gout of red blood into the air as it bore down on its actual target, Yao Jing.

The big man had reacted by instinct, trying to catch the creature and getting his arms raked by those long claws. Arms wide and akimbo, he had skidded back across the ground, tearing it up but somehow managing not to fall under or beneath the creature.

Over-developed muscles bulged and twisted as he bore the two or three tons of weight, the monster's long legs coming out to slash at Yao Jing. Only the bodyguard's armour managed to his insides from spilling onto the ground, the enhanced carapace that they had purchased recently managing to handle—barely—the attacks.

Red and orange light flickered around Yao Jing as he triggered his own buff technique, increasing his overall strength and defences. Bark Skin skin layered over him at the same time, and Arthur wondered how Yao Jing managed to get two buffs working simultaneously before he did. Frustrating...

Mostly though, Arthur was unleashing hell on the creature. Shadow tendrils had gripped its lower legs and bound them tight, again and again. Flames licked against fur as a fiery aura reacted against the creature, smoke forming and rising from its fur. As Arthur knew, the flame aura actually reacted against other monstrous auras and targeted ones, which was why the grassland wasn't necessarily burning.

Still dangerous to use, of course, but it wasn't Arthur's biggest concern.

The loud *whumpf* of a shotgun cried out, the slugs slamming into the monster. Blood burst from the wound, though it was less than you'd expect. Both because movies either showcased no blood or way too much from a shotgun spray—and also because the creature's own aura and innate toughness was defending against it.

Casey had fallen back, arrows following after Rick as she put arrow after arrow into the body. They struck deep, expanding on the wounded area as Rick pumped and fired. Arthur's own Refined Exploding Energy Dart also slammed into the same general area, adding to it.

Lam at the back, working with Uswah to help tie down those waggling tails. His shield catching blind attacks, his spear stabbing and cutting as they attempted to pin the tails down. Light ribbons, trailing behind the moving spearhead, helped to slow the attacks, bind them before they burst, but the Tower energy bindings were unable to do more than slow and hurt the tails.

All the while, Arthur closed in. Stabbing with his spear to dig into the shoulder joint, trying to cripple the middle leg that kept attacking his friend. Bleeding Yin Energy into the creature, causing that same leg to move slower, jerkier with each moment. He could feel his Imbued Strike working, though he had to refresh it constantly as he hadn't figured out how to actually make it an aura as yet.

Others were looking at ways of crippling it. Mel had shifted away and, thrown a hand up, and a series of lights flowed out, hovering over the monster's face. It was a familiar technique; the ability to conjure distracting lights that flooded the surroundings was both useful as a distraction and to see in the dark. It caused the monster to jerk itself around, its gaze hampered.

Her other hand, wielding a parang, hacked at a tail that kept waving at her, right at the maximum of its range such that she was slowly crippling it.

More blows, more attacks raining down on it till Yao Jing's arm finally gave way and slipped. Big paw smashed him down one side, his body curling under. He rolled, directly towards Arthur, desperate to get out of there before the monster finished the job as it landed, body curling downwards.

Weakly, the leg that Arthur had been attacking swiped at Yao Jing. Struck and glanced off battered armour, tore a strip out of his hairline and back of the neck before the man got out. The creature shifted weight in response to not being able to see its prey properly, twisting the front of the body around, putting its head suddenly in Arthur's face.

Hot air washed over his face, slobber and warm saliva splattering him along with a rank stench that made him really wish there were monster dentists. He could see deep within, all the way into the trachea and throat, his Enhanced Eyesight picking out the shivering motions as it roared in anger.

A deep sniff, as it realised what was there.

Instinct had Arthur leaping away. He wasn't some crazed hero in a book, intending to shove his hand into the mouth and unleashing a barrage of magic to kill it. That might work in the books, but it was just as likely to end up with him losing his arm. So, instead, he retreated as he formed and released the Refined Exploding Energy Dart. He'd been building one since the start, not needing any of his other techniques, not just yet.

He missed, of course. The creature had clomped down where he was, blinded by the still-spinning lights such that the Exploding Dart struck its hunched-over lower shoulders and neck as it leaned forwards. The explosion tore off skin and fur, leaving the monster rearing back as Yao Jing, now on his feet and rising, threw a full-power, Focused Strike uppercut into the side.

Bones crunched, the leg on that side completely sagging.

Arthur lunged in at an angle, using his spear to lead the way and sunk it into the side of the neck. He watched the Yin energy imbued in the strike slip deeper into the creature, tearing through its Yang energy, threatening its ability to function. More booms, and then silence as Rick reloaded, arrows still landing.

They were winning, which of course was when things went to hell.

Chapter 46

Their attackers emerged from the long grass, unleashing a series of ranged attacks meant to kill and cripple. Uswah, their rogue, was targeted by a pair of crossbow bolts that tore through the shadowed form. A pair of Energy Darts flew through the air, a last-minute twist saving him from one. The other struck him in the side, throwing him dangerously close to the tiger's mouth. It clamped down hard, powerful teeth skittering off his pauldron and tearing into the skin of his upper arm as it missed him by a hair, still unable to see properly.

More attacks landed, but Arthur was shouting now.

"RELEASE!" Arthur called, pushing himself away from the creature as he threw himself into a roll away from the body, headed for the back feet. Yao Jing backed off too, even as the lights shifted, giving unimpaired glimpse down one way. At the same time, the bindings around the tiger's back feet disappeared.

Freed, the monster's automatic reaction was to leap away. It did so in the only direction it could see, bunched feet sending it a dozen feet away. It didn't stop, jumping again as the lights disappeared entirely, allowing it to see fully ahead. Allowed it to spot a pair of crouching ambushers, desperately attempting to reload their crossbows.

"Reform!" Arthur shouted again, a hand coming up at the last moment to block the Energy Dart that flew at his head. He felt his hand slam into his face, throw him back. He coughed and spat, feeling the burns and the wash of Tower energy riot through him and his aura, even as he tried to rejoin the group.

Only to find something wrong with his leg. He couldn't tell what, didn't dare glance down, but his left leg didn't want to work anymore, some attack somehow slipping in to do damage in the chaos of the battle. Maybe one of those lashing tails?

"Reform," he kept shouting, eyed narrowed as he discarded the Imbued Strike and began weaving Bark Skin. Without mobility, he was stuck on the defensive. And while he'd love to return fire, he seemed to be the target of at least three of the ambushers now, which meant dodging and weaving as best he could with his gimpy leg was the best.

Luckily, Energy Darts were neither as fast as Refined Energy Darts or actual bullets. They were dodgeable, so long as he spotted them. And he wasn't entirely hemmed in. When he couldn't, his armour helped defray the damage, though it was like getting punched by a 300-pound boxer.

He'd done that for training. Once. It had not been fun.

No bark of the shotgun. He hoped Rick was okay. They had expected the attack, planned for it over the nights. Knew that the ranged attackers—himself and Uswah—were likely the priority targets. Casey had her own methods of protection, including Lam who had somehow managed to teleport himself in front of the pair who were now charging her. But Rick, he had nothing but guts and some armour.

Another larger Energy Dart was building out there. He saw it fire towards him and rather than risk taking the shot, he threw himself to the ground hard. Air was driven from his body, forcing him to roll to keep moving. It didn't take long for the rest of his team to arrive, the group returning fire at last as their attackers closed in.

Ranged attacks were great, but they rarely ended a fight. Which was why their attackers now came with parangs and swords and spears, ready to beat them down.

One last moment, propping himself up with his spear. Arthur readied himself for the fight, taking in the attackers and, somehow, was not surprised by what he saw.

Then, their enemy was on them, and it was once again chaos.

A last-minute lean, a yank sideways, and his spear dragged out of his opponent's chest, tearing it open. He caught the descending parang on his bracer, angling his arm to let it glance off even as he felt the jarring, shuddering pain as lightning sparked down his arm, making his arm senseless for a second.

Even with an open-chest wound, his opponent was not dropping. Arthur had only one hand, so he fell back, spinning as he built up momentum with his spear, using his initial movement to send it towards his opponent's leg. It forced the man to hop upwards, to dodge the strike rather than follow, and it gave Arthur time to regain control. He kept spinning, going through a combined staff-and-spear routine to create a zone that kept his attackers off him.

Their initial tight formation had broken up after a minute of fighting. Their opponents were good, smart enough to peel off individuals as they fought. Strong enough that individuals could overwhelm one-on-one at times, forcing his team to gang up when possible. Unfortunately for Arthur, they'd peeled his own bodyguards off such that he was forced to battle this man alone.

If not for his greater skill and armour, he would have lost already. The other was faster, stronger, tougher than him. Numerous cuts from the parang had dug into him, leaving trailing wounds on parts uncovered by his armour. The damn thing was getting a workout, but it was the cumulative effect of the shocking energy that was causing Arthur the biggest problem.

Bark Skin, surprisingly, was doing a good job at helping ameliorate the arcing energy. It helped him shed the attacks, and the passive healing of his other skill boosted his recovery rates such that within a few moments, he managed to pick up his spear with his other hand. It didn't stop his opponent from landing a stomp kick on his upper thigh though, leaving him leaning precariously to one side.

Too damn fast, his opponent. He hadn't even seen the leg come up as he finished blocking the parang with his spinning shaft. If he could activate his Imbued Strike, he could do the same—layer a debuff on the other. But dropping his Bark Skin to add the other was impossible.

Which left him with very few options but an old trick.

Arthur made the decision shortly, waiting for the right time. It didn't take long, after blocking two strikes including one that nearly cut off a finger or two. An overhead chop that he caught on the haft of his spear, a twist that put the parang into a bind that his opponent accepted. All to get in, to let the lightning arc into him.

Nearly face to face now, he released the Refined Energy Dart he'd built up.

Watched as his opponent jerk away, moving so fast that he dodged the first attack and using that motion to grip Arthur's own arm, to begin a twist and throw.

Shuddering with the lightning coursing through him, Arthur lowered his gaze and head just a little as he was turned and released the second Refined Energy Dart from his Poket Simpanan. It tore through the throat, just under the adam's apple of his opponent where no gorget or armour protected them.

Left them staggering back, head half-hanging on.

Unfortunately, Arthur was on the ground too, unable to follow up. Hurting too much and his limbs, his body no longer under his control. Heart beating erratically, his breathing short and pained.

A few moments, all that he could afford before he pushed himself up, finding his opponent finally dead and bleeding out. And the rest of the fight...

Well, not over; but mostly done.

Pushing himself up, pulling his spear to him, Arthur started building his Refined Energy Dart again as he staggered over to help. He had friends to check on.

Chapter 47

"Should have kept one alive," Leia said, prodding one of the corpses with her boot. Eric, squatting beside it and stripping the corpse of armour and other gear glared at his girlfriend.

"Told you," he said.

"I thought we'd have a chance later on," she replied, then grimaced. "Was wrong, *lah.*"

"Uh huh." He wisely didn't add more, knowing there was little to be gained by pushing the point. After all, the attackers were dead and none of Arthur's team were, even though none of them had notice the ambushers creeping up on them.

Arthur said as much, content to let the team peel the armour off their enemies. After all, he was still recovering, bandages slapped all across his body, tightened such that he was not in danger of bleeding out anymore.

"No need to ask either," Lam said, pulling the arm up of one of the corpses. He showed the inside of it where a tattoo had been done. "I bet you'll find this on them all."

"What is it with gangs and tattoos?" Rick asked, as he kept a lookout with his shotgun in hand. "They're so... ugly."

Arthur had to admit Rick was right. The stylized number four was a based on a Chinese character:

a basic rectangle—which was "mouth" in Chinese—with two strokes within like curtain drapes. However, the gang's tattoos were variations of this, like lips or a screaming face with teeth drawn over.

"So you can't leave so easy," Jan said. "Once in, you're in." Jan and Mel were over by the corpse of the seventh-floor tiger monster, finally freeing the massive beast stone that was within its corpse. They had also cut off the three tails, knowing that if they were lucky at least one of the tails would actually stay behind as loot instead of vanishing like the rest of the corpse. There were a few crafters who wanted it back in town, and the Tower would purchase it if not.

Jan grinned evilly a moment later. "You know you got one too, right?"

"I do not," Rick said, jerking his chin up. "I don't do tattoos."

"Seal," Yao Jing called out.

That froze Rick up, and Casey let out a high and tinkling laugh. "You didn't think about that, did you? What are your parents going to think?"

"They'll be fine," Rick groused, glaring at her.

Casey let out another chuckle, then stared at the surrounding grassland. After a moment, she looked at the silent Arthur. "So Harish lied to you?"

A grimace was his answer. It certainly looked like it, which was surprising to him. He'd thought he was a lot better at reading others. Also meant that Harish's promised favors were so much hot air.

"Maybe not," Uswah had been crouched over the attacker that had nearly gotten Arthur, the one who had led the charge. The strongest fellow, at least in Arthur's opinion. Though he hadn't seen enough of the fight to confirm that. She was tracing a finger along the neck, rubbing at the blood there before she finally sat backwards, rocking on her heels in the squat. "He's not 04."

"Then?" Arthur asked.

"Ghee Hin." She raised her hand, and through the blood, he saw some darkness. "Ink. He covered his own tattoo with some ink and ash, to make it look like a mouth." She grimaced. "Though it's hard to tell."

"Sorry, next time I'll stab him in a more convenient location."

She snorted at Arthur and continued. "Doesn't matter. I saw his face going in and out of their base. Followed him back to the Ghee Hin's headquarters and saw them greet him. Always something a little strange with the way he acted among the 04."

"So what? He's their liaison?"

"Or a mole." She shrugged. "Not sure."

"*Haiyoh*," Jan exclaimed in frustration. "Always the Ghee Hin."

"They're not a small group here..." Casey said, warningly. "This is their main floor. And outside..."

"Outside, they're going to be more of a problem," Arthur said, firmly. "If they're targeting me here, it's for sure because they don't want me out there. Which means, when I come out, they're going to be after me anyway."

Casey had no answer to that. A dour silence fell over the group as they realised their predicament. Arthur closed his eyes rather than look at the rest, turning over the new knowledge and his options. None of them were good, as far as he could tell.

Ignore the news, act like nothing happened. Keep them guessing a little bit, or maybe a lot if they hid the armour and goods. It might keep their attackers at bay, at least from direct confrontation. So far, the Ghee Hin had been using the 04 as catpaws; but after this attack, Arthur wasn't sure there were that many left of the group that were willing to work outside the bounds of Harish's orders.

Unless he was really just playing Arthur, and these guys weren't a splinter. At which point, things were even worse than he thought and no amount of prevacation would stop or slow the attacks.

They could come back, make no accusations and just showcase the goods and armour. A silent show of strength, acting as though putting down the group hadn't been touch and go. If they had focused on killing his friends rather than just targeting him, they might just have lost a few people.

As it was, it had been touch and go. Especially for him.

"Play ignorant? Or declare war?" Arthur muttered out loud. He couldn't really see many other options. Try to negotiate something, perhaps; but since they'd gone straight to trying to kill him, it didn't seem like that was much of an option.

"You could try talking to them." Casey received quite a few skeptical looks at her words, and she let out a sigh. "I could try talking with them for you. Find out what it is." She frowned. "It might not be all the Ghee Hin who have a problem with you."

"We can't fight them," Mel said firmly.

"Not alone," Jan agreed.

"So, we get allies, *lah*." Yao Jing said.

"Like the Sixes?" Uswah said. "From the first floor?"

"Exactly like that," Arthur said. "Except we double up." He frowned. "If they're not all in on it."

"The UN don't care. Not about Malaysia. They're just a branch," Lam pointed out.

Rick looked a little lost, which Arthur didn't blame him. After all, local gang politics probably wasn't something that his family had taught him about with any degree of thoroughness. Certainly not local gang politics outside of the Tower.

"The United Nations are an international group. They're more like, umm, a gang of gangs? Loosely affiliated, set up across the world, helping one another level up. They concentrate in Advanced Towers, don't do much in Beginner Towers except get their members through. It's why they don't have a presence on lower floors," Arthur said. "Even in the real world, they're more a North American thing. But they like having international branches because..."

Now he trailed off, because he had no idea about the reasons for that.

"Lets them test out new Towers and get a wider variety of skills," Casey said. "They're also focused on North America. Having different skills or cultivation techniques from the various Towers lets them develop their people more widely. Each Tower's challenges are different, so it's useful to have a wider variety."

Arthur nodded. There were some Towers that were entirely night-based or cave based, for example. And as such, you had to acquire quite a few night- or sight-based Traits and techniques to survive. A lot of rogues came out of those Towers, or sneaky warriors and mages. Then, you had Towers with platforms everywhere, that required you to climb, jump, and spin through the air. No surprise that movement techniques dominated those.

He had even heard of a Beginner Tower that was a series of arena challenges, one after the other. Climbers there were like gladiators, fighting through different cities. The cultivators that emerged from those were the deadliest duellists around but, quite often, horribly useless in most other scenarios till they ran a Beginner Tower or two.

Another reason why Arthur actually preferred the Malaysian Tower, though that might have been his nationalistic side showing up.

"So, you think the UN will help us here, ah?" Eric asked, getting the conversation back on track. "'Cause they're not scared what we can become in Malaysia?"

"Maybe. They might not want to get involved," Arthur mused.

"I can ask my family." Casey looked concerned as she continued. "But you need to be careful. I can't commit the Chins to the fight. Only my Aunt can."

"And you think she'll use it to tie us tighter to her, make her a benefactor like you?" Arthur asked.

"Yes."

"Well, good thing you're all part of the same group, right?" He grinned, unrepentantly. Which, of course, was a lie. The Chins might own Prime Group, but the large multinational company had multiple industries and competing groups within. Anything he committed to here would have effects in the real world.

But that was a problem for the future.

Though he couldn't help but note how Rick frowned even further.

Politics. Love them or hate them, you had to deal with them.

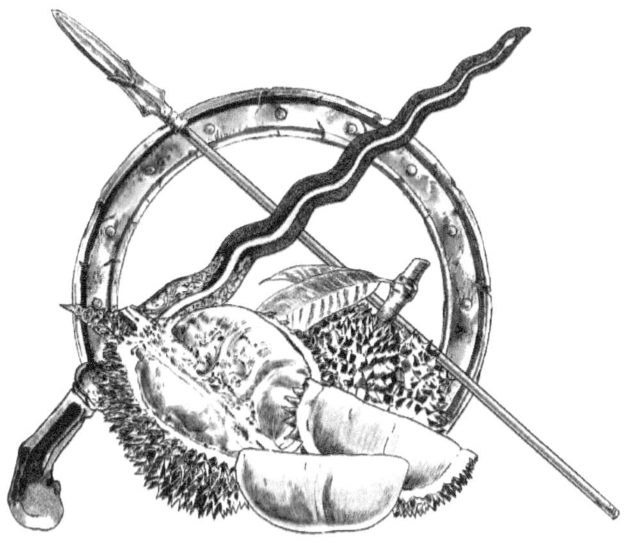

Chapter 48

With all the excitement of the attack, they chose to split the group once more. This time, Uswah and Eric made their way back to town, to warn the rest of the Clan about the ambush they had just encountered, verify that everything was well, and attempt to acquire further information on the Ghee Hin and their intentions.

The rest of the team had another objective, which was to continue acquiring monster cores out in the wild. Above everything, growing in strength was a necessity, though the team made one minor change.

"I can take one shift at least, every few days," Arthur protested. "I can work on my techniques while on watch."

"No. If you have the energy to be awake, you should be refining," Leia said, firmly. Mel, quiet this time and allowing his senior to take control of the conversation, was just nodding along.

"But..."

"No buts. You nearly died." Leia shook her head, eyes drifting to the deep stain in his armour that what little washing they had done had yet to remove. "We can't lose you."

"I know that—"

"Then stop taking risks!" Leia snapped.

"It wasn't that much of one..." Arthur trailed off, and then added, "It had to be done. We weren't even sure someone was going to attack us. And I have the best armour as it stands. How were we to know they were going to ignore everyone else and focus on me?"

"That's the point. You did something that put you in danger, and we had to all scramble to keep you alive," Leia said. "If you want to keep doing that, you need to be stronger."

"Unfair. I saved others too!" Arthur muttered.

Leia opened her mouth to continue the scolding, only for Mel to put a hand on her arm and pull her back. She stepped ahead of the visibly fuming woman, fixing Arthur with her brown eyes and speaking firmly. "Your senior is just worried about you. As we are all. That... was close. And she's not wrong. You need to get stronger." More softly, she added, "We all do."

"Fine..." Arthur sighed. He hated the fact that he was the weakest in the team, at least in terms of amount of attribute points invested. Most of the others were closer to third transformation than him, though they all lagged behind Lam and Casey for obvious reasons, lack of resources being the main one. Pushing ahead like they had, without having enough time to actually cultivate, had hampered their overall strength.

Funnily enough, old-timers like Noor and Li Sun were stronger, but not as much as you'd expect for people who had lived here for years. Part of that, of course, was the constant drain that existence had on the power pools. In addition, growing too much stronger beyond second transformation actually forced one to ascend because, otherwise, they'd be spending too much time cultivating rather than enjoying their existence.

"We got a specific number?" Arthur asked as they continued to trudge through the plains. One nice advantage of this terrain was that, given how flat everything was, they could orient themselves via the location of the town. The constant smoke trails that rose from various fires, whether for crafting or warmth or the occasional meal, was a telltale sign of where they were.

Smoke was also the method agreed upon by the group to signal any potential issues. Setting fire to a bunch of items to create purple smoke was not particularly environmentally friendly, but it worked.

"Five or six more groups," Casey said. "Give or take thirty stones more for each of us should do it."

By that math, Arthur figured she was looking at three to four more points before breaking through to third transformation. At which point she could have a few more points added to balance herself out and then she'd be at the theoretical maximum for the level—at least, if you didn't want to spend most of your time hunting and fighting but didn't have a whole organisation feeding you. Removing those concerns, she probably could add another ten points easily.

Of course, doing that would slow down her ascent, and he'd watched her keep a small notebook, counting the days off every time the sun changed. While it might be off a little, it was close enough. It did leave a question though.

"How long?" he asked, curiously.

"Another four months before I'm out of time," Casey said.

"Including the last few floors?" Arthur checked.

"Yes."

Considering the next two floors were expansive and the last floor just a fight, it left very little time for her to continue progressing. He figured he'd give her a week, maybe two, before she left to give her enough time in case of potential issues on the ninth floor. That was the trickiest one after all since actually ascending required the tracking and capture of the boss monster which fled through the ruins of an overgrown jungle city. Overall, a pain and a half to do.

"A month?" Arthur asked quietly.

"At most. Less if I can do it," she said.

He grimaced, remembering their earlier conversation. It didn't give him much time to use her to negotiate. Which left him at the mercy of Auntie Wen, if things went bad.

Resolved, he waved the group forward, speeding up a little. The faster they caught their next group of beasts, the faster they could get home and find out what the Ghee Hin were thinking.

"The other gangs didn't know. The Ghee Hin didn't tell them," Uswah said, days later. She had found them half a day's walk away from entering the city. They'd considered coming in at night or early morning but chose not to, not with the potential of not-so-friendly fire and the easy excuse that they were sneaking in. Add in fatigue from walking all day and it just made little sense.

"Will they help us? Do they know why?" Arthur asked.

"The UN want concessions." At the look he gave her, Uswah shrugged. "They wouldn't discuss it with me too much, but rooms were mentioned.

Maybe some cultivation techniques." She chuckled. "Our healing technique is getting a lot of buzz."

"Not surprised," Arthur muttered. "The basic healing technique available in the Tower is really... basic. Barely useful beyond a tactic-al level."

"Did you try to rhyme that?" Uswah said, looking disapproving.

Arthur shrugged, and she snorted. "Anyway, the UN are in. The Sixes are more hesitant."

"Really?" Now he was surprised.

"They want you to talk it out with the Ghee Hin first. Something about starting a war if they got involved," Uswah said. "I don't think they want to commit, not to us yet."

"Not even for rooms?"

A shake of the head and he sighed. The Clan hall rooms were a powerful draw, but they were only useful if he survived. The Sixes might be doing the math on whether he'd ever manage to make it into another Tower if he went out, being already engaged in a fight with a group like the Ghee Hin.

The triad had a lot more people out of the Tower than they did in here, especially considering how many rotated through. Even those that didn't get chosen to come in could be deadly to Beginner Tower climbers. You only needed to pump in enough bullets, or drive a car over someone, enough times to finish a climber.

It wasn't easy, mind you, but it wasn't impossible.

"*Celaka*," Arthur cursed. "So what, we have to go hat-in-hand and hope the Ghee Hin will stop attacking us?"

Uswah shrugged and he rubbed his face, trying to decide what to do. He hated the idea that he might have to go in weaker than he'd like. But without the backing of the Chins or the Sixes, he was not certain going in strong was the way to go. Which left him with not many options.

"I guess that makes it simple, doesn't it?"

At the look the group gave him, he shrugged.

"Got to have a word with a woman about a horse."

Somehow, he wasn't surprised no one got it.

Chapter 49

Leaving Mel and Casey to handle the various pieces of politics and speaking with both the UN and Double Sixes—and in Casey's case, to enquire with the Ghee Hin as well—Arthur made his way to discuss matters with Auntie Wen. After, of course, taking a proper bath and clearing the dirt accumulated over multiple days of camping.

It sucked, of course, that he was forced to visit immediately after returning. While he had managed to continue cultivating and refining energy from the stones while outside, the greatest joy after being out in the wilds was always the return. That moment when you were able to take a proper shower or bath, clean the accumulated layers of grime, put on fresh clothes, and flop onto a comfortable bed. There was no better way to really understand all the luxuries of civilisation than to be deprived of them, even with the barebone levels of civilized society life in the Tower.

Instead, with Jan and Yao Jing, he made his way to the Chin residence to speak with Auntie Wen. A quick runner had confirmed her presence and willingness to see him. And now, without Casey in the way, Arthur felt that they might actually be able to get to the heart of the matter.

So he was not at all surprised that he was shown into an office rather than a living room, his bodyguards left outside and pleasantries quickly discarded.

"You want me to provide aid against the Ghee Hin. Not just on this floor when my niece leaves but also in the outside world?" Auntie Wen said, concisely.

"I do, Ms. Wen." Arthur leaned forward on the large table separating them, bringing himself closer to her though the table was large enough that he could not loom. Especially while seated on this chair that was, he noted, a little shorter than average and put him below her height. "Though what resources you might have, in Kuala Lumpur and Malaysia in general, I still am uncertain."

"As you should be," she said, amusedly. "I take great pains to hide them. After all, most of my 'resources' are in the connections I have made and the favors owed me. Rather than outright ownership, like your Casey."

"Not mine," he said. "Though I understand your point. They do have quite the portfolio."

"Yet, they only utilize it so poorly." Reaching forwards, she picked up the cup of tea and sipped on it. Peering at him over the rim, she continued. "I have friends in many of their industries, and often can make use of their resources for minor things without alerting them. I also have friends in the government and police, including a few department heads. Only the deputy in the gang task force, at this time. But I have hopes."

"And they'll do you favors?"

"They'll do us favors. Within reason." She held the cup up, waving it a little as she continued. "So long as we do them favors too. Money, of course. Some prefer beast stones. Enchanted items, when you progress later, will be the best." Arthur nodded. "But other favors too, of course. Young ladies or men. Tickets or reservations. Meetings with the important. The favors can be quite varied, though..."

"Though?"

Her eyes crinkled and she sipped on the drink. After a moment, she answered. "There are three main reasons you can make another work for you. Do you want to know them?"

"Certainly," Arthur said, curiously.

"Ah, but what would I get out of it?" she said, tapping her lips. "Perhaps, shall we say, an answer?"

"An answer?"

"To one question. A truthful answer, to one question. Whole and complete."

Arthur grunted. "So long as it's not a secret that affects others or isn't mine to tell."

"Then we have a deal?" she said.

It would be a good test, to see how far she pushed it. How much she wanted, for something that might likely be quite simple. Sometimes, the initial negotiation was not about the actual deal itself, but what people did. "Deal."

"Sex, ego, and money." She lowered her fingers after each word, then did the opposite as she went the other way. "Or if you will, love, power, and resources."

"A little reductive, is it not? How about blackmail, fear, and pain?" Arthur said.

"We were talking of manipulating others to work for you. Fear and pain, blackmail, those work; but they are not consistent or good levers," she said. "Though, threatening another, you threaten one of those three anyway."

Arthur pressed his lips together, wanting to argue but realising it didn't matter. This was, after all, her viewpoint. Not a truth that mattered to him, but it gave him a glimpse of her worldview.

"Then tell me. Why does the sex lever not work on you? It's obvious you are attracted to women, but yet it seems to matter little." She glared at Arthur and he chuckled.

"Is that what you wanted to know? Have you not asked around already?" he said. "It's not as though it's a secret."

"Your Yin Body." She gestured at his face with her free hand. "The pale skin, the way you look but don't touch. Your lack of deep emotions. Is that what you're blaming?" He nodded and she snorted. "Bullshit."

"What?"

"A Yin Body changes you, but it doesn't make you sexless. It doesn't make you this cold. It is rare, but not that rare. You're not the only one that I've encountered. And they're all eventually pliable, in that way. You're... not."

Arthur offered a wry smile. "I've never been that interested. Call it a flaw or a twist in my makeup, if you want. It's nice, but it wasn't anything that made me jump up and shout. There's always been other things to do, money to be made, training and research to conduct. All the other things..." He looked away, returned his gaze to her. "The Yin Body, it's just been a bonus. Dampened it even more, but the fire was never really lit."

"Not boys or girls or anything in between?"

"If I was interested in boys, you think I'd say it? Even here?" Arthur knew many who had those inclinations escaped to the Tower. Without the government to control them, they could live the lives they wanted—if they survived, of course. Yet, the stigma hadn't disappeared, the rules and laws still existed outside the Tower, and the tattletales, the snakes, and moles were everywhere.

"How about to me?"

"It doesn't make a difference. I don't really get that interested anymore. No more than you would seeing a nice painting or a sunset. Beautiful, but that's it." He shrugged. "That answer your question?"

"I guess so. So, money or power then." She nodded. "And it seems, power is the lever right now."

"Not for myself. If it was just for me... well, it wouldn't matter. But I have a clan." He leaned forward, put the teacup down and placed one hand over the other. No lacing fingers, he had that broken out of him by his sifu a while ago. "So, do we have a deal then? Your help here, and outside against the Ghee Hin. In turn, we offer you...?"

"What lever would you use on me?" She asked. "What do you think I want?"

"Safety. No, security," Arthur said, firmly. "That's what you always wanted, isn't it?"

"There's no safety in our world. But added layers of protection..." She trailed off, then shook her head. "That can help. Once we start climbing, safety is over. But a legacy, a real one, that is possible."

"A real one?"

"My family. Money, security, stones. Cultivation resources." She stared at Arthur, leaned in and spoke softly. "He'll come, in a few years. Thinking that being a climber is everything, that this half-life is worth living. I couldn't—can't—convince him otherwise. This world, it's glamorisation of the Towers. Do you know, that the ones in power, many don't even bother coming in? And those that do, they only ever run a single Tower? Instead, they hire idiots like us. Keep control of the world out there. When my son comes in, he'll just be another tool for them."

"Unless he climbs high enough," Arthur said. "Better to be a well-shaped one, rather than something they'd throw away." He knew the truth of the world, but when you were one of the uncountable masses, who had no money or influence or opportunity, the Tower gave you a chance. A way to stand out, to pull ahead and keep doing so. "That's the promise of the Tower, at the end."

"You can only do that, only grow stronger, if you have the right tools." A cruel smile then. "Or you get lucky."

"Or if you get lucky. But you can't count on luck." Arthur sighed. "You want him to become a Durian."

"Maybe." Now Auntie Wen refilled her teacup, drawing the silence out. "If you're strong enough, good enough for him. Right now, the Durians are nothing more than an upstart organisation. But maybe..."

"Maybe." Arthur began to see how she was, how she thought. Auntie Wen didn't have a single plan, didn't choose a single path to victory. She scattered dozens of seeds, watered all of them hoping they'd all grow. Sent scouts on all those roads and if more than one became the way forward, she'd take them all. Unfocused, but he could use that.

So long as she offered him what he needed to. "We'll just have to see, won't we?"

Chapter 50

Details. There were a lot of them to hammer out. Things to clarify, resources Auntie Wen could bring to bear, both here and outside. Finally, communication methods, ways to ensure that she would support them when he asked for it, for when they had the meeting with the Ghee Hin.

It was all too clear, later that night, that a meeting would be needed. If a war was to be started, so be it, but Arthur refused to commit his people to that kind of danger and death without at least trying to get to the bottom of it. To see if he could avert the attacks.

If nothing else, he could at least draw out the people at the top. He might not be the strongest, but that didn't mean he was a slacker. And when it came down to it, while he was still green-ish compared to some here, he was still more skilled and trained at the outset than most who dared to come in.

He'd spent his entire life getting ready. To climb the Tower, without help, perhaps. Which, he figured, meant he was better, stronger than those who had expected help. Even if his own plans had been trampled over on the first floor, his training, his skills were still there.

"Tomorrow morning?" Arthur said, a little amused. "Fast, aren't we?"

Casey shrugged. "It has to be done. One way or the other." She hesitated, then leaned her head against the doorpost of his room. "You understand that I can't be there, right?"

"I don't," he said, surprised.

"Lam won't let me. It's not my fight, and I..." She sighed. "I can't take an active part. Not this close, not when I'm nearly out."

He stared into her eyes, seeing the regret lurking within. Yet, there was firm conviction too. "I get it. Don't worry."

"You do?" she said, surprised.

"I do." After all, Casey was, in the end, an ally. A business partner, someone they had used for her resources - and vice versa. Though there might be a real friendship in there, it was still tenuous. Hampered by her own needs, her own obligations. She was more than herself, and while committing to the fight might be within her right, her actions had more effects than an average individual's did. It meant something. "Anyway, Ms. Wen will be there." A slight beat and then he admitted, "Or her representative."

"You're certain?" Casey said, carefully.

"I am."

He could see the question in her eyes, the desire to know more. But in the end, she wished him the best of luck and closed the door, leaving him alone. After all, declining to get involved, she'd already declined the privilege to learn more. At least, for now.

To say he wasn't a little disappointed would be a lie, but it was only a mild feeling. Mostly, Arthur's mind turned to the morning. To how much rest he needed, how much he could refine in the time between, and what he would bring.

Everything else, well, that was for the day after tomorrow.

The warehouse they met in was similar, if smaller, than the one that the trio of gang leaders had sold him. Approaching it, Arthur noted how traffic in the region had dropped, almost devoid of everyone who had any sense and needed nothing desperately in the area. In fact, the entire town seemed to be holding its breath.

It gratified him, a little, to realise how much of an effect the Clan could have. Obviously, a gang war was nothing to be sneezed at, but the fact that others thought it might get out of control that they avoided being on the streets at all rather than assuming the Durians would be crushed outright was a good indicator of their strength. And importance.

Of course, it might also be because the UN and Sixes were here too, standing to the side. The Sixes still had yet to commit, only bringing people to watch—a half dozen that Arthur made sure to point out as people not to be touched unless they attacked first. The UN, with their varied members, was at least coming in strength, filling up one whole street.

Even if, at a glance, a bunch were hangers-on paid to bolster the numbers for a day. Then again, that was the way these gangs operated. Core membership, the hanger-ons, and the mercenaries—not all were committed fully but were up for a little violence.

Said something about climbers in general that there were a large percentage of them willing to throw down or just stand around and glare menacingly for a few stones.

Not that the Ghee Hin hadn't paid for their own people, hadn't brought their own numbers. Arthur noted members of the 04 hanging out with them, though much reduced in number, keeping to the edges. He met Harish's eyes before the man looked away.

Arthur stepped in and strolled to the makeshift wooden table in the center. The pair of rickety chairs there looked neither nice nor well-built.

Obviously, someone didn't want to put out the nice furniture in case it got broken.

Not a good sign for peace.

"Boss Fang," Arthur greeted the man who was seated already. He took a seat beside the Ghee Hin boss, eyeing the too-damn-handsome man as he poured Arthur a cup of tea.

"Clan Head Chua," Fang Chien said. "You called a meeting?"

"I did. Wanted to know why you're trying to kill me," Arthur got right into it, figuring there was no point beating around the bush.

"You're dangerous." He pointed to Arthur and then gestured to the people behind. "All of you." There was a shift and clatter of weapons, a low growl rising from Yao Jing. Arthur raised a hand, quietening his group without looking away from Fang Chien, waiting for him to continue. "You think a new Clan won't destabilize things?"

"There are new Clans and Guilds being set up all over the world," Arthur said, crossing his arms. "There's a half-dozen already in Malaysia."

"All controlled by government or one of their people." He shook his head. "None of them like you."

"Independent?"

"Yes." He leaned forward, fixing Arthur with a glare. "You think we don't see what you're doing? Who you're going to pull to you, huh?"

"Who?" Arthur asked, though he knew that answer.

"If you don't know, then you're worse than rude. You're also an idiot."

"Sticks and stones and words are all just hurtful." Arthur sighed. "So, you must want something more than just insulting me. Otherwise you wouldn't agree to this talk."

"You already got the UN to help, you think we don't know? What choice do we have but talk?" Fang Chien said, angrily. "Getting outsiders involved."

"Didn't mind them when you were all pressuring us not to take more land, but now they're outsiders because they're working against you?" Arthur shook his head at the hypocrisy.

"Different *lah*. But you, you want to know what we want?" Not bothering to let Arthur to answer, he continued on. "You join us."

"Now who's the idiot?" Arthur waved his hand sideways, past the warehouse walls in the direction that the UN were holding. It also, conveniently, included the rest of the city which meant it consisted of the Sixes. "You think we can do that, ah?"

"Of course not." Fang Chien snorted. "If you had done it right, come to us properly, we could have avoided this. Now, you can either come to us anyway, and make the Sixes angry. And maybe the UN. Or..."

Arthur didn't even bother asking what the or was about. This was the most frustrating negotiation he had ever been involved in. There was utterly no point to it, because he couldn't and wouldn't just roll over and let the Durians become a subset for the Ghee Hin. Never mind the fact that it was against what he promised those who had joined him—independence and working for the good of all. He wasn't going to tie the Clan to a criminal organisation. Even if they were just a feeder group to start, he knew eventually they'd be asked to do more and more unsavory things.

So why bother with the meeting at all?

"I see..." Eyes danced past Fang Chien to the men behind. A large number of men, only a portion of whom he recognised. Only a portion who were members of the Ghee Hin. Suspicion had him reacting, pulling at the cultivation technique he'd secreted in his second dantian. "You..."

Too late, as Fang Chien opened his mouth. Flames leapt from it, even as the secreted technique snapped around him. Fractions of a second ahead, as flames crept over his face and hair and around his armour.

Silence, as he crashed into the floor, the table flipping upwards as Fang Chien dove after him.

Then, pandemonium.

Chapter 51

Dragon's Breath met Bark Skin and if they were the actual things their names suggested, Arthur's trip through the Tower would have ended there and then. Luckily, one was more fanciful and descriptive than reality, the flames and heat emerging from Boss Fang's mouth nowhere near as hot as the rumored napalm-level flames that emerged from a Western dragon's mouth. The real thing might melt steel, but they were still Beginner Tower climbers.

Fang's could only burn flesh and boil eyeballs.

For the unprotected, that is.

Arthur had swapped out his Bark Skin before arriving, at the insistence of his people. Not that they had to push hard, as even he saw the advantage of keeping a defensive measure up on fast recall rather than his usual Refined Exploding Energy Dart. After all, he hadn't intended to start the fight, but the chances of his opponent doing so had always been high.

It was also why, when the attack happened, beyond the initial stunned moment when everyone realised that it really was beginning, his opponents did not have much of a surprise advantage. That was thanks to Uswah and a few others who had snuck their way around the corners and liberally applied their various rooting abilities, to the cries of surprise and confusion of the Ghee Hin and their hangers-on. He even saw a few fall over, knocking others into disarray, as stored and readied attacks flew between each group.

All that Arthur grasped as he kept rolling and threw his chair into the air. It bounced off the much bigger table, doing nothing to stop the furniture's trajectory and impact against Arthur's body.

It did have the advantage of slowing down Fang Chien for a brief moment, though he smashed it aside.

Furniture splintered, and a parang that the man had kept sheathed out now came down on Arthur. His own spear had been left behind; it clattered on the ground as he released it and flinched from the flames by instinct. Without a weapon, Arthur did the only thing that made sense.

He charged Fang Chien, bursting forwards to get under his opponent's grip. The blade and hilt and hand slammed into his shoulder, bringing a fresh burst of pain, but without proper leverage or angle, it could only clatter against smoking armour rather than cut.

At the same time, Arthur was weaving his Refined Energy Strike and the Yin-Poison Imbued Strike together, gripping his opponent around the chest as he tried to bring him to the ground. He might not enjoy grappling—it left his back all too open to being stabbed—but pushing the other away was the name of the game for now.

Chaos, as parang blade beat down on him. He felt his own hair and skin begin to crisp, his eyes watering and armour smoking further as Fang Chien triggered a flame aura. Much like Jan's, except much, much stronger. It burnt and licked at Arthur even as Fang Chien tried to get his strikes in the only open area vulnerable to him, the gap between helmet, gorget, and armour.

Dull thuds that kicked and hurt, that made Arthur wince and drove him down again to his feet, his grip threatening to give way under the onslaught of the stronger opponent. His own Imbued Strike triggered, washing in and contesting the Yang aura, the flames and strength of his opponent.

Sapping them, a touch.

More punches, more strikes. More poison, seeping in, more flesh burning.

"Arthur!"

The shout forced Arthur to open his eyes, briefly. Spot the oncoming trouble and drop, letting the latest strike drive him all the way to the ground. Moments before the woman—Zhiang Lin—was thrown into the pair of them. She bowled over Fang Chien, forced him to sprawl to the ground and scramble upwards, sinking the tip of the parang into a shoulder as he did so.

Zhiang Lin cried out, gripping at the wound and nearly losing a finger as he yanked the blade out of her shoulder.

Arthur would have helped, but he had bigger problems to deal with. Namely, the massive Northern Chinese hired gun that was stalking over. Tall enough to have done well in American basketball, easily over six and a half feet tall, maybe even seven. It was hard to tell, as he wasn't used to seeing people that tall in person. He scrambled to his feet and the other came rushing over, bent a little, hands like oven mitts held out and ready to grab.

"Big, sick!" Arthur muttered and released a newly formed Refined Exploding Energy Dart. He winced as the explosion caught his opponent in the face, made the other stagger back, bloody and missing a nose. He darted forward, barely escaping the blade that came tearing down his back in a Focused Strike—or maybe Penetrating Strike—that tore up his armour.

Dodged around big boy, grabbed his spear from the floor and then swung it around, tripping the slow-moving giant while pulling together another Refined Energy Dart.

And finally, finally ready to keep the battle going.

Fang Chien fell backward as Arthur swung his spear. He used all parts of it, sharp head, haft, and the body for blocking. Poured his Imbued Strike filled with Yin energy down the spear, through his aura into his opponents. He was focused not on landing the attacks but keeping his opponent on the backfoot, allowing the seeping Yin energy to invade his opponent.

Twenty, thirty seconds more into the battle, Arthur was pushing his opponent into the middle of the scrum. Trying to get them into the middle of the fight. He utilized his Bark Skin to take attacks, allowing the bruises and cuts to accumulate. When other combatants got in too close, he released a Refined Energy Dart, tearing through armour or bones or limbs.

Fang Chien—strong, powerful, and with his own techniques—was on the backfoot. Having released his flames just once more and caught a number of his own companions in the untargeted attack, he had fallen back on attempting to cut through Arthur's defense. Only Arthur's better armour and his opponent's focus on speed—a speed that was being drained by each moment's contact with the Yin poison—had allowed Arthur a chance.

A chance to push him back, all the way into his opponent's side where now the group was tangled, fighting one another, fighting Uswah and the other sneaks. Turned around, they compressed in a tight ball, a few even going so far as to give up and cast their weapons down.

They were winning, at least the battle within the warehouse.

The problem, of course, was that more Ghee Hin were coming in from the outside as well. And from the sounds of it, that battle was doing worse.

Chapter 52

They broke in from the right of where the Durians entered. Or perhaps it was left; Arthur had gotten quite confused and turned around in the last few minutes. He was just in the midst of crippling his opponent, slamming the butt of his spear into the man's hip hard enough to shatter the pelvic bone and paralyzing him with Yin Poison, when the wall exploded.

Ears ringing, he staggered to the side and bumped into an unyielding wall. Face bloodied and messed up, half-blinded with blood still pouring from his facial wounds, the tall Northern Chinese mercenary whose nose Arthur had taken out grabbed him with one meaty hand and then proceeded to punch him with the other.

Arthur tucked up automatically, keeping arms close to the side of his body and head, letting the body absorb the hits. His helmet had been lost somewhere in the fight, an annoyance that meant that the explosion had rocked him more than it should have. Worst, though, was that around the third or fourth swing, his spear had been lost from his grip.

He'd grab for his kris, but his left arm was numb and not gripping well. This giant had obviously dumped a ton of traits into strength and then used a technique to make himself even stronger. Add in the fact that he was easily second advancement and Arthur was feeling the real difference in cultivation for once. All he could do was take the punishment, pulsing his own Yin Poison into his opponent as he tried to cripple the other.

Stronger poison: definitely on the to-do list.

In the meantime, though, he was saved not by his opponent's exhaustion but the bodyguards that had been attempting to keep up with him. Yao Jing slammed a shoulder into the giant, tackling him to the ground and causing Arthur to fall to the side. After that, fists glowing, the pair of muscle-brains started tussling, managing to get a few boots into Arthur as he scrambled away.

Unhappily forcing himself up, casting around for his spear and not seeing it close by, he tugged his kris out instead. Recollection of the explosion, screams, and the smell of smoke and burnt flesh—though that might have all been just him—brought his attention to the hole in the wall.

Ghee Hin, streaming in. But they were fighting a rear-guard action, against the UN. The Sixes and a small number of his own people were behind. He felt his heart lurch at the thought of losing his own people, watched as a woman was cut down, and found himself running.

Screaming his head off, in anger and fury.

"Stop. Wait up!" Jan, just about finished throwing down her own opponent screamed, as Arthur rushed past her.

He didn't pay attention as he wove a Refined Exploding Energy Dart. Waited for the gap, released it, began it again. Dropped the Yin Poison, knowing that the next fight was going to need more than a slow-wearing down. No single leader to take down, just a lot of people.

Needed to get the damn dual cultivation methods working, and so he pulled at it. Drew up the Heavenly Sage's Mischief to run alongside his Bark Skin. Felt searing pain, but between being stabbed, punched, burnt and exploded, it was just another tally of agony. It was nothing, not when he was watching his people die.

A spear stabbing at him. He ducked low, stabbed with the kris, and left it buried in a throat. Stripping the weapon from his dying opponent, he spun the spear around, clipped another opponent in the arm. Used that moment of inertia to punch the weapon forward, clipping the corner of a neck and tearing open veins and arteries. He kept moving, feeling his body speed up as the technique took over.

Chaos and battle, a world that faded away to glimpses of motion.

He'd entered the zone, that moment, that state of mind where everything else faded away. Concerns about the future, pain from the body, and thrashing emotions all faded away. Only that moment, that second of movement and the next one. As though every movement was perfect, and when it wasn't, when a blow came in he never saw, an Energy Dart exploded and caught him and threw him backwards.

It didn't matter.

He was on his feet, back in the battle, rushing back in. He noticed motion, more people streaming in. Not attacking his people, so he didn't care, though they joined the battle with him, fighting on.

Screaming, shouting, aching.

Till the enemies were falling back, afraid of the blood-covered, unstoppable menace before them. Arthur might not have the sheer attributes of some, but he had more training, more practise fighting in battles and, most of all, a healing technique that was putting him back together as he was cut, stabbed, punched, and otherwise struck. That is, if they even managed to land a strike that mattered as his armour protected him from a large number of those attacks. In the meantime, he had trained over and over again on techniques to get his attacks through gaps, to grab and twist and slip a blow underneath the armpit, between gaps in the armour.

After all, his sifu might not have liked what they were doing, but the man was practical. And teaching techniques to grip and hold, to target tiny cracks and to set weapons so that it'd punch through anyway, that was just practical.

Even if, for example, some of those gaps were found in riot armour.

Some memories, like the riots of '69 and '29 died slow.

When the Ghee Hin finally backed off, when they started throwing down weapons and their morale broke, it was almost a pity. Because then, the adrenaline and that transcendent moment of movement and battle faded. When real life arrived, and all the pain, loss, and injuries came crashing down.

That's when he had to start counting the cost.

Groups of Ghee Hin, all squatting on the ground, legs crossed, arms raised and laced behind their heads. Like in the movies. Funny, the things you learnt. At least, Arthur figured that was where Rick and Eric had learnt this from. Various members of the UN and some of the Clan members were watching over the group too. Watching the triad members and each other, because tempers were running high. No one was killing anyone out of hand, just yet, but they certainly were a lot rougher than they could have been.

Arthur didn't even have the heart to tell them no. If anything, his hand itched to grab the kris and put it through a few throats, but that was why he was keeping his hands clasped behind his back. That and so the others wouldn't see them tremble, as adrenaline washed away.

In one corner, more gently and carefully, bodies were being placed. Even the dead of the other side were being treated more respectfully than the living, which probably said something about humanity if Arthur had the time to tease out such philosophical strands.

Mostly, though, he was too busy watching the pile grow. Or piles. One for the living, slowly fixing wounds. The other, for the dead.

Was it lucky, then, that there were a lot more of the first than the second? It took a lot to kill people, especially climbers. You could cripple, knock unconscious, force a person into shock and leave them on the battlefield, slowly dying. Emergency first aid, the passive healing from the Tower, and his Clan's healing benefits could—combined—bring them back.

If they were lucky.

"Our people are dying too!" A voice called, shouting at the group. Rick strode over, ready to cuff the speaker, but Mel raised a hand. She glared, speaking firmly and loudly. "We're treating everyone. If any of you have actual medical experience or a healing technique usable on others, put your hands up. We'll use you." A beat later, she added, "After you've been patted down."

Surprisingly, two hands went up. Arthur paid just about enough attention to note one was an actual nurse and the other had a healing technique.

Then, his attention was drawn back as Auntie Wen stared at him, turning his head by his chin. "Bad cut. You're lucky your technique removes the scars."

"Not something I care about, Ms. Wen." He paused, added, "Thank you. For the help."

"What? I'm chopped liver?" Jean, the UN boss, interjected. "My people nothing?"

"I already thanked you. Twice," Arthur said, patiently. Tried to, even as he saw the big, teasing grin. He watched as she smacked his chest, rested a hand on him a little too long as she leaned in. He swore he could literally smell the pheromones coming off her.

"I can think of other ways to thank me...."

"Later." Arthur exhaled, shook his head as the last of the adrenaline faded out of him. "There's a lot to deal with. People to count, injuries to sort out. And the Ghee Hin and their people to sort out."

"We need to take them, while they're reeling," Auntie Wen said.

"Wait... what? Take them?" he asked.

"Oooh, their businesses?" Jean said, perking up and grinning.

"All of them, yes." A head turned, taking in Raj who finally had managed to make his way over. "Though I feel it should be split among those who took part."

The leader of the Double Sixes snorted. "We helped."

"When you saw us join in and realised the Sixes were done," Auntie Wen said. "Utterly useless. We could have won without you."

"Could you now? And you think you are ready for another fight?" Raj said, angling his body aggressively. "You ready to start another war?"

Arthur raised a hand, stalling the conversation before they could get into it. "Raj, the Sixes can't take us all. But we don't want another fight. Nor could we all take the entirety of the Ghee Hin's stuff, not without a fight and not if you and I don't work together. Even keeping control of all their buildings, all the things they own or the businesses they're shaking down, will be too much."

"We don't..."

Arthur just spoke over Jean, ignoring her words. He really didn't care what Jean and Raj had to say. "I will say this. We Durians are taking all their brothels, all their nightclubs and massage parlors or whatever the hell they call it. The rest, you all work out, but don't expect to get an equal share, Raj. If nothing else, your people bled the least."

Then, voice dropping, he added, "But that can change."

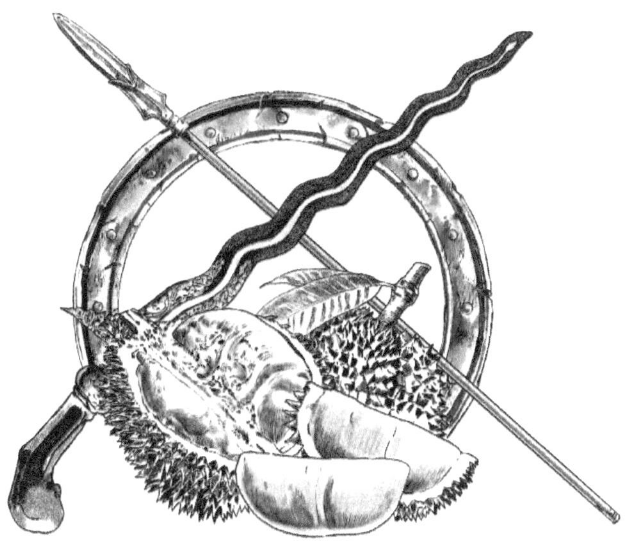

Chapter 53

Uswah found him, later. After all the horse trading, after all the subsequent battles and the taking of the businesses, and freeing—or at least, removal of women—from those establishments. Thankfully, the majority of them were not slaves, were not there against their intentions. Most just had debts, or were not able or were scared to progress further.

In any case, breaking into the establishments, bringing the people over and doing a check was necessary. Everything Arthur knew about the Ghee Hin, about the way they worked—and the way his own people were—he would have regretted not taking this opportunity. It wouldn't stop the Ghee Hin from rebuilding here, or another group from doing the same. But he could do what he could.

No surprise, then, that he was here, on the roof of his Clan building. Not even cultivating, not even practising. Just trying to let his mind, his nerves, his body to calm down.

Days of chaos and reorganisation. Of decisions and cold-blooded actions.

And it was not the end.

Fang Chien was downstairs, tied up. Arthur wasn't even sure why he had kept him alive, but he did. And now, he had to decide what to do with him. What next step to take. If he was going to hold a trial or just kill him out of hand. The problem when there were no laws involved was that decisions like this—the meting out of justice and the enforcement of rules—were all left to individuals. Groups and people like him who were in charge.

It sucked. There were numerous reasons why one should split the decision-making process of justice, from enforcement to judgement of guilt and punishment.

Everyone dreamed about being in charge, even for a brief moment. Even the most introverted. The smarter ones, the wiser ones, those who understood themselves well, or just had deepest insecurities shied away from that job. Leaving the power-hungry, the greedy, the selfish and arrogant, and the self-sacrificing to do it eventually.

It was why companies and governments all went to hell in the end. Politicians and professional managers and CEOs, all climbing to the top ahead of everyone else; all of them carrying around this innate arrogance that they were the best ones for the job.

Sometimes, they were even right.

A few were thrust into the position like Arthur. Some, even forced into such circumstances, declined to lead. Allowed themselves to be manipulated and moved around, allowed others to make decisions for themselves. Like the uber-rich who had money managers who dealt with their incomes and never cared what those managers did with it, whether to support terrorists or weapon manufacturers or mining companies that destroyed natives and enslaved others. All because the actual work of learning to do it yourself, to watch for what happened and accept responsibility for those decisions, was too much.

There was some delight in being the boss, some joy in doing the right thing, the ability to influence outcomes; but just as much, it came with days like these. Drudgery and decisions that had to be made. And the more powerful you were, the stronger you grew and the more freedom you had, the greater the weight of such responsibility. Decisions, piling up on one another, with the moral good somehow all kinds of grey and the right choice never actually clear.

The arrogant, the foolish, the diehard wannabes who never had a chance to actually make such decisions all declared it simple. For some, it might even be simple—for the narcissistic, the self-indulgent who cared only for themselves or those close to themselves. The worst of the worst saw the world in black and white and could not imagine a grey zone.

And when others saw such grey zones, tried to traverse that land and waffled between stepping over the line, they were happily insulted. Safe in their lack of power, firm in their belief, and often sheltered in their privilege, these children of the rich or the Western nations trolled others.

"Arthur." Uswah slipped onto the roof with him. Even knowing where she was, he found he could barely sense her, the shadows seeming to rise up around and wrap around her body.

"Uswah."

"You okay?" she asked.

"Fine."

Her silence was pointed, but he ignored it for a time. Just staring up at the sky as it wheeled on, high above. Idle thoughts about how those stars were formed, if they were real or just lights put in place, or if they had been transferred from a different dimension. Impossible to tell, few enough researchers willing to give it a go.

One day, they'd know, though right now the answer was all the usual.

It depends.

Eventually, when she realized he would not break, she spoke up. "*Terima kasih.*"

"Why you thanking me?"

"The women," Uswah said. "Three joined."

"Out of what? Forty? Fifty?"

"Not that many." A shrug. "Maybe more later. Now that we're watching. They have a chance. Even if it's to run it themselves." Obvious distaste at the words, but that was the thing with freedom. If you truly meant to let people choose, sometimes they chose in ways that you disliked.

Not that it stopped the hypocrites who then decided that you could then dictate how people could choose after.

"Whatever." Arthur waved a hand languidly. He had done it because it had to be done, but he had only made the decision and asked for it; the actual work had been put in by the Lotuses.

"No." Now there was heat in her voice, a rise in the tone that caught him by surprise. Uswah was not one to get angry, not with her Yin Body, not with her general temperament. "You don't get to do that."

"Do what?"

"Discount everything good you do, take on the bad." She pointed a finger at him. "You're angry and upset and tired of running the Clan, thinking maybe it'd be better if you didn't have it, right?"

"Not exactly…"

"Doesn't matter. It's close enough, yes?"

"I…"

"Then you don't also get to discount the good you do when you make the decisions. You do good, you improve lives. You make it possible for us to improve ours. And that's not a small thing, even if you think it might be." She shook her head. "You can't just see the bad, without end. Or else you'll break." Then her voice dropped. "And we cannot have that."

"Ah…"

"Yes, I'm worried about you. We all are." Her voice dropped, concern lacing her words. "I know the Yin Body helps, but it doesn't change the pressure. It just makes it easier to handle it. But we know, we know you didn't plan for this. Never expected this."

"How could I?" Arthur asked, then shook his head. "It was thrust on me and I'm just riding the current, doing the best I can because what else?"

"What else?" she said. "How about embracing it all and making full use of it."

"I am," he grated out. "I promised to make the Durians more than just another shitty Clan, more than another thing for people to grow rich, to trample on others."

"I know. And you're doing the job. But…"

He snorted. "I won't break. I don't."

"You don't know that." Uswah fell silent at the look he gave her and then she sighed. "Just, remember we are here to support you. And you are doing good. Even if this wasn't your dream."

He did not answer her, waiting for her to leave. Alone by himself, he could only shake his head a little. Not his dream. How could he have a dream? When the world took away all your choices, when your options were so small, that you could only take the craziest of risks to have any chance of something more?

His dream had only ever been to climb the Tower and exit it, with a chance to make a life for himself. Because he never had a chance for anything more. And now, he had that, and he wasn't sure he wanted it but he had it.

So maybe she wasn't wrong, that he hadn't embraced it all.

Because while he might have a dream for the Durians, he had none for himself.

Just the crushing realization of ever more work, for decades in a job that he had never asked for.

Chapter 54

"What you want?" Fang Chien ground out, tugging futilely at the ropes that bound his hands. "You ready to kill me, ah?"

"Not yet." Arthur sighed. "Though that option isn't off the table."

The leader of the Ghee Hin snorted. "You got no balls."

"Now that's an idea…" Arthur muttered, putting on a considering look. It was gratifying to make the man blanche and then glower at him. Not that Arthur intended to do something like that. He drew a hard line at tortute. Especially for something like this.

"So, *apa* you *nak*?"

"What I want from you? I'd like to know why you did it."

"You know already *lah*."

Arthur let out another elaborate sigh.

"Better to end you now, before you become a problem," Fang Chien stated, flatly. "That's why they keep me here. You think we're here for nothing?"

"No. You all need climbers too."

"*Ya, lah.* That's the Tower. Me, I'm here to stop you people." Fang Chien moved to gesture, came to a stop as the ropes kept him bound. He looked frustrated at them for a moment, then stilled. "Understand?"

"So, that's the Ghee Hin's viewpoint?" Arthur said, concerned. "They going to be a problem when we get out?"

"*Ya, lah.* Of course." Fang Chien sighed. "You don't want it to be a problem? Be tougher." He looked around, added, "Do what you did here. Be so strong, they don't dare come for you."

"Why tell me?"

"Because you beat me. I want you to succeed. Or else, I'm just a loser who lost to another loser," Fang Chien said.

"What happens now?"

"Your call, yes?"

"That depends. What happens when we let you go? What will you do to the Clan? We've broken the Ghee Hin here, though you still have your main building. We're not dumb enough to try to destroy you all," Arthur said, offering some information for free. Trying to get an idea of what the man wanted.

"I will rebuild my people. See what we can recover, once I take numbers." His eyes narrowed, as he continued. "You killed a number of mine."

"Quite a few, yes." Arthur shrugged. "Not that we were the major culprits, mind you."

"The UN." He grunted. "Bloodthirsty. There's going to be a price."

"So long as it's not us," Arthur said, warningly.

"We're done with you," Fang Chien said. "At least on this floor. My *tai kor* will handle you."

"That's it?"

A shrug, brought up short by the ropes. Arthur leaned back, considering. Fang Chien might be lying, but the thing was he had no way of telling. Oh, there were people with abilities that would let them sense truth or lies, that could play the role of lie detectors at a much better rate. In fact, some climbers specced for things like that and not necessarily those in law enforcement.

Problem was, the majority of those were Advanced techniques, not Beginner ones. The Beginner versions were just too basic, various traits and an enhanced sensing technique that was still reliant on the individual's ability to pick out such tells. End of the day, it worked for those who had trained in skills like that beforehand, whether consciously or not. The only reason Arthur had that side thought was because he remembered reading something about how individuals with abusive or semi-abusive environments were better at picking up clues.

Then again, he wasn't sure if that was another AI mangled garbage article or not. Wasn't like he had the money to pay for more than a few subscriptions to properly sourced information, and all that had been dedicated to checking on climber sources.

Another way that the rich, the West, managed to screw everything up for everyone else. A new way of extracting money and controlling the flow of information.

He'd be angry if he wasn't just tired of it all.

"I can make a contract." Fang Chien mistook Arthur's musings for dissatisfaction, hurrying on. "Buy one from the Tower. Signed between me and you."

"And then, once I get dealt with by your Tai Kor, you're free."

"Once you're dead, the Durians are gone."

Arthur grunted in agreement. That, sadly, was the truth. Till they managed to clear a few more Towers and upgrade the Clan itself, the members were dependent upon him. He still didn't know how much he would have to upgrade the Clan before it could sustain itself without him. As it was, he had a suspicion that needing to hand over control to each floor boss was taking up a degree of his authority that he could have saved up. Or at least, that was the way he envisioned it working.

The little he'd learnt from Casey had told him that much, how even Clans could have choices in how they evolved. She wasn't clear on the exact mechanisms, of course, and he believed her. After all, she may be from Prime Group and the daughter of the current head, but she was also still a kid in many ways. Just starting out.

Not someone you'd give too much information to. That she grasped even as much she did was entirely from her listening in to conversations between the adults.

"Fine. That sounds acceptable." Arthur knew he could push the man further, maybe even make the man subservient to them or something. He might be able to do it, but of course, that could easily mean Fang Chien being replaced or killed by his own people. Or just sidelined, such that there was no use making an agreement. On top of that, of course, was the concern about the Ghee Hin outside the Tower.

Even if he managed to get them to be peaceful, or to back off sufficiently, there was still a concern that him pressuring their people in the Tower too much could backfire. With the way information flowed too, details of such things would come after he had exited, most likely, unless he stuck around further.

On the other hand...

"But that's not just it. Peace alone isn't enough." Now, Arthur's voice dropped as he continued. "You got some of my people killed. There's going to be a price for that."

To his surprise, Fang Chien actually gave him an approving look when he said that. The man straightened a little, and they got down to bargaining. It made Arthur feel a little dirty, to be discussing lives as though they were just numbers that needed to be balanced or a line in a newspaper article, easily forgotten. But it had to be done, and payment—the blood price—had to be paid.

"So?" Mel asked, when he finally made his way downstairs. She had been busy dealing with some basic admin, handling the rest of the Clan's buildup while he was talking with Fang Chien. Even with the Ghee Hin and their main concerns faded, there was still a lot of work left.

"We need to start keeping a proper Clan roster. Names, family names, next of kin, and who we pay blood prices to," Arthur said. "We can't do much now, but later... we should try to do something for our people."

"Generous," Mel said, carefully.

"It's nice idea, boss. But what if they just joined and died quick?" Yao Jing said, concerned. "We could become real hard up."

"We can figure it out," Arthur said, waving a hand. "Maybe insurance or something, bought by others. A flat payment early on and then..." He sighed. "Then more if they get drawn into our shit."

"They knew what they were getting into," Mel said, gently to Arthur. Searching his gaze for the guilt he was too easily showing. "You know that."

"We can still do better." Arthur flopped down on a chair, glanced around the lounge and then continued. "We got a lawyer or paralegal or someone who knows contracts?"

"Uhh...." Mel looked flummoxed.

"Noor will know," Yao Jing offered. "I can ask?"

"Go." Arthur waved the man away and after Yao Jing shot a glance at Mel to make sure she was on duty, then took off to hunt down the woman.

"Why do we need one?" Mel said.

"We're getting a Tower contract between me and Fang Chien. No killing him, we get a couple of open favors we can call on, and they will leave the Durians alone for the next five years."

"Why five?"

"I wanted ten, but he pointed out he won't be here that long," Arthur said. "He's willing to commit to staying another five at most. After that, we'll just need to be strong enough that they won't mess with our people. Or come up with a new contract."

"Okay." Mel hesitated, then frowned.

"What?"

"Is that it then? All that fighting... and that's it?"

Arthur considered what she said, then eventually shrugged. "I guess? End of the day, not a lot more left to do. Casey's leaving tomorrow. And after that, it's just up to us to train and get out."

"Huh."

Arthur understood her feelings all too well. After all this rushing around, it felt almost anti-climatic. Then again, the entire operation of building the Clan was just secondary to what they were here for.

Climbing the Tower.

Chapter 55

Casey left the next day. Lam left with her as well, only staying long enough for her to visit the Tower administrative center, pay in the necessary contribution points, and then wait for the Administrator to wave their hands to make her disappear. Of course she hadn't collected the contribution points herself, instead just borrowing a large amount from the family. It was the point of having a lot of people around, gathering and farming such points to push someone higher when necessary.

Arthur, of course, didn't have that luxury. It was probably for the best, since he still needed to train himself with the changes that his body was undergoing. He could have asked for some of the points the Thorned Lotuses had acquired, but since most of them had no intention of moving upwards, they'd used most of their points for quality-of-life items rather than banking them.

All of which meant that while he might be able to scrape enough points together from the Clan to help a few of them ascend, it wouldn't work for the entire team.

But now, training was, in fact, easier to do than Arthur ever expected. For one thing, outside of the occasional dinner with Auntie Wen, there were no longer any major issues pressing on him. Their victory against the Ghee Hin and the actions they had taken meant that everyone started treating them with greater respect. Now, it wasn't to say that people were rushing to make alliances with them, as their long-term viability was still in question, of course, but they were certainly too dangerous for anyone on the seventh floor to handle right now.

No, things settled down really fast, and that left Arthur time to train, cultivate, and run the various quests that were necessary on the floor. As usual, they varied in kind from resource-gathering quests to straight-out kill-and-collect quests. Arthur much preferred the second, but he made sure to gather whatever resources he spotted. Even his meager additions helped, as the team would pool their findings and then at least one or two of them might finish the quest that trip.

Well, outside of Eric.

"Never knew you liked picking flowers so much," Arthur teased the man who had literally purchased boxes and wooden cylinders, often filled with dirt at the bottom, to collect the plants. Most of which weren't flowers, but who cared about accuracy when teasing?

"Good points, *lah*. Also, as sifu said. Do it, do it right." He patted the boxes slung around him, then grinned. "You're just jealous I got more points than you."

"If I decided to buy traits that let me see in more colors, I'm sure I'd...." Arthur shook his head, realising he was caught up arguing with his friend. "Whatever."

"Hah! I win."

"Uh huh. So. When are you and Leia leaving?" Arthur asked, curiously. He knew the pair were a lot stronger than him, already past the third transformation. They were, in fact, hitting the point where more cultivating was a bad idea. The quiet cap of the Tower was fast being neared and soon enough they would need to spend too many resources just trying to inch forward.

"Trying to get rid of us, ah?"

"No. Just asking." Arthur hesitated, then lowered his voice. "Also, could use some help, you know."

"Help?" Now Eric looked interested.

"Outside the Tower. Getting things ready. With sifu. But also with our seniors and juniors. And just in general."

"Oh... ohhh!" Eric brightened. "Leia said something like that."

"Yeah. If you are ready to go, best for you all to do that. Get ahead of me, get things sorted." He bit his lip, then continued. "You all are new, so there are fewer people who know you're connected to me. At least, in here." Arthur cocked his head to the side. "Not the same for others, you know."

"You think it helps?"

"I think it might. And right now, we're working on a lot of maybes and mights," Arthur said. "So, if you need to, if you can, move ahead. Both you and Leia. That'd be good."

Silence, and then Eric whispered, "I'm scared."

The obvious answer for Arthur was a fear for himself. But he knew Eric better, knew he wouldn't care, not for himself. Fear for himself, not a thing that had influenced the senior that he knew. On the other hand... "Leia."

"Yes. What if she fails? If I fail. She'd be hurt..."

"There's more Towers too, you know."

"I know." Eric hissed those words, then reined in his temper. "But it's more than that. It's hard to deal with it, with the fear for someone else. You know..." The last two words trailed off, hesitant.

"Rub my romantic failings in my face, why don't you?" Arthur said, making his friend wince. He waved it off. "I don't know what to say. Other than the fact that she's strong. She's the one who stayed behind, if you forgot."

Eric grunted, raised a hand to hit Arthur, and then dropped it.

"Fine. Three days." Eric paused, then added, "If she agrees."

Arthur nodded, dropping the subject. After all, he had gotten everything he wanted. He'd go over details, over the things he'd want from his friends, what they needed to set up. What might happen.

Possibilities, a lot of them.

Because the closer they got to getting out, the more problems he could see.

His seniors left without much fanfare. The few points they were missing were easily donated, Arthur promising to send over more. Now that he didn't need to rush as much, he felt the need to upgrade himself. Knowing he still had to weigh it all: the speed of his exit against the strength he would have as he left. The longer he took, the more time those outside had time to marshall forces against him, to build him up in their minds or tear him down. To decide, like the Ghee Hin to cut him down.

And the longer he took, the easier it would be for him to fight them off. At least, as an individual.

But one thing anyone with any real experience in this world knew was that you never could do anything worthwhile alone.

He wasn't the only one training, pushing himself. Gaining new abilities.

Uswah perfected her ability to shift through shadows, though the jokes about her needing to wear black and join a shinobi clan made her roll her eyes constantly. It didn't help that she had taken to carrying small knives with her, sharp and light such that her shadow tentacles could wield them for her, giving them an edge.

Jan slipped harder into her flame aura, building on that and her own skill with the spear. She spent time learning to channel the aura around her into a flaming attack, to hurt and burn those around. At the same time, she worked on greater maneuverability, quickly outstripping everyone else at the ability to conjure multiple cloud steps.

Mel, as always, was the most diligent. Yet, she kept her attention on the basics. The Focused Strike, the Empowered Attacks with her halberd. She had her ranged attacks, but those were secondary to her ability to fight and excel in melee. Like her personality, she was quiet and contained, but all so deadly.

Yao Jing, on the other hand, seemed to just be getting flashier. He used a parang, a small shield, a spear. But whenever he was pressed, he dropped them to get in close, to lash out with his fists. Now, his techniques and traits were finally allowing him to make full use of his propensity to get close, to grapple and punch and brawl. One of his favorite techniques boosted his strength, his ability to take damage. It was possible for him to ramp it up, quick and fast, but at the cost of his energy.

Rick... well, Rick was probably the one least changed. His focus was on his attributes, on using his guns. Empowering them, though as he pointed out, he could not learn many of the techniques he wanted because they was not available here. However, in the future, once they were out, that would change.

One after the other, his team grew stronger.

And then, it was just him. Just Arthur, who was still not certain he was ready.

But it was time to leave this floor, ready or not.

Chapter 56 – Floor 8

"Up, up, and away we go, wherever we stop, there's how we know we're slow," Arthur muttered, watching one after another of his friends disappear.

Only Yao Jing and Jan were hanging back, his erstwhile bodyguards till the last moment. He looked around, saw Noor and Li Sun, gave them a nod. It amused him a little, to see Fang Chien hanging back, Harish glowering beside him. The 04 gang had taken the worst losses, now just a part of the Ghee Hin. No one else wanted a group that small, prone to mistakes, and just overall incompetent.

The actual contract between Arthur and Fang Chien had been simple enough to sort out, after he had the wording and details passed through a lady who had been an actual lawyer beforehand. Not contract law but real estate, and certainly not magical contracts, though there had been some discussion about pushing her forward so she could help.

If she could get over her own fear of the last few floors.

Arthur shook his head, dismissing the thoughts for now. Later. It was his turn, and time to go. Handing over his seal, he waited for the contribution points to be deducted. He had exactly enough, mostly because he'd transferred over any extra to be kept by Li Sun, this floor's boss, to hold.

"Alright, any last-minute concerns?" No one spoke up, not that he expected it. "Then I'm off, like a prom dress."

Not that Malaysia did proms. But American culture and TV shows had a way of creeping in. Just like Bollywood and Tollywood movies. Or anime. Or, well, any major country that wasn't Malaysia with its still-struggling cultural exports.

Then, light. A twisting sensation.

And he was gone.

The last three floors of the Tower were weird. They deposited you at the bottom of a mountain range, and you had to climb it. Each floor was just a continuous land piece from the previous one, with the only demarcation being the presence of the floor monster boss in between. You had to climb your way through, doing battle with the monsters and collecting whatever resources you wanted and crossing higher till you hit the end. So it wasn't a single mountain he had to climb but a series.

Where a final battle awaited at the end; expect that one was another change in tune.

But he'd worry about that problem later.

The first question was whether he took the longer but easy route, the beaten-down path before him, and walked it, or if he intended to bushwack his way directly upwards. You could do both; the trial didn't enforce movement in any way unlike some Towers. There were advantages and disadvantages to both methods, and Arthur once more weighed the question in his mind.

Take the obvious route and it would be much easier walking. The ground was firm, the bushes cleared out on either end, and there was no chance of getting lost. However, the path went through a number of switchbacks, meandered back and forth, and did have offshoot pathways that could lead you the wrong way if you weren't paying attention. And, of course, the monsters were all waiting for you along the way.

Attacks were literally guaranteed and would be numerous. There weren't many places to rest, and even those resting places weren't guaranteed to be safe. Still, it was a proper pathway—if long. None of the monsters were going to be that difficult, including everything they'd fought before: the *babi ngepet*, the *kuching hitam*, the *jenglot*, and creatures from the platforms on the sixth floor.

Then, there was the bushwacking. Cutting upwards, heading straight instead of following the road. Cutting through areas where he might not want to do the trail. There were advantages: the total amount of distance he would have to cover would be less. Easily three to four times less distance, especially if he only needed to walk straight up.

He could do some of it, what with Cloud Steps and his willingness to cut his way through. He had a parang, and while it wasn't his favorite weapon, it was perfect for this kind of bushwhacking. Cutting his way straight up, pushing ahead with no intention of taking the main route.

Initially, it wouldn't matter, the trail would cut back and across from reports. However, at some point, the trail and the straight way up would diverge significantly. And that was the danger: because he did not bring with him a compass, did not have a cultivation technique to guide him through the wilderness.

Someone who had never cut through a forest might think it was simple, that all he had to do go was up. For the most part, that was right; but he was crossing and ascending a mountain range. That meant that there were times when he'd be going down too, times when he might have to deal with difficult terrain like cliffs that he couldn't ascend or rivers that couldn't be forded.

Worse, while the attacks were fewer theoretically, it was not guaranteed. At this point, they went from a relatively regular series of encounters to randomness. He might get by without an issue, just push his way upwards. Or, he might end up stumbling into a middle of a goblin village and have to fight his way through them.

"Make a choice, be the choice, if you aren't a fool, you'll never be able to find a soul."

Arthur sighed.

"Risk or reward, but at the end, where's my *lumpah* going to be?"

Head turning side to side, trying to figure out which way to go. He'd already had this conversation, over and over again, and eventually he sighed. Recalling everything people said to him.

Putting his feet on the trail, he started walking, spear held by his side as a walking stick with the metal butt hitting the ground, eyes searching for problems.

"Don't take risks, Arthur." Pitching his voice higher, a quiet mocking tone. Changing it up a little with each sentence. "You're the Clan Head. You cannot be killed." Growing gruffer, trying for Yao Jing. "Be good *lah*. We head up first, take care of it for you."

Then, laughing to himself, he discarded his mocking. He wasn't in a safe zone anymore, and monsters were out there.

The only question was when they arrived.

"Leeches! Leeches!" Arthur growled, jumping into the air and releasing a Refined Exploding Energy Dart at them. He watched the attack spin down into the ground and slam into the middle of the swarming pack. The explosion threw the leeches into the air, puncturing their skin and leaving globules of blood and meat to rain down.

Arthur spat, feeling dirt and other unmentionables in his mouth. Taught him a lesson to be talking while fighting. Still, for all his distractions, he caught the leaping *harimau hitam* with the tip of his spear that he'd been carrying next to his chest, shifting it a little so that the creature pinned itself on the weapon.

He tore it sideways, spinning it so that monster slammed into a tree nearby.

Legs bunched, he landed and struck out with his spear. Once, twice, thrice. Using it like a swirling, sewing needle to punch through the swarm. So many of them, but not an issue because he was stronger and faster than when he'd first met them. He was better than he had been.

He'd trained, he'd sparred, he'd gone through everything his sifu and seniors could throw at him. But there was no substitute, in the end, for real experience in the Tower.

In a blink, the monsters were dead, their bodies dispersing. No damage to him. The only thing he lost was a Refined Exploding Energy Dart. He now formed a new one and stored it in his second dantian. Then, stones to collect, and time to move on.

Chapter 57

Traversing the trail up the mountain with looming trees—many of them and the shrubbery alongside the trail itself filled with thorns—was a matter of patience and watchfulness and dullness. The only break in the routine were the occasional attacks by monsters, many simple enough to handle and no more intelligent than the overly large mosquitos that attempted to suck his blood.

The monsters and the traps: of the two, Arthur much preferred the monsters. After all, those at least provided beast stones that he could then utilize. Traps were just as dangerous, but yielded nothing more than pain and wrecked footing, as he found out upon missing a particularly cunningly wrought one.

He'd stepped over, carefully, the rope that had been strung across the trail, careful not to trigger it. Took a second step over and one more forwards, and found his foot sinking through the leaves strewn over the ground into a pit. He felt the scrape of spikes on his skin as he dropped, and when he automatically jerked his feet upwards, downward-pointing spikes dug into his flesh, basically embedding them in his leg. He hissed in pain.

It took the use of Bark Skin, some careful strikes against the wood, and a lot of pain before he dragged his foot free. Even longer to dig out the splinters from within his flesh. Thankfully, there were no monsters during this period.

Arthur found himself cursing quietly as he waited for the wounds to close.

"Got to be careful, this is a marathon. Make sure I'm not too fearful, when I'm not a paragon." He pushed himself to his feet using his spear, looked around, and carefully began his climb. He slowed down a little, just enough to keep a better eye on the surroundings and to tap the trail with the butt of his spear before he took a step.

In the meantime, he checked over his status screen to see his gains after weeks of training.

Cultivation Speed: 2.773 Yin

Energy Pool: 24/30 (Yin) + (7/7)

Refinement Speed: 0.1421

Refined Energy: 0.43 (40) +(0/3)

Attributes and Traits

Mind: 15 (Multi-Tasking, Quick Learner, Perfect Recall)

Body: 25 (Enhanced Eyesight, Yin Body, Swiftness, Fast Twitch Faster, Lightning Reflexes, Explosive Strength)

Spirit: 15 (Sticky Energy, From the Dregs, Strengthened Aura)

Techniques

Night Emperor Cultivation Technique

Focused Strike

Accelerated Healing – Refined Energy (Grade III)

Heavenly Sage's Mischief

Refined Energy Dart

Bark Skin

Seven Cloud Stepping Technique (189%)

Poket Simpanan Tua (135%) (Refined Energy Dart - 84% Integrity)

Imbued Strike - Yin Poison

Partial Techniques

Simultaneous Flow (181.7%)

Yin-Yang Energy Exchange (89.8%)

Yin Poison Darts (47.9%)

Yin Aura (67.3%)

As much as he would have liked to hit the third transformation, the time cost was too high. Already, with a ten-point spread between Body and his other attributes, he had found himself feeling a little unbalanced. He could barely keep up mentally with how fast he moved, the size of his energy pool was making it hard to fill at a decent rate and, overall, he just felt a minor sense of dislocation. It was, supposedly, worse when one particular attribute increased significantly more than the ten points. Of course, humanity was more than adaptable; it was literally their main trait. Given enough time, you could grow used to the difference in traits and push it even further; but it did lead to uniquely predisposed individuals.

Ten points was, of course, not a firm number. As one grew stronger and climbed higher, that ten point maximum spread increased as the relative difference between attributes decreased. 100 to 80 was very different from 15 to 5, in relative terms.

Even so, Arthur had no desire to be one of the weirdos with too imbalanced attributes. Considering he'd need to increase basically another fifteen attributes points, he realised he just did not have time to wait. Not with the problems that the Ghee Hin had already mentioned were waiting for him outside the Tower.

Sure, increasing his own survivability was important, but that came from allies and techniques as anything else.

Anyway, if he did this right, he would be able to cultivate outside the Tower with the beast stones he acquired now and had coming from the Clan, allowing him to grow stronger before he entered the next Tower. Less rushing around, unlike this entire damn Tower.

He had to admit, it was partly his fault too. He'd spent time working on his techniques—techniques he was trying to create himself, even—rather than purely cultivating. But there was only so much sitting down, meditating, and pulling on energy one could do before growing insane.

What he'd pushed hardest on was the Yin Aura, mostly because developing that had been required to make his Imbued Strike - Yin Poison more effective. He still was not able to keep it going continuously, but it now shorted out much less often. Which had quickly made him one of the most dangerous attritive duellists in the Clan. If he could survive long enough and land blows on his opponent, whether defended against or not, he would, eventually, win out.

Just like how Mel and Jan and the rest had collapsed fighting from the poison on the first floor, his own opponents in the arena eventually became punch drunk and easy to put down. The nice thing about the Yin poison was that, eventually, it disappeared without causing any long-lasting harm either, which meant he could utilize it constantly.

Of course, the biggest negative of the current poison was that it took time to build up. Unless he managed a critical blow, it took multiple attacks to inject enough of the poison to make a substantial difference. Considering the fact that the moment he managed a critical blow, most creatures were already dead or dying, it made the poison at first glance rather useless against monsters.

Which was fine. Arthur's major issue wasn't with the small individual monsters. He even had an explosive method of dealing with them, and once he got his aura working, an area effect technique. What he needed, and what the poison was geared towards, was boss monsters. The big, nasty creatures at the end of each floor that often required multiple attacks.

Just like the hydra that they'd fought before, which if he had the Yin poison working properly would have been dealt with more easily. The point of the poison wasn't to end things fast; he had Focused Strike, and eventually, he'd probably purchase something like Power Strike to combine the both.

No, the point was to take down those creatures that were immune to power attacks.

Or even better, deal with creatures who were immune to physical attacks. After all, working through his aura and Tower energy, it could and should affect non-corporeal creatures. Of course, that was theoretical. He didn't, after all, have any of those to deal with yet.

"Yin to pin, the kind of boss, that would be a loss," Arthur muttered to himself, eyes sweeping the floor. He'd dropped the rhyming a bit when he was with others, the business of work and cultivation keeping his mind focused.

Now, alone, it'd come back with force. Nervousness and a way to keep him busy and not utterly bored.

All good things.

Now, if only something changed along the damn walk.

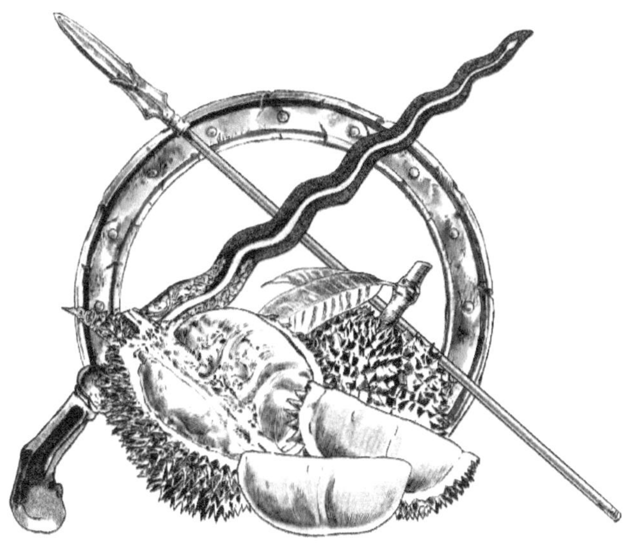

Chapter 58

It took Arthur two days before he was certain. He had begun to suspect after the first day, after he'd woken refreshed and ready to keep moving—or as refreshed he could be hunkering under a poncho and crammed into the side of a tree hollow. Rather than climbing the rather spiky and scrawny trees near him, he'd chosen to just use the hollow after killing the lurking badger-like monster within.

Two days and he was quite clear. He hard countered the entire damn eight floor. The eighth floor wasn't particularly difficult; it wasn't even particularly complex. It was just a slog. Day in, day out, you walked the trail, killed the monsters that came at you, took minor wounds, and kept going.

It was very much a marathon, and over the next three floors, the injuries he was supposed to acquire at each floor would slow him down. He'd known this, of course, what with the wiki having detailed the unchanging setup; but he hadn't realised how much of a counter his own advantages were till he had experienced it.

In fact, he was realising, his clan seal would make it easier for all his Clan members.

Injuries? Constantly healing. If he took a nasty enough attack, he just had to pull off for a few hours to have it healed up enough that he didn't have to worry about it. Rest? Sure, there had been creatures that had tried to get to him, but he'd blocked it off enough that the few he had to kill when he exited were no issue. And the side effect of the healing was that he needed less sleep.

He didn't suffer much of the pressure from knowing that there was a time limit—and it was an arbitrary time limit in the sense that a vast swarm of monsters would catch up with him if he took too long. After all, his Yin Body kept his mind calm, shifted his temperament to a more logical one. He didn't have the rush of adrenaline, the nerves that might affect others knowing there was a countdown.

More to the point, he was making good time. There was, obviously, enough time for most individuals to make it up the eighth floor without encountering the swarm of wolves. So long as you kept pushing, you never had to worry about them. Of course, the constant howls late at night, the knowledge something was coming for him, that could still wear on a person.

Then again, he'd been on a time pressure for the last few months now. Pushing ahead. So this was just another damn thing which he had to handle.

He could do that.

He was doing it. In fact, while there weren't any actual markers, Arthur could gauge from the descriptions and memorised landmarks how far he had come and he realised he was making good time. A week to get through the entire floor, and he was probably a day early if he kept at this rate. Nine days in, roughly, was when the packs of wolves that were hunting him would catch up. Give or take a day, since it was distance more than time that was the issue.

Of course, a small niggle of worry was that a climber might somehow get a little too slow and the monsters caught up. Presumably, there were cases when packs swarmed a climber and they never managed to make it out.

Hard to know how many, since there were only statistics for the number of climbers that had survived and exited, not how many had fallen to the Tower.

It was that minor niggle of worry that kept him moving, putting one foot in front of the other as he kept an eye out for monsters. He would have preferred to practise his techniques, but it was better to be safe than sorry. Especially as the number of ambush attackers and traps kept rising.

"No fair!" Arthur snarled, eyes widening as the latest trap came barrelling down at him. Whoever had decided that the giant rolling boulder trap was the ultimate in climber-killing had cheated, choosing to add in some magical railguards on the trail. In this way, instead of bouncing off the trail itself and disappearing, like pretty much any boulder might have in real life, it was forced to continue rolling down the trail in a bouncing vertical line of death.

Lips compressed as he considered his options, he felt time slow down as he watched the boulder bounce upwards and then again. Two options. Get off the trail—either sideways up the hill or into the air using Cloud Steps— or get under, sliding beneath the boulder as it bounced.

Unfortunately, there was never a guarantee of how high the boulder would rise or fall. It was, in fact, rather frustrating to estimate. He could risk it, but if he misjudged his sprawl and slide, he would be facing a couple of tonnes of angry stone. Better to take the easier method, even if did require cultivation energy.

Moments to look, analyze and decide, and then he was dashing sideways, leaping into the air to get out of the way of the boulder. Luckily, the magical rails that kept the boulder bouncing down the trail did not keep him from leaping away. One cloud, holding still for as long as he could as he bent his leg in before he jumped straight forward again to the next cloud.

The second one half-formed on the top of a branch. It was not enough, by itself, to give him traction. But with the branch on top of it, he was able to dig in, leap forwards at a sideways angle. It let him fly through the air even as the boulder kept bouncing, disappearing down the hill as he hit the ground, rolled and came up.

"Yes!"

Of course, that's when the lurking monkeys hanging on the edges, watching the boulder disappear, attacked him. A half-dozen of the damn creatures, some leaping at him, the others lobbing stones at Arthur. One missed, another smacked into his thigh, and a third stung his arm, numbing it and nearly causing him to drop his spear.

Bad timing as the howling monkeys, screaming and chittering and saliva splattering, struck. He couldn't get a spear upwards, so he instead shifted to raise his other elbow and allow the first monkey to land on it, elbow sinking into body. Another slammed into his lower body, the momentum bowling him over even as the third landed a little too short and had to scramble forward.

A scrum, a fight between the quartet as Arthur battled the creatures. They were weak, significantly weaker than him. It almost felt like an adult doing battle with a trio—no, a sextet—of toddlers. Except these toddlers were willing to bite, scratch, spit, and claw to do damage. With one hand he gripped a monster by the arm as he spun to smash it into another.

He staggered back, bleeding from a couple of minor scratches, but continued using the monkey as an improvised, furry mace. Slam, smash and swing; one after the other until the creatures fell down, bowled over. The flesh of the arm tearing, a hard swing pulling it right off, leaving him with an arm and no body.

That worked anyway.

Moments later, Arthur was done. As with any other battle, any fight on this floor, it hadn't been hard. A little annoying, what with the constant screaming, the spit on his face, and the long scratches on his arm. He could also feel a slight strain down his ribs, scratches on his arm and along his neck. Minor injuries, piling on. Infection would have been a concern if he didn't have his healing system.

They'd scab over in an hour, heal completely over in a few hours.

A few moments to open up the corpses, to find the monster cores within, which he dropped into his pouch. He scooped up his spear before moving on. Linger too long here, and there'd be another monster, most likely the kuching hitam. So he moved, using his spear to lever himself up.

Now he was scanning the ground. A few dozen steps, a pressure plate— and why there would be a pressure plate on a trail, he had no idea. He avoided it and went on.

Steps, climbing higher, wondering when the next shoe would drop.

Chapter 59

A giant babi ngepet, waiting for him at the top of a minor rise. It pawed the ground, snorting out loud, its proportionally small tusks tossed on the head as it attempted to intimidate Arthur. He considered the creature, the massive roaming mini-boss of this level and sighed at his luck.

Dealing with it would be tricky. He was on a ridge, one side nothing more than open air and the other a cliff face that rose up for another twenty, thirty feet before turning into a gentle slope. Arthur had a plan for what he intended to do, and the only question was whether to utilize his stored Refined Exploding Energy Dart now or when it attacked him. Also, would his attack have enough energy to blow pass its thick hide, or was he going to have to get in deep? Or utilize his Imbued Strike?

Of course, most importantly, he had to avoid its initial charge.

Feet pounding the dirt, the squat creature surprisingly fast. Before Arthur knew it, the creature had crossed half the distance and forced him to reevaluate his intentions.

One, two, three steps and then he leapt sideways. Same way he avoided giant bouncing boulders, Arthur leapt away from the charging boar. He turned his head as the creature barrelled past him, slowing down as it realised its prey was gone, tusk attempting to land a strike on the fast-moving flea.

The Refined Exploding Energy Dart smashed into its body in the space just behind the joint of the leg and about midway in the body. Flesh and blood and chunks of meat flew through the air, even as Arthur kicked off the formed cloud. Bouncing himself back onto the trail and landing with a flourish, taking one, two steps so that he could put his spear into the ground and ready for the attack.

At least, that was the plan.

What he didn't see until too late were the boar's mildly glowing footsteps. What he didn't realise were the increasing amounts of energy pooling in the steps.

When they blew up, it threw him sideways. By the time he recovered, legs aching, body torn up from flying rocks and shrapnel, ears ringing and mind blurry with smoke and clouds in the air, the boar had turned around and was charging him. Without time to actually set himself or his weapon, he threw himself away and to the side in the direction that he was leaning in anyway. He hit the ground, rolled and kept rolling, not intending to get caught by the trampling feet.

Forgetting, briefly, that he was on a cliff.

He remembered, of course, when he was plunging through the air.

Arthur hit the slope hard, bounced a few times into open air, hammered the side of his head into a branch of a damn tree sticking out as he careened off the side of the hill. He twisted, trying to reorient himself by pure instinct as blood from a torn scalp dribbled freely. He knew it was likely only a minor wound that was bleeding heavy, though the concussion that was exacerbated after getting blown up and smacked around wasn't minor at all, but the damn blood was stopping him from seeing properly and he had to get his feet right, get ready to hit the ground and...

Branches, foliage, his body striking a tree trunk. He slammed into it, bounced around, doing his best to keep his limbs in close and take the attacks on his armour. The helmet, the breastplates, greaves and all the rest helped, spreading the damage across him rather than letting it smash into one spot.

He had still fallen tens of feet, hundreds maybe, he wasn't sure. Enough, at least, that he was cracking branches of magical trees and being a bouncing ball himself.

By the time he slammed into the earth, he was all kinds of shaken and bruised and pretty certain that his hip had popped out of joint and he'd wrenched his back. Somehow he managed to be lucky enough only to crack a few ribs or maybe dislocate them, and leave his head mostly attached.

What wasn't attached? His backpack, his spear, and half his survival gear.

Also, his senses.

He just lay there, somehow still awake. Somehow, managing to keep himself functioning long enough to crawl and put himself against the edge of a still-shaking tree. To clean his face, just enough so that he could see what was happening around him. He grunted, finding the torn-open flap at the side of his head and pushed fingers into the hanging piece of skin, hissing as fresh pain bloomed. Sticky warmth, flesh sliding on bone, and skin underneath already swelling.

His head swam, twisting and turning and he found himself pulling at his energy, hunting for his healing technique so that he could begin the process of actively healing himself. His head was pounding too much, his focus drifting too often that he gave up. Realising he was best not managing his own energy now, not unless he needed it.

Instead, he leaned against the ground, the kris fumbled into his hand as he waited.

Lost and uncertain, without his various tools and resources. Not even his spear, which was going to be a problem. Or even his...

Oh. He did have his pouch, which had been secured over and over again because he was that paranoid.

So not that disastrous.

Just mostly.

His luck returned. He'd only had to kill four leeches and two carrion rodent-like creatures that had attempted to get to him, intent on swallowing him whole. Good thing, because even fighting them had left him panting and in agony; muscles and parts of him that he hadn't even imagined being able to hurt were throbbing. Who knew that there was a muscle right next to your tailbone that really, really didn't like it when you had a dislocated hip and moved.

Arthur did, now.

Thankfully, his body healed. Slowly, in fits and starts as energy had to build up before bones slotted into place or tendons tightened. Shards of bone were pushed out, cracks patched over, the wound in his head sticking properly. He didn't even want to know the type of scarring he would get, though thankfully, the Tower would eventually sweep that away, he knew. At least with his refined healing technique always running.

Still not fun.

Eventually, he managed to get his feet under him. Stand up, kris still in one hand, and limp around the vicinity, searching for his equipment. He found some of the pouches that contained his survival gear: simple pieces of string—metal and fishing string—and tent pegs, carving knives, a folding cup to drink water from. He found his pack that contained his first aid kit and used it to help keep parts of him together long enough for the healing to kick in.

Everything hurt as he moved around, his injuries nowhere near healed. Still, the healing technique was putting him back together, and he had managed to guide enough of it to his head to reduce the wooziness and pounding, so that his vision only blurred and shifted into multiples once in a while.

Moving around, collecting his goods, knowing he couldn't stay here too long. Tower monsters weren't regular creatures; they didn't run away from trouble but towards it. Eventually, something nastier like a harimau hitam or a pack of monkeys would arrive and he would have to contend with them. Not something he wanted to deal with. Maybe something he could *not* deal with right now.

The entire floor was meant to keep people moving, with only a few hours rest here and there before the attacks ramped up. So he needed to keep walking in a circle, widening it as he found his stuff, and hope that he could locate his spear. His lost backpack had a change of clothing, fresh underwear, comfort items, and things that would make life easier like ropes and pitons, more knives and plates, and some food to chew on to keep him sane. But it was not necessary.

His spear, on the other hand, that he needed.

Now he really wished he had some way of calling it to him, of locating the damn thing. Too bad there had been no enchantment that did that. Hoping it wasn't stuck in the foliage out of sight, all he could do was walk and search.

And figure out where he was.

Chapter 60

"There you are!" Arthur laughed as he finally spotted his spear. He limped over to it quickly, pausing as he was halfway there when he realized exactly where it was located. It took him a moment too long, for the creeping vines had managed to get behind him and grab his legs.

The vines pulled him forward, forcing him to slam into the ground. Head tucked in tight against his chest, he felt the air in his chest explode out of his lungs, only one arm managing to smack the ground just ahead of his fall to break it.

His head swam, the concussion that had been slowly healing grew worse again at the jostling. Blinding pain shot through him, his vision swimming as the vines dragged him closer to a large plant, red petals unfurling and the central stamen opening.

Arthur groaned, pushing himself upwards, focusing. He had rebuilt his Refined Exploding Energy Dart, stored it away, and it was a simple matter to release it. It surged forwards to strike the flower, burrowing within before exploding and spreading warm sap all across him.

The whole creature thrashed him around, bouncing him side to side in anger. On and on, it dragged him closer. Hands flipped around, Arthur managed to snag the spear from its resting place near the damn flower. After that, it was just a matter of stabbing around, again and again, and a few frantic moments to lever the spear into the creature's body to stop it from eating him directly.

Then, finally, the damn thing died, dropping him onto the ground to lie there, in pain once more.

"I hate this," Arthur said as he slowly pushed himself up. "But I got what I need. My backpack, my spear, and most of my gear. Now, I just need to put it in gear." A hesitation, then he sighed, realising he'd used the same word twice.

He was far down from where he had first fallen and certain that he was off the trail. A cliff face from here meant he couldn't actually make his way back up, unless he wanted to climb it. And considering the flying monsters out there, he knew it was going to be a pain and a half. Never mind the potential hanging vines that could grab him along the way.

Still, that was the most direct way up. He could see the cliff face, hanging towards his left. A long way to climb, such that he couldn't quite see the top of it.

The other option was to ignore the cliff face and look for the trail and try to reconnect that way, but he wasn't certain.

Or he could head more directly towards the end goal. He saw it, even now, the top of the mountain that he needed to reach. He'd have to figure out a way to get pass the current cliff face, head sideways a little, make it through the mountain ranges, and bushwack in the direction he needed.

There was one other consideration. The packs.

Either way, he was losing a day. Maybe more. Probably more. There was no way he could risk climbing today, which meant he needed to hunker up and wait. That started pushing the timeline with the packs getting too close for comfort, either way. If he bushwacked, if he did it right and headed straight for the mountain peak, he was sure he could make up time. Even if he was further down, even if he'd lost a day, two days by being down here.

But there was danger involved.

"*Tiu*," Arthur cursed and closed his eyes, trying to decide, trying to work out what he wanted to do.

In the end, he turned away from the cliff and started limping way. He needed to keep moving rather than stay still and risk getting attacked. More to the point, he was worried about how much time he would lose if he waited. He'd tried the safe and smart methodology, so now he was going to go back to what he used to do: run a risk and hope it worked out.

Arthur used his spear to aid his walk, eyes shifting from side to side as he kept looking for traps. He knew that, off the trail, traps and monsters would be fewer, but that didn't meant there weren't any. Keeping an eye on the peak and where he needed to go, he kept track of each step. Every time he had to walk around a tree, he moved back to his original line almost immediately after. He knew he needed to keep an overall straight line, what with the lack of a compass to use or any other form of guidance.

Eyeballing his way forward, Arthur kept moving, pulling at his various energy types to store another Refined Exploding Energy Dart. After all, it wasn't going to be this easy.

The first fifteen minutes was quiet, not a single damn creature to kill. He limped onwards, but soon enough the creatures that had been converging began arriving. Drying blood all across him, still limping, and probably smelling like a snack with all the various pheromones he was giving off from being in pain, he would likely have been a tasty snack even for normal animals. As it stood, the monsters on the floor were more than happy to come for him.

The first, he took with a fist to the face and then a stab with the spear. After that, he kept his spear leveled, not even stopping to grab the core this time around. As much as he'd miss the core, if the roamers were arriving already, then more and more of them would just come.

Better to put distance between himself and the fall, to force them to fight over corpses and decide how long they'd want to track him. Some would eventually give up and others would continue pursuing, but he would deal with them when it came to that. He couldn't stop them, but he could space out the attacks a little. So long as he kept moving.

The next was a giant green snake that dropped from above. Arthur hopped back, stabbed it once and then a couple more times till he managed to pin it to the tree. Since he needed to retrieve his spear from the still-dying creature, he managed to retrieve its stone as well whilst slaying the creature by opening it half-up.

Levering his spear out, he kept moving. He weathered the occasional attack from those monsters that chose to find him and only occasionally tore into corpses for their cores. He moved as fast as he could for the next hour. A semi-persistent use of Bark Skin kept him safe, or at least mostly protected, even when he missed a swooping bird with extended claws or the slashing attack of some molelike creature.

It drained his cultivation stores, and even with the significant stores he had, it wasn't enough to keep Bark Skin running constantly. By the time three hours had ended, though, he was out of the danger zone or at least so he believed. Attacks had grown less frequent, and he was able to avoid any encounters for the last half hour.

Arthur figured that was a success. At least for now. A few more hours and the sun would set. He'd find a place to rest up and would be significantly more healed, if not all the way back to normal.

Question was what tomorrow would bring.

Chapter 61

The thing about trail cutting was that it was never as easy as the movies made it look. Not through a tropical forest, not when every other damn tree had thorns long enough to scratch you up or embed in flesh or worse. Not when cobwebs and vines and branches dotted the landscape, when uneven root systems and mud and leeches were all part of the jungle. Those individuals who had never actually walked through a proper tropical rainforest from Malaysia or similar environs could never understand it, not when their idea of a proper forest was old-growth land in North America and Europe.

Enough space to easily walk around trees or between them? Sure, there was space between trees. Most of that was filled with prickly bushes and secondary growth, all of them fertile and often filled with thorns or with leaves edged such that even brushing your hands along them would elicit light cuts.

Clear vision fifty feet ahead? Hah! You wished. If you had about twenty feet of clear vision, you were in a good spot.

Then, there were the insects and bugs and creepy crawlies. Not as many mosquitos, mostly because humans weren't around throwing their garbage and offering easy meal sources. Not that they didn't eat other creatures, but there generally were a higher volume where mankind chose to end up. Same with flies and other carrion beetles and the like. Yet, it didn't stop a constant and vast number of other insects and ants and tiny scavengers from crawling, flying, and leaping onto you.

You got used to it, though keeping a pair of pants on helped—as well as tight underwear. No loose boxers here, not unless you wanted to make intimate acquaintance with tiny creatures.

Of course, that meant you were also hot. Hot, humid weather that drained stamina, that sapped the endurance of anyone unused to such exertions. A constant vigilance and the need to pick out the unusual, the strange, meant that mentally you grew tired, even as animals and monsters that blended into the foliage waited for their chance to attack you.

Spiders the size of your hand, that had venom injected into you when they dropped down. Snakes that were nearly as broad as your thigh, landing on your shoulders, constricting your body. Leeches that crawled up your boots, into your pants, between your toes, and sucked you dry. Centipedes, lying on leaves, their skin and hairs poisonous and irritating.

Dozens of problems and always, always, the need to keep cutting, keep swinging a machete to get through the blockages. Trying to move in the right direction, hoping you were going the right way and not getting turned around by the twisting slope and shifting undergrowth.

Thankfully, by this point, Arthur was more than a little experienced at forest floors. Even if he would never be as versatile and comfortable as an *orang asli* who grew up in a Malaysian jungle, he was no neophyte. He knew how to step right, how to check for sinkholes, to avoid walking into seemingly shallow puddles, and to watch for monsters or other tricks.

In its own way, without the regulated traps, cutting cross-country was also easier. He wondered, of course, what the wolves would do—or the Tower equivalent of them, since wolves really weren't native to these lands. He had fallen off the path after all. Would they leap down, chasing him? Back off and come around? Or did the Tower let them know where he was, to chase him onwards?

Hard to say, and he couldn't recall any particular wiki passage describing his particular situation. He was sure he wasn't unique of course, but there was only so much one could read, what with so many floors out there and climbers speaking and writing in three or four different languages. Even if English continued to be the main language of Climbers worldwide, the fact stood that many Malaysians just didn't speak it that well.

And while automated translations helped, it was still a pain and a half to use.

That being said, the first two days were relatively uneventful—that is, for days spent on an average Tower floor. Walk, fight, rest, and cultivate. Get up, walk, fight, fight, rest, and cultivate, and then walk more.

Repeated actions, one after the other, as he managed to cut through the landscape in the direction that he was sure would lead him to the next level, to the next stage of this marathon.

Typical.

Except, of course, for the appearance of the broken stone ruins as he came up the rise. A place of broken masonry, overgrown roofless buildings and a pyramid-like structure reaching towards the heavens, its presence hidden till now by foliage and a trick of geography.

Suddenly, Arthur wondered, if anyone had ever found this before and they'd just kept it quiet. Or if he really had found something new.

And what to do about it.

He watched the ruins for a good twenty minutes before even trying to make a decision. Pacing along the edge slowly, trying to get an idea of the size and circumference on it. If he was seeing an actual ruined city or just the large complex of a monastery or temple or otherwise far-off fort. Maybe even a single building, since the Tower did not have to play by sensible rules.

After stalking the outside for about fifteen minutes, grumpily pushing his way through and getting caught on vines and thorns, he came to a conclusion that there really wasn't a lot that he could learn without moving much more stridently. Trying to circumvent the building was going to take a while, and it certainly was much larger than a single tower.

With everything overgrown, it was nearly impossible to tell if it was the ruins of a city or complex, the surroundings blending in relatively well. No major outer walls though, so it wasn't a fort. More importantly, Arthur noticed no monsters or creatures lurking inside the ruins. There might be some deeper within, but thus far he'd yet to spot them.

Which guided his next choice, which was to cut through. Not only because there might be opportunity and treasure within, but also to reduce the amount of time he would waste trying to find the limits of the path. His movement, however, did offer one advantage: a pathway that looked and felt significantly less overgrown. Fewer trees, more low-hanging bush and tall grasses.

If he had to guess, he was now on an old road that had led to the complex itself. To confirm his guess, he dug into the earth and, after about half a handspan in, finally hit the paving stones. Rain and time had thrown new dirt over the entire thing, but despite the changes to the environment, it still offered some degree of ease for travel.

He took the path down into the abandoned ruins. Overgrown walls, pulled down by creepers and ivy, shrubbery growing out sideways or inside what were homes or other buildings. Sometimes, walls two, three stories tall jutted out randomly, somehow managing to survive the vagaries of time and nature. Mostly though, stone blocks randomly scattered around the walls they had fallen from. Remains of walls were a foot or two high.

Not too surprising, but a myriad number of small creatures lived in the ruins. What looked like a family of armadillos, rolling away the moment he neared. Smaller, darting rodents that boiled out of the ground, coming from what must have been a basement, to launch themselves at Arthur.

A Refined Exploding Energy Dart took care of them, the explosion leaving three dead and a half-dozen reeling. By the time they recovered, Arthur had speared and smashed another four, leaving the last few that tried to finish him to be stamped and crushed. One managed to get a bite into his calf, a flicker of notification appearing and disappearing as an attempt to poison him was enacted and wiped away.

The ruins themselves revealed themselves to be a full complex if not a city. By the time he had walked nearly thirty minutes in, heading towards the pyramid structure in the center, Arthur was certain that it was either of these—and if it was a city, a small one. Checking the ruins showed nothing of worth to take. Any valuables either never having existed in the first place or buried deep beneath the layers of soil that had formed.

"If there's a place to get anything, it's in that building," Arthur muttered to himself. It made sense, since it was the only building still mostly intact. On top of that, of course, there was the issue of how the Tower thought, and that too coincided with some degree of logic to its purposes. At least, sufficiently so, for Arthur to make that guess.

Question was, whether it was worth the rather significant risk of whatever lived inside those ruins to explore them.

Chapter 62

"This is a bad idea." Arthur muttered to himself once again. Even saying that, he was not moving away, he was not changing his plan. Instead, he began to strike his metal flask with the pommel of his kris. The enchanted poison kris had a wooden handle with a full tang that stuck out the end, the wooden handle coming in two parts and having been joined to the tang before being shaped. Thin wire laced along the handle itself helped keep it from slipping during fights as liquids were an issue in most fights.

The clanging of the metal echoed through the ruins, definite to draw attention. Standing right outside the opening of the pyramid—which he guessed to be a temple—he figured he would lure something out.

If he was lucky, just a few. But considering he had nothing to light the inside of the rather dark building, he had no intention of simply walking in and getting ambushed. Better to draw whatever monsters there might be out, especially since he was willing to put the two foot tactical withdrawal option into play at any moment.

A dozen strikes, over and over again, and then he stopped, slipping the flask back into its tied pouch. He locked it down and waited, ears straining for the slightest noise, cycling his breathing slowly and deeply. His eyes stayed still even as he turned his head from side to side slowly, keeping his gaze unfocused as he tried to catch movement.

No movement, nothing...

And then, something inside the doorway. One humanoid, then another. His eyes widened, at the numbers that slipped out, showing themselves to him. Hairy, large creatures—the shortest was over six feet tall. Bristly fur, with faces that looked like a mix between human and animal, and large mouths with teeth that looked like knife blades. Hands that looked like claws, too, sharp-tipped fingers on them.

"*Santu sakai!*" Arthur breathed the name of the creatures. Even as he made the decision to strike first, he waited for the right timing.

The Refined Exploding Energy Dart flew out to strike the one that had led the way. It moved, fast, dodging the attack. Others next to it stepped away too, moving aside from the fast- flying attack, leaving the one at the back to take the attack. What they probably did not expect was the Dart's explosion, which threw the group into disarray.

Immediately after his attack, he was running. Moving forwards as quickly as he could, pulling the energy for that Yin Aura to him. He needed to get the group slowed down, for them to suffer from the effects of the poison. There were six, no, seven of them. One had a large gaping hole in its chest right now. It was still struggling up, but Arthur wasn't going to pay attention to it.

Rather, he focused on the first one that had dodged. It was the largest, nastiest one. Smartest perhaps, certainly the leader but he wasn't sure it was enough to dissuade him from this. There were just enough of them to make this a challenge, a good chance he'd be killed in this fight. But at the same time, humanoid monsters meant treasure. It was a Tower given, pretty much, especially at these floors.

Another step, then another, then he dodged to the right as the creature lunged. Damn thing was fast, but Arthur took care of that by putting his spear in the way. It could lunge at him all it wanted, but Arthur had a spear and rather than impaling itself, it threw itself away, allowing him to track and get an easy strike in.

Blood splashed, filling the air with ruby droplets. Just as precious to its previous owner, if not more so as it lost its crimson lifeblood in droves. How apt, that we only miss what we had when we have less.

He drew his blade back, feeling trickles of power flow through his body and release into the air. The Yin Aura was no cloud, no diffusion of energy, though he had once thought of it like that. Only discussing the matter with Jan had he come to understand that the aura was a living thing, a projection of power and personality.

Once he began to understand that, he'd learnt to push his aura outwards to cover the necessary space around him. It had been slow growing, for locating his aura had taken him days. After that, if he pushed it too far, the entire thing snapped back. Nowadays, he thought of it akin to filling up a balloon with his Yin energy, diffusing the surroundings with poison.

Turning sideways, he saw that the group of santu sakai had neared him once again, clustering a little rather than spreading out. Rather than let them get away with that, he released the Refined Exploding Energy Dart he had stored within his second dantian. It flew through the air, too close for them to dodge successfully and caught his primary target in the arm. The Dart unleashed its fury, tearing the arm off and sending goblets of flesh and blood through the air. The explosion threw those nearby, crashing into one another.

In the confusion, he darted in.

The slowly expanding Yin aura took a bit to reach maximum potential, and even more for it to be effective but as he swept within, his body shifting through the spear forms to slice, stab, and sweep, he could feel portions of his energy leeching out as it came into contact with his opponents. Small trickles of power, entering other auras, other bodies. Those that were wounded or distracted were the easiest to harm.

He fought not to kill but to injure. Oh, he preferred and targeted fatal attacks when he could; but these were smart creatures. They protected the vitals, the parts of the body that would end them immediately. Heart, throat, head. Everything else—gut shots, slices along the inner thigh to take out a femoral artery—took longer. Even a shot into the lungs could be survived for a little while with sufficient strength.

Everyone who dabbled in martial arts had heard that hacksaw of someone dropping seconds after you cut the femoral artery or carotid. All of that, from what was an urban myth. Ask any actual doctor and they'd point out that if that really happened, not even the most gifted surgeons would be able to save as many.

In this case, the santu sakai were built to protect themselves. They had ways to survive fatal attacks, such as veins and arteries literally pulling into themselves to reduce blood flow, or the body going into shock and reducing the pressure. All of which meant that creatures could and would fight longer than you'd think.

It was why his sifu had pushed them to learn defense, to always watch for the follow-up blow, to go for the clean kill and retreat. Never to expose oneself for the follow up, because there would be. Especially in the Tower.

Especially with creatures that were humanoid but not fully human, whose lungs or guts or kidneys might be a little further away than you'd expected.

Defense, long cuts, pushing with his spear to slow them down. Dragging them to a stop, always moving, always backing away. Arthur was glad he was fighting out here, where he had space to move rather than inside the pyramid, where he couldn't see as well, couldn't be sure he had enough place to move.

Two of the monsters were flanking out wide, the leader coming up and gesturing them to attack. They kept trying to back Arthur up, to encircle him. The moment they did, he was in real danger. Aura continued to pulse, but he shifted his second weave, pulling at another of his techniques for the inevitable.

Unfortunately, the damn alpha was willing to sacrifice its own people to ensure he couldn't break free and run. Backpedaling as fast as he could, he still had to watch for steps that descended, for missing broken ground. He had to move carefully, pushing his opponents back with his weapon. Sliding his feet, shifting down carefully.

They came around, fast, loping into attack. He wanted to back off, but one santu sakai pushed forward and was stumbling a little—too good an opportunity to pass up. Spear tip pushed into neck, tearing a hunk of meat and blood as it exited. The foul smell of old, wet dog and blood filling the air, the musky scent making Arthur gag a little as he retreated.

Knowing he was too late, as the other two managed to make it around his back. Creeping up from the ground, hands lowered, head leading the charge a little as they gnashed sharp, knife-like teeth.

Surrounded and outnumbered.

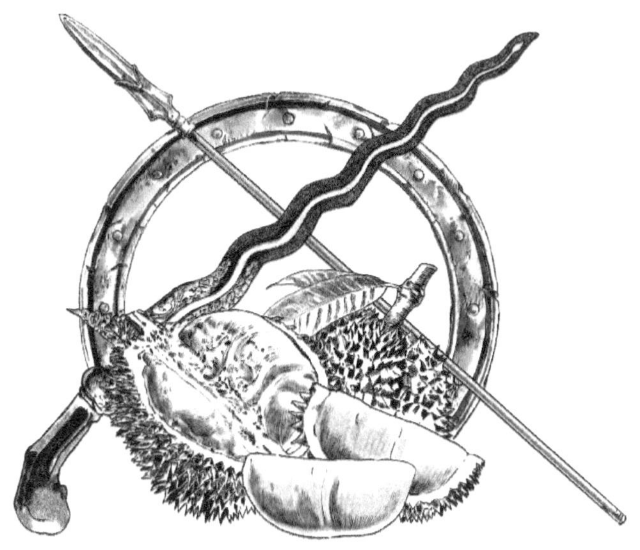

Chapter 63

The santu sakai pulled back a little, spreading out. The big one, watching from the back, paying attention. Unconsciously, or perhaps consciously, it had moved outside the range of his poison Yin aura that still leaked into his other opponents. It was slowing them down, a little. But the fight had barely gone on for a minute by now, if that.

Time was a strange mistress in combat, prone to exaggeration. Everything seemed to stretch out longer than it actually was. Only for you to come to your senses afterwards, battered, bruised, a little sore, and realise: no, it hadn't been that long. It was all, just... tricks.

A barking noise, closer to a dog or a hyena than the wolf that this creature resembled. Or at least, what Arthur imagined a wolf to look like. Not as though they were native to Malaysia. Zoo Negara, though it had resurrected visitor numbers with the opening of a KFC, had yet to draw him in. Something about how far away it was and the sheer expense, along with his need to keep himself fed and trained.

The bark was a signal, an indicator for the monsters at the back to attack. Or get ready. Hard to say, but they did use pack tactics. Two at the front, moving around the dying body of their friend, claws waving as they attempted to distract him.

He caught the second as it feinted, tore up its arm with his spear. Then, without even looking back, knowing they were coming, he leapt upwards. Calisthenics and training and the Tower upgrades meant he could easily clear over six feet, putting him well above the creatures that were coming from the stairs behind, clawed feet tearing up moss and dirt as they lunged.

He spun his spear around, thrust downwards. Caught one of the creatures on the upper shoulder, just beneath the collarbone. For a moment, he wobbled in mid-air, pushed a little higher with the impact and forces before gravity asserted itself.

Not before he saw the first feinter in front bunch up its leg, getting ready to leap at him.

Everything happening so fast, all in seconds.

A cloud, formed under his feet as he pushed away and backwards. Throwing himself into the air and higher, his spear pulling out as the santu sakai leapt to where he should have been if gravity had taken him. But he was still in the air, his spear licking up to smash into its body, sending him spiralling down.

Another cloud, briefly formed beneath his feet, let him stabilize and hop backwards, allowed him to push down and away from the steps. Over twenty feet of steps cleared as he flew backwards. Rather ridiculous if you considered it, but Arthur was more focused on landing properly and getting his guard up.

By the time he was set, the couple of creatures were on him again. Damn santu sakai were dangerous, fast, smart, and reacted well. No longer were they trying for the encirclement-and-kill, but more careful attacks. Pushing him and his spear to the maximum, forcing him to keep moving.

Wounds accumulated, on both sides. As good as he was, as much an advantage the spear and his armour gave him, there was only so much he could do. Especially when a lucky grab and yank stripped his weapon from him, leaving him to desperately scramble, punch, and kick his way out the scrum and roll away, his kris now in hand.

On and on, he cut and bled them, his Yin Aura poisoning and slowing them down. Attacks grew sloppy, missing him by inches and then feet. Charges grew uncoordinated, openings wider as he slipped his blade in, cutting again and again.

Until, at last, they were down and crawling.

And all there was left was the alpha.

Hanging back, grinning widely. Knife fangs dripping saliva.

Groaning, bleeding, Arthur set himself and took its charge.

Hot breath washed over him, blood dripping out of the creature's mouth as he felt his arm creak and bend and crack; it was trying to get Arthur's arm away. One of his arms was wrapped around the alpha's body, other hand shifting as it pressed the kris into the chest, searching, searching, searching.

A different feel, something a little firmer and harder than the flesh, empty space around lungs… his blade finally found the heart. He pulled back a little, plunged it back and felt it tear right in. Felt the monster shudder, twitch, the kris in his hand shaking and twitching as the heart continued to beat, tearing itself apart on the blade.

One last gasp, the mouth squeezing tight, pushing sharpened teeth into his arm. Then, finally, the creature collapsed and only a last-minute shift of balance on Arthur's side had it falling backwards rather than on top of him.

He was now all kinds of bruised after having crashed into the jagged edges of the stairs. Pulled himself free, wincing as he was forced to pry open the mouth and free his arm.

Only to find himself having to deal with smaller monsters that had been drawn to the battle. Buried under furry bodies, rats the size of his hand scrambling over him, tearing and biting. A snake, slithering along the ground, wrapping around his leg. A ferret-like creature, tearing into him with its larger-than-normal claws. A flock of tiny birds that blazed and burnt as they landed. And some damn lizard that was eating the rats as much as it was tearing into him.

So many, that he fought and tore off. Adding to his wounds, but most not able to get through his armour, just adding tiny injuries to him. Just enough to hurt him, to make it hard. Until, eventually, he was done, the pulsing Yin Aura he had never let go taking a toll on the small monsters.

Leaving him to lie there, panting, exhausted. Blood streaming from dozens of minor wounds and his arm, waiting for everything to clot and for him to get enough energy to pull out some beast stones.

"Closer than I'd like, but at least I'm not on a pike."

Silly rhymes. Always as a way to distract himself, to help him calm down. A distraction from the pain, from the knowledge that this had been a lot closer than he had expected. Funnily enough, he wasn't that injured, not like the last fight or his collapse. What had been dangerous was how easy it could have been a problem. If he had tripped at the wrong time, slipped on the stairs, let them surround him. If he had been crippled, or the alpha had joined the fight earlier rather than waiting until all his people had died.

Small things, big things; like walking on a high wire, always so close to falling. But so long as you didn't fall, you were fine.

Realisation, slowly creeping in, that this was his life now. That all his fights for the next while might be like this. So long as he did everything right, he was fine. But the moment he slipped, the moment he made a mistake, he might not get a chance to get back up.

Just like missing the explosive footsteps of the babi ngepet mini-boss. Except more fatal.

What would have happened, if he had been thrown into the cliff face. Knocked his head around? Knocked unconscious?

There was a persistent belief that so long as you got strong enough, smart enough, tough enough, you would survive. That the good made their way through wars or scuffles with barely a scratch. A lie told by movies and stories, over and over again. The reality was that luck played such a massive part.

The survivors weren't just the good or the best. They were also the luckiest.

Good thing he had always been the lucky sort.

Chapter 64

By the time he finished extracting all the monster cores and limped up the stairs back to his starting position, most of his wounds had healed. Only his arm was still healing and that one he had wrapped up tight with bandages after taking off his bracer. He had to adjust the bracer, push the leather back into place, and add some duct tape on the inside just so that it didn't bite into his skin since the alpha's mouth had pierced and driven the leather into his hand.

Terrible.

Pack back on him, Arthur made his way two thirds of the way to the main entrance of the pyramid cautiously. Ready to drop pack and back off if something came out, but he found nothing. Eventually he dropped the pack on the outside near the door and slipped in, not wanting to be burdened when he was attacked.

He needed to move fast. The sun was beginning to set and when that happened, he would not be exploring the inside of the pyramid. Right now, with the low-hanging sun shedding light, there was actually quite a bit more illumination than when he first arrived, just from certain angles.

Not great if he had to rely just on his mortal eyes, but Enhanced Eyesight once again came in clutch.

He poked his head in quickly, pulled back almost immediately after. Thought about what he saw and noted nothing tried to kill him. Still, he stuck his spear in ahead first, just in case whatever was waiting was smart. Still nothing troubled him, so he stepped in, stepped left immediately and put his back to the wall.

No hanging around the fatal funnel and highlighting himself in the door. It might work for gunslingers in old and bad Westerns but he neither had a gun or wanted to be like Rick. He much preferred not to die, no matter what people might think of him. Spear pointed at the interior, he waited for his eyes to fully adjust to the gloom.

Soaring walls, staggered inwards and held aloft by pillars. To his surprise, rather than multiple levels, it was just one giant pyramid. Nothing at all within but the pillars and an altar right in the center of the thing. Exit on the other end. A few shafts of light coming in from high above, just enough to illuminate things a little and not leave the place entirely gloomy.

He noted small figures on the ceiling, realised what the soft and slightly mushy footing was from. Not that the smell of guano was that hard to mistake, not once you had smelled it a few times. Surprisingly, nowhere near as pungent as bigger mammal droppings which was a good thing, considering just how much there likely was.

No other santu sakai that he saw, at least not immediately. No mewling pups or grieving female ghosts. A good thing, for a variety of reasons, none of which Arthur intended to interrogate. That way lay a lot of grief and moralising and whining.

He stalked in, pushing for action. Searching for their lair, for the place the santu sakai had slept and ate and done other things. Nothing within, though after a while, he began to pick out tracks in the earth. Not enough light in here for much greenery to grow, which made picking out where the creatures walked before easier.

Not much variation, mostly a circling pathway. Though a rather pungent-smelling corner spoke of a lack of hygiene. But everything else, all the tracks, they led to the altar. An altar, he realised that had been consistently cleared, even though droppings must have fallen on it.

That really didn't give him a good feeling.

Inch by inch, foot by foot, he crept closer. He drew a deep breath, slowed down as he came near. Grimaced when he saw the bones, stared at what kinds they were. Some were rather concerning: human-looking tibias, rib cages broken apart, even a skull. He couldn't tell if they were the real bones of climbers or something the Tower had created just to mess him up.

He looked away from them, walked the rest of the way to the altar. Saw how it had been set up, the channels cut into them all over the top. He stared at the way liquid would pool at the top and flow down the channels. Arthur frowned, scanning the surroundings again, and made his decision.

A quick spin around of the weapon, driving the tip of the spear into the soft ground. He reached over, dug deep into the side of the table-like altar and along the cracks. Fingers beneath the protruding edge of the table, strained upwards with his knees and back and arms. It stuck, hundreds of pounds of stone refusing to move and he eventually released it, frustrated.

Something was under there, he knew that.

He waited, pulling at the energies deep within him, and activated the Heavenly Sage's Mischief. Once he felt it fully activate, he reached again and gripped the altar once more. He surged upwards as hard as he could and felt a sucking, tearing feeling course through the table itself as what was sticking and gumming up the works gave way. Strands of dried blood and gum sap tore apart, pulling at the table top as he lifted and then threw it over, watching it flip over the edge.

Within, dark and dried black blood had pooled beneath. Gum and tree sap congealed, multiple tiny columns all across the surface to hold the table top aloft and offer a space for the blood to gather and flow. All leading into a central area where a dark heart lay.

When it beat, Arthur couldn't even say he was surprised. Not happy to see it, of course, but not surprised.

"That's rather messed up."

The heart beat again, dried blood moving in and out. He stared at it, wondering what he was meant to do with something like that. It was obviously an enchanted item of some form, but what it was, what it did, what it was meant for...

Well, nothing in the wikis had ever mentioned anything like it.

"Okay. Think this through. Enchanted item. Sucking in blood, using it because it's a heart. Will it die if it doesn't have blood? Will it die if I don't feed it blood? Do I have to bleed on it?" Arthur started speaking out loud and then jerked to a stop, realizing what he was doing. He reached sideways, grabbed the spear, and scanned the surroundings.

The bats rustled a little above, but none of them were coming down so far. That was a good thing, so he turned his attention back to the heart. He couldn't figure out what he needed to do if he wanted the heart. Well, he was definitely taking it, no matter how gross it was. The question was how to store it.

"My kingdom for a jar," Arthur said. Nothing in his backpack, he knew that much. He had his water flask but it wouldn't fit. He didn't carry glass, because he got beaten up too often. Without a choice, he wandered around the building hoping to find something. In a corner, a rather grotesque corner, he found what he was looking for.

"Amphora. Pretty sure that's the word..." Arthur picked up the clay jug with its cork stopper somehow still firmly sealed. Used to store the organs of priests in Egypt or so he recalled. Again, like so many things in his life, it came from glimpses and vague memories in thirty-second clips shown to him while he browsed social media or watched someone else do it.

Stupid-ass way to learn, though it did leave weird nuggets of information scattered through his brain.

He popped open the seal with the aid of his kris, managing to unseal the gum, and pour out what was, thankfully, only sand. No weird splotchy organs within. He grabbed another intact jar anyway, just in case it were useful or he ended up breaking this one, and returned to the heart. It looked like the heart would fit through the amphora's wide mouth.

After a few minutes of gross handling, he had the heart stored. Using the gum and dried blood, sealed away the entire thing, which was filled to the brim with still-gummy blood. Hopefully that was enough because he would not be feeding it his own blood. Or even opening the damn thing again anytime soon.

Water on his hand to clean it and after checking that the other amphora had nothing but sand, he took both over to his backpack.

All this, for a single magical item.

As he stood up after storing the jars away inside shreds of his clothing, he pulled up the notification again that had appeared when he'd grabbed the heart. Wondering if it was worth it.

Chapter 65

Seri Pahang Heart (Enchantment Item)

The heart of Seri Pahang has been preserved via powerful occult rituals. The heart can be utilized in magical rituals and to empower enchantments related to the creature's nature.

That was it. Not a lot of information at all, no indication of cost or price or anything else. It drove him nuts, and Arthur knew there was nothing to be done till he managed to make it to a Tower administrative center and have them make use of it. He might, perhaps, be able to buy something to store it away; but chances were, he would be better off getting the damn Tower to build him something with it.

Of course, it would help if he could recall more details about Seri Pahang. He knew it was a sea creature, Malaysia's version of the Loch Ness monster. Which, if he really thought of it, would be a rather sad thing. Also incongruous, since there were no large lakes around here, but again. Magical Tower.

More importantly, he could not recall any of its special abilities. Some control of water, of course, large size. Ability to breathe underwater maybe? Not particularly useful abilities, though... well. Playing Giant Man might be fun. As they said, size had a quality of its own.

In the meantime, as he mused about the potential new magical equipment he might have, Arthur had his backpack on as he traversed the inside of the pyramid. Rather than going around and triggering the appearance of even more monsters, he figured he might as well go in the direction he knew. More importantly, it gave him a chance to double-check the altar and surroundings for any additional magical or enchanted equipment.

To little surprise, there was nothing. Not at all unusual considering this was still a Beginner Tower. Finding even this heart was a stroke of pure luck, considering he would never have found this location if he hadn't been knocked off the trail by the babi ngepet. He'd have to thank the creature if he saw it again, preferably with the pointed end of his spear. Repeatedly and vigorously.

Exiting the other end of the pyramid, Arthur scanned the surroundings. The sun had nearly fully set by now, leaving him to stare at a gloomy, shadowed set of ruins. A sudden ill feeling poured through him, causing the hairs at the back of his neck to stand up, and he realised he had no desire to journey through the ruins in the dark.

Furthermore, as the sun set, the bats within the pyramid were waking and he had no desire to deal with them either.

"There..." No sooner had he spotted it that he jogged over, scanning the surroundings for trouble. Nothing attacked him before he reached the sloped-edge, half-tumbled-down building. The roof had come down at an angle, leaving him with cover on three sides and a sloped roof, though nothing to block entry.

Nothing for it.

He slipped within, pulled off his pack once he was certain nothing was coming and set up some simple rope traps right inside his current lair to warn him of approaching problems. Then, creeping all the way to back, bag propped against the side, he waited for the coming of the night.

Keeping an eye out and a hand on his spear, he began the process of cultivating. Pulling in energy to refill his empty stores of basic energy. He would have preferred to do some core cultivation—he had quite the collection by now—but that took more concentration than he cared to devote.

Not right now, not when every nocturnal creature was waking up.

Not when he was still shivering a little at the cold, the sense that something out here was not to be trifled with. Not at night at least.

Hours passed, and outside of one rather curious four-legged creature that ran off after a jab with his spear, Arthur was not disturbed. Yet the sense of being watched, of something lurking, only increased.

The first sign that his concerns were not the workings of an overtired, paranoid mind was the drop in temperature. Sufficiently so that Arthur's breath puffed outwards as he exhaled through his mouth. Not an everyday occurrence in most of inhabited Malaysia. His eyes widened a little, having only ever seen this happen one lucky day at Genting Highlands. A bachelor party for a schoolmate, one last hurrah that involved more gambling and drinking than strippers. A waste of funds in Arthur's view, but he could not say no to his senior, not even if the entire trip had taken a week of hard work to save up for. And then another two weeks to pay off everything they spent.

Still, the memory of stumbling out of the casino, holding his friend as they wandered down to the rental apartment and watching their breath plume in the cold night air was worthwhile. It had only ever been something he had seen in TV shows. And then, he had experienced it himself.

And here it was again.

Next, were lights. Pale, ghostly lights forming along the edges of the wall, passing through them. Making him realise that whatever was coming cared not for the physical.

Not a good thing, not for him.

He ran through his options. Refined Energy Dart might kill a few. He knew those attacks were partly energy-based. Usable against ghosts and wisps and things somewhat insubstantial. Most elemental attacks had the benefit of offering that kind of advantage.

He had meant to get more techniques like that, especially when he exited the Tower. The thing was, you weren't meant to face pure elemental or spiritual creatures now, not ghosts or spirit or their like. Not till later. That was an Advanced Tower challenge, not meant to be dealt with here. At least, that was the theory. Even when there were spirits and ghosts, you were supposed to be able to handle them.

Except the Tower didn't always play fair. Sometimes, things went bad, and if you weren't on the easiest path, these things could happen. Monsters that you weren't meant to handle, and all you could do was figure out how to deal with them.

The Refined Energy Darts, Exploding or not, couldn't take out so many of these ghosts. They weren't even that strong, he assumed. There were just a lot of them. He didn't think he would have enough energy to kill them all, and if he did, it'd be a waste anyway.

No. These creatures, they were so numerous he was better off utilizing something like his aura. Question was, if they were ghosts, would a Yin Aura kill them or make them stronger?

One of the lights drifted over, touched his shoulder before he could shift away in time. The skin and muscle around the part touched froze over, numbing. He shuddered a little, but the good news was that the light flickered and died.

He started counting inside his head, waiting for his body to warm up and heal. He paid more attention, trying to edge away from the lights, curious if he could just tank it over. By the time he hit thirty, the number of drifting lights, the tiny will-o'-the-wisp ghosts had more than doubled. With so little space to move in, another had landed on his leg, numbing his calf area.

Still, he counted, taking another on his left hand. It froze it over, made his fingers spasm a little though he still had a numbed, clumsy control over it. Not great, but viable. Out of curiosity, as one drifted near his face, he swung the same hand through it again. Felt the rush of cold wash over his limb, his hand spasming shut and gripping tight as tendons and muscles cramped.

He let out a little cry, nerves and muscles wide awake like plunging a hand into a bucket of ice. He couldn't even move the fingers anymore and only a hasty shove of it into his other armpit, a bit-off curse word, kept him from worrying about things like frostbite.

How insane would it be to get frostbite and lose digits in Malaysia? He might even get on the local Guinness World Record book.

Not the way he wanted to get famous.

Not that he ever wanted fame.

Cursing, he made note not to get hit in the same spot twice. It was painful, dangerous even. A push on his energy helped him begin the healing the process, electric shock and tingles rushing into his limb. Painful enough that he wanted to cry.

Seventy-eight seconds, and his shoulder felt back to normal. His calf was halfway there, but he had a feeling he had slowed the entire process down by getting hit more. All the while, he was shifting and twisting, trying to dodge the ghosts. It wouldn't work, not forever.

Making a decision, he pulled at his Yin Aura. He had been running it, prepping it to start all this time, and now he let it coat his other foot, push it out just a little further from his body there. It was a weird, uncomfortable bulge, but when the next ghost flowed through it, he'd know.

Chapter 66

What happened next was a strange juxtaposition of competing energies. On the one hand, he saw the floating light flare brighter, the energy within his Yin Aura dip. He could feel it almost literally sucking away his power, empowering the creature. At the same time, he felt unvarnished Tower energy—the portions of it that still were part of his body, his Yin Aura, the technique—attack the creature. Tearing at it.

Competing energies, both of them flickering back and forth till his aura, put under unusual strain from it all, collapsed. Moments later, the ghostly light brightened even further and then, to Arthur's surprise, disappeared.

"What in the hundred hells?"

No answer, but he was not waiting around to figure it all the way out. Two more of the ghosts impacted his body, flowed into him, freezing buttock and right chest. It made him groan, his lung straining for a second before warmth rushed in from the heart and dantian to cover it. Good to know his body automatically safeguarded the most important parts.

Could he maybe use what he knew about the Energy Dart, the way he could form it anywhere and make it part of his Yin Aura? He had not tried it, because he had always been focused on other options. The energy of the dart, the way it had been created was so different too. Not a steady state form of energy but more explosive.

It was why the Exploding Energy Dart was so easy to create. And why creating a weapon wasn't.

Not the time to experiment.

Instead he pushed his Yin Aura out. He had a feeling that what had happened was a matter of stability, that the ghosts—weak as they were— could not handle the full influx of Yin Aura. He was empowering them, but the same Tower energy was also hurting them, destabilizing them. Then, the absence of more Yin energy was enough to cause them to fail.

So, all he had to do was pulse his aura.

Not too fast though, otherwise they would just suck it all up and not be hurt. Not too slow, or else his control would fail. Energy expanded around him in a sphere, a sphere that he made easier to manage by crouching down, hugging his body close. The aura swept out, a globe of energy that he swore was purple but might just be his imagination.

It flared bright at multiple spots, coming into contact with the ghosts. His control of the aura churned and twisted, buckling in his mind and spirit and he fought to keep it smooth. To keep feeding energy into it, desperate to not lose it all before enough of the Tower energy had cracked these creatures apart.

He tried not to let the aura flow out too far, tried to keep it only a few feet around him. Watched as his Tower energy reserves dropped, every moment that the aura interacted with these monsters.

Pressure kept building, his control like holding onto a flopping, slick eel. Moments later, he dropped it rather than let it backlash against him. Once more, a few of the ghosts burned bright and then disappeared. Not all of them. A few of the lights at the far edges of his aura had brightened and managed to weather the storm and surge of power, continuing to exist even after the sudden loss.

They darted forwards, heading towards Arthur as though guided now by a living will. He threw up the Yin Aura again, finding that they were caught in it and slowing down as they absorbed his energy. He breathed out in relief, then turned his attention once again to the twisting of power, the way his aura continued to attempt to escape him.

He let it pour power into the ghosts, pulled it back, shrinking his own aura. Watched as they shuddered, twisted and then pushed again. That movement, that sudden change saw another flare, a destruction of the creatures' structural integrity.

More effective but harder to control.

Gritting his teeth as a second pulse failed, his threads folding backwards and making his meridians ache. He gritted his teeth, forcing the pain aside as he rebuilt his technique once more. By the time he got control again, a couple of the empowered ghosts had struck him. It left him cold, pained, and numb, their strength greater than the ones which had impacted before.

For a time, he struggled with his frozen body, at getting the meridians and energy to move properly. He only finalized it moments before he was struck by one of the ghosts. It paused, drifting back and forth before Arthur pulled his weave all the way back to his body.

Watched it explode and then poured out his power again.

He knew now what he needed to do for the rest of the night. Train his aura, control and empower and feed these ghosts, and kill them with generosity. If he failed, he would suffer. Fail too often and he would die. So that was his test.

Learn control, wield his aura. Or die trying.

Morning came slowly, the first signs of it the reduced number of ghosts. They had never stopped coming, all through the night. Sometimes, there was a break, a few less such that he would remove the flow of energy entirely and take the attacks on his body. Feel the chill steal through him, the numb pain that lulled him to rest. That break never lasted long, for soon enough ghosts would come once again and he was forced to utilize his Yin Aura.

Desperation and focus had him pour energy and attention to the technique. He had been stuck before this, unable to progress it meaningfully for weeks. Now, with no other choice, with death a moment away, he found himself tapping into a well of creativity, trying and testing ever more elaborate weaves and methods of control.

In the last hour before dawn, something had clicked. Something in the way he wielded all of it worked, and finally, a small insistent pressure appeared in his mind. His control of the Yin Aura felt easier than ever, the Tower aiding him as much as the simplified weaves he practised. Energy pouring all through him, giving him what he needed. The control to pulse his power as it rippled outwards and retracted, empowering and killing the spirits one after the other.

Now, with the energy gone, he let that insistent demand from the Tower blossom.

Yin Aura (Level 1)

Allows the extrusion of Yin energy into the user's aura. Yin aura has multiple uses and effects, most commonly including poison, lethargy, somnolence, and fatigue. Yin energy also promotes intuitive leaps, introspection, and cold energy states. Only one aspect may be used at this time.
Cost: 2 Energy per Minute

Fascinating indeed, that description. He had only thus far focused on the poison aspect of his Yin energy, drawing understanding of it from his kris. Now, however, it was clear that he could use not only the debuff effects of Yin energy but even utilize it as a buff. How that would work, of course, he was not certain. But he also knew how the colder, chillier, and more intuitive aspects of Yin energy had aided him during his trek.

Of course, all that would require training and testing. And after the night that he had, not getting an ounce of sleep through the day and his Tower energy stores low, he knew better than to expect to get any more training done.

Especially when he couldn't afford to waste time either, resting the day away. Not only just to get away from the ghosts in here, but also to avoid the impending pack of monsters.

Crawling out of his makeshift shelter, Arthur ran through a series of quick stretches before beginning his hike out. He still had a mountain range to traverse.

Chapter 67

Normally, skipping a night's sleep wouldn't be too bad. He had done it often enough, and with his new Tower infused and rebuilt body, it should have been easier. A couple of cups of coffee, or one good fight, and he would be right as rain to keep going. At least for another twelve hours.

Problem was, he neither had a cup of *kopi* or had a usual night. It wasn't as though he was running deliveries all night long or driven drunk socialites home—the latter he had done on one of the few occasions he managed to borrow a vehicle. No, the reason he was tired was because he'd spent the whole evening the day before fighting for his life.

Even for a climber, that was a bit much.

It was why his feet were dragging a little, his mind a little foggy. Twice, he'd nearly missed the attacks before they launched, forcing him to scramble at the last moment to defend himself. He'd picked up even more light wounds, much to his chagrin, but nothing that would slow him down further.

Once he exited the ruins, Arthur knew the attacks were going to come faster than ever. Still, he wanted to put some distance between himself and the haunted location, so he kept pushing. Dangling the prospect of a rest just fifteen minutes later.

Of course, like all good hiking leaders, that fifteen minutes was always just around the corner.

The next clearing, the next pond, the next place to rest.

That is until he nearly stumbled right into the middle of a *hong mama* nest. The oversized red ants with massive pincers forced him to scramble and run for a good ten minutes before they managed to scatter sufficiently. He still kept jogging for a bit, the last adrenaline jolt giving him a ninth wind.

Till, coming to a clear pond, one that was empty and—after prodding with his spear butt carefully—shallow enough to lack any nasty surprises, he flopped down beside the water. He quickly washed his face and skin, refilled his second water bottle after dumping its contents into his main one and waited.

He would drink once he was certain his skin wasn't reacting to the water. Never know what might be in it, though thankfully poisoned resources like this were rare. You could still get sick drinking stagnant water and, if you were really unlucky, pick up a few parasites. But the other side of having a Tower-remade body was that most of those ailments ended in a few hours rather than days.

Even so, no reason not to be careful.

Instead, he rested, backpack set aside, breathing slowing. He eyed the surroundings, debating if it was worth catching a nap here, if the danger of lounging beside the only water source around was too great. Eventually, he decided not to linger. Better to find a place a short distance away, but he did need a nap.

Fifteen minutes. Maybe half an hour. Just enough to wake him up, drive away the cobwebs in his brain.

In the meantime, he could cultivate some energy into his dantian while waiting for his skin to react. He should have enough energy and attention to spare, and every inch of power was necessary.

Waking up from his nap, rolling out from under the log after checking for lurking monsters, Arthur felt a lot better. He grimaced moments later when he realised his catnap had lasted longer than he initially wanted. Hard to tell just with the sun's positioning of course, but at a guess from the angle shown, he had slept for at least an hour. Maybe an hour and a half.

Obviously, his body had needed it.

Another grimace, a shake of the head, and then Arthur began walking, heading in the direction the set of stones he had laid out before he went to bed. Never know what might happen and what he'd forget, especially being as tired as he was.

He made it three steps out of the small clearing he had been in when the cat jumped at him. Reacting purely on instinct, Arthur dodged low, stuck his hand out, and grabbed it by the neck and spun, slamming the creature into the side of a nearby tree. The impact shocked the creature, causing feet that had begun to close to flinch open. Another throw, almost directly upward, had the cat flailing little limbs. The kuching hitam attempted to gather itself, only for gravity and an empowered thrust to catch it in the head.

A final twist of the spear head dropped the creature to the ground, the only damage some small scratches on his arm.

"Damn ambush predators," Arthur grumbled.

Bending down low, he quickly cut the creature open and extracted the monster core, wiped it down on the dirt and grass along with his hand and then strolled away. Warily.

The rest of the day was going to be a pain and a half, but at least his head didn't feel entirely clouded. Now, all he had to do was make his way up the mountain.

Not even an hour later, already looking for a place to camp with the sun beginning to set, Arthur came across one of the many cliff faces. He moved gingerly to the edge and grimaced, eyeing the large gap between him and the next cliff face. Over forty feet of open air between, and looking from side to side, he could not note any easy way across.

So.

Run and jump. Or climb down over a hundred feet and then do it the other way.

Forty feet plus was an impossible jump. He was pretty sure the world record, pre-Tower, was just over twenty feet. Quite the distance, and amazing, but he was no long jumper. He had trained a little, but the muscles and skill required was something else. He might, if he was good, have done about half of that he before entering the Tower.

Now, he figured he could clear twenty feet just by sheer Tower strength. He still had to cover twice that distance, though.

"Would a Cloud Step jump work as well?" Arthur asked the air. "Or will I be forced to have a spill?"

No answer of course. Well. Spell. Spill. Horrible rhyming sense.

"Doesn't matter, does it?" He sighed as he backed off, trying to get himself as much running space as possible. He couldn't afford the time to do this safely, so he had better hope his Cloud Step would work. First,

Heavenly Sage's Mischief, pouring ever more power into him to give him more strength.

Then, tightening all the straps of his backpack, making sure everything was strapped down, he bounced a few times on his feet, trying to get everything settled. Making sure he was ready.

Ready, he sprinted forward. Feet tearing into the dirt, leaving clods of soil behind him. Arms pumping as fast as he could, pushing his body to accelerate as fast as possible till one step from the edge he leapt. Upwards and forwards as hard as he could, spinning through the air.

Epogee.

A cloud formed beneath his foot. He slammed into it, feeling it give way just a little, robbing him of a touch of momentum. He pushed, as hard as he could, felt the energy he used to form it breaking apart. Puff of air and moisture behind him, as he rose ever higher.

He had done this, on numerous platforms on the sixth floor. Bouncing back and forth between platforms, defying gravity.

Leaping to a better future.

Higher and higher, till he was in the air and falling.

Cliff face rushing to him.

Howling: "*Celakaaaaaa!*"

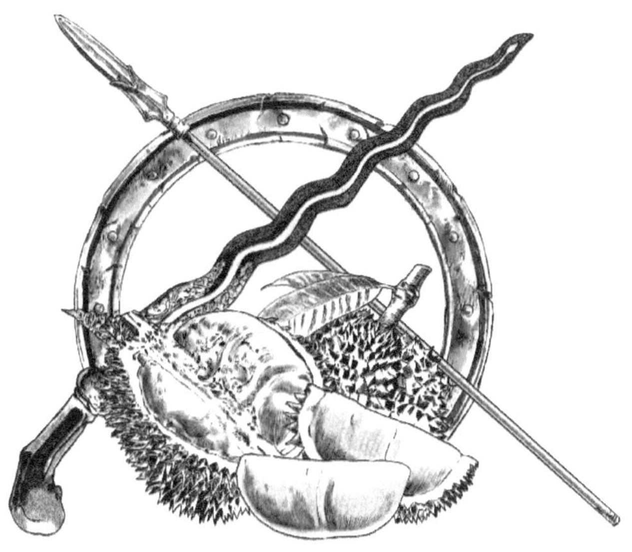

Chapter 68

Arthur slammed into the cliff a foot past the edge, rolled over and over onto his backpack and his face. Grimacing as he came up, feeling the edge of his pot and the other contents of his backpack digging into him. Hoping he didn't break the jar with the heart.

Hearing the crumbling of the cliff behind him.

That spurred him on, content to get away before it came crashing down.

Far enough away from the cliff edge to be safe, Arthur noted a small cave. He debated what to do, considered the falling sun. It was a little early. He could have pushed on for a few more hours, but if the cave was empty, it was a safe position to sleep. Better than hunkering under a fallen log or around a makeshift barrier or tied to a tree.

Decision made, Arthur moved towards the cave, poking his head in for a look. Not able to see much, he shifted his metal flask, pulling it out and using it to shine some light within. It offered a very badly diffracted beam inside, but with his Enhanced Sight, it was enough to pick the ferret-like creature lunging for his face.

Arthur didn't manage to get his spear up in time, only managing to flip the creature sideways as he raised the spear towards the charging monster. It crashed into him, unbalancing him for a moment and forcing him to drop the flask and scramble to keep his crouched footing.

A few desperate moments later, he managed to kill the damn thing, haft of the spear on its neck and his full body weight crushing the ferret's trachea. Or the monster equivalent of a ferret, anyway. Once it stopped trying to fight, he stabbed it open and extracted the small core before checking carefully for more monsters.

Thankfully, the rest of the cave was empty. He slipped in soon after, moving the couple of pieces of dried dung to the corner and covering it all with sand. Thankfully, it wasn't too fragrant, so sleep would not be too hard to acquire.

One last moment to set up a simple trap-and-alert system with bell and rope, and then he had his backpack off as his pillow. Eyes drifting close, he pulled up his status as the last thing to do this night.

Cultivation Speed: 2.773 Yin

Energy Pool: 11/30 (Yin) + (7/7)

Refinement Speed: 0.1421

Refined Energy: 0.27 (40) +(0/3)

Attributes and Traits

Mind: 15 (Multi-Tasking, Quick Learner, Perfect Recall)

Body: 25 (Enhanced Eyesight, Yin Body, Swiftness, Fast Twitch Faster, Lightning Reflexes, Explosive Strength)

Spirit: 15 (Sticky Energy, From the Dregs, Strengthened Aura)

Techniques

Night Emperor Cultivation Technique

Focused Strike

Accelerated Healing – Refined Energy (Grade III)

Heavenly Sage's Mischief

Refined Energy Dart

Bark Skin

Seven Cloud Stepping Technique (197%)

Poket Simpanan Tua (135%) (Refined Energy Dart - 84% Integrity)

Imbued Strike - Yin Poison

Yin Aura (Level 1) (108.4%)

Partial Techniques

Simultaneous Flow (189.3%)

Yin-Yang Energy Exchange (94.1%)

Yin Poison Darts (49.9%)

So close to being able to use multiple techniques at the same time. He needed to spend more time working on that, but splitting his attention while traversing the forest was a bad idea. Still, he could try some small degree of it later tomorrow. He certainly needed to cultivate to acquire some more energy. Even if he used refined energy more, Tower energy was needed to survive on a day-to-day basis, not to mention its use for a lot of his more basic techniques.

Tonight, perhaps. When he woke up, he'd cultivate.

Tonight's cultivation process was different. Perhaps with his constant use of Yin Aura and his expanded understanding of what Yin chi could do. But when he began to process the Tower energy into his body, filtering it out and changing it within his meridians as necessary, Arthur could swear he could feel the differences.

It was ephemeral at first, transient in nature, like the very ghosts he had fought before. By the time he focused on it, for one reason or another, it was gone. He did not try to push the matter, knowing that it was not the kind of energy he was attempting to create right now.

Instead, he tried to understand it, taste the differences in chi. Feel how it interacted with his body, where it was stronger in his meridians and where it faded. What the changes were as time went on, because he knew he would need to wield those changes at a later time.

A part of him wondered if it was worth it, if he could not simply purchase some technique or guidance from the Tower about all the forms of Yin energy there were. He had no time to train it here, but at least if he could understand some portions, he could push his understanding faster when he got to it. Then again, information coming from the Tower, manuals about techniques, provided an aid, but it was well known such information had limitations too.

No, better to do train when he could, especially if he could split his time, attention, and energy across multiple goals. Save time a little, because it all added up. Same with his attempts later on at cultivating this new energy and activating another technique. If he could do both, how amazing would that be?

Methods to do so were rare, expensive in the Tower if they were even available to purchase. And often, entirely unnecessary and a waste of time. Pulling only a single point of energy in an hour made little sense. Not when you could just sit down, cultivate properly, and pull multiple points especially as you grew stronger and acquired proper cultivation methods. Even worse, often these moving cultivation methods supplanted normal cultivation methods entirely.

There were a few who did it, but those few were either incredibly lucky to acquire rare techniques or enchanted items that sped up such a process.

Which was why, even if he did try to learn and figure out how to do it himself, he wasn't disappointed when he failed to get his other techniques working. The more important aspect of all this was learning how to move energy simultaneously. After all, when he could use his Simultaneous Flow technique properly, he could start channelling multiple full-body techniques. He could run Bark Skin and Heavenly Sage's Mischief at the same time. Or even the Yin Aura and the Bark Skin, making him much, much harder to kill.

Next step, of course, was to upgrade Bark Skin. Make it tougher, make it Bark Body or Iron Hide or whatever variation there was out there. He couldn't exactly recall anymore, never having paid that much attention to the next level. After all, he had so much to learn, and the exact variations were unknown. Not till he came in, not till he had actually tried everything and seen what worked for him.

That was the difference between practise and reality. You could plan all you wanted, but the moment you were stabbed and bitten, all those plans went out the window.

Then you adapted.

Just like he had to his acquiring his Seal and becoming a Clan Head. And how he was forced to adapt to traveling on this floor. He would improve, adapt, and move on—climb out of this damn Tower.

No matter what.

Chapter 69

Days traveling forwards. No further insane encounters, though he did meet a damn babi ngepet. This time around, knowing what it could do, Arthur made sure not to get near its explosive footsteps, instead using his spear to stab deep and then yank his spear out. Hitting the creature with multiple attacks, utilizing his Cloud Step to head upwards or sideways, while nearby trees shook and broke under the creature's assault.

The entire fight had taken minutes—which was long—and by the end, he had fallen over, panting and exhausted. This kind of fight, where he had to constantly be on the move, where a single mistake could end him, was draining to the extreme.

Even so, once the battle was over, he pushed on, days blending into one another. For Arthur, the process of climbing through the eighth floor fell into the same routine. Push as hard and fast as he could through the day, cultivate at night and listen to the howls of the wolf packs towards the end.

Twice, he had to backtrack. The first time was the worst, when he encountered a swampy piece of land and muddy lake stretching for as far as he could see. Without a craft to utilize and cross the space, nor with the ability to Water Walk, he could not afford to risk swimming and be attacked by the creatures within the lake.

There definitely were creatures within, not the least of which were the ubiquitous leeches. If he never had to fight them again, he would be super grateful.

Going around the lake had taken him over two days, with numerous battles as the lake itself was a major water source. He even had his first encounter with a kind of freshwater crocodile that was so uncommon these days in Malaysia, driven nearly to extinction except for a few remote places and the zoos. The crocodile came out of the lake, snapping at Arthur and forcing him to skip backwards before he embedded his spear in its head.

The second time he had to backtrack was when he ran into a steep cliff face that curved in such a way that there was no entrance to the other side. That one, luckily, had only cost him half a day. Thankfully, he had caught sight of the old trail to the east of where he was. He bushwacked over, cut across the trail, crossed its stone bridge, and then, afterwards, he went back to traversing the land once more and trying to regain lost time.

Each night he delayed, the howls grew louder. In the mountains, with the echoing rocks, it was impossible to tell how close they were. At times, it felt like they were over the next hill. At other times, many valleys away.

In the end, the only thing he knew for certain was that they were close.

Thankfully, so was he.

Cresting the latest hill, he blinked at what he spotted. A simple *paifang*, a free-standing arch that was used by the Chinese like a gate to mark the borders of a residence or property line. In this case, if he had to guess, it was the marker for the end of this floor.

Which meant, as he stood there, catching his breath…

There! Movement near the gate itself. What he had believed to be a rock at first glance was shifting, rising up, up, up. Its newly risen head brushed the bottom of the gate. Twelve, fifteen feet tall at the least, and a rocky and pale countenance the colour of bleached clay.

"An elemental? Come on, that's not even to theme!" Arthur grumbled. A bit of a lie, that, because mud monsters and the like were part of the folk tales. After all, the local religions were all about spirits, though few gave them humanoid figures.

The rather more important thing was how difficult it would be to handle the fight. Elementals were well known to be lacking in vital spots. Killing them was a slog, requiring you to carve away pieces of their main body till the energy animating the body fled.

"Yin Aura it is. Along with Imbued Strike, probably. Though maybe a bunch of Refined Exploding Energy Darts?" Arthur muttered to himself as he ambled down the way to the creature. He shifted direction a little, having spotted the trail that met up at the end.

No way to cross to the next level without going through the gates. Magical barriers made sure of that.

Arthur only barely managed to make it onto the road when another howl erupted. This time around, it sounded much too close, and casting around he realized that the creatures were visible. Eyes widening, he swore at the dozen or so wolves that were loping down the trail, coming for him.

Reflexively, he turned and began to jog away. Only long years of training and his Yin mind kept him to a slower pace rather than an all-out sprint. The damn elemental and paifang was too far away to sprint to and he would likely still have to fight it at the end. Better to reserve some strength.

At the same time, he started cudgelling his brain for details, trying to recall if he had to kill the final boss to pass through. Almost no one skipped them, of course, not without reluctance. If you wanted something good, like an enchanted item, a scroll, something useful from the Tower, then bosses were almost always guaranteed to be your best bet.

However, Arthur wasn't sure he had the time.

Feet pounding into the ground, kicking up loose dirt. Not a giant dust cloud; it was way too damp and humid for that. If anything, he had begun to sweat a little, the high humidity making it hard to dissipate heat. He would be sweating even more if he wasn't Yin-based, another nice side effect.

Still, he grabbed his flask, took a long and slow sip before placing it aside. All of it done at a light jog without looking back, so used to the motions by now, the warm water inside the flask only mildly refreshing. Disadvantage of a metal flask on a hot day, but it took battering around much better. There was a trace of metal in the spring water he'd taken, making it taste like iron and a little bitter. Limestone probably.

More importantly, his mind kept turning, searching for mentions in the wikis. There had perhaps been mentions of one or two "heroes" that had escaped a fight with floor bosses. The eighth-floor and ninth-floor bosses, maybe. Arthur was coming to a certainty that it definitely wasn't the tenth floor. Not that that was surprising. No escaping the Tower without dealing with the big final boss.

Ten minutes, he'd get to the elemental in ten minutes.

A glance backwards, and he figured he had maybe five before the lead members of the wolf pack reached him.

Five minutes was a lot of time in battle. It would be tight, but he could do it. Would do it. He still needed to get everything he could out of this Tower, and the beating Seri Pahang heart did not count as he had no idea how to utilize it.

Thinking fast, Arthur formulated his plan as he kept a close eye on the massive elemental. Not that it gave him much clue on its habits or movement patterns, standing mostly still in front of the paifang.

About a hundred feet later, any of his plans flew out of his head as the damn creature started bulging. Intuition had Arthur ready when it released the earth spike, forcing him to dodge.

"*Celaka!*" he swore.

Any chance of staying out of range and just lobbing explosive darts flew out the window and he sped up, eyeing the ever-growing number of bulges. In close and hard was the way to go, it seemed.

Chapter 70

Arthur rolled, feeling the spear of rock barrel past his head as he dodged underneath it. A moment later, left foot under him, he shoved off as hard as he could as he threw himself into another sideways roll, finishing with a one-handed kip up, throwing himself into the air and dodging another pair of attacks targeted at where he had been. For a moment, he was airborne, spinning through the air to reorient himself and see the elemental.

Staring at the creature, he released the Refined Exploding Energy Dart at the creature's groin. Once more, he was adapting to the battle, changing his battle plan as new information arrived.

He'd started out launching his Energy Darts at the creature's left leg, trying to topple it. However, as he landed on the ground and batted aside a hurling ball of stone with his spear, Arthur watched his Refined Exploding Energy Dart impact, explode, and send shards of stone skimming backwards and forwards and all around. Moments later, stone flowed towards the elemental from its surroundings, covering the wound.

Thus his change of targets and intent.

Chip the creature away, because one advantage he had was that the blasted rock elemental was not replacing its body with earth drawn from the ground. Not for the wounds he made, not for the projectiles it was hurtling at him. The once-massive creature had already shrunk by a good foot and a half, and it kept diminishing.

Problem was, it was also managing to score hits.

Hands still throbbing from the deflection, Arthur managed to dodge another fast-moving rock spear before he was caught in the backblast of an explosive cannon ball hitting just to the side of him. Shattered chunks of rock debris slammed into hip and arm, pelting him and leaving numerous bruises on open skin. Even through his armour, it hurt a little.

Didn't stop him from running closer, though. If he had the time, he might have tried to stay at a distance, but he just couldn't afford to wait it out. Nor did he know what other tricks the monster might have.

A second-wind skill to heal itself? A massive barrage of rocks? Or the ability to control earth at a distance if he stayed away?

Behind, frighteningly, the wolves had grown silent. Rather than howling and alerting him of how close they were, they ran for him, closing the gap. He couldn't even tell how close they were, not without risking a look back. And doing that was a good way of getting a spear to the face.

"Rock, spear, net." Arthur growled under his breath, ducking another attack as he worked on forming another Refined Exploding Energy Dart. "Like a lousy version of rock, paper, scissors."

Then, finally, he was there.

Leaf-covered ground the colour of bright orange, fighting on a slight slope, monster looming over him, and paifang behind it. Ten feet was huge, especially when said creature was almost twice his size. But now that he was this close, he switched out Cloud Step for Yin Aura, watching as the energy flow outwards.

Something in the ground...

He dodged sideways, moments before it erupted. Spikes of rock spinning upwards, barely a finger width in size but so sharp that it tore through the side of his armour into his leg, catching as he jerked sideways and broke the entire thing apart. He shattered more of the spikes as he moved, a two-foot radius of deadly ground half-broken.

He knew the ground was going to be weird.

No time to pay attention to the aching leg as he threw his spear at the descending rock hand. He slid across the leaf-covered ground as he battered the arm aside, his body and lack of footing betraying him. It helped him move out of the way though, so he took that as a win.

Shot his spear forwards, sliding it along the "head" of the creature. Chipped a bit of clay-like earth off, before he spun the spear, using the momentum to turn himself around and slam the shaft of the weapon into the middle of the monster.

Striking it as hard as he could, trying to see if he could crack or break the monster by sheer strength.

Rebounded, spun away, jumped into the air moments before the earth, trembling and twitching, erupted into more rocks. Took a bowling ball of a rock in his chest while releasing his own attack, tumbled down the hill as he flew backwards. Listened to the rumble and explosion of his Energy Dart, moments before he hit the ground, chest still struggling to work again, breathing interrupted and worsened by the impact as he skipped backwards on slippery ground.

Rolled sideways as he forced his body to work, just in time to get out of the way of another rock spear that impacted not too far from him. He ended up off the trail, slamming into a tree and then into a series of spiky bushes. Pain, as thorns drove into his body between gaps in armour.

At least the scream that it pulled from him got his lungs working.

Staggered back up, hid behind a tree as it got struck by a rock.

Glanced backwards to see how close the wolves were and realised that the two in the lead were much too close. Only a minute or two maybe, the pair of slavering monsters looking like they were about to fall over from the exertion but refusing to stop.

Pushed himself up, Refined Exploding Energy Dart still forming as he started running back in.

Noted that the elemental had shrunk by another foot.

An easy fight, if he wasn't pushing it. His body was patching up the pain and bruises, but his feet were not working properly because of a spike still embedded in it. But damn it. He wasn't going to, couldn't, stop now.

He dodged sideways as the elemental let loose earth spikes once again. Yin Aura all around him, so that even when he dodged the limbs, he was standing close enough to affect its body.

Keep moving, always moving.

His spear struck out whenever he could, and he began to notice the effects of the Yin Aura. The poison was affecting the creature differently from other monsters, making it more brittle rather than slowing it down directly. With each movement—as it rotated, or formed a spear or ball of stone—bits and pieces of its body were falling off. Spears that were shattered never rejoined the body, and even the ones left untouched by Arthur took forever to sink back into the earth.

Even the amount of injuries he took was decreasing. He was too fast, too skilled to get hit outright too often, and the few times he missed a dodge or had to suffer an attack, armour and enhanced strength and skill at collapsing inwards into himself helped defray the damage. Enough at least for his regeneration to keep him in the game.

Arthur was winning, without a doubt.

Which was, of course, when the lead pair of charging wolves entered the fray.

A couple of seconds of warning was all he got, before the first leapt at him. Arthur jumped backwards, watched as the erupting stone spears from the ground skewered his attacker.

"Gotcha!"

The words were more a slur, breathed out for his own sake than any attempt at getting another to hear them. No point, of course. And it still cost him.

The other wolf, a few steps behind, had skirted around and threw itself at him. His spear, twisting through the air was meant to catch and bat it aside. He didn't see—or perhaps didn't anticipate, hard to say—the ball of stone slamming into the shaft, sending the spear nearly out of his hands. Instinctive attempt to try to keep his weapon in control left him out of position for when the wolf struck him.

Bowled over, he struck the back of the elemental's leg. Wolf claws scrabbled at armour, gaping maw lunging at his face. He got out of the way, letting it strike the elemental's leg with a surprised whimper. Twisted and shoved, just enough to drop the wolf to the ground and get a foot properly under him.

Too slow, though.

More worried about getting booted by the elemental, Arthur was surprised when the arm grabbed him from above, crushed down on his body and yanked him upwards. Holding him aloft even as a pair of stone spears grew out of the body, aimed at him at point blank range.

No dodging, not anymore.

Chapter 71

Stone spears growing out of the elemental's chest were about to skewer Arthur. The hand that had reformed from a three-fingered fist into a giant putty hand locked him in place. Arthur stared at his impending doom. His mind raced for options, but his body knew what to do.

Refined Exploding Energy Dart, already ready for release when he needed it, exploded from his third eye, targeting the chest and upper arm section. Not the armpit, though close enough that it didn't matter. Even as it flew forwards, crossing the couple of feet, his body was twisting, his free right shoulder pulling backwards as his spear and arm drew back.

Focused Strike formed fast, embedded in the tip of the spear. His oldest technique, the one he had the greatest experience with. He could conjure and utilize it within microseconds, which was good, because that was all the time he had.

The explosion of refined energy buffeted his face, exposed skin, and eyes. Rock shards sent flying everywhere, his eyes tearing up as he tried to keep focused on the attack, his arm and spear rocketing forwards into the newly created gap.

It had slammed into weakened stone and earth, forming a hole twice the size of his fist. The creature was crumbling, assaulted by his Yin Aura already. The Focused Strike pierced all the way through, shattering rocks and bonds of magical energy. One of the two rock spears, all too close to the explosion stopped forming, the sharpened bulge halting.

The arm that held Arthur cracked. Freed, Arthur was pulling his spear back, even as that second rock spear fired.

It caught him high up on the chest as he fell. His leather armour, Tower-bought and enchanted for greater protection held out. Barely. The spear itself didn't pierce the armour, but the force of impact broke his collarbone and probably a rib, leaving his arm to hang helpless.

The armour also didn't do a damn thing about the momentum throwing him backwards as he fell to the ground. A leg, flailing about, kicked into rough fur as a wolf charged in, grabbing at his numbed right arm and yanking it sideways, eliciting a scream from Arthur.

He twisted, fought, tried to get some control back. He managed to do two things, even as he dodged a series of erupting rock spears. The first: holding onto his Yin Aura so that it kept robbing his opponents of vitality, the energy pulsing out of his body constantly. The second: grabbing his kris out of its sheath with his other hand.

Thrashed around like a rag doll, it took Arthur longer than he'd like to get the blade into the wolf. It skimmed off the skull, managed to slide into the side of the mouth and open it wide. It was enough to make the creature hop away into one of the elemental's moving legs, at which point it got booted to the side.

Not that Arthur did much better, because the giant foot booted him too.

Again, flying through the air. This time, he managed to keep hold of his weapon despite tumbling off the trail into the undergrowth. Pain filled him as he bounced off a tree and then another before he ended up crashing to a stop against the crumbled remains of another tree, ivy draping all across him. Yin Aura snuffed out. He was exhausted and in agony.

Thankfully, being bounced away far enough that he was out of direct line of sight meant there were no more attacks coming for the moment. Not so thankfully, he was certain half the bones in his body were cracked or broken. That thing hit like a truck, which made sense. It probably weighed as much.

Or at least a very large SUV, the kind that Americans drove who rolled coal even now when climate change was all too real because it was their God-given right.

Accelerated Healing wrapped around him, pulling energy from his core at a rapid rate to patch together his body. Crushed, bruised, and inflamed muscles. Damaged nerves and veins and arteries. Cracked bones. Overactive nerves.

Eventually, he pulled himself to his feet. He wasn't sure how much time he had lost, just lying there, letting his body fix itself and his mind to relax sufficiently that he wasn't entirely overwhelmed. No wolf coming for him, thank the gods, but he had no idea how much more time he had left before the rest of the pack arrived.

Instead, he began to inch forward, hissing with each breath. No way to use Yin Aura, not when he was healing himself, so he focused on forming a new Refined Exploding Energy Dart in his third eye.

Elemental in sight again, he let loose the attack and then hid behind the tree as a rock cannonball struck it. To his surprise, the creature was now half its initial size, barely larger than him and significantly thinner.

All that fighting, all the energy from his Yin Aura must have worn it down significantly. He could see how each moment as it shifted, its body continued crumbled as the lingering poison continued its assault on it. When his next Dart struck, it exploded and tore off a hand. Almost immediately, the hand began to reform but the body thinned further.

Arthur, pushing forwards after the creature had launched its next attack, knew he had to get in. Even if he only had his kris, he would have to kill it and take it down quick. He would not abandon the fight now. A glance to the side noted the whimpering, broken body of the second wolf, the creature still attempting to crawl forwards.

Time to finish this.

Slipped to the right, struck the elemental's arm. Smashed the pommel of his weapon into it, watched as Imbued Strike poured Yin energy into the body. A single pulse of Yin, hard and fast before he had to rebuild the technique. It infiltrated the body, causing the arm to slump and portions of it shatter as it tried to move.

A kick straight into the giant's leg. It felt like kicking a steel rod, or almost worse. Incredibly painful even after numerous years of training doing much the same. Incredibly stupid if not for the fact that his shin was covered with armour, blunting the impact somewhat.

That and the fact that his Imbued Strike and the Yin poison was making the body more fragile. Rather than unyielding stone, it cracked and shattered, leaving the creature tottering. Even as Arthur pulled back, the elemental tried to step forwards with the other leg, putting its weight entirely on the damaged side.

A bad choice, as it crumbled and broke beneath the weight.

The elemental fell, body crashing into the ground. More of its body cracked and shattered and Arthur hobbled over, exhaustion running through him as he grabbed for his spear. He desperately wanted to use Yin Aura again, take the creature all the way apart, but he had noted the other problem.

The rest of the pack were here, all of them streaming in.

He'd run out of time, damn it.

Chapter 72

Not Imbued Strike, that wouldn't work. Not right now. Instead, he got ready to utilize Focused Strike, knowing he would only get in a few of those attacks when they arrived. He'd need to make sure each of them actually was fatal. More importantly, he needed to create an opportunity for his attacks. Which was why when the first four closed in, he released the Refined Exploding Energy Dart he had formed.

Watched as it struck and blew the first wolf back into the another, fouling up two others on his left. Leaving the one on the right to keep charging, alone.

Arthur lunged, hissed as his leg collapsed beneath him; but Focused Strike helped him punch through the bones on the front of the wolf's body and embed the spear in lungs and torso. He rolled to the side, unable to stand as his body rebelled, pain washing over him as he extracted the weapon.

Another attack, swinging his spear to clip a wolf on the haft. Watched the wolf fall, bowl over another, messing up the charge. He managed to spin the spear around far enough to get his butt targeted and ready when the next monster lunged forward so that it took the blunt tip on its jaw, forcing it back.

Then, he was standing, swinging his weapon back around and down. Focused Strike to hammer the haft and blade in a downward strike onto the pair of wolves that were struggling back up, spear tip piercing skin a little but mostly intent on crushing bone. The already injured wolf that had taken his Energy Dart slumped, unable to get up.

Before he could rejoice, pain and pressure on his calf. Another wolf slamming into him, mouth clamping down, trying to pull him off his feet.

He let go of his spear with one hand, punched down with Focused Strike. Pounding the skull hard, crushing orbital lobe before he repeated the motion. The second punch pried the mouth off his leg, allowed him to stagger back and shorten his spear with a jerk and slide motion to catch a wolf as it leapt.

Cursing as his kris was nearly torn from his hand again.

His breathing came short and fast as pain and exhaustion threatened to overwhelm him. Already overwhelmed his training, such that he wasn't breathing right. Out of the corner of his eyes, motion.

Six more wolves, all of them rushing at him. He waited, backing off now, waving his recovered spear before him. Debating if he should fight short spear and kris together, as the creatures grouped up. Cursing himself and his traitorous body for failing to take out more than two of the wolves. He heavily injured another, the poor thing still pawing at its face. So call it three.

Leaving seven. One hanging back, six spreading out.

Before they could spread too far, Arthur released the next Exploding Dart he'd stored in the Poket Simpanan Tua. The attack took its target right on the snout as it began to lunge forward, causing jaw, teeth, and brain matter to spray outwards. The explosion of the attack caught the others by surprise again, allowing a Focused Strike to finish off an injured one.

Then, Arthur retreated, out of tricks.

Several wolves, including the Alpha, were coming in, circling him.

Spear entered the head of the wolf, piercing through eye and lodging in brain. Before Arthur could yank the spear head out, he was struck from behind by a pair of wolves, each of them going for his hamstrings. Only crouched low and turning was Arthur able to dodge the crippling blow, even as the mouths of the creatures bit into his leg, compressing around his thigh and the leg armour there.

Falling to the ground, Arthur rolled to the side, trying to get his legs free. One leg ripped free, blood spraying into the air as a tooth was taken along with it as his muscles contracted. He rolled onto his back, kris in hand, one hand blocking the lunging wolf going for his neck. The other hand, slipping into its chest, ripping downwards as he disemboweled it.

A shove, as hard as he could, popping the tooth out from his leg—along with more blood. He sat up, only to get another mouth clamp down on his right arm, jerking it sideways. Leaving him open as another wolf bounced forwards.

A Refined Exploding Energy Dart took it in the face, blowing a chunk of flesh out of the body too, but leaving the majority of the creature's mass to barrel into Arthur. Even as it knocked him back, another wolf was coming straight for his face.

Moving his head to the side, he felt teeth tearing near his face, ripping a portion of his scalp away. Blinding pain ran through him, and then it was just a mad scramble of his free hand swiping, punching out, kicking as he was held and yanked from side to side by the monsters holding him still.

Wounds accumulated, on both sides. Arthur could never manage to get his feet under him or free his other arm before another wolf grabbed him. Only the use of a Refined Energy Dart—no more explosions, not with the creatures so close—and the kris kept them from fully pinning him down and tearing him apart.

Even then, the creatures managed to strip a bracer away, the leg guard around one foot, and even a boot. A chunk of flesh from his calf and half his ear. He took wounds, once and again, but he dealt them too.

And unlike him, the wolves did not have a healing technique. One, then another, of the creatures were wounded, some fatally. Until eventually, he managed to get a foot underneath him. Then, onto his feet again, he buried the kris in a neck and ripped outwards, leaving the creature still gripping his arm to bleed to death.

The Alpha, lunging at him at the last, did the most damage. It managed to get its large mouth around his neck, bite in around the gorget and fling him around a little. If not for him sinking the enchanted kris into its side, a kris that slowly poisoned the Alpha, it would have been over.

But once the blade was planted, it was but a matter of holding on to the end.

Extracting his blade from the thrashing but slowing body and then replanting it, he searched till he found the heart and pierced it. When it finally collapsed, he tried to move the body away, but exhaustion left him unable to move his own body, forcing him to just lie there, half-pinned by the corpse as his healing technique worked.

Eventually, the technique gave him sufficient strength that he was able to push the body off him. He made sure to extract the creature's monster core first and then hobble over to the elemental's ruined body, pulling out the core from those remains too. To his surprise, he found something else, a hunk of twisted metal that just sat there, waiting for him to pick it up. Once he did, the Tower sent a nudge, one that he pulled up fast.

Enhanced Magic Metal Ore

Usable to create enchanted items. Type and variety dependent upon skill of the crafter and additional materials utilized in creation.

Arthur sighed, carrying the hunk of metal over to where his backpack had been dropped, depositing the ore inside it next to the heart-in-a-jar. He really wished he actually got an actual enchanted item like his kris, but he also knew that crafted items were more powerful.

Still, it wasn't useful at all to him right now.

Sitting down by the entrance, he began the process of pulling all his armour off, wincing as sticky blood tugged at his skin and open wounds. He grunted, stripping down to his underwear and then extracted his rag towel, wetting it down and began the process of cleaning himself off.

They never talked about this, but when you get beaten up a lot, with cuts, bites, and even entire bits of yourself torn off, things got bloody. Very, very bloody. And wandering around, bleeding and with parts not exactly in the right place even though they were healing, was painful in the extreme.

Arthur sighed again, pushing at the edge of his skin on his scalp, wincing as it shifted back on to his skull. He adjusted it a little, using the edge of his spear to make sure it was mostly in the right place before wrapping it with a compression bandage. The entire thing was bloody and disgusting and needed a good wash too, but it would do well enough for now.

After all, the Tower and his own technique would pull the rest of the skin into place properly and remove minor scarring eventually. It wouldn't, however, fix his biggest loss from the fight. A hand traced the missing part of the top of his ear, making him grateful that he didn't wear glasses.

Clean-up, a change of clothing. Washing down and then oiling the leather armour. Using brush, sandpaper, and duct tape to put his armour back into working order. It wasn't perfect and he wished he had bought a self-repairing enchantment for it rather than a durability one, but it was what it was. He'd never expected these levels to be so damn difficult.

But he was done with the eighth floor.

Finally.

Now to deal with the ninth.

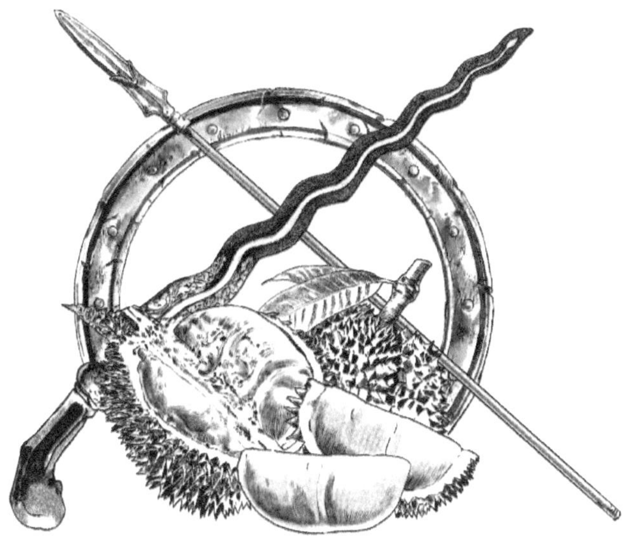

Chapter 73 - Floor 9

Stepping through the paifang that marked the difference in floors brought no trumpets or musical accompaniment. It only gave him a small mental nudge, a notification from the Tower

Eighth Floor Cleared. Entering Ninth Floor of Tower #STET

Nothing else, no useful information or anything. Still, it was good to see the change in floors confirmed, which was why he had bothered to even read it. Now, he dismissed it to check his surroundings. The ninth floor was much like the eighth, giving the very same options in terms of pathways, but it added the annoyance of puzzles, more traps, and even more roaming monsters.

The good news was, there was no timed event, no pack of wolves out to tear him apart if he took his time. The bad news was that the type, quantity, and quality of the random, wandering monsters would increase as time went on. Such that he would not just be fighting plain variations of the creatures but Alphas and mini-bosses soon enough.

Those who tried to farm the ninth floor for too long were likely to end up dying on it.

However, there was a reason climbers wanted to stick around, and that was because of the trio of wandering Tower personnel of the ninth floor. A merchant, a hermit, and a tinker were part and parcel of this floor. Of the three, the hermit was the most popular for he gave—if you passed his test—a cultivation manual or technique. The tinker, on the other hand, was much more variable, having a wide range of goods and services available. What you could get was always up in the air.

The merchant was simpler but the most problematic since he required payment. Trying to kill him was a good way to die. It was more a matter of luck to see what he had, though he also had a semi-regular set of goods available, unlike the other two.

The biggest concern was where one could find each of the three. The hermit—the highest risk, but also the highest reward—was off-trail. The tinker was most often found on-trail. And the merchant was almost always on-trail. Because of the increasing number of monsters, the question was where one wanted to take the risk.

And if one wanted to just head straight for the exit. This was where people like Casey, with her need to beat the clock, suffered. She would likely head straight along the trail, moving as quickly as possible and using the fastest trail, which was clearly marked on this floor. On the other hand, that wasn't necessarily the trail that either merchant or tinker would be on.

In the end, it was just a question of luck and persistence. And techniques. Certain cultivators went out of their way to build themselves up during this period, adding extra sensing techniques, even going so far as to add tamed beasts or trackers to help them locate the three wanderers.

It was a short-term strategy as far as Arthur was concerned, though for those who had the time to build up an array of techniques, it was much more viable. Not for him, so he could only trust to his luck.

"And I've been decently lucky so far…" Arthur muttered to himself. Even getting tossed off the mountain had ended up with him getting the Seri Pahang heart. On that note, what he recalled of the tinker drove him to think they would be the most useful to meet, since their ability to work materials together at a reduced rate could get him what he needed faster.

On the other hand, a new cultivation technique taught by the Tower's hermit was a long-term benefit. It was the one that real risk-takers loved to gamble on, but his recollection of the wiki details and the numbers showed that maybe only one in fifty climbers found him.

All of which meant, at least for him, that the trail was the way to go. If nothing else, he wanted a bit of a break before he had to fight again.

Evening, night, and morning again. Arthur had a late start, not because he was mentally recovering but because after his evening's rest, he had spent the rest of the time while waiting for daylight practising more vigorously the dual cultivation techniques. He tried, again and again, to force the techniques to combine, learning to guide flows of two full-body techniques together. Normally, brute-forcing it would not work; but in this case, he was able to pull upon moments of enlightenment, switching between his techniques swiftly and reforming one Refined Energy Dart or Focused Strike after another, in an almost continuous stream.

Almost.

That was what he was working on, why he was late in moving. Not being able to channel multiple full-body techniques had nearly gotten him killed. Perhaps he could have done alright with just partial ones, but it wasn't enough if he wanted to get through the next few floors.

Or maybe not. Maybe he would be fine. He only had issues with the big wolf pack. The elemental had actually been easy. Relatively speaking.

Either way, he had been so close, he had learnt so much, he had pushed. As hard as he dared, till at last, as dawn ended and the day truly began, he received the notification he'd been looking for. Moments later, he managed to hold two full-body cultivation techniques—Accelerated Healing and Heavenly Sage's Mischief—in mind, powering them through his meridians and flooding himself with both. Something clicked.

Simultaneous Flow Technique Upgraded (200.1%)

Allows the use of multiple techniques at the same time. Increased understanding will allow the utilization of additional techniques. User may now hold and control two full-body techniques at the same time.

That was it, but what it would mean for his fighting ability was significantly greater. Add on his increased understanding of the Heavenly Sage's Mischief, increasing the boost from just 2 Body points to 3 now, and the desperate fight on the eighth floor had helped tip him over on more than one thing. Almost worth losing a part of an ear for, really.

If anything, that loss might actually be good, since he needed to work on advancing his healing technique which had stalled for ages. He just had to find the time.

Later.

Right now, he had to keep an eye out for the wandering monsters of the ninth floor. There were the usual, including the troop of monkeys that had chosen to trade fire with him. A Refined Exploding Energy Dart into their midst and then a bunch of slung stones had taught them what happened when they tried to harass him.

It was a bit of an expensive lesson, though he did manage to acquire a half-dozen monster cores after chasing them off, so other than the loss of time, it was a net win.

No leeches, thankfully, but a bunch of grasping leaves of a monstrous plant laid across the ground that enclosed upon his feet when he stepped on them had him jumping away, barely managing to avoid be snared and pierced by their barbs. The damn road was also lined with a pit trap that he landed in the middle of.

Only quick thinking and the use of his spear to slow his descent before he managed to sink a hand into the earth long enough to climb out kept him from getting impaled on the stakes at the bottom.

The damn kuching hitam, on the other hand, he did not manage to dodge. Its leap and claw attack had torn out part of his throat and scored a deep cut along his jaw. If not for the fact that he was running his healing technique at the time and was able to patch his sliced pulmonary artery and vein together, he might have bled out quickly while fighting the creature.

As it stood, he still had to spend time cleaning himself off again.

After that, he kept Cloud Step running in the background, just in case he needed to get into the air again rather than hauling himself off the ground.

The ninth floor sucked, but so far, the monsters weren't too bad. After that fight he needed to reserve his power. So long as he did that, he would survive.

Chapter 74

Late evening and at the first major crossroads, Arthur found himself needing to burn through his resources at an astounding rate. Already, he was down one trump card with the Refined Exploding Energy Dart from his Poket Simpanan gone. He was flooding his body with the Heavenly Sage's Mischief and moving faster than ever, which was a good thing because he was barely able to keep up with the numerous attacks coming at him from his current opponents.

Whoever had decided that a hunting party of jenglot should be allowed to roam the roads sucked. Big time. He'd fought them before, of course, with help from his Clan mates on the first floor. However, fighting them alone was something else entirely, especially outnumbered as he was.

He could only be glad it wasn't a hunting party of orcs.

As it stood, Arthur was pouring Yin energy into the surroundings, blocking and slicing and retreating to ensure the group didn't manage to surround him. Between all the points he'd poured into Body since and the boost from Heavenly Sage's Mischief, Arthur was actually stronger and much, much faster than any single jenglot.

Which was rather amazing to think of, considering how much he struggled when he'd first encountered them.

Problem was, with a half-dozen fighting him, he was constantly turning away claws, stabbing his spear into exposed body parts, and slamming the shaft into legs just to slow them down. However, wounds and the Yin Aura were gradually draining them, making them slower.

A lean out of the way, the too-slow retraction of a clawed arm, meant Arthur managed to sink his spear all the way into the exposed armpit.

Drift backwards another step, use the haft of the retracted spear to push aside another attack, and then sidestep backwards while setting the spear on the ground to take the lunge of another. Watch as it sinks in, the creature coughing in surprise, hot air washing over your face with the stench of rotting meat and something sweet, and then shoulder charge.

Shove the body off the spear, spin it around to smack a jenglot in the leg, and sweep it off its feet, turn and elbow another as its claws scrape along armour.

Keep moving, keeping spinning and retreating, and then break through to retreat the other way, leaving dead and dying bodies behind. The Yin Aura constantly robbing them of energy, pulling those that were bleeding and suffering already into enforced slumber. Until, suddenly, there is only one jenglot left and it is charging you, and you only had to put the spear into its heart, the weapon extended so fast its attempts to block is for naught.

Arthur cleaned up soon afterward, pocketing the monster cores and heading for the crossroads. He stretched as he did so, rubbing his hands on his thighs to get rid of the last of the gumminess, and eyed both pathways.

As expected, there was a small sign right in the middle, similar to a hiking sign.

"Mountain peak - 34km. Scenic Route to Peak - 53km," he read out loud, rolling his eyes. What did surprise him was the extra note, at the bottom of the scenic route. "Kampung Baru - 24km."

"A new village, might have some... dirtage?" Arthur scratched his head. How did you rhyme village? Pillage? "Oooh, a new village, to pillage!"

Well, with that kind of rhyme and thinking, it was obvious which way he had to go. And it wasn't that much longer, right?

Who was he kidding. This was going to take him a few extra days at a minimum. He would need to speed up, but that was for tomorrow. Today, he was going to take it easy, until he was certain he had a good grasp of the kind of random monsters, traps, and nastiness that were waiting to mess up his day. Then, and only then, was he going to speed up.

Better safe than dead.

Half an hour later, Arthur was sprinting all out. Not because he was trying to catch up on lost time, or because he was running away from a monster. In fact, if he turned his head to the side, he would spot a half-dozen other creatures running beside him, from the *kuching hitam* and a small sounder of *babi ngepet* to a weird, warbling thing that was missing half its body but threw itself forward on its rotund other-half and pushed off with its sole leg and arm every time it finished a bounce and roll.

Every single creature was sprinting as fast as they could, all because of a ridiculous trap. Or geographic hazard. Hard to say what triggered the event, since Arthur was almost certain he had not tripped it or stepped on anything that would have caused it.

Even so, the landslide kept pouring heavy rocks and earth down at them all. Rocks that varied in size from tiny pebbles to chunks the size of his torso careened down around them, the initial edges of the rumbling mass striking with impunity.

A hard crunch, a pained squeal as a babi was taken down. The rock, twice the size of Arthur's own fist, had smashed into the monster's leg, leaving it crippled. Not even its own sounder slowed down, the animal panic of their impending demise gripping the group tight as they sprinted to get away from the rocky cliff.

In the distance, Arthur could see the line of safety. An unnatural cessation of the rockslide, a magical barrier that bounced rocks and other hazards away. That was causing its own problem, as the area just ahead of the safe zone began to fill with obstacles, boulders, and uneven ground that would need to be traversed at speed.

Something to concern himself with later, when he reached it.

If.

Ahead, the bouncing monster was half in the air. The creature was something from Chinese folklore, Arthur was certain, though he knew not its name. All of a sudden it was struck in quick succession by one, two, and then three rocks—diverting its path.

Suddenly, the creature was no longer headed for the narrow but firm trail; rather, redirected into open space to their left. As the dust from the stirred air choked him, Arthur could swear the creature met his gaze, despair writ large before it plunged off the end of the curving trail.

Arthur's own foot hit a hard rock. He stumbled, righting himself a moment later, ignoring the constant beat and ping of rocks striking him.

Something sharp cut across his face, drawing a stinging line across his nose and nearly taking out an eye, but all he could do was run.

A hundred meters had never felt so far.

Another strike, across the head, from a rock threw him off a little. He kept moving, arms pumping, his backpack swinging behind him as he tried to keep his spear tucked in close. Once again, he wished he had a magical storage ring, something to keep his weapons and gear put away.

None of that for him, of course, so he had to risk his spear getting yanked out of grip. His backpack struck his body with force as it bounced.

A particularly large boulder bounced ahead of him, slamming into the earth. Without thought, Arthur triggered his Cloud Step as he leapt, bounding off the formed cloud just moments before impacting the rock.

He knew it was a bad idea in a way, but with enough clearance above the ground, he was, he believed, safe enough from falling hazards. They were still coming down, all around him, driving into the earth. In mid-air, with nothing but his techniques to pay attention to, he risked a look upwards.

Saw the massive amount of rocks still coming down. If he got caught in that shower, he'd probably be so much squished climber.

Then, finally his feet struck the earth again. Ankle turned under the uneven ground, but adrenaline and fear kept him moving though a lightning bolt of agony raced up his shin. Around him, more of the creatures had fallen by the wayside even as a sharp S-turn came up before the end of this race.

A turn that was already half-filled with bouncing rocks, a choking cloud of dust that took out even his Enhanced Eyesight, and only a few seconds left before the entire mountain came down.

Chapter 75

Arthur raced into the cloud of dust and debris, falling stones and broken branches pelting off his body. Head bent low, eyes squinted tight, sucking in breath through his teeth in the hope of not choking. Heavenly Sage's Mischief was burning through him, forced to pour ever faster through his body, to soak muscles and tendons in energy to give him additional strength. Cloud Step was at the ready, for the inevitable moment when he needed to take to the air.

Didn't matter.

He saw the squat boulder, still rocking as it came to a stop, a moment too late. His front foot struck it, toe first sending a jolt of pain as he crushed his tiny appendage. Moments later, his forward momentum had him bowl over the rock. An attempt to turn the fall into a roll managed to have him slam his forearm into the ground, such was his momentum. He fell with a crash that transformed into a bloody slide through sheer dint of velocity.

One of the disadvantages of greater-than-human speed and velocity is that momentum and physics still played their part in the Tower.

He pushed himself upwards, was slammed into from the side and forced to roll as a sharpened tusk and maddened boar struck him. It luckily didn't pierce his armour, but it did cost him time once more.

Too much time, as he staggered to his feet and was struck by another rock on the shoulder, strong enough to almost crack his collarbone. Only twenty feet to his destination but clouds and rocks were all around him. Time slowed down as death approached.

No choice.

He ran, pushing forwards and sideways, edging as far away from the rock face as possible. Bouncing rocks all around struck at him, battered his footing, nearly took him out as he leapt into open air. A head turned sideways, his Explosive Dart blasting apart a boulder before it struck him, now only pelting him with shards of stone.

Falling, falling, falling, the world coming by him.

Five, six, seven feet closer.

Then, he triggered his Cloud Step, vaulting upwards with all the strength that he could pour into his jump. Muscles burning with Tower energy as it empowered his movement, the second cloud already forming as he neared the edge of the rock, open air beneath his feet as the second turn in the "S" shape of the trail came up: freedom lay just ahead.

Another leap, throwing him upwards only for an unseen boulder to strike him in the side and slam him off course, back into open air.

At least it pushed him forward.

The last of the rumbling ended, only a few final rocks falling down around the trail. Dust continued to rise but visibility increased, such that one might, if you looked close enough, spot a much put-upon climber. His spear was sunk deep into the clay earth of the trail, a bare twelve feet from the top of it, but with nothing to grip.

Right hand hung limp by his side, shoulder dislocated, blood running from minor cuts across his body. A foot juddered, trembling back and forth as adrenaline ran its course. Beneath the figure, a hundred-foot drop.

Arthur groaned, switching over to his healing technique once again. Within moments of the technique working, his shoulder audibly and noticeably wrenched itself back into position, eliciting a loud cry of surprise and pain from him. If you never had a body part slip back into place, outside of the pain, it was more of a surprise. The feel of bone moving against bone was disconcerting to say the least, like watching your mother kiss your adult brother on the lips.

Icky and weird and not to be repeated if at all possible.

Just as importantly, the healing technique helped refresh his muscles. The lactic acid buildup that had been ongoing had faded, the agony of holding over two hundred pounds of weight, all of which had been battered constantly by stone and branches and other debris, disappeared.

Now, all he had to do was figure out how to yank his spear out and get to the top of the ledge.

A real problem it would be if he didn't have Cloud Step.

But with his technique, the issue was significantly simpler. A yank on the spear as he got his leg against the cliff, then twisting around and reforming a Cloud Step beneath his feet to leap upwards directly. Once he reached the apex of his jump, he formed a second cloud and jumped ahead.

Somewhere in all that rushing around, fighting and surviving, the last little iota of knowledge had formed and the next step in his Cloud Step technique had triggered. Now, it was easier than ever to create two clouds. A third would take time, and he'd have to start practising, but he had a few more techniques that he needed to finish—including a whole new cultivation method to improve his mental defences he hadn't even poked at yet.

Later.

Cultivation Speed: 2.773 Yin

Energy Pool: 14/30 (Yin) + (5/7)

Refinement Speed: 0.1421

Refined Energy: 0.14 (40) +(0/3)

Attributes and Traits

Mind: 15 (Multi-Tasking, Quick Learner, Perfect Recall)

Body: 25 (Enhanced Eyesight, Yin Body, Swiftness, Fast Twitch Faster, Lightning Reflexes, Explosive Strength)

Spirit: 15 (Sticky Energy, From the Dregs, Strengthened Aura)

Techniques

Night Emperor Cultivation Technique

Focused Strike

Accelerated Healing – Refined Energy (Grade III)

Heavenly Sage's Mischief

Refined Energy Dart

Bark Skin

Seven Cloud Stepping Technique (200.7%)

Poket Simpanan Tua (139%) (Empty)

Imbued Strike - Yin Poison

Yin Aura (Level 1) (114.8%)

Partial Techniques

Simultaneous Flow (200.1%)

Yin-Yang Energy Exchange (95.3%)

Yin Poison Darts (50.4%)

No further improvement on the Simultaneous Flow but that wasn't surprising since he hadn't even tried to work on that. The Yin-Yang Energy Exchange continued to creep up. Eventually, he'd learn it and then shifting from his Yin energy to Yang or the vice versa would be much simpler. On a day-to-day basis, it made little difference, other than speeding up his cultivation technique a tiny amount. Or, using his very body to empower Yin-based attacks.

Considering he had not very many Yin attacks right now, there was no point in worrying about that. Even the poison-lulling effects were not so good that he was going to sacrifice portions of his very being for it.

It was interesting to him that Simultaneous Flow was still categorised as a partial technique. One wondered why, and if there was something else that he was missing by utilizing it in the manner he did. Was there an improvement, perhaps, that he was missing? In the end, he had no answer.

At least for now. It'd be a research project for when he exited the Tower, but to do that...

"I got to get moving. Or I'll be losing," Arthur muttered, levering himself to his feet.

One last look at the destroyed trail. There was an entire section that looked like a newly built slope. Potentially walkable, with the right kind of movement method, but his Cloud Step was not it. And considering exactly how unstable the entire thing looked, running for it was the way to go.

On the other hand...

"I got to get faster," Arthur muttered. Nearly being bowled off the side of a mountain was as precarious as driving on the fourth unofficial lane on the two-lane Sungai Besi highway. Which is to say, the "lane" that was actually grassy turf beside the emergency lane and a mere half foot from the concrete river.

Chapter 76

Wandering monsters, trapped trails, lurking ambush predators. All kinds of fun, really, especially when you started jogging down a trail. However, a day and a half past the crossroads and Arthur was figuring he had this.

Spitting frogs were dodged, Arthur not even bothering to slow down to kill them. Damn things had a habit of leaping away, and unless he wanted to waste precious refined energy, killing them with his sling took time and effort. Time better spent just jogging on. They didn't pursue, not too far, once you got out of range, so there was no point in pushing the matter. Better to keep running, heading for the next trap.

Pit traps, the occasional grabby vines, and explosive thorned roadside plants were either weathered, avoided, or outrun. His innate healing helped push out thorns on a regular basis and with his attention turned inwards a little as he ran, Arthur found himself learning how to manipulate his flesh and the flow of power a little better. Squeezing out thorns, fixing minor problems within him.

He even, occasionally, tried to work out what to do about the scarred-over missing portion of his ear. Once it was healed, he could not fix it further, and allowing his body to naturally heal things didn't exactly work. Sure, the Tower pulled you towards optimal, such that breaks and scars smoothed over eventually or even toughened up, but it wasn't the same thing as replacing missing bits.

A part of him remembered a little science he'd learnt, about how humans all had the same stem cells at birth which eventually became the different cells of the body. It had been a big idea in research—and still was—to make use of such things to basically rebuild organs and the like. Supposedly, there were even companies that provided replacement organs using that kind of research.

That is, in the West and other developed countries—and mainly for the super rich.

Nothing like that in Malaysia or other developing countries, no. They didn't have the money to pay for the necessary tests beforehand, much less for the individualised organs being grown. They had to do the usual thing: wait for an organ to come around through donations, pay someone under the table to go under the knife, or make friends with the triads or underworld and acquire said organs another way.

Of course, he'd only ever heard rumors of the last. Whether it was just a tall tale or something that could really be done, he'd never looked into. Didn't really want to find out, even if he could have asked. Some things, you didn't ever want to know.

Not if you wanted to continue sleeping or ignoring where some of your meal deliveries went.

The other option, of course, was the way *cicak* did it. They lost tails all the time. And it was even a common and somewhat cruel game played by children in Malaysia: catching the ubiquitous lizards—or were they technically geckos?—that were present in houses, then pulling their tails off and watching the tails twitch, even as the *cicak* ran away. No one actually killed *cicak* because they ate that most annoying of pests, the mosquito.

Of course, he had no idea how *cicak* grew back their missing parts. Jellyfish, or was it squid, had that ability too. Something in their genes, he vaguely recalled. Was it some chemical or lack of it that helped them do that?

He knew he had to work it out eventually since somewhere in there was the clue to pushing his healing skill ahead. Until then, he would try and try again with the various flows without a clue of what he was trying to do— much like a monkey might smack a bunch of buttons, except, unlike a *monyet*, he could sense the differences in chi flows.

Not that he could pay that much attention to all this pondering, what with the random monsters and traps.

Still, by the time it was late evening, he was beginning to get the idea he might be on the right trail. It wasn't very common, and it might have been weeks or months old, but Arthur had spotted tracks in the earth. Deep, rutted tracks that spoke of a heavy vehicle. A caravan, perhaps, or a wheelbarrow. Maybe a mini cart.

Either way, it was clear to Arthur that someone or something had gone through the trail before. It couldn't be months ago, since not long afterwards, a torrential downpour started. Arthur slowed down, what with visibility dropping from a good twenty or thirty feet to barely a few feet. It was hard to see where the trail turned, dipped, or otherwise shifted so that vegetation was in the way.

That was the thing with real heavy rain in the tropics. It came down so hard, you couldn't see your hand in front of your face. Try to run across the street, you get drenched in water. Within moments, just a dozen feet, and you might as well have taken a real shower.

From a slow jog Arthur slowed further again, till he was barely faster than a fast walk. He couldn't see anything, not even the sides of the trail next to him, just blurs of green and brown. The downpour made the earth muddy, every step sucking at his boots, causing him to exert ever more energy to walk. It grew slippery too, tiny streams of water turning into rivulets, which then became streams that flowed in small waterfalls all around.

Mud churned, traps that were set to capture him began to fail.

Grasping leaves curled up, reacting to the touch and pressure of the rain. Vines laid across the ground sprang into the air, shaking as branches retracted, and empty nooses abounded. Pit traps were revealed, open gaping holes all across the trail that he leapt over.

But there was a rumbling, not just the constant thunder that came from the sky but also rocks and mountain all coming loose.

Coming down.

Landslides that Arthur suspected only triggered on his arrival, instability all across the mountain set off by the heavy downpour. Environmental effects that, when Arthur realised what was happening, had him slow down further until he came to a full stop in the middle of the trail, simply feeling the rain pound down on him, washing him clean.

He stood there, head raised, his spear sunk into the ground tip-down next to him. Best not to be holding onto it, though he would have been incredibly unlucky to be struck by lightning considering the number of tall trees all around him.

Of course, he was also standing in rivulets of water, so it didn't need to hit him direct. Just close enough to burn.

Eyes closed, listening to the noise high above, listening to the patter of rain. He took his helmet off, felt his hair get plastered to his skull. He ran a hand through his hair, scrubbed at it again and again to clear some blood and dirt. Enjoyed the water running through him, the cold liquid.

For the first time, he relaxed. Not all the way, he couldn't do that. But significantly, because there was nothing out there, nothing too dangerous he could sense, nothing he could see. His world was drowned in water and thunder and that was fine enough, at least for now. It was peaceful, a sense of danger only lurking in the wings.

After a while, he shivered a little. Put the helmet back on his head, stripped the vambraces and elbow guards and rerebrace off his right arm. Then, he moved to wash the rest of his arm. Waited, himself as best he could, repeated the process on his other arm, around his legs. One by one, step by step, keeping only the cup and breastplate on. Knowing better than to remove those right now, as rain seeped its way through his breastplate, into his jacket and clothing beneath.

Rivulets of water, slowly dripping out from under his breastplate. Dirt and blood mixing together, dripping into his underwear and shoes. All of it squishy and disgusting but leaving him cleaner, finally, for the first time in a long time.

He exhaled, grateful. Relaxed. Thankful for the rain.

Of course, that was when *it* arrived.

Chapter 77

He did not sense it till the creature was barely a foot away. Not enough time to get more than his hand up to help protect against the reaching jaws even as long claws took him to the ground. At twice his size and about four times his weight, the black-furred tiger—a real tiger, not a puma—knocked him over with ease as it slammed into him.

Arthur crashed into the ground, the earth shaking, all breath driven from his body. One paw reaching for his neck was deflected by gorget and pauldrons, so that the claws only tore at the armour that protected him and not the tender flesh beneath. Its other paw found flesh, claws piercing in the gap between his rerebrace and pauldron and breastplate before being caught as it came down, snagging hard against the bindings that kept the entire thing together.

One hand extended to keep the lunging open-mouthed, razor-sharp, and surprisingly sweet-smelling breath-filled jaws of death from him, and the other hand caught by the claws, Arthur had no limbs to throw the creature off. Not while scrambling to the side, trying to avoid the monster's backleg claws from hooking into his lower body and tearing him apart.

Of course, considering how powerful the creature was, when it settled down for a moment to lunge jaws-first, he couldn't hold it off. All he could do was shift away so that it mostly tore into the ground and parts of his jaw and neck instead of his face.

"My turn," Arthur growled, waiting for the head to retract. Its mouth still open, it was the perfect timing for him to release the Refined Exploding Energy Dart right down the barrel of its exposed throat. The resulting explosion shook him, leaving his ears ringing, eyes tearing and dazed.

The *harimau hitam*, on the other hand, had fared even worse, the entirety of its back of its throat and neck blown away. A large gaping hole the size of a closed fist poured out blood, allowing him to see the still cloudy sky above.

Then, the creature slumped over, its body bereft of control entirely. Leaving Arthur to struggle to get the body off him, wincing at numerous wounds.

Was it the third or fourth floor where he had first fought this damn tiger? When it had nearly killed him with a surprise attack just like this? The harimau hitam almost had more success this time. Yet, he had managed to end it, by being strong enough and tough enough to take the full strike head-on before he'd dropped his hidden technique on it.

The Poket Simpanan was, as its name implied, really saving his fragrant durian ass again and again.

He let the adrenaline surge run through him for a few more moments, feeling his shortened breathing relax. His fingers stopped trembling. He unclenched his body, grateful that he hadn't eaten anything solid in ages because his body was sending urgent signals for him to take a dump.

All normal things after an adrenaline dump.

He noted them, accepted all of it, including the slight shakiness in his breathing and mind and then forced himself up. No guarantee after all, that there weren't other predators searching for him in the rain.

More importantly, the fact that these creatures were coming out was a signal that the floor was ticking up in difficulty.

Joy.

Traversing the rest of the trail after the rain lightened up enough that walking was viable had Arthur on edge a little. At least there were no more landslides. He unhooked his water flask from his side, sipped on the water and swirled it around his throat before spitting out blood and dirt that had gotten in while fighting.

Then, he took a bigger mouthful, grimacing as he noted how empty the flask had gotten. Water was one of the few things you generally needed, even as a climber. Oh, you could substitute for Tower energy, but it cost a significant amount more.

Kind of made it weird, really, that a climber could exist entirely on energy but… it was what it was. The physicists of course were all kinds of excited, pointing out how matter and energy were all the same anyway, so Tower cultivation and cores were just a more efficient process of transferring one kind of energy to another.

There was always this kind of discussion. For the most part, Arthur ignored it for the eggheads to theorise. He just knew that keeping hydrated was good—which was a minor problem when he was nearly out of water.

Now, mind you, he could try to collect rainwater. Nothing wrong with rainwater, so long as what you collected was clean. Wouldn't want the first rush, but if you were taking water from rivers or streams, you were pretty much drinking rainwater anyway. So long as there wasn't acid rain or the like, you were good.

Problem was, he was moving and not set up to collect anything.

As for the numerous streams around, even if the Tower was cleaner than real life, and random garbage and animal scat wasn't being washed into the water, it was never a good idea to drink or wade through water during a rainstorm or the hour after.

All of which meant he was going to have to stick to being thirsty, ration his water, and hope he came across a spring in the next few hours.

In the meantime, he had a lot of obstacles to avoid. The mud and streams of water and never-ending rain made footing treacherous. Overturned stones, or the occasional still functioning pea-shooter trap that decided that it really wanted a piece of him. And the landslides started up again.

"Run across or wait?" Arthur muttered to himself, seeing the massive muddy slope before him that had obscured the trail. He had no way backward. This entire section, a good few hundred feet of it, was just boulders, mud, and streams of water. He tried to remember if he ever heard of anyone having to traverse such ground, how long before a landslide became stable, if it did.

Came up empty.

Not as though he had expected to know any of this, and worse, full-out landslides and rockfalls like this had not been reported often beyond a few lines on the wikis. No one had mentioned or discussed how they got across other than a reliance on *qinggong* or movement techniques.

The water skimmers probably would be fine. Or air walkers. Or someone like Rick with his Gunslinger movement technique that used Tower power to shunt him as though he was sliding on rails. Arthur's Seven Cloud Stepping technique was more limited in that sense.

Arthur sighed, prodded at the flowing earth, noticed how much give there was. Grimaced and took a took step and then another half-dozen more, finding a comfortable spot in the middle of the trail to sit. Wasn't particularly great with the rain still coming down, but his body didn't feel the cold. Besides, hiding under trees when he was already completely soaked made little sense.

Best to wait it out before crossing the ground. Hope that the ground dried up enough to make a quick run across stable enough, without pulling him into the earth or sliding him away. He couldn't wait for the days it would take for it to completely dry, but the one thing about heavy rains in a tropical country?

They always ended. Eventually.

Unless it was monsoon season. Then he was hanging off the end of the Petronas Towers without a rope.

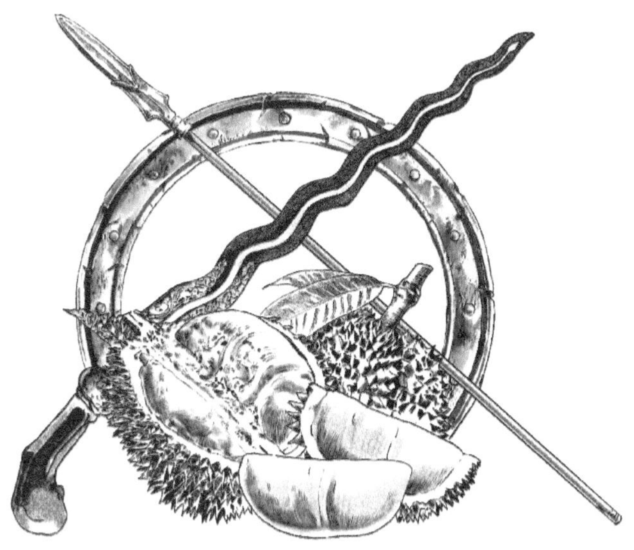

Chapter 78

Contrary to his concerns, Arthur made it across the first landslide without an issue. Oh, the mud had sucked at his boots, intending to entrap and slow his loping efforts across. The rocks and boulders and other debris he targeted for his jumps had a significant degree of give and variation, but when it became a real problem, Cloud Step gave him the perch he needed.

Something he learnt really fast was that if he only created a single cloud, he could hold the second in-abeyance within his dantian without forming it. He could then reform his first cloud much faster, ensuring it did not just disappear on him.

It was very much the pathway towards creating seven clouds, at least at the beginning levels, where one strode upon a single cloud and then formed the next one in front, layering the third cloud inside your dantian while discarding the first as you stepped. Theoretically, you could then just keep doing it forever; with multiple firm cloud options; but that was for the future.

All in all, he figured he was finally on the way to pushing for his third cloud, which was a nice benefit.

The second landslide had dried out after he had slept fitfully and coldly through the night, soaked as he was to the skin without a proper change of clothing. He figured it that crossing the second landslide would have been easier, but it was even more treacherous.

So much so that Arthur was currently riding a freshly toppled tree—ant nest, bright leaves, broken branches, and all— like a tree-board, sliding down the slope as the dried earth gave way.

Surfing was a non-starter of a sport in Malaysia. Not big enough waves generally, no teachers or trainers or general interest. He'd learnt to swim of course and even gotten certification to dive, but surfing? That wasn't a skill you needed. Not in a Malaysian Tower.

Or so he'd thought, until he found himself desperately trying to balance on the sliding tree, grateful for the handhold of a spear.

As usual, it was Cloud Step that got him through this, a leap that sent his impromptu surfboard sliding off the mountain before he leapt on clouds till he was back near the top of the landslide. After that, it was more prying himself out of the crumbling ground and then walking carefully, careful not to fall into the occasional hidden sinkhole.

Eventually, he managed to make his way out. Between the amount of time he had to take while traversing the land between landslides and waiting out landslides, Arthur pushed as hard as he could late into the night, risking even attacks by the damn *harimau hitam* and other nocturnal predators like the skimming owl with their near-silent wingbeats.

All of which was not at all fun. He eventually crashed after locating and killing the owner of a small burrow in the side of the hill. The burrow was not perfect, but it was small and warm, and he could strip down and dry himself off. He even went so far as to take his boots off and put on the pair of dry socks from his backpack, which had been carefully sealed in a sandwich bag.

Warm and dry socks slipped into slightly soaked boots were never great but still better than the squishy mess. Overnight, the blisters that had formed had healed, thankfully, which meant that he was mostly comfortable when it was time to get going.

The rest of his trip to the damn village was, to his surprise, uneventful. If you considered being occasionally attacked by monsters uneventful—which in the Tower, it was.

Of course, quiet was never the normal.

So when he turned the corner, weapon ready as he listened to the constant fighting, he was only a little surprised to find not a bunch of monsters waiting, but also the Tinker fighting them off. The slew of lizards, a half-dozen of them, were harassing the poor man while the pair of komodo dragons crept up on his still-trapped donkey. The poor thing was kicking outwards and defending itself as best it could, but being tied to the cart half-buried in mud, it wasn't able to do much.

Decision-making happened fast during a battle. At least after all the time he had spent in the Tower.

The Refined Exploding Energy Dart slammed into a komodo dragon in its side, blowing its chest open and killing it. The sudden attack startled the group. Arthur ran over, the Mischief technique and Bark Skin running at the same time. He skidded to a stop not far from the group, throwing his body into a full lunge that pierced the hasty block of a lizardman and punched into its chest. A pull and twist, and then he was spinning his spear around, retargeting.

Eight opponents against two dropped down to six and two in moments, with the last komodo dragon hesitating as it searched for answers. Its owner was taken out of the battle for a moment giving orders, leaving only four lizardmen directly engaged with the Tinker.

Simple enough for Arthur to deal with. He ignored one lizardman almost entirely, instead targeting another with his fast-moving spear, darting in and out until an opening was created and he put the spear tip into its leg and then chest in quick order. In the meantime, the pair of swipes his first opponent managed to get into his side were deflected by his armour and Bark Skin alike—the only damage being done to his backpack, which he had had no time to drop. Now one strap hung askew, pulling his balance off.

Swinging his spear around in a sideways slam, he pushed the lizardman off him. Its arms blocked the blow of the haft and hands grabbed at the spear. Arthur let one hand go, shimmying out of the pack as he fought for control of the spear with his other hand. Two hands against one should have been a simple win for the lizardman, but Tower mathematics and physics didn't always work that way.

Arthur was a lot stronger than he had been before, and holding onto his weapon was easy enough even if he wasn't strong enough to lift the creature up entirely with one hand. Once his backpack was off his shoulder, he did yank his weapon towards him, pulling the lizard closer. Then, he punched it with his free hand.

Once, then again, ignoring the way the creature tried to scratch him with its claws. Even when it pierced the gaps in armour, his Bark Skin was good enough to avert most of the damage. The rest wasn't crippling; it could heal later.

The first punch glanced off a weird bone protrusion that led to its more angular snout, the second punch coming in near the same angle struck properly along the side of the jaw and where the ear holes were. That dropped the already somewhat dazed creature, allowing Arthur to finish it off with a stab.

Then, he had to backpedal, fast as the remaining komodo dragon and more of the lizardmen arrived, with one last lizard keeping the Tinker busy.

A few hectic moments later and the use of his stored Explosive Dart, Arthur was pulling the spear out from the chest of the komodo dragon with his foot, eyeing the Tinker that had just finished its own opponent.

The Tinker was no human, just a humanoid-looking creature. The closest animal, or mammal, that Arthur could fit to it was a turtle, except, with proper hands. And with a shell that was made of hardened pockets that could inflate and have things stored within or extracted from, like it was doing now to pull out a cloth.

"I thank you, stranger." Surprising how the voice, contrary to his expectation, was rather high-pitched and not at all aged or wizened, even if the face reminded him of elderly cartoon turtles. "Your arrival saved Porta."

"Porta?" Arthur asked, then nodded when the turtle gestured at the pony. "I'm Arthur. And you are?"

"Dovgrey." A low bow, though Arthur noted that the large machete Dovgrey wielded was now clean but not put away. He also noted that the cloth used to clean the sword was not bloody, unlike his own spear which he shook out but still had blood dripping down the handle to stain his hand. "Would you be willing to help me extract Porta?"

"Sure," Arthur said, walking over and blatantly ignoring the machete. The thing was big and nasty, but the creature wasn't trying to hurt him. After all, everything he'd learnt about the trio was that they were harmless for the most part. Sticking his spear into the earth near the cart, he looked it over. "So, what do we need to do?"

"Simple. You dig it out, I'll guide Porta out."

"Why do I have to do the hard work?" Arthur grumbled, then glanced at the bodies. He gestured at the creatures, raising an eyebrow.

"Go ahead. You did the killing."

"Thank you." Grabbing his skinning knife out of the side of his belt, Arthur got to work on extracting beast stones. It didn't take him long, what with his prior experience. In short order, he was standing again and Dovgrey continued the conversation as though he had never been interrupted.

"Porta doesn't like strangers." A quick and pointed snap of the teeth from the pony made Arthur wince. Big flat teeth that could probably mush his hand. Or grab at stray hair and yank him around. None of it fun.

"Point taken." Walking carefully around the pony, he grabbed the shovel that was offered and got to work on digging the cart out. He made sure he wasn't near the creature's back feet, working in sideways first before he managed to get an angle to free up one side and then, eventually, the other.

A good twenty minutes later and the cart was finally free.

"So, traveler, care to tell me how the road is the way you came?" Dovgrey asked.

"Bad." A gesture by Arthur to the much smaller landslide they had just extracted the cart and pony out of. "Like that, but a lot bigger." A glance at the unstable earth and a frown. "Didn't realise things were still this unstable out here too."

"Mmm, I believe it was a trap." A nod to the dead bodies. "An opportune one."

"Ah…"

Now Dovgrey looked perturbed, staring into the distance. Arthur, on the other hand, was playing it cool, waiting. He saw no reason to push matters, not right now, not when the NPC owed him for the save and the work. It'd come, later.

"Frustrating, isn't it? When the Tower makes changes?" Dovgrey said, eventually. "As though I'm supposed to keep on going, when things are so… messy."

"No idea what the Tower is thinking," Arthur chimed in. "Or why it separates the last three floors into individual tests."

"Better for the final…" A shake of the head, its long sinuous neck shifting around on top of its shell before Dovgrey turned to Arthur. "Will you aid me, again?"

"Doing what?"

"I will need to get my cart across this barrier, if I am to return to the village." As Arthur glanced up, at the clouds and the fading sunlight, it added. "I can make it worth your while. Sleeping in the dark is not my preference."

"Nor mine," Arthur agreed. He was beginning to understand what was happening, and it wasn't great. Escort quests sucked, but at least this one had the chance of a good payout. So long as the man—or rather, turtle—did not die. "Alright, let's do this."

Chapter 79

The first problem with getting Dovgrey and Porta back to the village they just left was getting them over the minor landslide. Not a big problem, just arduous—except for the group of living peas that sat at the top, ready release their attacks whenever they crossed the fallen earth.

All of which meant that Arthur had to get to the top of the cliff that had fallen, dodging pea-shooter attacks while climbing upwards, mostly via the usage of cloud steps. Once he got high enough, it was just a matter of tearing into the plants with his spear.

After dealing with the peas and wincing at new bruises, he slid down the landslide and helped move the cart across the fallen ground. It mostly consisted of the pair of them carrying the single-wheelbarrow-like cart while Porta gingerly walked across the ground.

When they finished getting across, the sun was heading towards the horizon. The pair had to speed up, Porta thankfully taking on her job and

Dovgrey pushing the cart a little whenever it threatened to get stuck in the still-muddy earth.

Arthur found himself ranging back and forth, dealing with traps or wandering monsters. He could sense them arriving, in larger numbers than ever, forcing him to constantly be on the move. Once again, he groused to himself, wishing he had a gun or crossbow—not that he could use either well—to help with his ranged attacks. Or even wishing he'd spent some time learning the cheaper form of the Energy Dart.

Instead, he had to make use of the Refined Explosive Energy Dart he formed with care. He worried about running out of refined energy. He had thought he had come in with enough stores, but the constant need to move had drained his reserves down significantly, especially his long and brutal healing session.

Now, he picked his attacks with care, sometimes even reverting to his trusty sling when there were only one or two monsters that he needed to startle into a fight. Once they launched themselves at him, he would revert to his trusty spear.

Individual monsters—whether it was a *babi ngepet*, a *jenglot*, even the occasional *harimau hitam* or the weird flaming moose—were killable. The problem was that the longer he took to take one down, the more would gather meanwhile; and then suddenly he was dealing with two, three, or more at a time. Fighting them himself was, again, possible. That was the point of the spear, because it kept monsters at bay and allowed him to poke holes in them.

The problem was, more often than not, the monsters started heading for Dovgrey. Thankfully, unlike the stupid video games that sometimes the Tower seemed to model itself on, Dovgrey actually knew how to protect himself and his pony. A single creature he could fight off and delay, long enough for Arthur to deal with them.

Sometimes, Dovgrey even managed to kill off his foe. However, Arthur suspected that the more he relied on Dovgrey's help, the lower his eventual reward was going to be. Perfectly normal, after all. But frustrating.

Focused Strike came in clutch here. Which was just a weird saying, since no one used clutches anymore. Even the efficiencies for driving manual compared to automatic had disappeared, leaving only the racers and the enthusiasts as the only ones still learning how to use that old-fashioned system. Never mind the fact that, many times, electric vehicles accelerated so much faster and better. Even the most enthusiastic racer had to admit there was something to be said. There were even entire rival competing racing gangs using gas or modified electric motors, boosting the amount of power and torque given to a vehicle.

Made making deliveries across Kuala Lumpur a pain and a half, especially late at night when they chose to block off routes so they could get a few races in. And you didn't really want to get on their bad side either, since they were just as likely to find and beat you, or chase you down if you broke their cordons and thrash your vehicle.

Focused Strike helped Arthur punch through defences with ease, gave him a chance to kill creatures long before they could make trouble. The fact that Imbued Strike - Yin Poison was a long-term game meant that he couldn't use it at all, but there were aspects of the Imbued Strike that he began to see as a possibility for upgrading his own Focused Strike.

After all, they both focused on pushing Tower energy into another's body. Most creatures of the Tower had a natural resistance to that, some generic aura around the body and something deeper. Otherwise, without that barrier, one would constantly be cultivating and be over-flooded with energy.

Imbued Strike's goal was to push a foreign energy past that defense. Focused Strike pierced that defense and empowered the attack. Together, and guided properly, it might be possible to imbue a Focused Strike to pour sharpened energy straight into a body, bypassing the physical barrier.

In the best-case scenario, Arthur would basically get to use a Dim Mak attack—a death touch—that punched through a body without even worrying about the external threat. Wasteful, of course, because it was always easier to penetrate a body's physical defences first and then dump energy within.

But possible.

Idle thoughts, quick thoughts, minor explorations as he fought.

A horde of monkeys, throwing rocks and poo once again. He let Dovgrey and Porta run ahead, even as he loosened an Explosive Dart into the surroundings, exploding the tree that the leader was on, bringing it down and sending twigs and other splinters into a trio of monkeys. They screamed, shouted, one going so far as to rush Arthur.

He didn't even bother to kill it with his spear, already spinning up a stone with his other hand. No, Arthur just kicked the creature right in the head as it arrived, trading it for a stone thrown right into his chest in turn. The crack and twisted angle of the head was good enough for him.

Of course, the biggest problem was that, by the time he killed enough of the monkeys that they retreated, utilizing another Explosive Dart and a few slingshots, he had no time to collect the stones. Instead, he had to sprint after his pair of charges that had pulled off a good hundred-plus meters away, barely in sight.

Only to come across a group of orc-like creatures, all red-skinned and nasty. Four monsters, two of them harassing Dovgrey, two more around Porta, in their attempts to drag them away and pry open the cart.

Arthur ran forwards, pouring energy into the Heavenly Sage's Mischief to give himself a boost in energy. Too slow though, for a shout from one of the orc fighters alerted the one nearest Arthur. A feint downwards had the creature shift its massive maul to block Arthur's low-line attack, which was why it was surprised when Arthur leapt upwards and did a spin kick instead.

He rarely leapt and kicked. While he had studied the methods for fun—his Clan often practised such kicks—it was not part of his fighting repertoire. Being off the ground was a bad idea since you couldn't shift angles, normally. And learning to leap up to eight feet in the air and kick had little practical use unless your opponent was on a horse.

Or was a massive red orc that needed to be kicked in the head.

A Mischief-empowered and Focused Strike heel thudded into the orc's temple, cracking the soft skull and sending bone shards flying. The creature stumbled, but rather than dying immediately, it swayed around drunkenly. Concussed, brain damaged, it stumbled around, disoriented as Arthur landed and swept it off its feet as one foot struck the other's.

Then, he was running around the cart, spear pulled back and shortened.

Arthur dodged under the swinging hammer of an orc, feeling the brush of air as it passed over him. Stepped forward and thrust, angling the attack upwards. Watched as the creature dodge the attack going for its throat and neck, nicking the jaw instead. He cursed and twitched his spear so that the back end of the spear switched angles; he stepped in closer and slammed the shaft between the orc's legs.

When the haft bounced back, he controlled the movement a little by twisting his hand and stepping sideways, getting out of his opponent's range while catching the back of the orc's leg with the spear haft.

Felt the impact of the spear along that leg, the trembling reaction, the push necessary to drop the other onto the ground. Arthur stepped forward, kicked out, and broke the hand trying to grab his weapon. Twisted and attacked, moving, moving always. Because he needed to end this fight, and crippling and knocking the orc down was not enough.

So. Throat, head, or heart. He took an opening and put the tip of his spear between the eyes with another Focused Strike.

Ended up having to leave his spear behind though, as it got stuck.

Kris came out, even as he hard-blocked a descending mace, shortening the swing by stepping in tight. It hurt like blazes, but it did mean he could grab and yank the creature sideways, opening up a gap in the arm and elbow to sink the weapon within. Continued sidestepping all the way through, dragging the kris along the inside. Tore open the body as he did so, just enough so that it would cut various nerves and arteries and veins as he exited.

Spotted more monster, which to his surprise, he found dead. Trampled underneath by the rather angry Porta and then finished off by Dovgrey.

Arthur hesitated, scanned around, found the last living red orc and then finished it. He bent low, stripping the creature of its stone and then moving to do the same with the others, noting their size and glow. No reason not to harvest these now, especially since Porta was throwing a fit at the moment.

Something about nearly being taken away had upset the creature.

"How much further?" Arthur asked, forcing the words out as he breathed deeply.

"Maybe another half hour," Dovgrey answered as he stroked the pony, calming it. "Though, the monsters are getting feistier. When it turns full dark..."

"We'll be at the village by then," Arthur said, confidently. Under his breath, he added. "I hope."

Chapter 80

To Arthur's surprise, Dovgrey had delayed their departure by a few minutes to strip the orcs of their goods. Not that they had much, beyond some slipshod armour—pauldrons, greaves, leather skirts, and even a breastplate or two—as well as their weapons. All of that was piled into the cart, a small compartment unlocked long enough to store the loot before they moved on.

While the turtle-man was busy, Arthur ranged backwards and forwards to deal with gathered monsters, collecting the monster cores before they moved on. Being rather cognizant about his own needs, he intended to collect as many as he could, seeing the increased number of monsters as both a threat and opportunity.

In any case, once the Tinker was ready to go, Arthur had cleared the first few hundred feet well enough that they could travel together for a bit.

"So, where were you headed in such a hurry, anyway?" Arthur asked, curiously. "Surely you knew the ground was going to be a mess."

Dovgrey hesitated, then shrugged. "Well, I didn't actually. The landslides are uncommon—unusual if you will—to this event. And I must admit, I've only been through a half-dozen cycles of this floor thus far."

"Really?" Arthur said. "What were you doing before?"

"In building sales and purchasing."

"Oh, inside the Guild halls?" At the Tinker's confirmation, Arthur frowned. "So why do this?"

"Travel back and forth? It's the next step, of course. Looks great on the resume, if you're willing to do some of the more difficult jobs."

"Including potentially getting killed?" Arthur said, glancing at the scratch on the turtle's arm.

"The risks for us are low." Dovgrey hesitated, then added, semi-boastfully, "Not entirely absent, of course. Which is why we need to be certified."

"But what's the point?" Before he could get an answer, Arthur spotted a trio of bounding deer, all dark-skinned and nasty-looking. Evil-looking *sang kancil*, so Arthur made sure to murder them swiftly and with great prejudice. If folklore had taught Arthur anything about the tiny mouse-deer, it was that they were smart and tricky. Which often translated to magic users of some form.

A fact borne out by the slight pain on his exposed skin as the trio's minor aura of heat and flame had utilized bore out. If he'd let them stick around or fight long enough, he might have gotten more than a light sunburn.

"The point is to provide the floor users an opportunity for greatness, of course," Dovgrey said.

"Eh, boss. Don't get me wrong, I am happy you all do it, but why *lah*?"

"The Towers desire it." Dovgrey shrugged. "If you wish for more than that, I would ask that you ask another. Even old Tower inhabitants do not understand the will of the Tower entirely. We but learn how to work within it."

Arthur grunted. "Including working for them. Which humanity hasn't really worked out how."

"Time." Dovgrey said. "You need more of it. The Tower only recruits from multi-generational races."

"But I've seen - interacted - with others in the Tower?"

"In-floor are not part of the regular recruitment cycle. Same with promotion within the Tower," Dovgrey explained. "You can be promoted, of course, all the way through the Tower, but you'll never be transferred to higher levels." He tilted his head to the side, looking at Arthur. "Did you not study this matter?"

"Nope," Arthur said, cheerily.

Then, he was off, killing again. It took nearly an hour before he found another break to come back, cleaning off his hands and spear as he did so, trying not to gum up his own movements with all the sticky, drying blood.

"I learnt enough that if you got hired—and that was damn rare—you couldn't leave the Tower. Or if you did, you didn't get back home." Arthur shrugged. "Unless that's wrong..." A shake of the head indicated he wasn't. "There's no point working with the Tower for me, then."

"You don't like the Tower?"

"I don't intend to stay here." Arthur waved his hand upwards. "There's a world out there that I intend to return to, and more Towers."

"Ah, yes. Your Clan Seal."

"Exactly." Arthur tilted his head, considering and then added,. "So. You wouldn't happen to have more information on them, would you?"

"I do." A smile blossomed on that turtle-y face, pulled the mouth wide and crinkled up circular eyes. It made Dovgrey look even more adorable, almost causing Arthur to want to grab his cheeks and shake them. "But let us discuss this when we're safe, no?"

"Right, right…" Arthur sidestepped quickly to the side, bouncing high on a cloud he created and then thrust with his spear. He skewered the kuching hitam that had thought itself safe. Both Arthur and the cat dropped to the ground in short order. Out came the skinning knife, splitting the creature open, and then Arthur was back over.

"You know, I have something for that."

"For what? Killing animals?" Arthur said, then perked up as a thought struck him. "Or you mean the cleaning cloth?"

"Well, I do have some enchanted cleaning cloths, yes. But I was thinking more of monster core acquisition."

"What?" Arthur said, eyes opening wide. "You have something that automatically extracts the core?"

"A few things. One's a machine, if you will, that will locate and then remove said core from a beast. Quite useful, if a little slow. However, it will keep your hands clean," Dovgrey explained. "Really useful at more Advanced Towers too, where creatures might have bodies one does not wish to come in contact with."

"Acid, flaming hot bodies, that kind of thing?"

Dovgrey nodded in confirmation. "There's more, of course."

"Things that hurt? Yeah…"

"No—!"

Too late, since Arthur had to hurry backwards to deal with the swarm of leeches that had crept up on them, somehow managing to swarm on top of the cart and were in the midst of crawling towards Porta. Rather than kill them individually, Arthur utilized his Yin Aura, and the thin-skinned swarm creatures fell by the wayside soon enough.

He killed a few, of course, pinning those with his spear and extracting their monster core fragments, but with so many leeches and the cart never stopping, he could only collect a few.

Then, after the leeches were the hornets that came buzzing over, dozens of them. In this case, Arthur had to protect Porta more closely, pulling her along and watching her grow tired even as she was stung and harassed. Dovgrey pulled himself into his own shell, detaching tiny shields to cover the area around his head and arms to provide him cover. Didn't do much for his legs that had to be exposed, but soon enough the hornets were on the ground, unable to flap their wings hard enough to keep aloft.

Extracting the shards as they went along, dropping the Yin Aura the moment he could so that his companions didn't fall on their faces, kept them busy for a few more minutes. Eventually, though, Dovgrey returned to their conversation.

"More tools to collect. The best, well…" Dovgrey leaned over, whispering. "It just collects them, automatically. Pop, right into a secondary storage."

"Like dimensional storage?" Arthur said, eyes wide.

"Please, what Tower do you think you're in?" Dovgrey scoffed. "No, no. It'll just drop it in the same pouch you've kept it in. Or bag."

"Oh," Arthur said, disappointed.

"Greedy children," Dovgrey yawned, hiding its mouth and tapping idly on one of the shields on its front. He opened his mouth to say something more when those big limpid eyes blinked, once, and then again. Then, he cried out, "We're here!"

Not that Arthur needed the notice, what with having spotted it earlier with his own Enhanced Eyesight. However, the welcome sight and proximity to safety seemed to perk up even the tired Porta and the group sped up. Of course, all that meant for Arthur was that he grew even more wary.

Well-justified paranoia, as the trio of wasps slipped out moments later, lightning crackling along their bodies.

Chapter 81

"Typical," Arthur groused, as he hefted his spear. The trio of lightning wasps weren't moving, just hovering there in the middle distance and blocking the way into the village. The village was surrounded by high log walls which, of course, were utterly useless at keeping out flying attackers, but Tower logic likely kept the trio from going in.

Or maybe they just had general self-preservation, since there were a couple of guards watching everything, bows out but not loosing anything at the wasps.

"Couldn't be easy, now, could it?"

"Of course not," Dovgrey said, pulling on Porta's lead as he cinched the sides of his scale-mail breastplate tighter. "Just so you know, neither Porta nor I are particularly defended against lightning."

"Same here…" Arthur let out a long sigh. "I'll take them down, or at least bring them over to one side. You just get in."

"I do not believe the guards will open the door until the creatures are dealt with," Dovgrey said, but continued to keep moving. "Still, we will not be in your way, Climber Arthur."

"Thanks." Arthur trotted forward, putting some space between the two groups. He debated which skills to use, what he would need. Bark Skin had some minor resistance effects to lightning, but the keyword there was minor. Heavenly Sage's Mischief would give him extra speed, which would be useful against the wasps. Especially if he was going to be electro-shocked. On the other hand, considering these wasps might be three mini-bosses, this might be quite the long fight. Which meant he needed to deal with them via Yin Aura and just wear them down.

Lastly, of course, were his favorite quick shot attacks: the Refined Explosive Energy Dart—which he had come to think of as REED—and Focused Strike. Either of the two would be enough to land a fatal blow via surprise or at least a well-targeted hit, but there was no guarantee.

He'd have to make a choice of what to run and do it quickly. Some, like the Yin Aura, only worked if he pushed it onwards from the start of the fight. Which, if he thought of it that way, and the need to end this fast, saw it discarded. Same with Imbued Strike. Neither worked very well for mass battles, not just yet.

Eventually though, he hoped to make the Yin Aura so powerful he could knock out lower-level monsters with ease. It was getting there. Even the mass swarms of leeches or hornets weren't as much of a danger as before, especially coupled with good armour.

Which was the other side of the equation. He had good armour. Not perfect, but good enough that he didn't need Bark Skin. Anyway, if one of those stingers got through a gap, he doubted the short-term and specific boost of Bark Skin would save him. Their poison was the major concern here.

On the other hand, the goal was not to get hit. So Accelerated Healing, with its constant drain on his refined energy if he used the active version of the technique, was also a non-starter.

Options danced through his mind moments before he clashed with the trio. Two flew upwards, darting out of range, moving to surround him. The third lunged forward, butt and stinger leading the way. A quick sidestep took him out of direct line, the haft and spear tip shifting at the same time to deflect the attack while putting his own spear on target.

Focused Strike helped him punch through the defences, the creature's lack of stable footing making it easy for him to take the line. Problem was, before he could dig his spear all the way in, Arthur was already shifting directions, dodging the attacks coming in from other sides.

He spun sideways, focused and released the REED he'd been holding back to slam into the body of the already injured wasp. Moments later, even as the first Explosive Dart was sending goblets of flesh and chitin through the air, a second impacted the same spot. A giant gaping cavity where its torso was, forcing the creature to fall as nerves around wings failed and blood pumped out of the body.

As it died, it lashed out. Lightning, ignored till now as painful but not entirely crippling, exploded forth. Dancing between the dying body, the living wasps, and Arthur's body. It dropped him, muscles locking up and twitching.

Only a last desperate lean to the side had him fall out of the way of another attack and take the second hit on the edge of his armour, bouncing him off. He struck the ground hard, pain coursing through his side, unable to fall or roll with it, head bouncing off the ground a little and making him see stars.

The overpowered lightning attack died off, though not before a wasp darted down and stabbed him with its stinger. Targeting just below the edge of his breastplate that had ridden up and exposed his stomach and groin region as he thrashed around, it managed to impale him in the side above his leg.

New pain coursed through his body as toxins pumped into his muscles and bloodstream. Fresh agony as lightning, now given a direct entry to his body, poured itself through him. Arthur was regretting his lack of defence or active healing now as the barbed stinger tore out of him with a disgusting schlurp noise.

Even so, Arthur had enough energy and control to roll out of the way of the next wasp, barely avoiding the tip as it stabbed at his open-faced helm. Over and over again, leaving a trail of blood behind as Arthur tried to pull together the last edges of his techniques.

Buzzing high above, the two remaining wasps hovered around Arthur. He managed to get up on one foot, released the REED only to see the damn creature dodge his Dart in what was an obvious feint.

Good news was that it bought him time, enough that he managed to block the darting stinger of the other monster as it came for him, slashing with the kris as he finished the motion. He didn't manage to hit the body, angles all wrong, but the fast-moving wings on one side were torn up a little.

Not enough, not by far, to cripple it. But realizing he might be stuck on his knees, as lightning arcs danced through his body and the poison robbed him of fine control, he changed tactics. No more trying to finish this off.

Instead, Arthur used his skinning knife, the bracers on his arms, and his armour to block the darting figures. Threatening them, waving his weapon, targeting the wings. The creatures were wary of him too and his potentially fatal Explosive Darts.

Pain coursed through him as he dropped the Heavenly Sage's Mischief. No more time to worry about being stronger or faster, not when he was somewhat immobile from the lightning. Keeping his movements tight, his blocks and defences close, and not falling for their occasional feints. Threatening them with a bad look…

All the while, Accelerated Healing ran through his body, clotting the wound in his side, restoring destroyed nerves and flushing poison.

A small part of Arthur's mind pointed out what he was doing: soloing not one but three mini-bosses at the same time. Even if they were first-floor bosses, that would have been insane. The fact that he was now handling three and these were from the fifth floor?

Insane.

The buzz of the wings, the swinging dagger-like attacks. He leaned sideways, tore at a wing, pushing off the ground just enough to rise up, screaming in pain as his wound which had been closing tore open again. Dried blood, scabs, fresh burns.

Pain.

But the kris cut, tearing into another wing. Crippling the creature, sending it bobbing sideways. From the other side, he straight-armed the wasp darting in, feeling the hornet stinger slam into his breastplate, bruising his ribs and sending him over onto the side. He fell, rolled over, free arm pointed upwards as though to ward against the descending attack.

Not willing to give up its opportunity, the final wasp darted down, gathering lightning into its stinger. Hand, meant to block or slow, jerked upwards towards the creature's face.

Too late, the wasp realized there was a light, a glow in Arthur's palm. Moments later, the REED exploded outwards, catching it in the face, throwing it sideways as momentum and gravity took it down towards Arthur. He twisted, plunged the kris in, and took the body with him, kept rolling to get away from the crippled other wasp.

Didn't take long to kill this one, and then, staggering over to get his spear, finish the last. Leaving him standing before the village gates, victorious and bleeding and shocked.

Chapter 82

An hour and a half later, washed, mostly healed—but with a puckered scar on his abdomen and some lightning marks tracing across his body—Arthur sat down beside Dovgrey. The Tinker had managed entry and even the renting of the only rooms in the village for them, a major boon as far as Arthur was concerned.

But now it was time to get his reward.

"Thank you," Arthur said as he took the cup of water from Dovgrey. He looked sad for a moment that it wasn't beer or even juice, but you took what you received and were grateful. Placing the cup down after drinking, he raised an eyebrow at the still silent Tinker.

"Impatient. We should eat first," Dovgrey temporized. "I already ordered, you know."

Arthur opened his mouth to protest, then shut it before flashing a grin. "Sure, let's *makan*. Especially if you're buying."

"I am."

Smiling, Arthur took another sip of water, casting inwards for more information. This chance to talk to a Tower resident could be useful. There was, of course, a lot of information out there. Books and books about the Tower, the residents, the special place those who worked for them held. A lot of details... but the problem was, actually verifying that information was a pain and a half.

More than one scandal had broken out when information was proven to be untrue. If you trusted the self-named celebrity journalists and climber autobiographic tell-alls, some of the reasons for the differences in information was entirely due to the Tower residents themselves passing on bad information. Others were obvious fakes, lies about where and when climbers went.

So much, like today's meeting, would be unverifiable. Which also meant that any information he might glean from Dovgrey might be tainted too. Which then led to the question of whether it was even worth digging...

Never mind.

"You're thinking hard," the Tinker said, those big, round and soulful eyes blinking at Arthur. "About what to ask me?"

"About what's coming for dinner." Arthur grinned. "I'm Malaysian after all. Hoping there's a good laksa or curry. Or rendang. Kuih..." He said the last word dreamily.

The snort Dovgrey gave was skeptical, but he didn't call Arthur out on it further. Not that he could prove it. But now that Arthur was thinking of food, his stomach let out a loud rumble. A slow, amused blink, as the turtle-man stared at Arthur's loud midsection.

"What do you eat?" Arthur asked curiously.

"Many things. My favorite is jussap."

"What's that?"

Leaning forwards, Arthur questioned the other, learning about the cuisines of the Tower residents. The fact that he was genuinely interested in the foods that Dovgrey enjoyed, which were mostly vegetarian, probably helped. It also led to discussion of other species that lived in close proximity to the turtle.

"So, you don't cook at home then?"

"Food and cooking is not necessary. You know that."

"Yeah, but…" Arthur trailed off, understanding what Dovgrey meant. If he lived in the Tower as what was implied, on a floor in an Advanced or higher Tower, it made sense that restaurants were much less prolific. Even then… "That's kind of boring, *lah*."

"Cheap, though." Dovgrey waved a hand at the food that finally arrived. A few villagers tottered over with the plates held in hand. Arthur had counted about two dozen of these stick-figure humanoids that were a cross between a mantis and a human. The turtle added, "I eat when I'm working."

"Working, eh?" Arthur grinned. "Company expense account?"

A slow, languid nod. He clasped hands together, one on top of another and bowed to the mantises, and after a moment's hesitation, Arthur copied the motion. He eyed the food skeptically as Dovgrey dug in. At least the bowls of rice were normal, but the other items—insect-like meat fried up, vegetable hotpot that contained mushrooms and other unfamiliar items, including what might be tofu—had him looking a little skeptical. Mostly because the colours were lurid purples, oranges, and greens.

Seeing his host digging in, Arthur followed suit, marveling at the unexpected surprise of the meal.

"Nice." Not just that it tasted good, but expectations were thrown out of context as dishes he thought might be sweet or hot or spicy were instead sour or bursting with umami or just familiar. The hotpot, in particular, became his new favorite, and he lavished the gravy over rice.

For a time, discussion fell to the wayside, though occasional words were passed between the pair as Arthur savoured the meal. Only when the pair had cleared out the very generous meal and the various plates and utensils were taken away did Dovgrey sit forwards, hands clasped.

"Your reward." Dovgrey said.

"Yes…" Sudden apprehension clutched at Arthur, forcing him to breathe through the tension in his stomach.

"I could let the Tower decide. Or, I could do it for you." Limpid eyes blinked, slowly. "Which would you prefer, Climber Arthur?"

Trust that the other had his well wishes at heart, that he had not annoyed or unknowingly insulted the creature? That Dovgrey was, in the end, on his side? Or trust in the silent and impartial judgment of an unknown system? The Tower would weigh many things and come up with a reward, but there was no guarantee it would be personalized.

No guarantee that what would come from Dovgrey would benefit him either. There were enough stories out there where rewards were decreased, changed, or otherwise altered under the purview of the NPCs. They had a degree of leeway, more so when they allowed the climber to choose, as Dovgrey was doing now.

"Go ahead," Arthur said, choosing to put his reward in Dovgrey's hands. If there was one thing growing up in Malaysia had taught him, it was that one just had to rely on people and goodwill. Favours and connections were how you got things done, whether it was a run around endless bureaucracy and bribes or just locating the right mechanic.

"Then your present will be in three parts," Dovgrey said. "First, tomorrow, you can pick from my wares. Second, I'll do you a favor." A small smile. "Three options. I fix and improve your armour." Eyes drifted down Arthur's torso, what with him wearing only the breastplate and groin cup at the moment. "Which does require some additional work."

"Best I could afford. Or that they could do," Arthur said. The minor improvement to durability and cleaning that had been done weren't great, he knew that. But beginner human crafters were just that, after all.

"Not the best I can do," Dovgrey said with a shake of his head. "I can also replace your underlayer instead."

"Okay."

"Or, I can upgrade your spear." A nod to Arthur's black spear. "Give you an enchantment on it, something worthy of the material."

Arthur's eyes sparkled at the thought. He'd known the black spear could be so much more, but hadn't wanted to waste his money by upgrading the spear yet. He had vaguely intended to either upgrade it at the end, before he left the Tower, so that it was ready for the next Tower. Or at the start of the next Tower on its first floor.

But now... well.

"Third?" he asked, hesitantly.

"A new technique." Dovgrey smiled at the spark of interest. "Something that will fill in a gap in your current skillset."

"A combat technique?"

No movement, not even a blink of the turtle's eyes. Arthur huffed out loud his disappointment, but Dovgrey was unrelenting, refusing to give him a hint. Which was all kinds of unfair if you asked him, but that was what he got asking the NPC to choose. As it was, though, this was a better offering than he could have expected.

After all, he was being allowed to choose, not just get something dumped on him.

The only question was what.

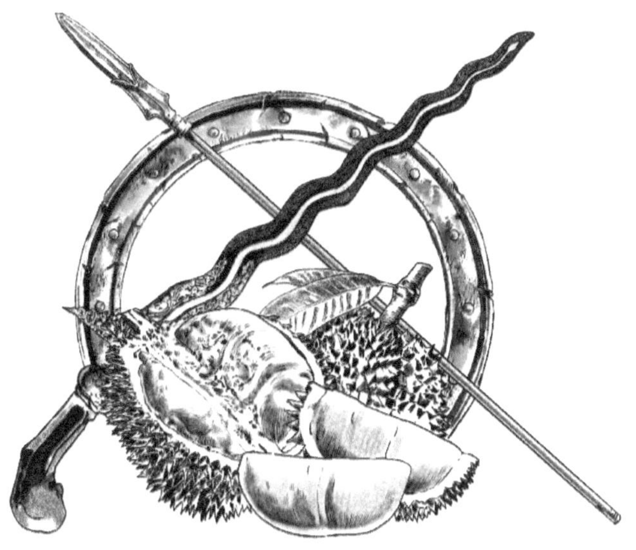

Chapter 83

Rather than make a decision immediately, and at Dovgrey's insistence that he would not open his cart till tomorrow, Arthur chose to sleep on his choices. It did mean that he woke up early in the morning, his enhanced body requiring only a short five hours to recuperate after all the beating it had taken.

Not that he had all the time in the world to think, what with the need to recover, then refine and cultivate ever more energy for his reserves. If he was stuck here, at least for a few more hours, he best make sure he top himself up. The fact that he was already facing the mini boss wasps meant that, soon enough, more dangerous wandering monsters would appear.

Time was running out.

Which weighed on his decision a little, Arthur had to admit. Getting either his armour or his spear fixed would cost time. How much, he wasn't certain; but enchanting in any form wasn't instantaneous. Of course,

Dovgrey was of a much higher level so he likely could do it much quicker, but still...

Defense, offense, or something new?

Enhancing equipment was always tricky. Most times, you tossed what you got from Beginner Towers soon after you entered an Intermediate Tower. The difference in quality and ability was just too great, that it was rarely worthwhile to keep old stuff. On the other hand, he still had at least one, if not two, Beginner Towers left to run before Arthur felt confident enough to run an Intermediate Tower.

If anything, all his original plans for once he left the Tower were now thrown away. Rather than just focusing on what was easy to get to—the Tower in Penang, and then, more dangerously, in Singapore—he could actually consider maybe doing another country's Beginner Tower. He might even have to start looking at the Tower rating scales at a more granular level, using some of the competing category classifications like the Adventurers Guild star categories or the competing Climber Tower Six Point Rankings.

Later, though.

If that was the case, if he was really going to have more options, than the use of either armour or spear—enchanted as they would be—would become much more important.

If he could get self-cleaning and repair on the armour, by itself, it would make a big difference. Increased durability would help too. Arthur's fingers traced the depression in his breastplate, felt along the scarred sides where spears, claws, and stingers had torn into the hardened leather.

This armor might last the rest of this Tower, but it wouldn't be much longer. The problem was the material. It just wasn't that great, and that was the major concern because even if he upgraded it, it felt like he was just putting a new coat of paint on a sixty-year-old Proton Saga.

No, the armour was not the best choice. He'd also noted the subtle hint offered, about something potentially available to buy in the Tinker's goods.

So, spear or technique. The first was rather obvious. Arthur picked up his spear, looked over the black wood shaft and the black steel spearhead, feeling the whorls on the shaft, the minor notches from blocked claws and weapons. For all that, the weapon was still in good condition, the shaft incredibly sturdy for something he had used and abused since the first floor.

He tested it then, checked the shaft for potential breaks, for places where it might bend and break and found nothing. Good quality, almost perfect really. It made sense to enhance the weapon, especially since there was no mention of upgrading the kris.

On the other hand, a new cultivation skill that filled in a gap could be incredibly useful. Equipment came and went, but skills… those would be his forever. Of course, eventually he'd upgrade or combine skills, discard the ones that he utilized for something better.

Seven Cloud Stepping might one day become a real flying technique, combined with something that made him faster. Maybe even a full-body movement and speed technique, making Heavenly Sage's Mischief defunct.

But what did he miss?

Something that could deal long-range damage repeatedly. A technique to capture or hold opponents. A buffing technique for allies, or a technique to heal others. Maybe a taming technique? He'd heard of those too… Sensory techniques would be useful. He was missing that entirely.

That brought speculation to a stop for Arthur. As much he might like to believe battle skills were being discussed, utility skills were just as likely to be added. Everything from skills that would make his cultivation grow faster, storage skills like his Poket Simpanan, sensory techniques, or aura boosting techniques were all on the table.

All of which were useful, but they had two major disadvantages. Firstly, it might push Arthur down a path that he didn't want to go; and secondly, any technique scroll given to him would still have to be studied. He literally had a mental defense cultivation technique that he hadn't found the time to work on.

"*Hun dan*," Arthur swore as he came to that realisation.

Well, if that was the way it was, that was the way it was. Setting his spear down, eyeing the shadows outside, he extracted another monster core.

Best to get refining, if he was going to be stuck here a little longer. Maybe he'd even upgrade himself a little, by the end.

"You're certain?" Dovgrey asked, picking up the spear that Arthur had offered to him.

"No. Especially since you won't let me look at your inventory till I choose," Arthur replied, trying for a slight wheedling tone. "Come on, boss. Please?"

"Nope." Tugging the spear closer, Dovgrey spun it around as his shell popped open, allowing him to slide the whole spear into one compartment. That, of course, made no sense physically but Arthur knew better than to complain. He did, however, feel a twinge of regret, wondering if he had just given up a storage technique or something. "Alright, come with me."

Trailing along like a good puppy, the pair reached the cart that had been left to dry under the simple open air stable, Porta happily munching hay alongside the vehicle. She was not tied up, a minor fact that surprised Arthur, but he assumed there were other things tying the creature to the village and stall.

Well, besides the hay.

"Here, you go feed her some corn." Dovgrey shoved the aforementioned bucket of feed at Arthur as he continued. "I will get set up."

"Uhh..."

His hesitation was entirely ignored as Dovgrey began the process of pulling his cart apart, extracting the hatches and then attaching it to the sides of the vehicle. In short order, he had the cart turned into a makeshift stall with numerous pieces set aside. He also had the various armour pieces and weapons propped up in a bag to the side.

"You look it over, don't touch. Because I'll know. I plan to get these sold." A gesture to the pieces. "Blacksmith will buy them for a good price."

"Really?"

"He will for me." Grinning wide, Dovgrey then shot a cautioning look at Porta and stomped off with his goods. Leaving Arthur to stare at the remaining goods laid out all around the stall on the makeshift tables.

All alone, but for a donkey. Which meant that a light-fingered climber with loose morals could take what he wanted.

"As though it's that easy..." Arthur scoffed, putting his hands resolutely behind his back. He knew exactly how these kinds of stories went, and they generally did not include a happy ending for the thieves.

Chapter 84

"What a display of junk," Arthur grumbled as he stared down at the items before him. There was a reason this NPC was called the Tinker, and it wasn't just because he could do enchantments on items and fix things up, but also because of the wide array of items he had.

At least the turtle-man had sorted them out into various sections. Books and scrolls in the top left; various trinkets right next to it including jewelry of various forms; then cooking items and other tools including a coil of rope and small pouches after that.

Then, moving down were weapons, everything from throwing daggers and darts to spiked ball caltrops and what Arthur swore was a grenade. Not that he'd actually seen a real one, but it looked like a grenade, with its egg-shaped body, handle and pin.

The smaller weapons took up much of the space. Knives of varying length. Spikes. Cudgels, one of which Arthur was certain was just a bunch of lead balls stitched into a leather hide. Useful, cheap, and quite effective. He'd seen them on the streets occasionally, at bars of a certain reputation when a knife and blood was less desirable but one had to deal with the regular rough clientele. Didn't want to kill them though, or else you'd never have any customers.

Down the cart, tacked on the end were the display for bigger weapons and bulky goods. Much fewer than the rest of his items, including a couple of packs, leather water bottles, a drinking horn from a creature that Arthur was certain was not a cow, a couple of swords, a mace in the shape of a sword and a large hammer. Then, two polearms: a guandao and a trident.

He obviously ignored the trident. Whoever thought that was a good fighting instrument was a fool. Great for spearing fish; horrendous balance otherwise and just as prone for your weapon to get caught and twisted out of your hand as you doing it to another. It was one of those anime or comic book weapons that looked better than it worked.

The guandao was pretty good, though. The large, curved blade on the end was great for sweeping attacks and for smashing through armour and chitin. You did not want to be on a horse if you were facing someone who knew how to wield one of those—or conversely, you wanted to be on a horse to use it. Much like the naginata, though it had a major disadvantage.

It couldn't thrust, and because it needed to sweep to attack, tight quarters were not where you wanted to take the weapon. Pretty much the reason why Arthur specialized in the spear, because he could always shorten his reach and thrust tight with it if he needed to. Though, depending on how tight things got, it could just as easily be dagger time.

"You have decided, yes?" Dovgrey asked, coming around at last.

"No." Arthur frowned. "You said there was armour?"

"Oh, but nothing that pretentious. Around the other side," Dovgrey said, waving him to the other side of the cart.

Rather than being laid out, the contents on that side were still seated inside the enclosed cart but the storage compartments all opened so that Arthur could peer within. He could see a bunch of makeshift bits and parts for weapons in a few of the locations. Also lots of clothing, including desperately needed underwear and socks, and then outer coverings of every kind. His gaze tracked over the contents, then glancing at the turtle while reaching out and receiving a confirming nod, he began to sort through them.

Not too long before he found what he had been looking for, pulling out the stretchy one-piece jumpsuit. He raised it, frowning a little at the warmth emanating from the suit itself, the tightly woven black-blue material almost seeming to pulse as he held it.

"What is this?"

"Underarmour, of course." Dovgrey blinked languidly. "Perfect to stop chaffing. It also has other properties." He waved a hand, and a notification appeared for Arthur moments later.

Complacent Mimic Underarmour of the Fool
Effect: Self-repairing, self cleaning, auto-sizing. Provides minor defensive bonus, resistance to cold and heat. Bonus to stealth. Can grow.
Caution: Mimic must be fed regularly

"This isn't clothing! It's a monster," Arthur protested.

"It's both." Dovgrey blinked again, looked surprised at Arthur's objection. "It is a self-repairing form of clothing and armor. Will last you years, can grow with you as you travel, and is in your color of choice."

"Black? I actually like wearing more colourful clothing, you know?" Arthur said. Nothing wrong with a good purple or red or green shirt. Made you stand out, in the sea of blue and blacks, especially when you went clubbing. "But it's the Tower. Black works."

"Yes, yes. You like being clean too, right? Well, the mimic will help keep you clean. It'll make all the dirt and blood vanish," Dovgrey said.

"You mean eat it from me, ah?" Arthur shook his head, folding it back. "What happens when I get wounded, will it try to eat me too? Because I'm not into that."

"Eh, you just have to train it properly."

"And how would you do that?" Arthur asked. He had to admit, the abilities of the clothing were great, but being eaten by your own clothing was not the kind of ending he envisioned for himself. At least, not by a mimic.

Okay, so he was grinning at the lurid thought, but it'd been months. He wasn't a monk.

"You drive a hard bargain, but I'll thrown in the acid and the brush too."

"Acid?"

What came next was rather vivid description of how one trained a mimic not to eat oneself. It involved self-harm, careful placement, and then the punishment via the application of acid to said mimic. Normally, such training took months, "But, it's a complacent mimic. It's already been trained and fed properly, so it'll only be a few hours."

"Of bleeding. Which is how you feed it."

"Exactly! Easy enough for a climber, right?"

"No."

"Come now, Climber Arthur. I told you I'll give you a discount, so for you, only eight stones from this floor. Cheap, right?"

"No." Arthur instead started picking out normal clothing including new sets of underwear and socks. Not too many, but even a couple of new pairs were worth it.

"I'll throw in the mundane clothing."

"*Tak mau!*" Arthur said, standing his ground. He wasn't going to bleed for this mimic.

"And I'll help you pick from the rest of the items, to fit your budget."

Now Arthur hesitated. That was the kind of offer that was hard to resist. Sure, he could try to look over the items available, figure out what he wanted. But this was, sadly, not a game. Things he picked up didn't necessarily come with much information, not unless the Tower or Dovgrey was being generous. A lot of the junk here was mildly enchanted or made of special material, so it wasn't just a matter of looking for Tower-made items.

"Fine, I'll take it." Arthur also reluctantly named the amount he was willing to spend. He still eyed the damn mimic suspiciously when Dovgrey shoved the clothing into his arms, but he had to admit the properties it had were really attractive. But again, it might eat him, which was why Dovgrey probably was desperate to get rid of it.

Or, was he just playing the part of a merchant desperate to get rid of it? Sometimes, trying to work out the intricacies of all that hurt his head. Which was why he ignored the entire thing for now. He had more important things to concern himself about right about now.

Like buying more stuff!

Chapter 85

Dovgrey moved immediately, not to the weapons or armour or bulk areas but the other side of the cart where all the trinkets and smaller items were. He reached out, shoving some of the merchandise aside before he began to pluck various items out.

An inkwell that looked to be made for stamps. Or perhaps had some solid ink within—hard to tell, with the case closed. An orange-yellow pouch with stitching all along the edges that had caught Arthur's eyes, because they definitely looked like enchanted embroidery. A ring and then a piercing, the kind that went into the nose or body or belly button. Finally, he plucked out two different knives and a small statue of a monkey made of jade and silver.

"That's... quite the collection," Arthur said, eyeing the statue in particular. Not something he would even have considered.

"Not done yet." Dovgrey next moved to the books and scrolls, flipping through them till he extracted two dumped them before Arthur. "Now I'm done."

"No weapons?" Arthur said. "No backpacks or packs?"

"Look first before you talk." A hand waved, and Arthur blinked as he felt something pressing on his mind from the Tower. Realising what it was a moment later, Arthur grabbed at the pouch, curious if it was what he thought it might be.

Pouch of Extradimensional Storage

Effect: Stores up to 80 liters of goods.

"Exactly what I thought," Arthur said. He touched the old pouch by his side, the one he got when he started, the one he kept all the stones in. The only form of extradimensional storage he had, and it was only really useful for small amounts.

On the other hand, 80 liters was about twice the size of a big backpack. Depending on how the pouch worked, he might even be able to store his spear in it. When he raised the question, Dovgrey snorted at him.

"Sure, but I wouldn't."

"Why not?" Arthur asked.

"It's a pouch. You pierce the other end, you destroy the enchantment. You put it facing up and stick your hand in, you're going to cut yourself."

"I could put a cap on it…" Arthur trailed off, shaking his head. He could see the impracticality of that. For one thing, he wouldn't even be able to use his spear if he extracted it, not immediately. The number of times he might need that would be high too. In addition… "This just a pouch?"

"Yes. Doesn't grow in size or change to fit whatever you can't fit."

Stretching the bands as far as he could, Arthur noted it was a good foot across. A decent size, but it wouldn't fit, for example, a foot-long haunch of meat. Made storing things difficult if he needed to extract more materials. More to the point, in general there just weren't that many drops in a Beginner Tower.

"Weight reduction?"

"95%."

"Damn…" Now that made a difference. Even if he only wanted to put the contents of his current backpack within, all his mundane goods and pots and pans and the like, it would make him a lot more maneuverable. No wonder Dovgrey didn't bother with the backpacks on display. This was better by far than any of that.

Arthur put the pouch back down, grabbed the monkey statue next. Let the pressure build a little before letting the notification that was waiting appear.

Howler Monkey of Warding

Effect: Creates multiple (fourteen) howler monkey simulacra that will spread out across the encampment and audibly warn owner of incoming threats.

"Oh, nice." Arthur didn't even need to ask why this was chosen. Protective wards while resting were very important, especially as one climbed higher and alone. Even if you were together with other climbers, an extra set of eyes—or fourteen—could be useful. "Let me guess, though: they actually have to see the threat. So something with good stealth could sneak past. But they're monkeys, so they'll likely take to trees or higher spots to keep watch?"

"Yes. They're simulacra so they're better than actual animals as their attention will not wander as much. However…"

"Still prone to wandering a little." Arthur grunted. No indication of how far they'd spread either, but he assumed that was mostly a question of geography. Not likely to go too far out, being pack animals. "Good choice…"

He put that one to the side, then started sorting through the rest of Dovgrey's selections a little faster. The inkwell came with a block which could be ground down to make ink. With the right skillset, you could create temporary enchantments. Someone who'd studied the right cultivation techniques could create talismans—one-off use enchantments—to suit the circumstances. No surprise that one of the manuals on offer was willing to teach Arthur how to do that.

"Tempting, but no." Not because he couldn't see how useful having such enchantments could be. Or because of how much time it would take to learn a new skill or master it. "Too expensive *lah*. Who's got money to burn like this?"

A shake of his head as he pushed it aside, continuing on to the other cultivation scroll that had been pulled aside.

Shadow Sense

Spiritual technique that spreads emanations from an individual's aura to provide a tertiary sensory method. Can be combined with other aura techniques. More powerful in shadows and darkness and those using Yin chi.

Effect: Creates a tertiary sensory technique via aura emanations. Range and fidelity of the shadow sense dependent upon strength of user and completion rate of skill.

Arthur blinked, reading over the description twice more before he found himself asking. "What's the range?"

"Starts out short, like a foot or two from your body. After that, it grows as you get better." Dovgrey let out a little shrug which made his entire shell shift. That brought to mind how the creature had not extracted a single item from the storage compartments of his shell, the place where Arthur was certain all the best stuff lay.

Could he have gotten something there, if he asked? Or did the shell simply store Dovgrey's personal items, to make sure he didn't lose them if he was teleported by the Tower out of danger. Another man, willing to risk the turtle's ire might ask. As for him...

"So, this is it? Not as though I can trade all in on for one good thing?" he said.

"You already did that." Dovgrey smiled. "You don't have enough, not with that budget of yours."

"And if I increased it.."

Big eyes drifted down to his pouch, before coming back up to Arthur. "Not enough, not yet."

"Yeah, I figured." Arthur sighed, moving on to the other items.

Ring of Piercing

Effect: Increases piercing effect of all edged weapons within user's aura by 15%. Reduces opponent's physical resistance by 10%.

Arthur grunted as he read the information. Simple enough of an enchanted item, similar in many ways to his own Focused Strike but providing an on-going effect. Not perfect, of course, because unlike his own technique, this worked only for edged weapons on the thrust and cut. Not so much use if he was bludgeoning anyone, which meant kicking or punching was out of the question for its effects.

On the other hand, that was only the first part of it. The second portion of the ring meant that even his blunt attacks or any of the secondary crushing or physical damage was going to be more effective. Add the fact that it was a persistent effect and this was much better than his own Focused Strike, even if less effective overall.

"This one's *mahal* too, eh?"

"Of course it's expensive." A nod to the pile. "All enchanted items are."

He didn't ask further, figuring they'd get around to bargaining once he was done looking it all through. Arthur noted that none of the items had prices on them, which reminded him all too much of wandering along Petaling Street with a tourist, trying to find a deal.

Surprising how much a single fake Rolex could jump in pricing, depending on who you were with or how they acted. He'd once played tour guide to a young lady he'd met at a club and winced when they'd exclaimed how badly they wanted a fake bag, especially when it was already four times as expensive as he knew he could have gotten it for. At that point, bargaining was not a question.

She'd still bought it and thought he was a genius for getting it at half off.

Piercing of Energy Enhancement

Effect: Increases use of Tower Energy by 5%

"Boss?"

"Oh, that one…" A lazy nod from Dovgrey. "It's good."

Chapter 86

Arthur let out a little hiss of breath as the damn turtle just stared at him after merely saying, "It's good." Impatient, he tapped the simple piercing with a sapphire embedded in it. It was a stud that went into the body, and he winced at the thought. He knew it was a given that he'd have to acquire a few at some point. Pretty much every climber ended up looking like a fashionista with bad taste after a bit, but still…

He hated the idea of rings or piercings or anything else that could get caught in clothing or weapons. It was bad form, and years of training without them, and after watching enough videos of what happened when you wore stuff like that, had him conditioned to hate the idea.

"So?" Arthur asked again.

"Overall efficiency increase in anything to do with Tower energy. Not refined energy, though." Dovgrey nodded sagely. "Why it's so cheap, and only here at Beginner Towers, is because it's the boost is so low in percentage."

"Since all you higher-level folks use more refined energy, right? And need a much bigger boost?" Arthur frowned. "But a percentage increase..."

"Caps." A wave at all the material on the table. "There's always a cap. Just not what you might see, because you're too weak."

Arthur grunted in acknowledgment. That made sense. Five percent on twenty was only like one point, or something. Five percent on a hundred was five. On five hundred, it was twenty five. By the time he had to worry about the caps, most climbers would have moved on. Which was why lower-level items like this one moved down to Beginner Towers.

"Okay. So anything to do with Tower energy. And cultivating too, *ya?*"

A nod from Dovgrey.

"Techniques?"

Another slight nod.

Arthur opened his mouth again, saw the look he got, and shut it. Everything was everything then. Maybe even refinement, which would be nice. If it meant efficiency in not just how much energy he used but also speed, it would be a big boost in a fight where fractions of a second could mean life or death.

Another winner.

Now for the dangerous cutlery. He looked both knives over at once, rather than drag it out further.

Enchanted Knife of Linked Harvesting

Effect: Enchantment links knife to a storage item, allowing speedy and clean harvesting of beast stones. When outer layer of a dead creature's defences are pierced, beast stone will be transported to linked storage item.

Ranged Throwing Knife of Return

Effect: Increased effective throwing range of knife. Enchanted to return to sheath after impact.

"Where's the storage item?" Arthur asked curiously.

"You can link anything you want." Dovgrey tapped the skinning knife's pommel, where a small jewel was socketed. "Put that jem the storage item, and your beast stones will drop into the storage slot. Has to be a storage item though. Can't be a plain pouch – it needs to have the enchantments on the storage items to work. Can't be too big either, or else it won't work."

"Oh..." Arthur rubbed his chin, and then asked the obvious question. "Why does the creature have to be dead?"

"Innate resistances. Might also not work on things too recently killed. You have to wait for the natural aura and defences to fade. This is just a Beginner tool, you know."

"Yeah. And it still requires me to stab things..." Arthur grumbled a little but could see how it would be super effective. The sharp tip would make harvesting much faster than cutting through bone or muscle or reaching into guts to pull things out. Meant that he wouldn't be leaving as many un-looted bodies behind just because he ran out of time to harvest their stones.

He wanted it, for sure.

"And this knife, there's only one of it?" Arthur tapped the Throwing Knife of Return. It was in a cross-body sleeve that would go under the lower rib on the outside of a breastplate. He assumed there were other carrying options, since it was the sheath and knife that were enchanted, not the belts. Still, it was a cool way to carry and use.

"You couldn't afford a whole set."

Arthur winced at the blunt assessment. "It fly back or just teleport in or...?"

"Reappears inside the sheath," Dovgrey said. "You don't have a good weapon for hitting things at range." Eyes drifted low to the pouch that Arthur carried his sling and the stones in. "And fast."

"Yeah, yeah... but a throwing knife?" Arthur snorted. "Contrary to video games, these things are an annoyance at best."

A shrug. "Best I have." Silence, then Dovgrey added, "Anyway, it's made of cold iron. Good for storing Tower energy."

Arthur narrowed his eyes at the addition, understanding beginning to penetrate his mind. After all, it wasn't an entirely unknown technique. Someone had named it the "Gambit gambit," which was a terrible play on words that, of course, became the commonly used name. Learn techniques and store them in thrown weapons, such that you could then deliver the attacks at range. Particularly useful since the physical object allowed one to store a higher percentage of Tower energy or refined energy inside the object rather than use a portion of it to create the container.

The downside was you actually had to study the technique and throw it. And while explosive enchantments were the most common, flame or other elemental enchantments were a possibility too. Given enough time, Arthur figured he could learn how to do it himself, giving him another aspect to his long-range arsenal.

Imagine storing a third REED in the knife, so that he could release one Explosive Dart after the other. Given enough time, he might even be able to lay a constant barrage of attacks on his opponents. A nice thought but...

"I guess I need to make a decision now, eh?" Arthur said and rubbed his chin.

Most of these were add-ons, things that were nice to have and might enhance him later on. The ink and the technique manuals were great but just too much work. Though the fact that the Shadow Sense technique tied into his Yin body had him leaning seriously towards purchasing it.

The throwing knife was useless till he learnt better techniques. Or, well, not useless but much less useful. More importantly, he only had this floor and one more to go before the big boss, which meant that his necessary utilization rate—before he spent time training himself out of the Tower and then coming back to a new one—was low. As a climber, he'd have access to a lot more choices in terms of what he could train in Malaysia.

No guns still, but bows and crossbows started becoming viable.

So, no throwing knife.

Storage pouch, harvesting knife, howler monkey ward, ring of piercing, and the energy enhancement stud. He shifted all those forward, pushed the rest back. Hesitated at the Shadow Sense technique and then, eventually, pulled it into the keep pile.

"All that."

"You are joking, yes?" Dovgrey said.

"Well…"

The turtle reached out with those weird, stumpy fingers. They were still small enough that he had fine dexterity. Dark and light green of turtle skin, with splotches of black. Nails that were hardened but blunted. Dovgrey pulled the harvesting knife, the energy enhancement stud, and the storage pouch aside, leaving the others in the initial pile.

"One of those three," the turtle said, gesturing down at the three expensive items, "and two of the others."

"How about two of the first row?"

"For another twenty stones from the ninth floor, sure."

Arthur grunted, "Fifteen."

"Twenty."

"Don't be like that, *lah*. You promised me a discount, boss." Switching to Manglish, Arthur tried his best to wheedle, only to get a flat look from Dovgrey. After a second, he sighed. "Eighteen?"

"Deal."

Considering how fast the damn turtle answered him, Arthur had a feeling he had lost out on that bargain. Taught him to show his cards. But, really, the difference between three and five stones wasn't that great. He had picked up quite a few already just escorting the Tinker to the village.

Now, the question was, which items to pick.

The Pouch of Extradimensional Storage was nice, but Arthur knew that the Merchant was supposed to have better quality items than that—if you found him. The fact that he wasn't in this village meant it was quite possible he wasn't here at all right now, which meant Arthur might be out of luck. Besides, it was unlikely he would have time to look further for the Merchant. Or the Hermit.

Even so, he'd lasted this long without a better storage pouch. A small part of him held out hope for learning a technique that gave him access to storage by creating an extra-dimensional space out of himself. That was the kind of technique you could get from the Hermit or other specialized quests. Basically not something you'd get in general.

He decided against the pouch. If he had to buy something, it wouldn't be that.

The sapphire stud—the Piercing of Energy Enhancement—was an overall upgrade, but he mostly used refined energy. If it upgraded that since instead of just Tower energy, the stud would have been a lot more useful for him. As it stood, a minor upgrade in cultivation speed just wasn't as precious as a major upgrade in harvesting time.

If nothing else, he wouldn't be covered in so much blood. So, the Enchanted Knife of Linked Harvesting it was.

Then, he just had to decide between the Howler Monkey Ward, the Ring of Piercing, and the Shadow Sense technique. As much as the ring was fascinating, he was already going to get an overall increase in his attack strength when Dovgrey enchanted his black spear.

Which meant…

"I'll take the harvesting knife, the howler monkey ward, and Shadow Sense technique," Arthur said. Even if he didn't learn the technique now—and there was something to be said about trying to practice it immediately—it was still a technique that suited him very well.

Best not to look the gift turtle in the mouth.

"Done." Dovgrey pushed the three items at Arthur and then began to put everything away, grumbling all the while. "Bargain with me and never actually buy anything."

"Needed to know what my options were. So… the spear?"

"Tomorrow morning."

"Right. Right." Arthur slipped the ring on, shivering as he felt the energies of the ring pierce him, sending little lightning shocks all the way through his aura and his body. He'd get used to it soon, but for now, it felt like tiny pinpricks all over him. Knife went into his new extradimensional pouch, knowing it was better to store it there than potentially lose it.

And then, he only had to go study his cultivation technique.

After all, he had a whole day to master it.

Chapter 87

Heading back to his room, Arthur made to lock the door and block it with the room's only chair. He didn't want to get interrupted, not if he was going to spend the day practising this new technique. After a moment's hesitation, he also went over to the windows and closed them, pulling the curtains together after shutting the heavy blinds.

In the shadows of the room, he took a seat on the bed, unrolling the Shadow Sense scroll to read. Soon enough, he was sprawled on his back, holding the scroll above his head as he read, charting the paths of energy he needed to utilize and explanations of aura control and manipulation. Those portions he found himself understanding and grasping quite quickly.

Within a few hours, he had mastered the first portion of the technique with only a few moments of energy backlash when he didn't get it right. Overall, minimal concerns. Even manipulating his aura was simple enough, what with his own experience with the Yin Aura that helped combine skills and even upgraded aspects of one another.

No, the real difficulty was something else. The utilization of a sixth sense that felt his aura at all times, that then noticed the layer between him and the escaped energy. It was a new area of study, one he had never thrown himself into before and required him to work on utilizing a sense that he had never truly paid attention to.

Much like proprioception or the sense that told you how fast you were moving or if you were up or down or sideways and where you related all across the continuum. Such senses were intrinsic to the human experience, but also so natural that most individuals never trained or noticed them.

Until, of course, your internal ear was knocked askew. Or you kept stumbling into things, banging your toes, wondering what happened and then realised you were holding yourself a little too tight or had grown an inch.

Children...

Once Arthur had that thought and ensured he could keep this portion of the technique running, he got up. Without his spear, he couldn't go through spear forms very well, but he had his dagger. Short sword and dagger forms were fewer in number, but he had done so many and worked so hard, he could instead play.

Which was what he did. The kris wasn't a weapon he had naturally trained in, though they'd been exposed to *silat* practice for about three months, which included practicing the kris. The martial art had nearly died out, what with the advent of other competitive sports and the focus on self-defence for the urban environment. Very few individuals kept up with training or teaching the old art of silat.

And then, the Towers came and suddenly, weapon use had become all the rage. Even silat had seen a bloom in interest, especially when people realised not only that was it highly effective, but that it was highly effective because it was painfully lethal. It still wasn't as widely practised as some of other martial arts with better PR, but it was no longer on the edge of dying either.

All of which meant that the guest teacher coming in had done so at his sifu's request. Three months of intense training in a different, harder style, with interesting rising attacks from the center line, movements that reminded Arthur of a striking snake at times, and a very controlled, tight fighting form.

Effective.

Remembering all that, trying to recall the motions and how they worked, he ran through the forms with his kris. A lot of it had to be adapted, of course. The scramble for survival in a battle between monsters and climbers ensured that forms which were merely elegant were discarded for what was effective.

Yet, going back to the basics was important. Teaching himself to keep his elbow in, to twist and push at the right time, turn the shoulders or rotate the hips correctly to generate that extra ounce of power. All necessary to keep his form and style efficient. Microseconds of improvement would one day make all the difference, especially if he kept climbing.

In addition, most of all, it was fun.

Children learnt by play. Adults could learn by play. Humanity in general was born to do so, but repetition and hard work were just as important. This, this was all three. Movement for fun and profit. Tight focus on the extension, on the feeling of his body and muscles and the air and the world outside of direct contact with his body.

Not just hearing, not just sight or smell or even taste, but the chi that suffused the darkened room. The way it throbbed with each moment as he moved, as his aura pulsed. So many points of failure, but most of all...

Most of all, he needed to feel it. To actually grasp and flex this sense and muscle that he had never even known was there. Shifting movements in this dark room were part of that, a way to force air flow and himself to extend and alter the environment. Small changes, as he struck or tossed his pillow or clothing about, letting them fall as he stabbed at them with the sheathed weapon, feel the clothing shift and turn, the outlines of it around his body.

Hours of repetition, over and over and over again until he got tired and thirsty.

Then, downstairs to acquire a jug of watered-down juice and a meal, all the while keeping his focus inward and tightly drawn in. The world throbbing, shifting, harder now in the daylight. The shadow realm gone, the bonus faded in all but the closest, darkest spots. The shadows under the tables, the chairs, in the movement of those around.

He went outside next, rather than back to his room. Returning to his forms, but with a greater challenge as the day ground on and on. He could keep moving, keep training because of his passive healing, and thanks to the Tower infusing his body with energy; and in this state of half-meditation and half-play, he could do it for hours.

And he did.

Past dinner, offering bare words to Dovgrey. The pair eating in silence, focused on a future and a world outside of each other's perception. The turtle-creature musing on enchantments, Arthur sensing the world around and attempting to understand what he felt, what sensation he could grasp.

It kept coming in fits and starts. At first, in the initial few hours, it was a ghost sensation, one that he almost believed was not real. So fragile that he was sure he imagined it. Later on, more consistently, more surely, as he grasped what this strange non-muscle movement was really like.

It wasn't seeing, not something so instinctive. Perhaps closer to hearing or smell at the moment. Not constant like touch or taste, but there in the background all the time. There were variations in this background. Like a sharp smell, a loud noise. Except that variation was between lighter and darker locations, where shadows pooled and darkness lay. Almost like he could feel light itself, even as it came falling down through the atmosphere to him. As it was shed by swinging lanterns or glittered off the edges of shiny metal or reflected off lighter-coloured clothing.

Except, those shafts of light were the opposite of sight for him. It was the darkness that was real sight, the shadows found at the base of feet, beneath tables, in the shifting movement of clothing.

He flushed red when he realised that. How he could feel his own shadows, in his own clothing… and the creatures beside him. Not that he had any physical desire, really. But sensing the shape of bodies, the outline between shadow and solid space... It made his mind race and offered too much information.

No one, no human, needed to know how well packed a turtle Tinker was.

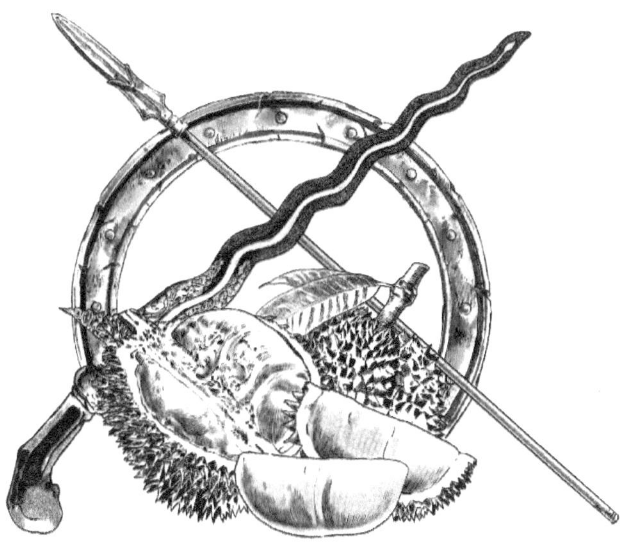

Chapter 88

Dawn, light filtering through. That moment between full darkness and early morning, the hour of the bear was it—or something strange and poetic like that. Funnily enough, the best time to practise his new skill, especially compared to full dark when there was too much darkness, not enough differentiation.

Later on, Arthur knew, it would be easier. He would grasp darkness and its gradations, understand how even black and night had shadows. For now, the dawn where light played across the horizon was perfect for his training.

He could feel it now the shadows now, consistently. Not far, mostly around his own clothing, with brief glimpses outwards. Maybe a few inches from his body, he could sense things around it. It was not consistent, sharpened by the amount of shadows present, varying by the deepness of a shadow and the degree of change.

Relearning how to see the world in a totally new way took a bit of time and effort. Thankfully, training in a sparring circle, two or three on one had helped. Feeling pressure, the sense of hands and body moving out of his sight, gaining a feel of where people were by instinct. Now, that secondary set of instincts was bolstered by the aura.

In time, Arthur knew, he'd grow more powerful, more confident in its use. In time, he would be able to track entire bodies and figures, because while it was called Shadow Sense, it wasn't confined only to shadows.

A powerful technique that he kept running, Tower energy bleeding from him each moment he utilized it. Thankfully, the initial portion of on-going aura was low cost and something he had mastered already.

Heading downstairs now, still holding onto the aura, having his meal with his backpack down by his side. Ready to go, because it was time to make a move. Now he just had to see what had happened to his spear. After half an hour of waiting, Arthur found himself drifting off, into himself as he paid attention to that shadow sense. A form of peaceful meditation that was interrupted by the sudden appearance of a spear landing beside him with a clatter and bounce.

"Here," Dovgrey growled.

"Wrong side of the bed?"

"No bed," Dovgrey growled, glaring at Arthur. "You bled too much on that damn thing."

"I did?"

"And the monsters."

Arthur frowned, uncertain what the turtle meant. He gestured impatiently for Arthur to just pick up his newly enchanted spear, so he did, allowing the notification from the Tower to filter through.

Sharp Black Spear of Wounding

Through continual use in an enchantment-primed state, this sharp black spear has gained an additional property.

Enchantments: Sharp – Increased Penetration by 25%. Wounding – Creates a bleed effect on wounded creatures, dealing additional damage per second until wound closes.

Arthur blinked, reading the first line. The Tower rarely added such descriptions, especially in the Beginner Tower, because it was unnecessary and just more work. However, this time around, it seemed his constant use of the spear and taking his sweet time in actually firming up an enchantment had a secondary bonus.

"Huh. That why you struggled?" Arthur said.

"Of course. We're supposed to only add one enchantment, and I was going to make it a good one." Dovgrey looked pleased with himself as he continued. "I did, too. Then, the spear started reacting with the enchantment when I tried to seal it all, and I had to work extra hard. Made me use all of my powdered enchantment core!"

"Thank you," Arthur said, standing up and hefting the weapon. No change in weight or balance either, at least not enough to make a difference. He could see how lines were now etched down the shaft and along the edge of the spear head. New sigils and runes that utilized Tower energy to empower them, stored within the monster core that had been ground and sealed inside those lines.

Outside of the Tower, he might have to enhance and increase the energy stored in the spear itself after months or maybe years. Depended on how well the Tinker had managed to do, the quality of his work. Unfortunately, Arthur wasn't the person to ask about that; after all, this was only the second enchanted weapon he'd ever examined up close.

"Well, that's fine." Dovgrey looked away, then after a moment looked at Arthur. "What are you planning on now? Finishing this floor?"

Arthur hesitated, considering. For all that he had complained about holding back on getting a second cultivation technique, he'd still picked up Shadow Sense. It had been the right choice, especially since he could now run two on-going techniques. Did he want to spend more time training?

Did it make any sense to still try to find the Hermit? If not him, he could try for the Merchant. The problem was, he had paid out quite a bit to the Tinker already, and if the Merchant wasn't on this trail, he either had to retreat back to the start—a lot of time he couldn't afford to waste. The chances of finding the Merchant further ahead on the trail was quite low, unless he was much further upwards where trails joined together.

That was the most likely scenario, if Arthur had to guess. If he delayed long enough, he might catch the Merchant further up on the hill, if he was heading to the peak. And not going down. If he was going down, then Arthur was entirely out of luck already and nothing he chose would matter.

So it made very little short-term, logical sense to go after the Merchant.

"Hermit." Arthur cocked an eyebrow. "Know where he is?"

"You sure you want to look for him?"

"Yes," Arthur said. "I have a week, probably, before things get really bad."

"I don't know where, but..." Dovgrey pointed towards the peak, vaguely at where Arthur had to go but further right. "Somewhere along that line I'd say."

There were a lot of questions that could be asked of why the turtle was sure. On the other hand, looking a gift horse, or turtle, in the mouth seemed like a bad idea. He had a feeling some rules were being bent, and it was possible Dovgrey was lying to him. However, Arthur figured it worked for two reasons.

One, there was no reason for the Tinker to lie.

And secondly, he was still heading to the peak.

"Thanks. I should get going then." Transferring the spear to his other hand, Arthur offered a hand shake, only for Dovgrey to do a horizontal handslap. Only quick reactions had him manage to repeat the actions without too much embarrassment.

"To meeting in another Tower."

"In another Tower," Arthur echoed, flashing a smile.

Then, grabbing his spear, he made his way out. After all, he had new equipment to test and a Hermit to find.

Chapter 89

The beast bounding through the woods was not what you'd normally consider an existential threat. The sang kancil were small, shy mammals, folklore leaning on their cleverness rather than their strength to win out against their various opponents. As such, the fact that the ones coming after him were coming in a pack and wielded Tower energy smoothly was a little bit of a surprise. Not a huge one, since they were a semi-common problem, but still a surprise.

No elemental energy, no wind or fire, but pure blue coursing power shot outwards from the mouse-deer pack, forcing Arthur to block and move. He swung the spear hard, watching the tip slow a little when it struck the pulsing blue light that defended the mouse-deer but shattering it moments later as its own enchantment worked.

A long slice, fur and flesh opening, blood leaking on the ground. A small plaintive cry, similar to a bleat but still quieter and would have been more endearing in a way if not for the fact that Arthur was also bleeding from a half-dozen other strikes that had punched through his armour—by virtue of bypassing it on an energetic level, rather than puncturing it physically.

So he was bleeding into his armour from the inside. Even if he had bought new armour, it would have done nothing to protect him in this case, which made him feel a little better about the entire thing.

Not that he was the only one bleeding. Most of the sang kancil now had at least one, if not a few wounds across their body. The small creatures were so fast that, even when he managed to break through the defensive Tower energy, they were still able to jerk their bodies out of fatal strike.

On the other hand, that also meant that he had a chance to see how the Wounding effect worked. Initial observations said very well. Their wounds, especially in the heat of battle, weren't closing, the constant movements increasing blood flow. Minor effects that would have clotted or slowed the bleeding down had stopped, meaning that the ground all around was pooling with their blood.

A minute into the fight, one of the kancil stumbled as it tried to attack Arthur, sinking to its four knees. He ignored it as it fell over sideways, unable to stand any further. Not long after, another dropped. A too-slow reaction saw Arthur putting his weapon into a third body and then crushing a head with the haft, as both opponents grew too slow to react.

After that, killing the few survivors was simple. Even better, his new enchanted harvesting knife yanked and deposited their beast stones with a simple cut. The knife worked very well even if he used, for example, the eye. Or any open wound. Which meant he wouldn't have to work too hard at sharpening the weapon.

"Nice..." Arthur muttered to himself. The only real difficulty had been keeping his new Shadow Sense out, because the vague impressions he got in battle were actually quite distracting. Till he got used to it, he would not be utilizing the aura for fighting. More than once, he'd dodged or twisted his body in anticipation of an attack he thought might come, only to be fooled by a dipping branch or a feint that entered his sphere of perception.

No, the Shadow Sense ability would be useful but, unlike what others might think or show in movies, such things took time to study and integrate. Which was partly why he'd wanted to acquire it earlier rather than later.

"Well, I guess I'm DOT man," Arthur said, turning away from the bodies. Between his Yin-poisoned knife, his poisoned Yin Aura, the Imbued Strike - Yin Poison technique, and now, the bleed effect from his spear, he was definitely a long-term, Damage Over Time kind of fighter. Sure, he could end the battle with brute force if he got lucky; but it was more likely he'd just end up bleeding and poisoning his opponents to death.

Not a bad thing but for the fact that he either needed to increase his evasiveness or tanking ability. Shadow Sense gave him better chances to dodge, but Bark Skin increased survivability against attacks. Of course, he always envisioned himself more like Sun Wukong—fast and powerful and deadly. He still had those skills, just that he didn't have the penetrating power of the monkey king just yet. One day…

"For now, got to move, and see if we will lose; to the monsters who wander, all over yonder." Putting his spear on his shoulder, he started walking again, cutting through the land. As he did so, he kept an eye out for signs, for anything that would give hint to the Hermit's location.

Unlike the stories that spoke of hermits in the mountains, cultivating away to gain immortality on air and cloud and nectar of the bees, the Hermit in the Tower needed a little more than Tower energy. They needed monster cores to keep them going, because they could not exist just on the paltry amounts of power that suffused a Beginner Tower. They also needed clothing and sharpened knives and wood to make fires. They needed water, to take the occasional bath in.

In other words, they left their caves to hunt or forage or travel. Which meant there were signs of their passage, if one knew what to look for. And while Arthur wasn't a tracker, in his time in the Tower he had picked up some skill at tracking, what with the need to find monsters, work out where his friends were going or had gone, look for potential ambushes, and most importantly, make his way back.

Familiarity helped as well. Over time, understanding what was unusual or different became part and parcel of one another. Like seeing a *gweilo* wandering near a squatter encampment, or a *dato's* daughter going to a sketchy KTV for a thrill. People in the wrong place, things misplaced.

Though, Arthur had to admit, all his examples were people. He always paid attention more to that than things, because people moved and hit and spoke out of turn. Wrong types of shoes, sporty cars, flashy mobile phones—those were interesting to note but not directly dangerous. Sometimes, they were just camouflage too.

Like the salamander on the tree that he pinned with his spear, punching through its body and then yanking it close to cut its throat with his harvesting knife. Holding it all together for a few more steps, waiting for the slight shiver in the blade to tell him that the creature had died enough for the stone to be teleported into his pouch, and then he tossed it away.

Funny enough, how mortal camouflage mostly went one way. Dressing up to look rich. Few tried to dress down, to look poor. Said something about their world, really, where everyone tried to get into the right places, where the few jobs that weren't automated still existed.

Idle musings, as he scanned the world around, hiking through the woods. Sweating and drinking of his water regularly. Never too deeply, never too much. Keeping an eye for the occasional fruit tree that he could pick from. Bananas and berries and maybe, if he was lucky, even durians.

Not that they were that common, all in, but it was better than nothing. He didn't need the salts, the potassium, and all the other minerals he sweated out, not when the Tower imbued his body with the necessary sustenance. But just like with food, consuming nutrients of some form, actual meals and water helped reduce the Tower energy cost.

Idle thoughts and an overall focus on the world around him. That was going to be his next few days, while he searched for the Hermit or signs of him, while hopefully avoiding any major encounters with a group of monsters.

At least, so far, those annoying fire moose weren't around. The most illogical of animals created by the Tower. Good thing he hadn't seen one on this floor. So far.

Chapter 90

The cave was hidden behind a shroud of trees and bushes, so overgrown with ivy that he would never have seen it, if not for luck. He would otherwise have been distracted by the pounding of a small waterfall nearby.

A need to piss had Arthur up late at night. As he stared up into the sky while depositing his golden gift to the plants around, a swaying branch had revealed the flicker of light.

It had been too bright, too unnatural to be anything but a fire or lamp. Or maybe a will-o'-the-wisp, though the Malaysian jungle had never been one for those creatures. Not to say the Tower wouldn't bring them over for the heck of it, but it was unlikely. And without a better lead, Arthur had made his way over.

That was two days ago, and other than some minor signs, he had not caught a glimpse of the light again. Still, muddy footprints and broken branches had guided him close, till he was here, standing before the cave opening. Wondering what was inside, for the darkness that blocked sight—along with a wall's sharp turn within the cave—hid much from him.

"Got to take a chance, if you're not in a trance…" Arthur shifted his grip on his spear, grimacing as he stepped within. Tight and dark: exactly the kind of place you wanted to have a spear. He just hoped that the cave opened up more instead of closing in, because otherwise he might have to abandon the weapon and his backpack.

He turned the first corner. To Arthur's surprise, another turn came soon after, though he was rather grateful that in neither case was the passageway too constricted.

After exiting the passage, noting how the moss and rock itself was brushed clean, smoothed out even in a few places from passage, he emerged into a much wider cavern. It was the size of the warehouse he'd left behind only a week or so ago, with a soaring ceiling and a half-dozen stalactites and stalagmites in the central area. Mostly though, those were along the raised edges, the entire cavern a bowl with one side having a lip.

On that lip, lounging rather than seated in a meditating position, was the Hermit. Instinctively, on seeing it, Arthur recoiled. There were many things he disliked, but rats—giant rats—were high on the list. Even the numerous attempts at reviving that 80s cartoon with turtles had not dissuaded or altered his lived experience of those disgusting, screeching creatures. Filthy, noisy, smelly, and all too prone to nibble on toes or fingers when one was sleeping or get into one's food…

"Are you here to kill me?" The voice was cool, a little amused.

"No… I…" Forcing himself to relax the grip on his spear, to shift its point away, Arthur continued slowly. "I just…"

"Do not like our little cousins." A sneer, from that humanoid rat face, red eyes glinting. Arthur almost raised his weapon again, such was the venom in its voice. "And kill and trap them with impunity. Poison too."

Arthur strode across the cavern, metal cap on spear tap-tapping against the bare stone floor. Moss, high above and luminescent was offering illumination, but it was a light green colour that gave a sickly cast off the rat and the surroundings.

"Don't forget boiling them alive, crushing necks, and various forms of testing," Arthur said. "But let's also not forget your cousins nibbling on toes and fingers of the sleeping and starving and ill, of bringing disease as they sneak into houses and eat our food."

"We are clean. It is your world that is a parasite-ridden place." The Hermit hopped up off where it lounged, landing down in the depression. "Your world mistreats anything smaller, anything different than them. Treats them as things to experiment on. Do not think we don't know of your lab rats…"

"Yeah, yeah, we're barbarians." Arthur shuddered as the Hermit came up to him, doing its best to loom but the twisted nature of its spine kept it from being able to stand at its full height. As it was, it came up just under his chin, which made it feel a lot less threatening. Not that height or size had anything to do with deadliness, but that was the logical side of him. The illogical side, the one that had full control as his fear and disgust ran riot even through his Yin Body, and he found himself recoiling. "But you're still caught in the same rules as we are. And that means I get a chance to learn something from you, right?"

Tiny hands clenched tight, brown eyes with that hint of red glared up. Then the Hermit nodded, once. Whiskers twitched as the creature breathed quickly, trying to contain its ire. Thankfully, the damn humanoid rat knew about dental hygiene, so the stink of rotting meat didn't fill the air. In fact, Arthur had to admit, overall the thing was quite fastidiously clean for something that lived in a cave.

"Then, tell me. What can I learn from you?"

"If it means you'll stop being a burr in my fur…" A shake of its head, then it continued. "Three options. You serve me, for a year max. Or you face a challenge of wits. Or a challenge of might."

"*Hun dan,*" Arthur cursed. The first option was, quite literally, the kind that climbers dreamed of. You stayed with the Hermit for the full year, basically playing the role of servant. Getting food, washing clothing, like any apprentice. Those who served at least a month gained at least a minor technique, for the Hermit would train them all the while. Those who came out after a full year could be powers in their own right.

The problem was, Arthur couldn't afford the time. If he was alone, if he had come here as himself, without the burden of the Clan, it would be perfect. As it was, leaving his enemies and his Clan to run around for a full year without him was a horrible idea. Never mind the skin-crawling vision of taking care of this particular Hermit for a year. Just the thought of sleeping next to it was enough to make him want to vomit.

Or get flashbacks of waking up to having his fingers nibbled on in an alleyway after a particularly bad run, when he'd gotten jumped during a delivery job…

That left the challenge of wits or might. Neither of which Arthur had a good feeling about. If he hadn't antagonised the creature, a challenge of might may have been viable. After all, how badly he got beaten—and he would be beaten—would depend on the Hermit. But he'd just pissed it off.

Wits, on the other hand, was an all-or-nothing gamble. Since it could be anything from a game of chess to having to do an intergalactic crossword puzzle, the results could differ significantly. There wasn't a lot to be done about it, and while Arthur didn't consider himself dumb—how many people did?—he wasn't exactly a genius of intellect.

If he was, he'd work for a corporation in a comfy office, doing something with numbers or code or unspooling AI machines or whatever. Instead of, you know, stabbing and punching his way up the Tower.

"I swear, you made this up on purpose."

Sadly, his accusation got him nothing. Which left Arthur no other choice but to actually make a decision, one way or the other.

Chapter 91

Somehow, the sickly green light in the massive cavern had grown in brightness. Perhaps his eyes had gotten used to it, or perhaps something in the Tower was reacting to the pair and the match that was about to happen. Arthur had no idea, but he had asked a few more questions—okay, a lot—before he had chosen to test his might against the Hermit.

Now, staring at his opponent across the space of the cavern, he was wondering if it was a good idea after all.

"Remember, you have to survive at least one move. It will be up to you to decide when to stop, but I will pause between each move to give you time to withdraw." The Hermit grinned wide, showing those sharp, almost needle-like teeth as it did so, and sending another atavistic shudder through Arthur's body. "The more you survive, the better the cultivation technique or system I'll provide."

"And it'll be the kind that is useful to me, *ya?*"

"I won't cheat you." The creature raised its hands up. Its claws began to glow with an ominous red light. "But you best get ready."

Arthur broke out in a cold sweat, rotating his shoulders and then setting his spear before him. He kept it in the neutral stance, mid-line and tip pointing towards his opponent, though he shortened the grip just a little to give him more flexibility. Keeping his opponent at range was unlikely, so maneuverability was most important.

His backpack had already been placed aside. While waiting, he had flooded his body with both Bark Skin and the Heavenly Sage's Mischief, the two most powerful and useful full-body techniques he had. At least, before he got injured.

While speaking, he'd also tossed aside the Refined Exploding Energy Dart from within his Poket Simpanan, instead going for an Imbued Strike – Yin Poison. Even if it slowed his opponent down a fraction, it might just give him a little advantage.

Worst case, it'd just annoy the Hermit.

"I'm coming!"

With that warning, the Hermit exploded into motion the moment he had finished speaking. He crossed the ground in quick bounds, going from side to side, moving nearly faster than Arthur could track. Every time the rat-man's foot came down on the earth, he'd throw himself forward, sometimes changing direction, sometimes continuing straight ahead.

Arthur made minute shifts of his body, forcing his eyes to stay unfocused, to track the motion out of his peripheral vision rather than lock on directly. Long years of training had taught him to do that, so that when the rat leapt into the air at the last moment, he reacted by instinct.

Legs tucked in, dropping himself downwards even as his spear tip shifted upwards. He felt the first claw impact the tip, pushing the point away. Arthur used the momentum of the push to twirl his spear around, the haft and backend of the spear impacting against the other reaching arm.

Too slow though. The Hermit's arm was already inches away from him when it did that. All he managed to do was push himself and the Hermit away from one another as claws scraped down the side of his face, catching and leaving deep gouges in the gorget around his throat before he was free from the falling body.

Arthur rolled, coming up and bringing his weapon tip back on-line to the Hermit, the sides of his face bleeding freely. He might as well not have bothered to use Bark Skin, as the creature's claws had torn right through his defense. As he stood there, he felt a wave of heat rushing outwards and causing his wound to throb.

"Poison…" Arthur snarled. "You dirty… rat!"

"You said it…" The Hermit let out a low hissing noise. It took Arthur a moment to realise it the rat equivalent of a giggle. "One move down. Coming."

The rat-man didn't waste another second before leaping at Arthur. Perhaps he considered that short conversation sufficient of a break for Arthur to pull out of the match, or perhaps he really did intend to kill Arthur.

After all, that was the greatest danger of the might test. While the Hermit was not supposed to directly kill a climber, they could push the matter as far and as hard as they wished within certain boundaries. Just like the Tinker might generously offer to help with product selection or enchantments, the Hermit could choose to not hold back as much.

The next attack was an explosive charge again, except rather than take to the air, the form was a series of fast-moving clawed swings that ended with a sudden tripping of Arthur via the creature's tail that had wrapped around his ankle. In mid-air, Arthur had no opportunity to dodge the full-body elbow slam that struck the center of his breastplate, sending him flying backwards through the air.

He impacted a nearby fully formed stalagmite, shattering it as he flew through, and then bounced twice more before ending up slumped against the edge of the cavern. His breastplate had caved in, the hardened leather bent inwards and compressing his own broken bones. But breath had been entirely robbed from his chest such that Arthur could not even scream.

Head swimming with pain, he dropped the Bark Skin, switched to the active form of Accelerated Healing to pull back his ribs, to give him space to breathe. A couple of yanks on the breastplate had it swing free as he popped it clear of his chest, the deep depression grinding open with each moment.

"You… what did you do to my tail?" Clutching his back appendage, the Hermit was staring at it, noting how it drooped and refused to listen to his own commands.

Arthur wanted to offer a pithy comment about how two could use poisons. Unfortunately, all he could actually do was get his breathing back in order and prop his weapon up, just grateful that tens of thousands of repetitions in breakfalls and rolls had taught him to instinctively keep his head tucked in. No concussion for him at least. But now, his Poket Simpanan storage was empty; he'd used his hidden Imbued Strike – Yin Poison.

Two moves down. Not enough by far.

Palpable anger radiated from the Hermit now as it dropped the tail. A blood-red aura swirled into being around the creature. Arthur could feel pressure from the Tower asserting itself, even as the rat hissed again, "Coming."

Arthur gambled, surging forwards and catching his opponent by surprise as he cut the distance between the two of them. Rather than trying to take the attack head-on, he crossed the distance and thrust with his weapon. When it was battered aside, Arthur kept moving, spinning with his weapon, his feet circling the creature as he struck at the Hermit.

Even as he spun past, a claw scraping along the edges of the flapping breastplate managed to nearly knock Arthur off his feet—it felt like dozens of giant red ants tearing into his flesh. The Hermit's blood-red aura sunk into his exposed flesh to eat into his skin. It was incredibly distracting, and if he wasn't already moving, already forcing himself to fight through another greater pain, he might have stumbled.

Spin completed, he pushed himself away, breaking off from his opponent as he swung his spear down to threaten the other. He felt the impact, and his eyes squinted tight as tears blurred his vision, feet stumbling across uneven ground before he finally managed to set himself.

Only to find the Hermit had stopped, anger all too easy to tell. The creature hesitated, then spoke again.

"Coming."

No more time to think as broken ribs popped back into place, bruised lungs filled with air, skin humming as streaks of burst capillaries all across his body faded a little. Now, the rat-man threw himself forward, bouncing high and then landing, rolling and springing upwards, tail still flopping uselessly behind as it sprung at Arthur.

Arthur retreated, shifting angles as best he could. Hoping he could break the form, the attack pattern, like he did the last time. It was a foolish hope, for each round the monster had sped up and the blood-red aura seemed to grow stronger.

By the time he managed to break free from this next encounter, one arm hung by his side, useless. His spear lay on the ground, a half-dozen feet away and another set of shattered stone columns lay across the floor. Only the use of that obstacle had managed to save Arthur from the bouncing rat, and even then, he'd had to sacrifice his arm.

Even as he shifted energy to heal his arm, and to flood his system with Tower energy to fill his body with strength to keep up with the ever faster and stronger opponent, that dreaded word rung out.

"Coming."

Chapter 92

Somewhere along the way, Arthur had lost his breastplate. Torn off after he'd loosened the straps. The most grievous of his wounds was close to his chest: a part of his ribs had been literally torn out by the relentless, non-stop attacks of his opponent. If not for the fact that his Accelerated Healing had managed to stop the bleeding, he would have gone down.

His left arm had been broken twice already; he'd sacrificed it a second time after it had finished healing.

One eye was glued shut from the blood that had pooled around it. The other eye was watering so badly he could not see out of it beyond minor blurs. Heavenly Sage's Mischief had been dropped in favor of Shadow Sense a few rounds ago, Arthur no longer attempting to dodge but to endure.

Rope a dope, except with a lot more blood and portions of the body torn off. The last attack had been a straight punch and rip, tearing the rib open, but somehow, he'd managed to keep on his feet.

"Comi—" the Hermit began to call out.

"Stop!" Arthur managed to croak out at last. He'd tried that a round ago, but the Hermit had not given him a break, much less time to recover from the wounds. He'd forced himself to focus his own healing such that he was able to croak the words out before the rat-man actually killed him.

The Hermit stopped, cocking its head to the side. He tried to move forward towards Arthur but stopped and his whole body jerked as though a live wire had been run through it.

Which it might have. The Hermit had gone out of bounds, taken steps outside of the Tower's normal boundaries of what was permitted, after its tail had been damaged. It had gone from irritation to vengeful anger, and only the fact that it was restricted by the Tower had stopped Arthur from dying almost immediately.

As it stood...

"Seven moves," Arthur croaked out further.

Not what he wanted. He had hoped for an even dozen. Surviving ten moves would have been fine too and quite acceptable. Four or five moves meant earning a medium-grade reward, the equivalent of a two-star cultivation technique. Seven was a high-grade two-star or maybe a three-star. Ten moves would have gotten him a four-star technique, and twelve moves might have gotten him a full five stars. A low-grade five-star technique, but still...

"Yes..." the Hermit hissed and then flinched. Arthur sensed the incoming notification moments later, even as he dropped Shadow Sense, slumping to his knees as the Tower demanded his attention.

Hermit's Test of Might (9th Floor, Tower #STET)
Result: Seven Challenges Completed

Difficulty: High

Rewards: Three-Star Cultivation Technique and additional upgrade (on Climber's choice)

"What?" Arthur blinked. He had never heard of the additional upgrade as a reward, and his surprise was so great he almost released his healing technique. Only a last-minute save and his ability to split his mind and hold onto that sticky energy of his kept him from losing it and causing an even worse backlash.

There was more pressure, more information coming down from the Tower. He knew it, but he shoved it aside for now, ignored the update. Knew that if he did anything, with his head so cloudy and his mind muddled from blood loss, that he would regret it. This was new, this was different. All his reading had never mentioned this...

Then again, how many idiots would annoy the Hermit or even take a much more difficult option when something simpler was offered to them. Not just that, but managed to survive?

Without his healing ability, he was definitely dead.

As it was...

The cavern floor was cool against his cheek. Cool and sticky. A rather nasty combination, but it was the chill that was making him shake, his teeth chattering, his muscles clenching tight. Energy swirled in fits and starts, every moment of his attention focused on it now as he tried to patch the numerous major cuts.

He was still bleeding out, he could sense it. But where...

Oh. His calf. Somehow, somewhere, the rat had managed to punch through the armour in his leg and open a vein down there. One that had continued to spurt blood as he walked, jumped, twisted, and stomped on it.

Arthur pulled and tugged at the area, forced the body to reattach torn parts of his calf before he lost his limb due to lack of oxygen. Or lose more blood that he couldn't afford to lose. His heart was beating hard, each moment a laboured thump. Occasionally stopping as though requiring a rest before it began again as energy flooded in.

His liver, producing blood, the Tower literally replicating the fluid in his system as refined energy rebuilt him, over and over again. Attention pulled in a thousand directions, wounds that needed fixing. But he kept his focus on those wounds that would otherwise end him immediately. Blood loss, shock, the gaping wound in his chest that needed to be closed and clotted.

Hand pressed against it, mind spinning, the taste of acid and blood in his mouth. The smell of dry stone and cinnamon...

One last stitch, one last artery to close up there. Then, after that, some veins, that gaping hole...

He could do it. He was sure.

Just one more...

Just...

Arthur was surprised to wake up with his head throbbing like a mini lion-dance troupe had taken residence within and was using the inside of his skull as their drums. Each moment, shards of pain and white light were dancing across his vision. Memory struggling to reassert itself fully, to piece together the last few moments of wakefulness.

Instead, a voice, an image staring at him. Mel...

"You idiot! We told you not take chances."

A mental wince, realisation that he was going to have to explain things to her. A lot of things, because somehow, he knew he'd picked up more than a few scars.

"What a pain..." Arthur breathed out, shifting himself to peel his face off the ground, sticky dried blood cracking as he did so. He noted he hadn't moved an inch since his impromptu sleeping beauty act. He really had pissed off that Hermit.

"You're lucky my tail started working again. Or else I'd have killed you. Climber or not."

Even the threat, or half-threat, couldn't rouse Arthur's emotions. He felt dead inside, too numb by his recent brush with death, too filled with throbbing pain and lancing agony to pay attention. Instead, he started up his healing technique again, used it to wash away some of the stars and fuzziness.

He was still bleeding, leaking out small amounts of blood here and there. If not for his Advanced Healing technique replacing the fluids and managing the last of the patches, Arthur knew he would have died. Too damn close for his liking, especially since this wasn't a video game where they gave you points for surviving near-death experiences again and again.

All you got was PTSD and a nagging.

Eventually, with his body much more stabilized, if not actually healed, Arthur managed to get an arm up to wipe his eyes clean. Then, and only then, did he focus on the Hermit.

"You're a real *sei baat gung*." Bastard was not enough, but a small degree of sanity stopped him from using even more inventive curses. "Now, what am I getting?"

"Up to you to choose." The Hermit was seated a distance away, stroking his tail, red eyes still glowing. "So choose badly."

"What do you..." Arthur stopped speaking, realising one of the reasons his head hurt was the Tower still wanting to push him information.

Reaching sideways mentally, he tugged on the notification. Curious what it had to say.

It had better be good, after nearly dying.

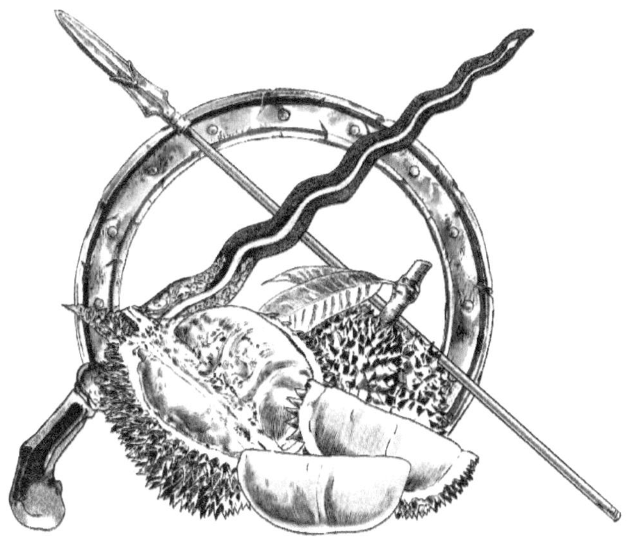

Chapter 93

Letting the Tower pass the information it had been wanting to was like popping a red-hot and white, inflamed pimple on the face. A pressure valve, relieved, that made one want to groan with pleasure, even as something horrible came out. Of course, it was just a matter of swiping it away later. This time around, the Tower actually had something useful to say.

Alert! Increased Difficulty Trial Test Taken
Alert! Original Clan Aspect (Guardianship) Found
Alert! Compatible Aspect of the Flame Phoenix Located!
Generating Reward Options...

"Do I even need your modlogs?" Arthur grumbled. It was a little bit of a silly complaint though, because the logs were giving him some interesting information. More so, when the options started coming down.

Reward Option #1
Increase Cultivation Technique Level

Reward Option #2
Improve Clan Guardianship Aspect

Reward Option #3
Enhance Flame Phoenix Seal

And that was all. "Now you decide not to say as much?" Arthur grumbled at the Tower. He knew he could be heard, but at this point, he was done caring about the Hermit. He was safe enough for now, from being killed outright at least. In any case, he wasn't going to choose to talk to rat-man, not more than he needed.

Of course, complain as he might, the Tower wasn't giving him any additional information. Which was exasperating, since Arthur had no idea what the three options would really result in. Then again, that was part and parcel of dealing with the Tower. So much of it felt like stabbing rats in the dark with a blindfold on.

Some things were clear. Firstly, as much as he wanted a better cultivation technique for himself, a single star rating increase made little sense. He assumed it would only increase by one star, though perhaps it might be more.

If it was two…

"*Hun dan.* Any hints of how much these rewards provide?" Arthur asked, not expecting an answer.

Good thing too, since he didn't get a real one.

"Hurry up," the Hermit said. "I want to got back to sleep."

"Not..." *Rutting with your sister*, Arthur said in his mind. After all, the Hermit could still kill him if he really wanted to; it just would be penalized heavily. However, being already dead, that kind of punishment was rather superfluous to Arthur. And really, even he might be a little guilty for his own prejudice.

Even against a rat.

"Not much help. Fine..." Arthur turned inwards, thinking it over.

The first reward option was individual. You couldn't really pass on the technique to others, beyond what you could write down. Depending on his level of mastery and his ability to explain it, the resulting documentation might be pretty useless. On the other hand, as the others had pointed out again and again, him growing stronger meant the Clan was stronger.

On the other hand, the other two options would make him stronger, he was sure. A small nudge had the Tower display his Clan Aspect and Sigil again.

Aspect: Guardianship

● *Minor increase in effectiveness of protective, healing, and shielding cultivation techniques.*

● *Trivial increase in effectiveness of precision, speed, and bonding cultivation techniques.*

● *Variable increase in cultivation and refinement speed dependent upon the number of Clan members within close proximity.*

● *Tower quest types have been expanded.*

Sigil: The Flame Phoenix

Sigil Bonus (Clan Head): Accelerated Healing – Refined Energy (Grade IIIb)

Sigil Bonus (Clan): Cultivation Exercise – Accelerated Healing – Refined Energy (Grade Ib)

Reading them over, Arthur had to admit he'd entirely forgotten about the variable increase in cultivation and refinement speed. The bonus rarely mattered until the latter part of his stay on a Tower floor, what with the need to recruit new members. It did make them pack together in their residences though, like... rats... but otherwise, the bonus made little difference to his day-to-day life.

On the other hand, he bet that, down on the first floor of the Tower, it was beginning to make a real difference. Eventually, he assumed they'd see a much larger percentage of their Clan members moving up the floor.

An overall increase to any one feature of their Aspect could be great, an overall boost of the Aspect itself was probably too much to ask for.

On the other hand, as for the Sigil... so far, it had only been leaning heavily into his healing technique. It was not the only thing the Sigil could do, though. After all, the Flame Phoenix was not just healing, or rebirth, or imperial grandeur; and now, he was wondering if it was Chinese or Western because healing could be both and...

He was spinning out of it, too tired and battered to really keep his thoughts in line.

"Conga line, bonga fine. Got to wisely choose, otherwise I'll likely lose..."

If he enhanced his Sigil, even if it just boosted his healing ability, it might provide quite the boost for himself and everyone else. He relied on his ability to keep taking damage like a cut-rate Wolverine. Or maybe, with his idiotic rhyming, Deadpool? He certainly was getting enough scars to be the second...

"Maybe I need to be talking to an imaginary audience?" He giggled to himself, though it came out more as a pained wheeze. He ignored the look he was being given by the Hermit, understanding that it was kind of insane of him. "Doesn't matter... just..." He coughed, moved his hand away from his side, feeling how sticky it was. Hoping his breastplate wasn't entirely destroyed but not having much hope for it, not after nearly having his chest caved in.

"Just got to gamble a little." The Aspect had a more quiet influence, boosting his cultivation techniques. Everything from Bark Skin to his healing techniques had received a generous increase, and even Focused Strike got a minor increase. Having that get better was more variable, more likely to come up bad.

So, it really came down to a choice between personal power or something for the Clan.

And after annoying the Hermit so much, Arthur had a feeling that any way the rat might have to make his life worse, the creature would take it. He could still feel the rat glaring at him, even as he channelled healing to make himself better.

"Option three. Enhance my Sigil."

It was kind of gratifying to see the rat startle. He quite likely had no idea that Arthur was a Clan head after all. It wasn't as though he had a big sign above his head, and his Clan seal was hidden such that no one could see it. The sigil was just part of the seal and more ephemeral as well.

Arthur waited, and waited, and waited. There was silence from the Tower, no indication of a desirable push for more information, that it had a notification for him. All the while, he felt his body healing, patching things together in an inexorable grind to have everything fixed, even as slices across his face and flaps of flesh knitted together.

He wondered, a little, how badly scarred he was. Tower climbers eventually lost most scars, but the eventually part was doing a lot of weight lifting there. Some scars, the most damaged, the worst healed, never went away, requiring one to subject a body to cosmetic surgery or fixes. And, of course, loss of limbs—

or tops of ears—were not coming back. Not without further effort.

Which was, partly, why he was pushing for the Sigil enhancement too. He had made a promise after all.

Time slid on and on, till he thought it might not come. That the Tower had forgotten or didn't hear him, as insane as that sounded.

Then, he felt it. A burning sensation where his Clan seal was located, writhing under his flesh as the magical tattoo shifted and twisted. He would have cried out, but he was out of breath and concerns, not about pain anyway.

Too tired to do more than just sit there, grimacing every few seconds as he kept the healing magic away from the seal.

Waiting for it to die down, waiting for the notification. Curiosity killing him.

Chapter 94

Sitting here in the darkness, Arthur extended his Shadow Sense a little, feeling it expand through the dry cavern. Funny how dry it was when a waterfall was but a stone's throw away. He wondered if that was a weirdness of geography or Tower insanity, then realised he didn't care. He tried to make himself think about it, to explore the cavern with his Shadow Sense. Tried to divert his attention from the pain of each breath that forced him to breathe shallowly, that had him sensing the way his shoulder itched and burned as the Clan seal shifted.

It seemed to take forever, a painful, uncomfortable sensation of ants moving beneath his skin that he had to forcibly ignore. Until...

Sigil of the Flame Phoenix has been upgraded!
New Sigil Bonus (Clan) - Enhanced Magnetoreception and Equilibrioception

"*Apa ni?*" Arthur wondered aloud, reading the esoteric words over twice more. Carefully, because he had never heard of either of those terms before. Just as interestingly, it was not splitting the Sigil Bonus, so it was being passed on not just to him but to the whole Clan at full strength. Of course, what it did was a mystery.

Equilibrio... Magneto... So, he had better sense of equilibrium, what . . . balance? And magnets? Waving a hand over his spear head, he didn't sense any difference. Not in the spear, nor how he felt sitting here. In truth, he didn't feel any change at all. But he had to admit, a large portion of that might just be because he was still seriously injured.

"Didn't get what you wanted?" the Hermit mocked.

Arthur glared at the rat-man, only to see it grab something from its side and throw it at him. He fumbled the catch, wincing as it landed away from his fingers to bounce on the floor. Thankfully, the paper did not stain on any of the numerous splotches of blood, the liquid seeming to slide off the material itself.

Sometimes, the weirdness of the Tower had some advantages.

Beyond giving him bonuses to things he had no idea what for.

Grabbing the document from the floor and moving away from the puddle of his own blood, Arthur sank to drier ground with a grateful sigh. Everything still hurt and he really wished that the Tower had given him an upgrade to his healing ability, but it was just a bonus. This was the reason had he decided to come.

Unrolling the document, he didn't bother reading it, instead allowing the Tower to pour the information of the cultivation technique into his brain. At least, the initial description.

Steel Skin

Toughen the cultivator's skin to make it as strong as steel while retaining the original flexibility. Offers greater protection against cuts, thrusts, scrapes, and crushing attacks. May be further upgraded in the future.

Cost: 1 Energy per minute

Arthur stared at the document, then looked up at the Hermit. He looked down again and then upwards, his sense of wonder threatening to break clear on his face.

"What?" said the Hermit.

"This is actually useful," Arthur said. "Would you have given me something even better if I'd chosen to go with a cultivation technique?"

"Of course. I know my duty," the Hermit said, nose wrinkling. "Though the technique would still be in the same line."

"So... Titanium Skin or Obsidian Skin or something better like that?"

All he got was a flat stare, making Arthur grimace. There was, it seemed, only a certain level of talkativeness his former opponent was willing to give. A moment later, he realised it was quite possible the damn thing was lying too... and just torturing him by giving him something that was good, but also...

An upgrade on something he already had. Admittedly, a significant increase since he was skipping Iron Skin entirely and going to Steel. Not just that though. The fact that he had studied Bark Skin before meant that actually making the technique work for him was viable. If he could find a safe place to train, of course.

Which meant...

"Eh, boss..." he ventured. "You know I don't really dislike you, right?"

"Drop it. You were more agreeable when you were truthful."

Arthur shrugged, figuring it was a good try. "So, I can stay here to train in this, right?"

"Why would you want to stay with me? Not scared I'll take a bite out of you at night?"

Arthur couldn't suppress the sudden shudder that ran through him, a motion that made the rat smirk and add, "So best you get going."

For a long moment, Arthur considered staying in the cavern anyway, just out of obstinance. But the truth was he wasn't likely to get much training done, not with the creature watching him. On the other hand...

"I need to heal. So you leave me alone, to cultivate and heal up, and I'll leave right after. Won't study this here," he said and waggled the document a little. "Deal?"

"And you think you have something to offer me in return?"

"My absence."

Silence, then a slight twitching shrug that started from the hips and rolled all the way up to the shoulders. It was alien and strange and set Arthur's teeth on edge, made him want his spear in hand even if he knew he was, theoretically, safe enough.

Silence afterwards, and realising that was the only answer he'd get, Arthur focused within on the healing. He still hadn't worked out how to cultivate or refine his body itself via body cultivation techniques, though at some point he knew he'd have to get there. For now, he started up the Bark Skin technique, just feeling out the flow in a conscious fashion before letting it fade.

Then, since he was waiting to heal, he looked at the Steel Skin document. He read it over, scanning for differences, overall conceptual changes, and to see how much he had to work upon.

Shifting of energy through various meridians and chi points—that was normal, not unusual at all. Easy to change, just had to memorise the order. A lot more branches, a lot finer manipulation though, so that would be difficult—but that was what his traits were for.

Next up, the way it bled into his skin, reinforcing it. There, there was a change. With Bark Skin, one just let it flow in, the energy pooling and firming and creating tiny warps and toughening areas naturally. It meant certain parts of the body were naturally more armored than others, and not necessarily areas you'd expect. Just like a whorl or a twist in the trunk might be a little harder.

When it came to Steel Skin, though, the infusion was much more regulated. There was a significant degree of fire chi—something that Arthur knew was going to be an issue with his Yin Body—that was utilized to get the initial metal chi to flow right; but afterwards, it was manipulation of aura and will and wood chi that smoothed and layered the Steel Skin.

As he kept reading, Arthur was surprised to note that, unlike Bark Skin, there were multiple levels to this technique. Just like how the Seven Cloud Stepping technique built upon itself, till one could create multiple cloud steps, Steel Skin could layer. Only three most of the time, before it stopped being worthwhile—because of a significant loss in mobility after that. And even with three layers, without proper caution, that loss in mobility could happen. With four layers, it was impossible to avoid.

Though...

"Huh. This is much easier to keep running than Bark Skin," Arthur said, out loud. "Like, the flows afterwards are easy to handle and simplified, once the initial switch happens. Is this just the cultivation technique or...?" Again he looked at the silent rat, and once again, his fishing was rebuffed.

Yeah, maybe that was a mistake.

Still, Arthur was beginning to see how higher grade techniques were more powerful, could be stacked on one another further and further because they actually required less work. His new Yin cultivation technique had been simpler to run and utilize than the ones he had learnt, or the zero-star technique that had been taught to others.

Steel Skin was significantly simpler than Bark Skin.

Even his Accelerated Healing technique, though it used refined energy, was also quite simple in some ways. Over time, he assumed, he could learn to simplify it further; but because he leaned heavily on the Body attribute and the Tower's manipulation, the actual flow and control of energy when he had first created it had been easy.

So... another advantage then, to the rich and connected. One that was a lot less easy to notice, but was significant. Especially at the higher levels.

As he waited for his body to heal, Arthur started planning, rearranging some assumptions. Not just for himself, but for the Clan.

Chapter 95

It amused Arthur that he was creeping out of the cave in the middle of the night. After he'd healed to a point where he was happy to allow the Tower to continue the rest of the process passively, he had begun to pull energy from the numerous monster cores he held and the Tower itself to top himself off. Unfortunately, while he could—and did—cultivate under the Hermit's stare, it grew increasingly uncomfortable doing so.

Eventually, he found himself needing to leave, the burning gaze that threatened to drill a hole through him disrupting his focus enough that he had slowed down significantly. He wasn't topped up, or even close to it, but it was good enough for now. After all, he still needed to find a place to train his new Steel Skin technique.

Which was why, creeping along with Shadow Sense up, Arthur was headed to the peak, climbing the rocky face not far from the waterfall. Not too close that the spray and loud crash of water would impair his climbing or hearing, but also not so far away that he couldn't follow the water back.

Up and up, climbing hand over hand, spear strapped to his backpack. A part of him missing the fact that he could have bought the Tinker's pouch of extradimensional storage, that would have made this easier. Having it knock into him as he climbed all the time was annoying, but that was the trade-off in the end.

Till he was up on the cliff and had a bit of a straight walk, though even here, the ledge was not far. He almost started walking again, when he realised that this might work. Not perfect, of course, but with some propping up and the use of his tarps and cut grass, he could hide from birds above and creatures below.

Add in the Howler Monkey Ward he'd gotten from the Tinker, Arthur was as safe as one could get on the ninth floor. At least for a while. Eventually, some monster would arrive but...

"That's later. Now I'm going to get bay-ter." Drawling a little didn't quite make the rhyme work; but that was fine. Arthur was more focused on what he had to read. First, he let Bark Skin run through him. He'd have to cultivate to draw back energy for what he was wasting, but with his much larger pool now, he had over twenty minutes of use before he had to stop and cultivate for another hour. And since he was stopping and starting a lot of the time, it wasn't even that bad.

The only real concern was if he was attacked. Which was why, for the first time in a while, he filled his second dantian with Tower energy before he began.

First step: modify the flow of Tower energy to shift it away from wood to metal. Or the Tower equivalent of metal energy. There were, supposedly, thousands of types; though sometimes that became a matter of cutting things super close. Like the difference between five or four elements, or how one might split earth and metal, and yet not have air.

Mattered little for practical purposes unless you were the kind to fixate on such details. Which Arthur, thankfully, was not. Instead, he just followed the lessons, pouring energy through him, adjusting the flow till he had metal-aspected Tower energy. Then, splitting it further to make steel, a specific kind of metal imbuement.

Once he had that down, which only required two cycles of testing and cultivating. did he get to the hard part. He took a break then, did a series of stretches, enjoyed the sunlight and made sure that nothing was trying to creep up on him and his tent. With the sun beginning to rise, Arthur even stopped to enjoy the giant ball of flame, amused at how large it was and yet not shedding near as much heat as the sun outside the Tower.

Made for beautiful sunrises.

Afterwards, he stepped into his tent again and began the process of distributing and welding the steel. He focused on small portions at first, getting it right in a patch around his arm, around his hand, creating a single layer at the top of his skin. Everywhere else, it clumped and bubbled, hurting a little and feeling stiff and ungainly. For the most part, he ignored it, allowing the Accelerated Healing that was part of his constitution deal passively with the clots that refused to go away, that required rejection or breakdown.

Like getting a burr in one's shoe but in random spots all across the skin and muscles of the body. The most uncomfortable area was just above his coccyx, forcing him to shift onto one butt cheek while he waited for it to fade.

Again and again, testing and learning and then cultivating. A part of him knowing that time was draining away, that monsters would gather eventually.

His first warning was the howler monkeys' screaming. Dying, as giant hornets attacked them. Arthur stumbled out of his tent, weapon in hand, to fight the creatures off. Amusingly enough, these were earth-aspected wasps and were hard to injure except for their wings. Not at all a sensible advantage, especially when Arthur was fighting them on a cliff ledge and all he had to do was cut off a wing and send them spiralling below, desperately trying to stay afloat.

The battle was over fast enough, though he only got two monster cores before he retreated back into his tent. Howler monkeys reformed as he utilized the ward once more. Useful thing: it used up its charge upon creation and then recharged. So if you stayed in one place, it mattered not. The monkeys would eventually fade, but they lasted over 24 hours each time.

Unless they got killed.

The second time was a day later. It was a wasp and not a hornet. He loosed a Refined Exploding Energy Dart at it, then took to battle against the wasp that was half his size, fencing with his spear till he managed to cut it enough times that it bled to death.

One-on-one, he was still their superior.

Time running out, like a hole in a bag of rice that you were totting home. Leaving precious grains behind, luring rats and other vermin that might follow you back. Never a good thing, especially if you didn't notice and your sifu smacked you on the top of the head for wasting money and then had you run a dozen laps till you were so tired that you collapsed on your face.

Then run another dozen after that.

He sped up the study, the testing, the learning. Pushing himself harder, running his cultivated Tower energy down to lower levels each time, such that it became more and more dangerous but something he could ignore, would ignore.

Till, finally, three days later, the notification came.

Success! Bark Skin technique upgraded to Steel Skin

Bark Skin technique removed from Status Screen

Steel Skin (100.2%)

Such a small thing, but important nonetheless. He pulled up his status screen then, because of course he had to.

Cultivation Speed: 2.773 Yin

Energy Pool: 7/30 (Yin) + (7/7)

Refinement Speed: 0.1421

Refined Energy: 0.17 (40) +(0/3)

Attributes and Traits

Mind: 15 (Multi-Tasking, Quick Learner, Perfect Recall)

Body: 25 (Enhanced Eyesight, Yin Body, Swiftness, Fast Twitch Faster, Lightning Reflexes, Explosive Strength)

Spirit: 15 (Sticky Energy, From the Dregs, Strengthened Aura)

Techniques

Night Emperor Cultivation Technique

Focused Strike

Accelerated Healing – Refined Energy (Grade III)

Heavenly Sage's Mischief

Refined Energy Dart

Steel Skin (100.2%)

Seven Cloud Stepping Technique (204.3%)

Poket Simpanan Tua (142%) (Refined Exploding Energy Dart 68% Integrity)

Imbued Strike - Yin Poison

Yin Aura (Level 1) (128.3%)

Partial Techniques

Simultaneous Flow (227.4%)

Yin-Yang Energy Exchange (98.3%)

Yin Poison Darts (50.4%)

Shadow Sense (54.2%)

He reveled in the improvements all around, then drew a breath and stood up.

Time to finish this floor and face that final challenge.

Chapter 96

"I. Should." Arthur leaned back, letting the attack bypass him, the creature's claws just missing his face before he pushed off with his back leg, pivoting from the hips as he thrust one-handed with his spear. He watched the weapon sink through dense fur into flesh and twisted his hand on exit, leaving a gaping wound that bled freely. "Have done. This. Earrrrrr-lier!"

Crashing into the ground, Arthur winced as his shirt gained another rent. He rolled with the momentum, came up, and set his weapon moments later, watching as the harimau hitam stopped before it crashed into his weapon.

Fourteen feet long from head to tail, and at least four if not five times his weight. Stronger than Arthur by far with the instincts of a predator and the speed of a Tower monster, the black tiger was an apex predator. But one that was now highly confused, one paw shaking itself out.

"Not easy, is it?" Arthur taunted, rising to his feet and stalking around the creature. Interesting to note his skin looked the same, even if he was utilizing Steel Skin, the enhancement entirely hidden beneath his flesh. More importantly, the tiger's swipes had only left minor cuts along his side, ones that had stopped bleeding already.

Meanwhile, the poor tiger had numerous wounds, the bright red blood staining its dark fur and creating muddy and sticky puddles on the ground where it wasn't covered by fallen and drying leaves. Arthur slid his feet along the floor, shifting over unseen roots, adjusting footwork as he circled the creature.

Funny how footwork and training changed over and over again as people put theory into practise and arguments slowly faded. "Lift your feet," they said, to give you speed and not ensure you didn't get caught on minor changes in landscape, to allow for lunges and explosive charges.

"Slide your feet," they then said, to handle significant variation in terrain, to ensure you didn't land on rocks or dips in the ground or slip on muddy patches when you came down. The ground could give way at any moment or pull your footing off course.

"Don't leap," they said, because you never knew what was above you and you couldn't change direction.

"Practise jumps and aerial combat," they also said, because monkeys and birds and hornets and other creatures existed up there, and if you waited below, you were at their mercy.

"Study multiple weapons and numerous martial arts to adapt," said some people, because you never knew what circumstances you might face.

"Specialise," said others, because a fool who spreads themselves too thin can never beat a specialist.

Everyone had their own ideas, their demands, their closely held opinions. The martial artists, the MMA fighters, the reenactors, and even the soldiers. Then, the Tower came and everyone had a chance to test it out, to see who was right in the greatest and deadliest testing ground ever.

Those who stumbled out years later were broken, haggard, and beaten. Hard-bitten and merciless, and perhaps most of all, adaptable. Specialist or generalist, single-weapon user or not, they had learnt and studied and took what the Tower gave them. And made it their own.

Just like Arthur, who had wanted to be a dodge specialist, who had never intended to tank shots or heal them like a Petaling Street knockoff of Wolverine. But he'd learnt to heal himself, to use different skills, lean on what he had and adapt, to change fighting styles and techniques, and to make best use of it all.

To get better and change, no matter what. So that even a mini-boss like this damn harimau, so much larger and faster, was wearing down. Blood was pouring out of it, Yin aura seeping poison into its body and leeching away strength. The monster knew too, for it came at Arthur immediately after, intent on finishing the fight.

Once more, Arthur went on the defensive, blocking again and cutting with the edge of his spear when he could, leaving long lines. Back and back till he was against a tree and unable to move away, a thorned bush one side and a steep drop on the other. Forced to hold, he managed to keep the tiger off, for a few seconds.

Before it chose to accept a deep cut as it lunged, ignoring Arthur's spear as it dug into its guts, in order to clamp its large mouth down on his shoulder. It bypassed the shoulder guards he had on, piercing the bare skin beneath. Even reinforced, Steel Skin could do nothing to stop the monster as it bit down, cracking bones.

Unfortunately for the creature, putting its body next to Arthur was already a recipe for disaster. Plunging his hand into an open wound, he directed a Refined Explosive Energy Dart into the cavity, yanking his arm back moments after it shot outwards.

The explosion cracked his own bones and dislocated fingers, but what it did to the insides of the creature was even worse.

Thrashing around and roaring, the tiger's wild swipes tore at his arm and chest, before he was thrown aside. Arthur crashed and rolled.

Spear ripped out of the body as it turned, more blood falling. Waterfalls of it, as the creature staggered, open wounds infiltrated by the Yin aura, poison seeping in and combining with blood loss to drive the monster to its knees.

It still crawled forward, such that Arthur had to give it a few kicks to get his feet away from questing mouth, but eventually, it stopped moving.

Leaving him to flop on the ground, panting as he waited for his body to heal.

"So that's why they still wear armour," Arthur groaned, patting at the open wounds that had scabbed over, new skin closing around them. They were still raw, a touch red, and seeping blood and other clear fluids, enough to make him grimace in disgust. Unfortunately, his clothing was shredded, a complete mess that made him regret not picking up the Tinker's mimic underarmour.

"I could…" Arthur trailed off, debating. He could go back. The Tinker might still be there. But truth be told, there wasn't enough time. In the end, he left it, content to wear this shredded clothing for now. He still had new clothing stored away. Later on, he'd dress in something nicer; but for now, he might even end up going bare-chested. At least until tonight, when he could start patching the rips.

Who said sewing was a woman's job?

He sighed and picked up his backpack. He'd strapped the backside of his breastplate to him; the front was a complete mess after the fight with the Hermit. Even after smashing it around and adjusting it, there was still a massive hole and weakness in the front that duct tape could not fix. Not to mention how uncomfortable it was to wear, with the edges and center chest caved in, constricting his breathing.

Add in the destroyed side straps that he could replace, but only badly, and it just hadn't been worth wearing anymore. At least he still had protection for his back, but it did little for where most attacks came from.

Still, with his Steel Skin ability, he was as protected as before, and he still had most portions of his armour left. He would just have to be more careful, and consider maybe purchasing fewer single piece armours in the future.

For now, though, he knew how effective his new technique was. And he had the rest of the climb to focus on.

Chapter 97

It wasn't really a surprise to find a boss at the edge of the trail, standing before the looming arch that marked the boundary between the ninth floor and the next. What did surprise Arthur, though, was the size of the thing. And, of course, what it was.

"Small. So lucky, it so small…" Arthur muttered, staring up at the 25-foot-tall creature. Skin like gray stone, with moss and small shrubbery literally growing out of it. Sang Kelembai was supposed to be so big that it could have walked from Kuala Tahan in Pahang to the state of Terengganu—a hundred or so kilometers as the crow flies—in a few steps.

The Tower version of it that stood before him was only small relative to its mythological size. Twenty-five feet meant that Arthur could barely poke it in the thigh if he stretched and mostly would be fighting around its ankles. Not that there wasn't a lot of theory about it. But practically, he hadn't had much experience.

Not many 25-foot-tall monsters to fight in the real world, nor practical ways to create such scenarios for practice. The best they'd been able to do was to use large statues and pillars, padding them out with specific locations to be struck at.

More importantly, Arthur knew he was going to have a problem with his current weapon. The spear was great for giving more range, but it made a lot less sense when you didn't have a range advantage. More importantly, a creature that big was more vulnerable up close.

"Going to have to get close and dirty then…" Arthur dropped his backpack, tightened the armour straps around himself one last time, and propped his spear aside. He could have thrown it, but looking at the creature's skin, he doubted it would pierce.

Kris, pulled out from the side. He kept it held close as he started trotting forward, waiting for the boss to spot him. It took a good minute, when he was over a hundred meters away, for it to open its eyes and focus on him.

Dark red eyes, gleaming with anger. Focused, as it reached sideways and ripped a whole tree out of the ground. Suddenly, a hundred meters felt a lot closer, as the creature started swinging the 30-foot-long tree around with one hand.

Cloud Steps thrumming through him, Arthur kept running, gauging timing and distance. Big weapon meant that its arcs were quite large too, which meant…

He let himself drop, sliding along the floor, flattening himself as the tree roared through the air above him. A jutting root brushed against his body, knocking him sideways a little and causing him to roll to the side.

Arthur groaned but ignored the pain and damage as he pushed himself up immediately. Time to go, to keep moving as he formed the first of the cloud steps, throwing himself into the air and sideways to avoid the descending tree, cutting the angle even as the tree smashed into the ground and embedded itself into the soft dirt.

Another cloud, formed sideways so that he could push off it. He slammed into the puffy obstacle, pushed off it and struck the edge of Sang Kelembai's arm that was stuck for a moment as it wrenched the tree upwards. He rode the movement as it rose, taking the angle and lift to kick off, throwing himself forwards right at the creature.

Dangerous to be in the air, right now. He couldn't dodge, not well, not while he was reforming another cloud; so he chose to distract his opponent.

A REED flew out, the Explosive Dart boring through the air for the monster's eye. A slight bend of the head, a twist, and the dart impacted the bony ridge of its sloping forehead, blowing apart a little skin and a lot of dirt and moss.

First blood, but it was barely a start.

The hand gripping the tree rose, while the other arm swung towards Arthur as it pivoted and tried to smack him. No longer in contact with anything, Arthur knew he had only one chance to dodge. A conjured cloud, barely formed in time, allowed him to change direction one last time, such that he flew—not at the face anymore but the neck.

Big, thick, meaty, and a perfect target as he utilized Focused Strike. He plunged the kris deep into the creature's neck, his momentum slamming the weapon and then Arthur's body into the creature, whipping him around its shoulder and wrenching his own shoulder a little. He hissed, scrambling a bit as the weapon sawed and then slipped free of the wound, gravity taking Arthur to the ground.

Swearing, he desperately tried to grab onto something as Sang Kelembai tried to swing around and grab him. The swinging hand and tree clipped him again in mid-air by pure chance, battering him with pure mass and sending him flying through the air to skip across branches and end up wrapped around a shorter tree, half-bending it before he tumbled off the thin sapling.

"Owwww...."

Lucky for him, the damn monster was now merely scrubbing at the bleeding scalp wound, getting blood out of its eye while casting around near its feet for Arthur. Its inadvertent strike hadn't even been noticed, so strong was the creature. Arthur, on the other hand, needed nothing more than the dislocated ribs and cracked bones in his body and leg to tell him otherwise.

"Need to upgrade muscles next..." Arthur complained as he leaned against another tree, hiding behind it as he tried to catch his breath. Upgraded muscles would mean less bashing damage, a necessity if he wanted to keep alive.

Pushing himself upright, he shifted his position a little. A part of him wondered if he could just sneak up close enough and lurk in the shadows, letting his Yin poison enter the creature's body in small increments. Of course, with something so big, it might take too long and he'd run out of energy before the poison really affected it. On top of that, he wasn't Uswah. He didn't have stealth techniques, and the ground around it was wide open.

No, he was just going to have to get in close and stay close.

A few moments to form the REED inside his Poket Simpanan, then he threw himself to the ground as the tree the creature was holding was thrown at his hiding spot. He winced as he was showered with splinters and broken branches, feeling something impact his back and bounce off the remaining armour.

No time to wait, though, as he scrambled upwards and started running, meeting the Sang Kelembai's charge.

Ducked to the side, skipped to the edge of the trail, hand extending sideways a little with the kris as the arm came crashing down. He felt the blade tug and yank in his hand, nearly causing him to lose grip as it tore and knocked against bone, but it pierced the creature's flesh.

Imbued Strike - Yin Poison triggered moments later, pouring poison into the monster. Mixing with its aura to slow it down, to decrease the speed of the vital energy that allowed it to move. Arthur kept running, twisting at the last second as the creature lurched sideways and threw a kick; he extended his body at an angle in an attempt to dodge the twisting and sloppy roundhouse.

Even as inefficient as the kick was, it was still being thrown by a giant weighing goodness knew how many tonnes. Its leg alone probably outweighed Arthur by two or three times and getting clipped by it threw him sideways, forcing him into a roll and then handspring into the air as the monster next tried to stomp onto where he was.

Twisting in mid-air, he got his feet oriented properly before he landed, running forwards once more. He wished he had his Cloud Steps but focused instead of keeping himself from getting killed and pouring more Imbued Strikes in, tearing into the creature with the kris each time it came close.

This entire thing was going to be a battle of attrition.

His opponent only needed a single, well-placed strike to win. Arthur needed dozens, each of them tearing into its body and leaving a trace of Yin Poison to fell it.

Every few moments the giant made an attack that missed by inches, sending shards of stone, of stamped earth into the air. His breathing was coming in deep and fast, pulling in the musky scent of forest and sweat, unwashed stone and moss as he danced near the monster's feet. Tearing into legs and the occasional arm that came down.

Not even trying to carve through to tendons and ligaments, but always, always, putting the weapon and his poison into it.

Step by step, wound by wound.

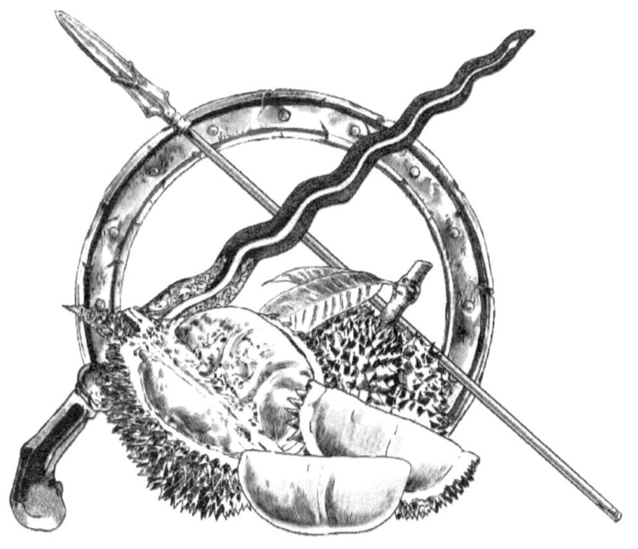

Chapter 98

Two minutes.

Just about long enough to make a good half-boiled egg. Not that any good Malaysian used something as lousy as a timer when there were dedicated egg boilers. The iconic yellow boilers were ubiquitous in *kopi tiam*—local coffee shops—and could be filled with up to four eggs. These plastic containers had markings for what level it was to be filled to with boiled water for each egg quantity. Once all the water drained out, you had a perfectly made half-cooked egg to dip into with toast, spread with butter and kaya jam.

Two minutes was such a short time, but in a battle, it was a lifetime.

Like a half-boiled egg, Arthur was battered and cooked, his body half-jelly by now after the number of near misses and glancing strikes he'd taken. More than one bone was broken, and it seemed the only thing keeping him upright were tightened armour pieces, constricted muscles, and sheer willpower.

Yet, in that time, he had only been booted away from under the monster once more, forcing him to cover that dangerous no-man's-land of the Sang Kelembai's reach once again. Another use of a stored REED, this time targeting a descending fist and its small pinky, had bought him time, especially when it had caused said appendage to drop away.

Of course, fighting with a monster raining blood onto you was just another disgusting part of battle.

No one ever talked about how disgusting being a Tower climber was. Not enough at least.

Two minutes and one second later, just as Arthur rolled behind the ankle and got ready to stab it as he rose up, it moved. So did the entire body above him, as the creature knelt over.

"Nice!" Arthur growled, jumping backwards and upwards at the same time. There was nothing dignified about stabbing an opponent in the buttocks, but it was a large, meaty target that had offered itself to him.

At least he didn't swing at the other pair of targets, which might have been less armoured but were more likely to enrage his opponent. While Arthur had few enough ethics while fighting for his life, attacking another creature's bananas and apples were just wrong, especially when a battle was somewhat stabilized.

He'd leave that for when he needed to enrage it.

More surprised than anything else that his kris stuck into the monster's buttocks, Sang Kelembai twitched the weapon aside and toppled over sideways over the same leg it had collapsed from. Arthur, who had been holding onto the kris at the time, was flung aside. Hitting the ground and rolling, cursing as he went through a bush filled with thorns that itched as he rolled over them—thank god for Steel Skin—he only realised what was happening then.

"About time," Arthur said. Gingerly retreating, dropping most of his other skills and refilling his Poket Simpanan as he retreated to find his spear, leaving only his Steel Skin active, he kept a close eye on the half-unconscious creature.

Attacks against the legs had piled up, the poison invading the body. While it normally affected the whole system more than just the point of contact, Sang Kelembai's limbs had fallen asleep first. He could tell the other leg was having trouble functioning, even as the poison spread through the entire monster.

It might not last long, but Arthur was certain he had a few minutes at least. Time he took to find his spear, to pause and breathe and channel his healing to fix the major concerns.

Crushed left foot, including quite a few pulverized bones that needed shifting back. He took his time on that one, dealing with the inflammation, with the fluid that had gathered, with crushed muscles and skin, pushing bone fragments back into place, rebuilding the bones.

It hurt, but since it had happened in his boot, it also meant that everything was roughly in the same place. No pieces of him had gone flying. He healed enough to limp the rest of his way over to the spear. Other injuries were being patched up in the background: bruised and bloodied internal organs, cracked ribs, herniated discs, dislocated bones including a pelvic bone or two. Kneecap, popping back into place even as it wobbled where tendons had been torn off.

Pain, but his body was holding together well enough. Switching stances, he pushed off with the foot that wasn't crushed as he approached the monster. Edging around to face its back, finding a spot that he could barely reach while he dropped Steel Skin and readied Imbued Strike - Yin Poison.

Then, a single lunge as threw Focused Strike from his Poket Simpanan into the lunge. Imbued Strike slipped in moments later as his spear slipped between spinal discs. Funny, how most creatures had those. Or not so funny, what with convergent evolution and just basic biomechanics taken into account.

Blade between the discs, slicing into the body as he wiggled it back and forth. His enemy twitched and tried to get at him but found its control further robbed. He sawed the weapon back and forth, now that he was sure it was not going to move. Even as jolts of adrenaline and pain roused the creature, it could not move.

He had crippled the monster's lower back, with a spear in the right place.

Then he extracted the spear and took a moment to breathe through the pain his movement caused, pain ignored during his own desperate battle and now aching all the more as adrenaline levels faded. Time to move on to the creature's neck.

After that, it was just butchery.

There were a few things that were different from a normal human body in the Sang Kelembai. Among other things, its skull was shaped differently, such that there was no soft spot at the back of the head to slip a spear into to end its suffering. Instead, he had to eventually put the spear into the monster's eye and then waggle the spear around enough to punch through to the head.

Butchery, if you will.

It got to Arthur, who now lay a distance away on his back. At least he didn't have to dig through the monster for its beast stone. He simply stuck his harvesting knife stuck into an appropriate wound and let the knife's enchantment transport the stone to his pouch while he healed.

Healing, in this case, was going to be tricky.

Delving deep into his body, he found himself working his way through the injuries, attempting to put it all back together. Accelerated Healing was meant to be a sped-up version of passive Tower healing, but he'd noticed after getting battered around so much that even Tower healing was not pure regeneration.

Not like ordinary human healing, which basically replicated the damaged bits and patched it over, taking information from nearby cells to help stitch things together as best as possible. After all, Tower bodies were half made— if not more—out of Tower energy itself. That was how they were transferred, between floors.

All of which meant that rather than DNA encoding alone, there was a certain degree of Tower encoding in the energy that was stored in him. Part of him was part of the Tower. Knowing that, he turned his attention to trying to sense that information, to pluck at it so that he could then force more regulated healing.

Already, he'd learnt part of this—how to focus his healing energy, how to encourage it. Now, he was just being even more focused, utilizing the Tower even more. Flashes of inspiration, of details that he understood or that the Tower managed to "click" with ran through his mind as he turned inwards, finding bone pieces that needed to be moved, to be slid back into place or replaced entirely.

One after the other, till he felt the edges of exhaustion and heard the clatter of his weapon falling to the ground. Forcing his eyes open, Arthur exhaled, curious what he'd see.

After all, now was the best part.

Loot!

Chapter 99

"Loot, got to get the loot..." Arthur hobbled his way over to where Sang Kelembai's body had been, noting it had disappeared after the Tower took its energy back. He grabbed his enchanted harvesting knife first thing, sheathing and storing it away before looking at the other item that had been left behind. He frowned, wandering over and poking at it, uncertain.

"This wasn't here, right?" Arthur asked the air. "Couldn't be..." After all, it was in the depression where the body had lain. It was pretty much exactly in the middle, still a little soggy from the blood released, the ground mushed up. So definitely a drop from the monster.

On the other hand...

"Why do I get all the weird shit?" Arthur complained as he limped over to his prize and picked it up.

A tapered, oval, cylindrical object with slight striations through it, rough and bark-like texture. The size of his elbow, which was unusual, because, of course, it was a seed.

Seed of the Kelembai

Effect: Unknown

"Very helpful, Tower." Arthur sighed, then carried it over to his backpack and stored it away safely in the center. Rubbing his face, he reminded himself to be thankful he even got it. Two boss loot drops so far in this Tower—this seed and the moose hide for his armour—was more than most people got. Even if they'd had to sell stuff like the wasp stingers, because they weren't technically usable loot, he had been luckier overall than most.

Even if all he got were weird shit like this.

"Well, I guess I'll just have to plant you somewhere." Arthur rubbed a hand through his hair, making note to spend some time reading up on seeds. He was sure someone else must have his idiosyncratic luck, so he'd just have to hit the wiki when he got back outside.

Of course, it might be secret knowledge too, but that was why he had friends who knew people. Casey or maybe Rick might be able to get that information if it was not publicly available.

Which, come to think of it.... "I wonder how they're doing?"

He hoped his team was alright. That they were all doing okay. He had faith in them, though. After all, this was just a Beginner Tower. While it was tough, it was mostly because he was new, still learning and rushing through. The others had advantages, both in training or experience.

They'd be fine.

Right?

Yao Jing was singing as he walked, keeping pace with the Merchant beside him. The Tower had given him a little gray man, maybe four feet tall at most, though he sat within this steampunk contraption of a skittering bug that contained his goods. The climber was in a good mood, a new pair of gauntlets on his arm that sparked with lightning every time he snapped his fingers in time to the music.

When he was done, he glanced over at his temporary companion. "So, like that, *lah*."

"The song was... interesting," the small creature said, shaking its head. "But I do not understand why it is about a wolf..."

"No *lah*! The hungry wolf is a man, *lah*, one who likes women!"

"But why call them a wolf?"

"Because we get all hungry, you know. Tight dresses, low necklines..."

"Ah... I have heard of this!" The Merchant brightened. "Uncontrollable lust in humanity, due to their year-long arousal unlike normal mammals. An evolutionary trait that increases aggression and enforces competition among males!"

"Say what?"

The Merchant looked over, shook his head. "It matters not. It's my turn, to sing, yes?"

"Sure, sure." Yao Jing's eyes narrowed as he noticed movement in the trees ahead. "But wait. Just let me take care of this."

Leaving his spear propped over in the cart, Yao Jing took off running, eager to continue testing his new gauntlets. The others were going to be surprised when they saw him.

Uswah hung in the trees, shadow tendrils holding her aloft and off the ground. Beneath her, the harimau hitam stalked, sniffing the ground, searching for its prey. The boss that blocked the way to the tenth floor had been playing cat-and-climber with her for the last two days, stalking her ever since she had attracted its attention.

After so long, though, even the massive regeneration of the monster was struggling against the rot and poisons she had embedded in it via her attacks. Patches of fur had fallen off, dark webs of criss-crossing poisoned veins and arteries highlighted across its body. But even now, the monster still moved with the savage grace that had nearly ended her life and took another limb.

As it stood...

Uswah flexed her left thigh, her eyes tightening a little as the pain flowed through her. The numerous bandages around the wound kept the still-seeping blood from dripping. She was not the only who could cause aggravated wounds, though in the last day the wound had finally started healing over.

She waited for the beast to be nearly out of range before she moved, casting a trio of fast-moving poison darts at it. They formed from her hand, flying through the air to impact the monster and splash across its fur, burrowing in through the monster's aura and into the skin beneath.

The creature spun around even as Uswah pulled on her Shadow Step technique. It was leaping through the air for her, reacting with blinding speed.

Not fast enough, for she faded into the shadows long before its reaching claws could get her.

Her victory. Now, she just had to repeat it another half-dozen times.

Rick cursed, spinning in mid-air as the Gunslinger's Slide took him out of the way of the massive, charging boar. His pistol shots continued to crack, burrowing into the massive, fatty body of the babi ngepet. Hollow point, pancake rounds weren't so useful when the damn thing was the size of a small house.

It didn't help that he couldn't shoot it head-on. The armoured head just deflected the majority of his bullets; they were crushed against the dense outer skull. Only by hitting it in the side could he do enough damage, and even then, getting it through the monster's tough skin and fat required careful target selection.

And a little boost from his skills.

Exploding Projectiles were never meant for bullets. It was the kind of technique you used with an arrow or crossbow bolt, infusing a single item that could burrow its way in and then do significant damage that way. Modifying it, or purchasing the modified technique, had cost a pretty penny, but his parents had been able to acquire it for him and had it delivered later on.

He just didn't have the energy to waste on it on the regular.

Skidding to a stop as his movement technique ended, he waited to see which direction the monster turned to face him. In so doing, for a brief moment, he had full sight of the parts his earlier shots had burrowed in and he fired, double-tapping in quick succession to put both charged bullets into the monster.

The resulting explosion was quite satisfying, causing the babi to buckle, front leg no longer working.

Hurrying backwards, Rick knew he only needed to wait for it to bleed out now.

Mel raised her spear again to her opponent. Handsome, tall, and elegant, her opponent copied the motion with its blade, saluting her in turn. She found herself sharing a small smile with Kosilia, the Hermit, before they flashed forward. New lover or not, they had a job to do, and training Mel in the use of the new cultivation technique superseded all other considerations.

She elongated her spear once more as she lunged forward, using the technique she'd studied to give her the edge in range. No surprise, Kosilia had recognised the attack, stepped aside to dodge it. But that had just been the start, as a moment later a phantom spear followed at a new angle that forced him to hop back.

Spear of a Thousand Angles was one part martial art, one part Tower technique, one part reality manipulation as far as she was concerned. With the technique, she could manipulate where the phantom spears could appear, but only if she had intended to attack along those lines. To make full use of the technique, it required her to understand her opponent well, to predict their movements, such that she could cover the openings they offered.

It was a technique that was easy to learn and would take a lifetime to master.

Which was why they fought, over and over again, pushing her to the limit.

At least during the days. At night, well...

The nights were another form of exercise and training.

Chapter 100

Cursing quietly, Arthur limped up the hill, using the spear to help hurry him along. He had taken too long, both between trying to draw more energy out of the stones to refuel himself and just to cultivate. So long that if the jenglot hunting squad hadn't sent out a scout, he would have been caught out by the whole pack.

Killing the creature had been simple enough: a single REED going into its chest at close range had finished the creature, though not before it screamed in death throes. The problem was now he could hear the rest of the hunting pack rushing after him.

Arthur was not certain if crossing through the archway to the tenth floor would stop the monsters from pursuing him, but he had to chance it. At the least, if he was on the road and across it, he could force the creatures to bunch up as they came through the archway. Make it easier for him to use his REED and other skills.

The fight was going to be tough, either way.

A glance at his resources made him wince even further. He would have to try to finish this fight without using his techniques, if that was even possible.

Energy Pool: 4/30 (Yin) + (7/7)
Refined Energy: 0.04 (40) +(0/3)

He would have to be careful, being so low in energy reserves. A tug on his refined energy formed another Energy Dart inside his Poket Simpanan in his middle dantian, stored away for when he'd need it next. He had eleven minutes of fighting energy, or eleven uses of Focused Strike, or a mixture of both.

Good enough to deal with the... eight jenglot, he counted after a quick glance back and a grimace. Among them was an alpha.

Yeah, that should be enough.

Passing through the archway, he received a small notification. Barely worth noting and dismissing, before he turned around and set himself just past the archway. Ready for the fight.

And everything had been going so well...

Leia crashed into the ground, rolling once and then again before she found herself flat on her back, staring up at the sky. Numerous wounds dotted her body, lifeblood flowing away from a stab deep in her chest at the upper part of her traps, a cut that had pierced her lung and was slowly filling it.

Damn it.

She coughed, saw the descending foot and rolled out of the way. Twisted her body so that her legs swung up and sideways, such that she helicoptered the attacking appendage, sending her opponent crashing down too.

Pain wracked her body and she gave up. Utilized her body technique, Full Throttle. Felt the pain fade away as adrenaline and other chemicals flooded her body and blocked off the pain receptors. She bounced onto her feet with a simple flip, ignoring the ripping feeling along her lower back where another wound re-opened.

Grabbed the pair of knives she had belted across her front, knowing her spear—a bare two meters away—was useless to her. She had a minute to finish this, before her body came apart and she did damage even Arthur's healing ability couldn't fix.

Fifty-nine seconds now.

Jan ran. Breath panting, the heat from behind blistering her back, her hair— or what was left of it

in complete disarray. Behind her, the forest fire kept growing, flames jumping from tree to tree without stop. Monsters and animals scrambled alongside Jan, their aggression disrupted by the natural fear of being roasted alive.

She understood entirely. One side of her body blistered still, clothing burnt off, her bra barely containing her after half of its strap having melted into her skin. The polyester blend being burnt into her body hurt like hell but was working itself out as she healed it away. Still, it would scar her for years, she knew.

"*Bodoh!*" she cursed herself out as she ran. Bad luck and bad use of her techniques had caused the raging inferno behind her, one that clouded the entire area with smoke and choked her with each breath.

Why did she have to get put into a too-dry jungle? What kind of rainforest was it, that was facing a drought? How did that even make sense? She cursed beneath her breath as she ran at the idiocy of such a thought.

But here she was. Running from a flame that ran along dry vines and across branches, even the mild sap inside trees burning off as the heat from the inferno swept onwards. She could run, but the flames were being fed by a wind, and she could see in the distance how it had started to rise ahead of her.

Forcing her to cut across the ground, to bushwack and hope that she could outrun the flames before it caught her.

Because that would be a really *bodoh* way to die.

The portal glowed before Eric, taunting him. All he had to do was get into it, crawl through, and he would be out of the Tower. His enemy was down, the final thing to block his exit.

It had been there for the last day. Hanging in space, waiting for him to exit. In the meantime, Eric was pulling energy into his dantian, cultivating and absorbing as much Tower energy as he could. No more monster cores to acquire, of course, but in the meantime, he could at least empower himself.

Get himself ready for the kinds of battles he expected to see when he exited the Tower. Buy himself time before his body began to break down and he would have to enter another Tower again.

Outside, there would be enemies and complications. A Master who would be angry and proud at the same time. And a girlfriend who, he hoped, would have made it out of the Tower as well. Exes, of course, that he would need to speak with and try to handle their appeal to him.

And, of course, whatever trouble Arthur had brought with him.

His damn junior was a trouble magnet . . . and still the best fighter of them all.

Chapter 101 – Floor 10

Focused Strike, right into the throat. He yanked the spear back, twisting as he did so to widen the hole as the weapon exited. The alpha jenglot staggered back, clutching at its neck. It bounced off the invisible barrier that had appeared, enforcing the rule that one could not go backwards to the ninth floor once one entered the tenth.

Once Arthur became aware of that fact—a situation that had occurred when his poor spear nearly bounced right out of his hands when he overextended a lunge—he had ruthlessly exploited it, using wide sweeps and threatening attacks to keep the jenglot moving, stumbling over each other, over corpses, and hitting the barrier when they tried to back away.

Now, their bodies were piled up before him on this side of the barrier. He bent low, using the harvesting knife to acquire the necessary monster cores before he sat down, against the side of the road, back against a stone arch. Cool stone chilling him, helping some of the blood in his wounds clot further.

He let himself catch his breath, a half-dozen times, breathing in and out, slowing his heart rate down, calming himself and waiting for the trembling, the nerves, and jitters to end. Then, slowly, Arthur began to shift his breathing again.

In. Out. With each inhalation, energy pouring in from all around him with each exhale, dregs of power pouring out of him that he didn't need. Yang energy, filtered away by his cultivation technique to give him the Yin side of the equation. Not that he only needed Yin energy, of course.

As he cultivated, he felt the energy coursing through him, felt the way he changed Yang into Yin energy, turning it from one side to another, over and over again. They were two sides of the same coin, and so all one had to do was just . . . turn it.

Yin-Yang Energy Exchange (100%)

He felt when it happened, when the technique switched on fully. Arthur was wracked with shudders, his body clenching and releasing over and over again, Yang energy suddenly forcing itself out of his body. Skin paled further as he broke out into sweat. Even traces of blood and oil seeped out from his skin.

Moments later, he opened his mind to the Tower, feeling the information course through as the Tower filled him in on things he had missed, on how the technique was meant to work, what it could be used for. His cultivation techniques had progressed, faster than ever. And the Night Emperor cultivation method was being refined by the Yin-Yang Energy Exchange.

Yin-Yang Energy Exchange was the methodology he'd studied under Uswah, and its effectiveness had fluctuated for a while as he got used to the Night Emperor technique, as one technique supplanted another. However, it was not just a cultivation technique—otherwise, it would have disappeared entirely—but a skill technique.

He'd understood that, because even a Yin body was still filled with Yang aspects. You could not, after all, function without some aspect of either form of energy. In particular, the Yin-Yang Energy Exchange tapped into the body mass, the formed energy that was his body, and allowed him to utilize that as a last-minute trade off.

It basically meant that he could, at the cost of his life and limbs—or even organs—trade out for more Yin energy if he needed it. Of course, he hadn't actually done that yet, but that was the new information poured into his mind by the Tower. More importantly and generally useful was that he could also adjust some of the Yang energy that floated inside his body, in his meridians and dantian, and even within the refined energy coming from monster cores.

Now that he had learnt it, not only had his own cultivation ability increased, but it also increased his refinement ability. Or, if he wanted to, it could eke out a little more efficiency during battle, though in some ways that felt even more dangerous than converting energy out of his body mass. After all, if he leached out all the Yang energy from his Yin chi, he could fall over and collapse.

There were other additional benefits, too, from finally understanding and having the Tower provide these details. For example, he could switch back to Yang energy as well, which would help during second transformation if he ever reached that, to help deal with the pain when it tried to "balance" him. Or, conversely, fight the change powered by the Tower.

The techniques also gave him a wider understanding of Yin and Yang energies, the various ways they worked. Not just the obvious life/death dichotomies or healing/rot but also the elemental levels of the pair, the associations involved and how they worked together. While it was not a guidebook, it gave him more understanding of things like his Refined Exploding Energy Dart and Imbued Poison that he might further refine and alter.

All that, of course, was for later. When he had the time and energy to do that, rather than spending his time leaning against a stone arch, waiting for his body to heal and recover and while he cultivated more energy to refill what was incredibly low reserves.

Cultivation continued to dominate things; he was forced to only focus on that. The rush of untamed energy into him did not allow him to pull other forms of energy away, even with a second dantian in play. He knew he wanted to learn to cultivate and utilize his energies, but now was not the time.

After all, doing so would be a good way of leaving himself damaged and crippled while monsters still roamed on this floor.

Instead, he kept focused for hours, pulling enough energy in until he was content with his supply before pulling up his status screen in full to see the numerical achievement.

Cultivation Speed: 2.943 Yin

Energy Pool: 22/30 (Yin) + (7/7)

Refinement Speed: 0.1614

Refined Energy: 0.17 (40) +(0/3)

Attributes and Traits

Mind: 15 (Multi-Tasking, Quick Learner, Perfect Recall)

Body: 25 (Enhanced Eyesight, Yin Body, Swiftness, Fast Twitch Faster, Lightning Reflexes, Explosive Strength)

Spirit: 15 (Sticky Energy, From the Dregs, Strengthened Aura)

Techniques

Night Emperor Cultivation Technique

Focused Strike

Accelerated Healing – Refined Energy (Grade III)

Heavenly Sage's Mischief

Refined Energy Dart

Steel Skin (102.3%)

Seven Cloud Stepping Technique (211.4%)

Poket Simpanan Tua (147.2%) (Refined Exploding Energy Dart 99% Integrity)

Imbued Strike - Yin Poison

Yin Aura (Level 1) (128.3%)

Yin-Yang Energy Exchange

Partial Techniques

Simultaneous Flow (229.7%)

Yin Poison Darts (50.4%)

Shadow Sense (59.7%)

Slow improvements, at least in those techniques he had utilized. Others, like the Yin Poison Darts, had sat entirely unused, because he couldn't afford the time to practise them, not in the middle of a fight. In time, perhaps, he would get around to utilizing them, but he doubted it would happen in this Tower.

On the other hand, with the new information about energy types, he had a feeling he would have some significant improvements the next time he had a few minutes to practise.

That wasn't going to be now.

Content with how much basic Tower energy he had, he extracted a monster core and began the process of refining it. This was going to take longer, a full hour by itself, but being a core from the ninth floor, it would give him just over 0.09 points of refined energy in an hour. Enough for 9 REEDs. More if he had time to train or empower himself. If he didn't worry that another group of wandering monsters would find him.

Two or three of these would have to do, he decided. Enough to give him a fighting reserve, for the last trial of the tenth floor.

He just wondered what his particular trial was going to look like.

Chapter 102

To his surprise, there were no monsters that came by to harass him, even after three hours of healing and refining. Even so, Arthur chose to move away from the stone archway, climbing the rest of the short hill upwards towards the peak. As the day was beginning to end by this point, he chose to search for a place to rest, but with the narrow peak and lack of cover, his options were tying himself to the top of a tree or just finishing the hill.

"Got a boss, at the top, who I might not, be at a loss," Arthur whispered to himself, as he climbed. He was tired, his body ached. Not because of any lingering injuries, but from the memory of such injuries. Not that he didn't have a few remaining injuries here and there, but nothing that would slow him down in a fight. If not for the fact that he recalled the pain, the way his body hitched.

It would take time and retraining, assessing and stretching himself out to relax those muscles before he was back at it; though the advantage of having adrenaline flood through him constantly helped to reduce the moments where he forgot that he was injured or had been.

No wonder so many climbers spent time doing things like yoga or slow stretching or tai chi, moving their bodies through full range of motion after they left the Tower. Or took part in things like dance competitions or showcases, or got involved with sporting competitions. It actually had practical effects, to force them to reacquaint themselves with their healed, undamaged bodies and to learn the full extent they had changed.

"Does that mean I should be joining the Climber Fighting Championships?" Arthur mused out loud.

It was a good way of making money. There was a lot of money involved, and not just in prize money or appearance fees but also the side bets. Many times, things like monster cores or enchanted material or even services were wagered, though Arthur really only knew of that by rumor.

Not as though he had the right to even get involved, prior to becoming a climber himself.

"Yeah . . ." He took a moment to regard how far he had come up the hill. He scanned the darkening surroundings, still searching for a place to rest.

Up a tree, or . . .

Light ahead. He frowned, slowing down. His jaw dropped as he got a closer look, surprise registering visibly on his face. His mouth didn't drop open like a cartoon character's, but it was certainly hanging.

After all, the last thing he had expected was an East Malaysian longhouse set at the top of the peak, lights glowing and welcoming. He stopped, considering his next steps.

Stop here and rest? In the hopes that whoever lived in there didn't come out. Or risk the denizens within, hoping that whatever the final test was, it wasn't going to trigger immediately. The fact that it was a house rather than a giant cave left him feeling hopeful that was the case.

It wasn't unusual for the final test to be something other than straight-out combat, though that wasn't the only possible scenario.

Of course, he also wasn't looking forward to the other potential options. Most of them he was even less suited to clearing. He was better off stabbing someone in the gut with his spear.

"Wait? Am I an idiot muscle head?" Arthur muttered to himself, then considered. He wasn't a tank, resolute and strong. He wasn't the sniper or the sneak or a mage or the Tower climber equivalent of all that. He definitely wasn't someone who made things . . . And while he was the leader, half the time in fights he wasn't giving commands so much as slotting in wherever help was needed while someone like Mel was ordering others around.

Though he did, occasionally, give the orders too.

So... maybe? At least, he wasn't entirely unaware of his role.

Arthur grimaced as he neared the garden area, which was a series of low bushes and then just open space. He glanced down at one spot that was just a large rectangle of beaten earth and could not help but guess it was a training ground, though that was his own bias. There were other obvious reasons for a place to be entirely bare of grass.

A loading and unloading section perhaps? Parade ground? He wasn't sure, but not everyone trained for hours a day and wanted a piece of land that was flat and bare like that.

As he looked around, he found his gaze lingering on one particular section of darkness. He slowed his footsteps a little as he stared at it, waiting for the shadows to resolve. As twilight deepened, more shadows spread out all across the surroundings and Arthur found himself reaching for his Shadow Sense, allowing his chi to spread through the surroundings.

Moments later, the shadow detached itself, resolving into a figure clad in nothing more than what some might call a skirt. Of course, the *sirat* was just a traditional piece of loincloth with a large "apron" in the front, wrapped a couple of times around the waist. Paired with an extra piece of cloth draped over the shoulders at times—or, as the figure before him showcased, nothing to cover the torso—it was simple and practical in the hot and temperate tropics.

Other things were more interesting to Arthur than the man's state of dress. The *kris* that was belted to his side, a hand rested close to the hilt, and the simple spear in his other hand. But also the headdress of hornbill feathers that he wore. Arthur blinked, trying to remember if this combination was culturally accurate, then dismissed it as unimportant for the moment. The Tower seemed to like cultural mashups, after all. In any case, he knew little about East Malaysian ethnic tribes and could not tell one from another.

"Hi, boss. *Kita boleh cakap tak?*" Arthur asked as he neared the man but stayed out of lunging distance of the spear.

"You are late," was the man's response to Arthur's request for a chat.

Closer now, Arthur was certain that the man was brown, tanned, and a good four inches shorter than him. That was good, though it did make the fellow a rather strange guard. Well-muscled, in the "I work for a living" kind of way, rather than the "I take steroids and hit the gym to look good in too-tight muscle shirts."

"I... what?" Arthur asked.

"Late. Tun Rahman is waiting," the man said. A guard after all, perhaps.

"Right, right. And, of course, I'm here to see him." Arthur forced a grin, offering a slight bow as he stepped closer. "It was a bit of a fight, getting here."

"Did Tun Lok attack you?" The guard shifted, staring behind Arthur.

"No. I..." He hesitated, then continued. "Just beasts. Big harimau. I killed it, though."

"So the rumors were right; you are a great warrior," the guard said, offering a nod. "Good. We need all the men we can get."

"Right, right. Of course, and there's a lot gathered already?" Arthur said, following as the man led him to the longhouse. "Lots of, you know, other warriors?" He was beginning to understand what was happening, and it was making his heart drop and his stomach hollow.

His tenth floor trial was a quest, a damn quest that had its own backstory and all. He would have to play a part, figure out what the objective was, and complete it in whatever way he could. Like a bad game of charades.

Of course, it was never that simple.

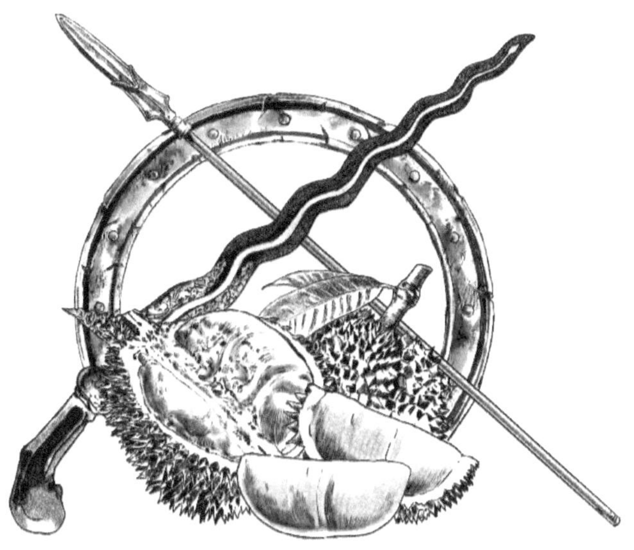

Chapter 103

The wooden longhouse that Arthur was led into was raised off the ground on stilts. Not too high, just about four feet off the ground, enough to ensure that a flash flood did not wash into the building though Arthur doubted that was even possible, with the building up on the hill. There was plenty of space beneath the longhouse, and that had the minor disadvantage of attracting snakes and other woodland creatures at times.

Of course, it also had the advantage of allowing one to keep chickens and other pet animals below, so long as one created the necessary fencing, so it was a bit of a give and take. Other than animals, the families living in a longhouse might use the space for storing items, even longboat.

In this case, Arthur noted that the entire ground space was left open, such that one could see beneath all of the longhouse. But the building was big enough that, even in bright daylight, there would be deep pools of shadows, probably requiring someone to be sent under to sweep for trouble on the regular.

But, of course, this was the Tower. This entire floor was created or dispersed as the Tower deigned. How much of it was accurate to real life, no one was entirely certain. The fact that these floors so often drew from local cultures spoke of a degree of customization, but the amount of energy required was staggering.

Entire fields of study were devoted to understanding how the Towers worked, how they bent physics, and how they powered themselves. There were a lot of new theories—and old ones, given new information—though the more popular ones revolved around tapping into unknown "dark matter" and the conversion of it.

All kinds of egghead things that Arthur ignored.

After all, he had his own problems. Like wondering what would happen now that he had come to a large dining hall slash reception room that was also the main entrance of the longhouse. A short table for squatting or sitting beside stood between Arthur and a man he assumed was Tun Rahman. At least, he looked similar to the bespectacled man in the history textbooks.

Eight warriors sat along the table, four on each side. Three women and five men, which was a rather significant departure from historical precedent. Then again, in the Tower, strength evened out, especially when one started getting to the later stages.

The warrior men were dressed only in sirat, like the guard, but the women had sleeveless vests and either skirts or pants. However, these were made of *batik* cloth rather than the dried bark of some East Malaysian traditional wear. Seeing the density of the weave and the myriad colours in the batik, Arthur wondered if they were distinguished persons.

Arthur turned his attention back to the man at the head of the table, older than the rest. He was dressed not in any traditional clothing of an East Malaysian tribe but in a silk *baju Melayu*. Worn by Malay men, it was better suited for formal events than combat.

The fact that "Tun" was part of Tun Rahman's name suggested that the man was either nobility or at least someone very distinguished.

Malay nobility and rankings were . . . interesting, to say the least. There were Tun, formerly nobility but now the equivalent of an old-time duke or commander of the forces. And then there were Tan Sri who were a level below. And then Datuk, which were the equivalent of a baron as far as Arthur could figure. And below that, which were all state-level people, there were Dato' who were the equivalent of knights—a title that was numerous as sin.

Anyone above a Dato' was someone very, very connected. On the other hand, it was a somewhat common joke—told by people like Arthur, of course—that anyone with a Dato' title (or Datin if they were female) had paid their way in and so were just too poor to tip.

Not exactly fair, of course. But then again, when the majority of Dato' titles were bought these days through favors and bribes, they were as useful in everyday life as an extra shiny gold watch, Arthur thought. He didn't feel particularly charitable towards that segment of society.

But he said, "My apologies for being late." And bowed a little—not much since there was never a huge thing for big bows in Malaysia.

For all his distaste of current day Dato' and their equivalents, those individuals seated here weren't lounge lizards, the pampered fools of modern-day life. These had the appearance and aura of old-time knights, warriors that kept a kingdom from being overrun.

Not people he was willing to annoy, not randomly at least.

"Unavoidable, yes?" said Tun Rahman. Unlike many of the others here, he was a little more on the paunchy side. Not surprising, given his age. The man gave the feel of an old warrior gone to seed, a man who had done it all and fought the battles that he now sent others out to wage. "Was it Tun Lok?"

"No," Arthur said. "Tiger."

A grunt, a few looks of admiration or caution from the others. Arthur took a seat at the man's gesture, sinking to the floor with gratitude and smiling as servants came out bearing a wood bowl filled with clear water and floating petals. The group returned to their conversations as he cleaned up as best he could and continued their meal.

The meal itself was interesting, a mix of older, traditional Malay dishes and more modern ones, in Arthur's admittedly limited gastronomic knowledge. Fried chicken dipped heavily in spices along with coconut-scented *nasi lemak*, cucumbers, peanuts, and roasted sardines. Large amounts of fresh fruit and vegetables, fried or grilled. And, of course, fish that had been baked or cooked with even more coconut.

Incredibly bad for one's cholesterol, if that was something he had been concerned about. Extremely tasty, otherwise.

"Harimau hitam?" asked his seat companion—a woman with short, curly hair—when Arthur was done with the bowl, leaving it muddy and dark with dirt and blood. Even after all that, his hands weren't entirely clean, but he did take a cloth to dry himself off as best he could while offering a nod in acknowledgment to the speaker. She smiled a little at his nod and continued moments later. "Took your time coming up?"

Now, his eyes narrowed. "You... know of the floors?"

"Of course." She gestured around, taking in all the other seated warriors. All of them appeared ethnically Malay just like the Tun—though Arthur sometimes found it hard to distinguish between Malays and those from East Malaysian indigenous tribes.

There seemed something different about them than the Tun, something that Arthur was unable to put a finger on, not just yet.

"We're climbers," she said. "Or were."

"Were?"

"We fell, during our trials," the man seated opposite Arthur said quietly. He had a scar over one eye. "This is just another damn play that we have to take, to get a chance to retake our own trials."

"You get that chance?" Arthur said, surprised. He'd never heard that before, and he had done a ton of reading. The serious nods from the pair and expressions of their companions nearby had him reevaluating what he had read. The problem with public message boards and AI chatbots was that, sometimes, details could slip past notice when they weren't the main narrative.

Or...

"Wait, you're second chancers?"

"We are."

Arthur shuddered, pulling away from the group instinctively. The looks of disgust and approbation they shot him for his instinctive reaction made him flush with embarrassment. Before he could shift his body language or explain, Tun Rahman spoke up.

"Do not fail me, for the consequences are dire, boy."

Eyes wide, another shudder ran through Arthur, even if in some ways, it was the best option too.

Just not for him, personally.

Chapter 104

Second chancers. They were the closest thing to resurrected climbers that you got. Or, if you believed the rumors, were actually reborn climbers. Or zombies. Or revenants. Or demons. Depending on your general worldview and the rumors you listened to.

The idea behind the rumors were simple: sometimes, depending on particular trial, or maybe for everyone who died on the tenth floor, one could be resurrected. Some people pointed out to Star Trek teleporters and various sci-fi stories of how, if one were just a bunch of data and energy packets transferred over millions of kilometers, then it would make perfect sense that you could make replicas of people.

Of course, various religions got upset at those ideas, went out of their way to try and disprove the very possibility. As usual, it wasn't something Arthur got into very deeply, but what he did know was that the idea of second chancers had always floated around—but actual sightings were rare.

Some people claimed to have met second chancers, of course, but many of them had been clearly disproven, shown to be outright fabrications or a stretching of truth.

If you were frozen or stuck in a long convoluted maze, was that considered a rebirth attempt? Well, for some, they'd agree. Others, disagreed. Vehemently.

Then, of course, the rumors and the concerns and the testing, on those that came out declaring themselves second chancers, the ongoing issues when they were out in the real world. Indiscriminate killings, murder of loved ones and families when said climbers snapped. Rumors of demonic summoning or sabotage of clans and guilds.

All that, in the initial years, before they became mostly a fanciful rumor. A suggestion of what the Tower might do, and less of an ongoing concern. Even in their heyday, Arthur knew of only a few dozen publicly acknowledged second chancers.

They went from something the Tower did to rumors, boogeymen that didn't really exist, crazed psychopaths and, in one case, a series of bad B-movies.

"We're nothing like that," hissed Arthur's first table companion, the woman with short curls.

"Don't bother. They all think the same…" sneered the man opposite. The deep scar over his eye somehow had not managed to leave it blind but did give him a rather frightening and menacing look.

"It's… you know," Arthur said, reminding himself that he wasn't trying to antagonize these people. Not yet, at least. Shifting his body closer, he offered them a smile. "All the rumors."

"I have my soul," the woman snarled. "I still pray to Allah and always will!"

Around the table, a number of others—including the Tun—chimed in with, "*Inshallah*."

"We are not forsaken, other than by people like you."

"I didn't..." Arthur spluttered.

"Then stop acting like I'm going to reach over and snatch your heart out!" she snarled again.

"Fine. Why don't we start by introducing yourself then?"

"Asman," said a hefty-looking young man sitting on Arthur's left. Since the others were still glowering, he introduced them. "This is Datin Nor," said Asman, indicating the woman on Arthur's right who had first spoken. Dato' Ramli was the man with the eye scar.

The names rolled out, one after the other, and Arthur did his best to remember them, knowing that it was going to be a little bit of a struggle. Finally, he introduced himself, offering them all a small smile before continuing. "So, uhh.... what's the quest?"

That caused Nor to snort and shrug one shoulder. When he glared at her, a little peeved, she continued, "We have some flexibility, but there are things we can't tell you."

"Or won't, eh?" Ramli added.

"Or won't." Nor grinned, almost seeming to take malicious delight as she spoke.

Arthur couldn't help but suppose that whatever was coming was competitive, then. Earlier, the guard had hinted at Tun Rahman's need for warriors. So if it wasn't a group battle—one of the major scenarios he could see playing out—that left a tournament, perhaps a series of hunt and kill quests. Or something he hadn't thought about as yet.

"So, can you tell me about yourselves instead?" Arthur asked as he reached forwards and picked from the meal. Everything was served family style, food being eaten with hands—well, with one hand in particular. One did not use the left hand, not unless one wanted to be ridiculed.

Long looks were traded between the group before they began to speak, offering their opinions and stories as Arthur ate a proper meal for the first time in weeks, if not months. Far up the Tower, even the seventh floor was pretty lacking in actual meals, especially for someone like Arthur who was focused on going up. The cost of procurement of materials was just too high, such that having someone else cook for you was a luxurious expense.

"Eight years, you know. That's how long I've been captured, though it doesn't seem like that," Nor was saying.

"Captured?"

"Resurrected," Asman offered. He was broad-shouldered, well-tanned and annoyingly pretty enough that the women were giving him looks whenever he spoke. Very familiar looks in two of the cases, ones that he traded back with them.

"Rescued," Ramli corrected.

"So you all don't agree on what happened?" Arthur said.

"Everyone's story is different, you know. I was caught, my timer ran out," Nor said. "Ramli was dying, he said."

"Or dead. And resurrected like me." Now Asman touched his neck, as though remembering a bad moment, before he continued. "We argue, we talk about it. But none of us feel physically different than what we were before."

"Damn. Do you age?"

Nods from those around, Asman in particular making a face. "My twenties will be over by the time I get out, if this keeps up. All my best party years, gone!"

"Can you cultivate?" Arthur asked next. If they could, they could easily be near the theoretical maximum of a Beginner Floor, maybe even more. If that was the case, fighting any of them head-on might be impossible—particularly Nor, who claimed to have been stuck on this floor for eight years.

Nor laughed at his question, as though she could see how he was fishing for information. Or perhaps she was just laughing at their circumstance, for it was rather bitter. But none of them actually answered him. And as though his questions reminded him that they were competitors, the group fell silent.

It took a while for the meal to finish, the entire group eating like they were starved for weeks on end, finishing plate after plate before they came to a stop. All the while, Arthur was cognizant of the glowering Tun Rahman, who was silent and listening. Something about the way he sat still or moved made Arthur wary of him. As though he was the living, breathing embodiment of the uncanny valley. Arthur wondered if the real Tun Rahman was anything like this.

Or was he, in fact, the real Tun? The Towers were magical, after all. For all Arthur knew, the Tower could have resurrected the historical Tun.

When the desserts—sticky rice and mango, cooked and soaked in coconut milk, delicious and so bad for him—was half-consumed, did the Tun lean forward.

"Good, you've eaten your fill, yes?" he rumbled. "You have eaten my food, pledged your loyalty to me. Soon, you will come with me, wage war against Tun Lok."

The group responded with affirmations, though Arthur noted more than a few sardonic glances shared among the second chancers. Arthur was a little slower to echo their words, and his delay had Tun Rahman glaring at him.

"Good! Then, sleep and rest." Hands clapped together, a dismissal that had everyone rising upwards. More servants appeared, individuals that all looked almost generically the same and gave even more of a strange feeling to stare at. These, Arthur knew, weren't really "real," more like programmed automations that took care of minor tasks. You could kill them, but they'd disperse just like monsters did. But unlike monsters, they would provide no cores.

Of course, depending on the scenario, killing them could end up with him losing, so, you know, no mass slaughter.

As they were led away, Arthur taking his time to move, picking up his backpack and spear from where he'd deposited them, one of the other second chancers, a short young man, stepped close and stumbled. He landed on one knee beside Arthur, who was still seated. Head bent low, he whispered quickly before he straightened.

"Don't sleep. The game begins now."

Then, he was up, moving away. Looking at the retreating back, Arthur could not help but spot Nor looking back and shaking her head at Arthur and at the young man. The latter was an older teen, really—more a boy than a man.

Then, Nor stepped through the doors and was gone, leaving Arthur wondering exactly what was going to happen tonight.

Chapter 105

The room that they put Arthur in was rather bare. It did have a few things going for it: for one thing, it was about twice the size of the closets he had been relegated to in the past; it had a bed and desk and even a small table. Of course, the bed had no mattress, only a bunch of blankets laid out on it. And the entire house lacked indoor plumbing, though at least there was a large washbasin filled with water. Cold, but beggars couldn't be choosers. Or, you know, climbers who had just fought through multiple floors and not taken a proper bath.

He was just grateful Tun Rahman hadn't chosen to get angry at his state of dress and the amount of dirt he was tracking in.

With the warning from the boy—and damn him for being unable to remember the name. Was it one of those "I" names, Imran, Ismail, Ishak? Whatever. Arthur definitely wasn't going to bed. Not that he wanted to sleep filthy either, so once he propped the chair in the way of the door, he stripped his armour off and began the long process of cleaning himself.

After the third time he had to ask for a change of water, he stopped blocking the door directly, just leaving the chair nearby such that he could toss it with his leg or kick it into whoever decided to charge in, if necessary.

Of course, that meant he left his back to the window which was propped open from the bottom, but what could you do?

Washing himself clean was a quiet and calming ritual. It allowed him to think over the events of the last few hours, his opponents, and what events might occur from now. Once he was done and clean, he dressed himself in a set of shorts and a shirt before he turned towards his weapons, finishing the cleaning process of those.

Funny, of all the things that he had, his weapons were the cleanest. Not just the edges, but along the grip and shaft where he held them closest, blood and guts wiped clean, brushed away over constant use. When he had time— and water—he cleaned them. Sharpened the edges, double-checked the points, and got rid of burrs and chips.

His equipment was a mainstay of his life here in the Tower. For him and most climbers who wanted to survive battle after battle. Indeed, it said a lot that it was his weapons were the best cared for. His leather armour, though, when he got to it an hour later, was still a battered mess.

He wiped the armour down with a cloth, noting how the cleaning spray he'd borrowed had done some work during an initial rub-down to help break down the accumulated filth. Leather needed to be oiled, after you used soap on it, rubbed down gently to give it back its suppleness. Burrs and scratches could be sandpapered away. Holes punched into sides could be banged out and then covered with duct tape later.

Too bad he didn't have better patches or strips of leather to replace broken portions. Bindings could be removed, grommets unpunched and pulled apart with the right equipment, but that took time. Even if he noticed a few straps were frayed, a couple ready to come apart, latches and buckles bent out of shape, he left them for now.

Instead, he finished the cleaning and inspection, wiped everything down, and set it all aside to dry. He would put it on, but armour was uncomfortable, especially when it had been beaten around so much. Uncomfortable and, especially in Malaysia, hot. There was a reason you didn't see warriors wandering around the South East Asian isles in plate armour.

Work finished, all his equipment sorted for the moment, Arthur stood up and stretched, walking around the small room. No balcony to walk out onto, just a window he could open. It was late at night, well past midnight now, and he almost wished he had taken some time to cultivate.

He was as ready as he was ever going to be, assuming he didn't have time to draw in more energy to refill his reserves. And yet, nothing was happening.

Sticking his head outwards, he looked back and forth. Searching for problems. Seeing nothing but a couple more windows, all of them closed but one. That was propped open from the bottom, a light burning within. It was two windows away from his.

He stared at it, hoping to gain some clue, but the angles were all wrong. He was in the midst of pulling himself back in, when he saw movement out of the corner of his eye. Craning his head upwards and sideways, he spotted a swinging shadow, moving across the top of the window and then—

A flash of eyes, narrowing under a masked face. He couldn't see much, just the silhouette and something glittering in one hand that flashed towards his face.

Instinctively, Arthur pulled away and into his room but just a touch slow. A burning line along his face, as the attack passed him by. Searing pain before a spreading numbness. He staggered back, kris appearing in his hand, legs landing against the edge of his bed before he collapsed against it.

Poison Detected!
Climber attempts to resist poison!
Poison partially resisted!
Poison partially resisted!

Numbness spreading through his body, the Tower providing details about what his body was doing. He understood this poison, this deadening of his nerves. It was not the same kind that he used, though it was a Yin-related poison, a thing of slumber and quiet, of energy lowered. It should have been simple to handle, what with his Yin body, his healing factor.

That it wasn't simple spoke of the potency of the poison. He shuddered, his body going into overdrive as it washed the poison away from the wound, Yin chi acting against the poison to reduce its effectiveness all over his body. From his wound across his cheek, blood still leaked. His vision swam a little as he focused on the open window intently.

Waiting to see if the attacker returned.

Wondering what they were doing now.

Then, voices. Raised voices, a scream, a clanging of a bell. The alarm was raised, and dread swept through Arthur as he tried to pull himself upwards, understanding running through him.

So that's what they meant by the game.

And why he should not sleep.

Chapter 106

Arthur forced himself to move, stumbling over to the door. He reached for his spear automatically, then hesitated. Socially, running around with a spear in the middle of the night was a bad idea, at least in someone else's house. Like drawing a gun and walking around with it unholstered.

Just not done.

On the other hand, Arthur had just heard someone scream. So, maybe it was more acceptable to carry his spear? Arthur found himself staring at it for a long time, his mind working ever too slowly for his liking. Another voice, more noises shouting from outside.

"Where are they? I want all of them here, now!" Tun Rahman's voice rose, nearing a shout.

Arthur groaned, realizing he was taking too long making a simple decision. He shoved the spear aside, grabbed the door and pulled it open, stepping into the hallway. He moved towards where the sounds were coming from, the main hall.

Not as though the longhouse itself was that complex, being a single long building with two wings on either side. One was meant for the guests, rooms on either side, a few of them with doors ajar. Arthur paused, long enough to close his own door at the visible reminder before he continued to stumble out.

As he entered the hallway, the gaze of those waiting fixed upon him, freezing him a step into the room. Blinking slowly, he looked between members of the group, more than a few offering him a rather intimidating stare.

"What happened to you?" Tun Rahman asked.

Killing intent spiked and Arthur gulped. "Uh… what?"

"You are injured. What have you done?"

"I…" Arthur held a hand up, forced his system to focus, cleansing the poison a little more, pushing it out of his head. He blinked, feeling himself stabilize a little, his head clearing out. "I was attacked. Someone . . . threw a knife. Poisoned."

"You saw something? Who was it?" the lord growled.

"I saw a silhouette, a shadow. It threw a knife at me," Arthur clarified. Touched his face, realizing that the cut had stopped bleeding, just leaving a sticky mess behind.

"How coincidental," Nor said.

"Agreed," Ramli added.

Tun Rahman looked over to the pair, narrowed his eyes. To Arthur's surprise, the short young man who had warned him earlier spoke up. "Or, perhaps, those throwing aspersions at a fellow warrior are more suspicious. After all, Datin Nor was here so quickly."

"Hameed!" Nor snarled. "How dare you betray us?"

"Betray? We're all on the same side, I thought?" Hameed said, putting on a look as though he hadn't stolen the last slice of *kuih* from right under their noses.

"You—!"

"Silence," Tun Rahman spoke up, holding a hand. "Dato' Hameed is not wrong. We should not be fighting among ourselves, not yet. We need every last man if we should hope to defeat Tun Lok. And now we are down by one warrior." His gaze roamed over the group, counting the numbers. Arthur did the same, noting there were... "Eight. Where is Datin Mahia?"

At the same time, Arthur wondered aloud, "Down by one?"

Hameed whispered, "Dato' Taufiq was just found dead. Didn't you hear the scream?"

Meanwhile, no one knew where Datin Mahia was and Arthur stepped aside as the lord moved to head for her room. Hameed followed, but the others moved aside like Arthur, before they were interrupted. A figure burst in from the front door, which was slammed open with a hard thunk. In came Datin Mahia, hair disheveled, harried, dirt showing on bare feet as she stumbled in, one hand clutching her upper arm which held a kris, unsheathed.

Everyone pivoted to her, weapons out. Dato' Ramli was the first to act, lobbing a throwing knife underhand at the woman. Mahia's eyes widened, her body flinching backwards reflexively but that was the wrong move. It didn't move her body out of the way of the knife that buried itself in her throat.

Staggering backwards, her kris dropping to the ground as she reached for her neck, eyes locked on the group, on Tun Rahman roared, "STOP!" But it was too late. She was dying, and though some of the others rushed over to help, the blade was caught in her neck. Any movement to pull it out would kill her all the faster as her carotid artery and potentially other blood vessels were bled out.

Arthur moved over, hanging back a little, watching the dying woman. He took it all in, the way she stared at the others, the dirty feet, the state of undress that she was in—underwear and light top, rope burns along the arms that scrabbled at the neck.

"Can anyone do anything?" Nor asked, looking around. There was a flatness to her voice, and she was already looking away towards the end of the sentence.

No one answered, not even Arthur, who did not have the skills to heal another person, only himself.

He was getting the idea now: Find the killer, or killers. Or kill everyone who wasn't you, but do it in a way that didn't arouse the suspicions of the lord. Which was something Ramli had failed at, based on the haranguing that was going on behind Arthur. On the other hand, Ramli wasn't yet in chains or ropes, nor had his hands been cut off. It sounded like he was getting a pass, though, with his protestations that someone coming in with a weapon drawn was dangerous for the Tun.

"No more! No one kills anyone anymore without my permission!" Tun Rahman raged, glaring at everyone as he strode over. He looked down at the woman, then gestured. Figures, his ghostly servants, swept in, pushing the warriors aside to surround her body. Funny how long it took someone to die, especially when everyone knew better than to yank out the blade that was partly stemming the wound. "My servants will care for her. Maybe they can save her."

"My lord, we should—" Nor began.

"I gave an order."

She shut up as he cut her off, allowing the servants to carry the body away. Not that anyone expected Mahia to recover. Unless she had an Accelerated Healing technique, dealing with a blade stuck in your throat was nearly impossible. Patching it together was not going to be easy.

"Well, it looks like we found your assassin, at least," Asman said to Arthur as the body was carried away.

"Are you stupid?" Arthur couldn't help but say.

"What did you say to me?" Asman snarled, a hand dropping to the parang by his side.

"Because if you are, you're forgiven. But otherwise, you think she was the one who attacked me?" Arthur shook his head.

"Why do you say that, Dato' Chua?" Tun Rahman asked before Asman could say anything further.

"Rope marks on her arms. Barefoot and underdressed." Arthur ticked the words off. "Someone tried to kidnap her or choke her with a rope."

"Why kidnap her, instead of killing her?" Hameed asked, reasonably.

"I . . . don't know." Arthur shrugged. "I can't guess at the motive, just point out the facts."

"Or she could be trying to fool us," Asman said, doubling down.

"Well, that answers the question," Arthur muttered.

"What?"

"You really are stupid."

"You!" The parang came half out of the sheath before a hand came down, hard, across his face, forcing Asman to stagger as Tun Rahman slapped him.

"I said, no fighting." Then, he turned to stare at Arthur. "And you, stop antagonising him. Or else, I will think you had something to do with all this."

"Apologies." Arthur offered a nod, grimaced at the splotch of blood on the ground. "I really wish we had a chance to talk to her. Maybe she—"

"We shall see. In the meantime, you all shall sweep my grounds again," Tun Rahman commanded, then eyed the group hard before adding, "In pairs."

Well, at least that made sense. Arthur surveyed the group, met Hameed's eyes and nodded to the boy,. Of them all, he seemed most willing to help Arthur out. Right now, what he needed most of all was information.

From the quickly rising body count, it was clear that being in the dark only ended one way.

Chapter 107

Arthur wished he had a chance to check out Dato' Taufiq's body, but they would get that opportunity later. Right now, since he was the one who had seen the assassin—or so he claimed, according to the others—he and his partner Hameed were sent to the roof to check on what clues they might find above.

The fact that it was the middle of the night and they were being tailed by another pair to keep them honest was rather off-putting, but Arthur figured that was for the best. At least he'd get a chance to understand his opponents a little further. Eventually, he might even be able to speak to Hameed alone.

"This way," Arthur said, leading them outside to his window. With it still propped open a little, it was easy enough to spot. All the while, he was scanning the surroundings, but without knowing what was normal around here it was a rather futile effort.

The fact that everyone else was acting the same way—clueless—had Arthur wondering how serious the group was about finding the killer. Then again, if his assumptions were correct about what was going on, there was a reason for that.

"Up there," Arthur said, pointing to where he had been struck.

"You said there was a dagger? A throwing knife?" Hameed said.

"Yes."

"Then we should find it. Not many use daggers, among our group," Hameed said.

"Yeah, too easy to lose them. It's… oh. Right. Evidence," Arthur cursed himself out quietly, turning his gaze over the surroundings. Mentally charting where the knife should have been. No glimmer of light, not even when one of the other cultivators came by, raising a hand filled with flame to provide additional illumination.

"Nothing."

"No knife here either."

"*Dia tipu, ke?*"

"Hey, I can hear you two." Arthur glared at the pair of cultivators who were accusing him of lying about the attack at his window. "They might have come back to pick up the knife, you know."

"And then got to the meeting before you? Not likely."

"Definitely trying to *tipu* us, aren't you?"

Arthur rolled his eyes, then walked away. He gestured to where he thought the attacker climbed back up the roof. He frowned at the window next to his, asking out loud, "Whose room is that?"

"Mahia's," Hameed said.

"Huh." He was sure the figure attacking him had clothing on. While Mahia might not be super fair-skinned, the lack of clothing she was flashing would have been something he'd have noticed. Too pale for the darkness…

"So, up there?" Hameed said.

"Yeah…" Arthur sighed and followed Hameed, leaping after the boy who managed to make the jump in one single, impressive leap. Arthur needed his own Cloud Steps to do the same, two clouds to reach the top.

On the roof, he teetered at the edge. Made of clay and leaves, the structural stability of the parts that weren't directly resting on the ceiling beams was rather horrendous, so Arthur was being careful not to put his foot in the wrong place. On the other hand, Hameed didn't seem to care, wandering over the ground as though he weighed nothing.

Considering his leap, maybe he did weigh nothing.

"Nothing here," Hameed said.

"You didn't expect anything, did you?" Arthur said, moving away from the edge carefully. Down below, the two other warriors that had followed him were continuing to search the surroundings halfheartedly, ignoring the pair on the roof.

A shrug from Hameed. "It would have been convenient."

"For what? Finding the killer? It's one of us, isn't it?" Arthur said.

"Most likely," Hameed said.

"So, this is what? A murder mystery quest?"

"You could call it that."

"And what would *you* call it?"

"Another Tuesday."

Arthur groaned, shifting forwards and then freezing as the roof groaned. "Seriously. Talk to me. What is going on?"

Hameed sighed and said simply, "The usual quest I get is a murder mystery. One of us—or in a rare case, more than one—is designated by the Tower to be the killer. We play our roles, while the climber fails or succeeds at finding the killer. Those of us who are not the murderer, if we figure it out without getting killed, we might get a chance to exit."

"Might?"

The boy shrugged. "Not as though we get a manual. No one shares what they know."

"So, why help me?"

A shrug was his answer, Hameed turning away so that Arthur couldn't see his face. A part of Arthur grew even more suspicious, but another wanted to believe the boy was just, well, a good hearted kid. Maybe someone who had been dragged along this far and was just trying to do his best.

Hey, he could hope.

"You said 'the usual quest,'" Arthur said. "But none of you seem to care very much. Other than to throw suspicion on one another."

"The Tower forgot one thing when it created the quest."

"Oh?"

"Humans are lazy," Hameed said, walking to the peak of the roof. He stood on the edge, swaying a little with the breeze, starlight highlighting his clothing and fluttering the sirat around his legs. Arthur followed along gingerly, crouched over rather than standing heroically like the other.

"Sure, but what does…" Arthur sighed, rubbing his face as he began to realise what the boy was implying. "They're going murderhobo, aren't they?"

"Yes."

Arthur sighed. He understood their reasoning, he just couldn't get behind it. After all, while it was easier to just kill everyone and let god sort it out, but that wasn't an elegant solution. It also meant that he wasn't only in danger from the designated murderer; everyone else was a danger.

At that thought, he glanced over to Hameed who was still standing there, hands behind his back, enjoying the night breeze. One of the advantages of being up a little higher was the reduction in mosquitoes, and along with the dark of the night, it made things quite pleasant really.

"Don't worry. If I wanted you dead, I'd have just kept my mouth shut." He smiled a little. "You'd be surprised, though, how many climbers die on the first night because they weren't careful enough."

"Yeah, fair enough." Arthur crab-walked over along the side, searching the roof for a little more before he sighed. "I am not seeing any clues. Are you?"

"No. And if there were any, I wouldn't trust them," Hameed said. "Most of those here have played this game a few times before."

"Red herrings," Arthur acknowledged. "So this really is a murder mystery?"

"As far as I know. You good at mysteries?"

"I wish..." Arthur said with a sigh. He never was one to read that kind of fiction. He assumed that was the case for most people involved—they didn't really have the skill, knowledge, or techniques to make figuring out a murder easy. Not as though there were that many places to learn actual detective skills in Malaysia. The homicides that happened were all too often gang related and/or rich people related. Which, of course, led to quite a few coverups as a matter of course.

Speaking of skills . . . Arthur asked, "Can you still learn new techniques? Increase your attributes?"

"We can't," Hameed said, glancing at him. "And there are penalties for when we try to break certain rules."

Arthur grunted at the venom in the boy's voice, strong enough that it made him shut his own mouth. He wished he knew what to say to the boy. Man. What do you call an 18-year-old who's been stuck in the Tower for who knows how long, unable to grow? At times, he seemed his age, young and impressionable. Other times, he looked and felt older.

A prodigy that somehow stumbled at the last step.

Arthur's heart ached for him a little, but nowhere enough to risk his own trapping. Whatever happened, he had no intention of being a victim of this murder game.

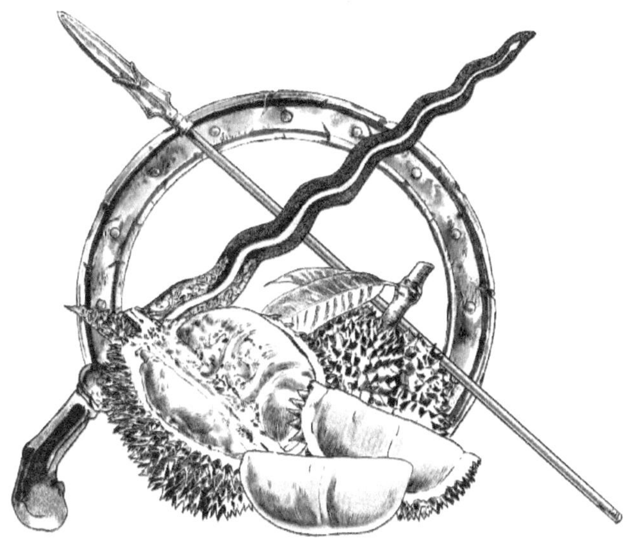

Chapter 108

After a few more minutes of futile searching, Arthur and Hameed were joined on the roof by the pair below. Arthur walked the entirety of the roof carefully but found no further clue about his attacker. Neither did any of the others, and so they swapped out with those investigating inside the longhouse. A quick check of each room showed that the second chancers had even fewer personal belongings than he did. Most rooms were bare, beyond the basics of weapons or a couple of changes of clothing. It made sense that the Tower didn't bother giving them much to work with. And after all, this scenario was focused on combat in a limited area, not trekking for days through the wilderness.

All of which meant that Arthur gathered absolutely no clues, other than noticing two individuals who had throwing knives in clear view—they were on his list of suspects now, one being the face-scarred Ramli.

Even Taufiq's corpse, still left sprawled on a bed with one leg off it entirely, the second leg half-propped up, and hair in disarray, told Arthur nothing. Well, beyond the obvious: clothed and armored meant that they were awake and ready. Weapon near their hand meant they had tried to protect themselves but failed. The angle of attack showed someone coming in from the window. The murder weapon seemed to have been a pointed weapon, not a skullbasher, and probably quite wide.

Which didn't narrow the case down at all.

What with no further information or anyone else being killed or otherwise found out, the group had returned to their rooms to rest. Arthur took the time—after barring window and door, and then stuffing his bed to look like he was lying under the covers—to catch a quick cat nap in the corner of his room. He didn't rest too long since he wanted to cultivate a little too, but being completely exhausted was also a bad idea.

Even so, he was forced to hide a yawn when he stumbled out for breakfast, joining the group that was already seated. He noted he wasn't the only one exhausted, though he was grateful that they were at least getting breakfast.

And tea. Strong tea, filled with milk and sugar. Not exactly *teh tarik*, but a close enough version of the drink that he wasn't going to complain as the servers pulled the tea through the air to add oxygen to the mixture. He was still a coffee man, but when in Malaysia you drank what you were given.

"*Nasi goreng* for breakfast?" Arthur said, eyeing the spread which included Malay fried rice. "At least some benefits to all this . . ."

"Yes, very much so. Eat up! Might be your last," Nor said, seated beside him again.

Arthur happily complied, scooping from the main dishes, adding peanuts and spicy *sambal* and fried fish and meat to his plate. He was careful not to take too much.

"No, no. Eat, eat!" Nor reached for the serving spoon, scooping a huge helping and moving to add it to his plate.

"No, thank you," Arthur said, blocking her arm. "*You* should eat though, need to keep the figure."

"You like?" She grinned, eyeing him.

Arthur shrugged. "It's not bad."

"Not bad!" she hissed in mock outrage.

"It's not the body," Arthur said. "You're fit and pretty enough. It's the personality."

Now she looked genuinely offended. More than one of the other second chancers was looking at him too, Hameed in particular looking amused. Even the Tun, who normally just glowered, was looking over as Arthur explained, "It's the desire to kill me. Just entirely wipes out any lust, you know. Just gone. Poof!" He gestured with his hands as he said that, a grin breaking out on his face.

Silence, then laughter filled the hall. The tension that had grown and kept the conversations somewhat suppressed broke, as people talked more animatedly amongst themselves. Nor, snorting, put the spoonful of rice down and went back to her food, only looking up after swallowing her latest mouthful to add:

"You're wrong, you know."

"About?"

"Me wanting to kill you. I just have to."

"Pah-ta-toe, Poh-tah-toe."

Nor shrugged, returning to her meal. Arthur noted few others were eating much, some eschewing the meal entirely. It took him half his small portion to realise why, as a tingling started around his lips. He raised a hand to his mouth, curious at the chemical taste that had begun to present itself. At first, he thought it was just the *sambal bilis* because, sometimes, you got that strange taste. Too much mining had led to the occasional destruction or pollution of breeding grounds, such that wild fish could be dangerous to consume.

Not that many people had the choice, and the small sardines that were used in the sambal bilis rarely had enough pollutants to cause trouble anyway.

His tongue was now numb. His teeth felt weird and swallowing was growing difficult. He stopped eating entirely and, glancing around, saw two others looking distressed.

You have been poisoned!

"Poison," he croaked out, once the notification confirmed his suspicions. He pushed the food away and the water too, coughing and spitting and wiping at his mouth to remove the trace amounts.

Two others staggered away from the table, grabbing at their weapons. As though they could stab away the threat. Tun Rahman was shouting, calling for people to hold still and calm, even as he pushed away from the meal as well. A growing hubbub, shouts asking who else had been poisoned and confirming that Arthur was not the only one.

Beside him, Nor looked fine. She was sitting back, calm. Ramli too, as well as Hameed, though both were standing up, hands away from their food or weapons. Ghost servitors had started approaching but froze at the shouted commands to not touch anything, leaving Arthur and the two who had jumped up to clutch at their throats and fight the encroaching numbness.

Yin energy surged, combating the poison. A part of him recognised it, the way the poison acted, the way it interacted with him. Not the exact same, but a close cousin. The Yin energy coursing through his body laid the necessary improvements to reduce the spreading numbness and the minor discomfort in his stomach.

He kept his energies focused within, leaving external problems like inflamed lips or numb tongue for later.

One of the other victims fell over, his breathing coming in jerks and stops. No one dared move close, in fear of being accused of adding to the problem. Or perhaps just reluctant to help another competitor.

A horrible way to die, Arthur figured, but the man seemed to slip into unconsciousness not long after.

The other victim was like Arthur, still awake, still looking around. One hand was gently glowing though, her body sweating profusely as she utilized whatever skill she had to counteract the poison. Arthur, on the other hand, had grown cold, colder than ever in his own methods of cleansing and transformation of the poison.

"So brazen! Poisoning our lord's food too," Ramli finally said, glowering. "Who is it? Which one of you?"

"Is Tun Rahman's food poisoned?" Hameed asked. "Was this attack meant for him?"

"How would I know?" Nor said. She waved at the food. "I don't have a skill to pick it out. And it all smells and looks fine to me."

"If the food was poisoned, why aren't we all affected?" Asman asked next, poking at the food with a utensil.

"Maybe they're just weak," Nor said, blithely.

"Or it's the drinks," Hameed offered, gesturing at the cups. "Those were prepared individually."

All eyes shifted to the servant that had been making it. The faded figure shrunk back in fear and uncertainty. Tun Rahman, silent till now, gestured and ghostly guards filtered over, grabbing the servant by the arms.

"We shall investigate," Tun Rahman said. "Still, that is but one possibility."

"If we look at what they ate . . ." Asman said, standing up and glancing at the plates of the three poisoned people. The now-silent body of the other climber had been picked up and taken away by guards. "Maybe there's a clue in the food?"

"I'm more curious about how it was snuck in," Hameed added, wandering over to where the cups used to make the teh tarik were at the serving station. "These three were the last to arrive, so . . . does that mean it's one of those who arrived here before?"

Now, cautious gazes turned to the four competitors who weren't affected, tension rising with each breath. Hands drifted towards weapons. There were only a few suspects now.

Chapter 109

"Stop!" Tun Rahman snapped, freezing the second chancers who looked on the verge of attacking each other. They glanced back to the older lord. Hands on his hips, he was flanked by a pair of ghostly guards. Not that they did more than flick a glance at those creatures, as though the ghosts were unimportant. Perhaps they were, because Arthur certainly didn't get the same sense of danger radiating from them as he did the Tun.

Then again, killing Tun Rahman would likely mean the failure of the quest entirely, which was why the entire group relaxed, moving hands conspicuously away from their weapons.

"Boss..." Asman started but was cut off.

"No. Unless you have evidence, there will be no accusations or attacks." Then, something flickered across the Tun's face, as he continued. "If breakfast is over, we must begin our next step." The second chancers nodded to one another. Ramli was grinning and Nor looked a little excited, a shift in stance that had Arthur worried. Moments later, it made sense as Tun Rahman continued. "Training will begin. Come!"

He strode past the group, ignoring Arthur and the poisoned woman, slowing down only as he reached the front doors. All but the poisoned ones had followed behind him quickly. The Tun suddenly turned and frowned, staring directly at Arthur and the woman, who had likewise been successful in combating the poison with a skill. "Are you shirking your duties, warriors?" the Tun boomed.

"No, my lord!" Struggling upwards, the woman moved to the door.

Arthur, caught out, took a moment more to follow. He might be confused, but he understood what was going on.

Outside, the group had gathered in a line before Tun Rahman, who seemed to be ignoring the entire issue about them being poisoned.

"…strongest warriors in the nation," the lord was saying. "We will show Tun Lok what it means to threaten me, and to do that, we must train and be led by the most gifted of you all. As such, you will pair up and fight one another for the honor of leading the raiding party!"

The moment he finished speaking, the others were moving. On his right, Nor pivoted to face him a fraction too late as Ramli got in front of Arthur first, smiling wide even though it lacked friendliness.

"Apologies, Dato' Chua," the last two words said with intense sarcasm. "But we all must win, yes?"

Arthur opened his mouth to answer, found his jaw still not working well, and just gave him the best, most skeptical look he could. Then he shuddered, feeling a wave of coldness ripple through him, then heat, as Yang energy replaced Yin moments later.

"Take your place, all of you."

Arthur nodded, sweating now as his body dumped the very last of the poison into the open air. He turned sideways as he walked forwards, vomited a little to remove some of the brackish and metallic taste from his mouth.

He took his spot opposite Ramli on the training grounds.

Not that the grounds were more than scratched-out space on the earth, but Arthur figured that was the way it worked. His hand drifted down to the kris he wore, regretting he didn't carry his spear to breakfast too.

Then he blinked as ghost servants appeared, each carrying a spear. Neither were his; they were training ones, the tips wooden and blunt. Ramli took his without even looking, pointing the weapon at Arthur one-handed.

"Begin," came the command from Tun Rahman as the other warriors got into position as well.

Arthur's hand was just on the weapon when the command was given, but Ramli didn't seem to care. He launched forward, his spear leading the way in a one-handed grip. Arthur snorted a little inside, though he took his time reacting, knowing he had to wait for the weapon and its wielder to close in before he moved.

Then, it was a simple matter of swaying to the side, raising his left hand upwards as he dropped the same side leg back, blocking and wrapping the spear up at the same time. His own spear he tucked in close to his body, aiming not for Ramli's body but the legs.

Somehow, he was not surprised when his casual deflection and block was dodged, Ramli managing to literally leap over his attack, using his greater weight and the leverage to rip the spear out of Arthur's grip. Ramli nearly sliced the back of his body too as he did so, forcing Arthur to jerk and twist as he spun, bringing his own weapon to safeguard against the kick that followed moments later.

Skidding backwards, his arms and weapon shaking a little, Arthur straightened as Ramli smiled, wide.

"Not as sick as you tried to show, eh?"

"Not as foolish as you seemed, charging ahead without a plan, eh?" Arthur answered.

Now, their weapons were pointed at one another. A small acknowledgment that their attempt at fooling one another had failed.

Now, the real fight would begin.

A flurry of blows, each of their spear tips and shafts used, a combination of elbows and knees and legs utilized when possible. Arthur cursed as he dodged an unexpected elbow, throwing himself into a roll and coming up with a sweep of his own spear, forcing his opponent to check it rather than follow up.

Ramli was untrained, his methods entirely unorthodox. Arthur could tell that his stance, his choices of how to react to attacks, and even the way he blended his attacks together came not from training but hard-won experience.

That was the trap, he realized. Second chancers might not be able to progress their cultivation bases or learn new techniques, but nothing stopped them from improving in combat experience. It was like fighting his sifu again, his master having acquired decades of experience and wiliness that made it hard to win against.

Times when Ramli felt open were shown to be lies, as Arthur had to frantically dodge and twist and block attacks. Openings that were just there to draw Arthur into different positions, setting him up for follow-on strikes.

The only advantage that Arthur had was that he had trained formally. He'd put in hours and hours of work, on days when he was tired, on days when he was in pain, because he knew he would need to fight in all such conditions. He'd practiced fast and slow, against newcomers and old hands. So even if his opponent's style was unusual, the body and the weapon could only move in so many different directions and ways.

The longer the fight went on, the more Arthur began to glean of his opponent's habits. He received numerous cuts, bruises, and stabs in the meantime. Never anything fatal, never sufficient for either party to call an end to the spar. Some of the wounds might have been crippling if they weren't sparring with blunted weaponry.

Most of all, Arthur was waiting.

"One minute!" Tun Rahman called, indicating a time limit to the spar.

He sensed it then, the sudden change in intensity. Now was the time, the time when "accidents" were going to occur.

After all, what better time to wipe the board clear than now?

Chapter 110

The first trick Ramli pulled when they next engaged was a simple one but nearly fatal for Arthur. When their spears engaged, Arthur pushing with the end of his to get his opponent's weapon off-line and away from his face, spider tendrils of power reached out from his opponent's spear shaft.

It grabbed Arthur's weapon, held it tight and froze it, such that Arthur could not move his spear like he'd expected. His own block, meant to parry at the outer line against his opponent's inner line crossing, should have been simple, a movement that did not require a significant amount of strength.

Now, without the ability to move properly, with leverage twisted, his opponent bore down and angled his body, throwing his weight behind the attack and pushing forwards.

Arthur grunted, suddenly in a really bad position that forced him to twist and duck downwards, angling his body beneath the incoming pair of bound spears. It was a bad move, though, for it placed him exactly where Ramli wanted him. A knee rose up, smashing directly into his face, crushing cheek and nose in turn and causing tears to spring to Arthur's eyes.

Another jerk and twist as he stumbled away and Arthur was forced to give up his spear. The moment it was torn free, the bindings holding the weapons together dissolved, allowing Ramli to use the spear with full dexterity once more. He didn't hesitate, jabbing at Arthur who had to scramble backwards, over and over again to get away from the weapon on his hands and knees.

As he stumbled, finally, while crab-walking backwards, falling on his butt, he saw the spear tip glow. Power coursed through it, sharpening the weapon with Focused Strike. What was a simple blunt spearhead, painful to receive but not fatal unless wielded without care, became a deadly weapon in a flash.

Which was what Arthur had expected.

Rather than try to block it or use another of his techniques, he conjured a Cloud Step beneath his right foot perpendicular to the floor. With that firm footing, he only need shove off hard with his feet to skim backwards even more, the weapon chasing after him as he basically slid across the earth on his butt.

It wasn't, of course, fast enough to dodge the attack entirely. The blade pierced skin and muscle, cut through his ribs, but that was when the momentum of Ramli's lunge ended. A second cloud, formed under the legs that had tucked in again had Arthur scoot off the blade and backwards, giving him a moment's reprieve.

Before Ramli could recover and lunge again, the glow of his own attack disappearing, Tun Rahman was there, slamming a meaty fist in a powerful backhand across the second chancer's face. It threw Ramli backwards, his voice roaring.

"Treachery!" the Tun snarled.

"No, my lord. It's not that! I was just overcome with the competition," Ramli immediately began groveling.

Of course, he wasn't the only one who'd taken advantage of that last minute. Arthur, clutching his wound, forcing himself to calm as he waited for it to clot and then heal, scanned the surroundings.

One dead. That poisoned woman, her neck snapped from what might seem to have been a bad fall if Hameed didn't look so calm about it. Both Nor and Asman looking the worse for wear, though at least they were alive. Sporting wounds on either side.

Excuses rang out one after the other from the group for their actions. Tun Rahman looked incensed, about to explode, and then, a flicker. He shook his head, looking around at the exhausted combatants.

"A pity," he said slowly. "But sparring accidents do happen. More importantly, we must still find the traitor and deal with them. We shall rest, for today," the lord said, leaving Arthur to stare after him as he strolled off after getting the half-formed servitors to grab the body left behind. When one came near to help Arthur up, he pushed the arm away, standing up with effort.

"You survived," Nor said, strolling up to him.

He raised the practice spear a little with his free hand for the moment in mock threat. She made no motion to guard herself or react as she continued, "I knew I should have taken you. Ramli's always terrible at finishing the battle."

"He's tricky, this one," Ramli said. "And you speak as though you killed your opponent."

"Hey!" Asman cried, looking annoyed as he worked on bandaging his wounds.

Arthur noted that Nor's own wounds had stopped bleeding, though he didn't see them closing. He, with his own grievous injury, chose not to speak, instead swaying a little as he staunched the bleeding and slowed it down with pressure.

"Anyway, he might still die," Ramli eyes narrowed at the blood around Arthur's hands. "Unless you have a blood healing technique like Nor?"

"Why are you telling my secrets?" she snapped.

"As though he has no eyes."

They began to bicker, a factoid that Arthur stowed away as he pushed himself to leave, heading for his own room. He got about halfway there before Hameed appeared, first moving to take the practice spear Arthur was using as a cane. When Arthur refused to let go, Hameed continued.

"Relax, we can't hurt you right now. Not directly; the rules don't allow it. Tun Rahman would kill us for doing so."

For a long moment, Arthur considered the piece of information, debating if he could trust it. Eventually, he let go, allowing Hameed to take the spear's place as support. Behind, he could hear the trio scoffing at Hameed and continuing their bickering.

"That's a messed up quest," Arthur said. "But why can we kill each other only while training?"

"Training, meals, at night. Outside of that, if you can get away with it, you can."

"Oh." It made sense that there were limited windows for when they were allowed to kill while the Tun was watching. It was probably why Ramli had been scolded when he continued attacking Arthur after their last minute of sparring was up. But he had gotten away with killing Mahia . . . Arthur supposed it was permissible in supposed defense of Tun Rahman. In any case, it seemed Hameed was telling the truth about there being rules of what they could or couldn't do—rules which aligned with the quest's story.

"When. Next?" Arthur grated out, his breath short as they took the stairs to ascend into the longhouse. It didn't help that something in his chest was moving, shifting under pressure as it healed.

"Will you survive?" Hameed asked.

All Arthur had to offer was a grin. It would have been melodramatic if he managed to do it with blood on his lips, but unfortunately—or fortunately—he'd managed not to bite his tongue or the inside of his mouth. Nor had the attack pierced his chest, such that he had blood to cough up.

Together, the pair made it back to his room where he was propped up against the bed, Hameed slowing down long enough to stare at Arthur's enchanted spear. An eyebrow rose as he regarded the weapon.

"Good weapon."

"Thanks." Arthur refused to say anything further, not seeing a reason to give away information that he didn't need to. Nor was he physically able to do so as bones clicked into place.

"Smart, to keep the healing ability hidden." Hameed said, before continuing. "But you should have bandaged your face too, if you really wanted to do a good job."

Arthur froze, remembering the cut across his face. It had scabbed over in a few hours and healed, and while he hadn't washed his face, it was obvious to those watching that it healed a tad too fast for anyone but someone with a good healing ability.

Arthur caught a glimpse of a smile on the boy's face, in the reflection of his spear. Their eyes met through the reflection, and again, that grin widened before Hameed left, leaving Arthur a little disturbed.

The kid was rather perceptive. And Arthur still wasn't entirely certain why the boy was helping him as much as he was.

Though he had a growing suspicion, born out of deep paranoia.

Which likely meant Arthur was right.

Chapter 111

Arthur didn't bother changing his bloodied clothing. For one thing, he still hoped that he could fool someone, even if it wasn't Hameed. He did, however, make liberal use of his bandages, now washed if still a little—okay, significantly—stained. He wrapped them tightly around his body. After that, he pulled his shirt back into position and began the rather painful process of finishing his healing.

He wasn't certain what else was happening outside his room, though his best guess was not a lot for the rest of the day. Chances were, the next opportunity for attack was their next meal—which he reluctantly skipped—then dinner, and then sleep once again. Each of those were when attacks were allowed.

He assumed some other activity would be called at some point tomorrow. Arthur tried to think of what kind of social activities or leisure things were popular with the Malay nobility but drew a giant blank. It wasn't as though that kind of information was covered in history classes. Most of Malaysian history lessons had focused on the time period when Malaysia was Malaysia, and maybe a little of the time when it was Malaya. Daily lifestyles before colonisation was a topic not significantly covered, at least not in the school curriculum.

Which, now that he thought about it, was a rather pernicious effect of colonisation. Why did he know more about how Victorian or even medieval Europeans lived than Malays or the Orang Asli indigenous groups who pre-dated them? Even decades after the British had been kicked out, some local students continued to take exams set by university boards not even from their own country. Bureaucracy and long-term change took forever, never mind the fact that there was just no funding of research about such historical periods, so that no one had anything to draw from even if they wanted to put together such a syllabus.

Not to mention, of course, the rather concerning degree of bias that crept into history books as it stood. It wasn't just the overuse of AI and the lack of primary sources when talking about events like World War 2 or the 1969 "Emergency," but also the desire to minimise or politicise events.

Like calling the 1969 civil war that raged through Malaysia an Emergency, so that international companies and interests could continue to do business in Malaysia and not pull out. Or characterising the conflict between Singapore and the rest of Malaysia that resulted in its separation as "minor disagreements." He'd literally seen that line before, in a plaque commemorating the event.

By this point, being able to cultivate and pull energy into his system and thinking silly thoughts was second nature. He was in the process of churning refined energy from the cores on hand into his dantian, swirling it around and around till it took the proper aspects. He made the energy part of himself before moving on, draining the core as quickly as he could.

The big advantage of moving to higher floors and getting better beast stones was that you could refine more energy from them, requiring you to hunt less and refine even faster, though there was somewhat of a hard limit due to one's own stats. Still, considering how little energy he had at the beginning, he was grateful for even the small amount of time he found to top up his reserves.

At the same time, he couldn't help but occasionally consider the remaining suspects. If he could, somehow, figure out who the killer was and lay out the evidence, he might be able to short-circuit the massacre and clear the tenth floor. Of course, he didn't need to be told that making a false accusation was one way to get his head chopped off.

So, do it right or don't do it at all.

Four people left—and of those, Ramli was the most suspicious. For one thing, he used a throwing knife, just like the person who had attacked Arthur. However, it didn't mean he was Taufiq's killer.

Taufiq's window had been propped open. Which meant that whoever had done the killing would have had to slip out without disturbing the stick that held the window open, a difficult thing with how narrow everything was, or take the time to reposition the stick after they had exited. Or come in through the door and then closed it again.

Since all the second chancers seemed to know something was up, the chances of someone opening the door at night was very low. The killer might have been a friend of Taufiq's, someone he was willing to open the door for.

So who Taufiq was friends with? Arthur made note to ask, though he wasn't sure he could trust the information given to him either. Which meant that, however he asked, he had to do it in a way to not raise suspicions that he was trying for a clue.

Next up: Nor and Asman and Hameed. He had nothing to suggest any of them was the killer, or was not. Nor had been fast to throw suspicion on him, but Arthur assumed such games were allowed—it wasn't a formal accusation.

If suspicious activity was a concern, all of them were potential suspects. Which, again, didn't help.

So . . .

"I got nothing, which is all kinds of sucking," Arthur groaned to himself as he felt the beast stone in his hand crumble away. He sighed, brushing himself off and reached for another. "This is why no one tries anything, eh?"

Maybe if he had a technique that increased his senses, if he had a way to become more sensitive, or had time to chart out the positions of where everyone was . . . If only the group wasn't out to kill one another, and had played the game the way it was supposed to.

As it stood . . .

"The killer might already be dead," Arthur grumbled as he returned to refining.

Unlikely, of course, what with the poisoning. But the poisoning might not even be the Tower-chosen killer's actions, but the opportunistic attempts of one of their compatriots.

If he couldn't work out who the killer was, did he have to become a murderhobo too, then? Try to kill everyone? More and more, it really did look that way, which was depressing to the extreme.

"You can whine, but if you do, you won't be fine . . ."

Groaning, Arthur made himself accept that this might be the only way forward. If so, he needed to stop reacting and start getting proactive. He couldn't just try to survive whatever was happening. He needed to start working out sneaky ways to assassinate the second chancers before they got him.

Unfortunately, for all his training, being a ninja or assassin just hadn't been something covered by his sifu.

But there was no better training than on-the-job training.

Chapter 112

Arthur watched as the next monster core crumbled away, the last dregs of its power sucked into his body. He swirled it around his meridians, following the cultivation method he had studied to help assimilate the energy as quickly as possible, while considering what his next steps were to be.

He had to go on the offensive, but the problem was that none of his skills or techniques were especially suited to doing that stealthily. Sure, he could conjure a Yin poison, but it was either stuck to his Imbued Strike or his aura. It wasn't as though he could infuse it into a liquid and make someone drink it.

More importantly, his self-made Yin poisons were not that strong. They lulled a body to rest, drawing down the energy levels of the victim and making them wish to sleep. Eventually, causing numbness and, to some small extent, even forgetfulness.

Similar, in some ways, to the drug used on him at breakfast. It didn't, however, forcibly paralyze a body. It didn't affect muscles in as direct a way, since it worked more on the overall energy pathways of the victim.

There were advantages to his technique, though: it was usable against almost any kind of monster, even those without highly active blood or liquid flows or muscles to freeze over. He didn't think that was the case with the poison that was used on him. He had a feeling that whatever poison that was, it was something natural, extracted from a snake or a plant or something of the sort.

"Crafters . . . always tricky, those fellas," Arthur drawled to himself, brushing the crumbs of the dissolving beast stone off his lap and standing up as he stretched. It was late afternoon now, close to time for dinner by the angle of the sun. There wasn't exactly a clock to set schedules, but eating as the sun started to set was common.

No point eating at night and wasting oil and wood if you could just time it right and eat as the sun began to set. Also had the advantage of pulling people indoors during the twilight hours when mosquitos were most abundant, which then reduced the number of fatalities and deaths from malaria and dengue.

You'd think that, after hundreds of years, someone would have come up with better malaria and dengue vaccines. But thus far, the few vaccines available only worked against a few strains. Worse, it wasn't even as though either mosquito-borne diseases had changed that much; but there just wasn't enough money in it for the big companies. If not for advances in vaccine development, they might never have bothered.

"I wonder if we could . . ." Arthur began but shook his head, dismissing the thought. One day, he and the Clan might be powerful enough to consider owning large pharmaceutical companies and the like. Do good and not just collect money; but he was far from that.

First, he'd have to survive dinner, and he still didn't have a way to go on the offensive.

"All defense here, no offense," he sighed. All his techniques were clearly good for up-front dangers. Uswah would be the perfect person for this kind of quest. He was more the kind to excel at a head-on melee battle.

Which, of course, led to the question of why he hadn't taken Ramli out, on the training grounds.

"Still too soft-hearted, old man."

Shaking his head, Arthur made sure he was properly packing and then, once more, hesitated over his spear. After a moment, he shook his head and left it behind. Since Tun Rahman laid out punishments for attacking another participant at the wrong time, bringing his spear was likely to attract unwanted attention.

In the main hall, he found to his surprise only Asman there as yet. Taking a seat beside the man, he cocked an eyebrow at the young Malay gentleman after his greeting, a silent query for more information. Or just an invitation to speak.

"Have you given up yet?" Asman said.

"On climbing the Tower?" Arthur shook his head vigorously. "Not a chance."

"Not that, *lah*. On the case."

"Oh, that. Eh . . ." He raised his hand and waggled it back and forth. "Maybe they'll slip up?"

"Maybe. You can guess who it is, can't you?"

Arthur snorted. He was definitely not going to guess.

"So you've all done this before?" Arthur gestured around the empty room. "This particular variation? Because I hadn't heard of it much."

"It's not common. But, when we're not here, we're—" He stopped, hissed, and clutched his head. After a moment, he shook it, returning Arthur's puzzled stare and stating, "Tower *tak suka kita cakap.*"

"The Tower won't let you talk about it?" Arthur clarified.

Asman grunted an affirmative.

"Huh. Never heard of that."

"That's because it only happens to us . . ." He smiled, wryly. "Normal climbers like you don't have to worry. Can live life, *syok betul, kan?*"

"I wouldn't call my life *syok*, exactly. Not so much thrilling as . . . heart-palpitating." Arthur then added, "And you guys . . . you know things we don't. Got any other juicy info?"

"I wish."

Arthur fell silent, looking around the room, watching the ghostly servitors come in and deposit plates of food, then move on after a bit. He couldn't help but wonder what was not being said. Why, if such a quest was not common, how the second chancers knew what to do. Had they all been stuck that long? Asking that question had Asman shaking his head, moments later.

"Don't ask. I'm not supposed to tell you anything."

"Can you . . . talk about yourself then?" Arthur gestured upwards, indicating the Tower.

"Nothing to say *lah.*" Asman said. "This my chance, and I failed, you know?"

"Friends? Family outside?" Arthur prodded.

"Takde." Asman shook his head in the negative. "I was a gamer, played a lot. But when my computer system fried, when people stopped playing, the UBI was not enough, you know?"

Arthur knew. It wasn't even enough to live on most times, not unless you were staying two or three to a room and didn't mind having a rather boring meal routine. Of course, the fact that Asman even had a gaming rig of some sort spoke of hidden depths.

Then again, they were on the tenth floor. Everyone here had hidden depths.

"So you came in, because . . . ?"

"I might have borrowed a bit," Asman said, grinning. "Had to. Then I couldn't pay it back. So I got in here. They collect the UBI for me."

"But the UBI stops when you register . . ." Arthur trailed off, realising how stupid he sounded. Of course there were ways for people to enter the Tower without being registered. Of course the triads and tongs and other gangs had figured out a way to bribe the guards, to enter information wrong or look the other way. Then, they could continue collecting money while the debtor was within the Tower and pad their pockets.

You had to admire it. It was an almost victimless crime.

"Then, you don't want to get out?" Arthur asked, eventually.

Asman snorted. "Of course I do. You know how much I miss a good *char kuey teow?*" Arthur blinked, since the lard in the dish – the very thing that made it so good – was haram. Of course, there were halal versions, but they just weren't as good. "Nothing here tastes right. And, if I'm out, I can live big, you know?"

"Yeah. I kinda do." Arthur sighed. "And the others?"

Before he could complete his thought, a voice cleared itself, making Arthur turn. Standing there, arms crossed was Nor, glaring at Asman and Arthur in turn. Asman smirked and Arthur, well, he just grinned.

Couldn't blame a man for trying.

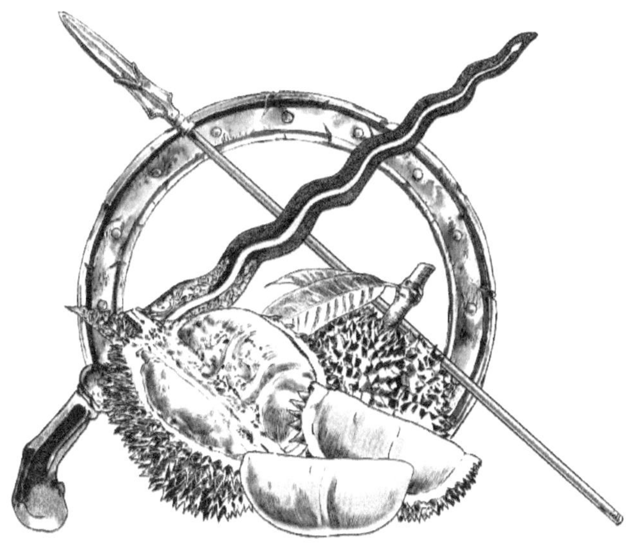

Chapter 113

Caught fishing for information, Arthur was prodded by Nor till he moved away from Asman to a different seat. Then, she happily took a seat in his old spot before ignoring any attempts on his part to strike up a conversation. Neither did Hameed offer any information when he stepped in, just a small nod before sitting down on the opposite side of the table.

When Tun Rahman arrived, everyone stood till he took his seat. A frown appeared moments later, as the Tun's gaze landed on the empty spot where Ramli should have been. Sudden intuition had Arthur looking to the doors, and then at Hameed who had most recently entered. The boy sat there, hands laced and resting on his legs, looking entirely too serene.

"You didn't . . ." Nor said, her voice suddenly hollow.

No answer from Hameed. No arrival from Ramli. After another few minutes of strained silence, Tun Rahman gestured to the servants who disappeared. Time stretched on and on, each breath in and out of Arthur's lungs a loud rasp in his ears. When the servants reappeared, they had only to glance at Tun Rahman before the man shuddered, that strange twitching and then calm appearing and disappearing on his face.

"Another death. The culprit is here, and growing bolder every moment!"

"Hameed, how could you?" Nor said.

"How could I what?" Now the boy looked up, still calm. "What are you accusing me of, Nor?" The way he fixed his gaze on her and only her might as well have added a large pointing sign above Tun Rahman's head instead.

"I . . ." She hesitated, shook her head, and looked between Hameed and Asman, before she suddenly made up her mind. "I am accusing you of killing Ramli. And of being the killer the Tower chose!"

"A dangerous accusation. Are you certain you wish to level it?" Tun Rahman said, fixing Nor with a flat gaze.

She gulped but nodded.

"Then, do you have evidence? If you do, I will review it now."

"Not enough, my lord. Not enough, but I know it's him," Nor's voice grew firmer with each word.

Hameed, watching the pair speak, just shook his head a little.

"Then, you know, you are staking your life on this accusation. If you are wrong, I must penalise you." Tun Rahman's voice was cold, remote, as though reciting a list of groceries rather than threatening her. "I ask, one last time. Are you sure of this?"

Nor licked her lips, her gaze fixed on Hameed. She seemed to be weighing something again, between the intangible weight of fear and whatever evidence she had so far. In the end, it tilted in favor of the accusation and she voiced her confirmation.

That was all the Tower needed, for light bathed the trio involved. Asman, watching all this, shrunk back, moving away from the sudden cones of energy—a movement that Arthur mimicked without thought. Energy pulsed for nearly a minute before the blinding light faded.

Eyes still watering, Arthur was surprised to find Nor gone, Hameed still seated in the same position, unconcerned. Tun Rahman, however, was looking grave.

"A false accusation has been leveled. Punishment has been meted out. Dato' Hameed has been found not guilty," Tun Rahman intoned from his standing position—and when had he stood up?—then sat back down.

Arthur reached out, gingerly, to poke at the empty space where Nor had been. Nothing there, no body, no indicator that she had ever been there at all. He looked to Hameed, who looked entirely pleased with himself now. All of which left Arthur wondering what the hell was happening.

Before, it sounded as if Nor thought Hameed would be on her and Ramli's side, whatever that meant for the other warriors. Were they planning to gang up and eliminate the others? But what if one of them was actually the killer?

And why did Nor make an accusation against Hameed when she had no real evidence? Why risk death when she had any other choice? It almost seemed to him that she had been afraid to fight Hameed.

Or was she gambling? Figuring that, at this point, it was a good bet? And if not Hameed, who could it be?

Well, by process of elimination...

"Will you do it, then?" Hameed asked, flicking his gaze over to Asman.

Arthur looked at the other second chancer, catching up only now to the implication. Asman stared at Hameed again, who looked back at Arthur.

"I . . ." Arthur said uncertainly.

"Well?" Hameed continued, his voice soft. "You wanted to solve the mystery, didn't you? Here it is."

Here it was, indeed.

Arthur opened his mouth, then shut it as he stared as Asman. For a man who was supposed to be the chosen killer, he looked almost puzzled, confused in the way he glanced between Hameed and Tun Rahman and then back to Arthur.

If Asman knew Arthur wasn't the killer and Hameed wasn't, then…

"Tun Rahman," Arthur said, suddenly. "Among those who were injured and taken away, do any of them still live?"

Hameed looked a little disappointed, as though he was expecting Arthur to jump at it immediately. He brightened a moment later, though, the shifting in his face miniscule but easy to catch if someone was watching for it, when Tun Rahman answered.

"The one whom Dato' Ramli injured did not survive the night," Tun Rahman said, sadly. "And now, there are only three warriors left. I fear it will not be possible to launch our attack against Tun Lok." Now he glowered at something in the distance, seeming to have dismissed the remaining trio.

"There, you see. It can only be Asman," Hameed murmured.

"So why don't you try it?" Arthur said, softly. He was suddenly hesitant about making the accusation. Something just did not make sense.

He was missing something, and till he could figure what that was, he wasn't going to make a move.

"Eat. We should eat. And afterwards, tonight…" Tun Rahman stopped speaking and looked confused for a time, before he shook his head. "Tomorrow. I will speak with you three and choose the right man to lead the attackers."

"Lead? Is the attack not called off?" Arthur asked.

"Of course not! We must make Tun Lok pay."

Looking into the Tun's eyes, he saw now confusion mixed in. As though he struggled to understand what he was saying, or why. That confusion, that trapped look in the man's eyes made Arthur shudder, break eye contact, and simply focus on the food before him.

Perhaps it was for the best, then, that the meal began to arrive. In strained and uncomfortable silence, the group ate. No poisoning, not this time. It made Arthur wonder if they'd killed the poisoner already. Was it Nor? Ramli? Maybe even the woman who'd died on the training grounds, poisoning herself to look innocent.

Or perhaps . . .

Now, he had another suspicion. One that might explain the reason for the lack of information on this trial, that explained the reactions of Hameed and Asman.

Arthur just hoped he was wrong.

Chapter 114

He was awake when the large roar that shook the building echoed through the surroundings, followed by a scream and grunts. Arthur rushed out of his room, carrying his spear and ready to do battle. Too slow, because by the time he threw the door open to Asman's room, the battle was over. Pinned to the side of the wall, veins of corruption and darkness extending from the spear that had been thrust into his chest, Asman's eyes were fading, staring into a sightless void.

Instinctively, Arthur wanted nothing to do with the weapon pinning the second chancer to the wall. Dark lines and smoke rose from it, malevolent and unsettling just to be in the presence of. He feared the curse that killed Asman—if it was a curse—and that, even now, rotted the walls.

Across from the open door, the window hung open, its shutters torn apart in the hasty exit of the killer. He listened as footsteps echoed above him, rushing across the roof to the other side of the longhouse. Movement behind him, and Arthur noted Hameed coming out of his room.

He backed up, spear leveled at the other. "Not you, then."

"No," said Hameed.

"*Celaka.*" Arthur fixed Hameed with a glare. "Is it always like this?"

Hameed offered a sardonic and world-weary smile that looked entirely out of place on someone so young.

Arthur's mind spun, trying to put together the clues and information he had been given. It was clear now that some of them had suspected, even known, that Tun Rahman was the killer from the very beginning. Arthur didn't think any of the second chancers could move so quickly and evade capture every time. Not unless Hameed could teleport, but Arthur didn't think that was likely in a Beginner Tower.

However, Nor had died making an accusation that she must have believed had a high chance of succeeding.

Was she dumb then? Did she guess entirely wrongly? Or could Hameed have been the killer but survived the accusation through some rule of the Tower? Arthur didn't know. Damn the Tower and its hidden rules!

"Why keep me alive?" Arthur asked, his weapon raised at Hameed as the boy stepped forward, his own spear held loosely by his side. "Why help me at all?"

"What makes you think I was helping you?"

"Your advice. You carrying me in to my room." A glance at his spear, verifying that it was still his and nothing weird had happened to it while it was out of his sight. He'd checked last night when he got back, just in case.

"Oh, yes. Couldn't have you die just yet."

"Just yet?" Understanding, some of it flowing through. "The quest, the Tower, needs me alive, doesn't it? To keep it running all the way."

"Until now. When there's only us left and you've all but failed..."

It clicked in Arthur's mind. Of course. No one ever said there had to be only one killer. In fact, Hameed had said it himself: the Tower could assign one or more killers. And there was no reason that the killer had to be a second chancer. If both Hameed and the Tun were killers, it was possible that the Tun could mete out false justice—hence eliminating Nor even though her accusation was correct. Meaning it was useless for Arthur to accuse Hameed; the Tun would not be on Arthur's side. So there was really only one way to clear this quest . . .

Hameed was strolling forward, weapon before him. Something in the way he looked, the way he moved, made Arthur take a firmer stance.

No longer the kid, he moved like a predator now. He reminded Arthur of his senior Bruce at the dojo, who lamented every day that his parents had spelled his name Li instead of Lee. Who'd worked longer and harder than even Arthur, just to keep up with his namesake. And became a first-rate killer.

"Now, hold still. I don't want to tire myself out too much before I kill Tun Rahman." Soft, the boy's voice was soft. Arthur felt something press upon him briefly, a pressure on his aura that he hadn't even noticed was happening till it was gone. His own aura infiltrated, his mind growing confused.

More confused, on top of everything that had happened.

"I . . . we . . . don't have to do this." Arthur whispered the words, knowing they were untrue but he was reluctant to kill the boy. He'd grown to like him. The thought of ending his life—possibly for good this time—sat ill with Arthur. They should, they could, find a way around this.

Their spears met, a gentle *thock*, as Hameed kept light pressure to open the way. He pushed the weapon out of line as he kept walking closer, voice lowering with each step as he got closer. "It doesn't hurt, you know. Dying."

Arthur hesitated, his retreat slowing down as Hameed continued speaking.

"It's true. You'd think, after being hurt so much, being injured so many times, that dying hurts too. But dying itself, it doesn't hurt. Not if it's done right. The passing from one side to the next, it never hurts. Don't even remember it, not the first time, and soon, not the ones after. Not unless they're special . . ."

So close. Hameed had gotten so damn close. Arthur's spear was entirely off-line, not in any position to block. The boy had taken a hand off his own spear, slipped a kris into it and smiled, keeping his gaze locked on Arthur as he closed that last few inches. The blade slipped in, and the boy was right.

"Doesn't hurt, does it?"

Arthur knew it had to be a mental assault. Some soporific that had gone in, just like the numbing poison. Causing his body to freeze up as the kris drove itself into him, turned, and tore him open.

It was Hameed's mistake, using the same poison again.

For a brief moment, as Accelerated Healing kicked in, sweeping away part of the poison and sending a lance of pain through his body, Arthur's mind cleared slightly. He found himself able to think at last, even as the boy continued to stare at him, all smiles.

So close they could kiss.

So, Arthur opened his mouth and let a REED loose, not even daring to give the boy a fraction of a second to evade—which Hameed might have if Arthur had shot the REED from his third eye.

The Exploding Energy Dart impacted his opponent directly in the nose and blew up, snapping both their heads backwards.

It was never smart to use explosives so close up.

Chapter 115

Arthur's head snapped back, even as blood and muscles and shards of bone and the fury of contained refined energy spread outwards. The blade stuck in his stomach slipped free, and he staggered backwards, his guts half-spilling out from the wound.

Coughing and spitting to the side, Arthur brought his weapon to guard, though his mind still woolly and confused by what had happened. Teeth rattled, one of them even managing to tear free of its socket, and a bunch of others rattling loose.

He cursed himself for not studying a mental safeguarding technique. For not giving himself some form of security against someone reaching within and influencing his mind.

"You!" Hameed clutched his shattered face and nose with both his hands. He'd dropped his spear and kris, nose gone entirely, blood streaming and chunks of flesh and bone missing from one side. He must have turned, at the last minute, to catch it on one side of his face rather than head-on.

Incredible reflexes.

Arthur's own kicked in now, long years of training having him stab at Hameed with his spear. It slipped in, one-handed or not. The spear went through muscle and flesh like a butter knife through kaya jam. When he pulled it out, blood splashed to the ground, squirting from Hameed's torso.

Arthur still wasn't sure what technique the boy had used on his mind, and he was still working out what had happened in this game; but when in doubt, attack again.

Spear went in again. And then again. The third attempt was partly blocked by waving arms, but even cutting along the edges of limbs, the spear's enchantments triggered, causing his opponent to gush. And not in the good way.

Shocked, Hameed backed off, blood still rushing out of him. He pointed a hand at Arthur, energy forming in it. Not blue or green or anything normal, but pale yellow and somehow sickly looking. Arthur threw himself to the side before it finished forming, dodging the blob of power that shot outwards.

To his surprise, the attack swerved, homing in on him.

A raised hand to block it did little as it splashed and then swung around his hand, like a glob of water flowing around a physical object. It kept coming, striking Arthur in the head, gluing itself to his aura before seeping in.

Just like the initial attack.

Fear coursed through Arthur, fear of the unknown. It motivated him to extend himself into a lunge and push, aiming to put his spear through Hameed's body. It made him forget that he'd been gutted himself not so long ago. When the pain of extending and twisting his body coursed through him, he shifted the point of his weapon.

It dropped, going through stomach and guts rather than chest. Still a badly damaging attack, especially as Arthur finished his collapse onto the ground, his lower body suddenly not willing to hold him up any longer. Hameed joined him moments later, but not before dropping another sickly yellow blast.

At first, Arthur wasn't sure what was happening. Unable to move, his body doing its best to put his stomach and guts back in place, to fix loose teeth and a torn-open, smashed nose. He only understood what was happening later as the energy burrowed into him, trying to lull him to sleep.

Anger had him utilizing his own Yin Aura. Anger and a little cunning, in the hope that by using his aura offensively, he could guard against additional strikes.

Mind closing off, he forced himself to focus on his technique, on just one thing. Pouring energy through himself, again and again, empowering that same attack. Pulsing it outwards to his opponent.

Unable to think of anything more, even as the mental poison threatened to put him to rest. Despite his partial resistance to it, it was still having the upper hand.

Not at all a noble sight, this fight.

Arthur lay there for a long time, pushing against the fogginess in his brain, focused only on keeping his Yin Aura technique working. He felt at the edges of the attack, noticed how it pressured him, how it interacted with his body and his mind and perhaps even soul. As much as he desired to move, it was all he could do to pour his energy into the Yin Aura and stay awake.

He wasn't sure how long they lay there—five minutes or thirty, it was all the same in his hazy recollection. Eventually though, the energy that had forced itself into him dispersed. His own energy stores that had been utilized to run the Yin Aura were almost gone. He dragged himself to his feet, focus still swimming, to look over at Hameed.

The boy lay by his side, a few inches away. He'd flipped over onto his face at some point, dragged himself over to Arthur before finally collapsing, the Yin Aura having soaked through all his wounds and past defenses to lull him to sleep. After that, he'd just bled out, the massive wounds Arthur's spear had caused and its bleeding enchantment finishing the job.

An ignominious ending to the fight and the second chancer.

Arthur understood he had been somewhat lucky. If he had utilized his REED at any other time, or if Hameed had known about the Poket Simpanan and his ability to utilize a stored attack, Arthur probably wouldn't have survived.

That initial mental attack had lulled him to lower his guard. Such that even getting stabbed was insufficient to push him out of it.

No wonder Nor had been willing to risk utilizing Tun Rahman to get rid of Hameed instead of fighting him head-on. Few climbers would have learned a mental cultivation technique or a defense for it yet. No monsters in the Beginner Tower wielded such gifts, and mental attacks—while highly useful against individual sapiens—did very little against a large swathe of common monsters. Not as though you could mentally influence a carnivorous tree or cannibalistic flower to stop it from eating you, or mind control leeches whose basic instincts drove all their choices.

The fact that Hameed had made it this far spoke to quite a powerful skill set outside of his cultivation techniques.

Too bad for him, he'd gotten used to one-shotting others with his techniques, leaving him open to Arthur's own attack.

Of course, he knew exactly how lucky he had been. Sure, his caution, his ability to suffer damage, and his Yin Body were all advantages, along with a degree of paranoia with regard to hiding his skills; but at the end of the day, if Hameed had been just a little more cautious, Arthur would have been dead.

Sitting with his legs pulled up, arm around his tender stomach, gritting his teeth as he finished pushing things around, massaging the parts that weren't in the right place, Arthur had to remind himself that the past was just that. Over and done with.

Nothing he could do to fix the past, though the moment he had a chance, he was going to learn a mental cultivation technique.

For now, though, he had a new problem, one that was stomping over.

The very last fight, and him with nothing more than a small amount of Tower energy in his secondary dantian. He still had refined energy, but it was being poured into Accelerated Healing to finish closing up his stomach wounds. Because the last thing he needed was for that to pop open, spilling his guts into the surroundings.

Again.

Chapter 116

He was tired, he was lacking in cultivation energy and, frankly, he was still badly injured. Fighting Tun Rahman, the final boss, was likely going to be a losing proposition. He didn't even have his usual tricks up and running, already having used his Refined Exploding Energy Dart from the Poket Simpanan it was hidden in.

He scooped up a tooth that had flown out earlier, jammed it back into his mouth, only to find the wound already closed.

Cursing a little, he kept pushing, not at all interested in running around toothless. A gap-in-the-teeth look was not at all sexy and he was still man enough to care.

Realising that all he was doing was injuring his gums, he gave up and dropped the tooth, noting another reason he needed to learn how to do regeneration. Now, it was getting personal . . .

Pushing that thought aside, Arthur made his decision. He ducked into the room with Ramli's body, shut the door hard and then dropped the closet in front of it, stopping the door from opening easily. Glancing down at the man's body, considering if there was anything worthwhile to grab, his gaze fell on a spear.

An idea flickered, and he quickly moved spear and chair around, adjusting them so that they were facing the entrance but back a few steps so that the door wouldn't swing open to smack into them. Then, his crude and simple trap done, he ducked out, cursing as he realised he'd left behind his own enchanted spear.

No point, anyway, since he couldn't exactly carry it outside while climbing up the roof. The spear had a lot of uses, but carrying it around while running away was not convenient. And running away was definitely what he was doing.

He leapt, gripping the edge of the window ledge, swinging himself backwards and upwards such that he spun through the air, landing on the roof. Landing with a hard thump, he hissed, gripping his stomach, pain radiating as his body pointed out how such movements were a bad idea. Breathing slow and easy, he started creeping along the edge away from the window.

A small jump afterwards, into a set of bushes not far away. He landed hard, hissing as the impact sent pain radiating through him again. Whimpering just a little as something broke apart within him.

He couldn't keep doing this, so rather than doing what he had intended to do—run away into the woods, after hopefully leaving enough clues that he was on the roof—he found himself rolling away. Under the building itself, moving such that he was out of easy sight so that he could have a break.

Small chance that he might get away with it; but he would take it.

He waited, forming a new REED within him, storing it away, and pouring energy as well into his healing, putting the retorn part in his abdomen together in case he had to fight. Running away was not at all courageous or manly, but if Arthur knew one thing, living to fight another day was the name of the game.

Anyway, he'd leave the big discussions of honor and morality and saving face for others; he was just a poor Chinese Malaysian given a chance at something more. In his view, you took what came, worked twice as hard, and kept going. Everything else, all the honors and applause, that was fleeting, momentary benediction until they found a new way to tear you down or take away what you had gained.

Footsteps above, crashing to a halt. A pause, a push against the door, scraping of the closet as it moved back a little. A frustrated growl, and then, an explosion of movement followed by a loud splintering when door and cupboard were pushed away as Tun Rahman charged through. It was punctuated by a howl of rage moments later, all of that causing Arthur to smile just a little.

He hoped that shout was because the spear had caught his opponent. He wasn't sure though, so he waited. For the sound of thumping along the roof. He listened as it faded away.

More noise after, as one very angry lord screamed his challenge.

A long moment, then he felt something from the Tower itself. A quiet insistence that he had no choice but to pay attention to.

Quest in Danger of Imminent Failure
Time to Failure: 23:59:04

Of course there was a countdown. Why wouldn't there be?

More noise, more shouts. Arthur tuned most of it out as he kept healing himself. He wanted to cultivate but dared not. Pulling himself into his body, turning off his attention to everything else going on around him would be a fool's move.

No, better to keep his attention here, while he lingered beneath the longhouse, while Tun Rahman stalked around, shouting imprecations and admonishments, daring him to come and do battle. Growing ever more unhinged by the moment.

"I know you. I know you're working for Tun Lok. You think I didn't? I'll kill you, kill all of you. Tear your guts out and string them out in front of this house, send your heads back to him! Eat your livers and have a *bomoh* make an effigy of your body. Make sure you can't ever betray me again like you did."

Arthur listened, waiting for the man—or monster—to run down. Probably a monster. One masquerading as the Tun, given that the real-life Tun probably wouldn't care for *bomoh*—local witchdoctors.

Eventually, silence, as Tun Rahman stomped away into the distance. Arthur exhaled in relief, allowing himself to relax a little before he turned his attention back to healing. He had less than a day—if he was lucky—before he would confront the other man.

In that time, he needed to fill some of his dantian at least and heal himself up.

Under the building, as pale moonlight streamed from above, Arthur pulled in Yin energy. A part of him noted the significantly stronger presence of Yin energy under the longhouse, even stronger than sitting in a clearing at night, drawing in the moonlight. You would think that would be the strongest, outside of perhaps a graveyard; but somehow, here, beneath the building, the Yin energy was powerful.

Flavored in secrets and death, in rot and damp and the quiet of lurking predators.

He drunk it all in, Yin energy swirling into his meridians, pouring through to lock into place in his dantian, one stream after the other. Drinking his fill into his parched center, feeling energy course through him and strengthen his body once again. He noted how even his healing technique worked a little better, now that he had a refilled dantian full of unrefined energy. As if the Tower energy he had just pulled in bolstered the refined energy, giving it more rigid and firm surface to work from.

Every minute, his breathing grew a little easier, the pain that he had shoved to the back of his mind faded away. At one point, he had to break off his cultivation and wait when a still-raging voice echoed. Coming back from searching the nearby woods, unable to locate Arthur, the Tun was returning to his residence.

Waiting for his prey to come to him.

Arthur understood that well enough. After all, that damn timer was running down.

20:47:18

He exhaled, pushed the concerns aside. Focused on cultivating, on his dantian, now that the man had given up the search.

Arthur focused on healing himself for the inevitable fight. Now that he was the only one left, it was clear that there was only one way to end this tragic story. To finish the quest.

A part of him cursed, wishing everyone had played their parts properly. Given him a chance to puzzle it out, rather than force him into a fight he never wanted.

If wishes were real, beggars would be full and the rich would be fools.

Chapter 117

Arthur rolled out from under the longhouse as the morning light finally began to filter into the clearing. He still wondered how the Tower managed to make suns so familiar. A giant light in the sky. An interdimensional pocket that rotated around its own sun. Maybe just a small opening, so that it was their own star in play but filtered through magic.

No one knew, though like everything else, there were numerous theories. Many of them adjusted again and again or competing for dominance as more information flowed out from the Towers.

End of the day, the Towers continued to be manifest mysteries that, in twenty years, no one had managed to find an answer to. It didn't help that even the most powerful and successful climbers were only in Advanced Towers—two levels above his own. That there was only two other Tower types after that—

the Master Tower and the Final or Legendary Tower—was little comfort.

After all, that single Legendary Tower, in the middle of the Antarctic Circle, was massive. Reaching so high into the sky and disappearing into a secondary dimension that no one even understood, no matter how many drones or planes or blimps were sent.

Musings about the state of the world were not particularly useful, beyond the minor advantage of giving him something to think about while he crept back to his room. He had not completely filled his dantian with Tower energy, having to split some time off to pull energy from the monster cores he never let out of his sight. But it had taken only a couple of hours to fill up near full, before he switched to refining. His biggest slowdown being the need to heal.

He could have waited a little longer, but just like he was healing, so was Tun Rahman preparing himself. And if he was right, and his little trap had injured the Tun, he wanted to start this fight now, when he still had the advantage.

Anyway, worst-case scenario, he figured he could run away again for awhile. But first things first, he wanted his spear back. Then, he'd find the man and hopefully launch a surprise attack, drop a REED on his head or something, just so that he could add to his advantages.

Which was why he'd crept out along the wall to his window, Shadow Sense unfurled.

It was only because he had his secondary sense working, that allowed him to "see" within the room without actually poking his head through the window, that he dodged the attack.

As he threw himself down and sideways, the explosion that tore the wall apart and sent massive splinters and broken pieces flying through the air, along with expanding energy and balls of power, had Arthur wincing. His ears rung from the noise, his aura registering movement moments later coming from within.

No time to deal with his surprise, he pushed off with an arm and shoulder to throw himself sideways.

Moments later, a series of new explosions on the ground as thrown darts or magical attacks landed where he was. He hit the ground again, rolling through a bush that slowed him down and diverted his course, forcing him to scramble backwards and onto his hands and knees for a second.

A body, flying through the air, shifting course from where it had been hovering by his exploded window. It crashed into the ground with a pained grunt, its spear slamming into the earth.

The figure folded over onto one knee, even as Arthur managed to stand and back off further. He was on full retreat as he swapped out Shadow Sense and began his full-body techniques: Yin Aura and Heavenly Sage's Mischief.

Wishing he could get a third up…

He reached for his kris, pulling it out.

Blinked as he caught a look at his opponent for the first time. Surprise had him staring as his opponent tugged the spear out and stared at the broken shaft and the remaining tip, all shattered from its own attack. The man—or creature—discarded it.

"What are you?" Arthur whispered.

Tun Rahman—or the being that had masqueraded as Tun Rahman—looked up. Ghost, perhaps. For he no longer had a full body and was growing indistinct and blue-white. It glowed as it stood there, then stalked forward, pulling out an all-too-real-looking kris.

"What kind of *hantu* are you?" Arthur growled, when Tun Rahman drifted forwards. He wished he knew about Malay ghosts and spirits. But by the time he'd grown up, a lot of that folklore had drifted to the side, forgotten in the rush to modernity. Then the Towers came, and what was real and authentic and what the Tower had decided was good enough had begun to mix itself up. Western stories and concepts came to the fore, mixing with their own local lore, such that sometimes it felt like everything was a hodgepodge.

And while Arthur liked the fusion concept in his meals, he wasn't so sure about hybrid monsters.

They just caused headaches.

"Were you always like this?" Arthur asked, trying again to get the creature to speak. He kept retreating onto open ground, finding firm footing as he figured bumpy ground was going to be more a hindrance for him than the . . . ghost. And ghost it was.

"Traitors. *Kita mesti bunuh semua pengkhianat.*" *We must kill all traitors.* The words were intoned without any real passion involved. It made Arthur frown, for it was this passionless recrimination that made him shiver, more than the way the figure drifted forward now.

As though all semblance at being human had been wiped away, it was behaving like an NPC—and a badly programmed one too. A part of him wondered if this Tun Rahman wasn't just a construct of the Tower, whether he had once been a person. Though, of course, the historical Tun had lived before the advent of the Towers. But you never know what the Towers could do, even with deceased historical figures. The Towers were magical, after all.

He wondered too if this ghostly fate awaited any second chancers if they kept failing over and over again. Forced to take different roles, forced by the Tower to play a mere role, having their true will stripped away? Already, they could not speak as freely, act as freely as they wished.

How much of them had been lost, as they respawned and were tested over and over again? How much of them was who they used to be?

What, if any, of him was really him?

Those thoughts nearly cost him his hand as the ghost of Tun Rahman darted forward at the last moment, crossing the ground swiftly and swiping with its kris. Only a last moment shift of his hand, a turning of his own blade forward, managed to achieve a block.

Then, there was no more time, as he was forced to do battle with the ghost.

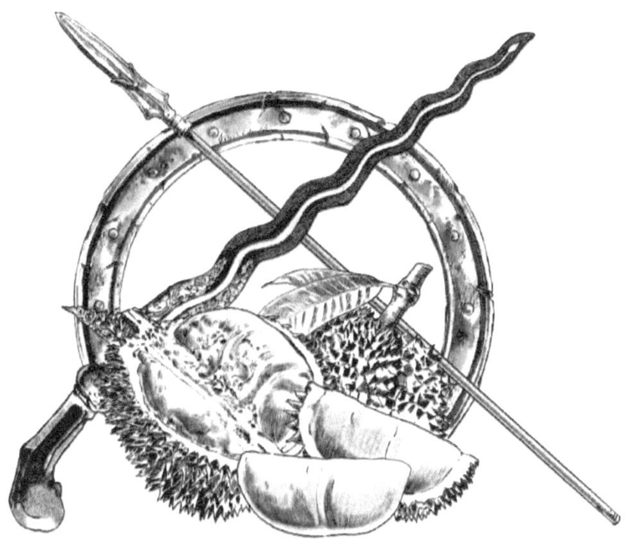

Chapter 118

The kris was an interesting weapon to use. Its wavy and slightly forward-curving blade allowed for easy stabbing, its sharp point allowing one to slip the long dagger within and tear a wider hole than a straight blade. It also allowed for certain kinds of blocks, as blades glanced off one another and skipped along the waves rather than sliding down to the hilt.

Which was good, because most kris didn't really have much of a guard. Some had none at all, others only a small circular guard.

Blocking, then, was more a case of parrying and beating, slicing against a blade as it came to push it aside or, more importantly, cutting or stabbing the arm that came in close. There was as much a battle of positioning, of shifting the body and using open arm blocks against the flat or the hand that held the other weapon, as it was direct strikes.

Add in a flurry of quick strikes with fist, palm, elbow, or foot to disrupt balance or positioning, to open up new lines of attack, and the pair of opponents were a blur of moving limbs. Arthur had no time to think, his body reacting to the attacks, grateful that he had spent months now using the kris, had trained with it relentlessly in that time.

Otherwise, he might have been cut even more, as his own reactions and majority of his training had been to use hilted weapons. He preferred hilted weapons himself, but there was reason his sifu had taught them to fight with and without guards—using kris, parangs, katanas, wakazashis, short swords, and more. Everything they could get their hands on, they trained in.

You never knew what the Tower would offer, what you might end up using, and beggars couldn't afford to be choosers. They were too poor to specialize or even hope to acquire a storied weapon, something passed on from one family member to another.

All they had was their training.

Back and back again Arthur was pushed away. Till a good kick sent his opponent backwards, the push-snap kick sending the somewhat lighter-than-normal ghost body flowing back. For a brief moment, they paused, staring at one another.

Then, they began to circle, searching for the opening needed.

Most people who had never dueled before, especially with weapons, didn't realise how dangerous that first step was. The moment one entered measure, that crossing of distance where one party or the other could hurt them. Full lunge or just a quick passing step, either way that moment of transition when one's momentum was captured, when there was no choice but to commit.

So the pair circled. In that moment, while looking for a mistake, for his opponent's attention to wander, Arthur also felt along his techniques, judged the way they were working. Heavenly Sage's Mischief was running well, only requiring a few more tweaks to make it flood into his body even more efficiently, further enhancing his strength and speed. Nothing to be improved there.

As it stood, Arthur realized he was faster than his opponent, if a little weaker. Tun Rahman had size and strength, and would likely have had more if he had his full body instead of a ghostly one. Right now though, each strike was only just a little stronger.

In a battle with kris, that marginal difference in strength meant little.

More importantly, after that first flurry of attacks, after he tried to wrap Yin Aura around his opponent so that it would interact with the Tun's aura and techniques, Arthur was coming to the conclusion that it didn't affect the Tun. It wasn't entirely surprising, what with the creature being a ghost of some form.

Yin energy was probably something ghost-like creatures resisted automatically, just like Arthur resisted poisons. He might even be empowering his opponent.

Knowing that, he let the Yin Aura die off. Imbued Strike wouldn't work either, so that left him with two options. Steel Skin or Focused Strike.

Before he could start up either technique, Tun Rahman was on him again. He missed that moment of weakness as his opponent snuck into range, slipping a foot an inch closer with each step, such that now he was right in.

A swing-by of the kris, a block. Passing blades, glittering in the moonlight and then slow-rising dawn. The pair struck and blocked and parried, blood running down one edge and ghostly light escaping from the other as blows that didn't manage to be blocked snuck past defenses.

There was a joke about knife fights.

At the end of a knife fight, the loser dies on the spot. The winner dies a few hours later, bled out.

It wasn't, of course, true. But the joke held a grain of truth in it. There was no way, when both parties were so close, so trained, to walk away without wounds. You accumulated them on the arms, on the outer edges which you used to block, sometimes on the inner sides or along the wrists or shoulders as you turned away. You picked them up as quick jabs opened up holes in the body and tore through muscles.

Long slices along the face, quick stabs upwards into the body, retreating cuts along the legs as you backed away. Bleeding your opponent out, one cut after the other. Taking out tendons, muscles, blood vessels.

Looking for that fatal blow, the crippling one.

A dozen more exchanges and Arthur fell back, clutching his arm. Pain, coursing through him, grateful that Steel Skin had managed to keep the attack from piercing all the way through his arm and forcing it to come out nearly at the same angle rather than turning and tearing.

It still left a wide wound, but his own attack had been just as damaging, if not more.

The ghost drifted back, a hand to its chest. Arthur hadn't managed to get the blade far up enough, not to its heart, not to slice or cut something important around that region or even pierce a spine. But the blade had still gone in where its right lung would have been, turned and tore apart the structure of the ghostly organ, and then ripped outward, snagging a little only on the rib as it came out.

In a normal person, that would have been a fatal blow. On the ghost, however . . .

"Why?" Arthur panted, his arm hanging uselessly, his other hand with the kris keeping his opponent back. He kept the blade in front of him, and both of them backed off. "Why attack your own warriors?"

"You, all of you . . ." the voice was unchanged, speaking just as firmly as before. No passion, as though the man was reciting lines it had no choice but to intone. "Betrayed me, in my own home. You let my enemies into my house, let them kill my family, kill my servants. Traitors, all but one . . ." Grief now, a touch of it breaking through the enforced carelessness. "And you killed him too, didn't you?"

"*Tiu.* You're replaying an event aren't you?" Arthur wondered if it was a historic one, or if it was just a conjured event. Both had been reported in the wikis. Quests based off historical events, many of them little known. Traitorous moments or resplendent moments of courage, battles that had been fought to the last man, and quests that showcased moments of quiet heroism. Or events that had never happened—could never happen.

Some climbers studied history, researched such events, hoping to get an edge. There were information packets available all over the world for different Towers, companies that were willing to offer detailed breakdowns or guesses, even printed sheafs of paper and books. All of it too much reading and research for Arthur's liking, not when there were other things to train.

Now, here he was, caught in one of those. And he was grumpy and bleeding.

"I will kill you," the ghost said. The hand holding the chest wound moved away, yet ghostly blood stopped escaping into the air. For a moment, Tun Rahman seemed to glow, then the brightness concentrated, focusing around the chest. The rest of it grew more vague, less solid. Intuitively, Arthur knew his opponent had just triggered an ability.

Before he could wonder what, it was on him. No more time to think as they clashed once more.

Chapter 119

Enhancement technique. Arthur guessed that was what it was, that caused Tun Rahman's ghost to grow more powerful. A berserk technique of some form. For over the next few clashes, his opponent came at him faster and more aggressive than ever. Berserk techniques didn't cause all fighters to go insane, frothing at the mouth. They didn't always take away thought and strategic consideration. Instead, they were so named because of the way they empowered an individual but at a cost later on.

Most generally allowed the user to keep their mind and focus, though the most powerful berserk techniques didn't. Regardless, there was always a cost, most empowering an individual for a short time frame and causing greater weakness afterwards. Some even did damage to the user, forcing the body to tear itself apart in an attempt to keep up.

Arthur's own boosting technique was no berserk technique, just a simple buffing one. Where he might increase his Body by four or maybe even five points, it was a regular, smooth increase. A berserk technique at rapidly increased Body by five points at the minimum, and that number could be doubled with practice or with better techniques.

Weapon sliding along the edge of limbs, a flurry of cuts. Some opening wounds along his face, along his chest and upper arm, stabs that pierced or left long streaks of blood along Steel-enhanced skin. Gratitude running through him, as he found the attacks only doing superficial damage for the most part, his reinforced body giving him an advantage.

His opponent was taking damage too, significant amounts. Still, not an equal trade of blows, because Arthur wanted to survive and a berserking ghost wasn't thinking about survival. Recollection and training guiding his attacks, as he fought defensively.

"How do we fight someone stronger than us?" One of his juniors, asking that question.

Mimicking his own sifu, he stepped forward. Two fingers, touching spots on the neck, the arm, the elbow, the wrist, and just above the knee. "Then, you take away their ability to fight," he said. "Remember, tendons and ligaments connect muscles and bones. Take them away, doesn't matter how strong they are, they can't use that limb. Dismantle, rather than kill."

It worked just as well against a berserker.

Slice along the inside of an approaching hand when it attempted to stab you. Rising slice on the inside, then twist your hand around, cutting down as you finished the ribbon, aiming at the inside of the elbow. Tendons and ligaments parting even as you fell back, away from the attack.

Angle to the side, watch as the ghost catches the weapon it drops from nerveless fingers. Duck low, cut sideways, behind the leg. Hamstring, torn a little, protected by long pants and bad angles. Later. He'd deal with it later, with a cut kick or roundhouse, put it all under pressure.

Tear it open.

Slice along the neck, tear at the muscles holding the neck aloft, that allowed the head to turn. He would have gone for a blinding attack, but the monster didn't bleed properly for a scalp wound and stabbing an eye was actually a lot harder than most people thought, especially when moving.

Dozen more attacks, quick passes that forced them both back.

One massive rising elbow that cracked a jaw and cost Arthur the use of his left hip as the kris ended up embedded in there.

His opponent had fallen back after that. Arms hanging by its sides, the ghost floated there, dozens of streams of ghostly blood floating away from it.

Leaving Arthur thinking he might be winning. Which was, of course, the wrong thing to think.

Before he could correct himself, the monster threw its head back. A rising scream, echoing around, assaulting his senses. His kris, and the Tun's one embedded in his hip, vibrated to the scream, one of rage and loss and death. Desperately, as the pain built, Arthur yanked the one in his hip out with his injured arm, gripping his own tighter.

The scream kept rising, higher and higher, louder and louder till suddenly, even with hands clutching his ears as best he could, his ears popped. Eardrums shattered, leaving Arthur suddenly deaf.

Not that it mattered, for the vibrations themselves continued in his very bones.

Eyes began to bleed, pain wrapping itself around Arthur. Rather than just stand there and wait, he pulled his own trump card, the one he had been holding back for just this moment. Wishing it was, somehow, stronger than this.

The Refined Exploding Energy Dart flew out from his third eye, skirting through space. Yet, to Arthur's surprise, its form began to come apart as it approached the screaming ghost, the energetic container peeling away as the sonic attack reached it. Such that, even before it reached the ghost it exploded, the untamed, highly volatile energy within escaping.

A roar of blue and white energy released into the air, transforming into white and yellow flames at the edges as it dissipated. Minor shockwave, enough to throw the hair back of both fighters and, thankfully, causing the ghost to stagger back, looking upset, staring back at Arthur as its scream was interrupted.

Before it could begin again, Arthur flipped the kris, held underhand and low at the ghost. He followed it as it staggered back, pushing off with one leg, rushing as best he could. Scared that he would never make it, Arthur dropped Steel Skin to begin empowering another Energy Dart.

The kris, a weapon not meant to be thrown, struck his opponent awkwardly. It hit center mass on the monster, but was caught half-flipped. Still, sufficient force made the ghost hunch over a little, indrawn breath exhaled as the kris clattered to the ground.

Moments before Arthur reached, that exhalation of air transformed.

No more plain air, but biting wind, chill and cold, seeping into the surroundings. White mist and fog grew, rapidly multiplying as Arthur plunged into the newly created cloud bank, swinging at where he believed the head to be, his vision blinded.

Fist connected briefly with something. Glancing off a chin or jaw or top of head, he couldn't tell, but the exhalation never stopped, the cloud billowing forth such that vision—even a foot away—was lost. Hip gave way, forcing him to fall over with a gasp. The cold froze over his ears, his extremities. His eyes began to hurt as did breathing. His body did not shiver, not yet; but he knew he'd be facing hypothermia soon enough.

Again, he pushed up, grateful at least that the cold slowed the flow of blood from his wounds.

Searching, hunting for his opponent, swinging arms wide as he listened. Everything sounded strange, thin and muffled. The cracking of branches, the chirp of birds, and the never-ending chorus of cicadas and grasshoppers and the buzz of insects had faded.

Frost grew on his skin, and his tongue ran across teeth that had begun to ache like he had eaten too much ice cream too fast. It ached all the way into his jaw, each breath a pain. Even his Yin Body could not handle such a sudden decline, though a part of him knew that he was mildly resistant to the cold because of it.

Yin Body or not, he was still mortal, he still needed his blood unfrozen, his muscles warmed, his tendons to work. His eyes hurt being open, from a biting ache and a swirl of frost.

"You know, if you wanted to retire and move to Genting Highlands or even Fraser's Hill, you could make some good money. Make the resorts actually cold again," Arthur called out, hoping to get something, anything. Global warming had done quite the thing to the poor hilltop resorts, reducing the nice chilliness of low twenties or even teens to mid-twenties at best most days. Well, global warming plus extreme development removing much of the trees, though some efforts to fix the tree situation had occurred.

Or so he heard, at least. He'd only ever been once to Fraser's Hill. A combined holiday and training trip, in an attempt to learn more about the wilderness and the cold.

Arthur was cursing now, wandering and desperate to find his way out. He wasn't even sure which way was he was going, not anymore.

With the Energy Dart stored away, he chose to switch techniques. If he couldn't find Tun Rahman soon, he was going to have to run off rather than stay.

After all, you couldn't kill what you couldn't see.

Another step, then another. Nothing—

Pain coursing as claws raked across his defenseless back, forcing him to stagger. Only willpower and training and his healing kept him standing, as he realised what the game was now.

And how greatly disadvantaged he was.

Chapter 120

When you can't win, cheat.

Fighting a ghost he now couldn't see, and on this gimpy hip, he doubted he'd make more than a few steps before he was attacked again. Better to get aloft, away from the attacker as fast as he could. Arthur crouched a little, jumped as high and as far as he could from standing.

He barely cleared four feet upwards before he began to fall, but Cloud Step gave him another boost, throwing him forward as he landed with the same leg he had jumped with. He flew through the air, ever higher and angled, a second cloud ready for his left foot to come down upon. Arthur nearly collapsed as the shock of pain raced up his body when it came in contact, but he pushed forward and leapt one last time.

Burning pain, like he had been stabbed, coursed through him once again. Only the cooler mind that his Yin Body offered him, and his prior experience with agony, allowed him to keep working on the next step. He couldn't form another cloud, not in time, but it didn't stop him from trying as he looked around, searching.

He was well over ten feet in the air now, his head even higher than that. Below him was a cloud bank that hung unnaturally close to the ground and was close to ten feet high. Already, out in the warmer air, his face and extremities that were clear of the cloud were stinging from blood rushing back.

More importantly, as he looked around trying to find his opponent, recollection came flooding back. He cursed himself, realising he had another option—he dropped the Heavenly Sage's Mischief and began another technique.

Slamming into the earth moments later, Arthur rolled to keep himself from hitting the ground too hard. He grunted in pain, feeling the wound that had closed after freezing over break open, a warm gush of blood that had cooled all too fast once again erupting from his side. As fast as his healing worked, it could not keep up with all the wounds and blood loss, so his head was spinning.

Crouched low, head bent down, Arthur forced himself to ignore his other senses. Touch, taste—he didn't even want to know when he threw up a little—and smell were useless. Sight was only marginally useful, and hearing was useless with the ghost floating. Instead, he had one last ability, and he just hoped it worked.

Shadow Sense.

It reached out from his aura, infiltrating the surroundings just like part of his aura did. He was realising now how powerful auras were, had been already thinking along those lines when he first found the interactions between Yin Aura and Shadow Sense, but now he was relying entirely on it.

He didn't know if he could make it work for him the way he needed, but he also didn't have a choice.

Feeling outwards with his technique, a sense of movement—a sixth, or seventh, sense—came to him, and he threw his hand upward even as he tucked and rolled. A little too late to avoid the attack entirely, but the hasty block meant that his left arm, already scored and damaged and somewhat useless anyway, took the brunt of the attack.

Cloth tore further, Steel Skin bending under the blow and parting. Swapping out from Cloud Step had been automatic the moment he knew he was committed to this, when he realised there was no good way to run from the fight. The freezing cloud bank was too broad, too wide for him to escape, not when he had only one leg that was working and no ability to see past the ghost's fog. He would freeze over, get ripped apart before he escaped.

Movement.

Rolling over his right leg, gasping as pain shot through him, arm hanging from the side. He felt the figure disappear again, but now that he had sensed it twice, Arthur realised he could track it better. He stayed down, letting his energy recover, waiting for his bleeding to slow, running options down.

He couldn't fight Tun Rahman in a kris battle. He was too wounded and blinded, and too reliant on his sight to win such a battle. Sure, they had done some blind fighting at the dojo, which group hadn't? It was a ton of fun, taught a series of great techniques and helped you understand where bodies positioned themselves in a way that most people who hadn't done it couldn't understand.

After all, most bodies could only bend so far. Tension and muscle positioning and rotational elements in limbs meant there were only so many variations.

If only he could get a hand on his opponent . . . but he was growing numb, muscles seizing up. He didn't have time to grapple for supremacy, not entirely.

There were too many maybes involved.

Instead, he waited for the moment when Tun Rahman drifted in again. A part of Arthur wondered why the ghost didn't just wait for Arthur to freeze over. Maybe it couldn't think that far ahead, maybe it just didn't want to wait. Rage seemed to be the watchword for this creature.

When it slipped close again, swinging at Arthur, he was ready.

The Refined Energy Dart exploded from his back.

The explosion caught the ghost in the center of its chest. Tore through its form, staggered it, and made the swinging blade skitter off the turning body. Arthur stumbled over, slammed his kris into the top of the ghost's knee and twisted, popping kneecap out of place with a squelch. It dissipated moments later, but the ghost collapsed.

Arthur caught the swinging arm with his own, hooked it under and pulled tight, used his kris as a piton to stab and pull, dragging his body the rest of the way upwards. Each attack left ghostly bleeding wounds behind, killing the creature slowly with each attack. Allowed him to cross upwards, such that he was on top of his opponent now.

Watched as the already significantly injured ghost thrashed, its desperate strength stilling, even as Arthur tried to finish it off faster. The cold seeping into his wounds was slowing him down, clouding his mind.

Somewhere along the way, the body stilled, dispersed, and dropped Arthur to the floor beneath. He didn't even notice it, the cold robbing him of his senses and his ability to move. What little energy he had, he turned to the Yin Energy within, rotating it such that could bolster the healing process, trying to close up the last wounds, to keep him awake.

He failed, even as the last of the freezing cold cloud dispersed, leaving him lying there, flat on the ground.

Victorious and dying.

Chapter 121

If this was a game, Arthur knew he'd probably have gained a Title or something along the lines of "By the Skin of His Teeth" or "Second? No, I'll Have More Chances" or "Just One More Minute, Death!" Since the Tower didn't give Titles like that, nor was this a game, Arthur figured he would just have to take the secondary prize.

Survival.

Pretty damn sweet prize, even if he still ached all over when he woke up. Part of that, of course, had to do with falling unconscious with a giant beast core underneath him, embedded in the ground and pressed against his chest while he slept. It hurt, though he was pretty sure that the pain in his chest was psychosomatic at this point.

Still, it was never fun waking up and realising he had been lying defenseless and dying, only held together by his healing technique. Not to say there weren't some gains from all that . . .

Variant Skill Created: **Accelerated Healing – Refined Energy (Grade IIIb) -> (Grade IVc)**

Passively increases base Tower healing rates by 97.3%.

Active use of technique increases base Tower healing rate by 301.2%.

Healing may now be directed.

Variant technique increases resistance against toxins and poisons by 49% (passive)/ 139%(active)

New variant technique increases resistance against elemental effects.

May not replace lost limbs or other permanent injuries.

Active Cost: 0.1 Refined Energy per ten minutes

A massive upgrade in his healing speed when he activated it, and a minor increase when he didn't. Actually not so minor—it was nearly double what other climbers got, and they were already healing broken bones in a week rather than months… So, well, that was something.

If he kept this up, his passive regeneration would make him like Wolverine. Or Hulk. Or Deadpool.

Yeah, he'd better work on that variant to deal with scars and dismemberments, because he was not witty enough to crack jokes to make up for his appearance.

"But that's not why you people read, right? My ability to be witty and break the fourth wall?" Arthur muttered out loud, then waited. He chuckled to himself as, of course, nothing happened. Not as though he was in a story, like Deadpool.

Though, he'd rather be She-Hulk than Deadpool. She at least got to climb out of her panels and beat the shit out of her writers who put her through stupid, hackneyed situations. Instead, Deadpool just cracked jokes and acted like a fool…

A deeper breath, as he turned his attention within and began the process of channeling his energy to heal his wounds. Time to see how fast his healing actually was, when directed. Since he hadn't been kicked out of the Tower just yet, he figured he had some time, and there was no point in exiting injured and tired.

And without his equipment.

By the time Arthur was healed, it was the middle of the day. The longhouse was now significantly less haunting in the full light of day, though it felt abandoned now. Not in the "gone out to Klang to get satay for the weekend" kind of abandoned, but the kind that you found in small towns, where people had left years ago, even decades. Empty and bereft of any of the energies that living in a building transmitted.

Wandering into his room, Arthur took the time to change clothing and then put on the remnants of his armor. He sighed, staring at what was left of it, knowing it made him look like a low-budget post-apocalyptic extra, but it was better than nothing.

Packing the rest of his gear, he took his time wandering through the house, poking his head into each room, looking for gear to acquire or anything valuable left behind. Not surprisingly, he found nothing of the sort in any of the second chancer rooms. His own experience earlier had shown that none of them carried much. Even their weapons had disappeared with their bodies.

The dining hall was not much better. He did, however, make use of the lack of servants or guards or anyone stopping him from raiding the cutlery and various plates and other utensils. He even picked at the various wood carvings around the building, grabbing whatever looked vaguely valuable to stuff into his backpack.

Depending on the work, he could potentially sell all this to collectors outside. It wasn't a lot of money, all things considered, not compared to selling a single beast stone; but he was poor and there was nothing to stop him from taking the stuff with him. It wasn't as though he was expecting to get into another fight now.

Quest Completed: Find the Killer
Difficulty: A+
Result: You found the two killers, after all the other participants in the event were slain. During the battle, you managed to understand a little of the reason for the deaths in this scenario.
Grade: D+

Luckily, it seemed that the Tower was using the Malaysian scoring system which was a legacy from the British. In this sense, a D+ was basically just slightly better than a pass, nothing amazing but good enough that he would only have gotten a small beating for the grade. Certainly, as far as Arthur was concerned, he was alive—so he scored himself an A+.

It was in the other wing, Tun Rahman's side of the building, that he finally found what he was looking for. At first glance, the room he was in had nothing of great value outside of some minor jewelry that he pocketed. He also found carvings that, to his untrained eye, were no better than what he had found in other rooms but swapped them with those in his backpack. Stood to reason that the Tun kept the more valuable items in his room.

After he was done packing wood carvings, some of the paintings, and even a bundle of batik, Arthur's backpack was bulging and full, with the last set of batik strapped to the top of it. Yet, for all that, it was not the greatest find.

Instead, it was a golden pendant with a pair of peacocks on either side facing each other, a single pearl at the center, and golden clasps on both sides. It had been on the dressing stand, the only item that triggered a notification when picked up. He pulled down the Tower information, surprised at the extent of details the Tower was offering for once.

Pendant of Everlasting Regret

The previous owner was betrayed by those he trusted most. Left to die and watch his people be killed, the anger and regret of the owner has seeped into the pendant.

Effect: Releases a massive sonic attack that affects all within a hundred feet of wearer.

Arthur grimaced, recalling the ghost's scream of rage that he had stopped by loosing his REED. Absently, he rubbed his ears where he imagined himself still hearing the scream, one of loss and pain that had reverberated through the surroundings.

Sonic attacks were uncommon, especially those loud enough to affect the entire body. Unfortunately, he was not foolish enough to miss the portion of the description which said "affects all". Being in the epicenter of the scream would be worse, he knew. Before he could use this, he'd definitely need to work out a way to shield himself from the consequences somehow. A technique perhaps, or another enchanted item.

Or he could sell it. No one said he had to keep it for himself. There were others who would purchase such a valuable item, and at higher levels, techniques to block sonic attacks or better manipulate them were likely available.

In any case, exiting with three enchanted items out of a Beginner Tower was heck of a find. Add in the Clan Seal and he likely had one of the more successful runs in ages. Of course, his fortune wasn't too surprising—there were numerous articles indicating that Clan Seal holders generally had better luck in Towers.

Whether that was just a matter of happenstance—Clan or Guild holders being naturally lucky—or something in the Tower system, who knew. Nor was it something that was statistically proven; there just wasn't enough public information to reach a degree of confidence.

No, it was more hearsay and rumors. But, considering his own experience, Arthur would lean towards believing it.

Arthur thought back to the quest completion results he had read. *Difficulty: A+*. With great reward comes great challenge, I guess," he mused. Maybe being Clan Head was what bumped up the difficulty of his tenth floor trial. While he had read of murder mystery scenarios, he hadn't expected the Tower to pit him against two killers instead of one.

Once he swept through the rooms one last time, Arthur finally made his way to the front door, looking around and willing his acknowledgment to the Tower that he was done with this floor. The request to exit pushed against the uncaring edifice through the weird, not-really-mental-but-sort-of-spiritual-mental connection he had with the Tower.

A glowing portal, so similar to the one he used to enter the Tower, appeared.

He didn't even hesitate before walking in. After all, this floor—this Tower—had nothing else for him.

Well, except for the final exit interview.

Chapter 122 – Exit Interview

White room, bland and featureless. Reminiscent of the very first room he'd appeared in at the beginning of this Tower. Except he wasn't being tested anymore—the entire Tower was the test. Now it was time for him to get his grade.

Or, well, rewards.

Arthur breathed in, making sure he could draw as much Tower energy as he could into his stores. He wasn't as worried about refined energy, but making sure he was fully topped up before he left was the smart thing to do. Once he left for the outside world, there was no more Tower energy to draw and he'd be slowly losing it, dying a bit each day and needing the monster cores to top him up until he entered a new Tower.

Cultivation Speed: 2.943 Yin

Energy Pool: 30/30 (Yin) + (7/7)

Refinement Speed: 0.1614

Refined Energy: 0.08 (40) + (0/3)

Attributes and Traits

Mind: 15 (Multi-Tasking, Quick Learner, Perfect Recall)

Body: 25 (Enhanced Eyesight, Yin Body, Swiftness, Fast Twitch Faster, Lightning Reflexes, Explosive Strength)

Spirit: 15 (Sticky Energy, From the Dregs, Strengthened Aura)

Techniques

Night Emperor Cultivation Technique (87% compatibility)

Focused Strike (114%)

Accelerated Healing – Refined Energy (Grade IVc) (0.4%)

Heavenly Sage's Mischief (148%)

Refined Exploding Energy Dart (162%)

Steel Skin (108.5%)

Seven Cloud Stepping Technique (227.8%)

Poket Simpanan Tua (173.7%) (Refined Exploding Energy Dart 99% Integrity)

Imbued Strike - Yin Poison (104.4%)

Yin Aura (Level 1) (133.3%)

Yin-Yang Energy Exchange (100.2%)

Partial Techniques

Simultaneous Flow (245.4%)

Yin Poison Darts (52.6%)

Shadow Sense (88.7%)

He stared at the large status screen before him, taking up one part of the empty room, just floating there with a slightly grey background so that he could differentiate it against the white room. Next to it were other details about himself and his clan.

The Benevolent Durians Clan Status

Organizational Ranking: 157,888

Number of Towers Occupied: 1

Number of Clan Buildings: 6

Number of Clan Members: 587

Overall Credit Rating: E

Aspect: Guardianship

Sigil: The Flame Phoenix

That was a rather nice bump up, really, for the number of clan members and their organizational ranking. Just as interesting, the credit rating had gone up, which was an overall indicator of how much funds he could borrow from a Tower when he tried to buy new buildings. It didn't matter in the first Tower, but once he started entering other Towers and acquiring out Clan buildings there, without his deal with the Chins that credit rating would become significantly more important.

Aspect: Guardianship

● *Minor increase in effectiveness of protective, healing, and shielding cultivation techniques.*

● *Trivial increase in effectiveness of precision, speed, and bonding cultivation techniques.*

- *Variable increase in cultivation and refinement speed dependent upon the number of Clan members within close proximity.*
- *Tower quest types have been expanded.*

Reading the last line about expanded quest types, Arthur bit his lip. Given the tough trial he'd just gone through—and which he suspected was more difficult because he was a Clan Head—he wasn't entirely enthusiastic about this reward. It might be a double-edged sword. After all, his knowledge from the wikis and forums of what might happen in a Tower was one of his advantages. If he were subject to rarer quests or scenarios, he might not have that knowledge to fall back on, simply because they were written about less.

Sigil: The Flame Phoenix

Sigil Bonus (Clan Head): Accelerated Healing – Refined Energy (Grade IVc)

Sigil Bonus (Clan): Cultivation Exercise – Accelerated Healing – Refined Energy (Grade Ib)

Sigil Bonus (Clan) - Enhanced Magnetoreception and Equilibrioception

He still wasn't sure what the new sigil bonus did, other than give him a slight sense of where everything was and a greater sense of balance. Arthur had noticed some of those effects whilst jumping around on his Cloud Step: a greater surety of his location and place in the world, but beyond that… nothing.

Notably, the increase in his own Accelerated Healing had not transferred to his Clan, unlike previous times. He wasn't certain why, as yet; but he hoped there was a good reason. He hoped there was a way to improve that healing grade for his Clan members, because the most recent upgrade was significant.

"Well, that's me. Not a lot to look at, see."

As though having waited for him to finish reading, the Tower pushed the information to the side, a new notification displaying itself before him.

Tower Run Duration: 11 months, 28 days, and 13 hours.
Speed Rank: 483rd
Calculating Rewards

Top five hundred.

Arthur debated how he felt about that. Top hundred was what they all wanted, that was what Casey had aimed for. She had a few months on him, what with having entered after him and his rather long slog on the first floor.

He hoped she had done okay.

Eleven months. Nearly a year, really. A lot of things could have changed in this time, a lot of information about him and the Clan would have leaked out. That could change what people wanted from him. Exiting would be a brand new challenge, one he was still not certain he was ready to face.

So, instead, he pulled up the next notification line as the rewards came in.

Rewards: Choice between increase in cultivation base, proportionate level of gear, or a new cultivation technique

Arthur stared at the information, spinning the options through his mind. Cultivation techniques, while tempting, were of less use to him since he had the Night Emperor technique. While not the best technique out there, it was still a 2-star technique which, historically, was about the best the majority of climbers could expect to acquire. Since he wasn't in the Top 100 where the rewards were actually pretty good, he doubted he would get anything that useful out of a cultivation technique reward right now.

With his Yin Body, it was even worse. It wasn't as though he could acquire the technique and then pass it on to his Clan, since it would not work for the majority. So that was out, right away.

New gear was useful. He desperately needed more gear. Whether it was new armour, better boots, gloves, or accessories, there were a lot of things that could be upgraded. Of course, the Tower might give him something he already had, like more weapons. Which was the downside of choosing gear, though there were mentions on the wikis that you could choose what kind of gear you got, though he recalled that was among the more speed-efficient climbers.

He just couldn't remember exactly where the cut-off was. It wasn't as though he ever expected to be part of that high-performing group. Hadn't even thought of trying a speed run.

Instinctively, he leaned towards the increase in his cultivation base. What that usually meant was an increase in his base stats. It was probably an overall increase in attributes rather than one that he could direct, so that all of his stats would bump up, bolstering him overall rather than allowing him to choose.

One of the major reasons he leaned towards this final reward option was because of how fast he had risen. Most climbers—a good eighty percent— who made it this far were at their second transformation. Arthur was a decent way towards reaching it, but he wasn't there yet. Which would make him one of the weakest individuals, at least in terms of attribute points, to exit the Tower.

That was, of course, the trade-off. His techniques were good, and he'd saved a lot of time by using and having his own Clan base with its greater concentration of Tower energy. But at the same time, it had still been a massive rush to get Casey up here for her Top 100 spot.

Maybe getting an increase now to his attributes would save him the one thing he desperately needed. A savings in time.

"Attributes, please."

The Tower notification flickered, disappeared.

Moments later, he felt Tower energy pour into him. Except, this time, it was more directed. Arthur dropped to his knees and sat on his ankles, breathing deeply as he cycled the energy through him, letting it pour through his meridians into his body, trying his darndest to keep it running and ensure that it was properly utilized.

For if the energy poured in and wasn't properly contained and run through, the overflowing energy escaped back into the Tower. Rather than let that happen, he churned his cultivation and poured energy into his body and mind and soul, feeling it soaking in, strengthening him with each moment. Guiding the refined energy where it needed to go, even if it was happening at a faster rate than ever.

Until, after uncountable minutes, sweat running down his body, his breathing like bellows, the energy stopped.

Leaving him changed, once again.

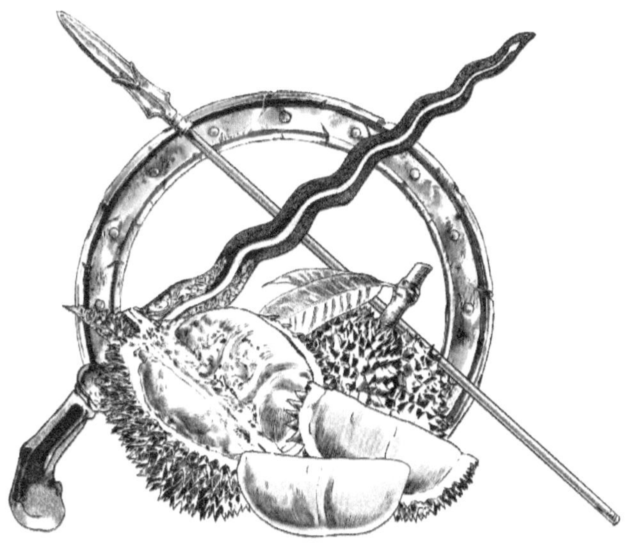

Chapter 123

Arthur stretched, feeling the energy within him and the clarity in his mind. He had been rather surprised at how much of a difference there was, but looking at the results that now appeared in the Tower notification wiped away some of that surprise.

Reward Received: +2 Mind, +3 Body, +2 Spirit

A total of seven attributes points. Much higher than what was generally received by those who took the reward. The lowest he'd heard of was around two points and the average around three. He had expected to receive more, since he had a higher rating overall, but it was clear now that the better cultivation technique he had had benefited him greatly.

Which was kind of unfair in a sense. Those with a great technique just piled on their advantages, such that when they finally got to the end, they were so far ahead of everyone else it was near impossible to keep up. Then again, why would the Tower be any different?

Before he could get grumpy about the realities of the world, the Tower began to form and display another set of notifications. This time, Arthur was surprised, having expected to be portalled out already.

Clan Head Arthur Chua of the Benevolent Durians has cleared Tower 2893 for the first time.
Result Grade: A+
Calculating Rewards…

"A+? I've never gotten an A+ in my life!" Arthur said, surprised. Which, he knew, made him a bad Chinese, but of course not all of them were eggheads. Some were samsengs and many others just not geared for an academic life.

Arthur had always found studying and learning about the Tower more interesting than dry studies about geography or the umpteenth retelling of colonial history or the Malay-washed retelling of contemporary 20th century nation building. As for math, beyond basic levels who needed it?

Still, he had to admit, a little glowing portion of his soul was chuffed at the sight of his very first A+ grade.

Rewards:
- *Upgrade to Clan Standing and Tower Communication Options*
- *Upgrade to Clan Aspect*
- *Upgrade to Clan Seal*

"Wah!" Arthur whispered his surprise, staring at the information. The first reward was easy enough to tap and verify details on. It was not too surprising. What little he knew—and the others had told him—confirmed that it was something he would have acquired just for completing the Tower anyway.

Clan Head may now designate Floor Bosses outside of floor and Tower itself
Reputation levels within Clan may now be displayed and adjusted
Floor income and holdings held by Floor Bosses now viewable
Communication between Floor Bosses and Clan Head is now possible
Clan Status is now viewable in all dimensions
Additional Clan roles now available
Additional Clan quests now available

Arthur's eyes narrowed at the last. He mentally willed the information to expand there and was only a little surprised when it did happen. Information cascaded outwards with that single prompt.

Clan Quest: Growth, Before All!
Requirements: Achieve 1,000 Members
Rewards: Additional Clan roles will be made available

Clan Quest: Expanded Foundations
Requirements: Clear and Establish Clan Buildings in three Beginner Towers
Rewards: Expanded Clan functionality, increased options for Clan buildings

Clan Quest: Keeping the Books Straight
Requirements: Designate a Clan Treasurer

Rewards: Additional functionality and access to Tower finances

"Tower finances?" Arthur asked, but the Tower was less than forthcoming with information. He sighed after a moment, discarding his prompting for further details and kept reading.

Clan Quest: Clan Advancement
Requirements: Establish and Clear an Advanced Tower
Rewards: Expanded Clan abilities, buildings, and quests

Well, that last one was not surprising. In fact, a little prompt actually showed that it was the first of a series of chained quests, many of them similar but with increased Tower difficulty. Skipping backwards, Arthur checked on the Expanded Foundations quest and realised that one was also the first in a series of quests, both in Beginner Towers as well as Advanced Towers.

Which, of course, led to the question of how he was supposed to do that. After all, he was only one man. If he tried to clear tens of Beginner and Advanced Towers, he could never do anything but spend his time clearing Towers.

Then again, the expansion of roles suggested the possibility of designating individuals who could establish Clan Buildings and clear Towers on his behalf. He vaguely recalled something like that happening in news reports of Guilds and Clans all over the world, though it was not something that was reported upon widely. Most people on the outside were not interested in news about a Guild or Clan establishing itself in another Tower. Certainly, he hadn't been that interested in such details back then.

Arthur sighed, gestured downwards, and noted a series of other Clan Quests. Many following the same pattern, so he discarded the information from the view screen before him. Then with a slight prod, had the Tower send it to him mentally for storage. Watching the same information appear, he closed it, satisfied he would have the ability to follow up on it later.

More importantly, since he was reviewing these details, he pulled up information on the newly available Clan roles.

Clan Roles available:
- Floor Bosses
- Treasurer
- Clan Trainer

He ignored the first one, knowing what Floor Bosses did. It was the minimum that was available to him, as a Clan Head. The Treasurer, to his surprise, had little further information other than that they managed Clan finances. Other than allowing someone to look at how much money the Clan supposedly had, Arthur wasn't certain what it was meant to do. Perhaps access some of that money to purchase things?

He wondered if they deposited monster cores for contribution points, or whatever form of money the Tower took further up, and if they couldn't take it out again. That would make sense. You traded in cores for contribution points, but you couldn't really do much with those points other than buy things.

If you could not extract that value and take it outside, then Clans would have to make sure they kept some cores for refining energy and trading.

If the Tower wanted people to constantly climb, then it ought to make cores difficult to acquire or bring to the outside world.

He'd have to check, of course, but it fit everything he knew.

More interesting than the Treasurer was the Clan Trainer. He wondered what they were supposed to do, how they were supposed to make things better.

Role: Clan Trainer

Effect: Increases training effectiveness of Clan.

Bonuses: Variable. Dependent upon individual designated as trainer.

"You couldn't be at least a little useful?" Arthur asked the Tower. Of course there was no answer. Just out of curiosity, he tried applying either role to himself and found that it was impossible. Made perfect sense, of course, but it was annoying since he could not then just pile all the advantages or even verify what the bonuses and abilities were by himself.

"I wonder if there's a cooldown in effect if I tried designating and then removing it from others?" Arthur muttered. He thought there might be, or some other hidden negative, because that was the way the Tower worked. But he could only wait till it was ready.

In the meantime, he turned his attention to the more exciting bonuses.

The upgrades to their Clan Aspect and Clan Seal.

Chapter 124

Featureless white room, his own status screen on either side of him. In front, finally, the rewards and details of his Clan Aspect upgrade.

Guardianship Aspect Upgrade Options:
- *Upgrade Healing Characteristics*
- *Upgrade Protection Characteristics*
- *Upgrade Community Characteristics*
- *Upgrade Quest Options*

Arthur blinked, reading the four options. That was not what he had expected, but it sort of made sense. It was not a direct upgrade to the Aspect itself, but an ability to alter how the Aspect worked and what he could improve within it.

Which meant that another Clan or Guild with a Guardian Aspect would not be the same the Durians, not after the first Tower and they certainly would differ further and further along.

"Couldn't make it a little easier, could you?" Arthur grumbled. In truth, he didn't mind having a variety of choices, since he assumed that this would allow him to increase that specific aspect more significantly than if it was just a general upgrade.

As it stood, right now the minor increase in protection and healing abilities was not something he truly noticed. Of course, he'd only learnt the Steel Skin ability after he received his Clan Aspect, so he didn't know how much the Guardianship Aspect boosted his Steel Skin. And while he might be healing faster, he couldn't tell how much. It wasn't as though there was a health meter with numbers that he could read. Wounds just closed, bleeding just stopped; it was hard judge the difference in how long it took.

"Focus on strengths or shore up weaknesses?" Arthur wondered.

Healing would, of course, be focusing on their strengths. Assuming the Seal upgrade allowed him to improve his healing aspect as well, he could make a minor increase into a moderate or major increase, perhaps. If that was the case, then his jokes about being Deadpool would start to come true.

"Huh… You know, DC doesn't really do characters with healing abilities," Arthur muttered to himself. Green Lantern, Wonder Woman, Batman, Superman, the Flash… none of them were characterized by massive healing abilities. Was it then that DC creators were just a lot more healthy than Marvel creators? Or was there another reason for that disparity?

Not his problem. Healing was definitely high on the list.

Next, upgrading protection would mean something along the lines of his own Steel Skin, which was pretty good. Almost every climber eventually studied a protective technique. You couldn't dodge everything, so having some protective characteristic—whether in the body or as a technique—was a necessity. While not as directly powerful as healing, it did increase your overall strength in combat.

Then, of course, was the community option, which was the most questionable bonus. He knew that they already received a minor increase in cultivation speed when in groups. The community option might also give some minor bonuses to shielding, perhaps. Maybe there were bonuses other than shielding that were possible. But in the end, a community option relied on others being, quite literally, around you.

As for increasing the type of quests available, Arthur discarded that thought almost immediately. For one thing, it was the least useful on an individual basis. Across a very large Clan, with multiple Towers, it might make sense. Especially if they had a large population of Clan members who were not interested in progressing.

But that wasn't the Durians. It wasn't what he wanted for the Durians.

So.

Protection or Healing?

"I wish there was someone to ask…" Arthur muttered. He knew it was still his own decision to make, but it would have been nice to bounce the decision off others and get additional input.

"Can I wait?" A gentle push had the Clan Aspect upgrade notification fade backwards. With another mental nudge, Arthur had the details of the Clan Seal upgrade arrive.

Flaming Phoenix Seal Upgrade Available:

- Increase in Flame Trait

- Increase in Regeneration Trait

- Increase in Fowl Traits

"Fowl traits? That's just . . . foul!" Arthur pronounced the last word proudly, then looked around in the silence and sighed. Of course no one was around to admire his pun. Still, the intent was there: no way was he going to increase his relations to birdlike aspects. What was the point?

"Wait . . . could we fly?"

No answer from the Tower, of course. That was kind of expected, but still... this kind of option was not a gamble worth taking. Not with the other options available. Not with the potential downsides—like feathers!

Well, probably he had nothing to fear. After all, there were no reported cases of climbers physically changing to look more like animals, at least from joining Guilds or Clans. There were cases of cultivation techniques and some rather esoteric enchantments and performance enhancers that did cause such a change, but all of them required a conscious choice and a lot of training.

Improving the human form, sure.

Substituting it? Much harder.

Which, now that he was no longer joking, made him wonder exactly what fowl traits could mean. Lighter bones, claws, flying . . . those were the things he could think of. You also had ostriches who could run really fast and penguins who could swim, but that wasn't common to birds. Great eyesight for the raptors, of course, and beaks that could tear.

Perhaps he was missing something, but he wasn't exactly an ornithologist, was he? He was lucky enough to pick out damn crows and pigeons. Oh, and sparrows. Living in a Malaysian city, one did not see a wide variety of birds.

"Alright, flame or regeneration?" Arthur mused. Regeneration might seem the obvious choice, especially considering he had the option to upgrade his healing characteristic via the Guardianship Aspect. Focusing on upgrading the Clan's healing abilities would make the group tougher, or at least pull more of his people out of the brink.

However, he could not help but wonder about the flame trait.

He didn't have much working experience with that. The flame trait was, if anything, the least directly impactful for him. But fire was always spoken of as a powerful element. Cleanser, destroyer, favored element of all too many *isekai* heroes. There was a reason Fireball was an iconic fantasy spell and dragons breathed flame in most depictions.

Fire was just plain useful too, even if they didn't need it to cook food anymore. It would give the Clan an offensive aspect, and while healing was all well and good, a good offense—the ability to kill their opponents faster— was always going to be a benefit.

However, the thing that worried Arthur the most was whether the Tower would take an aspect from his own cultivation techniques and pass it on to the rest of the Clan. The Tower had done that with his healing technique, so would it do that here? If not, would it just give him a low-grade cultivation technique that would then be added to everyone else? Like Flame Fist or something like that? If so, then a low-grade addition was only going to be helpful to beginning climbers. A short-term gain.

Then again, his entire Clan was made up of beginning climbers.

Healing, on the other hand . . . healing was going to be a useful boost, or so he hoped. He still remembered how his most recent upgrade to Accelerated Healing ability hadn't transferred over to Clan members. No reason was given, as yet; though he wondered if this was the way the Tower was hinting that he needed to upgrade his Seal first.

That would make sense, in fact, to Arthur. That there was only so much he could pass on, even if he upgraded his own skills further. It made some sense to him, that the Clan Seal and Aspect were limited by the grade of the

Clan itself. Otherwise, he could possibly just push ahead really far, ignoring the Clan Quests, and have a small but elite group.

"Then again, there are groups like that, no?" Arthur muttered.

Truthfully, he had no idea. He just knew he had a decision to make, and he'd been stalling long enough.

Chapter 125

Options swirled through Arthur's mind as he stared at the words hanging before him. He weighed them all, seeing the options for the upgrade bifurcate in his mind. A shrug of his shoulders reset the backpack on his shoulders again, the straps digging in a little with a large volume of stolen material resting in there. The straps were getting pretty worn. Multiple uses of thick sewing cord had helped keep the straps in one piece, but they were still rather damaged.

At least his store of monster cores were fine. Arthur patted his belt pouch where they were. While he had been diligent even before he got his enchanted harvesting knife, using the knife had sped up the number of monsters he'd been able to get cores out of—if nothing else, to make full use of the knife and get back his return. Of course, he was still in the negative; but that might not and would not last forever. Investing in the future was the way to go, or so he told himself at least.

"Apply upgrade for healing characteristic, please," Arthur said out loud once he had made his decision. He wanted to decide on the Clan Aspect first, because the healing portion of it was the most interesting element and the one most likely to make a difference for the entire Clan. He also wanted it upgraded because he hoped it could pull the increase in his own healing technique through.

It was a small hope, really; but it was one he felt cost him little to attempt.

Searing pain along his Clan Seal. He felt portions of it change, the parts that signified his Guardianship Aspect. He wondered if there were people who specialized in reading the crests on Clan Seals, who kept notes of the changes and the variations and could tell all the choices made just by glancing at a crest.

It felt like something that someone out there would do. Arthur hoped he never met them.

More pain, then a slight shudder, his body reacting to a flood of energy and a speeding up of basic processes. It was minor, not incredibly significant, except for the fact that his Accelerated Healing technique was always running, taking care of minor issues that cropped up, and so even a miniscule ramping up of it was noticeable.

Upgraded Aspect: Guardianship

- *Modest increase in effectiveness of healing cultivation techniques.*

Arthur waited for a slow count of ten after dismissing that notification, but to his intense disappointment, no additional notices appeared. He let out a sigh, raised his hand to tap the Clan Seal upgrade next and then let it fall. He shook his head after a moment, muttered to himself about being an idiot.

Opened his mouth to call out his choice, and then, after a moment, shut it again.

He tried, twice more, before he ran a hand through his hair.

"I really want the flame trait…" Arthur complained, to no one but himself. He really, really did. Even if, with a Yin Body, fire techniques were difficult to study, harder to utilize. He'd even tried, levels below when insects and wasps and the like had appeared.

It wasn't for him, he knew. But still, a man wanted what he wanted.

The difference, though, between a grownup and a child is that the grownup knows that want should not dictate action.

"Confirm regeneration trait increase," Arthur said, out loud.

Then, he sat back and waited. This time around, the flood was not physical, not energy coming in to interact with his body. It was a mental push against his mind that he allowed in.

He stood there, mind numb, jaw a little wide as he stared into space, information flowing in faster than ever as he tried to digest it all. Some of it quickly became second nature, details that he did not need to consider but were aiding him overall.

Others, well…

"That's how you regenerate body parts!?" Arthur said, reaching out to rub the nub of the top of his ear. Thankfully, he was not someone who wore glasses or the missing chunk of his ear would have been awkward. Those words were the only interjection he let himself have, before he turned back to focusing on the information streaming in.

It took quite a while, such that even his feet were aching a little, standing there unseeing as more information came in, enough to give him understanding of something that humans weren't supposed to be able to do and shore up assorted weaknesses in his variations.

After which, finally, it was gone and he had a chance to stretch, rotating ankles and hips and knees a little. Only when he was more comfortable did he look at the notifications, see what had changed.

Variant Skill Upgrade: **Accelerated Healing – Refined Energy (Grade IVc) -> (Grade IVd)**

Passively increases base Tower healing rates by 99.9%

Active use of technique increases base Tower healing rate by 311.8%

Healing may now be directed

Variant technique increases resistance against toxins and poisons by 49% (passive)/ 139% (active)

Variant technique increases resistance against elemental effects by 18% (passive)

Variant technique allows regeneration of minor loss to limbs and body parts at 0.2% (active)

May not replace major loss to limbs or body parts, or other major permanent injuries

Active Cost: 0.1 Refined Energy per ten minutes

Arthur eyes narrowed. He understood what it took to replace a full limb. He even understood why it was considered a major change and why it was not possible at this level. It required greater knowledge and a tapping in of Tower knowledge that he did not have at this time.

It was even more amusing to him that he had zero chance to make such changes actively. He had to wait, passively letting the Tower regrow his bits for him.

Of course, there was still some question about what might be considered active or passive. For example, a broken spine was small bits but big damage. Was that minor or major? He couldn't tell, not right now. Nor was he willing to test it himself.

Anyway, he had something else to look at before he speculated for no reason.

Upgraded Sigil: The Flame Phoenix
Sigil Bonus (Clan Head): Accelerated Healing – Refined Energy (Grade IVd)
Sigil Bonus (Clan): Cultivation Exercise – Accelerated Healing – Refined Energy (Grade IId)

"Yes!" Arthur pumped the air and then even did a little happy dance. So he was right! The Seal needed to upgrade before it could pass on more of his benefits to Clan members. Their version of Accelerated Healing was still a decent amount behind his, by two grades; but he now understood what needed to happen.

In time, he assumed, he might even be able to bring it up to a higher level. Maybe, even surpass the level he had now?

Before he could speculate further, he felt a shudder run through him, the information on the screens before him disappearing.

Leaving Arthur once more in a simple blank expanse. Moments later, giant glowing numbers appeared.

10

9

8

...

"Ready or not, I guess I'm coming out, eh?" Arthur said, realizing that the Tower was done with him. Time to exit.

Time to get back to the real world and handle all the problems that came with it.

Before he could say anything else, the countdown ended and he disappeared, leaving a white expanse once more. Bereft of climber or Tower presence.

Epilogue

The first thing Casey did, outside of her morning ablutions, even before she had a cup of kopi, was ask.

"Any word?"

"Nothing yet, miss." The voice was cultured, accented. Falsely accented, of course, as Casey knew. After all, her butler had never been to England or anywhere else in Europe. She'd picked up the accent from multiple reruns of *Downtown Abbey*, *Bridgerton*, and *Pride and Prejudice*.

Truth be told, it occasionally grated on Casey's nerves, the way Kristina put on airs. Yet, they'd been together for years now, and she understood the reasoning behind it, the deep sense of unease and insecurity that forced the other to put on such airs.

After all, while she might act as a butler and in all regards, ran Casey's small household, her main job was security for the residence. That had been the majority of her training after she had exited the Tower three years ago and proven herself to Casey's father.

"What is taking him so long?" Casey said, frustrated. "Any changes?"

"The same number of interested parties as before, miss."

"Well, make sure we pick him up before the others," she reiterated. "Even his Clan people."

"Of course."

Orders given, Casey turned to the next set of business. She'd gambled, heavily, on Arthur Chua. However, just because he was her biggest investment did not mean that she could avoid the rest of her work or investments.

Especially if he ended up dead.

Or working for someone else.

"You're sure, son? You've never been interested in the business before…" Rick's father stared at his son through the projection, the three-dimensional hologram flickering a little and casting skin the colour of the twilight night into shades of purple and black before stabilizing. Even after all these years, these 3D holographic projectors were still insanely expensive and rarely used, mostly still a toy for the rich and Fortune 500 companies. In the case of Rick's family, they were both.

"I'm sure. He's my Clan Head. And we're in on the ground floor. You always talk about that, right?" Rick said, eyes wide and hopeful.

"Well, yes. But this kind of investment, it's a long-term one. The profits are going to be miniscule for now…"

"Which is why we should use my trust, so we don't have to worry about shareholder reports," Rick said, adamantly.

"Your grandfather put the restrictions in place for a reason."

"And also left it possible for you to disregard them, if you thought it was right," Rick replied just as quickly.

His father turned away, looked down at the tablet that was beside him. He flicked his fingers across it, rotating through the business plan and report his son had sent him and then eventually nodded.

"Very well. I'll release the first batch of funds, as per your report for the first portion. But I expect you to hit the goals or else we'll pull our support."

"Yes! You won't regret it, Dad. This is going to be so lit!"

His father rolled his eyes, a quiet mocking of his son. But as the hologram faded out, Rick could swear his father was smiling a little.

"*Tak ada nama, tak ada apa* support," the Malaysian Minister of Tower Climbing said, flicking through the report before him. "*Kenapa tak* recruit *dia?*"

Of course, asking Mohammad why he had not recruited Arthur Chua or any of the Benevolent Durians—especially when they were underdogs who could have used the support—was rhetorical. After all, Mohammad had not been in the Tower himself; he was just the designated sacrifice sent to the Minister to report on this.

"*Maaf, boss. Saya—*"

Before the man could continue his apology or give any excuses, the Minister held a hand up, stalling his words. The florid and slightly overweight man leaned forwards, speaking firmly. "*Kamu mesti* recruit *dia. Tak boleh bagi orang lain ambil dia. Kerajaan malu sangat, dengar semua ni.*"

"Of course, boss." A slight bow was sketched. He winced at unconsciously switching back to English, knowing his boss hated that—despite the fact that modern Malay had adopted a large number of English words. Still, Mohammad had his marching orders; he couldn't let the government be outshone anymore. He would do his best to recruit Arthur Chua before anyone else did.

He'd start with extolling the benefits, but if not, well . . . the government had other ways of persuading a man. A lot of them.

Kow Sifu pulled the staff back from where it was pressed into the gangster's Adam's apple, dimpling it ever so gently. The man finished stumbling back, touching his mildly bruised throat, knowing that with just a little more pressure, it would have been crushed.

All around, different members of the Ghee Hin were picking themselves off the floor, more than a few cradling broken arms and ribs. Seven men to deal with a single old man, and they'd been beaten black and blue.

Worst of all, he wasn't even a Tower climber.

"Leave."

"You haven't—" The old man raising his staff was enough to cut the gangster off and he waved his group back. Not that the gangster really needed to utter threats. After all, they were all men of the street. Surely the old man understood what defying the Ghee Hin meant.

Watching silently, Kow Sifu waited long enough for the group to exit before he slumped, holding himself up with the staff that he grounded. He rubbed at his chest where one of the men had landed a blow hard enough that he was sure it was bruised if not broken.

Still, a small smile graced his lip. A wry, tired, but mostly happy smile.

Whispering to himself, he added, "He really did it, eh?"

Then, he limped off to find his bottle of *dit da jow* to rub on his bruises and other assorted injuries. And maybe put a few more bottles up for soaking.

After all, trouble was definitely coming.

###

The End

Want to continue Arthur's adventure now?

Read the next chapter in the free web serial on Starlit Publishing

www.starlitpublishing.com/blogs/climbing-the-ranks

Want to read a bonus short story set in the *Climbing the Ranks* universe?

Join my newsletter to get the exclusive content.

Final Character Sheet – End of Book 3

Cultivation Speed: 3.143 Yin

Energy Pool: 33/33 (Yin) + (7/7)

Refinement Speed: 0.1814

Refined Energy: 0.08 (40) +(0/3)

Attributes and Traits

Mind: 17 (Multi-Tasking, Quick Learner, Perfect Recall)

Body: 28 (Enhanced Eyesight, Yin Body, Swiftness, Fast Twitch Faster, Lightning Reflexes, Explosive Strength)

Spirit: 17 (Sticky Energy, From the Dregs, Strengthened Aura)

Techniques

Night Emperor Cultivation Technique (87% compatibility)

Focused Strike (114%)

Accelerated Healing – Refined Energy (Grade IV d) (5.8%)

Heavenly Sage's Mischief (148%)

Refined Exploding Energy Dart (162%)

Steel Skin (108.5%)

Seven Cloud Stepping Technique (227.8%)

Poket Simpanan Tua (173.7%) (Refined Exploding Energy Dart 99% Integrity)

Imbued Strike - Yin Poison (104.4%)

Yin Aura (Level 1) (133.3%)

Yin-Yang Energy Exchange (100.2%)

Partial Techniques

Simultaneous Flow (245.4%)

Yin Poison Darts (52.6%)

Shadow Sense (88.7%)

The Benevolent Durians Clan Status

Organizational Ranking: 157,888

Number of Towers Occupied: 1

Number of Clan Buildings: 6

Number of Clan Members: 587

Overall Credit Rating: E

Aspect: Guardianship

Sigil: The Flame Phoenix

Aspect: Guardianship

- *Modest increase in effectiveness of healing cultivation techniques.*
- *Minor increase in effectiveness of protection and shielding cultivation techniques.*
- *Trivial increase in effectiveness of precision, speed and bonding cultivation techniques.*
- *Variable increase in cultivation and refinement speed dependent upon the number of Clan members within close proximity.*
- *Tower quest types have been expanded.*

Sigil: The Flame Phoenix

Sigil Bonus (Clan Head): Accelerated Healing – Refined Energy (Grade IVd)

Sigil Bonus (Clan): Cultivation Exercise – Accelerated Healing – Refined Energy (Grade IId)

Sigil Bonus (Clan) - Enhanced Magnetoreception and Equilibrioception

Author Note

Thank you everybody for reading so far and following Arthur and the Durian's journey. I've had a ton of fun writing them, revisiting Malaysia in some ways and charting what might be. The next book or two will speed up a little, as we emerge from the Tower and Arthur has to deal with his new position. Expect politics, talk of Clan building and yes, more Tower climbing!

Rather than do each individual Tower and Tower level for new books, it's likely I'll just highlight specific sections and portions; the exciting bits. Now that there's a basic understanding of what it looks like, there's no need to watch us grind out every step of the journey.

On the other hand, Arthur's going to face a lot of new challenges. So expect intrigue and disaster to increase appropriately. I hope you're reading along on our site – Starlit Publishing – for new chapters, or just on your favorite retailer's website.

Once again, thank you!

~ Tao

About the Author

Tao Wong is a Canadian author based in Toronto who is best known for his System Apocalypse post-apocalyptic LitRPG series and A Thousand Li, a Chinese xianxia fantasy series. His work has been released in audio, paperback, hardcover and ebook formats and translated into German, Spanish, Portuguese, Russian and other languages. He was shortlisted for the UK Kindle Storyteller award in 2021 for his work, A Thousand Li: the Second Sect. When he's not writing and working, he's practicing martial arts, reading and dreaming up new worlds.

Tao became a full-time author in 2019 and is a member of the Science Fiction and Fantasy Writers of America (SFWA).

If you'd like to support Tao directly, he has a Patreon page - benefits include previews of all his new books, full access to series short stories, and other exclusive perks. www.patreon.com/taowong

Want updates on upcoming deluxe editions and exclusive merch? Follow Tao on Kickstarter to get notifications on all projects.
www.kickstarter.com/profile/starlitpublishing

For updates on the series and his other books (and special one-shot stories), please visit the author's website:
www.mylifemytao.com/

Subscribe to Tao's mailing list to receive exclusive access to short stories in the Thousand Li and System Apocalypse universes!

For more great information about great LitRPG series, check out the Facebook groups:

- GameLit Society

  www.facebook.com/groups/LitRPGsociety

- LitRPG Books

  www.facebook.com/groups/LitRPG.books

- LitRPG Legion

  www.facebook.com/groups/litrpglegion

And join my Cultivation Novel Group for more recommendations and to talk about the Thousand Li series:

www.facebook.com/groups/cultivationnovels

About the Publisher

Starlit Publishing is wholly owned and operated by Tao Wong. It is a science fiction and fantasy publisher focused on the LitRPG & cultivation genres. Their focus is on promoting new, upcoming authors in the genre whose writing challenges the existing stereotypes while giving a rip-roaring good read.

For more information on Starlit Publishing, early access to books and exclusive stories visit our webshop.

www.starlitpublishing.com

You can also join Starlit Publishing's mailing list to learn about new, exciting authors and book releases: https://starlitpublishing.com/newsletter-signup/